PROVIDENCE PARANORMAL COLLEGE

PROVIDENCE PARANORMAL COLLEGE

BOOKS 1-5

D.R. PERRY

BEARLY AWAKE

PROVIDENCE PARANORMAL COLLEGE
BOOK ONE

A charmed life can tumble down in an avalanche of problems.

Bobby Tremain's the first in his family to attend college, and also the first to see snow. A massive magical blizzard makes this not-so-average bear want to sleep all winter, but he needs to pass exams or risk flunking out of Providence Paranormal College.

Lynn Frampton's got a brain of epic proportions and an even smarter mouth. She went to college on the other side of the country to escape the town where everybody knows and fears her intellect. At college, Lynn's barely able to make friends, let alone influence people. At least she's at the top of her class.

Bobby needs Lynn's help to stay awake and pass his exams. She might just need his companionship, too. Can Lynn and Bobby find new hope together, or will their failures send them both packing?

CHAPTER ONE

Bobby

"Tremain." The desk shook under my head as something thick and solid made violent contact with its surface.

"Wha-huh?" I blinked, sucking in air like the wind got knocked out of me. It hadn't. The ecology textbook in my face trembled in the hand gripping it. Why had I fallen asleep again? "Sorry, Professor Watkins."

"Don't be sorry, just wake the hell up, Tremain. You can't afford to fail the final." Watkins turned on his heel and paced back to the front of the room. "Everything I lecture about is important to *you*, not me. I learned this stuff thirty years ago. Go ahead and flunk, all of you, like Tremain is going to. You know what I call that?"

The pair of giggling girls behind me snickered, saying something about flat-bottomed professors. They had a point, but I couldn't focus enough on it to even crack a smile. The tap and squeak of chalk on the board made my ears feel like they'd been making out with ice picks. I squinted at the words, trying to make sense of the chalky squiggles.

One giant snowfall and I couldn't concentrate. I could barely stay awake.

"For you miserable louts who can't be bothered to read what's up here, that says *Job Security*." Watkins tapped the chalk under each word. "Mine, not yours. I make more money when you repeat my class. Exam's on Monday, so you have today and the weekend to prepare. Find a study buddy. Read your notes and syllabus. Get it under control. Pass, so I don't have to look at you next semester. Now, scram, and hit the books."

I leaned down to pick up my backpack. A minute later, I sat up again, snorting out the tail end of a snore and wiping a thin string of drool off my cheek. Except it wasn't a minute later. The sky outside the empty classroom was dark. I didn't want to believe I could flunk out in my first semester, but that looked like my fate.

I gripped the desk instead of putting my head in my hands the way I wanted to. Shifters like me hadn't been able to get a formal secondary education until just five years ago. Before the Big Reveal, it was too risky to fake basic humanity and go to a regular school. Special colleges were for the Magi and Psychic kids only. After the entire world learned about Extrahumans, the mundanes and most of the Magi used any excuse to keep us out.

Providence Paranormal College was Ivy-League because it had existed undetected right next to Brown University since 1764. It had restricted admissions to the magic and psychic set, but now it was the first school to accept all Extrahumans on the Registry, even before we got protection under the Civil Rights Act.

PPC had everything a supernatural student could want, too: classes, clubs, and sports with shifter regulations. Headmistress Thurston was a Magus, so no wonder. Any Extrahuman seeking education for academic advancement or paranormal professional credentials was welcome. Humans could come here and study certain Extrahuman subjects, too. So far, only one had bothered to try.

"Dammit." I rubbed my eyes in the half-light, then stretched and got out of my seat. I staggered like my drunk Uncle Stu.

"What are you, some kind of sloth shifter or something?" I turned my head slowly, making out a curvy silhouette in the doorway.

"Nope, just your average bear." I yawned again. Couldn't help it. At least, I covered my mouth that time.

"That's weird." The voice was cool yet feminine. I smelled human, but no perfume or make-up. I decided she was the strange one, but in a good way. Most non-shifter girls at PPC splashed some on. I couldn't blame them, even if that wasn't my thing.

"Who do you think you are, calling me weird when you stand around in backlit doorways like a cheesy Bond villain?" I stuffed my book in the backpack I'd finally liberated from the floor.

"Oh, sorry." Her apology sounded mechanical, as if she used it an awful lot. "I'm Lynn. Professor Watkins practically ordered me to be your study buddy, but you were lost in dreamland." She stepped out of the doorway, letting me pass.

"Not interested." I dragged my backpack along the floor. Like most bear shifters, I'm built like a brick house. So was this girl Lynn but in an entirely different way. Even half-asleep, I noticed her hourglass shape.

"You really want to piss Watkins off, huh, Tremain? Ow!" Lynn hopped on one leg. I'd run over her foot with the backpack by accident. "Your bag hit me."

"Oh, jeez, I'm sorry." My first impulse was to whack myself in the arm to make up for it.

"Accidents happen. I'll let it go if you hit something else for me." She smiled. I caught the glint of her teeth in the light from the hall, and also the brassy sheen of her dirty-blonde hair.

"Wait, what?" I wondered how she knew I wanted to smack myself. Was this girl a psychic? Those smelled mostly human. I could have leaned in and sniffed her to find out but didn't want her to think I was creepy. "Sure, anything."

"Great. Let's hit some books, then. Together." She tilted her head, peering at me as I yawned again. "But not at the library. Somewhere noisier, like the dining hall. Come on, Tremain!"

Lynn left the doorway and was halfway down the hall before I could blink. "What's going on here? A bear shifter can't catch up to a regular human girl?" She tapped her foot. "Snap to it!"

I plodded along after the bossy girl at maybe an eighth of my usual speed. I closed a hand into a fist and scrubbed at my eye with it, wondering why the other bear shifters didn't have the same problem. An unseasonable snowstorm, over four feet, dumped all over half of Rhode Island, and I was the only guy whose bear side wanted to hibernate.

The aroma of food pulled me like a Looney Tunes character through the narrow tunnel dug along the sidewalk. Lynn's strangely hypnotic swaying hips helped. If she hadn't been there, I might have just laid down and gone to sleep in the snow.

"Move it, oaf!" Something solid slammed my shoulder, knocking me against a snowdrift at my right. My hand broke through the top crust of ice, saving me from falling in face-first. I grabbed a handful of snow and flung it ahead at the broad back of the wolf-smelling guy who'd pushed me.

"Ow!" Lynn turned around, eyes narrowing into glaring brown daggers.

"Oh, jeez, Lynn. I'm so sorry." I'd just apologized less than five minutes ago. Clumsiness had been sleepiness' constant companion since the skies dumped mountains of snow all over Providence.

"Again?" She shook her head, ice chips flying off in all directions from her hair. I let them hit my face, thinking I deserved worse. "You're a dangerous man, sleepy bear."

"Not as dangerous as your attitude, Frampton." The pushy wolf shifter crossed his arms over his leather-jacketed chest.

"Quit it, Josh. Seriously, will you ever let up on giving me grief? All by yourself, you're worse than every jerk-face back in my hometown." She rolled her eyes, then turned around with her hands on her hips. A low growl started in my throat, but a yawn cut it off.

"Keep mouthing off like that, and your new bear friend'll run off." Josh's smirk wasn't unkind, but it still bugged me. So what if Lynn had a sarcastic sense of humor? "Guys don't date grouchy nerd-women."

"I'll look for dates in a sack of trail mix. He's not one." She shrugged, kicking at the packed snow underfoot with her boot-heel. "Bobby here is a Watkins-mandated study buddy."

"And you're heading to the dining hall instead of the library with him. Why?" I blinked, rubbing a wet hand down my face as Josh cocked his head and raised an eyebrow. The guy was almost as tall as me but rail-thin with amber eyes and a shock of spiky blond hair.

"Because he'll fall asleep anywhere quiet, dog-brains." Lynn turned to stare Josh down, crossing her arms and tilting her head in a miniature mirror of his pose. "I don't have to answer to oblivious werewolves in any event."

"Wait." Josh looked over his shoulder to peer at me. "You're the hibernator?" He laughed. "Leaping Luna! I never met a bear shifter who couldn't keep his eyes open before. Where are you from, Hawaii? Wait." He scratched his head, looking genuinely puzzled. "Are there even bears in Hawaii?" Josh held his hand out.

My hand reacted automatically even though I hadn't intended to take it. I squeezed down hard, but Josh only laughed and pumped our arms up and down three times.

"I'm Josh—ing you. Nah, just Joshua Dennison."

"Bobby Tremain." I wanted to throw down a quip but had to yawn instead. "Hibernating oaf," was all I managed. I let go of the wolf shifter, then looked at the snowbank. It reminded me of a pillow. Was it soft? Maybe a nice place to have a quick nap? I rubbed my eyes, yawning again. "Someone tell the Sandman there's sleepy kids on the other side of the world or something."

"Come on, Tremain." Lynn grabbed the hand that was still kind of numb from snow and the handshake. It tingled a little. "We have books to hit. He has to pass, or he's out."

"You'll need a Tanuki's luck with that." Josh blinked, and the grin melted off his face. "The hibernation urge is bad news, bear."

"What's that supposed to mean?" I stifled yet another yawn. I was getting super tired of being tired.

"It means Frampton's got her work cut out for her. Later." He strode past us along the path to the dining hall at a pace power-walkers everywhere would envy. He could have been YouTube famous or on an infomercial with a walk like that.

"I guess we do have to go to the library, after all, Bobby," Lynn sighed, her shoulders drooping. "I need some books about your bear. Tell me about him on the way over, I'll check out whatever looks useful, then we head back here."

I meant to say that sounded like a plan, but it all came out in a yawny garble with only the last word spoken intelligibly. That didn't bother Lynn one bit. I followed her to the library, feeling like Princess Leia. Instead of Obi-Wan, this snarky girl was my only hope.

CHAPTER TWO

Lynn

I wasn't sure where I could leave Bobby Tremain without risking him falling asleep, but I needed books on brown bear shifters, not just stuff from the Internet about regular bear hibernation. I'd be getting my own crash course cramming session all about people who changed into bears this weekend. That was fine with me. Majoring in Alternative Therapies meant I'd have to learn that sometime, anyway. I didn't need a Psychic to tell me about all the extensive coursework in Extrahuman and Shifter Physiology in my future.

I sighed, poking Bobby's shoulder. His eyelids snapped open like window shades. He'd sat down on the top of the library steps while I'd been thinking. If he didn't get a B or better on that exam, Watkins wouldn't give me the extra credit. I'd slacked off in Ecology, so I needed it to bring my grade up from a B+ to an A. I had to keep him awake. At least, I was obnoxious enough to do just that.

"Come on, Rip Van Tremain. Don't sit anywhere to wait. No one should be sitting here, anyway." I pointed at the overhang above the

PPC library entrance. "I can't believe they didn't have someone clear that."

"Woah." Bobby stared up at the giant pile of snow and ice crowning the flat slab that protected the doorway. "I know nothing about snow, but isn't that a little dangerous?"

"Not really at this point." I shrugged. "The chances of it falling off are maybe a tenth of a percent. They'll probably clear it when the weather gets warmer. That's when it'll really be a risk."

"Aces Ecology and snow 101." Bobby yawned. "Is there anything you haven't studied?"

"Didn't have to study snow. Grew up in the frozen tundra outside Madison, Wisconsin." I opened the door and beckoned to him. "As much as I hate people hovering, just follow me in and around the stacks." I watched him stand up and stretch, the hem of his shirt hiking up a little to put his washboard abs on display. It was impossible not to stare. He waved his hand in front of my face.

"Lead on, supreme studier." He gave me a totally adorable half-smile, blinking sleepily at the same time. Why did all the guys at PPC have to be so intimidatingly handsome? It made me nervous, which turned my snark up to eleven. Not a good way to win friends and influence people. I couldn't remember making a single one the entire semester. The more things changed, the more I seemed to stay the same.

"'Kay," was all I could manage. Even if I wasn't so annoying, I'd always been shunned because of what I packed in the old noggin. I had a totally deserved reputation for being a brain and having an attitude. That's why I went to a school so far from home, to get away from all the people I'd pissed off just by opening my big mouth. But it hadn't worked. I hadn't been able to get a date or even make any friends during orientation. Half the school knew who I was and mostly avoided me unless they had an academic question. When that happened, they approached me with more caution than they showed testy types like vampires and dragon shifters.

I assumed the fake Valedictorian smile I'd used all last spring. At least, I had a high-octane thinker. If only I could use it to make my heart shut up about wanting friends, I'd be golden. I should be used to missing the mark socially by now. Story of my life and all. And now, Watkins had me helping Bobby Tremain of all people, the most high-profile student at PPC. At least, annoying comments kept most people from falling asleep. I only had to be careful not to care too much about him after the exam. He was an extra credit assignment, no matter how nice a package that came in. I had to stay focused, maybe even try to mean the cynical quips that came out of my mouth.

The PPC library still had an old card-catalog, something novel enough to use even though everything was also on the computer sitting right next to it. Even better, it was haunted in a good way. I'd always loved old-fashioned and spooky things, more negative points in the dating department. My max dates per guy in High School capped out at three. I'd never had a steady boyfriend, even though I'd had a more than friendly rivalry with the next best student in the school. That had been hot in more ways than one, but just a brief flash-in-the-pan. My younger sister had no boy trouble, even going out with more than one of the several guys who hadn't bothered texting me back.

"Um, Lynn?" The sleepy voice behind me shook the past loose from my meandering mind.

"Yeah, yeah. I'm on it." I reached for a drawer full of cards, which opened on its own, then spoke directly to the air above the open drawer. "Books about brown bear shifters, cross-reference hibernation. Vice versa" I watched fascinated as the cards ruffled with the touch of unseen hands. The library wasn't magic, but it had helper ghosts working in it. I'd asked for their help several times a week for the past three months, and it still hadn't gotten old. "Sleuthing out ways to keep you up."

"Woah." Bobby did a sleepy double-take, then winked. What right did anyone have to be so cute, even when he was this bewildered?

"Jeez, I didn't mean it like that." I tried not to let my hands shake as I copied down numbers, thanked the ghosts, and closed the drawer. Then I kicked myself for not laughing. I knew how it felt when jokes went over like lead balloons. I was so unused to people deliberately initiating jokes with me, I'd forgotten how to react when they did.

"Well, I'm glad your reputation's all about getting between pages instead of sheets, or I might think you were trying to take advantage." He made that sly sexy face again, this time without the sleepiness. He couldn't be aware of giving me a look like that, or he'd be horrified right after. I decided it must be another attempt at a joke.

"Oh, I've got a reputation for more than supreme intelligence." I almost couldn't believe Bobby was trying to kid around again. Probably just a way to stay awake, but that was my assignment. I could play that game. "Haven't you heard my big snarky attitude has been everywhere?"

"Just today. Mostly, you have a reputation for acing every subject." He yawned. "Rumor is, you're the type of girl who never gets Bs."

"Be glad I'm using my academic powers for good, then." I glanced at the shelf labels as I stalked past them, searching for the right ones.

"Oh yeah, I'm glad. I can imagine what might happen if you went over to the Dark Side."

"And that is?" I smirked at the Star Wars reference, imagining the Imperial March playing as I paced the stacks.

"Darth Lynn would convince every professor to use a pass/fail rubric. Guys like me would end up with our borderline grades force-choked." I snorted, barely stopping myself from belly-laughing in the library. That'd be almost sacrilege for me. A book slid out and then in again all on its own.

"Thanks, helper ghost," I said to the not so thin air. Just because some people in the library were dead was no reason to forget to thank them. Then, I looked over my shoulder at Bobby. "This is the place." I scanned the spines of some seriously old books. "Wow. Some of these should be in a museum."

"Yeah, kind of like Watkins." I couldn't believe he'd said something like that out loud. I turned to look at his face and saw a hint of seriousness in his eyes.

"Hey, I know he's old, but he's not so bad." I reached up, trying to grab the book I wanted. I missed, of course. "Height fail."

"I got it." Bobby handed me the book my fingertips had barely brushed.

"I'd thank you, but you should be thanking me." I hooked my arm around the thick volume, locking it against my hip. "Three more books and we can check out and hit the dining hall." The other books I wanted were all in easy reach behind me.

"Yeah, I'm starving." Bobby laced his hands together and stretched them over his head again. Holy boulder shoulders. I tried not to look, but then he patted his abdomen. "I've got a bear in there, you know." He winked like I was cute or something. "Your buddy said I shouldn't eat too much, though."

"My what?" I blinked, then shook my head feeling for all the world like I had water in my ears. Had I heard him right?

"Your friend, Josh, the wolf-man." Bobby leaned one elbow on the desk as the live and visible library aide scanned my ID and then the barcodes on the books. Not everyone working at the PPC Library and Media Center was dead.

"Josh isn't my friend, just a guy I pissed off at orientation." I clutched the books to my chest and pushed out the door.

"Oh." Bobby yawned again, distorting and stretching out his apology. "Sorry."

"Don't be. He's not." I slapped on that fake smile again and descended the library steps, glancing back at the snow pile on the overhang. I took a deep breath to get rid of the sense of some rude waterfowl walking over my grave. Feathery jerks should be on a platter at Christmas dinner, not freaking people out. "Neither am I, for that matter."

"Okay." Bobby followed me, then lifted his head and wrinkled his nose. "Hey, do you think they'd put bacon on my salmon?"

"What on your who now?" I kept walking. We both had a ton to learn and not much time. I should ask questions on the move. It might help keep the sleepiest were-bear in the world awake, too. Picking up the pace would be even better. I amped up my cold weather stride to a trot.

"Well, I smell both types of meat, but not together." He picked up his pace to keep up with me.

"That's some sense of smell you've got there, bear Padawan. Can you lift rocks with that nose, too?"

"Your geek is showing." He chuckled. "And only in a swamp. That's not a grizzly's natural habitat, but it's the only one I've known until this fall. All the Tremains are from Louisiana, which is an awful lot like Dagobah."

"Don't you dare tell anyone there's an X-wing under your back yard, Tremain. The Empire will be on us faster than you can yawn again." I surprised myself by giggling. Bobby was actually kind of fun even if it probably was just a temporary symptom of his woozy state.

"I swear I'll never tell." Bobby drew one finger in an "x" shape on the left side of his chest. That smile made his whole face light up, reminding me I'd better stop caring. He was so far out of my league he really might as well be on Dagobah. At least, I'd have someone nice to look at over remedial Ecology material. I told myself that's all he could be, extra credit and eye candy.

"Wow, if I'd known tutoring inspired this kind of loyalty, I'd have started doing it in Kindergarten." I rolled my eyes. Bobby opened the door to the dining hall for me. I tried not to let myself imagine this was a date. He opened the second door inside the vestibule, making me fail.

"You know, they don't have doors like this in Louisiana. It never gets cold there." His voice behind me was practically in my ear. I tried to hide the shiver at feeling his breath stir my hair. I made a beeline for the nearest table, needing to get away from him all of a sudden.

"There must be tons of differences for you." I plunked my books down on an empty table, my backpack too. "Culture-shock city."

"Oh yeah." He stretched his arms over his head again as he walked toward the food counters. I could get used to watching that, but shouldn't. After he passed this class, Bobby Tremain would probably never say a word to me again. We weren't likely to have many more classes together, either. We couldn't possibly have the same major.

"Hey, what's your major, anyway?" When he sent a puzzled glance over his shoulder, I shrugged. "It might help with how we study. If I know the context you need this class for, I mean, besides it being a basic requirement for half the non-magical majors here."

"Forestry." He gave me that sleepy half-smile again and picked up a tray. "I know, big surprise. A bear shifter studying for a career in the middle of nowhere."

"Well, that's actually good." I got a bowl and went straight to the rows of cereal dispensers instead of bothering with the hot meal line. "You really need Ecology in that major. It's the foundation for all the rest of your studies."

"I know." He held his hand out to take a plate piled with bacon and put it on his tray. He waited as the kid behind the counter went to the grill for something else. "I'm really kicking myself over my grades taking a nosedive. It's just like you said. Everything here is different from where I grew up. The campus is in the middle of a city, plus the climate."

"It doesn't help that Watkins is so old-school he only gives two exams and a lab grade, either." I shook my head as I poured milk over my cereal. "High stakes classroom is what he runs. I love that kind of thing, but not everyone can be Darth Lynn."

"I aced lab, but got a D on the mid-term." Bobby thanked the counter kid for his plate of fish.

We walked back to our table, plunked our trays down, then sat in front of our meals. He cracked his knuckles, then used his fork to transfer bacon onto the salmon fillets. After that, he tucked in, devouring fish and pork with a beatific expression.

"Well, there's hope for you yet, bear Padawan." I fumbled at the empty space on the right of my tray. "Crap on a cracker. I forgot my spoon. And you've got no napkins either." I headed back toward the condiments and silver-ware table to fix that, pronto. Surely, eating would keep him awake long enough?

CHAPTER THREE

Bobby

I watched Lynn go, my gaze going up from her hips to her shoulders. She seemed fun under all the sarcasm, so I couldn't figure out why she was always alone. Maybe her friends were all in her dorm or something. I noticed her drooping shoulders and realized the downward slant of them hinted that she was lonely. I took a deep breath through my nose, singling out her scent from the rest in the dining hall. For whatever reason, my already astute sniffer had gone into overdrive since the snow.

That's when I realized Lynn Frampton smelled unhappy. The joking, the can-do attitude about academics, was all some kind of mask. Underneath that, something told me she felt more out of place here at PPC than I did. I glanced around at the packed tables, but my nose told me more than my eyes. There were more shifters and changelings here than magi and psychics. Lynn Frampton seemed to be the only human enrolled this semester. Had she expected more human students? But no, she'd given no sign Extrahumans made her uncomfortable. She hadn't feared Josh the werewolf. I seemed like the only one who made her nervous instead of lonely or pissed.

"Think fast, Tremain!" A hand entered my field of vision, hovering over some of my bacon. I slapped it away without bothering to see who it belonged to first.

"No think, eat," I grunted, doing a decent impression of my dad's old Ultimate Shifter League persona. "Hungry bear is hungry." I picked the strip of bacon up and made it disappear.

"Yeah, I figured. Bears don't share." The tall man with shoulder-length brown hair sat next to me, crossing his ankles as he stretched his legs out under the table. He put his hands behind his head and leaned back. Women all over the dining hall stared in his direction. A few men, too. My roommate had that effect on anyone who appreciated the male form.

"And dragons want to own everything." I took another bite, chewed, and swallowed. I hadn't realized it was possible to be this hungry. "Kind of puts us at odds, Blaine."

"Yeah, but not really." The dragon shifter smirked. "If we weren't willing to be more than the sum of our instinctual parts, Providence Paranormal College would still be a tiny school for magically and psychically inclined humans. And Headmistress Thurston would have a much easier time running this place."

"So do your part for solidarity already, man. Stop stealing my bacon." I reached for another piece of stray bacon but realized I'd inhaled it all while Blaine talked. So, I picked up my fork and went to town on the smothered salmon. "Still can't believe the room lottery matched me with a dragon."

"I still can't believe you haven't figured out what's going on with your sleepiness." Blaine jerked his chin at the book pile on the table. "Looks like you're, at least, trying to." His gaze traveled over the books to the cereal bowl on the other side of the table. "And who likes soggy cereal?"

"I don't." Lynn had returned, brandishing a spoon like a sword and a tower of napkins like a shield. "There were no spoons, so I had to wait for the dishwasher. Now I need another bowl."

"Let me get it." Blaine stood up, his height making it seem like he looked down his nose at Lynn. He was a pain in the hindquarters, but not enough of a jerk to do that on purpose to someone he'd just met. "We shouldn't leave Bobby alone for more than two minutes, tops. We don't want him to fall asleep. I already read those, of course. They won't help you much."

"And I should believe you, why?" Lynn's frosty tone gave me a hint about why she might be lonely. The girl used her wit and intellect to wall herself in. "Because they didn't help you?"

"Because I'm his roommate and I watched this happen. The night the snow fell, I went straight to the library." Blaine put a hand on one hip, cocking his head to the side. Every head at a table full of girls across the room turned his way. "If you think you can outsmart a dragon, knock yourself out."

"I can, and I will. Outsmart you, that is." Lynn thrummed her fingers on the table once, her nails making four sharp taps in rapid succession. After that, she made a scoffing little snort. "You don't know what I'm packing up here." She pointed at her right temple, then dipped her spoon into her soggy cereal and took a defiant bite. "Has to be more than a dinosaur with delusions of grandeur."

"Guyyyyys." The word turned into one of my biggest yawns yet. I had to 'get it under control,' like Professor Watkins always said. The last thing I needed was my study buddy and my roommate fighting. Unfortunately, the stupid hibernation urge had me unable to do anything but inhale food and air.

"Jeez, no wonder you can't make any friends, Frampton. Cereal offer redacted!" Blaine turned on his heel and stalked out of the dining room. Wispy trails of white smoke flowed over each of his shoulders as he went outside.

I looked back at Lynn's reddening face, watching her swallow the mouthful of milky mush with a grimace. What could have caused that sudden surge of competitive anger? Did she have something against dragons in general? Her scent made me think whatever it was had been bothering her for a long time. Momma always said resentment festered. But the two of them had only just met.

She had to be self-conscious about her smarts, then. Had she been put down for it back home? I opened my mouth to let her know Blaine would come around, that he just wasn't used to being contradicted. But the angle of my head made me so sleepy. I could probably get away with resting it on the table just for a few seconds.

"No!" A rush of air blew my hair back from my face as Lynn clapped her hands in front of it.

"I'm awake, I'm awake!" Blinking, I pulled my head back, realizing I'd almost made a pillow out of the last of my food. My sigh escaped through a big smile. "Thanks, Lynn. Dinner's my favorite meal, not my favorite hat."

"Um, you're welcome, I guess." She sat down, twirling her spoon in the mushy cereal. Then she dropped it and picked up a book instead. "I'd better read this pronto."

"No, really, I mean it. Thanks for going out of your way." I took one of the last remaining bites of delicious fish and bacon heaven. "All Watkins wants you to do is help me with Ecology, not all this other stuff." I vaguely waved my fork at the stack of books. "Thanks for that. Everyone else besides you and Blaine just thinks all this is funny."

"Well, it's not. You're at school because you want to do something with your life." Somehow, Lynn continued talking as her eyes followed her right index finger rapidly along each line of text. "I've heard of your roommate before. Dragon from Newport, grew up in a mansion. Silver spoon, admissions on a platter. But some of us had to work hard just to get here. What's happening to you isn't fair, and we have to fix it."

"Wow, Lynn." I shook my head, partly to keep awake but also because this random brainiac girl was a real fighter. "You sound tougher than my own dad."

"Thanks." She still didn't glance up, but the tremor in her voice and her scent told me she took the compliment seriously. "I know who he is too, by the way. Also, what happened to him. For what it's worth, I'm sorry."

"You shouldn't be stuck with soggy cereal." I couldn't handle responding to that kind of sympathy. No one else had said anything like that the entire semester. People avoided talking about my dad in general, even when I brought him up. He'd been a champion several times over before the accident. But I didn't want to think about that just then. "You want some bacon? I'll go get you a plate."

"Wow, Bobby." This time, she did look up, but just for a second. "Thanks but no thanks. I'm a pescetarian. Means I—"

"Just eat fish. I get it." I stood up. "Salmon, then?"

"I'd rather have soggy cereal. It's poached, right?" She scrunched up her nose in a peculiarly endearing way.

"Yup, poached salmon. Definitely on the mushy side." I watched her reach out to drag the bowl closer. So, I put a hand on her shoulder, stopping her attempt to subsist on mushy cheerios. "I'll bring you a fish and chips plate. Nothing soggy about that."

"That'd be awesome." She tapped her current page, and I noticed she was already halfway through the thick book. "It says here that foraging for food helps keep grizzlies awake even in wintry temperatures."

"The more you know." I felt a little flushed when she cracked a smile at my remark. I didn't bother telling her that fish and chips weren't on the menu, or that the chef on duty owed me a favor I was more than willing to use for her. It seemed like the most natural and unremarkable thing in the world, helping Lynn Frampton. Despite what Blaine had said, she'd made at least one friend that day. Me.

CHAPTER FOUR

Lynn

The chair to my right creaked, and I wasn't surprised. Even though I was just a regular human, I'd spent so much of my life being glared, stared, or laughed at that I knew exactly when one of those was happening. I had a pretty good idea of who was engaging in the first behavior on that list.

"Beat it, tall, drake, and brainy."

"Wait, what's that? I thought I heard a pot calling a kettle a nerd." Blaine rested his elbows on the table, then sighed through the corner of his mouth to puff the hair on that side out of his face. "Look, I came over here to bury the hatchet. Bobby needs our help, and he'll be better off if we aren't pissing in each other's Cheerios."

"You're probably right." I stopped my finger as a phrase caught my eye. I pressed my nail into the page, my way of halting speed-reading progress. "Well, holy smokes."

"Wait, you found something?" Blaine sounded surprised. When I glanced up, his eyes were rounded and his mouth pressed into a thin line.

"It's only a hint, but it's got me thinking about something from one of my Shifter Anatomy assignments."

"Wings and talons, *you're* the human majoring in Alternative Therapies!" He leaned forward, trying to get a look at the page in the book I held. I rolled my eyes and turned the book his way.

"Right here, it says hibernation in grizzly shifters gets induced by drastic shifts in weather patterns from one year to the next." I tapped the passage.

"Yeah, I read that and then looked up the local almanac data. There wasn't snow, but the temperature isn't much different this year than it was last year." He shrugged. "It can't be that."

"Sucks to your almanac. They don't matter one bit in this case." I grabbed a notebook and flipped it open to a blank page. I wrote Bobby's name at the top on the left side, then drew a line down the middle of the page and wrote the words "other bear shifters" on the right.

"Okay, so think of the other bear shifters you know. Tell me some of the places they're from." I held the pen, ready to jot down whatever Blaine said.

"Well, Oliver's from Montana." Blaine tapped a finger for each guy he named. "Kyle's from right around here, grew up with Josh. Dave's from Maine. Paul and Lyle are from Vancouver. Jeannie's from Boston. That's all I can think of off the top of my head."

"Okay, how are those different?" I finished the list of places on the right, then jotted one word on the left. After I turned the notebook around, I waited for Blaine's jaw to drop in amazement at my genius. I only had to count to three.

"Tiamat's scales, it's not about the local temperature, it's what the bear's used to." Blaine closed his mouth. He turned a little green, then huffed a tiny wisp of smoke out his nose. "Bobby's lived in the Deep South all his life; same for his entire family for generations. He told me that the day I met him. What a lame mistake."

"What are you majoring in, Blaine?"

"Huh? Oh, Extrahuman Anthropology, with a concentration in Ancient Shifter Cultures." He ran a hand through his hair, eliciting a collective feminine sigh from a table of girls.

"So of course, almanacs would be the first thing on your mind for the weather." I still wasn't in much of a mood for smiling, and it probably wasn't a good idea to fake one at an embarrassed dragon shifter. "They're always telling me to think of the patient first and then the things affecting him. Anyway, I could still be wrong about this."

"Wrong about what?" Bobby pushed the book out of the way and put a plate of savory-smelling fried goodness in front of me. My mouth watered. *Now* I felt like smiling, so I did. It came out a lot wider and brighter than I'd intended.

"She figured out why you want to hibernate and all the other bear shifters here don't." Blaine leaned back and stretched his legs out again.

"Maybe." I bit into a crispy French fry. "It's just a theory, but check it out." I handed the notebook to Bobby and picked up a piece of battered cod. It was the perfect temperature, just under what would burn my tongue. Crispy heaven.

"So it's just because I never had a real winter?" Bobby didn't sit, opting to shift his weight from one foot to the other.

"Probably, but not for certain." I reached for a napkin to wipe my hands but opted for another piece of fish instead. "Still doesn't tell us what to do about it."

"Well, that's where I think maybe I can help." Blaine eased the biggest of the books from the bottom of the stack out of the pile. "This one here wasn't available the other day. Librarian said it was on loan to an alum." He held it up.

"*Aboriginal Shifter Migration in North America?*" Bobby stifled yet another yawn. I wondered if we should Netflix a loud action movie or something later on.

"Yeah. This book's about how Native American shifters coped with traveling across the continent in pre-colonization days. It's all based on artifacts and oral history research. That's my wheelhouse." Blaine patted the book like he was burping a baby. "I'll look specifically for stuff about south-to-north migration. Bear shifters back then must have dealt with that somehow. Maybe there's something you can try, Bobby."

"Make sure and—" I stopped trying to talk around the mouthful of delicious food, not wanting to rush my meal.

"I know, Frampton." Blaine's mouth made a little chagrined tilt. "I'll share what I find. For now, you and Bobby should go find something to do. I have a way to read extra fast, but it's definitely not something I want to do in the city. Thank goodness there's room for my dragon at India Point Park."

"Wait." I'd finally swallowed my fries. "What should I do if he starts falling asleep?"

"You seem to have handled that just fine so far." Blaine tucked the book into his backpack and stood up. "You're smart. You'll think of something."

I watched Blaine wink at Bobby, then turned my attention to the almost empty plate of fish and chips in front of me. Bobby stretched again, letting out a full yawn this time. I pushed the empty plate out of the way, sliding it over to make room for another book. My hand was halfway to the stack when I stopped to use a napkin. Returning greasy books to the library would only make me more enemies.

"I'll skim part of this book before we go." I picked up the medium-length volume about general hibernation. "It won't take more than a few minutes since it probably only has a few chapters we need."

"Okay." He just stood there, looking over my right shoulder.

"Um, I'm not sure I can do this with you being all loom-y, Tremain." I tried not to glance back at him, feeling the heat rise in my cheeks at his nearness. Blaine might be right that I had no friends because I was too forward, pushy, and competitive. At least now I could use those qualities to help someone for a change.

"Okay." He stepped back. "They had cookies. Want some?"

"Sure." I hadn't much liked the cookies in the dining hall. None of them were anywhere near as good as the hermits and snicker-doodles my mother made. Homesickness and culture shock hadn't helped my chances of starting over here. But I didn't have time for

Emo woolgathering. I opened the book and found the chapters I wanted.

I'd finished reading before Bobby was back with the cookies. Grabbing the notebook, I jotted down a few details we might need later. A tug at my sleeve almost made me jump right out of my skin.

"Hi, Lynn." A girl in flowing black garments with black curls framing her face and tumbling down her back sat down, crossing her arms on the table. I stared at her face, trying to remind myself where I knew her from.

"Wait, I've almost got it." Her name and identity were right on the tip of my tongue. I scrunched up my face. "M. Definitely something with the letter M."

"Yes!" The girl smiled, her eyes brightening. "Maddie. Your roommate."

"Remind me again why I always forget you." I hated that. I didn't forget in our room, of course. All her stuff was there, and there were signs on the door and over my desk to remind me.

"It's a thing that runs in my family. Umbral affinity." She chewed her bottom lip.

"Right, you're a Magus." I put the notebook down, trying my hardest to be polite. I had to live with this girl, so I tried to relax around her. It was easy since she was the serious type. I had no idea whether she genuinely liked me unless she was around. It had to suck more to be the girl everyone forgets than to be the one people always remembered. Maybe I didn't have it so bad with the foot-in-mouth syndrome of doom after all.

"Uh-huh." She twiddled her thumbs. "Anyway, I'm going home tonight. My exams are done except the paper, and that gets turned in by e-mail. Just dropped by to remind you and say goodbye until spring."

"Okay, Maddie. Thanks." I smirked, unable to help myself. "I'd like to say I'll never forget you, but..." I shrugged. She even giggled. "I think I might transfer back home, though."

"Wait, what?" Maddie actually looked upset. "Why?"

"I'm not making any friends here. My big mean mouth gets me in trouble no matter where I take it." I wanted to look away but knew I'd forget she was there if I did. "Might as well go to school back home in Wisconsin where I don't have my hopes up all the time."

"Well, I think your mouth is funny." Maddie put both hands over mine. "Wait, that came out wrong. You're funny. You always crack *me* up, anyway. And you're not mean-spirited, just sarcastic."

"Thanks." It figured; the one person who didn't think I was annoying was literally invisible for all intents and purposes. At least, I'd managed not to piss one person off during my time here. "You have no idea how much I needed to hear that today."

"Actually, I do." She sighed. "And that was what you said to me the last time we chatted about this."

"When was that, Maddie?"

"Last night." She smirked. "Don't worry, I'm used to reruns from everyone but my immediate family. They never forget I exist. You remember me better than most, probably because you're so smart. I'm almost afraid to stay here for Inter-session, but I really need that course for my major."

"Jeez, Maddie." I might have looked worried because I was. The longer I spent talking to her, the more I remembered. She was good company, and a decent person besides. "Is there anything I can do to help?"

"Not really." She shrugged. "My mom's out of the country. She said she's hired a guy to design an amulet that'll make people remember me for all the class hours plus a little extra. It's expensive but less than having to take the class over again."

"I'd stay too and take that terminology course if I was sure I wouldn't transfer."

"Do they even offer your major at schools back in Wisconsin?"

"Yeah, one school, but they're not as prestigious as the one here." I smiled . "This is the only Extrahuman Ivy-League school in the United States, and the only one in the world that accepts humans for a major in anything like health care for Extrahumans."

"Did you finish all the paperwork?" Maddie pulled at some lace edging her sleeve.

"Just the stuff here." I felt my cheeks get hot and my middle get cold. It was more than a little embarrassing, knowing this perfectly nice person had a case of the glums because of me. "The school in Wisconsin needs my signature in person. Until I sign that, nothing's final."

"Oh. Well, I'll miss you." Maddie got up. "I have a train to catch."

"Vermont, right?" It was a little sad, saying goodbye to her like this when we both knew I'd forget her once she was out of sight.

"Yeah!" She smiled brightly. "You remembered. Thanks, Lynn. You've been a great roommate, and a good friend."

"Same here, Maddie," I smiled back, trying not to look as down as I felt. "Whoever takes my spot in the room is getting the better half of the deal."

She hoisted a duffel bag over her shoulder, gave me a grin, and tilted her hand twice before turning around. I watched her leave the building, then looked down at the notes I'd scrawled for Bobby. When I looked up again, he was back with a plate of cookies and two glasses of milk, and he put them on the table between us and smiled. I had the feeling I'd just forgotten something important.

"Who were you talking to?" Bobby picked up what looked like a chocolate chip cookie.

"What do you mean?" I scratched my head. "Was I talking to someone?"

"No?" Bobby sniffed. "I smell human, jasmine, and a trace of myrrh, like the kind you burn on a charcoal briquette. A Magus of some kind?"

"I dunno," I said, shrugging. "I think I remember knowing a Magus who burned myrrh that way, but it seems like a long time ago."

"Weird." Bobby chewed his mouthful of cookie thoughtfully.

"Anyway, the information I got." I picked up one cookie. "You want to avoid bed. Like, don't lie down if you can help it. Sit in chairs, on the floor, stand up. You still might fall asleep, but it will be much easier for someone to wake you up again." I went back to skimming, unclear on why I'd stopped in the first place.

"Stay vertical, got it." Bobby crunched cookies, smiling with his mouth closed. "What else?"

"Avoid caves. That one sounds easy, but to be on the safe side, keep out of anything that might resemble one." I grimaced, thinking about the dug-out sidewalks until I realized Bobby's head and shoulders were higher than the sides. "That trolley tunnel over on Thayer's one example. So's most of Water Place Park."

"Hmm." Bobby swallowed his cookies "Okay, that shouldn't be too hard." He gulped down the milk from one glass and pushed the other across to me. "Is that all?"

"Nope. One more thing, super important. Don't shift, no matter what. Stay in your human shape, or else your train is headed for the Hibernation Station." I looked up at him, staring directly into his eyes. I had to get him to focus on what I was saying, which was much more important than the way his blue eyes threatened to weaken my knees. "Bobby, pay attention."

"Um, sure. I'm paying attention." He blinked a few times, and the tension between us cleared. "Why can't I shift?"

"Because the number one thing on the list for a Southern-climate bear right now is sleep with a capital 'S,' understand?" I turned the book around and put it on the table, then pointed at a paragraph that talked about how hibernating shifters always slept in animal form. "If you fall asleep in bear form, you. Will. Not. Wake. Up. Until. Spring."

"Okay, Lynn." He winced. "No need to stab that poor book to death with your finger. I get it. No bear form, no matter what."

"Do dragon shifters need to sleep like humans and other shifters?" I pressed my lips together, feeling inadequate. "I'm not very familiar with them yet."

"Blaine can pull an all-nighter without getting all punchy and weird like most people. Don't know whether that's just his family line or what, though."

"Do you have any nocturnal shifter buddies here? Maybe a vampire friend?"

"Not exactly a friend, but Blaine knows of one vampire. There's an owl shifter in one of my classes, too, but she's on some crazy pills that make her diurnal so she can attend day classes."

"Ask that vampire what there is to do at night to keep you awake. I'll need sleep in order to help you actually pass the exam, and Blaine's already been up from what I gathered. Looks like he's doing it again tonight, too." I got up. It was my turn to stretch and then bring the empty trays back.

"Okay." He furrowed his brow at the uneaten cookie sitting on a napkin in front of my seat. I saw him add two more, then demolish the rest on the plate. It was going to be a long weekend.

CHAPTER FIVE

Bobby

"What do you mean, you don't think you have a roommate?" Everything about Lynn confused me, but this was ridiculous. "I mean, you either have one, or you don't."

"I mean exactly what I said." Her grumble carried easily to my sensitive ears even though she walked in front of me. "I don't think I do, but I'm not a hundred percent sure. We go to a college for the strange and unusual. Things aren't as absolute as you might have had to deal with before, Tremain."

"Now hold on, Lynn." She did, so fast I plowed into her and knocked her into the nearest snowbank. "Jeez, sorry." I ran a hand over my face and held the other one out to her.

"I don't need a werebear to rescue me from snow. Just tell me why I had to stop if he was going to run into me." She sat up, shaking snow off her sleeves and mittens. "You think this is funny?" She held out her soggy outerwear.

"No." I shifted my weight from one foot to the other, then planted them. I'd finally had enough. "I just wanted to tell you to stop calling me Tremain."

"Can't handle my snark, huh?" She stood up, brushing off the seat of her pants as I watched, fascinated by the high color indignation gave her cheeks. "Or maybe this is a jock-versus-nerd thing? Only playing nice for your grade? Thought you'd get back at me by knocking me over?" Lynn snorted. "I've dealt with worse."

"Close your mouth and open your ears, Lynn. Let something from outside a book get through to that big brain of yours." I stared her right in the eyes, something that always got my kid brothers to shut up and listen. "You think I'm bullying you? All those extra books, teaming up with an arrogant dragon to figure out my malfunction, and implying you'll stay up with me half the weekend. All that right there says you're going above and beyond, helping me. You love Extrahumans so much that you're studying how to fix us when we get hurt. You thank the helper ghosts at the library, and you're not even a Medium, for Pete's sake. You're witty, brainy, and kind enough to help the guy almost everyone else is laughing at behind his back. So what if you're mouthy, too?"

The pink on Lynn's cheeks went scarlet. I could smell the threat of tears on her, making me wonder whether anyone besides her blood family ever said anything like that where she could hear it. She blinked a few times, and the tear smell faded. Even though she'd already stood up, she grabbed the hand I still held out to her. It felt good, and strangely tingly through the wet glove.

"I'm sorry for accusing you like that." Lynn didn't cut her eyes away when she apologized like too many other people had lately around me. "I'm just not used to having anyone like you around. You know, someone who acts decent and means it. It won't happen again."

"I didn't need any apologies, but I'll accept one, anyway." The whole anyone-like-me thing confused me, but now wasn't the time to ask about it. Letting go of her hand, I opened my arms. My family hugged things out. The way Lynn paled told me hers didn't. "That's okay too. As long as you call me Bobby instead of doing this last-name crap."

"Fine, Bobby." She cleared her throat. "Anyway, let's head to my room and solve the Schrödinger's roommate mystery."

"Never a dull moment at Providence Paranormal College, huh?" I chuckled.

"That's one thing I actually like here." Her feet crunched in the snow as I followed her. I yawned; the effect of having to defend Lynn to herself had worn off and I was sleepy again. Finally inside the lobby, she wouldn't let me sit while waiting for the elevator. She reminded me of Mom before Dad's accident, when she used to help him train. Taskmaster Tammy was what he always called her. Now, he just called her when he needed help to get into and out of his wheelchair. I stepped into the elevator after Lynn.

I wondered when I'd find my mate. It hadn't been in high school, like most of my family going back a few generations. On Mom's side, they'd found their mates later. One thing they had in common was the dreams. After meeting, every one of my shifter relatives had dreamed of his or her mate that same night—which reminded me of the sorry fact that I wouldn't be able to have any kind of dream until after the exam.

"Doesn't failure to sleep make people insane? Dammit." I sighed, glancing down at my study coach. "That was supposed to have been my inside voice."

"It happens to people who are overtired." She shrugged. "Be prepared for more of the same as time goes by."

The door opened on another generically painted dorm hallway. Even though dorms at PPC were renovated Edwardian buildings, they kept them simple and easy to clean with durable things like paint, fixtures, and furniture. We walked down to the end of the hall, where Lynn turned right and opened the door to room 566.

"Huh." I blinked sleepily at the two beds, only one made up. Lynn put her backpack on the messy one with the plain green plaid comforter and sheets. The other was much girlier, with a lacy coverlet in black and even some throw pillows that would have been at home in my grandmother's parlor if she'd been a Goth. "There's a roommate, but there isn't. I think you were talking to her in the dining hall, too. It smells like jasmine and myrrh in here."

"I hope she isn't sometimes dead like the cat in that crazy guy's theory." She sat in the chair in front of the desk, which was the opposite of her bed in the tidiness department. That was the only neat thing on her side of the room. It looked like a shrine to studying, with neat stacks of Post-it notes and index cards, one cup of highlighters and another of Sharpies. Lynn even had a dictionary, a thesaurus, and an MLA style handbook in a cubby. There was a wall-mounted stand for a laptop, which she removed from her backpack and hooked up. In contrast, the roommate's desk was bare except for a silver-embossed sketchbook.

"Think fast!" At the sound of Lynn's voice, I reached out, plucking a thick stack of rubber-banded index cards from the air. A sting on my pinkie made me wince. The hibernation urge had me off my game. Usually, I could catch just about anything in human form, and most things in bear. That was another thing I wouldn't be able to do this weekend—let my bear out.

"What are these?" I blinked my bleary eyes. The top card had one word on it, but the wide band across the middle blocked too much of it to read.

"My Ecology flashcards." She switched on and moved a wireless mouse, waking up her laptop. Then, she pulled open a drawer to reveal a USB keyboard. She plugged it into a port, then pulled up an audio app. "Shuffle them."

"Why do we need those if you're setting up your computer?" I sat on the bed to use the nightstand as a card shuffling surface.

"Study aids." Lynn looked over her shoulder and smiled. "I've got all kinds. Trust me, I'm a Valedictorian." She dropped a wink, and I laughed.

"Can you get more specific for the sleep-deprived among us?" I pulled the band off the cards carefully so they wouldn't go flying.

"This music ought to help keep us awake." I couldn't help but sigh with relief. Study tunes were like a last-minute pardon from listening to recordings of Watkins' lectures. With a few sweeps and clicks, a wailing voice backed by heavy metal thunder poured out of her speakers. I recognized it.

"Iron Maiden?" I had to think for a moment before trying to shuffle them. There were so many, I had to split the deck a few times and shuffle the sections. These cards were serious business. Once they'd been thoroughly mixed, I gathered them together and held them out to Lynn.

"When you want to stay awake, there's nothing quite like music that chases down your eardrums like a hellhound." She took the flashcards back from me and smiled. "Let's do this!"

And we did. We studied all night, only taking bathroom and vending machine breaks. Once the sky lightened, Lynn and I took turns washing up. The dorms had disposable toothbrushes in the medicine cabinets, thank goodness. I wasn't sure I'd be able to stop by my room without lying down. When I got back, Lynn had gathered all the books and cards. I grabbed my bag and got ready to leave.

CHAPTER SIX

Lynn

After we shuffled out of the room, I locked the door and followed Bobby down the hall. The sleep deprivation had me light-headed. For a moment, I imagined I could sail right out the window at the end of the hall and float to the dining hall. Some shifters and a few Extrahuman types could have actually done that. I, however, was just an earthbound human.

"Ye canna change the laws of physics, Jim." I rolled my eyes. "Stupid inside voice."

"Ha!" Bobby's laugh started as a bark but unfurled into something rolling in the deeps. It wasn't exactly contagious but damn was it good to hear something so genuine. "Blaine owes me ten bucks."

"When did you have time to make a bet with Trogdor the Burninator?" The elevator dinged at the end of my joke. "Ding, joke's done." We snorted together.

"I texted him when you took a bathroom break, what was it, like four-thirty?" He followed me into the elevator. "I told him you had a geek streak. Anyway, he accused me of bragging, and that was how the wager happened. He bet you were a one-franchise pony. I told him he was being an ass and would owe me ten bucks."

"I'm not a pony at all. I'm Lynn Frampton. But I'm not from Kansas, pal, so I ain't taking you to see a wizard." My mouth was running. Too bad I didn't have the energy to go out and catch it.

"You're cute when you're punchy." He put his hand on the fake wood panel behind me, leaning forward. "Champion studier and heroic tutor, too. I could kiss you."

For once, I couldn't say a word. Even my inside voice had shut up. He leaned in closer, tilting his head to one side. When his lips brushed mine, I thought maybe I was dreaming. The alarm on my phone would go off at any second, breaking the illusion that a guy as sweet and hot as Bobby Tremain would do anything with a mouth like mine besides cover his ears and run.

It didn't. He was still kissing me, but he'd stop if I didn't give him a clue I enjoyed it. Maybe it'd be better for him if he did. Some memory I couldn't quite put my finger on banished that thought from my mind. I tilted my head up, increasing the pressure between our lips, and raised one hand to stroke the strong line of his stubbled jaw.

One of his arms circled my waist, hugging me closer. I felt his firm torso press against mine, increasing my heart rate like I'd gone for a jog. The exhale that had started as a sigh morphed into a moan as his lips parted, tongue tasting my lips. I might not have been on many dates, but I'd done plenty of kissing, and even a respectable amount of necking. Usually punctuated by slaps or laughter, but maybe this time would be different. A girl can dream, right?

Bobby's other arm went behind my shoulders, supporting me as he pulled me even closer than before. His hand stroked my hair, which I'd brushed, thank goodness. I felt like the inside of a lava lamp, except a billion times sexier. I finally understood the appeal of that old Aerosmith song. We were pressed against each other in the middle of the elevator when it dinged again, opening.

"Oh, my GAWD!" A feminine giggle followed the strong New England accent. "Bobby Tremain the hibernator's been up all night with a girl?"

Bobby broke off our kiss, a growl starting deep in his throat. I turned my head to see a tall blonde punching a code into the vending machine, buxom up top, with skinny arms and legs. She clapped her hands excitedly, a smile with fluorescent wattage catching us in its harsh and unwelcome glow. In a second, Bobby let go of me and rushed out of the elevator, his stubble looking thicker than it had just a moment before.

"Stop that charge, Padawan!" The volume of my voice startled me. So did its confidence. Being kissed like that must be some kind of courage tonic. Maybe I actually *had* been to see a wizard. "No mauling the mall rat."

"Well, he could have tried to maul me." The blonde laughed, not unkindly this time. "I'm Jeannie, RA on Bobby's floor." She brushed past him, holding her hand out. I stood there shocked until the elevator started closing on me, then shouldered through.

"Hi, Jeannie." I grabbed her hand and let her pump our clasped mitts up and down three times. "Lynn."

"Oh, the human majoring in Alternative Therapies! I think that's awesome." She smiled. "I'm a bear shifter too, by the way."

"Cool." I kept my mouth in a straight line. Even though the situation was silly and my punchiness meant more snark on the Frampton Scale, I had something serious to say. "So, Jeannie. Since you're a bear shifter, can you tell me why you think Bobby's hibernation is funny? You know he could flunk his exams all the way out of this school, right?"

It was Jeannie's turn to stand there like a mannequin. She blinked a few times, reminding me for all the world of a deer caught in the middle of the road instead of a bear. Or Bear-shifter Barbie. I tapped my foot in a slow-motion expression of mock impatience, waiting for her answer. The elevator closed behind me, its ding interrupting nothing at all for once.

"I, um… Well, I guess…" Her lower lip jerked a few times, revealing bottom teeth like a white picket fence. "I guess it's not so funny. I'm sorry, Bobby."

"Um, it's okay." Bobby blinked at Jeannie, then at me. After that, he yawned so widely I saw tears at the corners of his eyes. "I knew Jeannie didn't mean anything by it."

"Come on. We should go do our morning coffee-summoning ritual." I held my hand out, and Bobby took it. As we left the building, I heard the whirr and thump of the vending machine behind us as Jeannie finally got her snack.

I might not have bear-shifter hearing, but her voice carried enough for me to hear her say, "Keep that one, Tremain."

Outside, the early morning sunlight still wasn't strong enough to give us snow-blind headaches. Even though I was used to lake-effect blizzards, this was ridiculous. I wondered whether it might be unnatural. Blaine had been right to check the almanacs. Maybe he should look again for more than just hibernation temperatures.

The dining hall had just opened, so there wasn't much more than cereal and beverages available. That was fine by me, of course. Cereal was my default food choice for any meal. I got a bowl and checked for spoons before pouring any milk. Plenty. I loaded my tray and turned, intending to find a table. I didn't need to.

"Hey, Blaine." I put my tray down across from him, plunking my bag of books on the floor.

"Spoons right away this time, nice." He hadn't looked up from his notes. I rolled my eyes even though he probably couldn't see them. *Dragons.* "So, I found some stuff last night. Want to hear about it?"

"Do kids like ice cream?" I took out my notebook, then had a few bites of my cereal. Bobby sat down next to me with coffees and a stack of Pop-tarts. He pushed a mug of deep-brown wakefulness in my direction and I raised it, saluting him before taking a much-needed sip. It was early enough not to taste burnt..

"Bear clans migrating north would make sure anyone too big to carry was an adult with a mate. Single bears did their family mate-seeking ceremony months ahead of time." Blaine grinned ruefully at Bobby, blinking slowly. Even with all the smoke trails last night, this was the first time Blaine had looked reptilian since I'd met him.

"Why?" Bobby didn't stop munching down Pop-tarts, just chewed harder. He didn't seem confused, just frustrated.

"Mates share a bond that helps them keep each other awake until it's safe to hibernate." Blaine sipped tawny liquid from a mug. I mistook a flutter of white at its side for a moth until I saw the string. Tea. The piquant aroma of bergamot wafted over. The dragon was drinking Earl Grey, hot.

"Oh." Now Bobby shrugged. "I can't do my family ceremony, if you can call it that. It's all about dreams, and falling asleep will defeat the purpose. There's no way to be completely sure who my mate is unless I take a vacation to Destination Dreamland, even if..." Bobby shut his mouth before he said anything else. Coffee must be reining in that inside voice . I drank as much as I could without burning my throat. I might need a little more brain filtering of my own soon.

"Yup. Mate's the only thing that can keep the sleep away or wake you up. You're S.O.L., my friend." Blaine shook his head, but I could see a flicker of mirth in the dragon shifter's eyes. "Almost."

"What do you mean by that, Trogdor?" I arched my eyebrow, trying to look more fierce than I felt. A deep yawn sank that effect like the Titanic.

"Wow, that's a jibe from the way-back machine, Frampton." He smiled. Bobby chuckled. I blinked. Back home, a remark like that would have ended with rolled eyes and an empty table. "Last night, I met a vampire."

"Well, go on." I twirled my spoon in a cranking motion, the universal sign for "Keep talking, you scaly jerk." I had to focus on Bobby's issue, not my own. "What's so special about a vampire?"

"He was a Psychic before he got turned. Makes memory amulets." Blaine reached for his tea, then leaned back in his seat. "I got you one last night. It'll remind you to stay the hell awake. It only works in one short burst, though, so you should only use it on exam day."

"If I make it that far." Bobby broke one of his Pop-tarts into pieces, not even taking a bite.

"You will. My new friend will bind the amulet to you later. He also said he'd help keep you company." Blaine spoke from behind his mug as though holding something back. I still didn't know as much about magical shifters as I should but remembered enough. Dragons weren't the shadiest shifters out there. That title belonged to the Tanuki. At least Blaine wasn't one of those. He meant to hide the cost, then. I wondered what he'd paid that vampire for a moment, then remembered how much money the Harcourts had.

"What's the name of this philanthropist?" I twirled my spoon in the cereal-sweetened milk dregs at the bottom of my bowl.

"Henry Baxter." Blaine handed the amulet to Bobby. "I'll introduce you all at sundown. Meet me at the library then, okay?"

"Okay." I yawned. "I need a nap before my last Anatomy lab practical practice session," I grinned. "Say that five times fast. Frail mortal over here needs a couple of Zs."

"Take some." Bobby's big hand covered one of my shoulders, rubbing gently. "I'll see you later."

"You sure he'll stay awake?" I glanced skeptically at him, then Blaine.

"I Dragon-Scout-Swear he will get no sleep in my company." Blaine held out one pinkie. I rolled my eyes but linked mine with his anyway. He let out a chuckle that sounded like a snort. Bobby's sleepy smile was worth a zillion Dragon-Scout pinkie-swears. "Fine, there's no such thing. But I won't let him sleep on my watch, or anywhere else either."

"Awesome." I got up, about to flip the cover back over my notebook. "Wait." I tore the uppermost page out and handed it to the dragon shifter. "I had a thought on the way over here about the storm. Might be nothing, but since your mate's probably an almanac, it could be fun to look into."

"Oh, this will be extracurricular. But you're right. Fun." Blaine folded the paper and stuck it in his notebook. "Later, Frampton."

"Bye, Lynn." Bobby stared at my lips. I leaned down and pressed them against his. Just before I turned to go, I caught the light of his huge grin. I dreamed about nothing but his smile and our kiss in the elevator until my alarm interrupted things just in time for lab.

CHAPTER SEVEN

Bobby

"Blaine?" The corners of my mouth still tilted up. There was definitely something that went both ways between Lynn and me, but I couldn't be sure what it was. I resisted the urge to snap my fingers in front of his face. "Blaine!"

"Huh?" He finally looked up from the almanac Lynn had joked about him being mated to. "What's up?"

"I have to talk to you about something." I still couldn't eat my breakfast, even with the grill sending the scent of eggs and bacon all over the place. My stomach growled, but my throat felt tight.

"Well, go ahead." He glanced up at me, then froze when our eyes met. "Wait." Blaine glanced around at the rapidly filling dining hall. "Is this a topic better left for a private conversation?"

"Yeah." I gestured at the frosted wreckage on my plate.

"Woah, you only ate half of those. Whatever it is must be serious, huh?" Blaine didn't wait for my nod. Instead, he gathered his scattered books and papers, sweeping them into his backpack. "Let's get out of here."

I followed him out of the dining hall and back across to the dorm, my feet dragging. The snowfall had left me a drowsy mess, but the weight of my thoughts that morning felt heavier than the four feet we'd gotten. I glanced down the way at the giant pile of snow and ice on the library overhang, but my shudder got cut short by a yawn. The urge to sleep had gotten stronger since Lynn left.

Once we were in our room, Blaine waved me away from my bed and my chair. He actually handed me a jump rope, the scaly jerk. I took it and stood in the middle of the room, wringing it in both hands as I got up the gumption to talk. Jumping rope might help me stay awake, but I couldn't bring myself to do it. The sudden rush of hot and cold anxiety worked well enough to pep me up, even if it kept my mouth shut.

"So, you spent the night with Lynn Frampton." The one time I could have dealt with Blaine dancing around a point, and he impaled the subject right on it. That maddening directness was probably for the best, though. "Is her mouth anything besides snarky?"

"Wow." I took a deep breath, the kind where you count to five. "All I did was kiss her."

"Yup, and then she kissed you when she thought I wasn't looking. I could tell." He tapped his nose. Sometimes I forgot Blaine's sense of smell was almost as good as mine. He waved his hand at me as though my nervousness was a PowerPoint slide. "And it's got you all worked up like this."

"Yeah." I shook my head, not in the negative, but to shake off the haze of sleep threatening to club me and drag me down until spring. "I thought she might slap me at first. Might have been better if she had."

"Huh." His face went blank like the window on a calculator. Blaine's thinking face looked like anything but. "Was this at the beginning of the evening or the end?"

"End." I twisted the jump rope more, wishing it was a long cord instead of beads on a rope. "Technically after sunup."

"Hmm." He rubbed his chin, and expression returned to his face like feeling to a waking limb. "Should have done it early. Then you would have had time to do the deed and see if your bear had the urge to claim her."

"Wait, what? No!" The urge to put my hands on my cheeks was strong, but I fought it. Bad enough I knew they were beet-red by then. Anyway, I didn't want to drop the stupid jump rope. Blaine had probably figured that in when he handed it to me. "I just met her yesterday. My momma raised me with manners."

"Mine did, too. Dragon manners." A wisp of white smoke trailed from one of his nostrils. "We're a pragmatic bunch, even when we're labyrinthine in our delivery. You need a miracle or a mate to get through this weekend. The memory amulet will help on exam day, but what about today and tomorrow? I'm betting a mate would make things way easier."

"Speaking of bets, you owe me that ten bucks." I still wasn't relaxed enough to crack a smile, but at least the muscles in my arms and hands had eased up.

"Which was it?" He pulled out his wallet, opened it, and tossed money on my desk.

"*Star Trek*." I closed my eyes, remembering her silly imitation. "She riffed on Scotty."

"See? She's perfect for you. Go upstairs now and bed her. What's the worst thing that could happen?"

I could think of a handful just off the top of my head. Some of them were good reasons, like the possibility that Lynn might not answer the door, or having to fight my bear while sleep-deprived. Blaine was being direct, so I decided to get right to the point of what bothered me.

"What if she doesn't want me?" I opened my eyes.

"That's just crazy talk, Bobby." Blaine puffed a faint smoke ring out of his mouth. "Human girls love shifters. They all want us. Look in a mirror. You're sex on legs, man."

"That ain't true." I shifted my weight from one foot to the other. It *was* true most of the time, but I'd never been comfortable with it. Sex shouldn't be something you did just because of how a person looked. I'd had my share of women hitting on me just for that, and I'd always said no. Without any feelings involved, sex just didn't excite me.

"Since when?" He glanced at me slyly. "How many human girls have turned you down?"

"None, but I don't…"

"No excuses, Bobby. You don't have the time or energy for them." I almost hated Blaine when he got like this, all single-minded. That kind of thinking would be dangerous to someone like Lynn, who from what I could tell, just wanted someone to care about her. I understood that all too well. So did my bear. He was so riled, I couldn't keep him down as far as I wanted.

"You listen here, Mr. Dragon Knows Best." I clenched my fists, the plastic beads on the jump rope creaking under the pressure of my fingers. "My dad's famous. If I wanted to just sex a girl up to run away from this problem, I'd pick one who's into that kind of thing. Trust me, I meet them every day. I could have a different girl every night if I wanted. You notice I've been single and home early all semester."

Blaine blinked, finally silent. The surrounding smoke thinned out, too. I waited. He was one of the smartest people I knew. He'd already made the connection. I was just standing by while his pride got out of his brain's way.

"Lynn's become different to you already." His face was composed, but his eyes blazed with draconic calculation. "Special?"

"Whatever I say, you'll twist it just like that." My bear's anger was up, and it wouldn't go down, no matter what I did. Blaine was implying I should do something that might hurt Lynn, not only physically but break her heart if I was wrong. I couldn't use words to convince Blaine he had a bad idea. He loved semantics too much. I let my bear have his way with my hands.

My fists clenched, twisting the jump rope one final time to send blue and white beads bouncing all over the room. Blaine's eyes darted from side to side, following them faster than even I could have. Dragons were magical shifters and had different abilities than the lion and tiger and bear types.

"I'm sorry, Bobby." Blaine sat perfectly still. "To be clear, I'm apologizing for pushing you, not for being who I am. I stand by my idea. It's what I'd do, but that doesn't mean it's the right strategy for you."

"Fine. Apology accepted." I looked down at the frayed hank of thin cord in my hand and the scattered beads on the floor. Just as I was about to pick them up, I yawned.

"There's really no other way your family has to figure out their mates besides dreaming or biting the bullet?" Blaine's eyebrows hunkered down in the middle of his forehead. I was glad to see him back in pondering mode.

"None that they've mentioned." I collected the bits of blue and white plastic, putting them next to the ten-dollar bill on my still-made bed. "I guess I could call and ask."

"Good idea." Blaine picked a few jump rope beads off himself and sent them soaring through the air to land next to the others. "You will spend a lot of time with her over the next few days. Get all the information you can."

"You're super-fixated on the idea of Lynn and me." I swept the bits of ruined jump rope into one hand and dumped them in the trash. "Why is that?"

"Just a hunch." He stood up, cracking his knuckles.

"Based on what?" I stuffed the money I'd won into my wallet, thinking I should have bet him twenty instead.

"Nothing concrete, unless I ask you a few questions. Nothing pushy, I promise. Is that okay?" He opened the closet and took out a basketball.

"Okay." As much as Blaine's arrogant delivery had gotten on my nerves, dragons were savvy shifters. Any clue would help, and I couldn't be picky about whether it came from my parents or my roommate.

"How many girls have you been around here in the illustrious halls of PPC?" He slung the hand towel he used at the gym over his shoulder.

"I don't even know, there were so many." Looked like Blaine

wanted to shoot hoops. I went to the closet to get my own towel. "Remember the first month? They wouldn't leave me alone."

"Yeah, I do. More than one tried to drag you upstairs at that house party." He gave me a pointed look. I hadn't gone to any off-campus parties after that. "And how many girls have you kissed since you came here?"

"Just Lynn." I sighed, remembering how her lips had tasted, and how her body felt pressed against mine. My bear had base urges, and while most women I'd met at school had tried their damnedest to play on them, he hadn't wanted any of them enough for me to give in.

"Look at yourself, man. You're all moony-eyed" He moved the door of the closet so I could see my reflection in the mirror on the back. I looked like a guy on the front of one of Momma's romance novels, gazing into the heroine's eyes.

"That tears it, then. It's time to call home." I pulled my phone out of my bag. "I'll meet you at the gym."

"No way." Blaine tucked the ball under one arm. "I pinkie-swore. My Dragon Scout honor is at stake here, Bobby." He opened the door, gesturing to the hall. "Call them on the way."

"Fine." Our room was on the first floor with the rest of the larger shifters on campus, so we didn't have to use the elevator. I think someone in the housing office had the idea that would help us get out in the open if we had a shifting emergency.

My feet crunched as I followed Blaine around a corner and down Hope Street. The urban campus meant PPC's larger buildings were spread out. At least Hope Street had been cleared better of snow than the side streets our dorms, classrooms, and dining hall were on. I tapped my phone, swiping to the house number. It rang a few times, then clicked as someone picked up. A long pause and a distinctly metallic creak told me it was Dad on the line.

"Bobby!" The lift on the last syllable told me he was glad to hear from me. I hadn't gotten him the last few times I'd called, so it had been a couple of weeks since we'd spoken.

"Hi, Dad." I'd needed to talk to him more than I'd originally thought. I took a deep breath of frigid air, vapor puffing out of my mouth like I was Blaine's cousin instead of his roommate. That was one northern novelty that never got old.

"Uh-oh." Dad's voice lowered, making me think everyone else at the house was still asleep. "This sounds like something serious. Let me wheel myself to the kitchen."

"Okay." I listened to a distant creak and squeak from his wheelchair, counting off the seconds I knew it'd take for him to get down the hall and away from the bedrooms.

"Go ahead, son." I heard running water in the background as he made coffee. Momma had redone the entire house just so he could get around. Before they married, she'd done historical renovations, but after Katrina, her work had turned more practical. She made nowhere near the amount Dad had while he was still fighting, but they were comfortable and had a solid retirement fund because of her. The medical bills had wiped out most of Dad's savings.

"Mom must have told you about the hibernation urge, right?" Last time I'd called had been the night the snow fell.

"Yup. Did that dragon friend of yours figure anything out?" I heard the coffee maker sputter then beep as it finished percolating.

"Actually, he needed help." I couldn't stop myself from smiling. "From a human. A girl, no less."

"That must have rankled." Dad chuckled. His tag-team partner had been a dragon shifter, so he knew their peculiarities well.

"Yeah, it did at first." I heard Blaine chuckle up ahead of me.

"Somehow, I don't think you're calling to let us know this is settled." A metallic clatter came over the line. I recognized the sound of him setting up coffee.

"No, because it isn't." I explained Lynn's theory and Blaine's, plus the potential solutions. "So, what I really need to ask is, do the Tremains have a way to be sure of their mate before making a claim? Mom's dreams won't help me since I can't sleep until after the exam."

"Shoot, son, you've got a situation on your hands." I heard the percolating drip of the coffeemaker in the background. "I bet that roommate of yours has already suggested you go full steam ahead and damn the torpedoes."

"Yeah." Blaine held the gym door open for me, and once inside, I shrugged off my jacket and hung it up. "I don't want to do that, though."

"Wait, you mean you don't want Lynn? She's the only girl you've talked about since Rochelle back in eleventh grade." Rochelle had been my only girlfriend. Her dad was famous too, but they'd moved away just before graduation.

"It's not that I don't want her. I think she's amazing. She's smart and funny. Got a good heart." I leaned against the whitewashed concrete wall. "But I bumped into her by accident, then hit her with a snowball when a werewolf dodged it. My bear felt horrible. If I do this and I'm wrong, she will get hurt. I don't think I could control my bear if that happened."

"Son, stop and think for a minute or five." I closed my eyes, imagining how Dad's face would look just then. The scar running down his left cheek was bone-deep, so the concerned frown I envisioned him wearing would scare anyone who didn't know him. Picturing it comforted me.

"Okay, but I need some help on which direction my thinker should take."

"How did I get myself saddled with this chair?"

"You pushed Momma out from in front of that truck. I still have no idea why you didn't move."

"It wasn't me who didn't move. It was my bear." Dad sighed. "He stayed there to fight that truck. I couldn't control him, because it was your mother, my mate, who was in danger. Do you understand, son?"

"But that was after fifteen years with her." He couldn't mean what I thought he did, could he?

"I'm going to have to agree with your pal Blaine. Give things a shot with this girl. I'd bet your bear's already sold."

"But Momma always says to wait for the dream."

"You want to know something about Momma she hasn't told you yet? You have to promise not to repeat it."

"Okay, Dad. I promise."

"She didn't wait. She had our mating dream the first night we met like she always says. The part she leaves out is, she had it wearing nothing but a blanket in the back of my pickup truck. With me right next to her." I heard him pause to sip coffee. "It was a crazy time for shifters back when we met. We couldn't court properly like our families did before the round-ups and registries. She only wants you to have what we didn't get, a chance to take your time and be prepared before starting your adult life. It's why we sent you to PPC even though we miss you like crazy."

"Wow, Dad." I wasn't sure what to say or how to talk more without my voice cracking. "Knowing the dire straits I'm in must be hard for you and Momma to deal with. I'm sorry."

"Listen, I didn't want to lay anything heavier on you than what you've already got going." He lowered his voice. "Anyway, you're the one in the situation. I trust you. You do what feels right for you and your bear. This is the time in your life where you need to find the balance you can both live with. You've got one hell of an urge messing with that, but believe me, you'll be stronger when it's over."

"Thanks." I heard Momma in the background, her patter on her cell with a client unmistakable. "I love you, Dad."

"Love you too, sonny boy. To the moon and back." I hung up with the man I admired most in the world.

Tucking the phone away in my hanging jacket, I turned around to find Blaine taking free shots at the human-height hoop. He got nothing but net, of course.

"Come on, Trogdor. Let's shoot some more appropriate baskets." I trotted across the polished wood, still slower than usual.

I was off my game the whole morning, not because of the hibernation urge, but because thinking about what I'd say to Lynn later took up most of my attention.

CHAPTER EIGHT

Lynn

After the lab practice session, I had to take a shower. Even though most of the stuff we had to identify was inside a jar or encased in a glass, the biology labs smelled like formaldehyde. After spending close to six hours in there, so did I.

I collected my basket of toiletries and headed for the bathroom, wondering why a magus or a psychic hadn't come up with some kind of scent charm or odor amulet to use in the labs. Maybe it was something they cast on themselves and not a location. They'd spent centuries hiding their existence, so why would they blow it by making formaldehyde smell like fresh linen?

For a moment, I thought I knew a magus I could ask, but her name and even what she looked like slipped my mind. At least I knew she was a Magus and not a Psychic, and a she and not a he. Maybe. And at least, I remembered where I knew her from. No, I didn't. I sighed, checking the water temperature before hanging up my robe and stepping under the hot spray.

The steam and wet surrounded me, relaxing shoulders sore from leaning over microscopes and black lab benches. I'd managed not to snark at any of my classmates by forgetting to talk. None of them bothered to try to speak to me, and I was too busy practicing identifying the supernatural creatures in jars. Okay, I had to admit to doing more thinking than I should have about Bobby. I didn't just remember that kiss in the elevator either, although that was definitely the main feature. His problem intertwined with my own. I couldn't be sure what his intentions were because of the hibernation drive. I'd been an idiot, kissing him in the dining hall like that. Blaine probably knew, even though I'd waited until he wasn't looking.

The extra lab practical study had given me something different to focus on, and it had also helped me realize I'd get bored back in Madison at a less challenging school. I was ahead of everyone else in the courses specific to my Alternative Therapies major. PPC was the best fit for me academically, but with the way things had gone socially, I still wasn't sure whether I could handle another three-and-a-half years. At least in Wisconsin, I'd go home to my family after classes. Even with sibling rivalry, I knew everyone there loved me. But in Wisconsin, there wouldn't be Professors like Watkins. There wouldn't be helper ghosts in the stacks and card catalog area. There wouldn't be Bobby.

I closed my eyes and rubbed mint-scented everything into my hair and over my body. A flush that had nothing to do with the water temperature made me wonder what Bobby would think of minty me. That morning, I'd only had time to brush my teeth before he kissed me. I'd see him at dinner when we met with Blaine's psychic vampire contact. I blinked, then rinsed my face. Blaine hadn't called Henry Baxter a friend. The dragon shifter was almost as sarcastic as me, and way more arrogant.

Did he have it easier, being a guy? Did he just not care as much about what people thought? Probably the latter. Being a billionaire who was able to turn into a dragon the size of a Little League field had to do something for one's confidence. Same thing probably went for being able to turn into a bear. If I left, I'd never get to see

Bobby do that. I'd always wonder what he would have looked like shifted. Even worse, whether anything might have happened between us.

I thought I shouldn't wonder anything about Bobby Tremain, though. The water went cold, so I got out, wrapping one towel around my head and drying my body with the other. Oddly enough, I used less lotion here than back home. Rhode Island was cold but more humid than Wisconsin. Maybe there were other differences I hadn't noticed right away, but hope was the heart-killer, worse than fear. That notable hadn't been able to kill my mind yet, and my name wasn't even Paul Muad'dib. A knock at the bathroom door was the executive deciding for me to dry my hair in my room. I opened the door and almost walked into Jeannie.

"Um, hi." I tried to shoulder by, wondering why she couldn't just use the bathroom on the first floor. Her first words told me there wasn't a janitorial emergency on the ground level after all.

"Can we talk?" I realized her usual grin had gotten bigger. It had the opposite effect of what she might have intended, more like baring her teeth than smiling.

"Depends." I took evasive action, but she countered it. Time to raise shields and try to survive the photon torpedoes.

"About?" That grin was giving me nightmarish flashbacks to all the times Aunt Sally had made me watch Miss America pageants. She always cried at the end.

"Will you stop blocking me from getting back in my room to keep an important appointment with my hair straightener?" I held up the small appliance that I couldn't imagine living without anywhere the temperature got below freezing. Frozen hair was no fun.

"Oh." She looked up at my terrycloth-turbaned head as though she hadn't noticed it before. "Sorry." Jeannie stepped aside, but I had a feeling she wouldn't leave me alone. I was never that lucky.

Stalking down the hall, the backs of my slippers thwacked against the tiled floor. I heard Jeannie's sneakers squeaking slightly as she followed. I walked through the open door and just left it open. She could find her own way in if she dared. Yeah, I'm rude when someone leaves me standing in a drafty bathroom doorway with wet hair. Sue me.

I went about the business of hanging up my towel and plugging in my straightener, waiting for it to warm and for her to speak. She didn't. Instead, she looked at the Goth decor on the other side of the room from my bed. I took a few minutes to look at it too until I remembered a bit about the girl behind the name inked on the dry erase board.

"That's my roommate's. Apparently, she's stuck in the 1980s." I brushed my hair as I waited for the wet-to-dry flat iron to heat. Did I mention that device was nothing short of a hair-drying miracle?

"You have a roommate?" She blinked, reminding me for all the world of those creepy dolls that shut their eyes when you put them on their backs. That was a step up from Barbie, at least. And yeah, I had hated Barbie growing up. I used to give them pixie haircuts and dye their hair with Kool-Aid, a practice that had my mom smirking and left Aunt Sally pale with horror.

"Is it so odd to contemplate the fact that another person could tolerate living with me or something?" I winced as I found out first-hand that my beauty appliance was ready. Maybe it had bitten me on purpose. A side-effect of the hypocrisy of extolling a grooming device while hating pageants and fashion dolls, perhaps?

"No." She looked at a sign on the wall above my desk. "Maddie May, Umbral magus. I've never heard of her."

"Most people haven't." I blew on my finger and grabbed a section of hair to dry. "It's nothing personal or intentional, she says."

"Yeah, that's kind of their thing, being unmemorable." Jeannie's mouth wore a smug little smile, as though her thing, whatever it might be, was better.

"Better than being remembered as a mega-bitch." I shrugged and rolled my eyes. By then, I'd remembered that Maddie was a nice person and my only friend here. Jeannie wasn't getting away with playing the Mean Girl in this room while it was still mine.

"Wow. Is that really what you think?" Jeannie put her hands on her hips. "Look, I came to talk to you about that, maybe."

"Memories or mega-bitches?" I tilted my head so I could glare directly into her eyes. "Probably the latter, right?" I figured her for the kind of girl who'd love to talk about herself, not me.

"Neither. Being remembered, actually." She dropped her hands to her sides. "I'm an RA, and I just saw the housing withdrawal form you submitted yesterday. That's why I'm here."

"Oh?" I patted my hair, then switched the iron to the side that was still wet. "Is there a problem with my form?"

"No, mostly just a question, because you didn't fill out the optional section." She took a deep breath. "Are you moving off-campus or leaving PPC?"

"Do you even know what 'optional' means?" She was in college, so yeah. That was definitely sarcasm. Wouldn't stop me from rolling on the floor laughing if it happened to be true. The RA looked like the girls who used to sit behind me and put gum in my hair during class.

"Wow, you really *are* as sarcastic as people say." Jeannie shook her head, but all the plastic had gone out of her face along with her smile. The corners of her mouth tilted down, and her eyebrows slanted instead of making golden arches. That weary expression looked almost genuine, but it might also just be resting bitch-face. Maybe she wasn't a bitch at all, and that was the best Jeannie could do.

"Of course, I do. But after meeting you this morning, I just had to try to find out."

"Why?" I blinked, trying to keep the rest of my face still to conceal my surprise. But Jeannie was a bear shifter. She probably smelled that on me, anyway. If so, she gave no indication.

"Because if you're leaving, there's something I want to say to you, and there're only a few days left." Her sigh was heavy and lower-pitched than I would have guessed.

"Well, okay, then. I'm not telling you the reason I have for submitting that form, so pick one and run with it." Reaching around the back of my head to get the last wet section, I twisted my arms awkwardly. "I'm a firm believer in just saying what's on your mind."

Jeannie turned to face the door. Her face got that Barbie doll look back, and her posture stiffened. She reminded me of a knight putting on armor instead of a woman whose biggest achievement in high school had probably been Homecoming Queen. She put her hand on the knob and turned it, but hesitated before pulling it open.

"My family and Bobby's go back a long way. We all went down to help the Tremains after his dad's accident. He's had it hard enough." She glanced over her shoulder. "So help me, if you break his heart…" She pressed her lips together, narrowing her eyes, the threat unfinished.

I stared wide-eyed at her face, for once stuck without a barb to throw in her general direction. Either Jeannie was mistaken, or I was. Occam's Razor had been one of my signature pieces of philosophy since I heard Spock quote Sherlock Holmes in *Star Trek VI*. She'd known him for years. I'd known Bobby for less than two days. If Jeannie thought he cared for me and I didn't, she was more likely to be correct.

"Okay." I put the flat iron down, no longer caring about the damp patch on the back of my head. "I'll do the best I can, being a sarcastic shrew and all."

Jeannie's whole face changed when she smiled this time. She didn't remind me of a Barbie doll anymore, or a pageant contestant, or even a Homecoming Queen. It was like watching a frightened cat finally approach, still unsure whether the outstretched hand in front of her meant ear scratches or being stuffed into a carrier bound for the vet. Jeannie got misunderstood too, just as much as I did, but for different reasons. She pulled open the door and let herself into the hall without further comment, closing the door gently.

Out the window, the sky faded to deep blue as the rest of the daylight ran out. I hurried through dressing, my disbelief at Jeannie's words still in evidence as I pulled on flannel-lined jeans and a bulky fleece top. Shrugging into my jacket and backpack took almost no time at all. I avoided the elevator because I had loads of energy to burn all of a sudden.

Outside, the snowbanks still loomed over me, slightly higher than my head. I navigated them with the cautious confidence of a girl born and raised in winter's natural habitat. These Rhode Islanders liked to freak out, stripping the shelves in every corner market of bread and milk. I'd seen worse. Maybe that was why I stopped and called to the clear, frigid sky above the precarious snow pile on the library overhang, "Do your worst, weatherman!"

I had no idea how bad it could get.

CHAPTER NINE

Bobby

"Are you sure that'll work?" The amulet seemed like the better bet. I believed Blaine, but not the vampire I still hadn't met. "I mean, the guy's not even licensed."

"Licenses are new for this kind of thing." Blaine twirled the straw in his soda. "Henry's been in business since the 1980s, before he even got turned. He helped my mom, two of my uncles, my cousin, and a complete and utter bastard I knew back in prep school. He's legit."

"If the Harcourts are doing it, so should I is what you're saying." I sighed, leaning my head on my hand.

"Oh, Henry's amulets are all the rage in Newport." Blaine winked, then blew bubbles through his straw. I was still amazed that a guy who could turn into a dragon big enough to take up the whole dining hall could act like such a kid. I wondered how many years he'd been alive. Surely dragons had to age differently than most other shifters. They might as well be immortal like their counterparts the Tanuki.

"Well, if everybody in Newport's doing it, then so will I." A low and muffled growl came from my midsection. "I really should eat something before he shows up, though. I don't think I could bear it."

"Ugh, I think that joke's more rotten than a petrified egg." Blaine wrinkled his nose as though the pun had actually smelled bad. "But anyway, good call on the food tip. You have to say a few words during the binding process, and it'd be best if that empty pit you call a stomach doesn't chime in with its own opinion."

I rolled my eyes and got up, practically knocking Lynn over as I stood. Instead of some sour and cranky quip, she blushed to the roots of her hair. I stood there blinking, wondering why she smelled different than before. When she licked her lips, I got it. This was Lynn swooning. Also freshly showered and rested. I smiled, couldn't help it. I was just that happy to see her.

She sat down before I could act on my bear's impulse to crush her to my chest in a public display of something that felt two sizes too big to be affection. Maybe Dad and Blaine were right. Either way, I'd do my damnedest to find out one way or the other tonight. My stomach growled again.

"Get some food you can eat while studying, bear-man." Lynn plunked a book on the table, cracking it open. "Ecology. Just because we're on vampire time doesn't mean we should slack off on your exam cram. Now go."

"You heard the lady," Blaine added a dollop of smirk to this new and improved wink.

I went. This time, there wasn't any bacon or salmon. I had to make do with cheeseburgers. A kid I remembered was some kind of feline shifter stood ahead of me at the grill, chewing his lower lip. The Changeling behind the counter, Seelie by his scent, wore a cruel little grin.

"No, I won't say it." The kid's arms and fists clenched tightly as he struggled to control his cat. PPC's buildings were reinforced to withstand shifter strength, but out-of-control shifting indoors would definitely get the kid in trouble even if he wasn't a large cat.

"If you don't, your food goes in the trash." I recognized a bully when I saw one. He still hadn't noticed me, so I stepped closer, leaning on the rail next to the kid.

"Is this going to take much longer?" I looked at the clock on the wall. "I've got a study date."

"Oh. Um, no." Now that there was a witness, the cafeteria Changeling backed off. He handed a plate with a cheeseburger and fries to the waiting kid. I gave him my order, and it was in my hands in record time. Someone tugged my sleeve halfway back to our table.

"Hey, thanks. I'm Tony. I owe you one." He put his hand out, so I shook it.

"Bobby." I yawned. "You don't owe me anything."

"No, man, I do. Not that a meowing shifter will be much help to someone like you." He touched his nose. "I can tell you're a bear."

"The nose knows." I tried to smile but only blinked sleepily. "What was his problem, anyway?"

"He thinks it's funny to make me act like I belong in an Internet meme." Tony rolled his eyes. "Anyway, I'll make it up to you if I see a chance. It's a cat thing. We don't like karma sitting so long it gets stale." I thought it sounded more like a Faerie thing, actually, but didn't comment. The only feline shifter I'd met before was a lion, and Tony didn't smell like anything so large. For all I knew, there was some kind of honor amongst smaller cats I hadn't heard about.

"You seriously shouldn't feel obligated, but I understand." I waved as I headed back to the table, feeling more awake as I sat across from Lynn.

The textbook she held out toward me had the distinction of turning what should be an interesting subject into a bland list of facts. A rainbow of neon-colored post-it notes graced the pages. One had a naughty mnemonic I learned the night before. Another, a doodle of Professor Watkins getting bound up in a spider web. I opened my mouth to yawn, but a laugh came out.

"Oh, this is awesome." I pointed at a yellow note with the words *Wake Up* underlined three times. "When did you find time to do all this?"

"These are the notes I usually make. I added that one while you got food." Lynn grinned.

"Huh." Blaine raised an eyebrow as he leaned to peek at the book. "No wonder you remember everything, Frampton. Your snark's good for something besides entertaining the witless masses."

"Huh?" She looked genuinely puzzled, as if she had no idea anyone thought she was a riot and a half. "What's that supposed to mean, Trogdor?"

Blaine chuckled and opened his mouth to answer, but he closed it almost right away. I didn't have to wonder why. I knew a vampire when I smelled one. I looked over my shoulder to see what Henry Baxter looked like.

He stood about a head shorter than Blaine, with dark hair and light eyes. Pale, of course, and he'd been turned in what looked like his late 20s. His leather jacket was open even though he'd just come in from outside. It was vintage, from the late 70s and punk. Vampires didn't put on outerwear because they needed to stay warm. Some did it to blend in, others out of habit. Mom knew a few whose clothes all had historical or sentimental value. I couldn't tell which Henry was, only that he continued to stand there, a little between and behind Blaine and me .

"Hi, there." Lynn's genuine smile surprised me. "Please, sit and join us."

"Thanks." Henry sat down in the remaining chair across from me. "You have no idea how many people don't understand about the invitation thing."

"Does this mean you can sit with us at any time now?" I didn't find Henry particularly scary as far as vampires went, but I was a little shaky on the exact rules. I couldn't tell whether he was being serious or pulling my leg.

"Nope." He jerked his chin at Lynn. "Just where she is. So, you're the one who's got to remember to stay awake for an exam?"

"Yeah." As if to prove my point, I yawned. "Hibernation urge. I have to pass that exam, or I'm out of here. I'll try anything at this point, even though it's hard to believe a memory amulet's going to help."

"They actually do quite a bit." Henry pulled a coin on a lanyard out of the inside pocket of his jacket. "I put memories of things that wake people up in here. Stuff like the smell of coffee, cold water in the face, fire alarms going off, whatever. Once I attune it to you, that stuff hits when you activate it. One like this will only last about an hour, but that ought to do it."

"Hold on a minute." Lynn sat back and raised an eyebrow. "They check for memory amulets at exams. How will yours pass that?"

"The proctors will look at it, but since I don't think Ecology covers hot coffee, they'll let it through. Blaine told me the subject so I can steer clear of anything they might find hinky. Also, there's this." Henry handed Lynn a small yellow paper.

"Ah. Registry slip." She nodded. "Part of the reason you're here, right?"

"Yeah. Johnny Law doesn't care that I've been making and selling these since before I got turned." The left side of his mouth pulled up in a lopsided grin. "Gotta learn all the red tape and yellow slips if I want to stay in business." He turned back to me. "You okay with this?"

"Sure." My stomach growled. "Uh, mind if I eat a burger or three first?"

"Knock yourself out. I still have to put the memories in before we do the binding." Henry palmed the amulet, closing his eyes and his fist around it. Then he held it up to his forehead and took a deep breath he didn't need.

"Why'd he breathe, do you think?" I didn't bother whispering my question to Blaine. Henry would hear me anyway, and whispering was hard to pull off with a mouthful of burger.

"All vampires with special powers had them before they turned." Blaine was the closest thing to an expert on the undead I knew. I wondered whether they counted as artifacts from his perspective. "I bet whoever helped him train his psychic ability did it with deep breathing exercises while he still needed air. He's been a Psychic longer than he's been a vampire, remember."

I wondered exactly how long he'd had the memory power and if so, whether it was the reason he'd been turned. Even though Mama knew a few vampires, she'd never asked them such personal questions. But I was at PPC to learn. Maybe I'd find out if I managed not to sleep all spring. I reached for another burger, not realizing I'd finished them already. Lynn handed me a paper cup with a straw. I took a sip and nearly dropped it at the unexpected contents.

"What's this?" I tried not to splutter too much around the question. Still, I stuck my tongue out after asking. Just couldn't help it.

"Iced coffee." Lynn's eyes flicked back and forth across lines of text. "Black, no sugar. You can't afford a crash."

"I'm cool with no sugar, but iced? Seriously?" I shook my head. "It's in the teens out there, snow higher than your head all over everything, and you Yankees drink iced coffee?"

"Yup." Blaine eyed my cup. "It's New England. If it was in the twenties, I might have worn shorts. Flip-flops, even. But not with socks. I do have *some* taste, you know." He grinned at my shudder. "If you're not going to drink that, give it here."

"No, I'll drink it." I took another pull on the straw and felt my eyes squint reflexively. It was that weird. Anyone who'd grown up in a subtropical climate would agree with me. "When in Rome, and all that jazz."

The coffee wasn't bad, just strange, even though I drank it in a heated building. I pictured Blaine in shorts and flip-flops, drinking one of these while smoke trailed behind him from his nose in the snow. So much was different here from back home, but just like the coffee, I went along with it.

Different was good. It meant I was awake and thinking instead of sleeping in the basement or a snowbank. No matter how good that sounded, I had to resist that desire. I looked over at Lynn. Now there was one temptation I could pursue. My bear wanted her enough to shut up about sleep for a while.

"Okay, it's done." Henry had his hand in the middle of the table between us, the coin on a string sitting flat in the center. "Just put your hand over mine like we're doing a secret handshake or something. Then repeat the first and last phrases I speak after me."

I nodded, then clasped his hand. It was the same temperature as the air in the room. The coin was cold, though, in an invigorating way. Henry gripped my hand in his, harder than I expected. Vampires have extra strength, but not as much as the bigger shifters. Maybe his psychic powers had something to do with that. He closed his eyes again.

"*Tempus fugit, non autem memoria.*" I mimicked him, then let him continue. "One time, for one hour, Bobby Tremain will remember things that keep him awake when he invokes this amulet. No other memories are stored in here, and once used, it crumbles. *Pulvis memento est.*"

"*Pulvis memento est.*" The coin warmed against my palm as Henry opened his eyes. He turned our hands until mine was on the bottom, then let go.

"You're all set." He rubbed his temples with his fingertips. "When you want to use it, just say that last bit again—*pulvis memento est.*"

"What's that mean?" I thought I should know, but couldn't place it. I put it around my neck.

"This memory is dust, basically." He shrugged, cutting his eyes away so no one at the table could meet his gaze. "I don't know Latin. It's just what they told me to use as an apprentice."

"But it'll still work, right?" Blaine elbowed me. "Sorry if that was rude or whatever, Henry."

"It's cool. Exact words don't matter for Psychics. It's all about the focus, and words in a language I don't understand let my mind do its thing without distraction." He smiled but stopped almost right away when Lynn gasped at the sight of his fangs. "Now it's my turn to apologize."

"No, it's okay." She took a deep breath, then let it out. "I've just never seen them before. I'd better get used to it."

"She's the first human majoring in Alternative Therapies." I patted her shoulder, watching her face for a reaction. She blushed a little, then smiled.

"Oh, wow." Henry blinked. "I knew there was one, but I never thought we'd actually meet. It's a big step, you know. Means a lot in the circles I used to run with that someone like you cares enough to want to help Extrahumans."

"Yeah, Lynn's got a big heart under all that sarcasm. No one else wanted to help a sleepy bear shifter pass an exam." A trail of smoke rose over Blaine's head. "Well, except for my nosy roommate."

"I'd love to stay and chat with you more, but I have another amulet to work on. It has to last the whole inter-session. It's taking a ton of preparation, and I need to get back on it. You can meet me at the Nocturnal Lounge later if you need help to stay awake tonight. I'll be working the whole time, but at least your friends can get some shut-eye. Good luck with your exam, Bobby. Looks like you've got it in spades everywhere else." Henry didn't seem like the type to wink, but he did.

"Yeah, I am. And thanks. I'll probably take you up on that offer of some company later." I watched Henry leave. "Blaine, how much did this thing cost you?"

"Oh, I got a terrific deal." He smiled like the cat who caught the canary. "I just owe him a favor sometime."

"I don't have to tell you to be careful with that, right, Blaine?" It was Lynn's turn to yawn. "Faeries are scarier about their favors than vampires, but--" She shrugged.

"No. I'll handle it when the time comes." He peered at her. "How long was your nap?"

"Like an hour." She yawned again, folded her arms, and rested her chin on them.

"You go get some sleep." Blaine thrummed his fingers on the table. "I will, too. Henry really seems to like you, Bobby. The Nocturnal Lounge is exclusively for the Night School students. They can only bring in one guest."

"You shouldn't be surprised, Blaine." Lynn lifted her head and rubbed her eyes. "He's a likable guy."

"That he is." Blaine flared his nostrils but no smoke wafted out. "You're not walking back to the dorm alone, Lynn. It's not safe in the dark with the ice and how tired you are. You're shorter than the snowbanks." Blaine's smirk was pretty weak, but I figured he was tired, too.

"I'll walk her all the way back to her room and meet you in the lobby later, Blaine." Standing, I closed her books and put them away in her backpack.

"I won't let him fall asleep." Lynn rubbed her eyes and reached for her bag. I offered her my arm instead. She took it, blushing again. I could get used to that. "Dragon-Scout swear."

They chuckled together as they linked pinkies. I looked over my shoulder, expecting Blaine to drop a wink. He didn't. Instead, his gaze locked on a spot to the left of Lynn's head. He looked more worried than I'd seen him since the time his parents announced a visit. I shut out any speculations and focused on being with Lynn. I could ask Blaine what had him spooked later.

CHAPTER TEN

Lynn

When the elevator doors closed in front of us, I almost expected Bobby to pull away. He didn't, instead, wrapping his arms around me and leaning forward to put his forehead against mine. Behind me, he reached a hand up and stroked my hair. I barely dared to breathe, wondering whether he'd kiss me again. I wasn't sure he would but decided not to care about it for now.

"I need to ask you something, and I don't know how without sounding like a cad." Bobby's mood couldn't be deciphered by looking into his eyes, but they were too close for me to do more than try not to go cross-eyed. Maybe that was his intention.

"Don't worry about how you sound to me." The left side of my mouth tilted up. "I dish out so many plates of fresh insult and injury, I'd better learn how to take it. And for the record, I can't believe someone in the twenty-first century actually used the word 'cad.'"

"Okay, then." He took a deep breath. "I want to try to find my mate."

"Get your hands off me, or whoever she is will think you're taken." Bigmouth strikes again. Filterless Frampton was out in full force.

"That's the thing, Lynn." He blinked slowly, then stared into my eyes. "Ever since we met, I can't stop thinking about you. That hasn't happened to me ever. I want to see if you're my mate."

"I thought you said the only way to find out for sure is in a dream." There was no way I'd let him sleep, big blue eyes and sweet talk or no. He had to know that.

"It's the way my mom's side of the family knows, yes." He cleared his throat.

"But it's not the only way." I didn't need to ask. I'd been studying ahead and already knew. Any shifter's animal would come forward and try to claim a potential mate in the throes of passion. "You're propositioning me, then."

The elevator dinged, its doors shaking slightly as they opened on the fourth floor. A girl with white-blonde hair and wide amber eyes blinked at us, her hand covering her Cupid's bow mouth and beaky nose in a gesture too fast to be human.

"Hoo, boy! I'll take the stairs." She backed away from the elevator, then turned on her heel. The last thing I heard before the doors closed again was a muffled "Sorry," punctuated by the stomp of her booted feet.

Bobby threw his head back and let out a laugh. I joined in, unable to help myself. He leaned against the wall behind him, and I stumbled into his chest. I turned my head, laughing so hard tears that squeezed out of the corners of my eyes. Laughing like that felt very good; I couldn't even remember the last time I'd shared that kind of mirth with another person.

There was no way I could be Bobby's mate. He was much too special for the likes of me. But then I looked up at him through bleary laugh-tears. He was right there with me, sharing the moment fully. That heart-killer had me by the throat. Of course, I'd want to give in to it here in Rhode Island, where the state motto was the word "Hope" all by itself. I was a nerd, so I also knew where the motto came from.

Maybe "Hope we have as an anchor of the soul" wasn't just another phrase in the Bible. I let it in.

When the elevator opened again on my floor, we staggered out like a couple of sailors on dry land after months at sea. Bobby escorted me to my room, our laughter mingling all the way. My hysterics made it almost impossible to unhook my keys from my backpack. After I fumbled at them for the fourth time, Bobby picked up my entire pack, put the key in the lock, and turned it along with the whole heavy bag.

"You're gorgeous when you laugh." He pulled the key out of the lock. "All the time, actually. When we're alone, it's hard to resist touching you, even though I know all elevators open eventually."

"That's the last time we embrace in an elevator, then." I held out my arms, and he gently placed my backpack in them. "We shock too many people."

"Oh, but Olivia always looks shocked." Bobby held his still-shaking sides as though girding himself for another bout of hysterics. "She's an owl shifter."

"Wait?" I almost dropped my bag as I wheezed with more laughter. "She's an owl shifter? And she actually said 'Hoo, boy' to us?"

Bobby rubbed one hand down his face as though he could literally wipe the grin and the giggles off it. He nodded, cheeks reddening so much I thought he might be unable to give me a verbal answer.

I could watch him laugh all night, and laugh with him all night, too. I felt better about myself just then than I had in years. Reaching out, I opened the door to my room, pushing it wide and stepping through. I dropped my backpack on my chair, then turned around. Bobby had his back to me, one foot raised to walk down the hall.

"Wait, Bobby." I leaned in the doorway like I had at Mr. Watkins' lecture hall. "We have a conversation to finish."

When he turned, his face was almost back to its normal hue, except for some red over his cheekbones. He didn't speak, just let his gaze roam up and down my body. Eventually, he stopped at my eyes, staring at them as though he couldn't look anywhere else. His eyes weren't exactly blue anymore, but brighter and lighter. I realized that meant his bear was coming forward.

"No shifting." I tried to sound as stern as I had while laying the ground rules for the weekend on Friday. It came out in a breathy, needy tone I hadn't heard myself use before.

"Just so we're clear, I know what you're trying to do." I swallowed past the lump that had suddenly formed in my throat. "If you feel the urge to claim me, resist it. I like you, Bobby Tremain. I like you so much, I don't want you chained to someone like me unless you're sure."

"So you're letting me in?" He licked his lips.

I had about a million innuendo-laced answers to that question, but only one counted. I lifted my hands off the doorframe, feeling their slight clamminess as the air met my palms. It would have been so easy just to step back and nod or brush one of his fingers with mine, but Bobby deserved something more definitive than sarcasm and coyness. Maybe I did, too.

"Yes." I put one hand on either side of his face, thinking I'd pull him in for a kiss. The moment I touched him, he surged forward, mouth on mine as he literally swept me off my feet.

I wasn't sure how Bobby managed to close and lock the door behind us, but he did.. His kiss was hot and hungry, and completely different from the questioning exploration in the elevator that morning. His eyes silvered over in a hue that could only mean his inner bear was close to the surface. He was utterly gorgeous. I thought I'd melt into a puddle the next time he touched me, but I didn't. And he'd been right about not much talking going on.

Afterward, I expected him to roll out of bed, put his clothes on, and leave. Bobby did no such thing. Instead, he turned on his side next to me, throwing his arm across my body to cup my cheek in his hand. He turned my head toward him, fixing me with his gaze again. I didn't want to look away as I watched the silvery hue leave his eyes, replaced by that gorgeous blue. He ran his thumb just under my lower lip gently.

"I'm sorry, Lynn." He sighed.

"Wait, what? Why?" I blinked. "Believe me, you have nothing to be sorry for in my book. I don't even have one word of snark to throw."

"I'm not apologizing for everything that happened, just the end." He brushed a wisp of hair off my cheek.

"It's okay, Bobby," I smiled, covering his hand with one of mine. "I'm on the pill."

"Oh." He breathed out another sigh, this one more relieved than the last. "Well, that's not all I meant."

"I'm not sure we could have handled much more of that tonight anyway, lover-boy." I dropped him a wink. "We got no sleep last night, remember?"

"Well, you should get some while you can." He bit his lip, face going brighter red than should have been possible right after sex. "Oh, jeez, that's not what I meant either."

"I will, thanks, regardless of how you meant it." I couldn't have stopped my smile even if I'd wanted to. "You can't, though. We probably shouldn't even be cuddling. Too risky in the snooze department for you."

"I know." He sat up, giving me a nearly monolithic view of his torso. "Cold shower time for me, then it's hanging with Henry and the other Night School people."

"Hey, I wonder if Henry's the one working on Maddie's amulet for the inter-session."

"Wait, who?" Bobby scratched his head as he adjusted his own memory amulet.

"Maddie." I pointed at the whiteboard with my forgettable roommate's name. "Schrödinger's roommate, remember?"

"Barely." Bobby looked down at me. "You're not just the smartest and most gorgeous woman I've met, but you're also amazing, Lynn. That's from my bear and me." He pulled on his jeans, then found his shirt in the pile of clothes. "I don't like leaving you after something so intense."

"I'm a big girl Bobby." Smiling, I enjoyed the view even more from the new perspective. "Thank you." I yawned.

"You're thanking me?" He raised an eyebrow as he lowered his shirt.

"Yeah." I rolled onto my side, curling one hand under the pillow. "I thought sex was kinda boring before. Also, you make me feel like this place isn't so bad. Like maybe I'm not so bad." I yawned again. Was Bobby's hibernation contagious?

"I've never thought you were bad, not even by reputation." Bobby stepped into his boots and shrugged on his coat. "Intimidating, yes. Your roommate liking you speaks volumes, even if you don't remember her much."

"Really?" I blinked, trying not to fall asleep while he was still here.

"Yeah." Bobby pulled the sheet and comforter up over me, tucking me in. "Magi of any type sense bad vibes. If you were a bad person, the other half of the room would be empty. But of course, you know that, Study Master." He changed the "y" sound at the end of study so it rhymed with Jedi.

"Find some balance in your wakeful Force tonight, bear Padawan." I couldn't keep my eyes open anymore. "I'll see you tomorrow for more Ecology cramming."

"Sleep well, Lynn."

I heard the tap of his bootheels as he paced toward the door. I also thought I heard him say something under the sigh of the hinges as the door opened, then closed. Two syllables, maybe, but I couldn't make them out.

Before I could think about it anymore, I fell asleep.

CHAPTER ELEVEN

Bobby

I stopped by my room for a quick cold shower. My bear didn't want to sleep. He wanted me to go back upstairs and let him put a claiming mark on Lynn immediately. My mind and body wanted to go back up there, too, but not for claiming. If I gave in to those urges instead of making myself presentable for Henry and the other night denizens, I'd snooze until spring for sure.

Water pressure in the dorms was mostly a joke when you wanted a hot shower. Cold was another story. I'd taken the ice-bucket challenge back during high school, and this was almost as much of a shock to the system. Cold showers in Louisiana were tepid compared to the water blasting through the cold pipes in the old basement and walls. We had buildings down there as old as the ones up here, but the surrounding temperature made one devil of a difference.

I left the dorm with wet hair, feeling like I'd funneled espresso shots straight from the machine down at Blue State Coffee. Heading away from most of the campus, I went down to the old trolley tunnel off Thayer Street. I stepped inside, counted fifty paces, then rapped out a special knock. I smelled the change in the air that told me a door had opened, even if I couldn't see it happen. Once I saw a faint light, I entered.

The air changed again, losing that sour aroma tunnels in cities always seem to have. A much more pleasant scent of hot cocoa, coffee, and biscotti replaced it. The warm glow of incandescent lights rose slowly to just a touch above movie-theater dim. I walked up the stairs now that I could see them, all three flights.

I came out next to a cherrywood railing around a large, square room. Bookshelves lined the walls to my right, filled with volumes older than my grandparents, judging by the smell. So this was it—the Nocturnal Lounge in the PPC Student Union.

I walked down a half-flight of steps to get out of the mini library and into the lounge proper. Comfy couches and chairs sat next to tables of varying heights. None of the furniture matched, even though it was all antique and decently maintained. I followed my nose to the kitchenette in one corner, the source of the cocoa smell. An electric kettle heated the water I poured over one of the better brands of the powdered instant stuff. I added a splash of cream from the tea station, feeling like I might need more calories than I could get from the beverage and a handful of twice-baked almond biscotti. The cheeseburgers were a fond and distant memory to my stomach.

I hadn't seen Henry on my way in but knew he was there. Vampires had a distinct smell that Henry actually took pains to try to downplay. I wrinkled my nose, trying to figure out what he used to balance it. Vampires smell sort of like diabetics to a shifter, but more dried out if that makes any sense. Blaine called it "Eau de blood-sugar mummy."

I didn't worry one bit about Henry or any other registered vampire biting me either. They could use blood from pretty much anything that had it, but the laws said that they had to get it from bags at hospitals. From what I'd learned, they considered blood from any kind of shifter similar to drinking one of those Slimfast shakes. I reached for the tray of biscotti, my elbow bumping someone.

"Hey." It was a man's voice, familiar from somewhere, and recently.

"Hey, yourself." I turned my head to see Tony the cat shifter from the dining hall. "I didn't think cat shifters were nocturnal."

"We are when we're at school for Nocturnal History. We're circadian chameleons." Tony crunched a cookie, not even bothering to dunk it in his coffee. "Half my Professors are vampires. The other half are Lords or Ladies in the Goblin King's court."

"Huh. How's that going for you?" There were two Faerie courts, the Goblin King's and the Sidhe Queen's. Those two had been married way back before recorded history, but now they had enough issues to make a whole library's worth of graphic novels.

"Pretty decent." He stepped back and gave me room to grab a pile of pastry.

"I'd heard that's a tough crowd." I stirred my cocoa, trying to break down the clumps of powder before taking a sip.

"Not for me." Tony shrugged, lifting the right side of his mouth in a sly half-smile at the same time. "I've got some bonuses to my Charisma stat."

"Good on you for listening to the DM, then." I tried not to let my nostrils flare. There was something about Tony that made me think he was more than just a regular cat shifter, but I couldn't place it just by the smell.

"So what's a nice diurnal bear like you doing in this Den of Darkness?" Tony jerked his chin toward the center of the room. I hadn't noticed before, but the people I'd taken for human sharing the space with vampires and nocturnal shifters weren't. They all had a slightly spicy scent.

"Are they all Changelings?" I'd met a few in some of my required courses, but none of these in particular. Changelings were young faeries who hadn't grown into their power yet.

"Yup." Tony was a shifter too, so he knew what I meant. "These are the Unseelie ones. And I know you already met the other kind."

"You mean—" I cut myself off at Tony's wide-eyed stare. I could almost see a long, bristling tail behind him.

"No. Don't say the s-word in here." I hadn't seen anyone with skin as olive as Tony's get pale that fast before.

"Okay."

"Seriously, didn't anyone tell you they almost had an all-out war right in the middle of Water Place Park this past summer?" Tony leaned against the counter with a casual confidentiality that made me realize he knew more gossip than my old neighbor, Mrs. Biddie.

"No." I avoided the rumor mill like the plague, just in case I was on it. Tony might be a good guy to stay on good terms with. He seemed even more in the loop than Blaine, especially with the Night School.

"Well, I'll tell you about it some other time." He shuffled his left foot a few times, then placed it firmly back on the floor., making it clear the silence wasn't comfortable. I remembered his insistence that he owed me a favor. Maybe Tony would feel better if I asked him a question.

"Have you seen Henry Baxter?" I sipped my cocoa, grimacing as the silty crunch of what had to be the last powder clump scraped the roof of my mouth. "I'm here to meet him."

"Oh, he's up there." Tony waved vaguely at the bookshelf walkway I hadn't bothered circling all the way around.

"Thanks," I grinned, hesitating over the biscotti. "I don't particularly like this stuff, but it looks like it's all I'm likely to get at this hour."

"This is the Night School. It runs on a totally different schedule than the rest of PPC." Tony grinned. "All the Changelings have to eat, plus shifters like me. Meals show up here three times a night. Those cookies were just what was left from breakfast. Henry might not think to tell you, but the skeleton crew brings in pizza at low noon."

"'Low noon?'" I wasn't sure I wanted to ask what he meant by "the skeleton crew."

"It's what they call midnight in the Nocturnal Lounge." Tony's smile reminded me of that disappearing-reappearing cat who kind of helped Alice.

"There's a whole subculture here, patois and all, huh?"

"Yup." Tony grinned again. "Totally fascinating, and hanging out here is as educational for me as some of my lectures. But then, I'm the guy who decided to take four years out of his life to study it all. You can't exactly consider me an unbiased source."

"That's okay. You're my only source." I smiled, realizing I liked Tony almost as much as I liked Blaine. The cat shifter was a little dodgy, but also joyfully enthusiastic about being here. He smiled back, letting a little chuckle out under his breath.

"Nice as it is talking to you, Bobby, you should go and see Henry. Vampires can get absorbed in complex stuff like he's working on tonight. He's safe from the sun in here, but the staff gets kind of miffed if the vamps stay here all day too often."

"Thanks." I waved to Tony at the foot of the steps, then went up. I turned left to cover the area I hadn't gone through on my way from the door.

Henry sat at a long table that was most likely from the library before they renovated it. He was tinkering with what looked like a pocket watch on a long velvet ribbon, using tools that were definitely not for watchmakers. I approached slowly, shuffling my feet on purpose as I went. It was a bad idea to sneak up on a vampire, even if I was the opposite of prime rib to their palates.

"Hello, Bobby." Henry didn't look up. "It can't be low noon yet because you've got biscotti."

"Does that mean you're making good time on that project?" I sat in the chair across from him, setting my cocoa and snack down before taking out Lynn's Ecology flashcards.

"Nope." Henry sighed, dropping a piece of amethyst on the table and running his hand over the top of his head. "This is the mother of all memory charms. I'm not sure I can finish it without something that belongs to the person it's for."

"Can you call your client and ask?" What Henry was up to looked much different than what he'd done with the coin around my neck.

"I was hoping someone here knew her, but no such luck." He forgot himself and smiled full-on, showing his fangs. "Sorry."

"I turn into a huge bear." I smiled back. "Fangs don't bug me unless they come with a threat."

"Let me guess. Nobody wants to see us when we're angry?" Henry's grin was closed-lipped but his eyes twinkled.

I just laughed, continuing when he joined in right away. For an undead guy older than my dad, Henry was all right. More than that. He'd invited me here to help me even though he didn't have to do anything but make the amulet Blaine had paid for. I had good friends.

"Anyway, I have to ask because you run in different circles than I do. Have you ever heard of a girl named…" Henry pulled a piece of paper out of his shirt pocket. "Maddie May?"

"Um, no." My nose twitched with the scent of jasmine, myrrh, and charcoal. "Wait. That paper smells familiar. Can I see it for a sec?"

"Sure." He handed it over, and I sniffed it.

"This smells like something in Lynn's room, but I can't remember what." I handed the paper back to him. "Maybe there's no connection."

"Lynn Frampton?" Both of Henry's eyebrows went up, making his widow's peak appear more pronounced.

"Yup, that's the girl." I couldn't help myself. I sighed.

"Hmm. She was there with you at the dining hall earlier." Henry checked some notes in a leather-bound journal, then looked back at the brass circle in front of him.

"Yes. She was with me, all right." I surprised myself by letting out another wistful sigh instead of a yawn.

"Nice. She's a smart girl." Henry glanced up, looking me in the eye. "Also, my client's roommate." He flipped the paper over, showing me writing I hadn't bothered looking at. There was Lynn's name, right next to Maddie May's.

"She's asleep right now, but I have something." I pulled a pen out of the side pocket on my backpack. "I borrowed this from her desk last night. Not Lynn's. The girl's." I snapped my fingers, trying to think of the other girl's name. I'd just read that card and already couldn't remember it. "Your client."

"Wow, dude." Henry took the pen, holding it point-down over the bronze disk he'd been working on. "This is kismet, you know that? I owe you one."

"No way." I shook my head. "You're keeping me from hibernating and flunking out of school."

"Are you sure?" Henry raised an eyebrow. "Favors are kind of a big deal in nocturnal circles, you know."

"I know." I rolled my eyes. "Tony goes on and on about it. But just like a favor's a big deal to vampires and Fae, it's not one to bears. I've got to be me."

"I get that." Henry bent his head over the amulet again, pressing a seam along one side until it popped open. Then he held the pen against a piece of smoky quartz inside. "What I don't get is how you've managed to stay awake at all. It's been what, two nights since the snow?"

"You try sleeping while an angry dragon shifter blows smoke rings at your face all night. And Lynn's even more of a taskmaster than Professor Watkins."

"Ouch." Henry sounded like something had actually hurt him.

"What just happened?" I looked around and saw nothing but a book a little out of place on the shelf behind him. The spine said, *Umbral Affinity and You: A Guide to Collecting Your Recollection.* I pulled the book down and set it on the table next to Henry. "I think this hit you."

"Huh." He flipped the back cover open, revealing a pocket with a card inside. One name in a curly cursive script was written on it over and over. "I wonder who Alice is, and why she couldn't write her last name legibly. Anyway, this book pops out at me just about every night I'm up here. Means the skeleton crew's arrived."

"Skeleton crew?" I'd almost forgotten Tony had mentioned them.

"Check it out down at the counter." Henry jerked his chin at the kitchenette. "I'll just lie low up here and keep an eye on this book until they're gone."

I stood up, not wanting to miss the chance to see something new. Down at the counter, the trash can emptied itself into a bin on a cart. Stirrers straightened themselves, and a cloth wiped the surfaces clean. The tray of biscotti slid into a cabinet on the side of the cart at the same time as a platter of pizza eased out and settled in its place. It was a relief to see that the Nocturnal Lounge's attendants weren't actual skeletons. Still, I hadn't encountered real ghosts before. At least, not that I knew of.

"Weird." I turned back around to see Henry bent back over his project again. "Do you want anything?"

"No thanks, but you'd better hurry if you want something. Fred Redford's here. He'll eat all that pizza if you don't grab a slice now." Henry waved his hand toward the stairs leading down to the lounge area. "Pizza's not my thing, remember?"

"Okay." I went back down, bringing my half-full cup of tepid cocoa and the crumb-filled napkin with me. As I tossed them in the bin, someone elbowed past me. He was about my size, with that spicy Changeling scent and a bright red hat perched on a head with shaggy nut-brown hair. From the way he piled half the pizza on a plate, he had to be the Redford fellow Henry had mentioned.

I squeezed next to him and grabbed three squares of bread, sauce, and cheese. When I reached for more, he glared at my hand. I growled, thinking maybe Unseelie types might respond like bear shifters. He grunted back and looked up, narrowing hazel eyes.

"Bear's not the only one with an appetite, Yogi." His voice was melodic and rich, not at all what I expected.

"Still got one." I glanced at the self-bussing tables. "Won't they just bring more if we take it all?"

"Maybe. I like the cut of your jib. Name's Fred." His hand tapped the bill of his hat. Maybe Unseelie Changelings avoided shaking hands, or maybe it was just his particular type. I didn't know anything about them except that they varied.

"I'm Bobby," I smirked, glancing at his plate. He'd taken three-quarters of the pizza. Combined with my share, the whole tray was empty. "I've got to respect an appetite like that. Mine's mostly my bear, but the rest comes from growing up in Cajun country. Where did you get yours?"

"I come from a long line of Redcaps. We do everything big." He shrugged. "My brother brought an Italian friend to lunch at our house once. She said we had more food than they do at Christmas dinner. Ate more of it, too."

"How much was that, exactly?"

"All of it." He chuckled. "You take every table in here and cover it with plates of food, then cover them again. That's how much food we had at lunch that day."

"Woah." Something invisible bumped me to the side. "Hey, look. They did bring more."

Fred and I moved over as another tray of pizza hovered its way to the counter. Once it had landed, he went back in for more. He'd already eaten half of what was on his plate by the time he stacked more on. I snagged a few more slices myself. The cart wheeled through a door near the counter. After it closed, I couldn't tell it was there.

"I've got studying to do," Fred said around a mouthful of pizza. "Later."

"Bye." I took a napkin out of the dispenser and headed back to Henry. He was still hunched over the amulet, tinkering away. I wasn't sure what he was doing, of course. Bear shifters had no way to sense psychic power or most magic. Blaine would know how Henry's work was going from halfway across the room. I had to rely on how Henry looked.

I saw a flash of white at his mouth—a smile. The pen must have helped, then. I sat down and settled in, munching pizza and studying flashcards. It'd be a long night, but at least the novelty of my surroundings and the good company would be more than enough to keep me awake. They'd also keep my mind off going back and curling up next to Lynn like I wanted to.

I'd wait until she was rested to see her. She was worth it.

CHAPTER TWELVE

Lynn

I knocked my phone off the nightstand when the alert sounded, opening my eyes to late-afternoon light. I'd missed my alarm. I reached down and fumbled the rectangle of glass and plastic off the floor. A tap and a swipe revealed the message that it would snow again later tonight. I didn't recognize the app. Maybe it was wrong.

"Joy. Not!" I nearly flung the phone across the room. More snow meant hard mode flipped into nightmare mode for Bobby. I had to drag my ass out of bed right away and get presentable. I definitely had to not break my phone over a stupid weather report app. It could be wrong. It had to be. The patch of sky outside my window looked too clear to turn stormy. Then again, this was New England, where people always said, "If you don't like the weather, wait a minute."

I dragged myself out of bed, unable to go back to sleep even if there'd been time and I wanted to. My adrenaline had kicked up its heels and was having a hootenanny all over my body. Hootenanny just made me think of Olivia the owl shifter and her "Hoo, boy" by the elevator the night before. And of course, *that* made me think about everything Bobby and I had done afterward. I shivered, realizing I'd forgotten I'd slept in the nude. Glancing around, I hunted for something to wrap myself in.

I needed a shower, although it should probably be a cold one. The memories from the night before had me hot and bothered. I wrapped my robe around me and picked up my bath stuff. It felt like I'd just had a shower, almost as though being with Bobby had been a dream. The pleasant, languid ache in my hips told me otherwise. I wondered whether he was thinking of me, and shivered because maybe he wasn't.

The hall was empty, so I sighed down it, rolling my eyes at my own stupidity. I wasn't even sure why I felt like such an idiot. I should feel like I'd won the dating lottery. Bobby definitely liked me, maybe even more than that. The feeling was mutual. The sex was almost as amazing as he was, and he'd implied he thought he'd underperformed. I didn't feel like an outcast around him and didn't feel like I'd scare him away with either my smarts or my smart mouth. So what was my malfunction?

I turned on the water, opting for scalding instead of freezing. Biologically speaking, cold showers did nothing for the female anatomy. My brain was being kind of a jerk, knowing all this stuff and thinking racy thoughts, anyway. As I stepped under hot water that had actual pressure because everyone else was at the library or dining hall, I realized a big personal truth.

My malfunction and my greatest asset were the exact same. I looked at every single thing as a problem. Not like an issue or an upset, but a puzzle. Anything and anyone I encountered was an equation to be solved, a piece that had to fit somewhere, an organism to be classified by genus and species. I was trying to be a doctor for people humans had not known existed until just before I was born with a scientific mind. I'd been forgetting all about my heart when an enigma had me in its teeth. At least my mental rambling considered them people and not test subjects or something.

Bobby thought I had a big heart. He'd come right out and said it to someone we'd just met. He trusted me, and believed I cared about him, not the unique mystery of his hibernation urge. No matter how friendly his baseline personality was, I got the idea that Bobby didn't trust easily. Children of famous people rarely did. I owed it to him to do more than just hope he was right.

Shutting the water off, I dried off, then put on lotion. I took my time in the bathroom, knowing no one else would need it for at least another hour. I hadn't washed my hair, so it wouldn't take anywhere near that long. As I went through the minimal version of my routine, I decided to test myself in the way that felt most comfortable. I'd write and answer questions about my feelings.

Back in my room, I could barely believe I was writing out a practice test for my emotions. I usually avoided examining my feelings like my sister avoided studying, but I couldn't do that now. Was that part of an answer? I'd told Bobby not to claim me even if his bear wanted to because he shouldn't unless he was sure. Had that been for his benefit, or because I was afraid? Was I was only drawn to him because he had an interesting problem? Was ours a Florence Nightingale romance, destined to fizzle the moment he got better?

My hand moved the pen across the blank page as I jotted down these questions, plus a few more for good measure. I always used a pen on self-practice tests. No, no lying to myself. It was bravado that made me choose ink over graphite. Fake courage. The real test was whether I'd stand by my answers for good or ill.

I got halfway through the questions I'd asked myself. The one that stopped me was "Do you even have feelings, Lynn?" Of course, I did. If not, none of the ostracism I'd faced over the years would have bothered me. Being left out, forgotten on guest lists—none of that would have mattered if I didn't care. I was on the verge of transferring to a crappy school from the only Ivy League I could attend because things hadn't changed. Was I wrong?

I glanced up at the dry-erase board with Maddie's name on it. She'd doodled little black daisies with heart-shaped centers in the corners. My roommate liked me, sticking around and expressing sadness at my plan to leave. Blaine was a scaly, egotistical pain-in-the-ass, but even he'd admitted to respecting my academic dedication. Jeannie had gone out of her way to try to convince me not to leave, and she only knew me as a random chick who had stuck up for Bobby.

I sighed as I thought of the most interesting man in the world. Not the one from those stupid liquor commercials. Bobby Tremain, the sleepy but utterly amazing bear shifter. He was the one with the big heart, the unexpectedly kind and giving nature in a sea of entitled alpha jerks. Had I sighed this much and gotten this angsty about any other guy? Not really. Not even the only other one I'd slept with.

Dan had been a study buddy, too. We never went on any actual dates, but we had spent a lot of time together at libraries and study halls. We'd had an academic rivalry going on, which I'd won when I beat him in the GPA department by three whole tenths of a percent. The big mystery about him for me had been how he got grades so effortlessly. We'd both lost interest in each other as soon as we'd scratched our hormonal itch. I never figured out his haphazard study methods, and I stopped caring almost instantly.

Bobby's issue was ongoing, yes, but he still occupied my thoughts and feelings, even after we'd gone to bed together. If anything, I was even more invested in helping him now than before. I was afraid of too many things to figure out which had priority. Fear of failing him, fear of how I felt, fear of how he felt. When a bear shifter claimed a mate, it lasted until one of them was dead, sometimes even after. I'd heard stories from psychics about how their ghosts would wait around until their mates died and they'd cross over together. His own father was in a wheelchair for the rest of his life because he'd pushed his mate out of the way of a truck. Even if Bobby and his bear were ready for that kind of commitment, was I?

I closed my eyes, feeling the trickle of tears I hadn't noticed before. I tried to imagine what it'd be like if he failed, got sent back home, and I never saw him again. That was too mixed up with failure in general for me to grok it. I shook that scenario off, replacing it with how I'd feel if he passed and I transferred back to Wisconsin.

I dropped the pen, slumping on my side and curling into a ball on the bed. My pillow smelled faintly and pleasantly musky, like Bobby. I felt something break within me, strong emotions rushing over and around like rapids against my flailing logic. I couldn't take thinking about just leaving and never seeing him again. Was that love? Did it matter if it fell a little short of that considering we hadn't had much time together? I definitely cared more about Bobby than anyone else here at PPC and everyone else back home I wasn't related to.

Sitting up, I grabbed a tissue and wiped my eyes. I glanced at the clock. It was time for the last round of studying over at the dining hall. I dressed and grabbed the already packed bag of Ecology notes and books. After that, I grabbed my makeshift emotional quiz and ran it through the shredder next to my desk. That was one lesson I wouldn't forget. I'd be a few minutes late, but at least, I'd be able to concentrate. Maybe. I'd have to see when I got there.

I walked to the dining hall, passing people on the way. Some snow had melted during the day, and a crust of ice had re-frozen on the top in the late-afternoon twilight. I glanced at the library. The snow pile on the overhang looked more precarious and dangerous now. It had icicles like the teeth I could imagine in Blaine's shifted-form mouth. More snow would just make it worse. Hunger derailed that train of thought. It was later than I usually got dinner, and my stomach sounded like a Sarlacc pit. Cloned mercenaries had better stay out of my way. I pushed through the door.

Bobby sat at a table near the food line with Blaine, who looked like he'd gotten some sleep. A bowl of cereal was in front of the seat next to Bobby, a spoon with a napkin on one side and a glass of milk on the other. I sat down and poured, then looked up and smiled.

"You know me too well already, Bobby." I picked up the spoon and practically inhaled the honey-nut oat goodness.

"They have veggie chili if you want that too. I didn't want it to get cold, or that'd be there instead of the one-letter alphabet cereal." Bobby stared right into my eyes. I didn't want him to stop, but my stomach demanded otherwise. I'd slept for close to twenty hours.

"Chili sounds awesome, thanks." I watched Bobby get up as I

finished the cereal and pushed it aside to make room for the books I pulled from my backpack. "Don't say one word, Blaine."

The dragon shifter just drummed his fingers on the table, biting his lip as he let out a faintly frustrated hum. He grabbed a notebook and scrawled a word across it. I glanced down to see "Taskmaster" pointed at me.

"Okay, you can talk, but not about sex." I didn't look up, just watched Blaine's notebook slowly slide away from me across the table.

"Tiamat's scales!" Blaine turned a color that might have embarrassed a beet. "Wasn't going to. Dammit, Lynn, I'm a dragon, not a counselor. I just wanted to tell you Bobby made some friends last night. You can actually study your lab stuff and sleep before the exam tomorrow morning if you want."

"Oh." I bit my lip. "Well, I guess that's one cat out of the bag. I have a bit of news that might be bad, though."

"Great, just what we need." Blaine rolled his eyes, then sipped soda through a straw. He glanced up at Bobby, who'd just gotten back with two plates of food. He spoke out of the corner of his mouth, reminding me for all the world of a person talking with a cigarette between his lips. "Hit me."

"Weather alert says it will snow again tonight." I pulled out my phone, showing them the message on the app.

"Looks like a bad prediction." Blaine peered at the screen. "What is that app, anyway? I've never seen that one before."

"It's one I got during orientation. Some Precognitive Psychic student made it or something." I shrugged. "I didn't think it was even set up to give me alerts, but that was what woke me up.

"Psychic, huh?" Blaine passed the phone to Bobby. "Let me go outside for a minute or three. There's something I want to check." He didn't wait for either of us to answer, just left.

"Lynn, this app doesn't have a way to toggle alerts." He swiped around a few times. "It really must be Psychic if it automatically informs you of weather events that might affect you."

"I don't know much about Psychic anything. Do you?" I twirled a French fry in my cup of ketchup.

"Just that it's individual to the person. Like, a Psychic might be able to talk to ghosts, but can't see the future. That kind of thing. They're one-trick ponies." He passed the phone back to me.

"So it's kind of like Magus power?" I stared down at the app displayed on my screen. A little red flashing cylinder in one corner gave me a bad feeling.

"A little, but also completely different." He chewed on a piece of fish. "You don't have any idea where you got it?"

"I think it was a table at orientation." I scratched my head. "The thing I really remember was the girl who installed it. She seemed terrified for some reason. Kept glancing over her shoulder."

"She was a student here?" Bobby pulled his own phone out and swiped through, shaking his head.

"The right age to be for sure, but I don't know. Definitely not professor age or anything. And she wasn't a vampire because it was broad daylight." I shivered a little, remembering how wild-eyed the girl had looked. "She was pale with black, curly hair."

"I think this is some kind of warning then, Lynn. Probably more personal than a weather report." Bobby looked up. "I don't have that app on my phone, so she definitely didn't give it to everyone. I do remember seeing a nervous girl like that at orientation, though."

"Give me that phone now, Lynn." Blaine leaned across the table, dropping his jacket on the floor. His skin should have been covered with gooseflesh, but instead, it looked a little scaly. Smoke trailed behind him, stretching in lines all the way back to the door he'd just walked through. I handed it over. "I did a partial shift to hone my magic senses for the next six hours."

Blaine's eyes went wide and changed color from brown to red. Not the bloodshot kind, but bright red like fire. His pupils were vertical, too. He glared at my phone, then traced one finger along the screen. A tiny spark flew up, shaped like a large snowflake.

"We've got a problem, Frampton." He set the phone down on the table, unconsciously wiping his hands on his jeans like the phone had been oily or something, even though I knew it wasn't. "That app senses magic-induced weather events better and faster than I can, but it's attuned to you like Bobby's amulet's attuned to him. Take a look through the history and tell me the last time it went off."

"Fine." I tapped and swiped until the information I wanted came up. "Hoo, boy. It was the storm that dropped all that snow the other night. You said that one was magic too, right, Blaine?"

"I think that Psychic wanted you to know this. That someone's messing with Bobby, wants him to flunk out." Blaine took a few deep breaths, his eyes and skin taking on a more human appearance. "Even worse, they might be messing with PPC in general."

"I'd say that's ridiculous, but you have a point about the college in general." Bobby looked pale, his mouth a flat line. "PPC opening its doors to all kinds is pretty recent, and I'm the highest-profile student here. If someone wants to make the school look bad by having the son of a famous but disabled prizefighter flunk his first semester because he can't control his bear, that might work."

"Well, we won't let them make it happen." I pushed my plate away, my appetite gone. "You're passing." I glanced down at his accurate notes covering half the table. He'd been working on Ecology even without me there. "You know the material. We just have to get you through until you can use Henry's amulet and you're golden."

"I hope so, Lynn." Bobby took a deep breath, the color returning to his face as he gazed at me.

"Me too." Blaine looked more fearsome than I'd ever seen him. "I think you and Frampton just painted a couple of huge targets on your backs, and once the magic snow starts flying, I won't be much use to either of you."

CHAPTER THIRTEEN

Bobby

I passed all of Lynn's old practice quizzes. I got every flashcard right. Maybe whatever Henry had worked on at the table with me the night before had rubbed off. Maybe I really *was* that good at the subject now. It was the foundation for my career of choice, after all, something I was interested in. At any rate, she'd been right, and I had Watkins' material on lock-down.

I also had a sick feeling in my stomach. Momma's side of the family had dreams, and sometimes the heebie-jeebies when something terrible was about to happen. She'd had a bad feeling on the day the truck almost hit her and got Dad instead. The way she always described it sure sounded a lot like how I felt that night. I waffled between not wanting to let Lynn out of my sight and getting as far away from her as I could so whoever was after me wouldn't be anywhere near her. Lynn was on edge, too. She kept looking over her shoulder or out the window.

Blaine kept both our heads in the game. His asides and tangents worked on our moods like pressure relief valves. I was surprised he had himself that together, with his dragon so close to the surface in partial-shift mode. Then again, maybe it was a façade. He might just be using his own defense mechanism, which also happened to keep Lynn and me from going all freakazoid.

"I can't believe I'm saying this to anyone besides myself, but I think you know everything, Bobby." Lynn yawned and stretched her arms over her head. "I don't think there's anything else for us to go over."

"What about the other classes?" Blaine raised his eyebrow.

"All those were papers or presentations." I gathered all the flashcards into a pile and banded them together. "They were done before the snow hit."

"This is the point where I tell study buddies to go get some sleep, but that won't fly here." Lynn glanced out the window again. "It looks like it's clouding up out there. I have that lab practical after Ecology tomorrow, and I should go over notes for it."

"Want to bring them to the Nocturnal Lounge?" At that moment, my anxiety pendulum was on the "keep Lynn close" side of things. "It's an interesting place to go. I've got invites from Tony and Henry, so we can both get in."

"There's a lab study group over at the library." Lynn tucked the flashcards in her backpack with her other books. "They're nowhere near as good of company as you, but maybe they'll let me join them."

"I understand." I stood up when she did, pulling her close before she left. "Be careful," I murmured into her hair.

"I will." She pulled back to look at me before stepping away. "I'll be perfectly safe, and I'll make sure it's not a white-out when I head back to the dorm. See you in the morning, Bobby."

"See you soon, Lynn." I watched her go, with that horrible sick feeling coming over me like Dagobah swamp gas. I sat down without really meaning to. After I'd taken a few deep breaths, I felt Blaine's hand on my arm.

"Wake up, man!" He shook me by the shoulder. "Should I text her and ask her to come back?"

"No." I shook my head, trying to clear it. "I could just head over to the Nocturnal Lounge. You want to be my plus one?"

"My partial shift means getting caught in a magical snowstorm would be bad news. I could end up going on a dragon rampage all over campus. Besides, I have homework too, Bobby." The red in Blaine's eyes deepened with frustration, even though his face wore a mask of droll boredom. His mouth barely moved when he spoke, making him sound like Thurston Howell from Gilligan's Island. "It's not the kind of thing they'll be happy with me doing in there." He glanced around, then leaned close and lowered his voice. "Seelie pictographs from the nineteenth century."

"Oh. Yeah. Don't come with me then." I wrinkled my nose. Whatever issue the Goblin King's Changelings had with even the mention of anything Seelie had already gotten old. More importantly, if Blaine was worried enough to admit he might lose his dragon's leash, I didn't want him to risk it.

"I'll walk you over there, though. The app says the snow won't start for at least another hour. That tunnel's dark, and Lynn told you to be careful of that kind of thing." He stood up and grabbed his satchel.

"How did you know where the night crew hangs out?" I rose and followed him through the dining hall and the doors. The cold air just made me sleepy, unlike last night. It was like my bear had no reason to stay awake with Lynn gone.

"I had to interview a Redcap for a midterm project." Blaine snorted. "He ate pizza the entire time."

"Wait, was his name Fred?" I was starting to think coincidence didn't exist, or if it did, that it didn't work the way I'd thought.

"Yeah. You met him, I guess." Our feet crunched across the layer of snow still on the ground.

"Kind of a difficult guy to miss, what with the bright red hat and him being almost my size and all." I felt the heaviness in the air and realized that Lynn's psychic weather app had been right. Oh yeah, it would snow big-time.

"True story." Blaine shrugged. "So, what do you have planned in there?"

"There's a group of fledgling vampire students doing a presentation on garlic and holy water. It's a whole musical act." I shrugged. "They might be terrible, but Tony tells me they're at least loud."

"Oh, is that the bunch who's in a band?"

"Yeah. The Night Creatures." I glanced at the silver-gray clouds covering the entire sky. "That doesn't look good."

"Doesn't feel good, either." Blaine shivered in a way that had nothing to do with cold air. When he looked back at me, his face seemed scalier. "There's magic everywhere. I'm kind of glad you can't feel it. My dragon wants *out*. I'll have to stay inside the rest of the night unless I want to risk going Godzilla on everyone."

"Look, thanks for walking me over here." I nodded down the alley at the trolley tunnel. "Go on and head back now." I started walking.

"Nothing doing." Blaine followed me. "I'm good to get you fifty paces in." We kept walking. "See, we're here already." Blaine knocked while I yawned. "Have fun, and stay awake, dammit. I don't get instant As if you flunk out."

"Ha, Blaine. Very ha." I rolled my eyes just as the light from the magic doorway illuminated us. "You're a pain, but a damn good friend."

"Thanks." He waved as I stepped through the door. "See you tomorrow."

The door closed behind me before I could say goodbye. I went up the stairs and into the Nocturnal Lounge, glad to have somewhere to go. I looked around but only recognized Henry up at the same table as the night before. Tony wasn't around, and I didn't think Fred bothered showing up until low noon when the skeleton crew brought pizza.

I skipped the cocoa on the counter, opting for some tea instead. The biscotti were anise this time, dipped in chocolate. I took my food and drink to the least cozy-looking chair, a shabby brown wingback. As I sipped tea and munched cookies, I watched the Night Creatures setting up. They had a full-sized PA and amp, with electric everything for the instruments and a full drum set.

One of the vampires picked up the bass and started plunking away on it. He had shoulder-length light brown hair and tattoos on his arms. I couldn't help but listen to him play since the amp drowned out every other sound in the room. Another vampire, this one with dark skin, a short goatee, and an earring, adjusted a dial on the PA. He went over and picked up a red guitar, then teased out a riff that rattled my teeth. This time, the bass player adjusted a dial. I figured it would be a long and sonic evening for Night Creatures.

Their presentation song was catchy, witty, and kept me awake. I never knew garlic had absolutely no effect on any type of vampire unless they'd had an allergy during their human days, or that holy water only worked on vamps who were Catholic. After a few hours, I knew the song by heart. They kept me so entertained, I forgot about getting pizza at low noon.

I had no idea Tony was there until he tapped me on the shoulder and practically dragged me away. I followed him to the staircase, where it was quiet enough to hear something besides Night Creatures. The frantic look in his eyes made that sense of foreboding from earlier come back with a vengeance. Before I could ask Tony what was going on, he spoke.

"You have to follow me and fast. It's Lynn." He grabbed my arm and tried dragging me out the door and into the tunnel.

"What about her?" I went with him. Otherwise, Tony would have had about as much luck moving me as knocking over a brick wall.

"I studied with her in the library because the jerks from her lab shut her out. After a while, she got tired and said she had to go back to her dorm. I smelled you all over her and I owe you, so I followed just to watch her get to the dorm safely. It was snowing like crazy out there. Still is." He waved his free hand vaguely over his head, swirling the fat, wet flakes as we came out of the tunnel.

"I see that." I let him keep the vise-grip he had on my arm even though I started to out-pace him on a course directly toward the library. "You still haven't said what happened."

"You'll know in a sec, but I'll tell you." He took a deep breath. "That huge pile of ice and snow got twice as big and fell off the roof." We rounded a corner. "She's under there."

A low growl threatened to turn into a roar at the center of my chest. The pile was high and deep, the snow heavier and more packed than I could dig or push through. Breathing through my nose told me next to nothing I couldn't see with my eyes. I couldn't be sure because I wasn't familiar with snow, but I thought it had happened less than five minutes before I got there. I stepped up to the edge of the pile. Chunks and spikes of ice stuck out every which way. Some of them were bigger than Lynn.

Tony was still rattling on about freak accidents and odd coincidences that make urban avalanches. I knew better. I'd seen that weather app and Blaine's reaction to the magic behind the storm. Someone had done this deliberately. She could be bleeding to death under there. Someone had to undo it deliberately, right now.

Blaine couldn't come outside without dragoning out and burning everything down. His dragon wouldn't fit in the narrow side street, anyway. This was a job for a bear. I didn't think about exams or failing. I didn't think about someone sabotaging PPC, or the media attention Momma and Dad would get when I went home in academic disgrace. Well, actually, I did, but my bear dismissed all those thoughts. I let him.

All I cared about was Henry's amulet and how it would keep me awake long enough to rescue the woman who was smart, funny, and probably my mate. I pulled the coin by its string out of my shirt and gripped it tightly.

"*Pulvis memento est.*" The weight on the lanyard vanished as it turned into dust and mingled with the snowflakes blowing around me. I smelled coffee and heard alarms. I felt the needle spray of a cold shower. I tasted Lynn's lips on mine and smelled a faint hint of mint just ahead of me.

As I paced toward the heavy, packed pile of snow embedded with ice chunks, I felt my feet fall more heavily. The tilt of my hips changed, and my torso lengthened and thickened. The palms of my hands morphed into pads with claws at the ends of my fingers. Scraps of fabric flew in a nimbus around me while keys, coins, my phone, and my wallet rattled to the ground. Tony padded behind me, collecting them.

I pushed my snout forward, grunting as it encountered heavy mounds of cold and wet. I tossed aside a huge block of ice that would have been impossible to move alone in my human shape. As a bear, I pushed it away as easily as I'd shot hoops with Blaine the day before. I dug, then pushed, then dug again, following Lynn's scent the whole time. I smelled blood, but only a little. My nose touched something soft and warm compared to the snow, but colder than it should be. Lynn, with a scratch on her cheek and an icicle beside her that had clearly been the culprit.

I sat back on my haunches, clearing snow to either side with the backs of my paws so I wouldn't accidentally scratch her. I tossed aside more ice, a thick sheet this time, that covered her legs. Once all the ice was off her, I could see she'd fallen face-down. I shifted back, not caring about the snow against my bare flesh. When I took her in my arms and turned her over, her breath just barely misted in the cold air. Even though she'd been dressed warmly, she was too cold. I had to get her inside.

I jogged naked across the street, my feet slipping a little on the ice. A sharp stab and scent of fresh blood meant I'd stepped on something sharp. I'd be fine since all large shifters healed fast. Once through the dorm doors, I headed straight for my room. The door was open, and Blaine was sitting at his desk with his mouth open in shock. He blinked a few times as I put Lynn on my bed and wrapped her in blankets.

"Tiamat's scales, Bobby!" He stared at the one thing still on me after my shift—the empty lanyard around my neck. "What did you do?"

"Saved her life."

"That's not going to be enough. Her lips are dark blue." Blaine pulled something from his desk. He pressed it between his palms and murmured a few unpronounceable words, then he handed me a red stone with blue striations. It was hot. "Make her hold this."

"What is it?"

"A firestone." Blaine swept the notes and books he'd been studying from his desk into his satchel. "It regulates temperature. I have to get out of here. All the snow and water in here is nearly as bad for me as going outside. Too much magic that clashes with mine. I'd better not be here until it evaporates. I'll be in the first-floor lounge."

"Thanks." I knew Blaine had heard me even though he'd shut the door before I spoke.

CHAPTER FOURTEEN

Bobby

I turned and stripped off Lynn's gloves, then put the firestone in her hands.

"Ow." Lynn moaned, turning her head on the pillow. She gripped the stone in her hand tighter. "Hmm. Firestone. Good call for hypothermia, bear-man. What happened?" Her eyes stayed closed, and her lips were still faintly blue. At least they looked to be a more human color than before.

"Urban avalanche. The huge snow pile on the library got you." I watched her eyes fly open as I spoke. "I had to bulldoze you out from under a literal butt-load of snow and ice."

"Bobby." Her eyes roamed over my body, then back up to my face. "You didn't use the amulet to shift without falling asleep, did you?"

"That's exactly what I did." I looked right into her gorgeous eyes. "I couldn't do anything but that. Blaine's partial shift means he can't be anywhere near this snow. Tony shifts into a little kitty cat. You would have died."

She said nothing, just flung her arms around my neck and pulled me as close as she could. Her clothes were soaking through the blankets, so I unwrapped them. She sat up and put the firestone in her lap.

"You're such a winter newb." Lynn shrugged out of her wet jacket and tossed it on the floor. Then, she pulled her damp shirt over her head. "Snowy clothes turn into wet ones pretty quick."

"Good to know." I couldn't do much besides watch her undress. Even though she did it fast, I stood there fascinated.

"I don't suppose you have any more blankets, huh?" She wrapped her arms around herself, gaze traveling around the room. "A robe, maybe, or a towel?"

"Something better." My voice came out low and rumbly. When her eyes met mine, she gasped. The look on her face reminded me of the night before.

I leaned over to climb into bed next to her and she put her arms around my neck, helping me and making room. My knee bumped the firestone, so I put it on the nightstand. I looked at her lips, noticing they were back to their usual pale pink color. I embraced her, wanting to taste them again. My bear and I agreed she needed as much contact as possible to warm up, but I couldn't lie down. I sat up and curled around her as much as I could.

Lynn surprised me by pushing me back down on the bed. Her assertive nature was one of the most exciting things about her. She was the most amazing girl I'd ever met, and I could tell she wanted me as much as I wanted her. There was so much I hadn't expected to find at PPC. I'd taken most of it in stride, just trying to keep up with the changes. Lynn was the one surprise that felt like a gift, like Christmas morning or turning a corner to find a spectacular view.

I tried to rein in my bear and keep him from claiming her. The last thing I wanted to do was hold back with Lynn, but she'd asked me not to mark her unless I was sure. I was, but that request might also have been about what *she* wanted. I wouldn't cross that line until I'd had a dream or she changed her mind and told me.

Lynn

I stroked Bobby's cheek. His silvery-blue eyes held nothing but tenderness and devotion as I gazed into them. I still could barely believe he had used the amulet to help me. Tony and Blaine hadn't been able to help, but he could have called Jeannie or Josh. He hadn't thought about that, though, only of saving me. I hadn't understood how much we needed each other until I woke with him standing there, naked except for that empty lanyard.

And that was why I turned my head, presenting my shoulder to him. He gasped, then let out a frustrated sigh.

"I'm sure if you are." I ran my hands over the closely cropped hair on the back of his head. "I'd claim you if I could."

My own eyes reflected back at me in his silvery gaze. He licked his lips, then bared his teeth. I'd never noticed how his bicuspids were pointer than most people's. He stared down at me, his eyes taking on a feral gleam.

"Love you." The words were slightly garbled by a growl, but they'd been unmistakable. They were also familiar. Those had been the muffled syllables he'd uttered the night before as he left my room.

When his teeth sank into the thin layer of skin at my collarbone, the pinch was painful, but just barely.

"Love you too." My voice had a higher pitch than usual, not surprising considering the tingling sensation the act of him marking me sent over my flesh.

He opened his mouth, let out a long growly sound, and pulled me closer. I pulled back. I had to thank him properly for saving my life, after all.

"Oh, no, Bobby." I sat up, shaking him. "Wake up." I glanced at the clock. It had been an hour and fifteen minutes since I'd left the library and the ice had buried me. Henry's wakefulness amulet had worn off.

I got up, searching Bobby's desk for something sharp. All I found was a pencil. I poked him with it, but he just let out a faint snore. Dropping the pencil, I felt like the world's biggest doofus for not bothering to check his pulse. I took a deep breath to calm myself, then pressed the tips of my index and middle finger against the inside of his wrist.

His pulse was slow and steady at a normal and perfectly human sixty beats per minute. No hibernating respiration to be found. All the books from Friday night said he'd be at twenty beats per minute if the urge won. When I turned my head back away from the wall clock, the mark on my shoulder stung a little. I put Bobby's arm down and walked over to the dresser to look into the mirror above it.

The claiming mark was only faintly red but unmistakable. Two punctures above the bone line and two below. I'd seen pictures, but none in person. Still, I knew they'd heal into shiny pink scars like small buttons. We were mates now, bound together for good or ill. Marriage at this point would simply be a legal formality.

I glanced at my mate, listening to his textbook-normal respiration. He'd wake up in the morning with his alarm like all the other bear shifters who had grown up in wintry climates. If he didn't, I'd be able to rouse him. Bobby could pass his exam without the aid of an amulet, just plain old coffee, like Blaine or me.

Think of the dragon, and he appears. I heard a knock on the door and his voice asking if everything was all right. My clothes were still wet, except for my bra and underwear. I put those on and rummaged around in Bobby's drawer for a pair of shorts and a t-shirt. His socks were ridiculously big on me but better than going into the hall barefoot.

I opened the door a crack to see Blaine's lizardly half-lidded grin. His skin and eyes still had their dragonish accents from earlier. He tapped his nose and winked. He'd known what had happened in there before I even answered the door. Blaine held out Bobby's wallet, keys, and some loose change, and I took the items, setting them on top of Bobby's dresser.

"Tony gave me these. He told me everything. Can we talk, Taskmaster?" He quirked an eyebrow.

"Sure." I stepped out the door. "Just let me use the restroom first."

"Of course." He shut the door quietly and leaned against the wall next to it.

Once I got back, he beckoned and headed down the hall toward the lounge. I followed, seating myself in the chair across from where he'd camped out with a stack of books and a few old scrolls. He took a deep breath and picked up one of the latter.

"Do you believe in coincidence?" Blaine unrolled the scroll.

"I didn't, not really. Now I do."

"Good." Blaine turned the parchment around. "This is a record of something that happened back in 1938, the winter after the Great New England Hurricane. Something similar occurred again in 1978 when we had one blizzard that was bigger than these two combined. I wouldn't have thought of it at all if my whole family hadn't been local since way back."

"Woah." I took the parchment from him, holding it gingerly. What could only be a magic-imbued image shimmered in brightly colored ink. It was like watching the *Wizard of Oz* right after Dorothy lands in Munchkinland, except this drawing had no Munchkins, cute dogs, or ruby slippers.

"Nasty way to go." Blaine gulped. "You almost rivaled it."

Two stockinged legs stuck out from under a slab of brownstone topped with snow instead of a house, and the shoes on the feet were black, but otherwise disturbingly similar to the Wicked Witch of the East's at the scene of her demise. I wondered whether one scene had inspired the other. I checked the caption, but it was in a language I couldn't read.

"Who was she?" I handed the scroll back to Blaine, shuddering.

"A Magus who threatened to go public about what she was." Blaine rolled up the scroll and set it down. "She was a student here too, known for her wit and for topping the Dean's List. She'd been Salutatorian at her high school, but still. Sound like anyone you know?"

"So this might not be anything to do with the school?" I scratched my head, still unclear about how destiny worked within the supernatural set.

"I wasn't trying to imply that." Blaine got out an oilcloth and wrapped the pile of parchment in it. "The opposite, actually. You're not magical, so you don't know this, but there has to be a coincidence in order for the really big spells to go over without a backlash."

"Did Bobby screw someone's spell up, then?"

"Yup." Thin trails of smoke curled out of Blaine's nose. "A spell that should have worked on you because it went off the last two times someone tried it. Whoever cast this is not going to be happy once they recover, but they can't mess with either of you directly anymore either."

"Really?" My eyebrow raised in a skeptical arch, more Bones than Mr. Spock.

"Technically, whoever tried to do this could go ahead and aim a big magic gun at you. But since those spells are pulled strongly by parallels like that other girl who died in 1938 and the woman in 1976, it'd be likely to fail and backlash all over again."

"Jeez, I'm glad I'm majoring in Alternative Therapies and not Magic Theory." I leaned my chin on one hand. "Sounds like a mess of trouble waiting to happen."

"Magic can be that way. Why else do you think they'd have schools for it? Psychics have it easier, but one thing they teach in every magic-related course here is to keep meticulous records for the heavy payload spells." Blaine waved the growing cloud of smoke away from his face. "That was one of the reasons so many practitioners were down with the licensure program. They'd been writing everything up already. It's also why bad eggs are so rare amongst Magi. Since records like that are essential for survival, it's too easy to get caught unless you're good at covering your tracks. And it takes a Psychic to do that with any certainty."

"So if Bobby and I don't have much to worry about in the future, why did you want to talk about this?"

"You're sharper than the oldest cheddar in the world." Blaine sat back and folded his hands in front of him. "Whoever it is might decide to take their frustrations out on your friends. I kind of have a vested interest in that."

"No kidding." I chewed my bottom lip, aware of the problem Blaine hadn't mentioned yet. "There's also their bigger plan. The reason they tried to make Bobby flunk out in the first place still exists. If the baddie is focused enough, he or she might skip any revenge attempts."

"Maybe, but probably not."

"Why?"

"Because evil is as evil does." Blaine sighed, shaking his head. I noticed he had circles under his eyes. "Whoever did this has a petty and personal imagination. Someone focused would have knocked out the school's power or taken out an essential resource like the library. Maybe even knocked a hole in the Nocturnal Lounge at midday. Straight-up acts of Extrahuman terrorism."

"I don't know if I should be relieved or not." It surprised me not to have a visceral reaction. All I felt about Blaine's news was numbness. Deciding how to think about it wasn't such a stretch.

"Go ahead and relax for now." Blaine packed up his books. "Like I said, you won't be the target next time."

"Doesn't matter. If you need help, you can find it here." I chewed my lower lip. "Also, if anything else like this happens to you or any of Bobby's friends, I'll go straight to the Headmistress. I think she'll have to listen to me, all things considered."

"Thanks, Lynn." Blaine stood. "Let's get your things out of the room. Then you should go upstairs and hit the hay."

"Good call." I yawned as I got up and followed my friend, and then his advice.

CHAPTER FIFTEEN

Bobby

The scent of hot coffee met my nose, making me aware of the warmth all around me. I turned my head, feeling the soft fabric of my pillow against my ear. More scents over the coffee drove me crazy—mint and something sweet. I opened my eyes.

"He lives." Lynn's lips didn't move, which was just as well since Blaine was the one speaking.

"Uh, I need to get decent over here." The sheets twisted against my bare legs.

"You ran halfway down the street naked last night, and you're still modest?" Lynn smiled. She put the coffee down on the nightstand and grabbed a pair of shorts from the foot of the bed. I took them and pulled them on under the sheet, then sat up.

"Did I miss it?" The clock said eight in the morning, but I didn't know what day it was.

"Nope. You've got an hour." Blaine leaned on the doorframe, as fresh as a dragonish daisy. His partial-shift scales and eye color had vanished. "Get dressed, get fed, get grades. Let's go."

"Coffee and water first." I took the paper cup and sipped from it. It was like a magic elixir of wakefulness and exactly the right temperature for hot coffee. I breathed the aroma and took a bigger gulp. Once fortified with a little caffeine, I pulled on my robe and shuffled down the hall. Five minutes later, the coffee was gone, and I was dressed. I headed to the dining hall with my roommate and my new mate.

"Had a dream last night." I slipped my arm around Lynn's waist.

"Oh?" Even though it was just one syllable, her voice came out all quavery.

"I'd say you were in it, but it was all you." I felt her arm slide under the back of my jacket and around my waist. "Nothing and no one else."

Lynn turned her head, slowing her pace as she looked up at me. She missed the curb when she turned to face me and I caught her, sweeping her into my arms. She threw her arms around my neck and hugged me tighter than anyone ever had before.

In the dining hall, we had breakfast and a flashcard review. I breezed through the material almost as easily as Lynn. Having a brainiac for a mate was awesome. The new connection between us helped me know when I'd gotten something right. We left together, Blaine staying behind because his exam started after ours.

Watkins was at the door to the lecture hall, eying each student as he or she passed. He held what looked like a magnifying glass. I knew it was a magical device that detected contraband cheating methods. A few of our classmates stopped to show him registry sheets for their magical and mundane assistive devices. In my pocket, my hand brushed against Henry's yellow registry slip. I'd have to remember to throw it out later. Then again, maybe I'd keep it for posterity or something.

"Good luck, Tremain." Watkins peered at me through the glass, then at Lynn.

I smiled, realizing I didn't need well-wishes from anyone. I'd gotten together with Lynn, and we'd made our own luck. We had to sit two or more seats apart, but it didn't matter. Once I had the test, my pencil flew over the scantron sheet as easily as my dad used to vault into the ring. It definitely hadn't been effortless, but it seemed that way. All the work had gone in ahead of time.

I wasn't the first one done. Lynn had that honor, of course. Still, I handed my test in before three-quarters of the rest of the class. Watkins did a double-take when he realized it was me. I waited for him to regain his composure, then watched him point at a block-lettered card to his right.

"Grades will be in your email by six o'clock tonight." I sighed as I read it, relieved that he'd let us know so quickly. Professor Watkins was harsh, but he cared. I'd begun to notice that trait in others a lot over the weekend.

Outside, I watched as Lynn threw a snowball at a familiar head of spiky blond hair. Josh whooped and spun around, scooping up his own handful of snow to fling back. The sound of Lynn's laughter carried a comfortable joy, even if it got cut off by what turned out to be an epic snowball fight. A sleepy-looking Tony showed up and joined in, along with Josh and two other guys, both with classic Italian looks but much bulkier than the cat shifter.

We flung snow at each other until our stomachs told us it was time for lunch. I waited in the dining hall for Blaine, and then for Lynn after her lab practical. I saw Jeannie stop her on the way in. They spoke briefly, then Lynn shook her head, and Jeannie smiled much more genuinely. I hadn't seen Jeannie being that obviously kind since she and her kin had come to help Dad and Momma after the accident. She'd been eleven back then.

"What was all that about?" Blaine pushed some books out of the way to make room for Lynn's.

"Just Jeannie asking whether I'd be staying at PPC." She didn't meet my eyes.

"What?!" Blaine blinked and stepped backward, nearly falling over. He was more shocked than I thought dragon shifters could get. I was right there with him, too. My stomach felt like it had been in a runaway elevator to the basement.

"Don't freak out, you guys." She blushed as she set her books down. "I'm not going anywhere. In fact, I signed up to stay on for a Winter Inter-session course."

"I wasn't freaking out." Blaine's eyelids went back to their usual half-mast. "Neither were you, right, Bobby?"

"Nope. Not even a tiny bit." The breathless laugh that escaped my lips said otherwise.

"Look, it was a thing I thought about. But that was so last week." She hung her jacket on a hook on the side of the booth. "Are you guys coming back after New Year's Eve?"

"I would, but there's nothing for me to take." Blaine sighed almost wistfully. "I'll just be over in Newport, though. If you need dragonish help for any reason, I can send my driver for you, or have him bring me here."

"I think I might." I slid closer to Lynn on the seat, letting her cuddle against me after she sat down. "There's a math class I'd have to take in the spring otherwise."

"Good." Lynn leaned her head on my shoulder. "Henry texted me, by the way. Apparently, he might need my help for that huge job he's been working on. I'm not sure why. Here, have a look."

"Huh. Weird." I took her phone and read the text, wondering what he meant about a roommate. I shrugged, and she smiled. Regardless, we'd find out after New Year's Eve. If Henry would be around too, it'd be fun.

By five, the sun had gone down, and the Night Creatures had just set up in the extra seating area where their class would present their final projects. I saw vampires, Changelings, and Tony settling in with notecards and posters. There was even one group with a fanged puppet that looked vaguely like Count Von Count from *Sesame Street*.

"They're loud, huh?" Lynn gestured at the band, then crunched cereal as they warmed up, leaning against me in a booth.

"Extremely. But they're also really good." I put my arm around her, feeling like I'd been with her for years and we'd only just met, all at the same time.

We sat through all the presentations before it was their turn, then the dulcet strains of *Garlic Sucks Less Than Us* met my ears. I felt Lynn's sides shaking with laughter as she watched me lip-sync all the lyrics I'd learned by heart the night before.

When it was over, everyone in the dining hall stood up to applaud and cheer. Even Blaine did a golf clap. The bass player went to the PA and turned the master volume down. Then he went to the mic and cleared his throat.

"This one was popular back around when we all got turned. Enjoy it. Two, three, four!"

I heard a riff that was familiar from my early memories of Dad's fighting days. I threw my head back and laughed, hugging Lynn tighter. Night Creatures was playing Blink 182's *All the Small Things*, which used to be Dad's entrance music. As soon as she recognized it, Lynn sang along with me.

SHIFTING GEARS

A PROVIDENCE PARANORMAL COLLEGE
SHORT STORY

SHIFTING GEARS

Blaine

In the alley next to The Brick End, I took a deep breath, then exhaled to get what I hoped was all the remaining smoke out of my system. Smoking's illegal at eating and drinking establishments in Providence, even dragon smoke. None of the cops here would care about my Harcourt pedigree if they thought I'd lit one up, either.

I didn't bother adjusting my clothes or hair. Dragon shifters don't have to worry about those things. Well, technically neither did any other type of magical shifter, but since everything in that department besides Tanuki and yours truly were extinct, it's a fine point. In any case, I found myself stalling instead of heading inside. My hesitation remained an utter mystery, however.

Leaning against the cold brick, I contemplated and found no answer. But I'd sort of expected that. We don't live lives of expository plot, tied up in a neat little bow of conclusion. We exist as if we're walking down a street, putting days one in front of the last instead of feet. On that note, I figured it was time to either put up or shut up. I opted for the former.

Rounding the corner toward the door, I shoe-gazed instead of looking where I was going. First mistake of the evening.

"*Oof!*"

I'd elbow-checked somebody solidly enough to displace my center of gravity. The ice underfoot gave no quarter to my fashionable snow boots and I went down, tangled up with my unknown and unintended victim.

"Fewmets!" I spluttered, bits of ice flying from my lips.

My hands and feet fruitlessly scrabbled against ice or dug into snow. I'd fallen, and I couldn't get up. Fortunately, I'm a dragon of the fiery variety. I thought of warm things until the ice and snow around me melted, then I stood up and evaporated what remained on my clothes and skin.

"Blaine Harcourt!" The guy on the ground let out a barking sort of laugh. He got up, snow clinging to his flannel-clad forearms and acid-washed shins. "Should have known I'd see you here. Playboy Blaine, love 'em and leave 'em, right?"

"What?" I put my hands on my hips, the question stoking my ire. You go missing for one hour with one Psychic at one party during your first week on campus, and nosy werewolves make assumptions forever. "I've never been to one of those speed-dating things in my life."

"Yeah, sure, fine. Whatever." Josh Dennison dropped a wink but grinned a little too widely. "So, you going in or what?"

"Um."

I almost didn't since the werewolf's low opinion of my reputation rankled. But it was cold out, and I had no other plans besides rattling around my mother's house in Newport like the last pea in the can.

"All right. Brains before beauty, then." Josh reached toward the door, but I got in his way.

"Brains, my tail." I walked in before him. Being outsmarted by a mere mortal at the end of Fall semester hadn't done my ego any favors.

Inside, garish pink decorations hung from every available surface in one corner of the bar. Pink tablecloths draped three round tables with numbers in the center. Pink's the worst color ever, an eternal fence-sitter, neither blazing red nor stark white. The Brick End wasn't brickish at all, but it sure looked like the end of something.

"It's the end of the world." The statement was growled through clenched teeth.

"As we know it?" My response came out automatically before I knew the speaker's identity.

I turned my head to find Tony Gitano, the most untrustworthy cat shifter I'd ever had the displeasure to meet. With his father's Mafioso gang running a brisk Extrahuman Black Market out of Olneyville, most people thought an honest cat shifter was as mythical as a unicorn. He sat on the bench near the door, wrapped in his ever-present black trench coat.

"Hey." Josh just sat down next to Tony like it was no big deal for wolfy dudes to hang out with feline people. He asked the cat, "How are you?"

"I feel fine." Tony turned his head and looked at me from the corner of his eye.

"How can you feel fine?" I rolled my eyes and talked with my hands like the good Italian boy Tony wasn't. I figured he could use the mockery. "Cats and dogs sitting together equals mass hysteria!"

"Yeah, and if you want to have a go at this speed-dating thing, you ought to sit down too." Josh jerked his thumb at the space on the other side of him. At least he didn't want me to sit next to Tony.

Glancing around for some concrete sign that this was, in fact, the place, I saw it. Taped to the wall above Tony's head was a Xerox with text and a big arrow pointing down, making the cat man look for all the world like an RPG quest-giver, or maybe a Sim. It read, *Wait here for your Speed Date!*

My hands clenched into fists, not because I wanted to punch anyone, but because I really love digging my nails into the palms of my hands for no good reason. I sat down. Almost immediately, a blonde woman with stick-straight hair, frosted pink lip gunk, and tracts of land far larger than I generally preferred bounced over.

"Here are your numbers!" She took her time smoothing a number one sticker on Josh's shirt, giggled when she stuck number two to Tony's trench coat, then wrinkled her nose and handed me the sticker that said number three.

"Hey—" I started, but she trotted away before I could protest too much about the unequal treatment.

The undecorated side of the bar was full of people watching Extrahuman College Basketball. That explained why it was just the three of us guys here for the Speed Date. I faked a yawn, trying to be subtle about checking for the missing piece of this puzzle and got a grumbled "Watch it" from Josh. I'd elbowed him by accident, but I'd spotted the ladies.

A redhead my height leaned against a wall next to Bianca Brighton, a Psychic Medium I recognized because of her purple hair. A blonde sat nearby with her nose in a copy of *Dragon's Blood* by Jane Yolen. I scratched my head, trying to figure out who'd come to a bar and hide in a trade paperback.

"Hairballs!" Tony stood up, pulled the number two sticker off his chest, and stuck it on the seat. "Gotta go."

He ran for the door like a cat out of hell. Josh blinked after him, then turned and shrugged. I shook my head, peering at the redhead and then the hidden blonde as though I'd suddenly acquired x-ray vision and could see through the book. But that was stupid. Concentrating on another sense, I used my nose to identify the two ladies I hadn't met.

Shutting my eyes helped me pay attention to what my sense of smell had to say. The redhead smelled like Faerie, the Unseelie kind. She had long hair with plaits in it, which I liked, but a solid and muscular build that was the opposite of my type. I turned my schnoz on the blonde, except that once I got a whiff, I realized she was a shifter, and I had met her after all.

"Okay, guys." The hostess' voice made me open my eyes. The ladies sat at the tables already. She sent Josh over to Bianca and seated me with the blonde shifter. After that, she set a timer on a red digital clock.

"Hi, Blaine." The girl put her book down, leaned her cheek on one hand, and sighed, her eyes on the door.

"Olivia, are you okay?" Some guys might turn mean at her unhappy-to-see-me tone. I'm not some guys, I'm a Harcourt, which means I'm never the first to dish out nastiness.

"I was." She still wouldn't look at me, just at the pink-enshrouded table.

"Cat got you down?" Almost everybody knew Olivia Adler had the hots for Tony Gitano, except for the paranoid neighborhood cat-man, of course.

"I'm sorry. I shouldn't let it get to me." Finally, she looked me in the eye. "I should ask you what your favorite movie is or something."

"Yeah, but it's okay." I shrugged, even though I'd have asked the diurnally inclined owl shifter out on a date under other circumstances. "You didn't come here to see me. You can do that on campus any day of the week."

"Thanks for understanding."

A buzzer rang, the kind that comes from the sort of alarm clock you want to chuck at a wall to shut off. The hostess with the leastest clicked over on her wannabe-Empire-State-Building heels and shut it off.

She made Olivia get up and take Bianca's place with Josh, who scratched behind his ear like an actual wolf instead of just a wolf shifter. The Medium sat on the bench, and the hostess directed the redhead to my table.

"Hello, I'm Blaine." I stuck out my hand, grinning. She wasn't my type, but I hadn't seen this lady on campus before and wanted to at least make an effort at friendliness.

"Gemma." She sat down and crushed my hand in hers.

"Ow! Um, I mean how. Are you doing?" I recognized her finally. From Newport. She'd been down at the precinct a few times for troublemaking as a kid.

"Meh." She let go of my hand, which was more of a relief than the damn buzzer getting turned off earlier.

"Meh?" I blinked. Blunt honesty wasn't what I'd have expected from a Goblin, but maybe she wasn't one.

"What are we, cats?" She smirked. "Meh, meow. Get it?" Honest, strong, worse than Dad's bad jokes. Gemma must be a Troll.

"No, but Olivia wishes one of us were." I winked.

"I don't understand." Gemma's expression went blank, which of course, it would. She didn't go to PPC or know its student gossip.

"That's okay. I don't either." I shrugged.

"So, a billionaire dragon at a speed-dating event." She snorted. "Sounds like an unrealistic romance-novel plot. You know, the kind with a healthy dose of smut."

"Basically fan fiction, then?"

"Something like that."

"I don't read it." I wouldn't admit that I'd written some of the bad Harry Potter variety back in high school.

"Okay. Do you like boating?"

"Um, no. Not really." I stuck my thumbs up. "Who's a Fire dragon that gets nervous in too much water? This guy." I turned the thumbs toward my chest.

"Ha." You could have called the sound coming out of Gemma's mouth a laugh, but if so, you'd have to consider snapping your fingers a valid form of applause.

"I bet you like boating, though."

"It's sort of my life." She pulled her blouse off one shoulder, showing off a tribal tattoo. I'd seen its like before, although not in the flesh.

"Are you seriously one of the Goblin King's Privateers?"

"Yup. A captain, no less."

"Well, I guess we're incompatible then."

She mumbled something that sounded like "Thank God," but before I could call her on it, the buzzer nearly shocked me into shifting. Good thing I didn't, considering the entire bar was half the size of me in dragon form. I'd have taken the building down like a one-dragon demolition crew.

The hostess peered at us, then shrugged. I watched her turn to look at the table Josh had been sitting at, which was empty. Bianca had also left the building.

"Um, it looks like we're the last Extrahumans standing." I fidgeted with the goofy pink tablecloth.

"Whatever." Gemma stood.

For a second there, I thought she might flip the table in a Fae version of berserker rage. Maybe her restraint was similar to what stopped me from shifting, but I always sucked at the whole empathy thing, so I didn't much care either way. I watched the literal pirate turn on her heel and stride out of the place. But I had to stay put, or it'd look like I was following her.

"This job sucks." The hostess stuffed her obnoxious timer into her oversized handbag. Her lower lip trembled, and her cheeks carried high spots of a pink that put her lip gloss to shame. "I quit!"

She slammed the door on her way out.

I tried turning my gaze heavenward for guidance or maybe some other form of comfort, but the gaudy tinsel hearts attached to the drop-ceiling got in the way. True love had come for my roommate Bobby, who was the most stand-up guy I'd ever met. I was a far cry from decent, so my situation seemed hopeless.

Miracles didn't exist. It'd take a metric ton of luck for a guy like me to find Miss Right. I had no idea that thought would come back to slap me upside my scaly head mere months later.

FANGS FOR THE MEMORIES

PROVIDENCE PARANORMAL COLLEGE
BOOK TWO

Memory is a tricky business.

No one remembers Maddie May. That's fine with her, since that's just a side effect of Umbral magic. Unfortunately, she has to take the Magic Theory Lab at Providence Paranormal College. Maddie won't pass if the Professor can't remember her.

Henry Baxter's a psychic vampire who can store total recall for himself and others. He's been in business since 1986, but new regulations mean he needs a degree to keep operating. Going back to college after sixty years on Earth is definitely a drag, especially since society treats vampires as second-class citizens.

The woman everyone forgets and the man who remembers everything seem like a natural pair. While Maddie's all for it, Henry keeps pushing her away. But what if the only way they'll survive is together?

CHAPTER ONE

Henry

The bronze circle looked burnished in the dim mezzanine light of the Nocturnal Lounge. I'd been exhausted when I finished it, and I couldn't remember that happening to me before. I wondered whether it had. I might have wiped the memory, storing a copy in some object not too different from this one. Memory was my business; copying, recording, sometimes deleting.

I could wash my hands of this project after sunset when I bound the amulet to the magus I'd made it for. She had Umbral Affinity, a rare talent that went with her magical energy. I'd had a friend with that talent up until 1989 just before the Big Reveal happened and the whole world found out about Extrahumans. She ended up dead in the same incident that made me a vampire.

"Hey, Henry!" I glanced into the lower level at a wiry dark-haired guy in a trench-coat. I wrinkled my nose, getting it used to the gamy scent of a shifter. With the amulet in my pocket, I headed down, trying not to look as reluctant as I felt. Being an introverted vampire with psychic powers wasn't usually a problem. Being one who had to go back to school after over so many years was a whole different ball of wax.

"Tony." I grinned at the cat shifter with my lips closed. He'd never seemed disturbed seeing vampire fangs before, but I didn't like showing them off.

"Lynn sent me. I'm here to bring you to your client." Once Tony Gitano stopped talking with his hands, like a good Italian boy, he poured a cup of coffee.

"Oh. Okay." I watched him dump five packets of sugar in his cup. Sometimes he took it with just milk and other times black. Nothing I knew about Tony made sense. That was par for the course with most feline shifters. I never knew back then exactly what type he was or how much he'd been through.

"You want some?" He stirred the cup briskly, then tossed the stirrer and empty packets in the trash.

"I don't drink…coffee." I leaned against the counter, still feeling the languid heaviness in my limbs which meant the sun was still up. "It's too early to leave. Not sunset yet."

"I know. But I figured It'd be nice to have coffee without all the estrogen." Tony smirked. "Your client's there with some female friends."

"I'll be good to go by the time you finish that." I glanced at the coffee, glad he'd poured it. Eating and drinking regular food worked, but all tastes paled in comparison to scent. Being a vampire was sort of like having a slightly burnt tongue all the time unless blood was on the menu.

"Figured as much." He splashed cream into his cup, making clouds in his coffee. "I got a question for you."

"Go ahead." I hoped he didn't have a terminally ill relative. That kind of thing was always awkward. Turning had strict regulations, and it didn't get rid of the effects of most diseases the body couldn't eventually heal on its own. Turn someone with stomach cancer, they'd be in pain for eternity. Turn someone with Alzheimer's, they'd never recover their lost memories.

"Why are you even here?" He blew on his coffee. "At school, I mean. Don't want to get metaphysical this early in the day."

"I need a license if I want to keep my business." It was mostly that simple, although I could have just gone to community classes. But I knew the Headmistress here and she'd arranged a scholarship.

"Yeah, I've heard that. But how do you still take clients?" He sipped the hot beverage, glancing up at me over the rim of the cup.

"They can't stop me from doing piecework, but the law says I can't advertise or claim any business expenses." I shrugged. Even with Extrahumans added in, tax law was boring.

"Fred's dad didn't have to get a degree to keep running Redford Renovations." Tony raised an eyebrow. "Uses magic and enhanced materials, too. Unfair, huh?"

"It is." I grinned, trying to lighten the mood. "I can handle it."

"Seems lame. I mean, you're a vampire and a Psychic which means double limits. You can't go out in the daytime, and you're a one-trick pony. Fred's dad is a full member of the Goblin King's court, with a pretty high rank. Redcaps are bad-asses. Way more there for them to worry about."

"You know an awful lot about this stuff for a freshman cat shifter." Redford Renovations had big connections, which went a long way in Rhode Island as far as licensing goes. Being Unseelie just made him more powerful. The King's power grew with every new changeling who tithed to him, and Unseelie was the way to go since the Extrahuman status quo changed with the Big Reveal.

Tony laughed so hard he would have spilled his coffee if it wasn't already half gone. He took a deep breath, then shook his head and ran a hand through his hair.

"School of hard knocks." He sipped. "I was an employee. Took two years off after high school to work there and save money. Also, I'm more curious than the average cat."

"So I've seen." It was my turn to chuckle.

Tony's mouth stretched into a flat line. He crossed his arms and tilted his chin slightly up, a hard glint in his narrowed eyes. His coffee stuck out in the hand under his left elbow, still upright.

"Not in a Psychic way, man." I sighed.

"It's not you, Henry." Tony's voice came slightly muffled through his clenched jaw. "Turn your ears up and have a listen. Someone's trying to break in here."

I tilted my head and focused my minimal daylight energy on amping up my hearing. I heard scratches and splintering wood. Someone was almost through one of the walls in the stacks directly across from where we stood. If they broke through, I'd be standing right in the last light of the sun.

I would have leaped out of the way, but the best I could do was a trot. I was slower than a regular human in the daytime, even with one of my senses enhanced. Tony did better. He sprang off in a burst of Extrahuman speed. Then, he leaned forward and rushed me. I hit the opposite wall underneath the mezzanine.

"Blanket!" I glanced up at the emergency box on the wall above my head.

"On it!" Tony shattered its glass front, then pulled out the leaden tarp inside and covered me with it.

I huddled under a safety blanket for the thirteenth time in my unlife, wondering how one cat shifter could protect me from whoever wanted me dead bad enough to literally tear down a wall in the magically warded Nocturnal Lounge. That took raw physical power and strong magic. I thought I'd have just a few seconds, but time stretched on.

I breathed to measure its passage, hearing more splintering crunches, shattering glass, and the noise of upholstery being torn. Some sounds were less than a yard away. Who or whatever had burst in was literally tearing the place apart looking for me. I had no idea how the attacker didn't see the bright red blanket.

After four minutes, the effects of the sun vanished. I leaped up, throwing the blanket aside to see a snarling jet-black form in the middle of the room. Wisps of dark smoke or soot curled up from its ears, tail, and claws. It went on four legs but wasn't shaped like any natural or magical animal I'd seen. Its mouth was pitch-black, too, its roar a hollow sound more like wind through an alley than anything living. It had no eyes, only emptiness where they should be.

Tony stood next to me, staring at the thing. He didn't move, and the thing didn't seem to see him. Tony slowly raised his arm, pressing a single finger to his lips. I didn't dare open my mouth. Magic. How in all the Realms did a cat shifter know how to cast a spell? I held my tongue, watching and waiting. And Remembering.

The best way to counter an unknown creature like this was to make a Psychic impression. I could erase regular memories, but not an impression. I'd never forget this particular attack for the rest of my nights, but an impression would let me find out what this thing was and how to stop it if it showed up again. Even better, I'd be able to share the experience with others as though they'd been there. I could get help as long as I could find willing people . Most just avoided vampires like me.

I watched the thing sniff Tony's fallen coffee cup, then the spot on the floor where I'd been standing. It raised its head to nose the counter-top, then followed my scent back up the steps and around to my usual table in the mezzanine. Its footsteps made no sound at all, but trails and tendrils of shadow clung to the spots where it placed its feet. Those shadows rose and dissipated in moments. Maybe a Magus would still be able to see them, but I was just a psychic.

I saw Tony shake his head, pressing his finger even more firmly over his lips. Overhead, a crash and howl carried down to meet our ears. Scattering paper and sharp cracks echoed through the wrecked Lounge. For a creature that seemed insubstantial, it sure did a lot of damage.

I breathed again to mark the time, straining to hear anything or anyone outside the breach in the wall. Normal traffic sounds from Thayer Street came through, plus the bleat of a siren further down College Hill. After another minute, I couldn't hear the creature anymore. Tony kept his hand over his mouth but beckoned with the other. Then, he went up the stairs to the regular exit. I followed but looked over my shoulder at the hole in the wall. I made an impression of that and the completely decimated corner I used to work at. Almost nothing was where it had been before the attack.

Tony increased his pace once we got outside, still gesturing for quiet. He led me down Thayer, then across to the dining hall. He went around to the back of the building and ducked behind a dumpster. After that, he snapped his fingers. I watched a particolored translucent membrane appear and then pop like a soap bubble. I remembered from a summer afternoon over forty-five years earlier.

"We need to talk now." Tony stepped back out from behind the dumpster but stopped at the corner of the building. He put his hands on his hips, elbows pushing the sides of his trench-coat out to either side. "I just saved your life. Not a peep about how I did it to anyone."

"You have my word." I followed him, watching his shoulders and gait ease into their usual relaxed tilt. "How did you do it? I've never heard of a cat shifter with magic before."

"How'd I do what?" He stared at me, unblinking. "Make up whatever story you want, but keep it to yourself."

"Do you have any idea what that thing was?"

"Grim." He dropped his arms to the side, looking tired out all of a sudden.

"Well, yes." I rolled my eyes. Tony, like most cat shifters, was frustratingly dodgy when asked a direct question. "That's a decent adjective to use for it, but—"

"No. That thing's called a Grim, an elemental, summoned, Pure Faerie creature." Tony turned his head to look me in the eye as he opened the door to the dining hall. "They'll be back two more times." He stepped into the vestibule, then went through the second door.

"Well, that's not so bad." I followed him, glancing around the dining hall to see a trio of girls at a table in the corner. One of them looked familiar.

"Oh, yes, it is." Tony shut his eyes. "Every time Grims show up, they kill someone."

Before I could say anything about neither of us dying, the familiar-looking girl stood up and waved at us. It was Lynn Frampton, mate of the bear shifter I'd helped just before Fall exams.

"Hi, Henry! " She sounded much cheerier than usual. "Happy Winter Inter-session!"

She had no idea. Then again, I barely did. All I knew was, things sure hadn't started out happy.

CHAPTER TWO

Maddie

I'd sat with Lynn and Olivia, having coffee and giving the re-hash of who I was and why I was there. Re-run introductions were boring but essential. Nobody except my immediate family remembered me because of Umbral Affinity, the lamest magus enhancement ever. Lynn was my roommate, so her memory caught up with a bunch of the things I had to tell over again, but Olivia didn't. She kept apologizing about side-effects from the medication to keep her on a diurnal schedule.

"Seriously, I'm cool with repeating myself." I curled my nearly always cold hands around the hot porcelain of the cup. "It's just part of being me."

"I just didn't want to be rude, is all. I should remember, too, with my photographic memory." Olivia twirled a shiny teaspoon in her already empty cup. "If it were me everyone forgot all the time, I don't know what I'd do."

"It's not rude, it's magic." Lynn had a book as usual. She read out of it. "An enhancement to Magi of the Umbral school, Umbral Affinity is the tendency to escape memorability."

My roommate closed the book and looked up. Her face lit up a little, but I knew whoever had arrived wasn't her mate Bobby. That would have made her eyes brighter than a Christmas tree. I watched her call out to Henry and Tony, waving them over. I didn't bother turning around, just shuffled my chair over to make room for them.

A strange tingle came from my right side as they sat down. I looked out the corner of my eye, wondering why Henry Baxter, the Psychic memory vampire, felt like Umbral magic. I turned in my seat to scrutinize any residual energy traces. Anyone who'd been around a spell in action or a magical creature had them.

His gaze met mine only briefly, then he cut his eyes away. I saw wispy traces of shadow no one else at the table could sense except maybe by smell. Bright scraps of some other magic I couldn't identify shimmered, fading just as rapidly. Under that, the gray static hum of unliving vampiric energy made a constant yet faintly pleasant drone. I couldn't find a trace of Henry's Psychic energy, which was normal with a side of regular sauce. Only dragon shifters and Tanuki saw both kinds. Magi like me needed a magipsychic device to get a look at that.

"So where's your roommate, Lynn?"

I couldn't help it. I laughed. Henry turned to look at me again, startling slightly so his mouth opened and I could see the tips of his fangs. I smiled back. My dad had been turned when I was little. Plus, I'm a little desensitized to anything dangerous. I'd grown up with an inherent fearlessness that comes from no one remembering who I am.

There were a few exceptions, but unless my own family decided to go on a rampage, I'd be safe from just about anyone or anything besides Pure Faerie creatures or natural disasters. And if a Magus with Umbral affinity ever went rogue, anyone they wanted dead was a goner, anyway. No one would see or remember them coming until it was too late.

All those thoughts happened in an instant before I was conscious of taking one breath. In the next, I noticed everyone staring at me.

Tony was across from me next to Olivia. Both of them wrinkled their noses as though they both smelled something strong at the same time. I glanced back at Henry's face only to find myself eye-locked with him. Vampires don't have to blink, but he did.

"I'm Lynn's roommate, Maddie. Before you forget me again, I have to ask why you and Tony are covered with Umbral energy."

"That's not important." Henry kept looking at me right along with everyone else. I was a little south of comfortable.

"It is." I didn't want to blink, so I used the trick Mother had taught me and narrowed my eyes, then glanced up. "I'm not letting you do the Psychic wooj on me until I know you didn't tangle with anyone I'm related to."

Henry sighed. I could tell he didn't want to deal with this, and I felt a little bad. He probably thought this was more discrimination, and that maybe I was a bigot. Circumstances during the Big Reveal had caused a rift between vampires and the rest of Extrahuman society. I'd heard the humans were even worse.

"We had a brush with a Grim about fifteen minutes ago," Tony answered. "You want proof, head over to what's left of the Nocturnal Lounge."

"There won't be proof." Lynn twirled a pencil against a blank page in her notebook. "This happened at sunset, right?"

"Before, actually." Henry gazed into my eyes, but I got the feeling he wasn't just seeing me. He was Remembering. "About five minutes between when it broke through and sunset."

"Even worse, then." Lynn's pencil scratched more purposefully against the paper. "There won't be any evidence it was a Grim. All the Umbral residue will vanish into the ether in a couple minutes. Heck, they might even try to blame you guys for all the mess if you're there before the authorities."

"Even worse, the Campus Police probably won't do much." Olivia leaned her chin on her hand. "They don't care much for nocturnal anything, just like the regular police."

"Yeah, cops sure like to overlook things like that. But I have a string I could pull." Tony leaned back in his chair. "A Grim is serious business. I'll need some kind of proof I can show my contact, though."

"I'm proof. I did my psychic 'wooj' back at the lounge." One corner of Henry's mouth tilted up, but the smile didn't touch his eyes. "Is your friend the type of person who'd listen to a vampire?"

"He wouldn't even let you try to prove anything without someone trustworthy vouching for you, a description I don't fit, by the way." Tony didn't meet anyone's eyes. "He's a werewolf."

Hisses, boos, and even an outraged choke came from everyone around the table. Only Henry and I kept quiet. No respectable werewolf would believe a vampire about anything nowadays. They'd been the most at odds during the Big Reveal exactly because they'd been the most friendly before. Alliances going back centuries had crumbled when old friends sold each other out to save their own skins. I wasn't sure how bad things had gotten, but the only groups with more enmity were the two Faerie courts.

"Would he listen to Blaine?" Henry raised an eyebrow.

"Oh, definitely." Tony smiled, then let out a chuckle. "If you can convince a paranoid dragon shifter to head over here when he doesn't have to."

"Blaine owes me a favor, remember?" Henry folded his hands together, leaning back in his chair.

"He's over in Newport for Winter Break, but said he'd give dragonish help on the phone." Lynn pulled out her phone. "If Henry's calling in his favor, he'll have to show his scaly face."

I saw Lynn get up and walk away with her phone, watching her face brighten as her friend picked up on the other end. Olivia stared almost blankly, probably because of the Adderal forcing her into a diurnal pattern. I couldn't tell where Tony's attention went, but cat shifters couldn't resist eavesdropping. Henry turned his head toward the exit, then glanced back at me.

"If you want to wait until this is settled before I bind your amulet, Maddie, I understand." He put his hand in his pocket, then opened it to reveal what looked like a brass pocket watch on a chain. I didn't care one bit about that.

"How did you remember me?" No one did without a reminder once they'd looked away. I'd need to join a shifter pack, make friends with Faeries, or have a baby for someone to know who I was. He'd forgotten me earlier. But what if that had been an act? Vampires couldn't turn shifters or Tithed Faeries. I couldn't hide my shiver. At least Henry was the only one paying enough attention to notice.

"It's what I do, this Psychic memory thing." He glanced at the amulet in his hand. "I made a psychic impression, just like I did with the Grim. I'll never forget you now."

"Did anyone ever tell you making Psychic impressions of girls who were born after you got turned is a bit creepy?" I winked. What was wrong with me? I'd gone from freaking out to making jokes in less than twenty seconds.

"People tell me vampires are creepy a hundred different ways every day." He leaned his elbow on the table. "If I let it bother me, I'd stay home even more than I already do."

"I wasn't saying it to bother you." I felt like a total twit with no idea why I should care that much about what a guy I'd just met thought of me. "Sorry."

"You were joking." He shrugged, grinning mildly. "Most aren't. They don't care if they bother a vampire." Henry shrugged. "Anyway, I figured it'd be better to remember a client with Umbral Affinity. If you need another amulet, you won't have to explain yourself over and over."

"Makes sense." I shook my head to clear it of the banter. "Wait, you made a Psychic impression of the Grim? Is that the proof you were talking about?"

"Yup." He tapped his nose with one finger. "I can put it in a penny or something, let everyone have a look at it. They'll get a front-row seat to the Grims' performance of *Tear Down The Lounge* without any of the risk."

"If you can make amulets with impressions in them, then why worry about convincing a werewolf? Shouldn't the police just believe something like that?"

"That's a logical way to think about it. Problem is, distrust isn't so rational. Let me show you something." Henry pulled a phone and a touchscreen glove from his pocket. "The technically dead need these." He put the glove on his right hand, covering his thumb and first two fingers. Then he tapped and swiped the phone.

"I totally already know vampires can't just use a smartphone without those." I smiled. "You're not my first."

"No wonder you don't mind sitting at the Goth kid's table." He chuckled a little.

"I sit at any kind of table I want. No consequences, no regrets. I learn better when I see something up close and personal."

"Speaking of that, here." Henry handed his phone over. "I completely disagree with the website I'm showing you, but I think you'll understand my point and reasoning."

I blinked in near-disbelief at the page full of misinformation. The header had a motif of Nazi symbols, and the sidebar's lettering stood out against an old, grainy photo of people in pointy white hoods. This was a website for a white human supremacist group. One "article" on this page refuted the Holocaust. Further down the page was a baldly revisionist five-paragraph "essay" legitimizing slavery. The last one told how vampires were just the gay people who'd died of AIDS in the 1980s and 90s, back from the dead to spread the disease. I checked the fine-print information at the bottom, hoping to see the tag-line of a satire blog. I didn't. The site's followers actually viewed the world this way.

"I can't. There are no words for this." I pushed the phone away like it was poisonous.

"I do." Henry took his phone and closed out of the browser. "Insulting. Sickening. Depressing. Terrifying."

"This problem of yours with the Grim will be tough to solve." Lynn's voice came from over my shoulder. "Blaine will help, but as you just showed…um, your friend here, most people will think a Grim hunting a vampire is the vampire's own fault."

"True story." Henry shrugged, then took off the glove and pocketed the phone. "Sad, but true."

"Jeez, sorry." Lynn walked around me and hunkered down to look at my face. "I definitely know you, but forgot your name again." She blushed a little.

"Maddie." Recognition made her eyes twinkle.

"Yes. My roommate." Lynn sighed, looking like she'd just scratched an itch on the inside of her skull. "Blaine and I will help Henry with this Grim problem. Bobby will, too, once he gets here. I can handle all the research we need, along with my terminology class. You other ladies don't have to worry about it."

"I'll help." I watched Henry start, and thought it was because he'd forgotten me. Then I remembered he couldn't. It was my turn to blush. "I wouldn't even be able to take this course if it wasn't for you, Henry."

"I'm in." Tony put his fists on his hips. "That Grim tore up the whole Nocturnal Lounge. I fracking love that place. Whoever summoned it deserves a piece of my mind and anything else we can bring against him."

"I'll help, too." Olivia crossed her arms over her chest. "I'm in the same class as Lynn, so we can study together and research Grims and Summoners."

"Great." Lynn stood up and stretched. "Let's hit the library. Blaine will meet us there. Grab books, notebooks, computers or whatever from wherever you stash them. I need a few things from our room. Maddie, are you cool with the Psychic wooj now?"

"Yes, but not here." I got up and shouldered my backpack. "This place feels like a fishbowl." I glanced at the wall of windows that made up the front of the dining hall. "Let's go to the fifth-floor lounge."

"Lead on." Henry put his hands in his jacket pockets. We headed out of the dining hall and over to the dorm.

CHAPTER THREE

Henry

I sat in the fifth floor common room, waiting for Maddie to come back from the restroom. I wasn't sure what got into me back at the dining hall, over-sharing with her like that. It had been years since I had a friend to talk to. Had I spilled my guts because no one would remember anything Maddie might say about me? No. I'd told her because her interest seemed genuine.

I wasn't sure how to feel about that. I'd always kept things like that disgusting website secret. There was something about Maddie. Of course, it could simply be the fact that I thought she was gorgeous. I hadn't been around a woman I'd found attractive since the Twentieth Century. She would have fit right in with the old crowd from before my turning.

I stopped reminiscing and got the amulet out again. I held it as though I could warm it even though that was impossible. Room-temperature was my default setting until I drank blood from a living creature. No one did that anymore unless it was a serious emergency.

I'd kept my head down, played by the rules. Being a good little psychic vampire hadn't gotten me anywhere special. It also hadn't gotten me killed.

"Okay. I'm ready for all the wooj you can throw now." Maddie sat on the low coffee table between us. She held her hands out, palms up.

"Under the circumstances, do you think it's a good idea?" I stuck my hand in my pocket, fingertips brushing cold metal.

"It's the only idea. I can't do this lab without your amulet, Henry." She shrugged. "I guess you could let me fail if you're mean or something."

"But I had the amulet on me when I got attacked." I gripped the amulet, still hesitant to take it out of my pocket. "Had just finished it, in fact. Aren't you worried about the Grim?"

"Not really. They can't do anything to Magi with Umbral Affinity, you know." She smiled. "We always see them coming, and they have a hard time tracking us. Our magic smells too much like theirs."

"I didn't know that. Never learned much about anything besides my own abilities. I knew an Umbral Magus once, but back then everyone kept their powers secret."

"That's okay. I'm kind of odd because I like talking about magic. They won't be able to teach me anything about Umbral magic in particular. My parents say I could teach them a thing or five."

"Doesn't it bother you, that you're here to learn and it's not really relevant?" Maybe she felt the same way I did about being at school.

"I'm majoring in Magic Theory, and that's always relevant. I need to know how magic works because my parents are both Psychics. My aunt was the Magus." Maddie clenched her jaw so hard I heard her teeth grind. "She died when I was little. I'm mostly self-taught, so maybe that's why I want to be a teacher. Why in all the Realms am I telling you this? Oh, jeez, did I say that out loud?" Maggie's dusky complexion would have hidden the color in her cheeks, but no one can secretly blush around a vampire.

"Maybe for the same reason I showed you that website."

"Which is?" She leaned forward like I was about to put on some kind of performance.

"I have no idea." I held the amulet in my pocket, wondering whether a class was worth Maddie risking a Grim attack. "But that's okay."

"Coincidence?" She stared at my hidden hand, waiting for the not so big reveal.

"Not my area of expertise. That's a Magus thing unless I'm mistaken." I raised an eyebrow.

"Yes, and one I need this amulet of yours in order to study. I'll be happy to share what I learn, especially since Blaine still hasn't taken this class." She rolled her eyes. "Did you hear about his wacky conspiracy theory? He thinks some kooky Magi are messing with the school? It's truly tinfoil-hat worthy."

"Blaine's an overachiever." I pulled the amulet from my pocket, opening my hand. I wanted to help her. If the amulet put her in danger, I'd just have to help her more. "Also, not nearly as easy to talk to as some other people I've met."

"True story. Speaking of Trogdor the Burninator's imminent arrival, let's bind this amulet already." Her smile was easy and relaxed. "Lynn doesn't like being late to the library, whether she's meeting temperamental dragon shifters there or not."

"This binding will be a little different from most others I make. This is supposed to last three weeks of inter-session. You must turn it on and off yourself, so it's not running while you sleep or do anything you'd want Umbral Affinity for."

"Okay." The amulet could have been solid gold or a moon rock from the way Maddie looked at it.

"When you want to use the amulet, put it on, then say *'ex umbra in solem.'* And when you want to shut the effects off, say *'ex solem in umbra.'* If those phrases aren't okay for some reason, we can agree on something else. Just speak up now about it."

"No, that's fine. They don't use Latin in this class. Should be good."

"Great. So, when you're ready, just put your hands on the amulet. When I say the Latin mumbo-jumbo, repeat after me. I'll have to touch you the whole time. Is that all right?"

"You know, I was there when you did Bobby's binding." The little curve of her lips would have seemed shy if she hadn't been looking me right in the eyes.

"Oh?" I tried not to look as stunned as I felt. How she could be this calm around a "bloodthirsty vampire" was beyond my comprehension.

"Yeah. I know the drill. It's fine, I won't freak out about touching a vampire or anything." Her smile brightened until it put the moon to shame. "You're just a guy with a sun allergy on a liquid diet." She dropped me a wink, then took the amulet.

I had no idea what to say to any of that. If only being a vampire was that simple. She knew it wasn't. She'd seen the website and said I wasn't the first she'd met. Maddie had seen more than most anyone would imagine, too. Being effectively invisible meant she could watch or listen to just about anything without being noticed.

Any Magus with Umbral Affinity could walk unseen, hidden better than someone under Faerie Glamour. Some old legends said the sun couldn't penetrate a properly enhanced Umbral shield. I wrapped my hands around hers, feeling a slow, nervous fear that usually only plagued me in big crowds. I pushed it down since I had to focus. I looked straight ahead, meeting Maddie's deep-brown gaze. No, that wouldn't work. I cleared my throat, closing my eyes instead.

"This amulet will make Maddie May, Umbral magus, memorable while it's active. Those who encounter her for the next three weeks will remember her and previous interactions while it's working, even if they look away. Her name will be connected with her identity on coursework, and grades assigned will go on her record permanently. This amulet will cease to function when the Inter-session final grades are submitted, or after three weeks and one day, whichever is longer. *Ex umbra in solem, ex solem in umbra.*" I opened my eyes and let go of her hands. Maddie repeated the Latin with a much spiffier pronunciation than I'd ever managed.

"What did you do, go to some fancy prep school or something?" I clasped my hands together, not liking how they felt empty all of a sudden.

"Nope. Home-schooled." She peered at the amulet, then shrugged and undid the clasp on its chain. "Mom's a polyglot. I get all my languages from her, even the dead ones."

"How many do you know?" I was fascinated that someone this young had learned so much more than me.

"Only four." She slipped the amulet over her neck.

"Only? Most people just know one." I looked away as she tucked the bronze circle into her shirt.

"I have a lot of time to myself, whether I want it or not." She shrugged with one shoulder, the opposite corner of her mouth tilting up in a half-grin.

"Do you?" I was surprised. If I could walk around without people knowing I was a vampire, I'd be out all the time. It was dangerous to go alone as I was.

"Usually, it's fine that people forget." Maddie pulled her satchel's strap over her head to cross her body. "Sometimes, it's a giant pain. I learn tons, though, and that makes up for it."

"Bet that takes a lot of patience." I tried not to look too disappointed that we'd part company soon. I wanted to stay and talk longer. Instead, I held the door as we headed down the hall and toward the stairs.

"It's the very first thing I learned. That and recaps. I have to repeat myself every time I talk to someone." She chuckled. "Social interaction feels like the first minute of a Supernatural season finale."

"I hope you don't have Kansas singing Carry On Wayward Son stuck in your head every time." I smiled, , watching her curls bounce as she went down the steps ahead of me. "Do they ever get déjà vu?"

"Lynn sometimes does. We live together, plus she's super smart. Notices things." She pulled the door at the bottom of the stairwell open and held it for me. "It makes her more likely to realize something's wrong or missing."

"I know. She solved Bobby's hibernation problem when no one else could figure it out." I couldn't help smiling but turned my head in time to hide my fangs. "Outsmarted Blaine, even."

"Yeah. Blaine was spectacularly jealous. I watched him fuming outside the dining hall for almost twenty minutes straight, the night they met." Maddie's laugh rang out in the blandly decorated dorm foyer.

"Same night she met Bobby?" I wondered how she'd sound in the superior acoustic environment of the Nocturnal Lounge. Then I remembered that place was a total mess now and frowned. We pushed through the door to head for the library.

"Yup. And we know how that went." She sighed. "Cornily romantic, but it's nice to see people happy. Way too much of the opposite lately, you know?"

"Sometimes I think it's all I see. The downside. The clouds." I didn't dare tell her how much just being in her presence turned all that around for me. I'd sound like a psycho vampire instead of a psychic one. Bad news in the romance department.

"Means you'll be the first to recognize the silver lining when it shows up." She turned at the top of the library steps, standing at exactly my height. If the steps hadn't been so wide, I might have run right into her.

"Yeah. I think I will." I stepped around Maddie and opened the door to let her into the library.

Maddie gasped, then smiled as I held the door like she was savoring a piece of gourmet chocolate. Any chivalric gestures must be just as novel for her to receive as they were for me to give. Had I compared her smile to the moon before? Something other girls might roll their eyes at made her face glow like the last sunrise I'd seen. I didn't need to make another impression of Maddie May, but I did it anyway. Vampires like me had to take light where we could find it because we never knew when we'd see any again. At least my ability meant I'd never forget the singular beauty of that moment for the rest of my existence. The fact that a Summoner wanted me dead made any connection I could get that much more precious.

CHAPTER FOUR

Maddie

I'd had no one besides my mom and dad deliberately hold a door open for me. No one remembered to. As soon as their backs turned, people forgot. Blaming them would've been like holding a grudge against fish for swimming. In one of my many recaps with Lynn on this subject, she said I was too easygoing, and that I deserved better and should stand up for myself. I'd nodded and smiled, understanding that that was what worked for Lynn. It wouldn't for me. But that'd be different with everyone for the next few weeks, at least. And Henry would remember me forever.

I glanced back, a hot flush taking over my face. It was like having the flu last year, except my stomach felt fluttery instead of queasy. I'd read enough of Mom's corny romance novels to know what that was. I finally had my first crush. On a Psychic vampire who couldn't forget me. I'd talk to Lynn later about it, maybe more than once. For now, I headed toward the back of the library's ground floor, where my roommate usually studied.

A cloud of whitish smoke hung over the large table where they sat, a sign that we had a dragon. Lynn leaned against a sleepy-looking Bobby on a bench with a book in front of her. Tony sat on a backward chair with his arms crossed on top of the backrest. Smoke-rings wafted over Blaine's head as his fingers tapped out staccato beats on his laptop's keyboard. None of them looked up until Henry cleared his throat behind me.

"Henry?" Tony looked narrowed his eyes. "Why did you bring a random chick?"

I explained, resigned to an evening of recaps. But then I pressed pause and smiled so hard my face hurt. There's an amulet for that. It'd be worth using to stop a Grim from wreaking shadowy havoc on campus. I put my hand in my shirt, without a second thought for the raised eyebrows around the table.

"*Ex umbra in solem,*" I said. Then I sat down in a seat and pulled out a notebook.

"Excuse me?" Blaine peered over his screen, raising an eyebrow. Then he blinked and shook his head as though trying to clear it. "Woah. Trippy. Psychomagic."

"Huh." Henry peered at me too. "Yeah, the effect is a little odd, and I only see the psychic stuff."

"Lynn, why didn't you tell us your roommate could be a movie star?" Blaine might have had a sense of déjà vu, but likely no other indication he was repeating himself.

"I dunno. Maybe because she's fun and a more decent person than scaly playboys." Lynn rolled her eyes at Blaine, then stuck out her tongue and blew a raspberry in his general direction. Bobby laughed so hard he almost choked.

I laughed, too. That was my reaction whenever Blaine met me for the first time, so it did just fine this time. He shocked me by winking at Henry. The last time, he'd asked me on a date, then promptly forgot doing any such thing, which was fine by me. Blaine might be a dragon shifter, but he was more interested in the Extrahuman equivalent of Antiques Roadshow than breathing fire.

"So, Maddie here saw the Grim's energy." Henry's tone was all business. He'd leaned against one of the Reference shelves, hanging back from the others at the table.

"Makes sense." Lynn stuck a neon green flag to the page she'd been speed-reading. "I've got a book here that says they're Umbral creatures."

"If only we had a book on Umbral Affinity." Tony lifted the top book off the pile in front of him. "I thought I saw one around before, but can't remember where. Definitely not listed in the library."

"Nocturnal Lounge." Bobby stretched. "It hit Henry in the head the night I got my amulet last semester."

"Sounds right." Henry nodded. "Nice memory. Are you sure you're not a bit Psychic, Bobby? Most people just rationalize away the ghostly phenomena."

"I think some on my mom's side of the family. We get dreams about our...um, life changes." Bobby tucked a stray strand of hair behind Lynn's ear. She leaned her head on his shoulder and kept right on reading.

"Go look for it then, Cat Man." Blaine made a shooing gesture with one hand at Tony. "It's not like you're actually doing any reading."

"Nothing doing. I ain't going back there alone." Tony's voice lapsed back toward his classically nasal Rhode Island accent. He'd never remember telling me how he only did that when he was spooked. "What if it comes back?"

"It can't." I, at least, knew a thing or two about Grims. "They get summoned, kill, then vanish. They can't come back until the summoning magus calls them up again."

"Yeah and said Magus only gets to summon a Grim three times." Lynn probably knew a thing or three about Grims by now herself. "I'm still shaky on exactly how or with what. Everything I'm reading says 'unspecified anchor material' and a bunch of jargon about Summoners. Summoning's Ph.D. material, you know."

"Well, if you're safe for the rest of the night, why not head on back to the Lounge and find that Umbral Affinity book?" Blaine waved his hand in Tony's general direction again. Tony homed in on it like a house-cat on a laser pointer.

"You don't have to be so bourgeoisie about it, Trogdor." Lynn rolled her eyes. "Jeez, I'll go."

"Nope. We need you here speed-reading." Henry turned, and I finally got a good look at the minimalist image in white paint on the back of his black leather jacket. I'd know that logo anywhere. "I'll go."

"Me too." I stood up. "If there's anything magic going on there, I'll sense it."

"It's dangerous to go alone. Take this." Lynn glanced up at me over the top of her book. She tossed me a pocket-sized notebook with a pencil stuck through the spiral binding.

"I love danger." I caught the dead tree parts and put them in my handbag. Even though she used computers like everyone else, Lynn believed in the power of tangible backup. I agreed. "I'll be sure and take plenty of notes if I see anything."

I trotted to catch up to Henry, who held the door again. That was so awesome! I slid down the rickety banister, almost twisting my ankle on a patch of black ice. I got a bit ahead of him, then turned around and started walking backward. I didn't care about the ice. The risk just made things more interesting. And I was about to kick risky business up another notch and flirt with a vampire. What was a little ice compared to that?

"Bauhaus, huh?" I gave him my biggest smile. "You paint that jacket yourself?"

"Yup." Henry covered his mouth with his hand, laughing behind it. "The foibles of youth. That's a lie. I repaint it every year or two."

"At least it's not The Cure." I stuck out my tongue, then winked. "I love them both."

"Only reason it's not is that I'm a lousy painter." Henry rolled his eyes at his self-deprecation. "Thanks for coming with me. Tony's." He shrugged.

"He seems more like a chicken shifter than a cat shifter tonight." I wondered whether cat shifters like Tony Gitano were the origin of the term "scaredy cat."

"Maybe, maybe not. A Grim's like a Great Dane on Umbral steroids. Can you blame him for being scared of one?"

"Not when you put it that way. Anyway, I didn't mean to insult your friend like some kind of nearly invisible mean girl. Sorry." I felt like a giant jerk, realizing I'd been running my mouth because I was nervous. Being alone with the only guy who'd actually be able to remember me was more than a little crazy-making.

"That's okay. Thanks for coming with me. I'm not used to having help, but there's a lot of that going around tonight for some reason." Henry glanced at me, his eyes meeting mine. I tried not to blush. It was probably nothing personal, anyway.

"Want to know a secret?" I glanced to either side, breaking eye contact while pretending to make sure no one else was listening.

"Always." Henry's voice was low and soft, not at all what I'd expected.

"You should get used to it. Bobby and Lynn are both convinced your wakefulness amulet saved her life last semester." I sighed. "If he hadn't had it, she'd be dead, and he'd have flunked out.

"Wait, what?" Henry stopped walking.

"You didn't know he used it when all that ice fell off the library and buried her?" I stepped in front of him, looking up at his face even though it was back-lit by the street light. "They're mated now. That's why he didn't hibernate. I thought you knew."

"No. I did not know that." He took a deep breath, then let it out slowly. "Did you hear about Blaine's theory?"

"Which one? He's got about seven at any given time." I smirked. "Lynn loves discussing Blaine's crazy theories. I've heard about them at least five times since I got here this afternoon."

"I'm talking about the one where he thinks some Magus manipulated the weather to make Bobby flunk out." Henry stepped to the side, then continued down Thayer Street.

"That'd be an Extramagus. Those are super-rare." I turned and trotted along to catch up to him. "And Bobby stayed awake, anyway. He passed."

"I know. But that's only half of Blaine's theory. He thinks the Magus wants to shut down PPC." Henry put his hands in his pockets, shivering a little even though vampires don't really feel the cold. "That'd be an insane Extramagus."

"Uh-huh." I shrugged. "More likely Blaine's dragon is showing off a little paranoia. They're known for that, after all."

"Maybe. But there've been some powerfully insane and insanely powerful Extramagi in Providence before. Partly because of all the Faerie gates in proximity to each other. One Extramagus got taken down when I was your age before the Big Reveal."

"Don't they all have to register now?" Everyone knew what the new laws said, even though plenty of people bent and broke them.

"Not all. Some got turned, went into hiding, or left the country. A few others went missing, presumed dead. Anyway, we're here." Henry turned a corner off Thayer Street.

The rounded entrance to the Trolley Tunnel framed a dark passageway. I faced forward and walked on eagerly. I never met a shadow I didn't like. My Umbral Affinity gave me a bit of night vision. Not as good as a nocturnal shifter's or a vampire's, but better than most people. The heels of Henry's boots struck pavement behind me as he trotted to catch up this time.

"Wait up, you'll go too far." He tugged at the sleeve of my jacket, stopping my advance. "The door's here." Henry's fist tapped hollowly against what looked like concrete but sounded like wood.

"Petrified?"

"Just so." After Henry finished knocking, a portion of the wall swung away from us. I saw stairs leading up. "It will be a mess in there, especially where that book kept falling on my head. The Grim annihilated that corner. But still it's worth a shot if it has information we need."

"Okay." I followed Henry up the stairs. The mezzanine was half full of splintered wood and torn up books. There were more stairs leading down to an area with old broken furniture. Broken was too kind a word for the state of those tables and chairs. Maybe they could be recycled into matches.

"Hi." A female voice came up from down in the mess we surveyed.

"The Lounge is closed, I'm afraid. I should have put up a sign, but the ghosts needed me."

"That's okay, Bianca." Henry knew this lady. "Are they all right?"

"Mostly." A frazzled looking blonde woman with pink streaks in her hair stepped out from under one of the overhangs. If she was checking on the ghosts, she had to be a Psychic Medium. "I've still got a lot to do here, but I'm exhausted."

"Hey, I see an intact coffee pot down there." I pointed at the far end of the counter behind Bianca. I patted Henry's arm. "Go look for the book." I headed downstairs. "I'll get you a cup of Joe, Bianca."

"Oh, thanks." Bianca's dazed and weary smile spoke volumes. She'd thought only of the ghosts since she'd gotten here, not herself. "You're a lifesaver."

"Nope, but I have some of those in my bag if you want one." I grinned, rummaging in a low cabinet for a paper cup. No cream or sugar remained in the rubble, so I poured her coffee black. "Thanks, by the way."

"Horace here says I should be the one thanking you." Bianca gestured at what most people would think was an empty space to her left. "He says my aura looks like I need caffeine."

"You're definitely welcome. If it wasn't for Mediums like you, the poor ghosts would have some serious problems, especially after something like this. Do any of them know what happened here?"

"Not really. The sun got in, and the Skeleton Crew ghosts don't like that." Bianca sipped her coffee, then made a little smile.

"I still only know the most basic stuff about Mediumship." I glanced to her left where the ghost was supposed to be. "This must be awful, though."

"You still know more than a lot of other students here at PPC." Bianca squinted at me and blinked a few times. "What's that, Horace? Ah. A Magus. Most of you guys and many of the shifters don't understand what goes on with the ghosts here."

"Both my parents are Psychics, so I'm used to taking their word for things I can't see. But believe it or not, my roommate told me about the ghosts on staff here. She's human."

"Wow, far out." Bianca held up one finger, then glanced to her left again. "Hold on a minute. Horace says there's a problem—" A loud crash came from up in Henry's general direction. "Upstairs! Go!"

Bianca dropped her coffee and took off up the steps, her long tie-dye broomstick skirt flapping behind her. I'd gotten there before her, wondering what kind of trouble Henry might be in up there. Once I got a good look, I realized trouble had found him instead.

"Dahlia, stop!" Bianca stepped carefully past me and over chunks of plaster and wood splinters the length of her feet. One of those hovered in the air, Henry's heart directly in the path of the business end.

"Dahlia? You're the one who's been dropping books on me all semester? Please put the stake down." His hands were out in front of him, flat and outstretched with the palms up. "I only want to help catch whoever did this."

"What's going on?" I stepped between the makeshift stake and the only guy capable of noticing me for more than a few seconds. "Leave Henry alone."

The cool factor of my wannabe daring rescue attempt got completely ruined when I tripped over a thick, old book. I plucked the offending volume off the floor and sprang up, brandishing it against the makeshift levitating stake.

"Oh!" Bianca put both hands up to her face, covering her cheeks like that painting The Scream. The jagged wooden pointy thing clattered among the rest of the rubble on the floor. "Dahlia finished her unfinished business, just like that." Bianca snapped her fingers. "Last thing she said was, her grandma's book is in the right hands now."

I hefted the old tome, its canvas cover pitted and scarred by use and time. It had probably lost its dust jacket decades ago. I couldn't make out the worn words on the spine, so I flipped it open, turning past the flyleaf. The pleasantly dry and musky aroma combined with indented type and crisp, matte pages filled my senses.

"Well, we found it. Umbral Affinity and You." I turned around and held the book out to Henry.

"No. You keep it." He stuck his hands in his pockets. Henry strode over all the mess on the floor as though it couldn't trip him. "That's what she wanted."

"Who was Dahlia?" I scrambled after him, trying to walk where he did. Since he was taller, it was a lost cause.

"Another Umbral magus I knew a long time ago. We teamed up with some other Extrahumans to stop one of those powerfully insane people I mentioned."

Henry picked up the piece of wood the ghost had almost staked him with. He pricked his finger with the tip, blinking. He dropped the huge splinter and his face twisted with pent up emotion.

"We got him, but she died. Her fiancé got sick, and I ended up like this." He grimaced, showing his fangs. "Coincidence sucks. Stay away, or it might happen to you." He hurried from what was left of the Nocturnal Lounge. I hesitated, glancing back at Bianca.

"Go. I'll talk to you some other time." Bianca waved the backs of her hands at me in a shooing gesture.

I nodded, not bothering to try to explain to Bianca that she wouldn't remember me next time. I had a vampire to catch. Coincidence made certain events more likely to repeat, but it couldn't be that absolute. Lynn had beaten that devil only two weeks earlier. I had to hope I could, too.

CHAPTER FIVE

Henry

My thoughts were in the past, remembering the night Dahlia died and the book found its way back to Providence with me. My feet were on auto-pilot, and I focused my hearing on the tinny Walkman headset's tones of Bela Lugosi's *Dead by Bauhaus*. I kept on walking down College Hill all the way to Weybosset Street. I headed further down into the city until the rattle and thud of a drum set and seriously amped-up bass guitar drowned out my music.

I turned left on Empire Street and stopped in front of a bank of flier-festooned windows. The chalkboard sandwich sign in front of the AS-220 billed a cover band, The Mission of Sisters. They were a Goth tribute, covering all the classic Post-Punk pioneers. I laughed so hard I coughed, leaning on one hand against the red brick between entrances. Irony was a church, this bitter laughter my solitary prayer. When I got some semblance of control over my hitching sides, I pulled a black cardboard pack of clove cigarettes from my jacket's inside pocket. My Zippo followed.

A flick and a puff sent me even further back in time. The memory shift was like the one time I'd been given morphine in the hospital, all leg-loosening wobble and white-cotton haze. Drugs didn't affect vampires unless we fed on someone inebriated enough to need medical attention. I didn't want or need them. Memory was my poison, the only substance I could use now.

With my eyes closed to the high-polished flat-ironed hairstyles and yoga pants as clubwear, I could almost pretend it was still 1985. The illusion would break the second I opened my eyes to find an empty wall instead of her and Neil leaning nearby, limbs a tangle of comfortable affection. Neil was a Null Magus, whose powers saw through and stopped other spells. He'd been the only one of our old circle to keep in touch after she died and I turned. Cancer had gotten him back in 2004. Nothing I remembered or imagined would ever bring them back.

I held the clove so loosely, I could barely feel the papery filter between my fingers. At first, I thought I'd dropped the cigarette. When a puff of smoke and unmistakable vapor of living breath met my nose, I knew better. I opened my eyes to see Maddie, of course. Her satchel bulged with the weight and breadth of the book Dahlia's ghost had entrusted to her. I wondered why she'd wanted Maddie to have it instead of her sister, Headmistress Thurston. She had no idea how heavy that book really was, and she shouldn't be carrying it. I should be nothing to her but some guy who helped her pass a class. I was dangerous, not just because I drank blood, but because of coincidence. She risked potentially fatal bad luck just by having me around.

"Sorry for stealing your smoky treat." She took another puff. "They remind me of home. Dad smokes these."

"He shouldn't. They'll kill him." I held out my hand, a wordless request to get my cigarette back.

"They can't." She shook her head, puffed again, then exhaled a stream of smoke through her nose. "He's a vampire, like you. Turned back when I was two."

"I'm sorry." I pulled the pack and the Zippo from my pocket, lighting up a replacement for the smoke she'd bummed.

"Why?" Maddie's gaze pinned me with frank curiosity, like a bug to a specimen card.

"All the natural and man-made restrictions. The world is cruel to vampires, with good reason." I stared back, wounded by her interest. If she wanted the truth, I'd give it to her. "Kind of sucks for your family, doesn't it?"

"Dad's worth it, dealing with all that." She turned her head to take another drag, but still managed to keep her eyes on mine the whole time. "Doesn't your family feel the same way?"

"I don't have a family anymore." Even though I barely whispered it, she heard my confession.

"I'm sorry."

"I'm not." Closing my eyes, I kept a tighter grip on my cigarette this time after taking a drag. "They're all in a better place than I am now."

"You have friends."

"Not so much." I opened my eyes, stared down into hers as though I could find what she meant in there.

"Tony, Bobby, Blaine, and Lynn are good people." She arched one eyebrow. "Even though I have to repeat myself every time we meet, I consider them friends. Why not you?"

"They could be if I let them. In the ever-popular words of Tony, 'Ain't happening.'"

"Fine. If the people busting their behinds to figure out how to stop a Summoner from trying to kill you aren't enough, what about me?" She stubbed out her cigarette on the wall, then tossed the butt in a can. "I went back to where you got attacked, then chased you halfway across town. Pretty friendly, huh?"

I had nothing to say to that. She'd stepped in front of a stake for me. I'd never really understood why anyone did that sort of thing. I froze up when things got dangerous, relying on the bravery of others. It wore me out. Maddie gazed up at me through a haze of smoke, her eyes shining between thick, dark lashes. I felt like I owed her an answer.

"Surgeon General says being my friend is hazardous to your

health. The reason I don't have any from back in the day is that the ones who stuck around ended up dead." I took a drag, grimacing as I tasted filter. "The ones who ditched me went on to do very well for themselves."

"Hazardous friendship is better than none at all." She plucked the stubby butt from me, tamping it out and tossing it to join the one she'd finished. "And the last time I checked, you were the one getting attacked, not me."

"Grims go after anyone around. You saw what it did to the Lounge." I crossed my arms over my chest.

"It'd have a serious problem attacking a Magus with Umbral Affinity, even one as inexperienced as me." Her smile wasn't punctuated by fangs like mine but looked just as predatory. "Grims are pure shadow. I could hide from one for years, and with more study, I could eat one for breakfast. And if I had its Anchor, it'd be toast."

"Good point. But still. I drink the blood of the living. Not exactly a safe friend to have."

"Oh, please." She rolled her eyes. "I brought my dad his sundown pick-me-up until I left for school. No one sees me coming or remembers where I've been. If I wanted to, I'd be more dangerous than you. Next argument."

"I remember you." I slouched against the wall. "Always will. And there are other types of exceptions to your forgettable rule that could happen."

"Yeah, but I'm not likely to join a wolf shifter's pack or trade in the brainiac roommate for a Faerie one. Even you wouldn't be able to see me when I'm hidden."

"Touché." I was still too depressed to smile, but I stood up straighter.

"Are they playing *This Corrosion?*" Maddie glanced over her shoulder at the chalked sign. "Suffering Shadows, they are!" She dug around in her bag.

"What are you doing?" I pushed off from the wall.

"Getting five bucks so I can pay the cover and go dance." Maddie pulled her hand out of her bag, gripping Lynn's notebook instead of a wallet. She dropped it back in and tried again.

"Stop that." I put my hand on her arm.

"I'm going in there and having fun while people can still see me, Henry." She stopped rummaging, blinking up at me. I could sense her blush even though I could barely see it.

"As you should." I held out my arm. "But I'm paying. It's the least I can do for someone who followed me all the way down here just to drag me out of my funk."

"No Funk. Post-Punk." She smiled and took my arm. I thought she felt feverish even through the thick leather of my jacket. We walked up to the entrance and through it, then past the bar and to the door leading into the venue. They asked for our ID, and I tried not to look too relieved to see them put a yellow plastic bracelet on Maddie's wrist. She was over twenty-one. At some point, I'd ask her why she started school so late, but now wasn't the time.

As we stepped into the dim room where the band played, she immediately moved to the music. I straightened my arm, letting her go to the middle of the space in front of the stage. I hadn't danced since the Twentieth Century. It'd take more than this to get me out on anything resembling a dance floor after all that time.

I headed off to the edges of the room, nearly running into the table with the band's merchandise on it. I picked up a card with a web address on it, shaking my head and musing. Even five years ago, they would have had stacks of CDs instead of cards with QR codes and coupons for downloads. I could read in the dark that they had both covers and original material available online. Maybe I'd check out some of their original music. They seemed to know and love the old-school stuff, and I had found nothing new I liked listening to in a long time. Even the campus band Night Creatures hadn't impressed me much. They sounded like Fall Out Boy.

After pocketing the card, I glanced up at the band. They looked more Emo than Goth, but that probably had more to do with their budget than tastes. This Corrosion ended, and I recognized the opening riff of *Swamp Thing* by The Chameleons. A head of riotously curly black hair turned. My eyes met Maddie's and her smile nearly blinded me, even in that dim room. I only closed my eyes for a second, and then I stepped across the invisible line that divides those who do from those who do not. I danced.

Decades fell away again. The only real difference I felt between past and present was the lack of an aridly fragrant stale smoke atmosphere between us and the drop-ceiling. I couldn't forget everything that came after the days I breathed for reasons besides speech or meditation, but I decided I'd take what I could get. Close was enough for me. My lips moved along with words I thought I'd worn out over the last thirty years.

This time, I was the one who made eye contact. She looked away first, but only as far away from my eyes as my lips. I glanced down to see hers moving, too. We lip-synced in unison about whether storms came or just showers.

The music took me and I spun on my heel, my body making movements nearly as automatic as the shapes of the lyrics on my lips. When I turned back again, I tried to find Maddie. She'd vanished. It wasn't just a trick of the light or an Umbral memory lapse. A spike of fresh and cold wintry air met my nose. It came from the back of the room. I followed it and found a door marked "Exit Only." I shouldered through.

It only took a moment for the red to overtake the edges of my vision. I had to get my blood-lust under control before I killed someone and got myself exposed to the sun. Rhode Island didn't have capital punishment, but people willing to "daylight" a vampire lived all over the world. They didn't care much about the laws on the books. Ironic that I had to watch every move I made while people like that got away with a slap on the wrist for murder.

The heady copper scent of human blood threatened to distract me as I dragged the rubberized nose clip out of my pocket. My Extrahuman sense of smell was always on, but not breathing wasn't enough to block out the scent of blood. Sometimes it was more like a curse than a special power.

I'd just about gotten myself under control, still following the anguishing and familiar blood scent. I focused on enhancing my hearing just in time to pick up a muffled cuss word. I stopped trying to move like a human and made a leap for the source of the sound. Rough brick walls whizzed past on either side until I landed five feet away from Maddie and the piece of shit who had her pinned against the wall.

"Your wallet's in here somewhere, freak." The mugger's free hand rummaged in her satchel.

"You're never finding it, bozo." I could barely believe my ears. Maddie' sounded more like an angry shifter than a frightened magus. "If I want, I can make it so you'll never find anything again."

I had no idea whether she was bluffing. My psychic powers had never leaned toward lie detection. I stepped closer, hissing and baring my fangs.

"You think your vampire pal's going to scare me?" The thief flipped his hand over, revealing a tattoo in the shape of a crucifix. His middle finger shot straight up in the air as though for good measure.

"Oh, give me a break." I rolled my eyes. "Really?" I pulled my arm back and curled my hand into a fist, ready to give the attacker a right hook. "After all this time, people still think that works? I'm Protestant, and fisticuffs never go out of style, pal."

"Don't you dare touch him. I won't be the reason you go to jail." Maddie's eyes flashed with deep, dark anger. And then, that deep darkness grew.

I had to step back to avoid it, but still, I peered toward them as the darkness emanating from Maddie's eyes enveloped them both. I heard a choked cry and then the staccato bass sound of sobbing. With my vampiric hearing, I knew right away that was the attacker.

The softly hollow click of chunky boot heels was the next sound I heard, then a murmur as she deactivated the amulet. A shadow emerged from the bruise-purple cloud of darkness at the end of the alley. Its shape sharpened and clarified into a petite feminine form. Maddie slipped her arm under mine, forcing me to either turn and leave with her or let go. I chose the former.

"I'm sorry." She adjusted her satchel strap on her shoulder. "I was trying to improve your night, but got the opposite result."

"I'm a little scared to say this to you right now, but you're wrong." If my heart could beat, it might have broken out of my chest just then.

"Oh?" Maddie glanced up at me.

"Yeah. This is the most interesting night I've had in decades." I grinned down at her.

"Interesting in the Confucian sense?" That eyebrow and one corner of her mouth tilted up in tandem.

"All that and a bag of Eastern philosophy." I let her escort me all the way up Empire Street to Weybosset. "Thanks, by the way."

"You're welcome, I guess." She pointed to the chain still hanging around her neck. "I thought I shut this off. Wearing it to go out dancing was probably a bad idea."

"How so?"

"I'm not used to watching my surroundings like that. I thought that guy was marking someone else." A little rill of laughter escaped her throat. "I forgot I wasn't forgettable."

"Aren't you worried he'll want revenge or something?" I looked over my shoulder.

"Nah. He won't remember me." She shivered a little. I resisted the urge to put my arm around her.

"Wow." I walked on with her in silence, unable to come up with the right words until we passed The Arcade. "You weren't kidding about Umbral magic. If you're this competent, why bother with lab classes? The Headmistress would probably let you test out of those."

"I want to take them, learn more about Magic Theory first-hand, and see other schools of magic in action. I need to master control, too. I can only really use my powers when something's got me upset. That's sloppy, not competent."

"I understand."

"Of course, you do. It takes vampires at least two years to get a handle on things, right?"

"Even longer if they're on their own."

"Is that what happened to you?"

"Sort of." I wasn't sure how much I wanted to tell her. "Things were different before the Big Reveal. Some vampires back then thought it was a measure of strength to see how long the newly turned could fend for themselves. Kind of like free-range parenting, but completely different."

"Oh." Maddie gripped my arm tighter. I'd expected the opposite. "Dad had help the whole time."

"And of course, he had your mom to help him."

"Nope."

"Wait. So he's the Magus and then got turned."

"Guess again." Maddie's lips wore a smile, and her tone was still light. "Mom's a Psychic. Precog."

"Huh. I'm stumped."

"It's okay. My great-aunt was the one who inherited Grandma's powers, but she died before I was born. I've had no training at all. Grandma pissed off the Sidhe Queen. Some Seelie hound called a Spite ate most of her powers. She tried showing me a few little things, but I learned more from her books, to be honest."

"So that's why you're here at PPC."

"Exactamundo."

"Gesundheit."

Our laughter mingled all the way up College Hill. I walked her all the way to her dorm, reminding her to keep the amulet off until she needed to use it for class. She nodded, backing up on the steps outside the dorm until she was my height. Her smile was open, genuine. I hadn't even wanted to kiss anyone since last century. I couldn't stop myself and leaned in, brushing my lips lightly against hers.

Maddie ran her hands lightly down the back of my head, brushing through my hair before coming to rest gently on my shoulders. I wanted more from her than I could even imagine asking. The pricking of my fangs against the inside of my lower lip warned me not to let this go any further. I hadn't fed in over twenty-four hours and drinking from a human in public could get six months in prison.

I tried not to notice the way she watched my face when I mentioned I had to go home and get a drink but failed miserably.

Maddie looked as hungry as I felt. Her disappointment was palpable as I excused myself for the rest of the evening. I ought to try to avoid her in the future, but I had one problem. The psychic impression I'd made of her was indelible. I'd never be able to forget Maddie May, no matter how much I wanted to or what I did.

CHAPTER SIX

Maddie

"Jeez, Maddie. What are you, hungover?" I hadn't heard my alarm going off until Lynn picked up my phone. "Get dressed and down to the dining hall stat or you won't make it to class on time."

Instead of turning off the chime blaring out from my phone, she dropped it next to my head on the pillow. I sat up and tapped the button on the screen to shut it down. Rubbing my eyes and yawning, I wondered why I felt so tired. I hadn't had time for a drink. Then, I remembered the mugger, and Henry kissing me. That worked on my drowsiness like intravenous coffee.

"Okay. All right. I'm going." I shuffled into my slippers and then to the door.

My bathroom basket sat where I always left it. The halls were empty, which made sense. Only Lynn, Olivia and I were on this floor over the break. So much hot water came from the pipes, it was almost a shame I had to shower so fast. After dressing, I slipped the amulet over my head, tucking it inside my shirt. It felt slightly cool and tingly against my skin, reminding me of Henry's lips on mine the night before. If I kept that line of thought up, I'd be too distracted to focus in class. I shook off the tactile memory, twisted my hair at the back of my head and clamped it down with a clip.

I headed to the dining hall, where Lynn was present as usual. There was just enough time to wave at her, grab coffee in a paper cup and buy a granola bar. I also snagged the holy trinity of dining hall fruit, tucking them away in my bag. The apple, banana, and orange would get me through as long as I could manage to eat them during whatever lunch break Professor Brodsky decided to give us.

The lab building was out by the gym over on Blackstone Valley Parkway. It was a way to go, but I liked walking. Watching people swerve out of my way and then scratch their bewildered heads afterward never got old. My feet crunching against the icy sidewalk ground out a counterpoint with the crispy breakfast bar between my teeth.

By the time I reached the PPC Magical Laboratory building, my coffee had cooled enough to chug. I gulped half down, then checked the room directory and my watch. My class was on the second floor, and I had five minutes. I took the stairs slowly, finishing my coffee at the top and tossing the cup in a bin. No one watched as I put my hand down my shirt and fingertips against the smooth bronze surface of the memory amulet.

"*Ex umbra in solem*," I murmured. Then, I opened the door to the lab and stepped inside.

Long, white tables met my eyes. They appeared to hover over the black and gray speckled terrazzo floors, but upon closer inspection, they sat on thick Plexiglas bases. The air in the lab had circulation, but the room was windowless. I looked all around for a fan and finally found one in each corner. They were half-circles on sticks, made of wood, glue, and white peacock feathers, swirling lazily on filaments so thin I could barely see them from the floor. Magical fans for a magical lab.

I took a seat at the front table closest to the door. Only the one in the back corner was occupied already. I never sat in the back because, usually, it helped the Professor to remember I'd just asked a question. Also, sitting closer helped me focus and keep my mind on the subject instead of whoever sat in front of me. I also liked being by the door, but that had nothing to do with study habits. I wasn't exactly sure where that habit came from, actually. Doorways are just so interesting. You never knew what might come through them.

A couple of guys showed up arm-in-arm, laughing together. They plunked their bags on the table front and center. One of them noticed me and smiled.

"Look at that. We won't be all alone up here." The one who'd spoken had olive skin, brown curly hair and horn-rimmed glasses over hazel eyes. He leaned toward me and stuck out his right hand. "I'm Ian, and this is my boyfriend, Charles."

"Maddie," I smiled and shook his hand. Once we let go, I waved at the purple-haired guy with the nose ring and blue eyes. "Hi, Charles."

"Hi." He pulled a workbook and some pencils out of his bag. Then, he blinked a few times and glanced back at me. "Have we met before?"

"Yup. Magus History with Feldercarb last semester." I smiled, relieved that this would be the last time I'd have to do a rerun with Charles for the entire inter-session.

"Huh. That was a big class. Sorry, I don't remember meeting you." He shrugged.

"Don't be. I'm Umbral."

"Oh, wow." Charles deliberately looked away and then turned back. "Woah. And you're Maddie from Magus History. Making me remember you is way advanced for this level of Magic Theory. Is it going to be a cakewalk or what?"

"Nope. I have a little help from a psychic, um, friend. An amulet. If I shut it off, you'll forget all about me."

"Hey, thanks for not saying 'again,' okay?" Charles chuckled. "Ian, can you believe this? We get to be in a class with an actual Umbral magus and remember her the whole time."

"That's awesome!" Ian smiled even more brightly. He opened his workbook. "Brodsky is fifty times tougher than Feldercarb. He gives quizzes before every class, and if you don't pass, you have to leave.

They say he's harder on the students than the creatures he summons. Did you get to look over the material for the first class last night, Maddie?"

"Yes and no." I got my already marked up workbook out. "I read over it back at home. Spent most of yesterday on the bus and then did some other stuff with friends."

"You don't make friends with Umbral magi." I absolutely did not like the tone and timbre of the throaty voice coming from the back of the room. Still, I turned around before Charles or Ian did.

The person sitting in the back was rail thin and lanky, with glossy though unkempt black hair that looked surlier than what I could see of his or her face. I had no idea whether the owner of the voice was male or female, or what kind of magic they had either.

"And you are?" I wasn't scared of a surly classmate. Maybe I should be, but whatever.

"That's enough, Miss May, Miss Phillips." The voice came from the doorway. I glanced over my shoulder to see a woman with silver streaks in her chestnut hair adjusting bottle-green cat's-eye glasses over her gray eyes.

"Yes, ma'am." "Miss Phillips" sat up straight, her voice taking on a decidedly more feminine pitch and timbre. She sounded less antagonistic by leaps and bounds, too. I almost forgave her for being so blatantly insulting. Almost.

"Let's refrain from judging each other before we get acquainted." The woman paused on her way toward the front of the room, raising one ruddy eyebrow at the girl in the back of the room.

"Yeah, I'm sorry. Name's Nox." Nox ran one hand over her head, shuffling thick hair out of her eyes. "I was born without a wall between my inside and outside voices. It gets passed down in my family."

"Apology accepted." Almost doesn't count, but witty apologies do. "I know someone with a couple of sandbags where that wall should be." I shrugged. "I can handle knowing one more, I guess. Why not come and sit with me? The workbook says practically every project needs a partner."

"'Kay." Nox collected her workbook and backpack, then got up and sauntered over to the empty seat at my bench.

When I turned to face the front of the room, the middle-aged woman stood behind the high, white Professor's bench. She put down a clipboard and made four marks on whatever document graced its top. She glanced around again, then shrugged and smiled. Her teeth were just a tiny bit crooked and whiter than I expected for a woman going gray. She looked familiar, but I couldn't place where I'd seen her before. This was definitely not Pavlo Brodsky, the Professor who was supposed to be teaching Magic Theory Lab.

"Some of you may already know me, but I should introduce myself formally." She turned her back on us, uncapping a smelly dry-erase marker. The name she wrote on the whiteboard made Ian and Charles gasp almost in unison. I would have laughed at them, but was struck speechless by the three nouns: Henrietta Thurston, Headmistress.

"I'll be replacing Professor Brodsky for the duration of this course." Her grin was guarded but gentle. "He's gone on emergency leave, but don't think you're off the hook. Although I'll be running this lab more hands-on than he does, your workload will be every bit as intensive and hectic as you'd expect from him."

I raised my hand as she took four sheets of paper from the bottom of the clipboard. She nodded at me but didn't speak until she'd passed all the papers out face-down.

"Yes, Miss May?"

"Should we refer to you as Headmistress or Professor, Ma'am?"

"Professor will do for the duration of this course." She turned the corner to get back behind her bench and sat down. Then, she pulled a deck of large cards out of her bag and shuffled them three times. "You have five minutes to complete the quiz. Go."

I bent my head over my paper, pencil flying. Lynn took all her tests in ink, but I wasn't that confident. Served me right for not being such a genius. Still, the three questions were easy. Most of it was common magical knowledge as well as common sense. I mean, if there was anyone in the class who didn't know psychics couldn't see magic, they probably shouldn't have gotten into PPC in the first place.

I was about to turn my quiz face down when I noticed my mistake. There was less than a minute on the clock, barely enough time to erase everything I'd written besides my name and the date. I blew wormy, pink eraser crumbs off the paper, so they marred the shiny white surface of the lab bench instead. Then, I flipped the page over and took a deep breath, trying to relax. I wondered whether anyone else had made the same initial mistake I did.

Professor Thurston's heels clicked solidly against the floor as she went around collecting everything. She spread the quizzes face-down, then turned one of her cards over in front of each finished test. They were Tarot cards. Mom had those, used them to see whether I was a magus or a psychic back when I was little. I recognized the Ace of Cups, the King of Pentacles, and the Page of Swords. The last card she turned over was The Tower reversed. Bad news, that one.

"One of these grades is not like the others." Professor Thurston tapped The Tower. "The quiz that got this card is the only one that either passed or failed." She turned over each of the quizzes after that. A series of blinking and brow furrowing got replaced by what I guessed was only a veneer of calm.

"Miss May, you passed. Everyone else did not. Don't worry, it's only worth two extra credit points." I heard the sound of one round-toed shoe tapping against the tile. "This will be the only quiz you get until next week, but its purpose was to make you remember the most important thing about magic. Follow the instructions."

"But how did we all fail? Those were such easy questions." Nox hadn't even raised her hand before speaking.

"Miss May, answer that please." Professor Thurston busied herself with corralling her cards.

"Right under where we put our names, there were two sentences. Instructions. Do you remember them?"

"Yeah. Something like that's on every test. 'Answer these questions in the time allowed' or whatever."

"Right." I cleared my throat. "But on this test, it said 'don't answer any of these questions in the time allowed' so we weren't supposed to write down anything besides our names and the date."

"Great Goblin's Garters." The way Nox said that was almost like how Blaine said Tiamat's Scales. I wondered what kind of magic Nox was packing and whether she'd been raised by Changelings, Faeries, or both.

"Magic Theory is all about the rules of magic, regardless of the course's unfortunate name." Professor Thurston shuffled her cards again. "You're not here to learn which theories are contested, have wiggle room, or memorize exceptions. You need to pay attention to the rules, how they affect spell instructions, learn them as though they're completely immutable. After that, you can start thinking about how all of them might still be up for debate."

"Is that why you flipped over Psychic cards even though you're a magus?" Ian lifted his chin off his folded hands.

"Yes and no." Professor Thurston stepped out from behind the bench, fanning the cards as she went. She held them out to me, and I took one. Then, she did the same for the other four students. "Psychics with Precognition use cards like these to predict things. Humans use them for the same purpose. They get oddly accurate results, coincidentally, according to most Extrahumans. But coincidence isn't just a fancy word for an accident. Each of you sees and manipulates magic, limited by your schools, just like the Psychics. Nox, put these on and tell me something about the energy on these cards."

"You didn't use any Psychic energy at all." She held the Professor's glasses up to her eyes, squinting through the lenses. "It's all magic around those cards. The only Psychic thing in this room is on Maddie." Nox pointed at me like the tallest toddler in the known universe.

"Yes. So, how did the cards predict that one test wasn't like the others if I'm not using a Psychic power?"

"That's easy." Charles leaned back in his chair. "Coincidence and magic are related. We're all magical, and that rubbed off on our papers with the graphite and ink. You tapped into magic, allowing coincidence to act like Psychic ability when you used the cards."

"Interesting idea, but that's not what the rules say. Hold on to that line of thinking for when you take Advanced Magic Theory, though, Charles." Professor Thurston nodded at Nox's raised hand.

"According to the reading from Chapter Two, you didn't use magic at all. You used the cards like a human would. Magic's everywhere, just like coincidences. The cards worked because they're around both those forces. The coincidence in Maddie's quiz pulled that reversed card to it like the moon pulls tides."

"Exactly." Professor Thurston got up, holding her tarot deck. "Now, look at your cards."

I blinked, bewildered to see The Tower again in front of me. This time, it wasn't reversed. I knew from Mom it was worse right-side up. I glanced over at my classmates. None of their cards were the same as earlier. Nox had The Fool. Charles had the Nine of Pentacles. Ian had the Nine of Cups. Out of the corner of my eye, I saw movement from Professor Thurston's direction. I looked up.

She held one hand over her mouth with the other on her breastbone. I caught a glimpse of the upturned card just before she swept it back into the deck. Ten of Swords. Another bad-news card. Actually the worst ever, according to Dad. Something horrible was in store for Headmistress Thurston, and if her readings used coincidence, it had something to do with this class. Then again, maybe it had already happened. With the Nocturnal Lounge trashed, she shouldn't be this surprised. But then, maybe she thought whatever was going on had passed by now.

I ran my fingertip down one side of the card. Not even a sting. These were some well-used cards. If the Professor did readings with them in the right place at the right times, she'd have a much better idea of the situation than a non-trad freshman like me. Unless someone was blocking her. That'd have to be someone who knew her well, practically intimately. I remembered Blaine's theory about the snowstorms and Lynn's icy adventure by the library last semester.

Professor Thurston collected the cards to begin her magical forces demonstration. I took one last look at The Tower before handing it back. The image of the two people falling from its parapet haunted me for the rest of the day. If Blaine was right about someone attacking the school, whoever helped Bobby and Lynn was next. Henry had given Bobby the amulet that let him save Lynn. I'd convinced Lynn to take a chance on making friends. The Grim attacked the Nocturnal Lounge. Blaine's next theoretical victim had to be Henry.

Maybe it was time to start taking Blaine's fears a bit more seriously. After all, it wasn't really paranoia if someone was actually out to get you. But the only person who believed the whole thing was Blaine. Lynn, Bobby, and Olivia had insane cramming to do, plus more research on the Grim and the Umbral book. Tony was on the crew fixing the Lounge. And Henry didn't answer my texts until Friday.

CHAPTER SEVEN

Henry

I sat in the PPC library boiler room the Friday after inter-session started, waiting to meet Tony's werewolf contact. It was dingy and dark, but at least dry and safe from the sun. I'd have preferred the Nocturnal Lounge, but it was still a wreck. They'd probably warded it, but with holes in the walls and ceiling, I couldn't go in until after sunset.

My building had a door in the basement leading into the watery tunnels under Providence. The only tunnel exits on campus were the from the Lounge and the Library. I heard the shouts and strikes of a construction crew from the former. It was Fred Redford and another gruff voice that had to be his dad.

The boiler room was all concrete walls and copper pipes. And the eponymous boiler, of course. It blasted out heat that made me feel like a cat in a room full of rocking chairs. At least if it malfunctioned leaking water would put me out if I caught fire. Still, boiling water was no fun even as a vampire.

I'd spent much of the day failing to sleep. I kept waking from a daymare I couldn't remember, which almost never happened. Most of my day terrors came from psychic impressions. There'd been plenty for my subconscious to choose from. The Big Reveal's survivors had all kinds of issues, from physical injuries to mental scars like General Anxiety Disorder, my own personal demon. And before you go asking, the existence of literal demons hasn't been proven by either the human or the Extrahuman community.

Finally, I got up mid-afternoon and pulled an all-dayer. I didn't bother feeding. We don't need blood unless we do something strenuous and specifically vampiric. I hadn't, and probably wouldn't need to do much more than amp up my hearing. That kind of thing barely made a dent in my reserves. Instead, I brewed up the last of my coffee.

I can always tell a vampire-friendly house by its aromatic potential. That and the fact that there's always at least one decently furnished sun-proof room. Nothing tastes good to a vampire except blood. Everything else tastes like paper. We have complex senses of smell, though, and coffee is one of the most calming scents to pick up. Another one is Earl Grey tea, which led to geeks everywhere wondering whether Captain Picard might have been a closeted vampire. I cleaned up, dressed, and gathered my things, sloshing some coffee into a travel mug to take with me.

It was a good thing I did. More than boilers and hot pipes made the library basement nerve-wracking. A crack under the stairwell door meant a scimitar of sunlight slid across the area next to the exit until twilight. I stayed way back near the tunnel entrance, which smelled almost unbearably musty. Everything down there had either that dank aroma or rust and steam.

The sword-like sunbeam had just started sheathing itself under the door when my phone beeped. It was Maddie, so I read it right away. I'd read all the texts she'd sent me about tarot cards and Blaine's crazy theories, too. I just didn't respond because it was better to avoid Maddie and keep her out of harm's way. The whole mess made me want to hibernate like a bear shifter until the problem resolved itself.

Need to talk. You up? I closed my eyes, intending to just ignore the message again. When I did, I remembered the soft heat of her lips against my own cold ones. That was strange. I hadn't made an impression of that kiss though I definitely should have. I pulled on my touchscreen glove and tapped out a reply.

Down, actually. Library boiler room.
There in 5.

I waited until I heard her footsteps on the stairs to go back in the tunnel even though I could smell whatever she wore that made her smell like jasmine and myrrh as soon as she walked into the library. That was a scent for sore olfactory nerves. Thinking of nerves had me fidgeting. I realized I'd been doing it since getting her message. What could she want now? She'd stopped texting about the cards and the theories on Wednesday.

"Henry?" I stood in the shadows, not daring to look up until I heard the door close behind her. The last thing I wanted was to be sun-blind the entire time and unable to see her.

"Maddie . What can I do for you?"

"I might be in a bit of trouble." The corners of her mouth turned down. I realized I missed the smile she'd worn most of the night we met.

"Meeting a vampire in a dark basement kind of trouble?" I stepped out of the shadows with my hands outstretched in my best Bela Lugosi imitation. Then, I waggled my eyebrows like John Belushi.

Her laughter echoed off the pipes. It was a little strained and frayed around the edges, but good to hear. I couldn't help but join in. The idea of a twenty-something woman getting my dated pop culture references was giggle material for sure.

"Olivia would say 'hoo, boy,' but I'm no owl shifter." She let out a satisfied sigh. "Thanks. I needed that."

"Thought you came here to talk, not laugh." I leaned in the tunnel doorway, knocked back by a wave of guilt. I should have at least answered her once. She'd been stressed all week over what was probably just a random tarot card. I'd have done anything to make up for it.

"I did." Her eyes roamed over everything in the room except my eyes. "Heard you're meeting Josh Dennison later. The wolf shifter."

"That's not what you're here about." I knew a subject change when I heard one.

"No, it isn't." She sighed, the smile vanishing from her face. "It's been a rough week."

"Is it your amulet?"

"Not really." Six of Maddie's steps took her across the small space. I knew the start of pacing when I saw it. "I mean, I think it might need a recharge before week three because I use it in the dining hall. Can you recharge it? Is that even a thing that's possible? How much does that cost, anyway? Do I have to call Mom or Dad for more money?"

"Maddie." I stepped closer to her, not just because I wanted to but because she looked like I felt, at the shoreline of a panic attack. "Don't talk about it yet if it's doing this to your nerves. You need to calm down first. Here."

I pushed the wooden crate I'd used as a chair closer to her. She sat down and gratefully looked up at me. After that, I heard her inhale, then count to five under her breath and let it out slowly. That was the same breathing exercise I did though I couldn't remember where I learned it.

"Maddie, you said your dad's Psychic?" Maybe talking about her family would help.

"Yeah. He's clairvoyant." She looked up again, her face calmer than before. "Jade scrying bowl is his weapon of choice."

"Wait. You're Shi May's daughter? I should have figured that out when you said your mom was a Precog." I felt like such an idiot. There was only one Psychic turned during the Great Reveal who used a jade bowl, and he had a Precognitive wife who figured out where he should use it to look. "Your family probably saved half the Extrahumans in the Northeast back in the 90s."

"Yup." She grimaced. "But now, you're the one changing the subject. I think Blaine's theory is right and your amulet helped Bobby save Lynn. You're the target, Henry."

"You believe Blaine?" I raised an eyebrow. The only thing most people believed about Blaine Harcourt was that he was loaded and a huge flirt. "But Blaine did tons to help Bobby. More than me."

"Right, but you got attacked." Maddie sat up straighter and folded her hands together so tightly her knuckles went nearly white. "Henry, it's been five days. The Grim can come back anytime. Maybe even right now."

"Oh. Well, that sucks. Maybe I should go home, tell Tony I'll meet him and Josh somewhere else."

"Look, I'm not sure the Grim's after you."

"Wait, what?" I blinked. "You think it's after Tony?"

"No. I think the Extramagus wants to mess with me, too. Hurting you would do that because..." Maddie blanched, shivering a little. She pulled the amulet out of her shirt like it was a last-ditch effort. "Well, never mind that. All week, weird things happened to me in class."

"Really? I've heard Brodsky's lab experiments are pretty tame."

"Except Brodsky's not teaching the class. It's the Headmistress."

"Okay, so what happened?"

"Professor Thurston uses Tarot as one of her coincidence demonstrations. I keep getting The Tower reversed and the Nine of Swords, and so does she. It's little things, but lots of them keep happening to both of us. I kept a tally." She pulled a sheet of paper out of her bag.

"Wait, are you sure it's nine? That's your tally?" I shook my head, handing the paper back to her. I wasn't sure how to tell her that I knew the Headmistress's unlucky number was nine. She'd lost her sister, and her aunt had gone missing on September 9, 1989.

She tucked the paper away, but before she could say anything else, the light under the door vanished utterly. I froze. Maddie turned, following my gaze. She gasped, then stepped in front of me. I was thinking she had a death wish or something.

"It's here."

I didn't need to ask what she meant. I grabbed her arm and ran down the tunnel at a fast but still human speed. But I couldn't do any of the vampiric stuff until the sun went down. Maddie followed. She had no choice with the panicked grip I had on her arm.

I heard the groaning of bending metal and splintering wood as the door caved in behind us. I didn't have to look back to know the Grim had come crashing through the door. My ears picked up claws screeching on metal and the hiss of escaping steam. I pushed Maddie ahead of me just in time. Wet heat blasted my back, hotter than a mortal could endure.

I bared my fangs, turned around, and planted my feet. After that, I screamed as daylight pierced my eyes. This time, Maddie dragged me away. Sun splotches danced in my line of vision.

"How did you get it to stop last time?"

"Hid." I almost said how but remembered my promise. I couldn't blow Tony's cover, even if I had no idea what it was actually for.

"Okay. Hush now." Maddie took a deep breath, then turned right. The floor sloped down, and the air got staler. She murmured the Latin to turn her amulet, off and the surrounding darkness got almost tangibly inkier. She clutched my hand in hers. I gripped back tightly.

She took two lefts. I couldn't tell her this new passage curved to the right without risking the Grim. She figured it out eventually. If we kept going this way, we'd end up in Water Place Park. At least it was January. Even so, the park would still be relatively crowded with downtown workers heading out for drinks on Thirsty Thursday.

I tugged her hand, slowing our pace. Maddie responded by stopping. I bumped into her this time. She might have thought I was waiting for the sun. It was down, but I needed to heal the steam burns. I could get arrested for having a fatal-looking wound in public. Yeah, there are laws against that. Since vampires are the only Extrahumans that happened to, it's a pretty bogus law. Still had to follow it.

I closed my eyes and focused on the welts on the back of my head and neck. The plus side to being scalded instead of burnt is your clothes survive. I stifled a groan at the idea of repainting the Bauhaus logo on my jacket. I was starting to hate Grims with the fiery passion of a million burning suns.

My injuries were worse than I'd thought. I also had to heal the sun-blindness. Those two things made me hungrier than I should be around the living. When Maddie turned around and looked up at me,

I could see her clearly. Her mouth dropped open, making a little 'o' of concern.

I realized I had the impulse just after starting to act on it. I managed to stop leaning toward her with less than an inch to spare. She threw her arms around my neck and closed the distance herself. I put my arms around her, hands pressing against her back as firmly as I dared. She might be a powerful Magus, but she lived in a fragile mortal body. As our lips parted, I ran my hands up her back until one went on her shoulder and the other to the nape of her neck. Her hair was just as lush and soft as I'd imagined.

Last time I was this close to a living person while hungry, I'd intended to feed. Back then, that's what vampires did. After the Big Reveal, publicly feeding on anything living would get you jail time. They had a three-strikes system with a ban on concurrent sentencing. If I got caught kissing her, we'd be taken to the nearest hospital to determine blood-loss. If any was missing, they'd read me my rights.

I pulled away before anything illegal happened, but it was still too late. The scent of her enveloped me more completely than the shadows she'd drawn around us. I hadn't even focused and yet I'd somehow made the memory of her lips on mine as indelible as the first time I'd seen her smile. That loss of control was bad news.

She leaned her head against my chest. I wondered what she thought about the fact that no breath or heartbeat stirred within. Then, I remembered she said her dad got turned when she was barely more than a baby. I put my hand on her shoulder again. Maddie responded with a little sigh. I wasn't sure whether it was contentment or relief. One thing I did know was that the Grim had given up its chase by now.

"It's crowded out there, and I'm too hungry to be around people unless there's something legal to drink." I looked down to find her peering at me through her eyelashes.

"Luxe Burger has bags." She pulled back and took my hand again. "I know a shortcut."

She really must have a death wish if she'd spent last semester in these tunnels. I let Maddie lead me out of the passageway and through a narrow underpass. We came out just across from the restaurant. I still had to walk by people heading around Water Place Park and toward their pubs of choice, but knowing I'd get a drink soon helped me endure it.

The hostess took one look at me and seated us immediately. I figured she'd seen hungry vampires before. She leaned over and passed us our menus.

"I'll bring you a drink right away, Mr. Baxter." The low tone of empathy was the last thing I'd expected from a stranger.

"Um, thanks?" I blinked at the woman, watching her set a menu in front of Maddie.

"You don't recognize me because I was only eleven last time you saw me. Your amulet helped my Nana remember us all during her last five years." She clicked away, making a beeline for the bartender.

I rubbed my chin, remembering a pudgy blonde girl with pigtails clinging to the skirt of an old woman with kind but vacant eyes. Those eyes had sparked with recognition when I slipped the coin on its string over her head and activated it. She'd hugged the girl as they murmured pet names to each other. Maddie reached across, covering my hands with hers. The hostess set a filled hurricane glass complete with garnish on the table instead of the plastic cup and straw I expected at most restaurants.

"On the house," she said as I reached for my wallet.

She was gone before I took a sip. Another surprise; this wasn't animal blood. I looked over my shoulder to see the hostess toss a Rhode Island Blood Bank bag in the trash, human. The corners of my eyes stung. Having this kind of drink in a restaurant cost over fifty bucks.

"You went away for a moment." Maddie rubbed my thumb with hers. "You okay?"

"Better than I've been in ages." I smiled, not caring whether anyone could see my fangs. "Text Blaine and tell that skittish dragon to get down to campus. We're going to sit down with everyone, including

Tony's friend, and figure this out. That Extramagus isn't getting either of us."

Even after the side-trip, we had a little time to kill. The walk back to campus was longer over land, but I didn't mind. She hadn't said a word about that kiss in the tunnel, but when I slipped my hand in hers as we left the restaurant, she gripped back. She hadn't looked at me like I was crazy, either. Maddie's hand was warm, of course, because mine was cold. I wondered whether she found that creepy or refreshing. Maybe she thought nothing of it in the cold winter air.

We went to the dining hall, looking for Lynn. That was where she'd said she'd be meeting Blaine. She wasn't there, but we saw Bobby in the food line. Maddie led me over to the table where he'd left his backpack and we sat. Apparently, she was hungry even though she hadn't ordered a burger earlier. Running from a Grim and an exploding boiler could do that. I wouldn't flatter myself by thinking it had anything to do with me. Then again, she was still holding my hand under the table.

"Well, crap." Maddie rested her head on her free hand as she looked out the window over my shoulder.

"Where?" I grimaced and lifted my foot, looking at the sole of my shoe. Yes, it was a bad joke. That kiss had me feeling awkward.

"Very funny. But not literal crap. Look at the library."

I turned my head, then sighed and covered my face with one hand. Another PPC building trashed because I was in it. Yellow and black saw-horses already barred the entrance. I saw Campus Police let Bianca the Psychic Medium in. Helper ghosts lived in the library, too. That girl was dedicated. I wondered what her story was. All mediums got their ability to commune with the other side via some near-fatal trauma.

"Well, there goes that idea for a meeting place." Bobby plunked a fully laden tray on the table between Maddie and me. The aroma of stuffed scrod and baked potatoes wafted up from the bear shifter's meal. I wished it was coffee. Fish hadn't even been something I liked smelling while human.

"So, now what?" I crossed my arms on the table.

"Blaine and Lynn will figure it out." Bobby speared a forkful of fish and chewed thoughtfully. "Hey, Henry? I just thought of something. With the library and the Lounge closed, doesn't that limit your daytime access to campus?"

"Yup." I sighed, feeling my eyebrows draw closer together. "Good thing I'm not taking inter-session classes."

"Still, it cuts you off from everyone." Bobby took another bite.

"I know." I stroked my chin. "Hmm. I wonder if that's been the whole point of the attacks all along?"

"Attacks? Don't you dare tell me it's plural now." All three of us watched Tony approach with a tall blond man with slicked-back hair. His posture was straight and bold, implying confidence that would outshine Blaine's bravado. He dressed in light colors like some kind of anti-Goth. Even his leather jacket was light gray.

"The ones on the Nocturnal Lounge and the Library, of course." Maddie looked him right in the face, staring daggers at him.

"Was afraid you'd say that." Tony shook his head.

"I'm calling them accidents until there's proof otherwise." The blond man crossed his arms over his chest.

"You'll get that soon enough, Josh." Tony leaned on the table. "So, where are we meeting now that the Library's off-limits?"

"Let me text Lynn." Bobby pulled out his phone and started tapping.

"Hey, I wanted to ask who's been fixing the Lounge? Same guys who are out there?"

"Yeah. That's why they're here already." Tony glanced out the window. "Redford Renovations. I worked forty hours already, and they don't want to pay overtime. Otherwise, I'd have to be there."

"Now, why does Redford sound familiar?" Bobby put his phone down on the table to wait for Lynn's reply.

"Fred. It's his dad's company." Tony waved. Maddie looked out the window. A guy in a red baseball cap waved back. I should have known the Redcap would want as much work as possible. He was only a few more jobs away from being able to cover all four years of tuition at PPC.

"Oh." Bobby picked up his buzzing phone. "Lynn says to come to the dorm. Blaine can meet us there."

Bobby shoveled the last of his dinner into his mouth, then picked up his bag and the empty tray. He dropped that at the dish-washing window on the way out, the rest of us trailing along. This time, I kept my hands to myself.

CHAPTER EIGHT

Maddie

"So who are you, anyway?" I hadn't seen Josh shoulder into the space Henry had left between us.

"Maddie May."

"I've never seen you before," he said, shaking his head.

"Oh, yes, you have." I smiled like a packet of Sweet & Low.

"No way. I'd remember if I'd met you." His grin could have gone in the dictionary next to the word wolfish.

"Not a chance." I glanced past Josh to drop Henry a wink. "I'm Umbral."

"Leaping Luna, get out!"

"That's what we're doing." I stepped under Henry's arm as he held the door for us. Josh had to go around. He didn't look too happy about that.

"So, do you believe this story about a Grim?" He crossed his arms, stopping just inside the door.

"Yup. Saw them myself less than an hour ago." I smirked at Josh's incredulous blinking. "I was in the library when they attacked and everything. And they trashed the heating system down in the basement." I walked down the hall, pausing to wave at Blaine, who was by the stairwell.

"Well, there's one good thing about another Grim attack, anyway." Henry's voice echoed down the hall.

"What could possibly be good about something like that?" Josh trotted to catch up with me.

"It can't attack again for another five days," Blaine answered, figuring out in seconds what it took Henry and me a whole conversation to grok.

"Any ideas on what the Grim is after, Trogdor?" Bobby punched Blaine in the arm.

"Two of them, actually. Maybe three." Blaine waved to Lynn, who was at the elevator. We all squished in and she pushed the button for the basement.

I found myself crammed in the back corner. I felt the weird stomach-hitching that comes with vertical movement, and then the elevator made a soft *bing*. The doors rolled back.

I hadn't been in the dorm basement before. There was laundry on the fifth floor where I lived and the odd hours I kept between diurnal and nocturnal classes meant they were always available when I needed them. Lynn led us to an old wooden door. She pulled out an equally old iron key and turned it in an antique brass lock. The doorknob was old fashioned with a big cut-glass grip. When Lynn opened the door, the whole crowd of us stood there for a few moments just staring.

The basement lounge was one of the few rooms on campus that hadn't been redone when Headmistress Thurston opened Admissions to anyone. Previously, only Magi and a few types of Psychics could apply to PPC. This was a room for them. I walked in first, feeling instantly at home in the space. All the wood paneling was real, not printed press-board from the 1970s and not whitewashed like the rest of the building. The floors were wood parquet, variegated boards making a meticulously laid herringbone pattern. Built-in shelving lined one wall even though all the books were old Reader's Digest condensed volumes. Six wing-back chairs sat in a semicircle with small tables between them. I chose the chair in the middle, opposite the door.

I watched as the others entered the room more sedately than I'd have expected. Even Josh looked around in clear fascination. I couldn't blame them. This room was like a time capsule, a look back at what PPC used to be like, beautiful and needlessly exclusive. I could see why there'd been some resistance in the magical community when Henrietta Thurston diversified the school, even though I thought she'd made the right call.

"How did you get the key, Lynn?" My question snapped her out of her reverie.

"Jeannie. She said we'd better respect this place like the antique it is." Lynn glanced at Josh.

"Yeah, yeah." Josh sat down near the door. "I know how to respect people, places, and things. I'm not the son of two Alphas for nothing, you know."

"Just quoting Jeannie." Lynn took the seat on my left.

"She's the RA." Bobby shrugged and sat next to her.

"For the rest of the year, at least." Blaine sat on the other side of the room.

"Sorry I'm late." Olivia stood in the doorway, a turquoise blue robe wrapped around her pajama-clad frame. Her platinum hair stood out starkly against it. Tony gestured at the seat he'd been about to take. She sat down, grinning up at him wearily.

"You're a real trooper, Olivia. Thanks." Tony sat by Blaine.

Henry shifted his weight from one foot to the other, then ambled over to the last available chair between Blaine and me. Once seated, he glanced at the dragon shifter instead of me.

"So Maddie, let me see this Umbral Affinity tome again." Blaine raised an eyebrow at me.

I pulled the book from my bag and watched Blaine's mouth stretch in a wide, toothy grin reminiscent of a crocodile. I waited until he grasped the binding before I let go. Henry pressed back in his seat as we passed the book.

"You had this with you in the library?" Blaine flipped through it absently.

"Yes. I've had it on me since you guys finished taking notes."

"Okay. Remember those ideas I mentioned outside?" Blaine's eyebrow quirked.

"Yeah."

"Okay. I'm brainstorming here." Blaine looked around the room. Lynn pulled out a notebook and nodded. Blaine nodded and continued. "The lounge got attacked. Tony and Henry were there. So were Maddie's amulet and this book." He patted it.

"Wow." Tony leaned forward, putting his elbows on his knees. "I didn't even think a Grim could be after an item."

"All by themselves, they're not." Blaine flipped to the back of the book. "But the book and the amulet aren't regular items. They've both got Psychic energy and Magic energy, plus some other things in common." He handed back the book.

"Of course." Henry ran a hand down his face, almost as though wiping away his neutral expression and replacing it with wan sadness. "Me, their owners, and an Extramagus."

"Tell us more, my fine fanged friend." Blaine leaned back in his seat.

"This book belonged to Dahlia, another Umbral Magus I knew. A group of us found out about an Extramagus who was trying to get turned so he could lose his magic limit. We were hiding the vampire he'd captured after some of our other friends broke him out. The Extramagus caught us, though. Dahlia died taking him out."

"Wait. I heard of a guy trying to rule the world right before the Big Reveal." Olivia shivered. "He was a nutcase. Read a little too much Lovecraft way too seriously if you ask me."

"Yes, same guy." Henry closed his eyes. "He could do any school of magic, but the more he mastered, the worse his asthma got. He'd spent twenty years tracking down the oldest, most powerful vampire he could find, then he kidnapped that vampire's wife to make him agree to the turning. She's who we rescued. Me, a Null Magus, an Air Magus, and Dahlia." Henry tapped his pinkie, his brow furrowed. "No, I guess there really were only four of us."

"There were only a few ways to get a binding contract back then." Tony shook his head. "It's one reason people don't like owing favors to Faeries."

"Yeah. He had a relative who'd just tithed to the Sidhe Queen sending ransom notes disguised as contracts back and forth."

"Wait. A Seelie backed this guy?" Josh's eyes went round and wide. He blinked.

"Yup." Henry sighed. "According to Extrahuman law at the time, everything was by the book. That's why the older Magi didn't help. Seelies love the Old Law."

"Are you serious? They wouldn't help stop Magus Mussolini?" Lynn leaned forward, nearly jumping out of her seat.

"You have to remember that not everyone thought Magi rule was a bad idea. Just a handful of us with nothing much to lose stood up to the guy. No respectable Magus would have dared break the Old Law like that." Henry sighed. "Times were different back then."

"You have a point, even if I'm not technically supposed to listen to it yet." Josh shrugged. "Whatever. I like a good story. Go on."

"Anyway," Henry continued, "After Dahlia died, I brought her book back here. Her fiancé, Neil, said it was what she wanted. Bequeathed in her will and everything. That's all I remember. But I didn't know it happened until Maddie got it back at the start of inter-session."

"So, I think whoever sent this Grim either wants the book, the amulet, or Henry." Blaine shrugged. "Maybe all three."

"But why send a Grim? Isn't that a little excessive and pointless considering how destructive they are?" Olivia scratched her head.

"The fact that it's a Grim just hints at a bigger picture." Blaine took a deep breath, then blew smoke trails out of his nose. "The stuff that happened last semester was excessive, too. Do all of you know about that?"

"I think I need a little filling in." Josh steepled his fingers and leaned back in his chair.

"Basically, someone dropped snow on Providence, and then a load of ice on my head." Lynn fluttered her hand in front of her. "I'm fine, thanks for asking."

"Wait. Someone can make a snowstorm and drop ice?" Josh's forehead crinkled.

"Has to be an Extramagus." I shook my index finger at his nose, pretending it was a rolled-up newspaper.

"Well, yeah." Now it was Josh's turn to scratch his head. "But aren't Magi one-trick ponies, like Psychics."

"We are, except when we're not." I winked. "An Extramagus can do more than one school, but there's always a drawback. An illness, or a limit on when or where they can use their extra powers."

"Like how the guy in Henry's story had asthma?" Josh rubbed his chin.

"Right." I nodded. "Most Extramagi are born that way. Usually, they come from families with a long line of different schools in the same family and a bit of Faerie or shifter blood thrown in for good measure."

"How many families are like that in Rhode Island?" Lynn had a pen and notebook out, ready to make a list.

"Hold on a minute there, brainiac." Blaine held up his hand. "It's an Extramagus with a PPC grudge. Magic families from all over sent their kids here. He or she could be from anywhere. That's not the best way to narrow it down."

"Well, how else then, Trogdor?" Lynn rolled her eyes.

"List magic families with Summoners, maybe?" Blaine smirked.

"It's not magic." Henry shook his head. "Summoning's Psychic. It's just the creatures they call that are magical, usually Pure Faerie."

"Back to square one, I guess." Bobby shrugged. "So the Extramagus can't even be calling the Grim."

"Hmm." I put the book back in my satchel and got up to pace. It always helped me think. "What about Mind magic? Doesn't work on Faeries, or long-term on shifters or Magi, but could an Extramagus control a Psychic?"

"You know, maybe one could." Blaine sat up straight. "I did a project on Mind magic artifacts. They were a thing back in ancient Greece."

"This sounds complicated." Olivia cradled her head in her hands. "Should we take this to Headmistress Thurston?"

"Probably. But again, it'd have to be someone she'd listen to. Like someone from Campus Police." Lynn leveled a glance at Josh that was almost a glare.

"Cool it, Frampton." Josh's lips twisted into something like the second-cousin of a grimace. "I'm sold. There's only one problem here. It's just a matter of finding something to convince my mom and dad."

"So you'll help?" Blaine grinned. "Tony owes me some money now."

"Yeah. I'll help you find something to help you with." He scratched stubble so light it was nearly invisible. "If you think Headmistress Thurston will believe you, go ahead and talk to her. I'd advise against telling her where you got your information from, though."

"Why? She seems approachable." I leaned on a bookcase.

"For you, maybe, since you're a student. If you can find a way to bring it up theoretically in class, go for it. But she clams up like crazy outside of a classroom setting.

"You know a lot about her." Bobby raised an eyebrow.

"She's my Godmother."

"Oh. Wow." Blaine rolled his eyes. "Someone here's an even more fortunate son than me. I might have a silver spoon, but Josh Dennison's got a magical Godmother."

"Please, no alpha-hole one-upmanship while I connect the dots." Lynn shook her head, scribbling down notes on her paper. "I need to hear myself think in here for about five minutes, mmmkay?"

"Whatever Lynn needs to get her brain in gear." Bobby leaned back in his chair.

The room was silent except for Lynn's pen. I felt something like a goose walking over my grave. The Grim couldn't attack again right after busting up the library. Still, something nagged at me like crazy. I glanced around. Henry spun a coin on a string. Bobby folded his hands over his belly. Olivia blinked at Tony, who peered at a speck of nothing just over my head. The toe of Josh's boot wiggled, as though he wanted to tap his foot but didn't dare piss Lynn off.

I shut my eyes, trying to focus my attention on whatever bugged me. It was behind and slightly to my right. I stood, keeping my eyes closed and felt my way along the bookshelves. The energy was close, but higher. I stood on my toes and reached up with my left arm. My fingertips traced a fine and fuzzy layer of dust. And then my touch met cold metal. I opened my eyes just as a brass oil lamp tipped off the shelf I'd knocked it from.

"Eek!" My arms flew above my head, making a circle. The lamp clanged to the floor. I heard a low, angry growl from Josh's direction.

"You okay?" Henry's voice was right in my ear.

I blinked, glancing around. I was on the opposite side of the room, looking at the entire half-circle of wingback chairs. Six pairs of eyes blinked at me, the faces housing them tilted up higher than usual to gaze at me. My feet dangled in thin air. Arms supported me under my shoulders and knees.

"Um, Henry?" Of course, it was Blaine opening his big mouth first. "Didn't your mother teach you that it's not a good idea to meddle in the affairs of Magi?"

"He's not meddling in my affairs." I cleared my throat, glancing from Henry's face to the ground. "He just kept that lamp from knocking me out."

Henry put me down. I smoothed out my skirt and straightened my top. I was less mussed than after our adventure in the tunnels earlier. Henry put his hands behind his back and stood up straight. He didn't move or even look at me. I didn't have to wonder why. Josh glared like a basilisk, his upper lip curled back in a sneer.

"Lamp?" Bobby blinked and looked around. "What lamp?" He wrinkled his nose. "Wait. I smell old oil."

"Yup." Tony got out of his chair and strode across the room to where I'd been. "This old thing was hiding up there on the shelf, I think." He pulled a long scarf out of his pocket and wrapped his hands before touching the lamp. Then he looked at me. "It's not dusty. You touched it. Well, crap."

"Yeah, but just barely." I looked down at my left hand. It seemed normal enough, no purple polka-dots or nails growing at an alarming rate. "Why? Is that a bad thing or something?"

"Maybe, maybe not." Tony shrugged. "You won't know until something weird happens."

"Awesome. Because nothing weird is already happening to me." I rolled my eyes. "What is that lamp, anyway?"

"Djinn house." Blaine peered at the lamp once Tony put it down on a table. "They're imprisoned Faeries."

"Are they, um." Bobby took a deep breath and looked around. "Seelie or Unseelie?"

"Dude, don't worry about saying either of those words around anyone here. None of us are in either of those Courts. It's all good." Tony shrugged.

"Oh. Okay, then."

"Anyway, there's no way to tell which flavor until the Djinn comes out. Which, hmm." Blaine examined the lamp. I watched ruddy scales cover his hands. He picked it up, turned it over, and shook it. The lid stayed affixed. "It's in service already. We can't even talk to this Djinn until either its term is up or whoever it's serving decides to fess up."

"Well, we should leave." Tony had packed up his things faster than I could track. "Put that damn lamp back on the shelf. We shouldn't talk around it."

"Wait, you think this lamp is spying on us?" Josh blinked, then turned his head to stare daggers at the lamp instead of the vamp.

"Better safe than sorry, especially since we're dealing with a Summoner." Blaine sighed and shook his head, getting up to return the lamp to the shelf. "My parents have the biggest hoard in this hemisphere, and even they don't want a Djinn's lamp. Too risky, according to Mother."

"Oh, for goodness' sake, let's just go already before Cat Man has kittens." Lynn waved her hand over a head still bent over her notebook. I recognized the beginning of her bossiest tone, which it seemed we needed just about then. "Trogdor's right. Olivia, go get some sleep. I'll have something for you to do tomorrow. And Blaine, can you go back to your parents' library? Make a list of things Summoners call up and send it along. All the Summoning books are on reserve all of a sudden."

"Will do." Blaine shouldered his backpack. He opened the door for Olivia, then followed her out. Tony watched them go, an inscrutably catlike expression on his face.

"I'm going to order a pizza." Bobby stood up and stretched. "We can have it in the first-floor lounge. By the time it gets here, we'll want a break."

"Maddie, I need to go upstairs and get more books. A lot of them." Lynn put her notebook and pen down on top of the already substantial stack of books. "Help a girl out."

"Sure thing." I followed her out of the room, realizing I'd be leaving Henry and Josh alone in there. Not the best idea, maybe, but it probably had to be done. Twenty years of bad-will between vampires and werewolves would just hang around like a rotten smell until they cleared the air.

The tension in the room was palpable as I reached out to shut the door behind me. The two men stared at each other, looking like negative images, dark-haired Henry clad all in black and blond Josh in a white t-shirt and acid-wash jeans. I hoped they wouldn't trash the room and give Jeannie a reason to go all bear-form on them once they got done with their chat.

CHAPTER NINE

Henry

"Okay, Wolfenstein, out with it." I had to tilt my head up just slightly to glare directly into Josh's eyes.

"You touch another mortal in my presence again, we will have a problem." He put his hands on his hips.

"I didn't see you rushing to help." I raised an eyebrow.

"Because Umbral Magi can take care of themselves. They don't need undead blood-drinkers putting their hands all over them to avoid getting hit in the head."

"You may be right." I couldn't shut off the internal Billy Joel sound-track about how I may be crazy but it just may be a lunatic she was looking for. I did stop the smirk it inspired from touching my lips. "What's your problem with me, anyway? You don't freak out about the guys in Night Creatures."

"They were all turned near the end of the Big Reveal." Josh bared his teeth. "I know you've been operating much longer than that. How old are you anyway?"

"Not really that old. Turned in 1989." I held his gaze. In a staring match, vampires have a distinct advantage. Biologically , we don't need to blink. I'd made a habit of it, though, so it took a little focus.

"And how many did you turn in the 90s?"

"None."

"How about before and after that?"

"None."

"Bullshit. Vamps always want to turn someone. It's part of your biology, after all."

"Still, I haven't." I'd almost forgotten that Josh was a sophomore here at PPC. He'd probably taken some kind of Extrahuman Biology class by now. He'd know vampires can only reproduce either by turning people or mating with other vampires. The latter was a long and complicated process.

"How do you manage that when vampires much older than you went on a turning spree all over the world?"

"Because I never got into the business of making and pulling strings like the really old vampires. I was a Psychic first, back before basic focus training got integrated into regular schools. I learned how to control myself before you were even a twinkle in your mother's eye."

"Huh. Who trained you, then?" He raised an eyebrow, lifting his head so he could look down his nose at me.

"One of the best Psychics in Providence from back in the 60s." I hoped I was right. The identity of my mentor was something I must have put in the memory bank and then wiped.

"I don't suppose you have proof?"

"Ask Professor Watkins. He signs off on all my papers."

"He's a Projection Psychic, not the Memory kind." Josh's surly tone made me struggle against shooting back some old Star Trek quote at him.

I know. But he vouches for me all the same, and it's easy enough for you to check. Are you going to argue with an old Navy Seal?"

"Fine. I'll believe you for now. But you have to admit you're pretty damn dangerous."

"So are you." I put my hands on my hips. "Do you need a lecture about all the Magi and Psychics you dated last semester?"

"I can control myself. My parents are Alphas who expect me to follow in their footsteps."

"Just like a vampire trying not to get arrested or, worse, has to control himself, or are wolf shifters deadlier than undead blood-drinkers?"

"Point taken." His concession came through clenched teeth, but the fact that it came at all told me Josh was probably more easy-going than typical Alpha heirs. I didn't have time to delve into the reason for that but made a mental note that it existed all the same.

"So, can we just agree to disagree now and focus on the truly creepy conspiracy theory that two out of two brainiacs agree on?"

"Not just yet. Still a hatchet to bury."

"And that is?"

"Maddie." Josh's lip curled again. I blinked, surprised he still remembered her after she'd left the room. The amulet would have lost its effect on him once she left. "Don't be so surprised I remember her. It's a wolfy Alpha thing. Memory Psychics aren't the only ones who can trump Umbral Affinity. Faerie magic can do it, too."

"Ah." I knew wolf Alphas remembered everyone in their packs. That meant either Maddie had wolf shifter blood somewhere in her family history, or Josh was forming some kind of pack. That gave this conversation more weight than I'd initially thought. Maybe this was a dominance contest with Josh trying to protect a potential pack member or establish a pecking order. "So, what is the problem with Maddie, exactly?"

"Like I said, you're all over her. You spent time with her before this meeting. Alone time. Touchy-feely time." He narrowed his eyes. "Explain."

"We ran from the Grim together. It attacked us in the library basement, just like she said." I scoffed. "Thought you said you believed that."

"What else?" Josh would know if I lied. Wolf shifters could smell everything vampires could.

"She kissed me." I took a deep breath, trying not to lick my lips.

"Don't let her. You're no good for someone like her." He crossed his arms over his chest. "It's creepy for old vamps to hit on chicks more than half their age."

"You're right." I thought about the first time I saw her smile and how her first thought after the attack had been for me. Someone with that kind of light inside should never have to consider an eternity without the sun. I should back off and give her room to make her mind up about that.

"Huh." Now it was Josh's turn to blink. "So what are you going to do about it?"

"You're the big Alpha on campus here, Josh. I'm not challenging you on that. All I do is jog memories and give advice. You tell me. What should I do about it?"

"Stay away from her." He barked it like the order it was. No mere suggestion from the likes of Joshua Dennison.

"Can't really do that, since the Grim seems to be after both of us and we're all working on this Extramagus thing."

"Okay, you have a point." Josh glanced at the shelf with the Djinn lamp. "So, stop rushing to help her. Stop acting like Prince Charming when you're Count Dracula."

"Fine. I'll quit with anything that might remotely resemble flirting. I answered your question. She's like your pack-mate now, right? So what are you going to do about keeping her in check?"

"Shouldn't that be enough?" He raised an eyebrow.

"Nope." This time, I let the corners of my mouth tilt up. Giving in to Josh's play for dominance over the group had been freeing, lifted a huge weight off my shoulders. All the same, I wasn't going to play Omega. I'd call things as I saw them even when it wasn't what he wanted to hear.

"Why?"

"Because Maddie's strong-willed. And she's lonely. That's not something you're going to understand right away, so let me lay it out for you. She's spent most of her life with only her parents and maybe her grandparents able to remember her. When I gave her that amulet, she looked at it like salvation. Do you know the first thing she did once she had it?"

"No. Tell me."

"She followed me downtown and went to a concert." I looked him right in his reddish-brown eyes. I kept staring, not blinking or indicating in any way that my next admission felt like a knife to the gut. Josh had my support in taking control of the Grim situation. Now, I was about to put my chances with Maddie in his hands. It was the best thing I could do for her, the safest thing, what she deserved. "Right now, she thinks I'm the only guy who will remember her, ever. She doesn't care that I'm undead and dangerous and twice her age."

"Huh." Josh's lips stretched out in a wide grin that shifted into a bright smile. "I know exactly what to do about that." He ran a hand through his hair and popped his collar. "Thanks, Henry. You're not so bad. If all the vampires acted like you, there might be a chance at rebuilding the ties between our people."

I watched him turn on his heel and stride out of the room. If rolling over for an up-and-coming wolf Alpha would keep Maddie safe from the Grim, I'd do it a hundred times over. Maybe he'd even help protect me in the process. And as much as it'd hurt to watch Josh court the first girl I'd cared for since the Cold War, I knew it'd be less painful than watching her torn to pieces by the Grim or whatever else got summoned. She might end up rejecting him anyway, stubborn as she was.

There wasn't a future for someone like her with me. Her own parents were a testament to that. Her mother was still human even though her father had been a vampire for most of Maddie's life. The approvals board for turning was an endless nest of vipers disguised as red tape. If they hadn't given her parents approval, they'd be unlikely to grant it to her.

I shouldered the leather jacket that had been my only physical comfort for what seemed like forever. As I headed out of the room, I took one last look at the Djinn's lamp on the shelf. There was no way to tell whether it was already in use like Blaine and Tony had said. Still, it was tempting to go over and give it a rub, anyway. A few wishes might help us. But I couldn't risk it. The Djinn might serve the summoner. It also might be Unseelie, which would make its wishes more like something out of *The Monkey's Paw* than Disneyland.

I pressed the bottom button on the old-fashioned light-switch, then stepped out of the room. As the door closed behind me, I understood that another portal had shut during my earlier conversation with Josh. The saying about a door closing and a window opening was a crock of bull. Vampires were supposed to shut themselves up in lightless rooms after all. I'd have to just stick with my decision to do what was best for everyone. For Maddie, especially. I already cared too much.

CHAPTER TEN

Maddie

There wasn't much to do at the first-floor lounge. I watched the door for Henry, but only Josh appeared. He wolfed down slices of pepperoni pizza from Caserta's. Ha, "wolfed." I didn't blame him. It was good stuff. Blaine even took a few slices on the road back to Newport.

I listened to Lynn ask Tony way more than twenty questions. He described some other creatures that Summoners could bind. Seelie Brownies were physically weak but excellent spies. They could make bargains with either Unseelie Gnomes or the Seelie Imps who twisted time or made miracles. Pixies did everything through water, with Sprites their airy counterparts. Spites were Sprites morphed into Spectral hounds the Queen had made to counter the King's Grims. Spectral magic was the opposite of Umbral, like fire to water.

I wondered how a cat shifter had all this information about Faerie creatures. Lynn's left eyebrow would soon get stuck in the upright position if it hadn't already. I had a feeling she'd figure out what was up with Tony sooner or later.

Later on, Bobby and Lynn walked ahead of me toward our room. She went back down the hall with him after a murmured conversation I tried not to listen to. I went to bed, remembering those risky stolen moments with Henry. I'd been at his mercy, but he'd controlled himself. That had to mean something.

I gazed at the shadowy ceiling, reached out with one hand, made swirls and eddies in what everyone thought was the absence of light. Shadow play was the most common way Magi discovered their children had Umbral talent. Mom told a story of how she used to find shadowscapes above my crib. My earliest memories were of shadows and the other stories Mom told when she thought I wasn't listening. The sad one about how my aunt died alone because no one could remember her long enough to save her life. Would I end up like her, or like Grandma? Grandpa Joe was a wolf shifter, able to recall her because of their pack ties.

Eventually, sleep turned the shadows into dreams. My alarm went off what felt like a minute later. I got ready for class, then headed straight down to Thayer Street. I wanted to see my friends that morning but needed my thoughts more. The snow from before winter break had melted. It was weird to walk down streets with just an occasional dingy gray snow pile in January. In Vermont, the snow stuck around longer. I stopped at Au Bon Pain for a croissant since I'd skipped the dining hall. I relished the quiet anonymity of interacting with people who wouldn't remember me even with my amulet. The staff in the cafe had no idea a Summoner was messing with the school down the street.

I was used to Umbral Affinity for the daily minutiae of living. On a contemplative morning like this, activating the amulet to get breakfast would just make me feel like a falcon with wet wings. That reminded me to spend the rest of the walk thinking about my notes. There'd be a test at the end of class today.

I was ten minutes early, so I said the incantation to turn the amulet on before walking into the classroom. Charles and Ian were already there. They passed their notebooks back and forth, getting in some studying I'd neglected the night before. Being chased through the catacombs and then finding a Djinn lamp had put a monkey wrench in those plans. Last-minute studying seemed like a good idea.

"Do you mind some company?" I smiled as Charles and Ian looked up from their work.

"Drag a chair over." Ian waved at the empty end of the bench. "We're on device activation, figure it'd dovetail nicely with the activity today."

"Oh, yeah, we're making simple gadgets today." I pulled up a chair and sat.

"Have you ever done that?" Charles ran one hand through his blue hair. "No one else in my family has magic, so I've never even seen it done."

"I made some shadow pictures before. Never lasted more than a few minutes, though." I shrugged. "It will be interesting, trying to channel Umbral energy in such a bright room."

"Oh, yeah. Wow. I didn't think of that." Ian shook his head, wincing with the movement.

"I'll manage. It's about getting the theory in this class, anyway." I shrugged. "I can always make shadows around a small object with my hands."

"Yeah." Charles breathed out a sigh that probably sounded more relieved than he'd intended.

I glanced up to see Nox hurry into the room alone, looking more put together than usual, though her eyes seemed slightly vacant. It reminded me of the time I'd seen Olivia after she had her Adderal. She pulled a jet-black patch of what looked like fur from her bag and tucked it under her shirt, pressing it to her stomach. I blinked, barely able to believe my eyes as it melded with her skin, vanishing entirely. Droplets of water beaded up on her face, smelling distinctly of a dank fen or riverbank. Her hair dampened and increased in volume, taking on that unkempt appearance I'd thought was just her desired look. She dabbed her face with a small gym towel. Her eyes gleamed with an awareness they'd lacked before.

"Sorry about the swamp smell, guys." Nox's face reddened a little as she hung her head.

"Oh! I had no idea you were a Kelpie until now." Ian just barely stopped himself from clapping his hands. "I've never met a Faerie shifter before."

"It's okay. I usually keep it down on low, but that's what I get for hitting the snooze button too many times. I've been wiped all week. My magic feels sparse. Usually, Unseelie energy's all over the place this time of year. It's why I'm taking this class over the inter-session."

"Huh, what could possibly be displacing seasonal Faerie magic?" Ian chewed his bottom lip.

"Hmm." I tapped my pencil against my book. "A bunch of Seelie creatures in the area, a Magus who can siphon Fae energy, unseasonably warm weather, a Seelie artifact washing up on the beach. Stuff like that."

"Wow, you know more than I'd think about that kind of thing, Maddie." Nox peered at me from under her long, thick bangs.

"I spent most of last night studying magic creatures and energy. Some friends are taking Terminology and Creature Classification." I smiled, hoping she wouldn't ask for a list.

"Study buddy osmosis learning, huh?" Nox actually smiled.

"Something like that." I looked up at the clock, saw it was time for class to start. "Where's Professor Thurston?"

"Maybe she's getting things for us to make gadgets out of." Charles flipped over a flashcard. "Ugh, will I ever remember this coincidence postulate?"

"Which one?" Ian leaned against Charles' shoulder, picking up the card. "Oh. Coincidence Denial. That's tricky because it should really be called Coincidence Defiance."

"How so?" Nox dropped her workbook and pencils on the bench without even looking at them. She headed over to flip over the flashcard, then read off the back. "One way to attempt breaking a coincidence pattern, Coincidence Denial is the attempt to change a likely magical outcome by repeating the pattern with one or more major changes."

"That's a vague and confused way of putting it." I shook my head. "No wonder you have trouble remembering it. How about thinking of it like lucid dreaming? Instead of waking up, you stay asleep and give yourself a weapon or some friends to fight the danger."

"So, Coincidence Denial is to recognize the pattern and doing something about it that the last poor sap didn't get to try?" Charles smiled. "Except I'll think of The Dark Tower. Like when Roland had the horn at the end of the series, you know next time it'll be different for him. Thanks, Maddie. That helped me get my brain around it way better."

"You've got lucky study buddies." Nox turned her head toward the door, but not before I caught the weary look in her eyes. "I think the Professor just walked in downstairs."

"Thanks, Nox." I faked a smile. Something was bothering my lab partner. It occurred to me that maybe she'd be helpful if the summoner had Faerie creatures at his disposal. Maybe she'd even know something about that Djinn lamp. I banished the thought. She had her own issues. It'd be insensitive to just jump in asking for help without finding out if she felt up for anything besides classwork.

Nox ran her hand through her hair, giving me a better look at her eyes. They looked bloodshot and a little puffy as though she'd been about to cry. It was awfully early to be that down in the dumps. I wasn't exactly a morning person, but sleep always sort of reset my emotional state. Either Nox had bad news that morning, or she hadn't slept. I'd want to talk to her later. Just as I was thinking I should text Lynn and ask her whether a Kelpie might be helpful, Professor Thurston arrived.

"Today's activity is important but difficult. I don't expect any of you to succeed at making a permanent gadget. That said, if you can't understand the principles behind imbuing an item with your particular school, you're going to have a rough go of things this session." The Professor set a large cardboard box on the instructor's bench. It rattled, as though it contained a collection of things. "Come up and get an item to work with."

I dragged my chair back to the bench next to Nox. I waited with her, letting Charles, Ian, and then the Kelpie go up first. She rummaged in the box with her eyes closed. That told me she knew a thing or two about coincidence herself. It seemed like the sort of thing Blaine would do. I'd have to ask him about it once he'd taken his own Magic Theory class next semester.

I copied Nox, looking away instead of closing my eyes as I felt around in the box. It wouldn't get me in trouble since this wasn't a test. The item that met my hand felt long and cold with a sharp point on one end. Its texture wasn't metal, but some other rigid substance. I didn't look at whatever it was until I got back to my seat.

"Woah." Nox had looked before I did. "That's seriously creepy, Maddie." She recoiled from my hand and the object it held. "You have to give it to Professor Thurston, like now."

I looked down and saw a vampire fang attached to a chain by a jump ring. I shuddered but managed to keep from flinging it away, then got up immediately. The croissant threatened to leap out of my throat as though my body itself was trying to eject the horror of what I held. The only way a vampire fang stayed intact once pulled was if he or she was awake and aware throughout getting defanged and was killed directly afterward. Necklaces like this had been trophies during the time just after the Big Reveal, their makers prosecuted for crimes against Extrahumanity and imprisoned for life afterward. What was one of these doing in the lab box?

"Um, Professor?" I held the necklace out to her, shivering as though I stood in an arctic wind instead of a climate-controlled magic lab.

"I'm calling the Police." Professor Thurston pulled a handkerchief from her pocket, plucking the fang from my hand with it. I was struck by how pale the Professor's face got, but nothing else besides her short words indicated her alarm.

I stood in front of her bench as she took the room phone from the wall to report the grisly discovery. The Providence Police had a Magical Forensics unit. Maybe it was old, a relic of a more turbulent time. There'd still be an investigation. There was no statute of limitations on murder. Professor Thurston placed the handkerchief-wrapped fang in a warded bag and set it on her desk.

"I expect the rest of you to begin imbuing your items. Miss May, with me please." The Professor gestured to the space beside her. I walked behind the bench, waiting as she described a semicircle over our heads with one finger. A privacy spell, Air magic. I'd had no idea which school she had until then. Now, where had I heard about someone using Air magic recently? Last night? I almost had it when the Professor spoke.

"Now that we won't be overheard, tell me when the last time you saw the fellow who made your amulet was?" She sniffed, jaw clenched. "Henry Baxter, I believe is the name on your amulet's registry slip?"

"Last night, probably around eleven. And yes, that's Henry Baxter. Memory Psychic. He's a vampire too."

"I'm well aware of Mr. Baxter's talents, his state of being, and his history." Her gaze met mine, gray-blue and airy. "He's been a positive force in Providence's Extrahuman community since the late 1970s, decades before he got turned. I went to High School with him, you know."

"Is he okay?" I asked her the only question that mattered right then though her statements raised fifty more in my mind.

"If you saw him last night, then yes." She sighed, her voice carrying a relief her posture didn't reveal. "I could tell by looking that the fang you found is nearly a week old."

"Wait, what?" I shuddered. "You mean it's not from before the Equal Rights trials?"

"Most certainly not." She glanced down at my right hand, which had held the necklace. "It's in a warded bag now, but take a look at your hand. There are residual traces, still visible. Check closely."

I did as Professor Thurston asked, turning my head so I could squint out of the corner of my eye. Then, I gasped. A trace the approximate shape of the fang hovered squarely in the middle of my palm. The magic energy was a combination of types, but unmistakable. All three types were familiar, after all.

"Death, Unliving, and Umbral, all recent." I blinked, feeling tears prick the corners of my eyes. "Umbral stuff's all mine. And something fuzzy that I can't make out."

"Psychic energy. Telepathic." I looked up to see Professor Thurston holding a monocle over her left eye. "Here. Have a quick look." She handed the device over.

I took it gingerly with my left hand, not wanting to disrupt the energies I'd be looking at. I closed my right eye, unable to make my sight multi-task the way the Professor could. Age and experience were huge advantages in that department. It's why we went to school, after all. I saw the shimmer resolve into a smoky violet hue. Telepathic Psychic energy. I couldn't figure out why that was there. Unliving energy was key to preserving pulled fangs. The Death energy came from the vampire's demise. Was I looking at the Summoner's handiwork? They had a sort of telepathy with their creatures through the anchors binding them. My mind wasn't officially blown, but it was a near thing.

Professor Thurston held out her hand. I placed the monocle in it, blinking a little more. This time, I had to wipe the corners of my eyes. The Grim hadn't gotten Henry, but had killed someone else instead. There had to be two dead vampires by now. The summoner was killing on campus, but why?

"Is there something you want to tell me, Miss May?" Professor Thurston pursed her lips, expectant instead of puzzled. "It's an interesting coincidence that fang went to your hand. There's a reason for it."

"Yes." I couldn't tell her the details of the first Grim attack. Only two people could, and only one would matter. "You need to talk to Henry Baxter as soon as possible. A Grim attacked him at the Nocturnal Lounge the night before inter-session started, and again last night at the library."

"Grims can't preserve fangs, Miss May." She drummed her fingers on the benchtop. "The police will not believe a vampire, not even one as upstanding as Henry Baxter. They will require nothing less than hard evidence."

"I know." I looked up, locking gazes with her. "But it happened.

The Grim's Summoner could have preserved the fang. I have no idea who'd be able to control one, though. Definitely not a student, not even at the graduate level. Summoning is Doctoral work, according to all the PPC guidelines, right, Professor?"

"Astute observations, Miss May, but they don't explain the Telepathic energy being on the fang." Professor Thurston raised an eyebrow as her watch beeped. She held my gaze but tilted her head at the box of items. "I truly appreciate the extra knowledge and life experience non-traditional students bring to the college experience. For now, please take another item and do the activity. I've got more calls to make."

She snapped her fingers, and the privacy spell popped like a bubble. She walked to the door, heels clicking hollowly against the white floor. I reached into the box again, looking down as soon as I withdrew my hand this time. The circular object in my hand was a medallion stamped with a wolf on one side and a set of fangs on the other. The chain it dangled from was old, definitely from before the Big Reveal. It was an old alliance medallion, the kind that bound a vampire to a wolf shifter pack.

Now, what kind of coincidence could that tie me to? I pushed the question away for the time being. I had a lab to pass after all.

CHAPTER ELEVEN

Henry

I'd been sleeping when the phone rang. Yes, vampires can sleep even if most don't. It conserves blood, letting us feed less. I'd wanted an actual break while PPC was mostly closed, but recent events meant I'd spent as much time out as during the Fall semester. I was the school's oldest freshman, so I had my habits. Supposedly I'd liked them, but I jumped when that phone rang. It could be Maddie. I woke up smiling at the thought.

I shook off the emotion along with any trace of drowsiness. Last night, I'd made that promise to step back. It didn't matter that I'd been happier with her around. Friends could make each other happy from a nice, safe distance. She deserved a chance to meet someone who wasn't a second-class citizen, to have more than one choice.

"Hello?" I picked up my dumb phone. I preferred that to the smartphone in my apartment.

"Henry, I've just been told you were attacked by a Grim. Twice. And you didn't bother notifying me." I'd know that voice if I unlived a thousand years. Henrietta, my old friend from High School. Also, the stopping point for any buck passed around PPC.

"Yes, Headmistress Thurston." I figured that was the way you greeted an old friend who'd abruptly stopped speaking to you decades earlier.

"Don't you dare Headmistress or Professor me, Henry Baxter." Her voice came through in a whispery yet still strident tone. "This is life-or-death business, and you didn't tell me. Why?"

"Didn't want you stuck with that kind of mess again. Or have you forgotten the last time that happened?" She knew I meant the hostage situation that had ended in Dahlia's death and my turning. The Extrahuman authorities hadn't believed her then, even with her new husband's sterling reputation and deep connections.

"I haven't." Her voice didn't exactly soften, but the edges blunted at least. "This is different. One of my Magic Theory students pulled a fang out of the amulet box."

"Please don't tell me it was Maddie May who found that terrible thing." I held a breath I didn't need. "She's a good egg, shouldn't get involved in something like this."

"Too bad. She already did. Like most Umbral magi, Miss May's got a sleuthing streak a mile wide." Henrietta sighed. "I know you two are acquainted."

"Not so much. I just made her the amulet that lets her go to this class of yours." I scratched my head. "By the way, doesn't some Russian guy usually teach Magic Theory?"

"Don't lie. You spent more time with her than that." I could picture the face she'd be making to go with those words—a coy little lopsided grin. Henrietta had always smiled more with the left side of her face than the right.

"Fine. I've seen her off-campus twice. The rest of the time was just studying in a group." I tapped one finger against my nightstand. "Don't avoid the question about that Professor you're replacing, though. I've got one of my hunches."

"Fine back, then. Hold on." I heard shoes clicking on tile and a faint echo as Henrietta moved away from what or whoever she'd been standing near before. The faint squeak of a hinge told me she'd gone through a door. "He took an emergency leave two days before classes began. Didn't give a reason except to say he had to take care of some sleep issues he's been having."

"And this is Professor Brodsky, right? The double Ph.D. who also runs the Summoning research lab?"

"I'll send someone from Campus Police down to look in on him." A faint scrape and clink sounded, then Henrietta took a deep breath. "Since he's on medical leave, they won't even raise an eyebrow about that sort of thing." Her exhale was unmistakable.

"Hey, you should re-quit with the smoky treats. Those things'll kill you."

"You try integrating and running a school where your star pupils get walloped by a snowstorm one session and two buildings get trashed by a Grim the next." I heard her take another drag. "You'd get back on whatever your worst habit was, too."

"Insane amounts of coffee milk isn't as fatal as the cancer sticks. It's also not the same on the palate as it used to be." I surprised myself with a little snicker. "Quit them."

"Why don't we talk like this more often, Henry?" She'd turned a faucet on to cover her laughter. She had to be in the restroom.

"Because you're Professor Henrietta Thurston, former Prom Queen and Headmistress of the only Ivy League school for Extrahumans in the United States." I leaned back against the wall behind my bed. "I'm just a two-bit Psychic who happened to be friends with her crew, then went and got one of them killed and himself turned."

"Quit with the self-deprecation, Baxter." Her voice was still thready and breathless after all the giggling, but her tone had gone back from High School reminiscent to serious business in a second flat. "You risked your neck to stop that Extramagus. You'd have died just like poor Dahlia if the vampire you rescued hadn't had enough energy to turn you."

"Maybe, maybe not." I stared up at the bare wall on the other side of my one-room apartment. "But I wasn't forgettable like she was."

"That whole event's right there in the texts we assign for Local Extrahuman History, I'll have you know."

"Too bad they don't name the Extramagus or the vamps along with the champs in any of those books."

"Sometimes, a curse is a blessing, Henry. At least that's what Rick used to say." I heard the unmistakable muffled squeak of gritted teeth. Smoking wasn't the only bad habit she'd reverted to, then.

"I'm surprised you brought him up." Rick was her ex-husband, former Prom King and Dean of Students before PPC got integrated. He'd tolerated me while I was still really alive because Henrietta loved her friends, but was the main reason everyone besides Dahlia's boyfriend Neil had cut me off after I got vamped. I thought I remembered him believing us about the Extramagus though. "I was really surprised you two didn't last, all things considered."

"Well, sometimes you have to choose between your home life and your job." Henrietta sighed again. "No. That's not true. I just couldn't do it anymore. Put up with his bigotry. It got worse after I integrated the school." I'd thought she shunned me because of Dahlia's death. That would be easier to take than her giving in to her husband's bigotry. "Sorry, I didn't intend on saying anything about all that."

"Look, you should talk to someone about it, maybe more frequently if you already do." I couldn't imagine she didn't have a therapist. "But I'm not remotely the best person to be your sounding board."

"For what it's worth, I'm sorry."

"For what it's worth, I'm not." I pushed my feet into the slippers I kept at the edge of my bed. "Keeping a low profile once I got back probably saved my life. It would have been dangerous getting involved with Rick's brand of Extrahuman politicking. Anyway, I bet Maddie already told you to look around the Lounge and the tunnels by Water Place Park."

"She did. But if that fang turned up in the box today, we probably won't find anything until whoever's doing this gets caught."

"Or until it happens again."

"Yes, that." I heard her turn the tap off. "Maybe whoever Campus Police sends will find a clue at Professor Brodsky's apartment."

"We can hope." I shuffled into the kitchen to warm up some water for tea. I still hadn't been out to get more coffee.

"Call if you discover anything else." I heard the hinge squeak again, and the echo of her footsteps in the hall. "Goodbye, Mr. Baxter."

"Bye." My old-fashioned flip phone let me hang up before she did. There are no small victories, just small victors.

I filled and plugged in the electric kettle. My apartment just had a refrigerator, counters, and cabinets. Technically it wouldn't be legal to rent a place without a stove to anyone living, but for me it was fine. The last thing I wanted was a gas fire caused by an appliance I didn't even use. I got the tea tin down from the cabinet above the microwave. Someone came in through the door upstairs, into the hall. I scooped loose tea into the infuser over my favorite mug, then froze at footsteps on my basement stairs. What kind of unhinged person would visit a vampire before noon?

The knock on my door was light and unexpected. I'd just braced myself for property destruction and a fight-or-flight situation. Then, I breathed in deeply through my nose. Of course. Lynn had given Olivia an errand for today. No one mentioned it'd have anything to do with me, but I caught the dry feathery scent of owl shifter outside. I knew it wasn't some other bird shifter because she was the only one taking an Adderal and Ritalin cocktail every day. Those had a distinctive smell, too.

I unlocked the knob, the bolts, and the chain. When I opened the door, I caught Olivia in mid-yawn.

"Sorry." She blinked. "For yawning in your face and bothering you at this ungodly hour."

"If it's ungodly, why aren't you sleeping?" I gave her a sideways glance, waving her in. "Tony's nocturnal too, and he sleeps until at least two in the afternoon every day." I pulled out one of the chairs at the small table doubling as a kitchenette and room divider. Such is life in studio apartments.

"Tony's lucky. Lynn sent me on a mission today. Our Terminology class just has a test on Fridays, so once I finished, I went all over campus." Olivia pulled a series of paper bags from the big brown satchel she always carried. "I found some things. Only touched them with gloves on. Lynn wants to see if you can get anything from them." She shuddered even though I kept my apartment ten-ish degrees above what keeps pipes from freezing. Her eyes were wider than usual.

"What's wrong?" I glanced down at the brown paper bags on the table.

"You're not going to like some of this stuff." Olivia yawned again, looking like she'd rather be anywhere but here.

"There are tons of things I don't like. I won't freak out or anything, but if you want to, you can leave." I nodded at the unlocked door. The fact that I hadn't redone even one of the bolts pricked at my mind like a waking limb.

"I'm not supposed to until you're done. I have to bring them back so Blaine can do his dragon thing with them tomorrow."

"Okay, then." I got up to shut off the boiling kettle. "You want some tea?" I glanced at the door instead of Olivia. I was a lousy host.

"Tea?! Definitely." She got a hungry look on her face that I'd begun to associate with Bobby Tremain in the dining hall. I pottered around the kitchen, rummaging at the back of the cabinet for sugar and non-dairy creamer. I never used it myself, but my landlord did. The tea always went on when he came to collect the rent.

Just as I'd finished setting her infuser up, I heard the snick of the lower deadbolt. Owl shifters were perceptive, but I hadn't expected one living diurnally to have much awareness. She'd noticed my discomfort. Maybe that said more about me than Olivia. All the recent socialization had shaken something loose. It'd take a while to settle down and fortify the armor I usually wore against the world.

The tea steeped as I brought the sugar and creamer to the table with some spoons. I set out saucers and napkins, avoiding the ominous bags for as long as I could. When I turned back with the mugs, Olivia headed back toward the table after taking a detour past my bookshelf. Owl shifters loved books like dragon shifters loved their hoards.

"So, what do you think?" I watched her pull the infuser out of the mug and set it on the saucer.

"Not enough High Fantasy, too much proto-horror. I'm not a Lovecraft fan, but Poe is nice." Olivia sprinkled sugar in her tea, then heaped two teaspoons of powdered ersatz cream in after it. "You ought to try Robert Howard."

"I have. An absent friend swore by his work, but it just never caught on up here." I pointed at my temple, then took the infuser out of my own tea, inhaling deeply. Black, like my vampiric existence. The thought made me smile just a little.

"Do you have a lot of those?" Olivia gazed down at the light tan tea thoughtfully. "Absent friends, I mean."

"More than I'd like."

"Listen, one of the things you're not going to like is from the Nocturnal Lounge. Fred Redford found it."

"I figured." I took another sip. "What about the rest of them?"

"One's from the library."

"How did you get in there?"

"Work-study. I digitize stuff in the media lab. I told them I had to get some homework, and they let me in." She tasted her tea, made a face, added more sugar. "I found an amulet. Round brass thing, the size of a pocket watch."

"Wait, what?" It was my turn to blink like a sleepy owl.

"I shouldn't tell you more. Lynn said your impressions should be as unbiased as possible." She tried the tea again and nodded at it this time. "Maybe I already said too much."

"No, it's okay. I'll do a mind-clearing exercise before I start." I inhaled the scent of bergamot again, bracing myself before starting. "Glad they're separated. I won't know what I'm getting with my eyes."

"Exactly what Lynn said."

"It's comforting when a super-genius agrees with you." I set the paper bags in a line, then reached out to pull one closer, opened it, and stuck my hand inside.

The object in my hand was instantly familiar. I remembered working on that amulet for the better part of three months, making mistakes and having to undo my impressions several times. Even the ribbon it hung from felt like an old friend. The energy coming off it was distinctly psychic but bonded to magic. Umbral magic, because no one else would need an amulet like this. Thing is, there weren't any other Umbral magi at PPC, or even registered in Providence. I shook my head. The magic on the amulet held a feel of age and experience.

"This is an amulet I made for suppressing Umbral magic." I took my hand out of the bag, leaving it inside. "But I don't remember who it was for."

"Is there a way to check that?"

"Maybe, maybe not. Depends on whether I made it before or after the Big Reveal. There'd be a registry slip if it was after. I might have stored the memory of binding it in an item, but that's somewhere I can't get to until Monday." Olivia didn't need to know I kept a collection of trinkets in a safe-deposit box at the Providence Underground Bank.

"Well, you got some information to start with, anyway." Olivia leaned back and sipped more tea.

I shrugged and grabbed the bag in the middle. At first, I thought nothing was in there, but my fingertips brushed something warm and diaphanous. I closed my eyes, trying to get my hand around whatever it was. A thin and delicate netting wriggled against my palm, its warmth less unsettling than its stickiness. It clung, wrapping itself firmly around my fingers, binding them together. It could only be one thing.

"Spider shifter silk?"

"Crazy, huh?" I couldn't see Olivia, but she was smart. She'd be leaning away from the table. No one wanted to tangle with this stuff, literally. It'd let me go since I wasn't technically alive. "That's what Fred found in the rubble of your table, by the way."

"And he gave it to you?" I opened my eyes, all done with my impressions.

"Well, he made me bring Bobby." Olivia shrugged. "Wouldn't give it to me directly. Thinks I'm untrustworthy because I stay up all day."

"Ah. Everybody loves the all-American bear shifter." I waited for the silk to uncoil and settle back inside the bag, then folded the top over probably more than I had to. "Even Changelings likely to tithe Unseelie."

"Fred hasn't taken his mantle yet?" Olivia blinked. "I wonder why."

"No idea. Maybe ask Tony." I leaned my elbows on the table.

"Um, no rush on that." Olivia's cheeks pinked. "Anyway, what did you get?"

"It wasn't put there by a spider shifter. It's a spy device. Like a magical nanny cam."

"So that means checking the registry's not going to help us?"

"Probably not. You can get spider shifter silk in half the magic supply shops in Rhode Island." I wiggled my fingers, then paused to take another slug of my tea. "Mainly, this just tells us we're not looking for a spider shifter. Would a shady Extramagus or his Psychic friends register spyware?"

"No way. So what are we looking for?"

"Magi or Psychics who can make that kind of device and are connected to PPC." I took a few calming breaths as I gazed at the last remaining bag. I had a hinky feeling about it. "Might want to start with Professor Brodsky, who went on medical leave just before inter-session started. He's a Summoner, you know. They're Psychic."

"Okay." Olivia jotted a few things down on a small notepad, then held her tea in both hands between herself and the last bag. I didn't blame her.

"Well, here goes nothing."

As I extended my hand, the clock across the square from my building struck twelve and my phone rang again. I grabbed that instead of the bag. That had to be a sign.

"Hello?" The connection sounded like the caller was outside in the wind.

"Henry."

"Maddie." I cleared my throat. "What's up?"

"Are you okay? You sound like you got a stay of execution." She seemed to just get me, but then again she might just get vibes. Having two psychic parents does that to people.

"It's been a hectic morning." I held one finger up, signaling to Olivia that I might be on the phone a while. She smiled, curling her hands around her mug.

"I know. Professor Thurston called you." The connection cleared like she'd gotten out of the wind.

"That was a cakewalk compared to the errand Lynn has Olivia on." I grimaced at the bag, then shrugged at Olivia. "Memory psychometry isn't anyone's idea of fun."

"Ouch."

"None of that's the reason you called." I hoped she didn't call just to hear my voice even though I was way too glad to hear hers.

"Yeah, um, I guess." The hemming and hawing didn't bode well for putting distance between us. "Look, the fang had Telepathic energy on it. I can't figure out why. Does that fit with Summoners? I know they get something like it with their creature contracts. But on a fang, it doesn't make sense."

"Not that I've ever heard of, unless Mind magic's involved. Why not talk to Lynn about it, or Blaine?"

"Yeah, I guess I should." I could hear the smile in her voice. "Thanks, Henry. Sorry for bothering you while you were busy."

"Don't be sorry. Psychometry's like a grab bag full of broken glass and venomous snakes. I'm glad to get any kind of break from it. Bye, Maddie."

"Bye." I kept the phone open until she hung up. After that, I put the device down and set my head in my hands.

"You've got it bad." Olivia's voice made me sit up. I'd almost forgotten she was there. Her face wore a slight but wistful grin, her eyes dripped with empathy.

"Um, what?" I shouldn't have let Olivia see that.

"Never mind." She glanced at the most awful brown paper bag in the entire city of Providence and shuddered a bit. "Might as well get it over with, right?"

I groaned like I used to the morning after a night at the clubs. At least hangovers didn't happen to vampires. I reached for the bag again. I got a tingle just from putting my hand inside. Whatever was in there had a familiar feel to it. I couldn't help myself, I trembled a little.

Once I held the wider-than-average card, I knew exactly what it was, where it had been found, and why it was here. I gulped, a reflex left over from my mortal days. An image came up behind my tightly closed eyes, one that should have been heartwarming but gave me a deep chill instead. I dropped the card back in the bag and closed it, understanding I'd get nothing else from it. Blaine probably would. I'd want to know exactly what he got off it right away, too.

"That's Headmistress Thurston's. It's The Lovers, a tarot card her ex-husband gave her on their wedding day." I shuddered. "Trouble is, the emotion in there is all wrong for her. It smacks of regret and missing someone, but I know that's absolutely not true."

"So why'd I find it at what Providence Police are now calling a murder scene?" Olivia turned her head and looked at me out of the corner of her eye.

"Someone's trying to frame her for a hate crime." I explained about the vampire fang in the lab box. "And if I'd been the victim, it'd make perfect sense."

"Who'd want to do a thing like that?" She blinked slowly a few times. "And who'd believe it?"

"Her best friend got killed rescuing a vampire. You're an Extrahuman Law student. You know any detective worth his salt would pin that motive on her." I took a deep breath, but it fell far short of calming. "There's nothing more I can tell you until Blaine has a go at it." I pushed the bags across the table toward her. "I have to be there when Blaine does his thing. We'll need to talk."

"Blaine wants to do it alone." She plucked the bags from the table, then stowed them in her satchel.

"Tough." I crossed my arms.

"He'll be a dragon. Scaly. Massive. Big teeth." Olivia fastened the clasp on her bag and got up, heading toward the door.

"Nothing I haven't seen." I rolled my eyes, leaning back in my chair.

"He's a fire dragon." Her eyebrows tried to make friends with her hairline as she undid the deadbolt.

"Okay, scary. I'll manage." I uncrossed my arms and shrugged. "You tell them."

"I will." She turned the knob and pushed the door open, standing in it for a moment. "Owl shifters always leave pellets of wisdom for their hosts. Here's yours. The best-laid plans of Magi and monsters often go awry."

"What's that supposed to mean?" I stood up, collecting the tea things.

"I think part of you knows already. Bye, Henry. Thanks for the tea." She shut the door behind her. I bolted it before finishing clearing up.

CHAPTER TWELVE

Maddie

I pushed through the door at street level, finally done with class. I'd imbued the charm with Umbral energy that still hadn't worn off. No one's had. Our homework was to record how long the energy lasted and one more attempt over the weekend. Nox hurried out the door with me. I stopped short, and we collided. I ended up on all fours with scraped palms. Nox tripped right over me, stumbling headlong into Josh Dennison.

They were a tangle of limbs at the bottom of the steps. Muffled exclamations of surprise and annoyance had me stifling laughter as I stood up and brushed myself off. They looked like a giant amalgamated spider. I reached a hand down and grabbed one of Nox's. It was cold and a bit clammy, exactly what I'd expect from a Kelpie.

Josh's eyes followed our movement as I helped her up. Her breath plumed out white in the cold air, carrying a stammer of laughter along with it. I held my hand out to help Josh up, but he shook his head and rose on his own. I also laughed. Couldn't help it.

"Great Goblin's Garters, that's hilarious!" Nox held her shaking sides with one hand and pointed at Josh's chest with the other.

"I know, right?" I leaned on a lamp post to steady myself, gasping words out between giggles.

"What's so funny?" Josh put his hands on his hips, feet shoulder's width apart. His face wore the most menacing frown he could probably manage. Other people might be scared of an angry wolf shifter, but it didn't faze either of us. After all, Nox could turn into a magical Unseelie horse, and I could hide if Josh wolfed out.

"Didn't look before you put your shirt on today, huh?" I pressed a hand to my breastbone, trying to suppress the giggle fit.

"Leaping Luna, I did it again?" He pulled down the hem of his t-shirt, peering at it. I watched his lips form the words "Fuck you, you fucking fuck." He rolled his eyes, reminding me of Lynn on an extra-sarcastic day.

"Yup." I shook my head. "You wore the rudest shirt in the known universe again."

"Wait, again?" Nox's question came complete with a curious glimmer in her eye. "You mean he's worn that in public before?"

"Yeah, I did. That was the worst presentation grade I ever got." Josh sighed. "I'll have to do something about that before I go on my Campus Police business."

"And how." I blinked. "Wait. You have Campus Police business?"

"Yeah. Gotta check on some professor on emergency medical leave. No one's heard from him and the Headmistress is worried."

"Hmm." I wanted to tell Josh more, but probably shouldn't in front of Nox. She didn't know about the Grim problem.

"Oh, wow." Nox put one hand over her mouth. "The only Professor on leave is Brodsky, the guy who was supposed to teach Magic Theory. Can I go with you? I had him last semester and actually liked him."

My voice mingled with Josh's as we spoke simultaneously. "Sure, let's all go—" "Um, that's not a good idea—" We stopped, glaring at each other.

"Look, I have to go change my shirt before heading over to Brodsky's anyway." Josh still held my gaze like the Alpha heir he was, but it softened a bit. "Why don't we all go and Maddie can tell me what her issue is with having company on a mission like this."

"Okay." I re-settled my satchel on my shoulder.

Nox just nodded and hitched her backpack up her arms. We followed Josh along Hope Street, heading toward Swan Point Cemetery. He took a left toward the hoity-toity houses between Hope and the Blackstone Valley Parkway. Those were multi-million dollar properties. I hadn't imagined someone like Josh living here. No wonder he didn't have a room on campus. Then again, his dad headed PPC Campus Police, and his mom was the Extrahuman liaison to the Rhode Island State Police. Of course, they lived in an exclusive area. This was Rhode Island, and any position of power came with benefits. And I thought Blaine was the only rich kid I knew.

Nox's eyes practically bugged out of her head when Josh stopped at a wrought-iron gate. Her power came from an Unseelie Faerie object. No wonder that gate freaked her out. It had spikes in front and on top, definitely the fashion at the turn of the twentieth century. Nox swallowed audibly, gripping the straps of her backpack so tightly her knuckles blanched.

"Sorry about the gate." Josh grinned more gently at Nox than I expected. "We'd take it down, but we're on the Register of Historic Places. They won't let us without a ton of red tape." I felt my eyebrows knit together, wondering why Josh would fib about something like that. Umbral Affinity sometimes let me know when people hid the truth. He must have told her a whopper.

"It's okay. I'll be fine in a sec." Nox set her backpack on the ground at her feet. She unzipped it and pulled a small oilcloth pouch from inside. Then, she put her right hand under her shirt and murmured words in a language I couldn't recognize.

Josh blinked as she pulled a slick black rectangle of pelt from under her shirt. She tucked it into the oilcloth pouch, a few drops of swampy-smelling water dripping to the sidewalk in the process. After that, she put the pouch back in her pack and zipped it. I'd seen the difference the pelt made in her appearance that morning. What really struck me was the change in her attitude.

Nox's lips pulled back in an easy smile as she put her backpack back on. Her hair lost its wet and bedraggled look, and when she tucked it behind her ears, it stayed put. Her eyes were blue-green, something I hadn't noticed before. As she walked through the now open gate, her stride was long but more tentative, with a hint of feminine sway she'd lacked before.

"You two have your talk." Nox glanced over her shoulder at us as she ambled ahead up the long tree-lined driveway. "I'll meet you halfway up."

"Well, that was unexpected." Josh turned around to close the gate behind us. "She's something else. How long have you known her?"

"Just since the first day of class." I grinned at Josh. "And that's part of the problem."

"Oh?" He walked slowly toward the house.

"Yeah." I followed. "This Brodsky thing's more than what it seems. I was with Professor Thurston when she called Campus Police. She thinks he knows something about the Grim."

"He's the Summoning Professor. That's not a huge mental leap to make."

"I know. I think she suspects him, but needs hard evidence."

"So this might be more dangerous than checking to see if the old guy had a coronary. And we shouldn't bring a Kelpie as powerful as Nox seems to be. Why?"

"Because she doesn't know about all this. I believe Blaine's tinfoil hat theory, that there's an Extramagus messing with the school. Nox shouldn't get mixed up in that unwittingly."

"I get it." Josh shrugged. "But not everyone reacts the same when the going gets tough. If she's like me, she will welcome a distraction. But Brodsky can't call the Grim again for five more days."

"Who knows what else he could call up, though."

"Gotta check his apartment to find out. If he's there, he'll cooperate, wouldn't want to blow his cover by messing with us. If not, we might find Thurston's evidence." Josh shook his head. "Look, I'm not a brain like Lynn or a Boy Scout like Bobby. I'm dangerous in a fight, but that's not all there is to being a wolf shifter. I know how to play a mission like this. Both Mom and Dad are Alphas. I cut my teeth on double-speak. But I don't know Faeries. Bet you dollars to donuts Nox does."

"Okay, fine. I still have a weird feeling about bringing her in on this, but I'll let you decide. It's bad enough Lynn got Olivia involved. She's half-asleep all the time."

"Why an owl shifter wants to be diurnal is beyond me." He shook his head. "Crazy bird."

"True story."

"Leaping Luna, you sound like Baxter." He shook his head, then walked along in silence briefly. "You should spend time with someone else for a change."

"Huh?"

"Come out with me tomorrow night." Josh turned to face me, walking backward when side-stepped and continued up the driveway.

"Um." I chewed on my lower lip. I wasn't sure about how Josh looked at me. It wasn't romantic or lusty, just protective. Definitely not the way a girl wants to get asked out. "Where?"

"Dunno. Wherever." He stopped at the circular part of the drive, near the huge house's entrance. Nox stood with her back to us, gazing at the intricate woodwork on the top of the gabled roof.

"Hey, Nox, want to come out with us tomorrow night?"

"Sure!" She looked over her shoulder just as Josh turned. And there was the spark that had been missing from Josh's face before. He said nothing, turning his head away from her before she could look him in the face. I was struck by how controlled he was. If that was the life of a wolf shifter Alpha, I felt more than a little sorry for him. Nox and I waited while Josh went inside.

"I didn't expect this much of a difference." I glanced at Nox's backpack. "It seems like there shouldn't be one at all."

"That's because our skins carry more than magic and shifting ability." Nox scuffed the pale gravel coating the driveway with the toe of one boot. "They have ancestry in them, too. Little quirks and personality traits from generations back, compliments of all my forebears who wore it. The more ancestors, the stronger the magic."

"Wow. Is it distracting?"

"Sometimes. It's not like I hear most of them all the time, they just affect my mood. That and my appearance." She smirked, then gestured at her torso. "I'm the first woman in my family to inherit it after twelve generations. My grandpa's not happy that number thirteen's a girl. His influence in there is the hardest part. He fights me on anything too feminine."

"And I thought my life being forgotten by half of everyone sucks." I realized that if she'd inherited it, she must have lost her father already.

"Guess I'm still getting used to it. The magic's a huge benefit." She smiled, but not with her eyes. "I was mundane before, so I love that part. I took to Water magic like a duck."

We laughed together easily, a heartrending change in light of that morning's horror. I still thought Nox shouldn't get involved countering the person trying to wreck PPC. I thought about coincidence. Maybe involving Nox wasn't up to me. I'd call my mother tomorrow, ask her about the future.

Josh came out of the door, wearing a navy-blue Campus Police shirt. He smiled, but the expression didn't really touch his eyes until he glanced at Nox. That was another puzzle. Why ask me on a date when he was clearly more interested in the Kelpie? For some reason, I thought it'd be a bad idea to call him on the carpet right here and now.

The walk down the drive was quicker than the one up. We headed across Hope Street and down the hill on Rochambeau, then turned up a narrow driveway. We stood at the side door of a yellow sided triple-decker. Josh rang the bell for number three, the one with Brodsky's name beside it. He waited, then rang again. No response. Then, he pressed the button for number one next to the name Kazynski. A voice came over the intercom.

"*Preevyet?*" The Russian greeting crackled with age and intercom static.

"Hi there. I'm from Providence Paranormal College, just here to check on Professor Brodsky upstairs."

"Oh, go on in." The words carried through on a heavily accented voice. "He not home, but you leave the note or something for him, *da*?"

"That's right. Thanks." Josh grabbed the doorknob just after it buzzed.

The narrow stairwell smelled strongly of wood polish. The door marked number one was on the left. A violin-shaped welcome mat sat in front of it, reminding me of a guard dog. We went up creaky stairs with low-pile carpet cushions on the risers. At the top, the door to number three stood open just a crack.

"Huh, odd." Josh made a gesture from his forehead down to his chin. I had no idea what that meant, but Nox seemed to.

"Hide us," she whispered.

I gathered shadows around us. Josh blinked, then gave a smirk and pointed at his stomach. Nox pulled her Kelpie skin out of the oilcloth pouch and tucked it under her shirt. The change was weird even after her explanation. After that, Josh turned toward the door, beckoning for us to follow as he pushed it open and went inside.

Brodsky's apartment was dim, the only light coming through drawn shades and the door behind us. It was nearly silent, too. I almost jumped out of my skin when the refrigerator compressor came to life. Nox put a hand on my arm, calming me instantly like I was relaxing in a warm bath. No wonder she liked Water magic if that's what it was like.

"Professor Brodsky?" Josh stood next to a combination coat and umbrella stand. A hat, coat, and long, black umbrella occupied half of it. "PPC Faculty sent me to see if there's anything you need." Josh glanced around, then leaned toward the hat on the rack. He closed his mouth, taking a long, deep breath through his nose. He'd be able to track Professor Brodsky if he got a recent enough scent, but he shook his head and ventured further into the apartment. We followed.

The living room had a sagging vintage couch in the middle. A crooked bundle of something brown and stick-like lay across it. I couldn't figure out what it was until it moved. It was a Brownie, a Pure Faerie. They didn't mingle with humans or reproduce by making changeling offspring. They were dangerous to talk to. If you asked them too many questions, they'd rope you into a contract just by answering. It was part and parcel with their inability to lie. A direct question counted as a contract. I hoped Josh understood that Seelie didn't mean benevolent.

"Why does the scion of the Sons of Dennis smell like, Unseelie scum?" The Brownie sat up, blinking eyes that looked like knotholes. "Does he want to anger his parents?"

"I'm not angering anyone, wood-child." Josh put his hands out, palms up. "It comes with going to college."

"Yes, they let anyone in now. Not like the good days." The Brownie's voice was like twigs cracking underfoot. "Don't you wish things hadn't changed, wolf-child?"

"Days are days. We live how we have to." Josh stared at the creature, unblinking. "I'd tell you to stay in the Under if you don't like it, but you're in a Summoner's house."

"Yes. His dreams are troubled and his night hours restless. Are you here to interfere with him?"

"What he does in his sleep is no concern to me."

"Perhaps it should be. I smell the unliving on you, too. Another reminder of the old days." The Brownie stood, stretching to its full and spindly height. It looked like a bunch of extra-long bamboo come to life, like the Sawhorse in L. Frank Baum's Oz books, except vertical. "Are you turning back to the old ways, courting an alliance with a vampire?"

"Just going to college, like I said." Josh chuffed out a breath. "Vampires are more trouble than they're worth." Josh's grin matched the condescending tone he cast at the Brownie. I understood the kind of bait he used here, but wasn't sure it'd work. The Brownie hissed, its limbs crackling. "Surely your host has better control of himself than a vampire."

"You're wrong, Son of Dennis. Control, yes. Of the self, no. Don't you want to know what I mean?"

"Of course, but I'll never ask while a Summoner binds you." Josh's smile was as cold and distant as a crescent moon. "That just means he gets to control what you do with my contract."

"You think you're wise." The Brownie's posture became more rigid, a sign of relaxation for their kind. "But you err. It would be a Magus who'd own any contract we make this day."

Time seemed to slow down as I watched Josh's eyebrows raise quizzically. Just as he opened his mouth, Nox surged forward, breaking free of my hiding spell. She slapped him hard across the face before he could speak.

"How dare you?!" She glowered at him with such a show of anguish and raw pain that I almost dropped my shadows.

"I'm sorry. I don't know what I did wrong." Josh looked as surprised as I felt, eyebrows like apostrophes accenting his wide eyes.

"We had a deal, and you go slumming it with a Summoner-bound Brownie?" She tapped one booted toe heavily on the hardwood floor, making a hollow, dead, wooden sound. "Don't let the creature's flattery go to your head. But with a target that big, how could it miss?"

The Brownie clattered and rustled and snapped in its unique expression of distress. It backed away, tumbling over the couch to land behind it. I heard a wooden skitter as it rushed to escape the confrontation. A hint of movement only I could see in one dark corner of the room told me it'd gone to ground. Brownies were earth-aligned Faeries. Water magic wielded by an Unseelie creature was the only thing that could banish them from this realm for a year and a day. If that happened to this one, it'd breach Brodsky's contract. The Sidhe Queen would punish the Brownie harshly. It'd do anything to avoid such a fate.

"Is that enough information to satisfy our contract, Kelpie?" Josh stared Nox right in the eye, his upper lip curling in a snarl. His fists clenched in rage. He wasn't faking any of it. Her insult had stung more than the slap. I wondered whether she knew.

"Not yet. You look around and find anything you can. I'll keep this sorry excuse for a chip off your shoulder." Nox turned to face the corner, hand outstretched in the Brownie's direction.

"Fine." Josh strode toward the small hall leading to the bath and bedrooms. I followed him, knowing the Brownie wouldn't notice Umbral magic while Nox stood over it.

In the hall, he paused, then took the left door into a bathroom with a shower stall. A single shelf held towels, soap, and anti-dandruff shampoo. The medicine cabinet contained Tylenol, a toothbrush, and a series of sleep-aids. These ranged in strength from over-the-counter to prescriptions that got heavier the further forward in time the dates got. Whatever trouble Brodsky had with sleep started in midsummer.

Josh picked up the most recent bottle, dated December 1st. He shook it, holding it up to the light. It was half-full. Professor Brodsky had stopped using pharmacological sleep methods after exams. I made a mental note to add that to the tinfoil hat notebook.

I had to step into the shower to let Josh out of the bathroom, then followed him across the hall, into an office. A shelf of textbooks and lab manuals lined one wall, all from classes Brodsky taught. Nothing out of the ordinary there. The desk had a paperweight with Umbral energy inside it. I'd recognize that anywhere, of course. Something about it was familiar. It shimmered like my amulet, an item crafted to let Psychics use magic or let Magi be Psychic. It might connect to the Grim, but its energy was faint. I pulled out my phone to tell Josh to check the paperweight.

Josh moved along to Brodsky's bedroom before he got the text. He tapped his phone, then hit Send. He'd check it after the bedroom. Josh had already taken off his jacket and shirt before I realized what he was doing. He was going to scent everything in wolf form. I looked away to give him privacy. When I heard the click of wolf paws on hard-wood, I turned around.

Josh sniffed everything he could reach, which was most of it. He was rangy as a wolf which made him about my height on his hind legs. After he checked the bedroom, Josh went back to the office. I watched him sniff the paperweight, then flinch away in a backward half-jump. I stayed in the office as he checked the bathroom then went back to the bedroom. When he appeared in the hallway on two legs and fully dressed, I followed him back to the living room.

Nox hadn't moved from the spot she'd taken up earlier. Even her arm was in the same position. Just as I was about to check for magical influence, she lowered it.

"Don't ask the twig any stupid questions, wolf." She strode to the front door and stood by the hat rack. "Say bye-bye and get out of here. Once you answer my questions, our deal is done."

Josh turned to face the Brownie's corner. They crept out of the shadow, creaking and crackling as they crawled to the couch. The Brownie reminded me of a stick bug. Once stretched out across the threadbare cushions, they looked up at Josh again.

"Until we meet next, Son of Dennis." They quivered like a bird's nest in a strong breeze.

"Yes. Hopefully, under very different circumstances." He grinned.

"Indeed, we shall. And the Kelpie, too." It stiffened.

What could the Brownie mean? I wracked my brain, then remembered that Brownies had the Faerie version of Precognition. Mom always said they knew which way the winds of fate blew.

I kept to the shadows until we got back to campus, which was better than getting in the middle of the weird tension between Josh and Nox. We made plans to meet down at The Coffee Exchange on Wickenden the next night. Josh spoke with a stiff formality that hung on him like a necktie, or maybe a noose.

I wasn't going out with him alone. Nox might not come after the spat in Brodsky's apartment, but that made no difference. I sent texts to the rest of the tinfoil hat crew, then went back to my room to check my homework. The Umbral magic in the alliance medallion faded as the moon rose. I recorded it in my workbook, wondering whether I'd have time to repeat the imbuing exercise over the weekend. At least Professor Thurston would have to accept my excuses if I couldn't.

CHAPTER THIRTEEN

Henry

India Point Park was cold on Saturday, but I didn't care. I had to do something besides think about Maddie and pushing her away for her own good. I wasn't sure she was the type of girl who'd let herself be pushed. Maybe when this Grim business was over, I'd leave Rhode Island. Greenland was a decent place for vampires, and I'd never seen the Northern Lights.

I walked across the bridge over Interstate 195, following the zigzag ramp leading down to the park. The red brick steps at the bottom were new since the last time I'd been there. I didn't bother following the path bordering the greenish-brown expanse of late-winter grass. The snow had mostly melted though gray and black mottled piles edged the area. India Point Park was open, with no shade, not a good place for a vampire to hang around after three in the morning. Luckily for me, it was only thirty minutes after sunset.

Blaine stood by the dock facing the water. If he shifted where he was, his nose would rest on the wood, leaving the rest of his body on the oblong lawn that hosted sunlit festivals and concerts I'd never attend. I let my boots stomp and squelch in the damp so he'd hear my approach. Even though he couldn't breathe fire in human form, I didn't want to startle him. That'd just make him regret agreeing to accept my help.

"Hey, Henry." Blaine's voice blew back over his shoulder, carried on the harbor breeze. "Fangs for joining me."

"Aww, how cute, Trogdor. That's the oldest vampire joke in the history of the English language." I stood next to him, crossing my arms in a parody of his posture.

"Knock it off, Baxter. We need to get this done pronto so I can meet everyone."

"Oh." I sighed. "It's a group outing, now?"

"Seems like you almost want Maddie out with some other guy on her own." Blaine shook his head. "What's your beef, man?"

"None." I shrugged. "I'm a vampire. Beef tastes like cardboard now."

"You poor thing. Still, you know what I mean." He gave me a side-long glance.

"I'm not going to the shindig or hootenanny or whatever you youngsters call it." I crossed my arms over my chest.

"Not even with Maddie doing the inviting?" His eyebrow did the Mr. Spock shuffle. "I'll bet she sent your text first."

"She shouldn't have invited me. I'm bad news." I managed not to sigh by clenching my jaw.

"Oh, please. Don't tell me you're going to do the whole brooding-vampire thing. That trope's more tired than a hibernating bear shifter."

"There's a reason we brood, you know." I shook my head. Blaine couldn't possibly understand.

"Yeah, yeah. I know. The whole 'I'm dangerous, stay away from me and find a nice normal guy' thing." Blaine chuckled. I blinked, surprised because he sounded about as rueful as I felt. "I get it. I turn into a scaly beast with fiery halitosis. Almost everyone I meet is highly flammable. Danger, Will Robinson."

"So why get on my case if you get the whole threat-to-your-loved-ones thing?"

"Because it's more bull than a Minotaur. Ladies know what they want, and in this day and age, they go after it. The guy from the wrong side of wherever nobly giving up on love so the girl can 'stay good' is so 1985. Of course, you came of age then, so I shouldn't be surprised." Blaine kicked at the ground, rucking up some grass under the toe of his boot. He stared down instead of out.

"Woah, dude." I shifted my weight and put my hands on my hips. "I came to help investigate, not get dating advice."

"Package deal, my friend." Blaine turned his head, smirking at me. "You bring it, I advice it."

"Millennials." I sighed.

"Gen X-ers." Blaine's eyes rolled so far back in his head that he could probably see his brain.

"Whatever." I blew my bangs off my forehead.

"I just. Can't. " Blaine held his hands out in front of him like he held an invisible basketball.

"Are we done now?" I tapped my foot.

"Nope." Blaine dropped his hands along with the invisible basketball. "You want to help this investigation? You accept that invitation. Let the girl decide. Everybody knows you're into her. The two of you have the luxury to decide whether to date in the first place. You're lucky. Some of us, not so much."

"Fine, I'll go." I blinked. "I'll just hang out, let her choose like you said. But I've got competition now."

"It's your mind, think what you want in it." Blaine opened his backpack to reveal three familiar-looking brown paper bags on top of a pile of clothes. I realized why he'd chosen the location he had.

"Nice idea, putting them over water so they can't affect you." I stepped around to the other side of the bags, putting my back to Narragansett Bay.

"Well, if any of them have Water magic, they could." He squinted down at the bags even though he wouldn't see anything more specific than the presence of magic in human shape.

"I think that's not too likely." I put my hands on my hips.

"Well, what did you find anyway?" Blaine shook his head. "Never mind. We'll compare notes after. Stand back a little more. You don't want to be this close to me when I shift. Air displacement might knock you down."

I went where he directed. When Blaine transformed, I couldn't look away. Scraps of fabric flew around him in a nimbus before drifting back down to earth. I'd seen other shifters do their thing, but most of those were regular-sized and changed out of their clothes ahead of time. Wolves, bears, coyotes, some birds. Shifters came in all sizes, but dragons were the biggest. Blaine took up the entire lawn, and it would have been more if he hadn't doubled up his tail and kept his wings folded. His scales were reddish and edged with some lighter color. Trails of smoke curled and twisted up from nostrils the size of my hand. Blaine turned his head and blinked. A clear inner eyelid closed over the vertical slit in his orange iris, followed by an opaque scaly outer lid. When they opened again, Blaine glanced at his backpack.

I stepped closer, taking the bags out and lining them up on the deck. I tried to sense which was which. No dice. I grabbed the one to my left and opened it. Blaine stared at a spot on the deck. I peeked in, seeing immediately that I'd have to upend it carefully. Good thing there wasn't any wind that night.

The net of spider shifter silk drifted down, coming to rest on one wide wooden board. The smoke from Blaine's nostrils got thicker and whiter. If he kept that up, it'd get hard to see. I almost fell over in shock when his voice sounded in my head. I had no idea dragon shifters did telepathy. No wonder they could see magic and psychic energy. They actually used both in dragon form.

"Supernatural spyware, huh?" Blaine blinked again. I watched his eye swivel back and forth in the socket. "Imbued with Air magic, a classic choice for listening in. Where'd this come from?"

"Nocturnal Lounge, right where I work on stuff." I shrugged. "No trace of who it came from, or who built the device. Whoever imbued it was a Magus careful not to touch it and definitely not a vampire.

We're just about the only people who can handle spider shifter silk without having to remove it with scissors."

"You sound like a cop." Blaine blinked with his clear lid.

"Worked with them a few times before the certification requirement." I shrugged.

"Ah." Blaine watched me put the gossamer filament back in the bag. "Next."

I tucked the bag back in Blaine's backpack and opened the next. This time, the tarot card slipped out, face down. I turned it over so Blaine could see the image of two people in love. I waited for his telepathic commentary.

"Psychically , the emotions on this make me think of lost love, but you already knew that." He opened his clear lid again. "This belongs to the Headmistress. It's got her Air magic all over it, plus a few traces from the PPC Magic Lab. She's the only one working there right now."

"Are you sure? I mean, can you tell how old the energy is?" I refused to believe Henrietta had anything to do with the attacks or the fangs. Not after the conversation we'd had on Friday. Still, she'd let the most experienced Summoner in the state go on medical leave. No. She wouldn't murder vampires, harvest their fangs, and leave them in her lab. She wasn't that evil or that stupid.

"Hmm." Blaine tilted his head, peering at the card. "Huh. Her energy is older than the lab's. That's weird." He blew a pair of smoke rings. "Where'd this one come from, do you know?"

"Crime scene. Dead vampire." I shivered.

"Tiamat's Scales." The epithet came through my mind at almost a whisper, not thundering like I expected. "Someone's trying to frame Headmistress Thurston for murder?"

"That's what I thought, too." I shook my head.

"How? You can't see the magic." He lined his left eye up with my face.

"Those emotions are all wrong for her." I didn't dare move. The background feelings coming through Blaine's telepathic link were tense and guarded. One angry breath from him and I'd be literal toast.

Now it was Blaine's turn to look at me like I was from Mars or something. His gaze would have been unsettling if he hadn't been humming the latest WBRU earworm. I wondered whether all dragon shifters used music to focus, or just Blaine. I'd have to get him listening to something better than the navel-gaze hipster stuff the local alternative station played.

"I'm not going to bother asking how or why you'd know something like that. It's pretty obvious you're about her age and this is a small state." More smoke rolled up and out of his nostrils. "I'm guessing the police aren't bothering with a formal investigation because the victim's a vampire."

"Nope. They're investigating all right." I shuddered despite my efforts not to. "A fang was found. In the PPC Magic lab. By Maddie."

"Shells of the Mother's Egg." That was just about the strongest oath a dragon shifter could invoke. "A crime against Extrahumanity? Now what I really want to know is, how'd our plucky little gaggle of college students end up with something that should be in an evidence locker?"

"Olivia's way sneakier than anyone suspects. She found these things on Lynn's hunch-based errands." I jerked my chin at the last remaining one. "I hope they give these to someone official once we're done here."

"So Josh believes." Blaine blinked. "No wonder Chief Dennison wants to meet me on Wickenden later."

"Yeah. Made a deal with him for it." I looked at my feet, the water between the deck's slats, a nail in one of the boards.

"Said deal didn't involve you avoiding a certain Umbral magus, did it?" I put the tarot card back in the bag to avoid meeting his heavy gaze.

"You're too good at guessing these things, Blaine." I sighed. "You're like the sitcom character who tells people to just kiss, already."

"Somebody's got to do it. Anyway, there's just one left. Out with it, already." He set his head back down on the edge of the deck. "Why put it off?"

I didn't tell Blaine the reasons for my reluctance. Maybe he could sense them, anyway. It felt like fear, doubt, and anticipation all joined hands in my heart to play ring-around-the-rosy. I shook my head to settle myself, then turned the last bag's contents out on the deck. The bronze amulet clinked slightly, hitting a crooked nail as it came to rest.

"Wow." Blaine raised and lowered his inner eyelids a few times. I watched his pupil widen, then narrow. The amount of scrutiny he gave the amulet made me uneasy. He even flicked his forked tongue out a few times like a snake, as though scenting with it. "This is crazy-go-nuts."

"How?"

"This amulet is designed to help suppress large amounts of magic energy. It's a little like Maddie's, and it has your Psychic energy all over it. But it's old, and has no unliving energy. So that means you made it before you got turned. And it's definitely you, not some other Memory Psychic operating at the same time. I'm comparing the energy right now, and it's an exact match except for the stuff that comes with being a vampire."

"What's that mean?"

"First of all, you're a strong Psychic. This amulet still works." He tilted his head again, peering at me and then the amulet one more time.

"If it still works, why'd the owner get rid of it?" I raised an eyebrow.

"I can think of three reasons." Blaine flicked his tongue out again. "One, owner's dead. Maybe even the dead vampire. Two, owner figured out how to suppress their magic energy some other way. And three, which is my personal favorite because I'm paranoid. The owner wants all that magic now. They could have dropped that just so we'd know how powerful they are."

"I think you're wrong on number three, Blaine." I sighed. "I don't think villains get that mustache-twirly in the real world. You sound like Tony, not a big, bad dragon shifter."

"You're right. But that's not too surprising." Blaine's tongue flicked out again. "The big whackadoodle about this amulet isn't on the

Psychic side of things. It's the magic. Whoever you bound it to has just about every type of magic energy except Unliving."

"That's impossible. No Extramagus on record has ever had that many schools of magic."

"On record. You're a Memory Psychic. You know records aren't always the whole story. They're limited. There are sealed records of Extrahuman Council trials where the only things on file are a case number and a memory amulet. One of these from back during Prohibition was about an Extramagus, actually. The identity was sealed, something about protecting the family from the sins of the forebear. This Extramagus had a physical limitation—paraplegia. Kept trying to get turned to keep all that magic and lose the limitation. When the vampires refused, he started picking them off during the day. Extrahuman Council agreed to take him out. I only know about it because my mom was part of that squad."

"So how come I don't remember making this?"

"No idea. There are too many ways you might have forgotten." Blaine turned his head to put his eye next to my face again. "Some of them might even incriminate you."

"You mean I might have agreed to wipe my own memory, or let the Extramagus do it with Mind magic? Not as incriminating as you might think. I agree to that kind of thing all the time. Keep a stash of amulets hidden away. Evidence galore in case someone decides to screw me over later." I sighed. "All I'd need is time to go through them."

"So the right amulet might tell us exactly who the Extramagus is?"

"Yup." I straightened, finally feeling like I might be useful in this whole mess.

"And there's a whole new reason you're the target, my friend." Blaine blinked slowly with his outer lid. "You might be able to out this Extramagus at any time."

"Not really." I sighed. "The thing is, I don't remember which amulet is which. It could take months to find the right one. Years even."

"Then start working on that as soon as you can." Blaine blew three more smoke rings before thinking at me again. "If you helped the Extramagus before, that explains why it's a Summoner attacking you now. Big bad Extramagus has to use a cat's paw. Get the clothes out of my bag, please. It's time to shift back, and I don't want to get arrested for indecent exposure."

I nodded and dragged out stacks of Blaine's not-so-neatly folded clothing. Then, I repacked the amulet. I didn't have to look up to know Blaine had shifted back. The surrounding air got cooler and felt emptier without the huge dragon on the lawn. I zipped the bag, waiting until the rustle of fabric ceased before standing and looking up. Blaine shouldered his backpack.

"Hey, wait, what's this?" Blaine trotted over to the edge of the deck. He rolled one sleeve all the way up his arm, then reached down to the water.

I approached, watching him fish something round and about the size of a bocce ball out of the flotsam on the water's surface. It glimmered faintly with a naggingly familiar iridescent energy. Blaine turned around, pulled a small towel out of the front of his backpack, then wiped the orb.

"What is it?" I scratched my head. I couldn't remember seeing anything like it before, and the strange energy had me puzzled.

"Japanese sea float. Kelpies, Selkies, and Tanuki think they're lucky. Can't hurt to have in a pinch, even though I don't know anyone who can use Faerie and Water magic." He passed it to me. "Check it out."

"What's that weird haze around it? Not the magic, the other golden glowy stuff?" I turned it over, watching its energy swirl and twist over and around the other magic like an oil slick, only much more pleasant-looking.

"Gold, you say?" Blaine raised an eyebrow. "Sounds like luck energy. That's something I can't verify without shifting back, and we're out of time and wardrobe for that sort of thing. I'll check into it tomorrow or something."

"Okay." I peered at the sea float, then handed it back and let Blaine stow it under the paper bags. The object held me transfixed in a state of fascination until Blaine zipped up his backpack.

"Let's meet Chief Dennison and go have fun, old man." Blaine slapped me on the shoulder, snapping me out of my reverie. He strode away across the winter-yellowed grass, breath puffing out of his mouth in the cold. The fact he was a dragon added to the volume of vapor trailing behind us as we crossed the bridge. I could almost pretend I was really alive.

We headed down the ramp on the Fox Point side. When we got to the street, Blaine waited. A PPC Campus Police car pulled up, and the window rolled down. The guy inside looked a lot like Josh, but older and with a buzz cut instead of a spiky hairdo. He asked for the bags.

"Here you go, Chief Dennison." Blaine set his backpack on the passenger seat, unzipped it, and let the Chief take the three bags out.

"I expect a formal report from each of you by tomorrow afternoon." He looked straight ahead instead of at either of us. "Bring it in-person."

"No problem." Blaine pulled his backpack back through the window and waved. I just nodded even though Chief Dennison hadn't looked at me once.

CHAPTER FOURTEEN

Maddie

"Yes, Mom. I'm actually going out with people who remember me." I spritzed my hair with just a little water, wanting my curls to perk up, not freeze.

"That's awesome!" Mom's squeal made me jump and squirt my face instead. I even heard her hands clap in the background.

"Mom, your eighties is showing." After patting my face dry, I gave my eyeliner an appraising look. I'd have to fix it now.

"I don't care." She lowered her voice and cleared her throat. "Is it a guy? It's a guy, right?" She reminded me of the seagulls in Finding Nemo.

"Yeah, Mom." I sighed. "There's a guy."

"Oh, now that doesn't sound like something you're happy about." She clicked her tongue against her teeth. "What's wrong?"

"It's just *a* guy, not *the* guy."

"Oh. Sounds disappointing." I could picture her, pulling at one of her springy curls and letting it go. I'd ended up with a hair type somewhere in between her tight, natural curls and Dad's straight, thick tresses.

"It is." I rummaged in my cosmetic bag for my eyeliner. "This guy, when he asked me out, it was like he had to or something."

"Then don't go." I heard the clink of a teacup on a saucer. Even out of town, Mom always settled in with a book and a cup of oolong. "Don't put up with that, Maddie. You deserve better."

"I know." I uncapped the liner. It'd only take a few seconds to fix the smudge. "I invited friends along, so I don't care that Josh is being weird."

"Wait. Which one's Josh?" When I heard Mom's tiny gasp, I pictured her clutching the front of the robe she'd tie-dyed herself before I was born. My mother was too earthy-crunchy to clutch pearls. She said flannel was just fine for her, thank-you-very-much. "He's not the fellow I hired to make your amulet, is he?"

"No, Mom." I blinked, nearly poking myself in the eye with the brush. I don't mess around with a pencil for that. Liquid all the way. As I braced my elbow on the counter, the real meaning of my mother's words sank in. "Did you see something about Henry?"

"Sweetie, I couldn't tell you if I did." Her sigh might have carried wistfulness over Mount Everest if it hadn't come through the phone first.

"Yeah. I figured it had something to do with your Precognition." I fixed the line on my upper lid and put the brush back in the bottle, twisting the cap. "Josh is a wolf shifter. Kind of Alpha-jerky, but does the right thing most of the time. His dad runs Campus Police."

"And he's the indifferent asker-outer?" She muffled the slight slurp as she sipped tea.

"Yeah. I think someone put him up to it." I chuckled, so she'd think it wasn't a big deal, but that effort fell flatter than a pancake from the Empire State Building.

"Lame." Mom clicked her tongue again. "And yes, I did say that back when I was your age."

"It applies." I had to get her off her tangent. "Mom, I called to ask you something serious, and you've avoided it the whole time we've been on the phone."

"Okay." I heard the rustle and rattle of cards being shuffled. "What's your question again?"

"Mom, put the cards down. I don't want a tarot answer, just a Mom one. It's not about the future."

"Oh?" I heard a hollow thud as she set her deck down. I could almost see her, leaning on her elbow in a mirror-image of the posture I used to apply all the makeup she never bothered with. Her brown eyes would be slightly unfocused, traveling the room until they rested on her deck again. "Fine, then ask away, sweetie."

"Mom, why hasn't Dad turned you?"

"Why didn't you tell me it was a personal question?" She was dodgier than cat-form Tony in a room full of rocking chairs for some reason.

"Oh, come on, Mom. Please just answer me." Her side of the family had Changeling blood, so sometimes it was hard to get a direct answer out of her. Other times, she just spouted things I wished I could unhear. Life with a precog was interesting.

"It's not time yet."

"Have you ever thought that if you wait much longer, you won't get the license approved before it's too late? They can take decades to finalize, Mom, you know that."

"We already have the license. Had it since you started Kindergarten."

"Wait, what? Then why aren't you turned already?" I spritzed my hair with water again. Yay, speaker-phone.

"Like I said, it's not time yet. Close, but we need to wait a little longer."

"What are you waiting for, Haley's Comet? Another solar eclipse?"

"Nothing like that." She sighed. "I can't tell you yet, either. Don't feel bad. No one knows why, except me and Dad."

"Oh. It's one of those thingamabobs." I snapped my fingers, trying to remember the word. "A psychic whatsis. Starts with the letter c, I think?"

"Yes. A contingency." I heard the clink of stone on stone. She'd be charging her crystals since I'd asked her to put down her cards. "If I mention the thing I'm waiting for, it might never happen."

"Yeah. Oh, and thanks. I passed a test because I know so much about coincidence and contingency. I told Professor Thurston I owe it all to you."

"Sorry I can't tell you, but we've got what we need." She sounded more relaxed now that I'd dropped the subject. "Your grandma used to think we'd split up if I kept waiting."

"I learned last semester how the turnings during the Big Reveal split a lot of families up." I put the spray bottle back in my bag. "You and Dad are outliers, you know. Weird, huh?"

"There's nothing wrong with that, Maddie, especially when you're both happy. If something improves your life, helps you feel cared for and less alone, then it's right for you. When a place or person makes you feel like that, it's a keeper."

"Thanks, Mom." I packed my makeup away. "I have to go now, meet people."

"Well, thanks for calling. I always love hearing your voice." Her voice brightened instantly. "Have a good time!"

"I think I just might now, Mom." I picked up the phone and tapped the icon to turn off the speaker. "Love you."

"I love you too, sweetie." She hung up.

I walked down the empty hall to my room. After I'd put away my cosmetics and hooked my phone to the charger, I glanced over at Lynn's side of the room. She'd found someone and gone for it, even though she spent the better part of last semester thinking she couldn't make friends.

I'd spent the better part of my life thinking no one would remember me long enough to care the way Dad and Mom cared for each other. Last semester, I'd asked Lynn to stick around at PPC because hope was important and she was worth it. It was time to follow my own advice.

The intercom buzzed just as I started scrolling through my phone contacts to find Henry's number. I set the phone down and pressed the intercom button.

"Hello?" It had to be for Lynn.

"Hi, Maddie." Nox's voice surprised me. Should she be able to remember me?

"Nox. What's up?" Of course, she'd remember. She had Faerie magic.

"Figured I'd walk over with you if that's okay?"

"Sure." I pushed the button to open the door downstairs. "Fifth floor. Meet me in the lounge. Left off the elevator, you can't miss it."

"Cool, thanks." I heard the door downstairs open over the static-filled connection, then let go of the intercom button.

I put my wallet and keys in a smaller satchel than the one I carried to class. I added lipstick, my spray bottle, and the Umbral Affinity book. Brodsky could send the Brownie after us. It couldn't do much to hurt us, but it could spy and try roping people into bargains. Water might scare it off. It'd be able to sense the trail of my magic if I hid after it saw me, but the book might have some tips on how to mitigate that.

Nox was already in the lounge when I got there. I'd called Henry, but he hadn't answered, so I sat next to Nox, tapping my foot. I stopped that as soon as I noticed. There had to be a reason he hadn't picked up, right? A reason that didn't involve some kind of attack or disaster. The sun had set almost a half-hour earlier. I glanced at my phone, then away again.

"Waiting for a message?" She tilted her head, a slight smile tilting the corners of her mouth.

"Maybe." I shrugged.

"I'd be worried, too." She nodded.

"Huh?" I blinked.

"About whoever you're messaging. We were like Captain Obvious and his In-your-face Band of Obviosity Pirates over at Brodsky's."

"Yeah, I was just thinking about that when you got here." I pulled opened my satchel, showing her the spray bottle. "Check it out, brownie repellent." She laughed.

"Josh and I have big red targets painted on our backs now." Nox smirked, eyes sparkling. I only just noticed she wasn't wearing her Kelpie skin. "Trouble with a capital T. T is for taunt, drawing aggro for you guys."

"You say that like it's a good thing to pull the boss without your armor." It was my turn to laugh. I got the reference even though I'd stopped playing World of Warcraft a few years back.

"Maybe it is. It might take the heat off Henry long enough for him to figure something out. He's the one with psychometry, right?"

"It's a little like psychometry, but really he's reading old memories."

"Isn't that the same thing?"

"Not really. A Psychometry Psychic can touch something another person hasn't and still get an impression. It'd be all about the object and its history. Henry can't read something unless someone touched it. And what he gets has to do with the person who touched it, not really the object."

"Wow, you know a lot about Psychics." She raised her eyebrows.

"My parents are Psychics."

"Cool. We have Magi in our family. I was born mundane, though, so that's why I got the pelt instead of my brother. He's an Earth Magus."

"Wow." I wasn't sure what that meant, but Nox seemed to be in an explanatory mood.

"Yeah. Incompatible magic. It'd be amazing to have both if they didn't cancel each other out, though."

"Yeah, it'd be like a Magus with more than one school who could also shift. And had Faerie powers."

"Totally broken." She smirked. "GM would hit it with the nerf bat."

We laughed together, then stopped when my phone beeped. The screen said **Josh Dennison** instead of **Henry Baxter**. The corners of my mouth dropped like rocks.

"Not who you wanted to hear from, huh?" Nox didn't even try looking at my phone. My level of respect for her skyrocketed.

"No." I checked the message. *Here already, where r u?* I sighed. "Let's go. Josh is already at the cafe. Lynn, Bobby, Blaine, and Tony are going to meet us there. Maybe Henry." I tried to look as nonchalant as possible. "Olivia decided she needs sleep more than a night out."

"Is she really a diurnal owl shifter?" Nox pushed the lounge door open.

"Better living through chemistry." I ducked under her arm and out into the hall. "You should meet her sometime. She's read just about everything in the universe. Remembers it all, too. Like a walking trivia bank."

"So you're saying she's a hoot?"

We laughed together all the way down the stairs. I'm not exactly sure why Nox headed for the stairwell instead of the elevator, but I didn't mind five flights down. Up would have been another story with my short legs. Outside, I saw a familiar long, black car standing at the curb in front of the building. As we started walking by, the window rolled down.

"Mr. Harcourt sent me to drive you to Wickenden Street." Nox blinked and stared at the liveried driver. I didn't blame her. The chauffeur was like a movie trope, with a shiny hat, white gloves, and a pristine uniform.

"Blaine's the only person I know whose family has more money than the Dennisons. It's legit."

"Okay, then." She reached for the door, but the driver shook his head, got out of the car, and did it for her. "Swanky." She climbed in. "I never imagined."

"I haven't been in one either." After I got in, I bounced a little to test the springy, plush seats.

Nox sat across from me, long legs stretched out in front of her. I seriously envied her shiny oil-slick leggings. I'd never have the guts to wear those without a skirt over them. She put one hand over her mouth, giggling at my antics. I found a radio and switched it on. NPR talk. I rolled my eyes and pulled a cord out of my bag. Once one end was plugged into my phone, I connected the other to a jack next to the radio. A few swipes and taps got us some decent music. Peter Murphy's voice crooned about how Bela Lugosi was dead. Undead, undead, undead.

"Wow, this is an old song." Nox shut her eyes and swayed. "My mom loved this stuff."

"Mine didn't. She's kind of a hippie." I chuckled. "Listens to Jimi Hendricks, Fleetwood Mac, Janis Joplin. She and my dad both wonder where I got the Post-Punk bug."

"You never told them?"

"I'm not sure myself." I shrugged. "Just that when I heard this kind of music, the first thing I thought of was my shadows. This stuff sounds like how they feel."

"After being in them myself, I can see why."

The car stopped. I put my cord away, and we got out. The cafe was half a block down. We thanked the driver and walked over. Josh opened the door. He held it, standing with his back against it as we passed. He barely looked at me because his eyes were glued to Nox. It was nice to see my new friend getting some attention, but downright weird that he'd asked me out when she'd been standing right there. Hopefully, he'd rectify that and leave me alone, already. All I could think while he held the door was how he'd unknowingly left the house in a shirt with the "f" word all over it.

The scent of coffee and wood polish surrounded me like a warm hug. I remembered how Henry said he loved the smell of coffee. Lynn and Bobby leaned together on a less threadbare couch than the one at Professor Brodsky's. Tony sat on an ottoman which didn't match the chairs. They waved us over. I plunked myself down in a chair-and-a-half, leaning on the arm so no one could share it with me. The only comfy seats left were two spots on a loveseat. Josh pulled a hard wooden chair over from one table, turned it around, and straddled it. Nox took the love seat, stretching her legs out under the coffee table. I watched Lynn's left eyebrow do its Spock imitation at the seating shuffle. She opened her mouth to say something snarky, but Bobby's impromptu shoulder massage put a stop to that.

"What do you want?" Josh propped his elbow on the chair back, then leaned his chin on his fist. His eyes focused on a spot somewhere between Nox and me.

"Coffee, black like my soul." I spoke in a sing-song voice with the brightest smile I could manage. Tony burst out laughing, Bobby joined in, and Lynn chuckled behind her hair.

"Light and bitter for me." Nox smiled across at Josh, her expression somewhere between flirtatious and predatory. "That's exactly what I like."

Josh got up and turned toward the counter pretty fast, but I still noticed his reddening cheeks. Once he was up there, Lynn put her serious face back on and gave me a pointed look. I smiled and shrugged. She lifted her eyebrows and shrugged back.

"Hey, look who decided to show up!" Tony stood smiling at the door. I turned to see who was there.

Blaine and Henry shouldered into the shop. I watched Henry inhale through his nose, his eyes going half-lidded just as I'd imagined. I shifted my weight to make room in the chair, kicking myself for choosing the smaller seat. Blaine made a beeline for the other half of the loveseat, plunking himself down next to Nox. He smiled at me.

"This is your friend from lab, right, Maddie?"

"Yes. Blaine, this is Nox. Nox, Blaine."

"Thanks for sending your car around, even though it was ostentatiously swanky."

"I'll need it over here for later, anyway." He gave Nox a toothy grin. "My walk was much shorter. It was the least I could do. And everyone should get to ride in one at some point. Same goes for other kinds of rides."

While Blaine played out his particular brand of not really humble demurral and flirtation, I looked for Henry. He was at the counter, speaking to Josh in low tones. Both had their hands on their hips. I wondered what they were arguing about, so I tried reading their lips.

"It didn't work." Josh clenched his jaw, shaking his head. "It's like trying to mix up oil and water."

"So, now what?" Henry shifted his weight from one foot to the other.

"Go." Josh jerked his chin at the door.

"Blaine brought me. He won't like that." He raised an eyebrow.

"Tough." Josh crossed his arms over his chest, tucking his chin to hide his throat. He stared directly into Henry's eyes. I knew an Alpha stare when I saw one. "You said you'd quit."

"I did." Henry smirked.

"She didn't." Josh sneered.

"Tough." It was Henry's turn to cross his arms, though he didn't tuck his chin.

I stood. They had no right to talk like I couldn't make my own decisions. As I stepped around the love-seat, Blaine glanced up. He winked, then gave me a sly little smirk. I tilted my head, raising an eyebrow. He responded by jerking his chin at the vampire/werewolf standoff and waving one hand at me in a "move along" gesture. I went. Henry was already out the door by the time I got to Josh.

"Don't go to all this trouble on my account, Josh." I immediately crossed my arms and tucked my chin, glaring up at him with upturned eyes. "I'll determine my own dating prospects."

"He's dangerous, Maddie." Josh met my eyes, reminding me of half the arguments I'd seen on TV between brothers and sisters.

"So am I. Umbral magic's no joke." I gestured at myself. "Poison hides in pretty bottles."

"Prove you can handle him and I'll get out of your way." He glared down his nose at me.

I focused my energy, marking an invisible circle around Josh's head. Then, I filled it with shadow. I heard Blaine's voice choking out choice words about Tiamat. I glanced over my shoulder where the rest of the group looked puzzled with one other notable exception. Tony. How in the world could he see magic? That was a question for another time. I peered back through my shadows at Josh. He turned his head, nostrils flaring as he scented the air. His head cocked to either side, ears wiggling slightly as he listened. He got nothing, of course. The sphere of shadow had cut off all of his senses except direct touch.

"Proven." The rest of Josh's breath whooshed out in a relieved sigh. "Now knock it off."

I called back my magic, smirking up at him. His slight frown upended itself, spreading out into an easy smile. Josh dropped his arms to his sides.

"Let's go bring him back." Josh turned toward the door.

"No, I got this." I shook my head, hoping my bouncy curls didn't make me look like an intractable toddler.

"Nothing doing. I'm responsible for this whole business." Josh narrowed his eyes.

"So am I, and—" Just as I was about to break the truce and call Josh a third-wheel, I heard a feminine gasp and a low male chuckle. Over on the love-seat, Blaine had turned on the charm. He was putting some serious moves on Nox, one arm around her shoulders as he grinned. He smiled, then turned a challenging glance on Josh. So that's what he'd meant with all the pantomime. I felt like I was stuck in a production of As You Like It.

"Handle it yourself, then." Josh's eyes glimmered. He handed me the black coffee. Now, Josh had something more important than a brooding vampire on his mind. He strode over to the rest of the group, turning his back on me.

I headed out of the cafe, glancing through the window to see Josh approach the love-seat, then stop. He'd forgotten Nox's coffee. Blaine got up to get it. Lynn and Bobby looked on in confusion. Tony grinned like he was from Cheshire, knowing he'd have some extremely juicy gossip for Monday.

Once on the street, I shut my eyes. I couldn't track the unliving energy that made Henry what he was, but I had my amulet. I reached in my shirt and focused on the connection between it and me, the one he'd helped me make. After that, it was easy. I ended up in front of the Wickenden Pub. Ninety-nine beers, one sign said. I read another one: Top Ten Reasons You'll Not Feel You Belong at the Wickenden Pub.

I smiled and went in.

CHAPTER FIFTEEN

Henry

I stared at the scarred table, not realizing what was carved in the wood next to the unfortunately, sweating glass that contained my stout. I'd nearly forgotten that the Wickenden Pub served all their beer cold. While drawing a line down the condensation with my pinkie, I sighed. I dragged water through the letters H and T. That was when I remembered why the x under the initials hadn't been a mistake. Rick had meant to make a multiplication sign between Henrietta's initials and his. He'd wanted a whole tribe of children with her back when we celebrated his twenty-first. All he had to wait for, he'd said, was her graduation.

But Henrietta had kept going and going, like an academic Energizer Bunny, until she had two Ph.Ds. I remember waiting and watching for birth announcements in the paper after Rick exiled me from our social circle, finding nothing. Even though they wanted nothing to do with me, I still cared about them. Back in 1999, hospitals were the only place to get legal blood. When I'd seen Henrietta over at Women and Infants, crying on the shoulder of a nurse with a Maternity Ward badge, I understood. Some things weren't in the cards for everyone.

The Wickenden Pub smelled like beer, stale beer, and old pizza with a slight hint of bathroom disinfectant that got stronger the closer you sat to the back exit. That's why the trace of myrrh and jasmine puzzled me. I had to stop thinking about Maddie so much, even though I'd never be able to forget her. I'd been an idiot, making an impression of her like that. I should have known it'd come back to bite me.

The warm hand covering mine was a total surprise. I looked up, so startled I almost knocked over my untouched stout. She steadied the glass, then picked it up and took a sip. She grimaced.

"Ugh. Why do they serve it cold?" Maddie stuck her tongue out, closing one eye.

"Maddie, go back to the cafe." I closed my eyes. She was still there when I opened them.

"Wow." The round O of her mouth broadened into a hard smile. "Just so we're clear, I don't take orders from baby Alphas or vampires who idolize Buffy The Vampire Slayer's boyfriends."

"Are you challenging me?" I raised an eyebrow.

"You think you're Josh's Beta or something?" She smirked.

"Ask him." I shrugged.

"You'll need this, then." She pulled what looked like a half-dollar on a string out of her pocket, plunking it on the table between us.

"An alliance amulet?" I'd never seen one before. "Where did you get this?"

"Lab. It was the second thing I fished out of that box. Nice little coincidence, huh?"

"No such thing as a nice coincidence." The phrase was automatic. I hadn't intended to lead her on at all, at least not consciously. I recognized the defeatism in that line of thinking.

"Most of the time, you're wrong." She rubbed the side of my hand with her thumb. Why hadn't I shaken off her touch? "Coincidence is the only protection anyone has from a Magus. Resist enough times, you're safe. What tends to happen the most keeps on happening when magic affects people."

"I'm not exactly people anymore, Maddie." I shook my head.

"Magic Theory says you are. So do I."

I didn't say anything. I could try to argue with her, but she had the Magic Theory facts right. Coincidence meant that all Extrahumans had more concrete confirmation of sentience than anything the humans had come up with. The Extrahuman Rights trials had set a precedent for using magical tenets to help define our legal rights. A Brownie or a Djinn would fall under those rules, for example. The Grim wouldn't.

"Listen, Henry, because I'm only going to say this once. I'm falling in love with you. I don't think there's a way to stop it, and I don't want to, anyway. You've done a whole world of good here, and I have a feeling you could go on to do even more. I want to be there with you for all of it."

"I'm a vampire, Maddie. You already have to deal with one person in your life living like a second-class citizen. I don't want you to have to deal with one more."

"You'll make two more, actually. Mom has a license for turning."

"Then things will already be hard enough for you in the near future."

"I don't think so. This right here," she tapped the medallion, "represents an old traditions of belonging and respect. That tradition went on for ages. The way society treats vampires now will pass, eventually. The world will see that you're like any other people, with the potential for horror or honor. Honor won most of the time back in the day until technically immortal people had to worry about death. It'll win again, if only you expect it of yourself and let people appreciate it when they see it on you."

"That doesn't happen very often."

"I think the hostess over at Luxe Burger would disagree."

"The opinion the two of you share about me is an unpopular one."

"But it's not wrong. And if you don't let people express it, no one with the wrong idea will ever know about the right one." Maddie's grin was gentle when I'd expected smug. She had me with that argument. Be the change you want to see.

"And what idea is that?"

"Just the slightly unhinged notion that any type of Extrahuman is part of humanity. It's right there in the term, after all. We're all worthy of dignity, respect, belonging. And love." She squeezed my hand. "Especially that. No one should have to resign themselves to eternity alone. Especially a man who can't forget."

"Heady stuff from the woman no one remembers."

"I'm afraid. Someday, I'll be alone forever and no one will remember me." Her smile dimmed down, darkening with the loneliness that hounded her as tenaciously as any Grim.

"Look, most people can't remember you, but you've been here just over six months and already found a score who want to." I took the alliance amulet off the table, pocketing it. After all the decades of change and danger I'd been through, it was time to let my guard down.

"Maddie, you control your actions, how you treat people. You could be awful to the lot of us, lie about what actually happened, hide things we need as a prank. If you were that kind of person, all the memory enhancements and coincidence in the world wouldn't make any difference. That's all on you. Only some of your fate gets decided by coincidence. The rest is a choice."

"Unless it intersects with a contingency." Her eyes widened suddenly like she'd just had a eureka moment. I watched her shake inspiration off. "Oh!" She blinked at something over my shoulder. "Don't turn around. Act natural."

"What is it?" I kept gazing at her.

"Brodsky's Brownie."

"What do Russian baked goods have to do with anything?"

"Professor Brodsky." She leaned close to my ear and lowered her voice. "The Summoner. He had a Brownie guarding his apartment."

"Wait, you went there?" I murmured back, finally at ease with being this close to her.

"Yeah. With Nox and Josh." She drummed her fingers on the table.

"Oh. What should we do?"

"Get out of here. Try to shake the Brownie so I can hide us."

"Why not hide us now?"

"If they see me cast, they'll track the spell."

"Okay, then. We walk out through the back. Pretend you're on the way to the restroom. I'll follow you in a minute."

"Fine." She leaned in and kissed me. This time, it didn't last nearly long enough.

I watched Maddie walk past the scarred tables, ratty chairs, and long, dark bar to the far end of the room. The narrow hallway had a sign over it that said Restrooms. Her nose wrinkled, then she stepped into the darkened hallway and out of sight. I picked up my stout and chugged it down without worrying. It couldn't make me drunk or even tipsy. The taste was barely there, like anything a vampire drinks cold. Maybe the next time I tried drinking alcohol for taste, it should be Irish Coffee or something.

I picked up the empty glass and stared into it, letting my shoulders droop to put on a good show for the brownie. Then, I shrugged at no one in particular and brought the glass back over to the bar. By this hour, it was crowded and dark enough for me to blend in. No one else had a jacket with smeared white paint on the back, but that wouldn't make me stand out in the barroom murk. I set the glass at the far end of the counter, then squeezed past some kids who could only be from the Rhode Island School of Design. They could give Blaine's hoity a run for its toity. The guys had beards and pompadour hairdos atop tight flannel shirts, suspenders, and skinny jeans. The girls wore a mosh pit of pastel colors screen-printed with birds and feathers.

"Hey, buddy!" One of the guys called out to me. I looked over my shoulder at him. "Haven't you heard Bela Lugosi's dead?"

"Yeah. Undead." I gave him a smile to shame the day-star.

I ignored the surprised noises they made and the air of their backward passage as they all scrambled to avoid me. One of them looked past me and did a double-take. He'd seen the Brownie, but the tilt of his head told me the Faerie was still at the front of the pub.

The hallway was a malodorous new world. People should be full of piss and vinegar, not my nostrils. I didn't have to breathe, but the ghost of the Wickenden Pub's bathrooms would haunt me for at least five minutes of outdoor walking. I didn't have much reason to pray anymore but gave thanks that the Grim couldn't be summoned for four more days. That beast could smell us from a mile away.

I pushed through the door outside. At first, I didn't spot Maddie at the back of the courtyard. She stood near the corner where the wall was lowest. I'd forgotten there wasn't an exit back here. The staff wouldn't want people using the back patio to skip out on their bills. The wall was an easy jump for me. I could tell right away Maddie didn't think she'd make it over.

"We'll have to jump it."

"I can't." Her curls bounced when she shook her head, eyes glimmering with imminent tears.

"Sure, you can." I glanced over my shoulder.

"Nope, no way." I noticed her shivering. She shouldn't have been since it wasn't too cold for her warm jacket.

"Okay, I get it." I lifted her in my arms, trying not to get lost in the rush of emotion as her body pressed against mine. It'd been decades since I'd done anything that felt this heroic. "You're scared of heights.

"Caught me. I'm not perfect."

"Good. Neither am I."

I jumped to the top of the wall, planting my feet firmly to absorb the shock with my knees. Here's where the extra strength and durability from being a vampire helped. Usually, a law-abiding person like me didn't leap too many walls. At the top, I looked down. Good thing I hadn't vaulted completely over and into the throng of trash cans behind the Pub.

I trotted along the top of the wall easily. Better balance was another vampiric perk. How had I forgotten I could do all this? Had I really been too scared and miserable to have any simple fun? I jumped down, setting Maddie on her feet. She adjusted her shirt and jacket, then smiled up at me.

"That was kind of cool, but only because I didn't look down." She closed her eyes and stepped back into the shadow of the wall, then leaned against it. I joined her, listening while she murmured the same words she'd used in the tunnels under the library. Shadows gathered around us. We'd be hidden now.

"Heh. Maybe we'll do it again sometime." I held out my hand, and she took it, walking back toward campus. I didn't want to drop her off at home. Maybe we should stay out.

Maddie tugged my hand. I stopped, looking down at her face full of fear. She stared across the street. This was a night of firsts for me. The creature peering through the shadows was a Spite.

I'd only seen a sketch of one. When a Sprite displeased the Sidhe Queen, she'd turn them into a hunting hound. Their wings became prehensile spikes with stingers on the ends, which could paralyze even vampires and dragon shifters. Spites could see magic because they ate it. If the Spite caught up with Maddie, they'd drink her magic. She'd only get her power back if she got away before a complete drain.

Spites were summonable like Grims and Brownies, but the Summoner needed a Seelie oath, tithe, or fealty in order to control it accurately. That meant either Brodsky or the Extramagus was hooked up with the Queen's Court.

"We have to get someplace safe." I racked my brain, trying to think of something.

"Needs a physical barrier." Maddie was right. Spites eat wards.

"Yup. Do we run?" As a Psychic, I didn't have much to fear from them. Unless they'd had been given orders to stake and behead me, of course.

"Not from a Spite. The faster you go when they can see you, the stronger they get. Walk like a normal person."

We continued up the street and the hill. I couldn't think. We had to get somewhere fortified. Magi warded places instead of buying good locks, including most buildings on campus. If I got through all this, I'd be having a talk with Josh about the common-sense of mundane locks. There'd be no shelter anywhere on campus with the Nocturnal Lounge still under construction.

I headed for my apartment. If it'd keep Maddie safe long enough for the Spite's time or energy to run out, I'd take it. My building was old, so I'd risk it trying to dig through the brick. But if the Spite broke through after sunrise that'd be the end of me. It'd take most of the Spite's time to do it, though, so it couldn't get Maddie after that. My landlord would be pissed, but I wouldn't be around to get evicted, anyway.

I bolted the front door and the basement door, then rushed downstairs with Maddie in tow. The Spite must be padding around outside of the building on feet with opposable thumbs. That was one of the creepiest things about them. The Sidhe Queen turned the Sprite into a killing machine, leaving just enough sentience to make victims pity it as they died. Have you ever seen a mastiff in pain? I learned that night that a Spite's eyes look like that all the time. I turned the key in the deadbolt, then followed Maddie into my tiny apartment.

"Don't worry, I'll get the lights after I lock the door." I threw the deadbolt, then did the chains and latches at the top and bottom of the door.

"Won't just shutting it work? I mean, it opens out so the Spite can't batter it down." Maddie's voice came from somewhere behind me and to the left. I turned on the lights just in time to stop her from tripping over one of the chairs and into the table.

"They can work latches and doorknobs, but can't pick locks." My fangs pricked my lower lip. I hadn't realized how hungry I was. But how had I used that much energy jumping on and off a silly little wall and doing up locks at Extrahuman speeds?

"I was afraid you'd say that." She set her satchel on the table, then took her jacket off and hung it on the back of the chair she'd almost tripped over. All I could smell was her blood.

"I have a book on pure Seelie creatures if you want to look at it to pass the time." I headed straight for the fridge and opened it. Nothing. I couldn't understand. I'd just stocked up at the Providence Animal Rescue League on Wednesday. I always got a week's supply. There should be at least five bags in there. Where could they be?

"I can think of other things I'd rather do." Her voice didn't sound low, purring, or husky. I had to hope she didn't have anything physical in mind.

"Um—" Before I could protest, Maddie crossed away from me.

"I haven't seen this much vinyl ever." She looked over my music collection with her back to me. I leaned against my empty refrigerator, unsure whether I'd be able to stay on the other side of the room from her. "Is it okay if I play a couple of these? I've never seen some of these EPs and imports."

"Go ahead." The words came out slightly slurred. Vampires always have fangs, but the hungrier we get, the more they stick out. They were at an awkward length for speaking by then.

Maddie froze with her hand hovering in the air next to a Siouxsie and the Banshees record. She looked over her shoulder and narrowed her eyes. Then, she stepped slowly sideways, crossing the short distance between the records to my bookshelf.

Without turning her back to me, Maddie eased out the book on pure Seelies. She checked the index, flipping through some pages. Her eyes flicked from side to side across the pages, slower than her brainiac roommate's but still respectably quickly. When they stopped, her eyes widened and her eyebrows went up.

"Henry, you're in trouble."

"Yeah, I know." I shut my eyes, trying not to look at her to stop thinking about biting her. I opened them, realizing that only made it worse. With my eyes closed, all I could hear and smell were her heartbeat and blood. "I don't know why."

"The Spite drains all kinds of magical energy. When you feed, the blood you take turns into Unliving magic. That's why it fuels you. When we walked here, you got between me and it. Must have been just close enough for it to steal a bunch of what keeps you going."

"I did not know they could do that." After all the times I'd complained about going back to school, I finally understood why the Licensure Board required it. Too bad I'd be dead in the morning.

"Well, the good news is, it can't do it until it can see you. So when you get a snack from the fridge, you'll be all set."

"It's empty."

"Move over." I stepped in front of the sink, letting Maddie wrinkle her nose and furrow her brow at half my kitchen. She shooed me away from that, too. After looking back and forth a bunch of times between the sink and the refrigerator, she nodded. "Water magic with little tiny foot and hand-prints. I just saw that in the book. Pixie. Looks like Brodsky has quite the crew at his beck and call."

"I don't understand." I shook my head, moving back in front of the sink again. "What's Brodsky got against PPC or vampires or us in particular?"

"Don't know. Maybe call Lynn and Blaine about that?" Maddie flipped through the book again. "Pixies. They're tiny, elemental, and summonable. They could get in through the sinks." She headed to the bathroom, looking over her shoulder before going in. "I'm warding the faucets."

"Good idea." I sat down at the table across from Maddie's jacket and tried not to think. With the Spite outside, she couldn't run from the hungry vampire inside. Coming to my apartment had been a bad idea. It was too small for me to get far enough away from my temptation. What made it worse was I felt exactly the same way Maddie did. I was falling in love.

Vampires had the drive to turn people they loved, especially someone who'd be genetically compatible afterward. After Death Magi, Umbral were most likely to be. And Maddie had grown up with a turned dad, meaning she'd been exposed to more than enough of the right kind of magic. Within just a couple of hours, I'd barely be able to control myself. If I turned her without a permit, she'd be lucky to spend eternity in prison. I'd be executed.

"That's everything. There's only one thing left to do." Maddie stepped away from the counter. I'd been so lost in thought I hadn't noticed her warding spell.

"Yup. Go open the top drawer of my dresser." I watched her cross the room, nearly mesmerized by the steady, strong pulse under the smooth skin on her neck.

"Stakes?" She raised one eyebrow.

"You have to use one. It's the only way I won't go nuts and try to turn you in a couple of minutes."

"Not the only way. If that Spite or anything else breaks in here and you're staked, they'll take your head, and that's the end for both of us. We'll need to be able to protect each other." She dropped the stake back in the drawer and closed it. Then, she pulled her sweater over her head, draping it over her jacket as she approached me. "You won't be at full power with what I can give, but this way we won't have to fight each other or leave you paralyzed. Relax. My mom and dad do this all the time."

"Maddie, we shouldn't." I shook my head. "I haven't done this all the time. All my blood came from bags or donors who used knives. I've never even bitten anyone before."

"Huh." She put her hands over my shoulders, gripping the back of the chair behind them. "I've never been bitten either."

By then, I couldn't say anything else. She'd draped herself across my lap, leaning against me in a way that reminded me of leaping the wall. Had I really felt like a hero then, like something more than a parasite? I needed that confidence back. I lifted one hand, stroking lush, dark curls back from her neck. Gazing into her eyes was like contemplating the vast potential of a new evening. They held nothing but hope and promise. The confidence I needed was right there, with her.

Finally, I understood. Like Rappaccini's daughter, Maddie had grown up tending a garden of shadows and unlife, fatally poisonous to most. She knew the consequences and risks that came with affection for my kind, maybe even better than I did. What I'd written off as parasitic, she'd watched work as symbiosis. I'd heard stories of Shi May as a kid, how he used his scrying to help people. I'd thought of him as a hero. His own daughter thought I could match his example. If I believed in her, I had to believe in myself.

I tilted Maddie's head down, kissing her lips tenderly as I recalled the focus training that kept me sane and controlled all those years. I'd need all my mental armor for this, like I'd used on her amulet. My memories from that time seeped up like groundwater in a drought, except now I understood why crafting that amulet had been such an emotionally draining task. I'd done it before, under enough duress to wipe the memory. But the only way to beat fate was to break cycles.

"Let's make some positive coincidence," I murmured against Maddie's throat.

The sensation of her flesh parting under my fangs and the sweet, hot taste of magically infused blood threatened to drown my focus. I'd left my island of carefully controlled solitude in a desperate attempt to reach civilization. I'd never make it by myself. But I wasn't alone.

"We already have that." Maddie's voice was a lifeline, her words a rope to cling to. The tide of blood washed me up on dry land. My calm returned. After I disengaged and licked her wound closed, she blinked sleepily at me, running her hand down the side of my face to stop at my chin. She kissed the corner of my mouth, then leaned against my shoulder.

I carried her to the bed and set her gently on top of the quilt. Her pulse was steady, but not as strong as earlier. I kissed the inside of her wrist before putting it down, then brushed some stray curls off her forehead. She'd need sleep, then food. I could give her that. Maddie dozed off just as I covered her with an extra blanket. I put on the Siouxsie record she'd reached for earlier, then flipped idly through the Seelie creatures book and waited.

CHAPTER SIXTEEN

Maddie

The incandescent light was almost too bright when I opened my eyes. The staccato clatter of boiling water rattled in my ears, followed by the slosh of pouring. Henry stood in the kitchen, clinking a teacup against a saucer. That sound was pure comfort. He bent at the waist as he set the tea and a plate of graham crackers on the table.

I sat up with a heaviness in my limbs like I'd slept under a lead blanket. My throat felt dry and my stomach rumbled, but nothing hurt. I shuffled toward the table. Henry pulled the chair out for me, smiling. His fangs were normal length, and his color better, even if not as sanguine as back in the cafe.

"Thanks." I sat.

"No way you're thanking me." Henry glanced at the plate and cup in front of me. "If I served you fillet mignon and lobster a thousand nights in a row, maybe I'd deserve thanks."

"Actually, this is exactly what I want right now. My stomach's still fluttery."

I inhaled graham crackers so fast the tea was still too hot when I finished. As I blew on my cup, Henry brought over another stack. I ate those too, sipping between bites. The kitchen clock read a quarter to five in the morning. Something about that bothered me.

"They're still out there?"

"Yeah." One corner of Henry's mouth tilted in a half-smile that avoided his eyes like the plague.

"Shouldn't they be gone by now?" I glanced at the clock again. "It's almost sunrise."

"Check the book." He opened it to the Spite page then pushed it across the table.

"They stay until full sunrise? That makes no sense. What kind of summoned thing does that?"

"Seelie ones, apparently. Makes perfect sense to me." Henry glanced at a spot high on one wall, practically near the ceiling. "You can't hear it yet, but the Spite's been working on getting in here for the last twenty minutes. They can chew through stone, so even though my landlord bricked up the windows, they'll get through, eventually."

"When?"

"Sometime around six, maybe earlier."

That can't happen." I flipped open my satchel, grabbed my phone. "I'm making some calls."

"Don't."

"Why not?"

"We don't know what kind of spies Brodsky might have on the rest of the group. If they're overheard, he might send something even nastier after them."

"What can be worse than a Spite?"

"More Spites."

"Okay, good point." I pulled my portable keyboard out and propped my phone up. "I'll text instead. Can Brownies read?"

"Nope."

"Good." My fingers tapped messages to Blaine, Lynn, Josh, and Nox.

Henry dragged out a battered old Dell and fired it up. In a minute, his fingers moved with blurred speed.

"What are you doing?"

"Getting in touch with the Nocturnal Lounge crew. Fred Redford and Tony. Maybe they know how to distract it."

"I can see why you'd call Fred for that since he's a Redcap Changeling, but Tony?"

"Tony's a gossip. He works for Faeries and pays attention."

"Why not just use SMS to talk to them?"

"This is better, especially since Brodsky seems to favor using Seelie creatures."

"Nocturnal Faeries are Unseelie, huh?"

"That's a myth. When a Changeling takes a mantle, they can pick either Court. Seelies are traditional, and they like things to stay the same. Unseelies push rules to the limit. They've adapted better since the Big Reveal, so younger Changelings tithe to the King instead of the Queen. It's shifting the power balance pretty steadily. Add in centuries of bad blood and the stories each Court spreads about the other, and you've got a tempest in a teapot."

"Are the stories true?"

"Exaggerated. The only cure for that kind of misinformation is hard proof." Henry sat back and cracked his knuckles. "It's one reason Headmistress Thurston opened PPC to everyone."

"Education's the only way to fight hate." I glanced up at him. "It's why I want to teach."

Henry opened his mouth to say more but closed it when my phone beeped. The message was from Josh. Made sense. He'd be the only one remembering me. But then one came from Nox. I checked his first.

Mom's raiding Brodsky's now. I showed the message to Henry before reading Nox's.

Spites hate water. I showed that one to Henry, too.

"If they find the Grim's anchor they'll arrest Brodsky."

"Spites hating water isn't going to help us, though. I can't do Water magic. Best I can manage is hide a puddle and run through so it follows me."

"No puddles in here, especially with the faucets warded." Henry leaned back over his keyboard again. "Tony says to check that book. What's he mean?"

"No idea." I scratched my head, unsure why he'd mention that. I sent lists to Lynn and Bobby. Another message came in from Nox.

Evidence Achievement unlocked, APB out. Police tracking Brodsky now. I showed that awesome news off.

"But will they find him in time?"

"What's that noise?" I glanced at the clock again. It was half-past five now.

"That is the sound of bricks in a Spite's jaws. I've been listening to it for the last two hours now."

"But the sun's coming up. How much time do we have?"

"Maybe twenty minutes."

"Sweet Dark Night, what does Tony mean by a book?"

"Dahlia!" Henry bolted out of his seat, reaching across the table for my satchel. "She tried to stake me so you'd pick up her old book." He held up *Umbral Affinity and You*. I hadn't had a chance to look at it since the night in the basement lounge. I opened the cover, feeling a tingle as I picked up the corner of the flyleaf. Instead of flipping it, I rubbed it with my palm. An inscription showed up, all shadowy purple letters.

"Dear Dahlia," I read aloud, "someday, a dear friend will need a dark in the lightness. Make sure the right one gets this book when the time comes. Contingency and coincidence demand no less from our family. Love, Grandma Josephine. P.S. p.138." I thumbed through to the indicated page.

"Henry, look at this." I pointed at the entry.

"Sun Shield?" He blinked, his mouth wide open. He reached down and brushed the tip of his finger across the typeset-indented words. A thread of golden energy I'd never seen before surrounded the title. Gold was Luck energy, according to my textbooks. That stuff had no alignment to any magic school, element, or planetary influence. Only Tanuki could turn it. I blinked, and it vanished.

"Grandma used to tell stories about this spell. If I can figure it out, we could go for a stroll down College Hill in broad daylight." I turned my phone and keyboard toward him, then went over to the turntable. I changed the record from Siouxsie to one by The Chameleons. As I sat on the bed studying the old Umbral spell, the bass thud of *Swamp Thing*, the first song we'd danced to, filled the room. "Man the messages. I'll figure this out."

The spell needed something that absorbed sunlight, something that cast a shadow, and something sunlight would destroy. I grabbed Henry's solar-powered calculator off a stack of bills. That'd do. I'd need to attach it to something I could hold over our heads. I read that the reason I'd need something sun-vulnerable was that this spell only worked in life-or-death situations. This totally counted and meant I could use Henry as that component. I got up and pulled a big, black, bat-like bundle of metal and polyester from the umbrella stand.

"Got any super-glue?" I'd need to attach the calculator to the outside of the umbrella, then imbue the whole shebang with Umbral magic.

"Drawer under the bathroom sink." Henry didn't even glance up from typing.

The glue was right where he'd said it'd be, but so was something else. Someone, actually. A short, squat little figure with a scarred leathery face and patched conical hat rubbed their eyes sleepily. They stood, clicked its heels together, and gave me a salute. Then, they handed me the glue.

"Um, thanks." I held the tube between my thumb and forefinger. "Who're you?"

"Gee Nome, Lady." The little creature adjusted their pointy green hat and puffed out their chest. "I watch this house. Good to see a Lady with the Gentleman."

"You might want to hide a little better and then go back to sleep." I literally kicked myself for not recognizing a Gnome. Those were pure Unseelie creatures, the kind responsible for missing socks and misplaced glasses. I'd asked them a question without thinking and if I asked two more, I'd owe them a favor.

"Why should I hide, Lady?"

"A Spite's about to break in here." I peered behind Gee to see if there was anything else useful in there, while also checking for more Gnomes or whatever. "You don't want to be around when that happens."

"A Spite? Really? Who sends those anymore?" Gee rolled its eyes and tapped their foot three times on the bottom of the drawer. "I could help the Gentleman. Sun's rising, you know."

"Oh, I know. I'm Umbral, so I'm doing the Sun Shield spell." I held up the glue. "This is to put my sun absorber on my shield."

"You can't fight Spites while you do magic, Lady. And the Gentleman's weaker while the day-star shines."

"I know."

The Gnome looked up at me with a mildly expectant smirk. They knew something, maybe even had an ability that could save Henry. I'd have to ask them directly.

"What can you do to help, then?"

"Glad you asked, Lady." The Gnome smiled, displaying rows of sharp metallic teeth. I'd read somewhere that didn't have their own teeth, just whatever they could steal. This one must have gotten them from a hardware store. "I can make sure you have help. All you must do is ask for it."

"I don't imagine you'll get more specific without me asking another question." I looked into the Gnomes eyes, trying not to blink. My time was running out, but I'd know whether they'd volunteer that information in the next few seconds.

"Two items, and four of your friends to bring them."

"Fine, then." I took a deep breath. Saving Henry and my magic were important enough to owe a pure Unseelie Faerie. At least they were only a Gnome. "Will you help us?"

"Yes, Lady." The Gnome rubbed their hands together. "Make your shield, then leave this place with the Gentleman. Help will find you in time." It held its thumb and middle finger up and winked, then snapped its fingers, vanishing in a small cloud of greenish smoke.

"Who were you talking to?" Henry's voice came from the other room.

"Gnome." I closed the drawer and carried the glue out of the bathroom, shutting off the light as I went.

"Oh. Gee. Did they give you the glue?" He glanced up from the screens.

"Yeah." I waggled the plastic tube at him, then went across to the bed and opened the umbrella.

"Good." He turned my phone toward him. "Huh. Nox said she just found something that might put a dent in a Spite."

"Awesome." I coated the back of the calculator with glue. "Anything else?"

"Oh, Josh said Tony snuck away from the crime scene, talking to himself." Henry shook his head. "That guy. You never know what he's up to."

"Maybe I do, but there's no time to talk about that now." I had to focus on umbrella-imbuing and tell him about Gee. I gestured at my little project. "Once this is done, we should get out of here."

"Yeah, good point. We should keep at least a five-foot distance from the Spite if we don't want it stealing our magic." He typed something again. "Olivia says we'd better make that six feet and head west. Well, duh."

"Wow, she's up?" I had glue all over my fingers, but the calculator stuck to the fabric. Restarting the record helped me focus. "I hope they track Brodsky fast. How are you at running in the daytime?"

"Regular human speed." Henry typed one more thing, then shut down his computer. "That's one of the Spite's problems. They move at a human pace because as Sprites, their wings gave them extra oomph. Getting a head start at vampire speed will help us."

"Let me imbue this. We leave immediately after. We need as much of a head start as we can get." I put my hands on the umbrella.

The song's intro guitar riff hooked me, tightening my concentration. When the bass drum thudded out its steady beat, Henry turned up the volume. I felt the music now, in the umbrella under my hands and the bed under my crossed legs. I let all my thoughts and feelings about darkness pulse down my arms and out into the hastily crafted device.

Henry's voice mingled with Mark Burgess's as he sang along about a tune calling to him.

Shadows had been my friends for as long as I could remember, their shapes appearing on the wall between my hands and the night-light I turned on just to create them. I summoned them all to my memory and let them power my magic. The duck and the bunny, the cat and the owl—creatures of comfort. The spider and the shark, the wolf and the dragon—creatures of predation. The church, the steeple, the tree with stubby child-finger branches—sites of safety. I gave the energy these forms and willed it into a new shape, one to protect me and the man who'd never forget me, no matter what.

My lips moved, forming words without sound around the lyrics we'd sang at the AS220 weeks earlier.

The magic enhanced mere fabric and aluminum into a shadow construct to protect us from the inevitable dawn. Shelter we could take with us, hold over our heads out in the open instead of waiting in here for that Seelie demon to tumble the wall down on us. I opened my eyes. It was done. I'd imbued my second magical item. I had to hope it'd last long enough under the sun's relentless eye.

The lyrics implored me to leave, to go now. They were right; it was time.

Henry had packed everything back in my satchel and had his own backpack over one shoulder. I took the umbrella in one hand and slung on my satchel with the other. Keeping continuous contact with the shield was a must, or I'd risk it running out of energy at the worst possible time. I stood in front of the door while Henry undid the locks.

We pounded up the stairs. I smirked at the irony of the old superstition about opening umbrellas indoors. Doing it now felt like good luck. Everything was turned on its head, by a kindly Professor who'd inexplicably turned murderer, to Seelie creatures spying and hunting us down. The street door pushed open under my hand.

The faintest hint of light tinged the horizon, its glow bloodying the sky. I went west, as Olivia advised. We'd be moving toward Brodsky's apartment, and the police were still investigating. Maybe they had emergency sun-proof blankets or light-free transport.

Henry scooped me up once we got out the door and ran as fast as he could. I heard the scrabble of broken brick and mortar behind us. Over Henry's shoulder, I saw the Spite begin their pursuit slower than I'd be at a dead sprint or even a jog. Their belly was distended, probably from eating the concrete that made up the building's foundation.

The distance between us and the creature increased as they stopped to regurgitate amalgamated stone. I wasn't sure whether Spites could digest it eventually, but this one didn't want to try. I looked away, not wanting to watch any creature throw something up. At least we'd get a better lead while they purged.

Henry's feet carried us down Brown Street until it became Camp Street. After that, his pace slowed. I tapped his shoulder, and he put me down. Behind us, the sky was a cloudy light yellow, like a week-old bruise. The sidewalk under our feet was dark with morning dew. I linked my free arm in Henry's, and we jogged ahead. We'd lose our lead at this pace, so we'd have to stop and make a stand at some point.

When we passed Doyle Avenue, I knew there was no way we'd make it to Brodsky's building before the Spite caught up. The only park we passed had no cover at all. Everything else was closed. Even Holy Name Church was locked up like Fort Knox. Too bad. pure Faeries of any type couldn't get into churches, temples, mosques, or synagogues without an invitation from the presiding clergy.

We were on borrowed time. We'd have to buy as much more as we could. At least I knew help was coming.

CHAPTER SEVENTEEN

Henry

I put one foot in front of the other as fast as possible. The sun about to rise behind me was pure terror compared to any fire I'd seen in my unlife. It was the difference between starting at a fish jumping and having your boat capsized by a great white shark. No contest in the fear factor department.

If Maddie hadn't kept going, I might have just given up. She'd shown me more kindness, treated me more like a normal person than anyone had since the battle that claimed my humanity. Being with her felt like peace and plenty in a constant state of skirmish and scavenge. This short time with her was precious. I couldn't let the Spite take her powers. She wouldn't lose half of herself on my watch. I was ready to make a stand.

I realized she'd already been looking for a defensible place. Nothing on Camp Street would give us the advantage in a direct confrontation with a Spite. I almost wished the Grim was chasing us. At least then, Maddie's magic wouldn't be at stake. But, of course, the fact that she'd been helping me was the reason Brodsky sent a Spite this time.

Billy Taylor Park was the only choice for a battleground. The paved basketball court gave no cover, but we'd have a clear line of sight and room to run it in circles. I nudged Maddie, indicating the park. She frowned at the open area but crossed and hopped the fence all the same.

I saw an added benefit: two buildings east of the park were tall enough to cast shadows for a few minutes. This would let me fight the Spite far enough away from Maddie to make a difference. I had to stay in the shadows or fall back to the umbrella. Vampires could drink Spite blood. I could grapple them into the regular shade and not worry about getting hungry. I'd need to bite fast so it couldn't drag me into the sun, but even if it did that, Maddie could still get away.

We ran to the west end of the paved-over park and waited. The Spite climbed the fence with some difficulty. Their back had been broken multiple times to deform it for eternity and cause them to walk on all fours. They'd been changed cruelly, robbed of intelligence and autonomy. I couldn't help but pity them. Their limpid eyes rolled, looking at us. Once they got to our side of the fence, they sighed. I got the idea the Spite didn't want to fight. I glanced at the lightening sky, sending out a prayer for them even though my old church had denied the existence of my soul.

Something white bobbed in the new light, hurtling toward us. It swam on air, but that was all I could make out with the sun behind it. I pointed. Maddie and the Spite peered at what I'd singled out in the sky.

"Olivia!" Maddie let go of my arm, waving as she called out. "Down here!"

The owl shifter folded her wings to dive. Something draped in fabric hung from her talons. She banked, dropping the item in a shadow on the other side of the basketball court. Then, she ran straight into a window, knocking herself out. She looked like a little white pile of snow on the ground by the building's back stairs. Maddie and I ran for the object she'd dropped and I pulled off the cloth. A shiny purple glass paperweight rested in my hand. I had no idea why Maddie squealed and jumped up and down.

"Give it here!" She held out her hand, and I placed the paperweight in it. She curled her fingers around the dark glass, then took a deep breath and let it out. The shield got stronger and more light-resistant as purple-black energy swirled up from the object in her hand.

The Spite paused, one foreleg in the air as hesitated. Their eyes focused on Maddie, terror as vast as mine for the sun in their gaze. I finally understood what she'd done. She'd plugged into the Grim's Anchor, tapping it like a battery. The shield would last longer, but we still had a stalemate on our hands.

I peered at the bottom of the building to check on Olivia, but she was gone. When I looked up, Josh and Nox had hopped the fence. Nox wore a pair of elbow-length dishwashing gloves. She held a shimmering sphere, her hand as far from her body as she could get it. Golden sparks whirled and pooled on its surface, sparkling in the new morning light like flying fish. Luck. Blaine's glass float.

"Stop, Spite!" Nox called to the Seelie hound as though they would listen to an Unseelie shifter. They clacked their spikes against the ground, whining eagerly like she'd brought salvation instead of demise. Beside me, Maddie gasped.

"That fishing float." She elbowed me. "It has Seelie Water magic. That's the only thing that breaks Seelie enchantments."

The Spite turned their back on us, taking slow, steady steps like a fly fisherman wading against a strong current. They got within three feet of Nox, the closest a pure Seelie could get to anything Unseelie without instinctively attacking. Nox gazed down at them, nose red and cheeks streaked with tears. She pitied the Spite, too.

Josh's jaw dropped so far he could have caught every fly on the east side of Providence. He stared at Nox with a mixture of envy and admiration. I understood that as a young Alpha wolf, he'd wanted to save the literal and figurative day. He was about to be upstaged by a Kelpie, of all things.

Nox pursed her lips and blew a kiss at the glass float. It sailed like a soap bubble toward the Spite, drifting until it burst, spraying gold-tinged glass shards and seafoam all over the creature. They whimpered, shivers claiming their entire body. Their spikes drooped and their hunchback straightened.

That whimper became a series of screams as bone broke and reformed. Stripy scars melted, leaving smooth oatmeal-pale skin behind. A thick mane of white hair sprouted from the back of their head. Their fingers lengthened, along with arms and legs. The creature stood on two legs now, facing Nox. I watched them stretch each limb one at a time, examining them. They bowed to her, then turned toward Maddie and me y. They weren't a Spite anymore. The sea float had undone all their deformities. Well, almost all of them.

Wing bones lifted tattered strips of iridescent gossamer. This Sprite was flightless now, but at least they wouldn't live forever in pain and on their knees.

"I'm sorry for attacking. I was enslaved, but now I'm free. I owe you each a great debt, but the only thing I have to give is information." They stepped to the edge of Maddie's Umbral shield. "The Summoner is also the summoned, his will controlled by a more powerful Magus."

"Who?" Josh shook off his shock and awe, stepping forward to question the creature. Since the Sprite had agreed to pay us with information, he could do that without risk.

"I do not know, but I see that you will find out. Once enough of you turn coincidence in your favor, you will find him. Each of you four has earned three questions. The Son of Dennis has two left."

"I'll want to ask mine at some point in the future," Nox said.

"That is your right, Kelpie. But know that the Sidhe Queen will track me down at some point. Do not wait too long."

"Understood."

"I think I'll wait, too." Maddie had pocketed the Grim Anchor. "If you need to hide, find me, and I'll do what I can."

"Thank you, Shadowmistress."

"I want to use one of mine." I stepped to the edge of the shield. "The Summoner's Brownie. What's his Anchor?"

"The vampire inquires wisely." The Sprite smiled. Had I thought them so terrifying just minutes ago? "A wood cane of birch. The Summoner kept it on the floor under his bed."

"Thanks. I'll wait to ask the rest of mine if you don't mind."

"Very well." The Sprite turned back to look at Josh. "Son of Dennis?"

"I have one question no one will have the answer to yet. I want you to answer me when you've discovered it."

"Very well. Ask, and I will deliver your answer when the time comes." The Sprite gave him a pointed look. "Know that coincidence prevents me from answering a question you've already asked."

"Who will the Summoner attack after me?" Josh's jaw clenched, his eyes unblinking and intense.

I nodded. Of course. Josh had done a lot to help Maddie and me, so he had to be next on the Extramagus's list.

"Understood. I'll bring your answer when it exists and falls into the scope of my knowledge."

"I'm going to get Henry somewhere safe now." Maddie beckoned to the Sprite. "I'll hide your trail until it parts from ours."

"Thank you, Shadowmistress." It bowed at her. "I'm sorry his home isn't safe anymore."

"The basement Lounge has everything you could want." Tony leaned against the chain-link fence near where Olivia had fallen. "Go there. The Sprite can get to a bunch of hiding places from the old trolley tunnel on the way."

The Sprite froze when Tony spoke. They didn't turn around, just stood there with their back to Tony. Their facial expression was inscrutable, but their eyes held fear. When I looked again for the cat shifter, he'd gone. One white feather settled to the ground where he'd been. The Sprite finally turned their head, gazing at Maddie expectantly.

"You have to invite pure Faeries under a ward, Maddie." Nox's tone was gentle, although a little hoarse. Ha.

"Oh, right. You can come under here. You have my permission." Maddie beckoned the Sprite. They took one long step, placing them-selves at my side under the Umbral sun shield. I wondered what it looked like from outside. I'd ask Josh later. There was no way I'd dare try to find out first-hand.

Our motley group made its way back to PPC on Camp Street. It had gotten late enough for the church to open. A man in a deacon's habit blinked from the steps as we walked by Holy Name. I wasn't sure whether I was the first vampire to take a shielded stroll outside during the day, but I was definitely the only one that particular deacon had seen. I smiled and waved, unsure of whether he could see me clearly or not. He rewarded me with one briefly upraised hand, then dropped into a slow-mo genuflection.

Faces peeped between blinds and curtains all along the street. Josh took point and Nox brought up the rear, making us an intimidating spectacle. One old man, bald under his black Greek fisherman's cap, stepped out the door to stand on his stoop. The slow clap of his hands as I approached accented his genuine smile. He was missing his two front teeth and seemed familiar, but I couldn't place him.

We made it to the trolley tunnel without further incident. The Sprite left so silently I couldn't imagine how anything but the Queen herself might track them. Nox went upstairs, mumbling something about helping Lynn. Josh watched her go, then shook his head like he'd been in a daze. Maybe he had. Kelpies were known for their ability to mesmerize. Once we got into the basement stairwell, Maddie dropped the shield.

"I guess this is where I say good day?" I smiled full-on, finally comfortable with that expression.

"No way." Maddie brushed past me, heading down the stairs. "Come on."

"Huh?" I followed her, even though I wasn't sure why she didn't go back to her room where she'd be comfortable.

When she opened the door to the lounge, I understood why she'd messaged Lynn and Bobby. While I'd been thinking about turning to dust, she'd been preparing for my survival. An air mattress sat in the corner farthest from the door. A mini-fridge with a Shifter Fighting League sticker on the side held a few days' worth of animal blood. There was even an electric kettle, cups and saucers, and tea. It was only bagged Bigelow Earl Grey from the dining hall, but that little touch broke me. I sat in one of the chairs and set my elbows on my knees and my head in my hands. It was all I could do to keep from crying.

"Henry, what's wrong?" I could feel the warmth of Maddie's hand through the thick leather of my jacket. I took a few deep breaths I didn't physically need before speaking.

"Nothing." I met her concerned gaze with the full force of the hope surging in my heart. "Finally, nothing. I don't feel like I'm all wrong just for being me."

"I hope you get to keep that feeling for a long time."

"As long as you're around, I think I can." I stood up, tilting my head so I wouldn't break eye contact with her. "You make me feel normal, Maddie May. I love you."

She didn't say a word, just flung her arms around my neck. Her lips met mine with no hesitation or fear.

As we headed together to my temporary bed, I realized that Maddie accepted me for who I was, knowing what that meant for me and anyone close. I used to find the night magically fascinating until I got confined to it. Since then, I'd gone through the motions and just existed. Maddie brought me back to life that morning in more ways than one.

I'd lived in a cold gray fog since I'd turned. In Maddie's arms, the color came back into everything. Drab hues brightened until I could begin appreciating the light again. Without it, darkness was stark instead of lush. I'd lost my balance, but that morning with the woman I loved, I took the first steps toward regaining it.

All it had taken was coincidence, convergence, and a little golden sliver of Luck.

CHAPTER EIGHTEEN

Maddie

We came together at the intersection of hope and despair. In the moments after, when I fell back breathing as he lay still, I remembered what Mom couldn't tell me. Convergence. I wondered whether this was it. My eyes slipped closed like a canoe slips into a creek. I drifted on sleep's current, Henry's cool hands soothing my overheated ones.

When I woke, I knew it'd be obvious that I wasn't really asleep. Still, I kept my eyes closed. The room would be pitch black, and even though I could technically see in the dark if I focused, it wasn't the same. Everything was green and gray when I did that, and I wanted to remember how Henry looked in something other than monochrome. Vampires were lucky; they saw muted colors when it got dark.

I heard the sharp click of the light switch and the soft rush of the heating electric kettle. After I rolled over and opened my eyes, I saw Henry placing teabags in the cups. I sat up, pulling my comforter around me.

"It's three in the afternoon already." He smirked. "Even Tony doesn't sleep that late."

"Well, I stayed up all night and most of the morning." I grinned, and my stomach rumbled.

"You need food." He shrugged. "No one thought I'd have a guest, I guess."

"I don't want to leave you here alone after all that." I shuddered.

"I'll be fine." He grinned.

"Hey, is that Djinn lamp still in here?" I peered at the bookshelf where I'd found it before.

"No, it's gone. I have no idea where it went." He glanced over his shoulder at the shelf, too. "We all agreed to just leave it here, right?"

"Yeah. I wonder whether one of us came back for it without telling the others, or if Brodsky came and got it after he realized we'd found it."

"What makes you think it was Brodsky's?" Henry raised an eyebrow. "It could belong to anyone."

"Aren't Djinn summoned creatures?" I sipped from my cup.

"Not exactly." Henry breathed in the scent of tea. "They're tithed Faeries, bound to serve a purpose."

"More like Fred's dad than that poor Sprite?"

"Sort of. Djinns are like magical hermit crabs—they need a home. They all got bound when the King and Queen split. It's a cool story. I wish I remembered who my Psychic mentor was. He's the one who told it to me."

"Why don't you remember him?" I couldn't imagine not being able to remember someone so important.

"I must have taken those memories out, put them away." Henry leaned his head on his hand. "The only reason I can think of is he went into hiding."

"That's sad. Maybe we'll work on finding him some time."

"Maybe. I have to go through some of my old amulets." Henry sighed. "There might be something in there. A clue. I also think it'll help with Blaine's tinfoil hat theory."

"You're waiting for Monday, huh?" Only mundane banks opened

on Sundays. No one would keep amulets or magic items in one of those.

"Yeah. They have a tunnel entrance for vampires. I'll head over first thing tomorrow, see what I can find." He shrugged. "Maybe my mentor's memory is in one of the amulets. But mainly, I have to look for anything I can find on the Extramagus, Brodsky, too."

"Well, yeah." I scratched my head. "So they arrested him. But Olivia had the Grim's anchor. How'd the Police get evidence for an arrest?"

"The fang. They also found two sets of remains." Henry curled his hands around his teacup. "Horace from the Skeleton Crew made a statement last night. People forget ghosts are legal witnesses if their Mediums support them. He saw the Grim attack the Lounge."

"Is the Lounge fixed yet?" I raised an eyebrow. It had to be done by now.

"I don't know. I'll ask Tony or Fred next time I see one of them." Henry wrinkled his nose. "Ugh, I forgot. I have to give a report to Josh's dad. With Blaine."

"When?" I sat up, stretching my arms over my head. Henry stared, licking his lips. I blushed and pulled the comforter back up to cover myself. "Sorry. Didn't mean to be that distracting."

"You can distract me like that later all you want." He winked. "Supposed to be this afternoon. It's still technically afternoon, right?" Henry put on his shirt, then his jacket. "And how do I get to the tunnels from here to make it to Campus Police?"

"Why go down there? Just call."

"He said I had to do it in person."

I wrapped the comforter around myself and got out of bed, stepping over to the chair where I'd left the umbrella leaning. One touch told me it was completely depleted. I thought about recharging it, but when I picked it up the calculator clattered to the floor. I shrugged, grinning apologetically at Henry. No one would have brought super glue down here while setting things up earlier.

"How about we call him over here?" I tucked the calculator in my satchel, losing my grip on the comforter. "He could meet you in the basement."

"We could try that." Henry's eyes roamed slowly down and up my body before he looked me in the eye. "You'd need to wear something a little less revealing, though."

"Oh." I felt my cheeks heat up as I gathered my clothes. "Um, yeah."

I got dressed while Henry called Chief Dennison to explain the situation. They agreed to meet in the laundry room, which also had no windows. Henry got a bag of blood from the mini-fridge and drank that from a mug while I had some tea. After he'd finished, he poured the rest of the bag into his cup. My stomach growled again.

"You really should have some food." Henry reached out and patted my tummy.

"After you make that report." I pulled his hand up to my mouth and kissed it.

A knock came at the door. Too early for Chief Dennison. Henry went to it, asking who was there. He opened the door for Lynn.

"Nox called and told me to bring food, but you're a vampire. Isn't that the weirdest thing ever?" Lynn blinked at me, then shook her head after I activated my amulet. "Oh, okay. The food's for you then, Maddie. Here you go."

"Thanks so much." I opened the bag to see a bagel with some peanut butter and a plastic knife to spread it on. In moments I went to work setting up the super tardy meal, then tried not to eat it too fast.

"I'm going across the hall to meet Chief Dennison now. See you when it's all done, Maddie." Henry leaned down and kissed me on the mouth. Nothing super-passionate or anything, but it was enough for Lynn's eyebrow to reach new heights. Once he was out of the room, she dragged a chair next to the one I sat in and leaned forward.

"No wonder your date with Josh was so weird." She shook her head. "I mean, I thought it was strange that you were out with him instead of Henry in the first place, but still."

"What happened after I left?" I swallowed the last bite of my bagel. "With Nox and Josh and Blaine, I mean?"

"Oh, boy." Lynn shook her head. "Blaine's got a reputation and Nox was just giving him grief about it. Definitely no interest there on her part. Josh almost went ballistic, though. I've never seen him like that about a girl before. What kind of Magus is she?"

"She's not one. She's a Kelpie."

"Oh, no." Lynn sighed. "Poor Josh."

"Why?" I blinked, wondering why Lynn looked so sad. "They'd be great together. Wolves marry other shifters all the time."

"But Alphas can't marry Faerie creatures. If they get together, it'll look like the Dennisons took the Goblin King's side. The pack has to stay neutral, or it might implode."

"There's really no way?"

"Maybe. If another high-ranking pack member got together with a Seelie, then there'd be a balance. It'd have to be a sibling. I don't even know if Josh has any of those. Which rules out other options like passing on being the Alpha or going packless. If he's the only heir, he can't do either of those things."

"Well, there's a bit of hope then." I wiped my hands on the napkin from the bag.

"Dunno, Maddie. Not everyone gets a happy ending. I mean, look at Professor Brodsky."

"Him? He's got to be better off now, right?" I bit down on toasty bread and nut goodness.

"What, in jail for crimes against Extrahumanity?" Lynn gave me the Mr. Spock look while I chewed. "He'll go to trial by autumn and spend the rest of his life in prison. How's that better?"

"Better as in out from under the control of whoever had him." I ran my tongue over my front teeth, making sure they didn't have peanut butter all over them.

"Wait. I didn't hear about that." Lynn put one hand over her mouth.

"We just found that out this morning." I told her about confronting the Spite, how Nox had transformed them and the information they gave and still owed us.

"Wow. Maybe Olivia should intern with whatever legal firm is representing Brodsky. We might want a woman inside on that trial, and she's an Extrahuman Law student. Anyway, that's more info for the Blaine tinfoil hat theory pile."

"You're calling my hunt for an evil cabal of Magi a tinfoil hat theory?" Blaine leaned diagonally across the doorway, the back of his hand on his forehead. "Oh, the indignity!"

"Move it, dragon-breath." Henry shouldered past him.

"Anything for the big vampiric hero of the morning." Blaine arched an eyebrow at Lynn. "Did you hear about his stroll through the rosy-fingered streets of the dawn?"

"Maddie just told me." Lynn smiled.

"Good. Stick it in the tinfoil hat files, will you?" Blaine stuck his tongue out.

"I kind of need some actual rest, and Maddie needs more than a bagel to eat." At Henry's words, Lynn stood up.

"You sleep?" Blaine glanced at the rumpled bed. Then, he winked at me.

"Yes, actually." Henry smirked at Blaine.

"Okay, then." Blaine stepped out the door, waiting. Lynn left , brushing past him.

"I'll see you later, then." I gave Henry a kiss worthy of a Psychic impression and went off with my other friends to let him rest.

CHAPTER NINETEEN

Henry

I headed down the tunnels an hour before sunrise after confirming I could go to the Nocturnal Lounge after the bank. I waited until the teller came to unlock the tunnel entrance at seven. He opened the door, ushering me inside.

"Mr. Ricci, hello." I nodded.

"Henry Baxter. I haven't seen you since the twentieth century." The wrinkles around the little man's mouth deepened as he smiled. I grinned back, understanding that not everyone was as comfortable seeing my fangs. The gloom that thought usually caused was nowhere to be found.

"I'd like to see my box, please." I handed him my I.D. and showed him the key.

"Of course." He nodded, beckoning as he limped down the hall. I thanked Mr. Ricci when he set my box down.

Once he'd settled me in a lightproof safe deposit room, he left me alone. The box was small because my amulets were never big. Any memory, no matter how detailed or important, would fit in an object of any size. It'd be easy to become a packrat, collecting items to put memories in. That's why everything in my box was necessary. The memories in the bank were too painful or too dangerous to keep in my head. Still, there were more than I'd have the energy or emotional fortitude to check out that day. It'd take months to get through them.

I used my key to open it and reached inside, letting coincidence guide my hand. The object I touched was smooth and almost flat, except for a concave depression on one side. Without looking, I knew this was a worry stone.

The memory came back as I pulled my hand from the box. Images of the past flooded my mind, walking down Camp Street in the morning past Holy Name Church, except it all seemed bigger. Memory me was seven years old, and I looked up at the overcast sky to the west as I walked. The sun had risen, but storm clouds kept its light at bay.

When I got to Rochambeau Street, I stopped in my tracks. One man stood over another, hunched on the ground. Bloodied fists and a pile of polished wood shards stood stark against the gray concrete. The man on the ground scrambled to pick up the pieces of a violin. He was past middle age, and when he reached out, I saw a row of numbers tattooed his arm.

"Beat it, kid." The man standing glared across the street at me. I felt a sick powerless futility, along with the understanding that no one around could stop this guy. I looked up and down Rochambeau Street, certain it'd be empty. But it wasn't.

Another kid stood on the corner diagonally from me. He was blond and tall, but my age. The kid shook his head, then extended one hand. Even across the street, I felt the chill air that knocked the attacker flat on his back. The attacker snatched a gold chain with a ring on it off the ground, then got up, and tried to run away. The survivor with the broken violin called out something about giving his mother's ring back.

A blond boy across the street dropped me a wink and extended his arm again. This time, I saw a shimmer of heat rising over his hand. He aimed his pointer finger like a gun at the thief, who screamed, dropping the ring like it was on fire. He sank to the sidewalk, clutching his blistering hand. I crossed Rochambeau, heading toward the scene as fast as I could. As I went, I did a deep breathing exercise.

"I'll keep him from bothering you ever again, Mr. Kazynski." The boy strode toward the thief, gesturing with his hand again. A stream of water shot out, and I blinked. I knew he was a Magus, but I'd never seen one who could do more than one type of magic before. "I'm way under eighteen, and my grandpa's got major connections."

"No! I'll never come back, I swear." The thief shivered in fear as the water hovered in front of his lips and nose. Mr. Kazynski looked on in abject horror. It was the expression on the victim's face that made me think the other kid's threat was genuine.

"Uh, I have a better way to stop him than that." I wasn't sure why I'd interrupted a dangerous and probably batty Magus, but it felt like the right thing to do.

"Oh, really?" His smile glittered like the grill of an oncoming truck.

"Yeah. I can make him forget he's ever seen Mr. Kazynski."

"Go for it." The kid arched an eyebrow. "Better make everyone forget while you're at it. Bad tempers and long grudges run in my family."

I nodded. As I approached the thief, the water moved out of my way. I clutched the worry stone Mom had given me and focused on everyone present. I started with the thief, touching the stone lightly to his right temple. He blinked, then headed down the hill toward North Main Street in a daze. Next, I turned to Mr. Kazynski. He'd put all the pieces of his ruined violin into its case by then. I noticed a pair of seals embossed on the velvety lining. This musician was talented enough to be honored by both Faerie Courts. I hesitated.

"What's the problem?"

"I don't want to piss off the Sidhe Queen and the Goblin King by messing with their fiddler." I pointed at the seals.

"Huh. Maybe you want to piss my family and me off even less."

"Dunno." I shrugged.

"I guess if someone has to remember it, Mr. Kazynski can." The kid smiled at the flustered violinist.

"Okay, then. You're next."

"No. You get both of us at the same time."

"What do you think I am, a master-level Psychic?"

"I think you must be to come running over here."

Again, I didn't answer him. My hand trembled a little as I held the stone up to his head. If I couldn't remove both our memories at the same time, he'd never know he'd told me not to. Then again, he seemed like the kind of kid who'd throw a fireball at my head for kicks. I went ahead and siphoned more memories into the stone, his through his forehead and mine through my hand.

The scene faded out, and I finally understood why I'd been on the wrong side of the street to catch my school bus on the first day of second grade. I felt exhausted because the stone held three perspectives. After that, I had to stop checking for the day. I thought about taking a few amulets with me, but with Brodsky in police custody, who knew what the Extramagus might throw around next. After tying the ring and worry stone together in a bandanna, I locked the box, then rang the bell to call Mr. Ricci.

I headed for the Nocturnal Lounge. Josh was in the trolley tunnel, leaning against the wall. He smelled like cloves, and cigarette butts littered the ground at his feet.

"Those things will kill you." I leaned next to him.

"Not really." He blew out a smoke ring that rivaled some of Blaine's "Wolf shifters resist the ever-living hell out of diseases."

"Huh. Who knew?" I smirked.

"Maddie did. She's up there, by the way." Josh jerked his chin at the hidden door.

"Oh?" I raised an eyebrow.

"Yeah. Tony and Fred brought her and Blaine up to look at some books." He pushed off from the wall, stretching.

"Well, what are you doing out here, then?"

"Waiting for you."

"Please don't tell me we need to have another talk." I rolled my eyes.

"Sorry." He dragged the glowing end of his nearly burned cigarette over the patchy brickwork of the tunnel wall. "We do. I swear it's not like the last one, though."

"Okay, so talk."

"It'll be a while before this happens, but my parents expect me to be the Dennison Pack Alpha someday. There's some wolf politics stuff I don't want to bore you with, but I need to run a pack before then for experience."

"What's that got to do with me?"

"We're both elbows-deep in Blaine's crazy theory. Like Nox said, we painted giant targets on our backs by helping you and Maddie, so I'm stepping up. Blaine's too out-of-touch to be in charge. Frampton and Tremain aren't leaders. It's on me to keep us focused."

"Josh, your head's going to be too big to get through the door if you don't stop pumping your ego. Get to the point already."

"See, that right there is why you're the ideal Beta." He chuckled.

"But I'm a vampire."

"I don't care. We're at PPC and handling a PPC problem. If they accept whoever's qualified, so will I." He gave me a lopsided grin. "Maddie told me she gave you a medallion. One of the old kind."

"Yeah."

"Give it here." Josh held out his hand.

The string trailed behind the bronze disk like a long tail. It rested on my upturned palm. I didn't have to wonder whether Josh could see it, either. He reached out and clasped my hand, pressing the medallion between us.

"This is a formal alliance between the vampire Henry Baxter and the Tinfoil Hat Pack. Our territory is PPC campus, India Point Park, Swan Point Cemetery, and this tunnel." Josh's voice was clear, his tone carrying unquestionable authority. "Do you accept this alliance and rank as Pack Beta?"

"Yes." I felt the unmistakable tingle of a supernatural oath. Wolf shifters had a weird type of energy, somewhere between Psychic and

Magic. They say it comes from the moon. "Let's get upstairs and go to work."

"Fine." When Josh took his hand away, he left the medallion behind. I blinked, watching him slip one around his neck. The magic in the alliance pledge had split it into two pieces. I put mine on, then knocked to open the secret door.

Josh and I went up the stairs and into the Lounge proper. All the furniture was different and half the shelves new, but most everything else was the same. I thought we were alone until I saw people in my old corner of the mezzanine, heads bent over books.

Blaine looked up from his scribbled notes. He nudged Tony. Maddie sat across from Blaine, her nose in the Umbral Affinity book. Fred Redford stood off to the side, eating a foot-long steak bomb. I didn't mind. It was better for a hungry Redcap to eat food instead of the furniture. Olivia peeked out from one of the stacks, amber eyes wide as she looked at Josh's chest and then mine. Her little gasp of surprise sounded more like a sleepy hoot than anything else.

"Finally, the X Generation arrives." Blaine scribbled something else. "I'll need to know if you found anything about weird Magi at the bank, Henry."

"Hi, Olivia." Josh ignored Blaine and nodded at her.

"Hoo, boy, you've gone and done it this time."

"What?" Blaine looked up at Josh and me, then paled. "Oh, no, you didn't."

"What's the big deal?" Fred rolled his eyes. "It's only a couple of bromance necklaces."

"No, it's not, but you wouldn't know." Blaine shook his head. "You can't see that magic."

Tony stared at the medallion halves like he could see something. I remembered back to the first Grim attack, how he'd made a Glamour. I almost asked what he saw, but I remembered my promise. One of these days, someone would figure out what his deal was.

"Magic's probably mine, from when I worked on it in lab. Wait, did you say necklaces? Plural?" Maddie looked at the medallion halves. "What kind of magic is that? It's definitely not Umbral."

"It's an alliance medallion. I used it for its intended purpose." Josh put his hands on his hips. "Things will get crazier around here the more we find out, so I formalized things."

"I ain't a pack animal." Tony practically bristled.

"You don't have to be." Josh's tone was full of bravado. He knew as well as I did that we'd need Tony's help.

"So, you want to know what I saw at the bank, Blaine?" I had to change the subject before we ended up with a cat and dog fight on our hands.

"Yeah. But first, look here." He flipped open an old magazine. Old as in published when I was still in diapers. "Check this guy out. He might be our mysterious magus."

The article was from a 1972 Magiczine, a publication that looked like gibberish to anyone but Extrahumans. The man in the picture was blond, tall, and haughtily imposing in a way that put both Josh and Blaine to shame. He looked familiar. If I'd seen the article the night before, I'd have thought him some random Alphahole.

"Richard Stanhope, Extramagus." I read the caption aloud. "He looks a lot like someone I saw in a stored memory I found this morning." I described what I'd seen to the group. Olivia watched without blinking the entire time, the pen in her hand moving back and forth across a moleskin journal. She held it up for everyone to see the drawing she'd made.

"Wow. This could be that kid's grandpa."

"Yeah. Too bad I have no idea who that kid is." I sighed. "I bet he's the Extramagus causing all this trouble."

"Well, why not this Stanhope guy? It says here that he doesn't like Magi and Psychics mingling with us rabble." Tony pointed at one of the article's quotes.

"Because he died right at the start of the Big Reveal." I stepped over to the bookshelf behind Maddie. "It's in here. He died hiding magic artifacts when it looked like Extrahumans would be outed. Says House Harcourt had something to do with it, too, Blaine."

"What?" Smoke came out of Blaine's mouth with the word. He took a few deep breaths before speaking again. "Mom and I are having a talk later." He looked back down at the table. "Um, whenever she feels like it."

"Anyway, at least we can try to look up all his relatives." Maddie tapped her phone, entering the name in her Evernote app. "I have a subscription to Ancestry dot com. I'll check it once I'm at an actual computer. In the meantime, do we have any idea what Brodsky's telling the police?"

"He can't remember anything." Josh rolled his eyes.

"Makes sense if our Extramagus was controlling him." Blaine tapped his pencil against the magazine. "Any idea how?"

"We saw a bunch of sleep-aids in his apartment." Josh ran his hand over his head, spiking up his hair. "Maybe that's got something to do with it."

"But sleep help is a Psychic thing, not magic." Olivia peered out from behind the bookcase again.

"Amulets can be Psychic and Magic at the same time." Maddie glanced up. "Mine sure is."

"So you're saying you think the Extramagus took a sleep amulet and put Mind magic in it?" Blaine blinked.

"Why not?" Josh shrugged.

"Hmm, I don't know. More mysteries." Blaine stroked his chin. "You think I could get a look at it sometime?"

"That's the problem. There wasn't anything like a psychic sleep aid at Brodsky's apartment." Josh shook his head. "Not even in the secret compartment the Sprite told us about. They found the second fang in there, though."

"Maybe you didn't look hard enough." Fred's voice came out muffled around the last of his sandwich. "He was a Summoner with Faerie minions. A Brownie, a Spite, and a Pixie, right? So the amulet might be under a Glamour or in a Faerie Circle or a Gnome's junk pile."

"Could you check that?" Josh scratched his chin.

"I could, but it'd be stupid to bother." Fred swallowed. "If your Extramagus was careful enough to work through that poor Brodsky guy, he would have gotten that amulet back by now."

"Good point. Mind magic's super regulated." I sighed, glad I knew all the illegal things for once. "The police would trace that fast."

"Leaves us at a temporarily dead end." Blaine flipped the magazine closed.

"So, what now?" Maddie shook her head. "We've still got a problem. He'll come after Henry and me again, right?"

"Um, no. Because both of you were direct targets of the Extramagus, just like Lynn and Bobby were last semester." Blaine sighed. "It's someone else's problem now."

"So one of us is next?" Olivia glanced up from stowing the journal and pen in her bag.

"Awesome." Josh cracked his knuckles. "Let him bring it. He'll have to go through me first."

"Not you. Nox." Maddie tucked her phone away. "She's the one who neutralized the Spite. It would have gotten Henry if it hadn't been for her."

Josh looked like a sail on a day with no wind. I punched his shoulder. His jaw tightened.

"Hey, you have help. Isn't that what a pack's for?"

"Exactly." Blaine smiled, then chuckled over Tony's second attempt to insist he wasn't no pack animal for nobody nohow.

CHAPTER TWENTY

Maddie

The sky looked like lapis lazuli to the east and boulder opal to the west when I met Henry at the tunnel next to Water Place Park. I took his hand, and we walked along the mosaic wall toward the park proper. I ran my hand along one and found a paw-print made by a shifter artist when this wall went up.

Even though Providence is on the coast, I smelled no salt in the air. Henry probably did, though. The park's eponymous water came from the Woonasquatucket River. Our footsteps mingled, echoing across the round man-made pond on the cobblestones along the RiverWalk. The braziers were empty, unlit at this time of year. WaterFire didn't start until mid-March. I looked forward to seeing it with someone who'd remember me this year.

I stopped walking when we got to a bench. Henry sat down, pulling me close to him and looking into my eyes. I smiled. I'd left the bronze amulet at home, saving the rest of its power for the remainder of my class. Everyone we were meeting would remember me.

"I'm not ready to go over there just yet."

"Agreed." He pulled me closer, sweeping a stray curl off my left cheek. His kiss took my breath away. It was a few moments before I found my voice again.

"Why me?" I stroked the back of his neck.

"I'd forgotten how to feel until you came along." He smiled. "My life was like Kansas at the beginning of *The Wizard of Oz*. That happens to vampires sometimes, but you already knew that."

"Yeah, I do. If Mom and Dad hadn't been destined before he got turned…" I couldn't finish that thought. I couldn't even imagine how to.

"You said something about a contingency the other night. Something about your mom mentioning it." Henry was a Psychic. He knew what that meant to a Precog.

"Yeah, well, she says that's why they're visiting." I leaned my head on his shoulder and sighed, looking out at the untroubled water.

"They really didn't tell you they were in town until after they got here?" Henry put his arm around me.

"That's life with a Precognitive mother. I'm used to her knowing where I'll be before I do." I looked up at him.

"Harsh during the teenage years, huh?" He rubbed my arm.

"Yeah, no actual sneaking out of the house or anything since she was immune to my Umbral Affinity." I ran my hand through the short hair at the back of his neck. "Anyway, are you nervous?"

"You'd better believe it. At least I don't have to worry that they hate vampires or Psychics. But it's unsettling how they have something they need to tell me. Should I be worried?"

"I'd say no, but…" I shrugged. "Who knows?"

"Then let's find out already." Henry stood up and took my hand. He led me around the rest of the RiverWalk, back toward Luxe Burger. He waited until we could see the door. "You ready?"

"Okay." I took the lead. We headed into the restaurant together like we had just four nights before. At least, this time, Henry wasn't starving.

I saw Mom and Dad seated, and they waved us over. Just a handful of years ago, I might have been embarrassed, but now I understood. They seemed corny in their enthusiasm because they'd been through some strange times together. They appreciated what they had so much, they didn't care what people thought when they acted happy about it. Folks like them made people like the Extramagus even more mysterious. Why reduce happiness when it was so hard to come by in the first place? Why not foster it, let it grow and spread instead?

Dad kept his mouth in a straight horizontal line but winked at Henry, anyway. Mom pulled me close, whispering about how cute a couple we made. She asked too loudly whether I'd been eating enough. He laughed and said he could tell it must be the perfect amount. Mom didn't order anything. Dad sipped a Bloody Mary.

"You're wondering what we had to tell you that was so important we couldn't do it over the phone." Dad stirred his drink with the stick of celery that even living people never ate.

"It was the contingency, of course." Mom leaned her cheek on her hand. "I saw that you'd find someone and he'd do something momentous. And it happened, so we're here to tell you that it's time for us to use that license."

"Wait, what?" Henry's brow crinkled in confusion. "I don't understand. I didn't do anything. It was our friend Nox, the Kelpie. She freed a Spite."

"Oh, Maddie told me about that already. You did something more important than just win a battle." Mom fluttered her hand. "You took a step toward stopping a war."

"It's that." Dad nodded at the middle of Henry's chest. "Your alliance with the wolf shifter."

"But I didn't tell you about that." It was my turn to make my face do a confusion gymnastics routine.

"You didn't have to." Mom tapped her temple. "I saw the whole thing before it happened, of course."

"And I saw it once it did." Dad smiled. "It's been decades. Well, you know exactly how long ago the last vampire-wolf pack alliance dissolved. You've got a bit of a reputation, Henry Baxter. Everything I've heard is good."

"That's a huge compliment coming from Shi May. Thank you." Henry blinked, smiling back. I squeezed his hand under the table.

"All the same, I'm still Maddie's father. I'm also a vampire, like you. I know what it's like to love a mortal woman and have to wait. You'll take your time with her. Let her have her education uninterrupted. Make sure everything is done within the law."

"I will, sir. I know how the laws for turning work, and still remember what it was like to be a fledgling."

"Good, then we won't have a problem." Dad took the celery out of his drink and laid it on a napkin.

"Dad, seriously?" I rolled my eyes. Henry froze, looking more than a little frightened. "Okay, obligatory embarrassed-daughter act all done. For now."

"She gets that from me, you know." Mom's conspiratorial wink started everyone at the table laughing.

I spent way more of my time laughing after that. Knowing for sure that I had people in my life who remembered me made all the difference. When the rest of my friends came through the door in a raucous group, it only took a few moments for them to notice I was there. Lynn and Bobby blinked and scratched their heads, taking the longest to remember me. Olivia glanced at a journal and smiled, then took the first chair she got to at the table across from ours. Nox sat next to her, leaning back in her seat and making herself at home.

Tony shrugged out of his trench coat, draping it over his chair before sitting down. He made a snide remark to Bobby about cheeseburgers and Internet memes, then dropped me a wink. One corner of Josh's mouth tilted up as he mock-saluted Henry. He turned his chair around and sat backward on it across from Nox.

"So, what do you call this ersatz pack of ours anyway?" Blaine took his seat almost primly by comparison as though trying to prove that some shifters had decent table manners.

"You're going to love it." Josh lowered his voice when he spoke, so I didn't hear what he said, even though I knew the answer already. His reply had Lynn giggling and Bobby slapping his knee. Olivia cocked her head to one side and blinked, and Tony smirked. Nox whickered a laugh.

"Really? Tinfoil Hat?" Blaine blew a tiny wisp of smoke out his nose. "Can't you take anything seriously?"

"No reason to. Everything else is serious enough. Gotta grab a little light while we can." The waitress interrupted him, coming over to take their orders.

He was right. A little light made a big difference. Without it, what was darkness anyway? I leaned against Henry and looked at my parents again, certain I had all I'd need, even if we lived for centuries.

SAY WATKINS

A PROVIDENCE PARANORMAL COLLEGE
SHORT STORY

"Now get out of my lecture hall and hit some books before your grades hit Ground Zero."

I watched the second-semester sophomores shamble out like a zombie horde. Spring semester always began with a sort of mass somnolence. I yawned.

"It better not be contagious."

"It's not."

"Who said that?"

"Ahem."

I peered up into the nosebleed seats, but no students lurked. After turning to check behind the whiteboard, I almost tripped right over something. Leaning over for another look, I saw that the impossible had happened. I was wrong.

"Gnomes. Just what I need." I rolled my eyes and lifted my foot to step over the little Faerie.

"That's absolutely right. Well, almost." The Gnome winked.

"I'm not asking you what you mean by that." I kept my foot in the air, looking around on the ground for more Gnomes.

"Really?" The Gnome chuckled. "Then get off my lawn, whipper-snapper!"

"That's usually my line." I put my foot down safely on the other side of my annoying little visitor.

"I know. I'm a fan."

"No, you're a Gnome." I rolled my eyes.

"You're not funny, you know."

"I don't care. I'm not here to be funny. I'm here to teach too much material to too many students. Usually, they're the ones who can't get things under control." My shoulders sagged. "But now I'm in their shoes, thanks to old Brodsky being sloppy and getting himself arrested."

"Right. It's why I'm here." The Gnome gave a snappy little salute. "To help."

"Gnomes don't help projection Psychics for no reason." I tucked my folder of lecture notes into my satchel.

"I have a reason." The Gnome's eyes cut away to the right.

"Lay it on me, then." I jiggled the giant steel-coated Bubba travel mug that I kept my high-octane coffee in, found it still half-full , and took a sip.

"No."

"Huh." I scratched my head. No self-respecting pure Faerie did mortals favors unless it was payback. And I didn't have any IOUs from Gnomes. But someone I knew did, once upon a time. And hadn't a Gnome been involved in the debacle over inter-session with said person's old apprentice? "Edgar, that memory-bending bastard."

"Not a nice thing to call your brother." The Gnome grinned, showing a mouth full of steel bits and bobs.

Gnomes had no natural teeth. Instead, they made them from items related to whoever's debt they'd dealt with recently. My missing brother had used metal for most of his memory trinkets in his practicing Psychic days. This little Unseelie Faerie must owe Edgar something. I wondered whether it was from way back or more recently. Could the Gnome have information I wanted? The simplest explanation always makes the most sense, even in Extrahuman affairs.

"In any case, there's no point in using me to satisfy your debt. I haven't seen Edgar for decades. He never calls, he never writes, he's not been seen since floral prints and flannels were all the rage." I glanced at my watch, in a near-panic because I was exactly one minute late to Brodsky's next Extrahuman History section. "Good day."

"But you need help."

"I said, good day!" I stamped with one foot perilously close to the Gnome. Not a flinch from the Faerie's direction.

"Gnomes are Unseelie, so there's nothing good about a day for my kind." Tiny fists socked themselves against mini hips. "And I'm helping you whether you like it or not."

I opened my mouth to say something else, I don't even know what. Everything around me streaked and flashed, like when The Enterprise goes Warp except in reverse. I blinked and held my hands out in case I was falling. But no such thing had happened. Everything went back to normal seconds later. Almost.

Light from the ceiling flashed back from the face on my watch and into my left eye. But my right eye saw and my brain comprehended immediately.

"You moved us five minutes backward."

"Ayup." The Gnome winked, then clapped their tiny hands together. "Now get it under control and move your backside, so you're not late."

"That's my line!" I pulled my fingers apart to keep from making fists. After that, I filled them with the satchel and bucket of coffee. Slinging the satchel over one shoulder freed up one of my hands, essential if I expected to open the door once I'd scaled Mount Classroom.

Marching up the aisle of the lecture hall, I passed row after row of empty seats. The sophomores might have been figuratively zombified, but at least they picked up after themselves. Then, way up in the back, I found something.

"Phillips!" I couldn't clap to wake the sleeping Kelpie, so instead I balled up a fist and clanged it against the stainless steel jug/mug hybrid in my other hand. Under my breath, I mumbled, " Why do I always have to get the sleepy ones?"

"Say wha—" A long snort and a short jolt interrupted her words.

"Watkins! I mean, what? I mean, Professor, sir." She sat up, flinging dank hair out of her face in a completely futile effort to make herself presentable.

Nox failed miserably at that, of course. She'd drooled over half her chin, and her coat had left an impression like a line of stitches on her cheek. Her eyes were so bloodshot I could barely discern her iris color, and she had a puffiness about her visage that hadn't been there during Fall semester. The Kelpie was not okay.

"Listen, you don't have to go home, but you can't stay here, Phillips." I tapped my wingtip-clad toe in her general direction. "I've got students waiting for me across the hall, so scram."

"Oh." Nox pulled the lapels of her coat closer together, then hoisted an unusually large rucksack up to her right shoulder. "Uh, okay." She blinked, and her lower lip trembled.

I didn't have time for this. But Miss Phillips looked like she'd been sleeping in lecture halls instead of wherever she was supposed to. Even worse, she looked like she was about to cry over it. I'm harsh and stodgy and like it that way, but I'm not heartless. Kids at the College should never be left without options. As far as I'm concerned, the only person who had any right to limit a student's choices was said individual.

"Listen, you're Unseelie. The Nocturnal Lounge is technically open twenty-four seven. Nobody bothers going there in the daytime except the ghosts on the skeleton crew and their hippie Medium, though." I pushed the door to the lecture hall open with one hand. "Now skedaddle already."

"Um." The lanky kid somehow managed to duck under my outstretched arm. "'Kay. Thanks." Phillips scuttled along the corridor, reminding me for all the world of one of those water-walking bugs.

Crossing the corridor, I made a mental note to have a chat with Jeannie La Montaigne, the Resident Assistant. She'd be able to figure out Nox Phillips' damage way better than a crusty old professor like me.

When I put my hand on the latch to open the door, I yawned again. Glancing down at my watch, I wondered how four of the five gnome-stolen minutes had gone by already. Was my brain old enough to perceptually warp time? What had I just been thinking of doing? Could it be Alzheimer's, like poor Mr. Meyer?

"Ahem." The Gnome peered up at me, showing off their steel smile. I realized that the makeshift teeth looked a bit crooked, which meant it was about time the Faerie replaced them. I wondered what, or potentially who, the Gnome's empty gums waited for.

"Er—" I wanted to ask. One more question would be safe. But there wasn't time. I walked inside the other lecture hall and strode down to the front, fully prepared to begin class but grouchier than usual about it.

That entire year was turning out to be one of my worst in so many ways. Temporal obligations were only the beginning of my troubles.

OF WOLF AND PEACE

PROVIDENCE PARANORMAL COLLEGE
BOOK THREE

If you don't own your mistakes, they'll own you.

Wolf shifter Josh Dennison shouldn't tempt coincidence, or he'll end up ill-fated like his missing brother and maimed sister. The wolves pledged neutrality when the Goblin King and the Sidhe Queen split up centuries ago, but he's falling for the one woman he can't have—a Kelpie whose magic comes straight from the Goblin King's court.

Nox Phillips has hidden on campus since she undid the Queen's punishing spell. When she and Josh work together again, their mutual attraction can't be denied. But for any favor shown to one Faerie court, a price must be paid to the other, and the pair already walk a thin line. Nothing can erase Nox's guilt or prevent the Sidhe Queen from putting her on trial. How far will Josh go to save her?

CHAPTER ONE

Josh

"Get up, Josh." The voice was loud, intense, and familiar. But I couldn't place it, not even after opening my eyes. The room was pitch black.

"Fine." I sat up as fast as I could, swinging and hoping my fist would make contact with whoever wanted to drag me out of bed at zero dark thirty in the morning. No luck.

"Out the window." Some invisible force pushed the middle of my back, propelling me out of bed. Magic? At least I wore pajamas a week into February. I still couldn't place the voice. Male, for sure.

"Light." If I saw who it was, maybe I could put up a fight.

"No. Get out of here right now." The voice had lowered to a near whisper, but all the intensity was still there. Someone I knew from school?

"Clothes." The hair on the back of my neck stood up. The rest of the house should have been dead silent at this hour. Instead, a whole slew of people stomped around the living room, the kitchen, the parlor. It was worse than the night our parents went to Block Island

and Derek threw a party. This didn't sound like a bunch of 18-year-olds trying to get their illegal drink on, though.

"No time." The voice was on the other side of the room now, in the shadows near the closet.

"I'll go if you fess up to this later, man." I reached under the bed and grabbed the strap of my bug-out bag. After that, I stepped into my boots, not bothering to lace them.

"Fine. The window." I heard soft footfalls in the corner, then tumblers in a lock and a door opening. But my closet didn't have a lock. Heavy footsteps on the stairs killed the urge to investigate.

My room had a wannabe balcony, but I didn't use that. I'd need more than just stucco to get three stories down. I went to the smaller window, jerking on the shade to get it to snap up. It fell on my head instead. I pressed my lips closed, not daring to shout the string of epithets that had only gotten more colorful since I'd started at PPC.

Once I'd flipped the latch on the window, I wriggled out. The trellis had held my weight the last time I'd tried this, but I'd been fifteen and at least twenty pounds lighter back then. The top held up, but once I got to the second floor, it gave out. I thought of Tony Gitano the cat shifter as I fell to the ground, not remotely on my feet but relatively unharmed. I'd landed in the roses, all bare branches and thorns—the opposite of a comfortable landing. The cuts and scratches on my arms and face would heal in a few minutes. It was good to be a shifter.

I looked up. No one was at the window. The light went on upstairs in my room, along with shouts of surprise and barked orders to find me. I took off across the back lawn as fast as I could on two legs, and that was pretty damn fast. I'd won all the shifter-designated sprints they had in Track and Field back in High School.

The wall at the back of our property was too tall to hop without shifting. The last thing I wanted to do was turn into a wolf in the middle of Providence. It'd make me easier to track, I'd lose all my stuff, and I'd have no idea when I'd be able to come back here. I hoped my parents were just doing a drill or something, but this could also be mutiny. They'd made a few unpopular decisions, and I hadn't helped their image lately. I turned right to beat feet toward the old garden gate. It was covered with ivy and I'd have to crawl through, but I should make it. I'd gained only twenty pounds since I was fifteen, not fifty.

The tiny gate still didn't have a lock, but the latch was on the inside of the wall. No one outside could reach it. My sister Beth always called it the Alice gate because it reminded her of something out of one of Lewis Carrol's books. I looked back at the house. Her room was lit up like a Christmas Tree. They'd gotten her, then. No way she could have put on her prosthetic in time to bug out unless whoever had warned me went to her first. Derek's windows were dark. He'd been missing since 2008.

I wriggled through the Alice gate, dragging the bag behind me. Once through, it clanged shut like a mouth full of metal teeth. No going back now. I looked at the sky, to find not even a trace of dawn. Time to visit Henry Baxter, then. He was my Beta though an unconventional one. Henry was a vampire, and wolf shifters'd had nothing to do with them since the early 1990s. I'd thought it was time to change that. My parents couldn't outright say they agreed even though I knew they did. I went down the street as fast as I could without attracting attention, doubling back so I didn't walk past the house.

My family estate was on the Upper East Side of Providence, a swanky neighborhood. Henry lived in a basement apartment most of the way down College Hill on the Lower East Side. It had just been renovated after a freaky Seelie hunting hound called a Spite tore a hole in the wall trying to get at him. We'd had trouble with a mind-controlled Summoner over Winter Break. Yeah, Extrahuman society was a bitch, but we dealt with it, my family especially. Mom and Dad did police work, and I'd be expected to follow in their footsteps.

I walked down Rochambeau Street, the most direct and often used way to get down to the Lower East Side. The more well-traveled my route, the better. It'd be easier to hide my trail. As I turned down the cross-street that would take me to Henry's place, a stream of intricately gorgeous music flowed from the first-floor window of a familiar triple-decker house. I turned around to see the light on, warmly incandescent and inviting. Usually, I didn't like violins, too squeaky, but whoever was playing managed to eliminate that particular sound from the mix.

I stepped forward, feeling a strong need to go and listen more closely. I didn't stop to think about why anyone in their right mind would give a masterwork solo violin performance on Rochambeau Street at who knows when in the morning. It smacked of compulsion, something you do in a dream or see in a horror movie, the kind where you yell at the screen about how dumb the guy walking toward the monster is, then roll your eyes and sit back to wait for him to die gruesomely. Yup, I was doing the future dead guy shuffle.

"Josh? What are you doing out at this hour?" I hadn't known my eyes were sore until I saw Nox Phillips. The sight of her snapped me right out of whatever weird trance the music had put me in. "Are those pajamas?" She blinked, almost as though she'd been enthralled by the music, too. I thought of something else that got people killed in horror movies.

"Um, yeah." I took a deep breath, trying to keep from blushing. The Kelpie was just about the most gorgeous girl I'd ever laid eyes on, tall and lean with dark hair and deep blue eyes. Unfortunately, dating any type of Changeling or Faerie was absolutely forbidden, even the shifters. Packs couldn't take sides in the conflict between the Unseelie Goblin King and the Seelie Sidhe Queen.

The pit of my stomach sank as I realized Nox had majorly crossed the Queen and I'd been standing right there while she'd done it. Maybe the home invasion had more to do with me than I'd originally thought. At least I could ignore the fiddler now. "Had to bug out. Something nuts is going down at my house. Was on the way to find Henry."

"He's out of town until tomorrow, remember? Went to Vermont with Maddie for the weekend." Nox shook her head a little more vigorously than most people do when indicating the negative. Was she shaking off the music's effects, too?

"Crap on a crap cracker." I ran my hand over the top of my head, hoping it'd stand up in a less bed-head kind of way. "I got nowhere to go, and I need to figure out what happened, why people are chasing me."

"Why not come back to campus, then?" She put one hand on my shoulder. "Wait for the rest of Tinfoil Hat to wake up and talk to them about it. Whoever's looking for you wouldn't think to check the Nocturnal Lounge."

"Good idea." Tinfoil Hat was the temporary pack I'd made during the Summoner situation. It was a motley crew but still had mostly shifters as members. "Lead on."

I walked, trying not to brush against Nox when the sidewalk narrowed halfway to campus. It wouldn't be right to give her the wrong idea. Then again, I wasn't even sure whether she thought of me that way. Kelpies were Unseelie magical horse shifters, freshwater versions of the Seelie seal shifter Selkies. They could be inscrutable, especially while wearing the magical pelt that gives them their powers. Some of them had magic or psychic powers as well. I had no idea whether Nox did or not.

"Hey, Nox. I just remembered you never said whether you had any magic or whatever before the Kelpie thing."

"No, I didn't." She pulled out her phone, tapping out a text message.

"So? Dish." I put my hands on my hips before realizing how ridiculous that looked while walking uphill in pajamas and combat boots.

She just laughed. We turned up Angell Street, heading toward Thayer Street and the old trolley tunnel. The entrance to the Nocturnal Lounge was in there, with a secret knock to open the hidden door. They ran the place like they thought it was the Bat Cave or something. Maybe there were actual bats or bat shifters or even Batman, and I just didn't know. I'd only been in there once, right after a Grim had wrecked it in more of that Summoner business. When the door opened, and we went up the stairs, I knew this time would be different from the last. I heard music and smelled pizza. My stomach growled almost as viciously as I could while shifted.

Henry's usual study and work spot in the mezzanine was empty, of course. Sometimes, Tony was up there, but not now. The vampire band Night Creatures practiced on the bottom floor, blasting out riffs behind Lane belting out *Of Wolf and Man* by Metallica. A mixed crowd of Unseelie Changelings, vampires, and nocturnal shifters stood or sat, listening. I finally saw a familiar face and headed down the stairs. Nox followed. She'd have to keep an eye on me because only the night people could be in here without an escort.

I headed straight for the counter at the side of the room, grabbing the last slice of pizza before Fred Redford could. The Redcap Changeling frowned at my hand, then grinned when he saw who it belonged to. He didn't bother trying to talk over the band, just picked up the Leaning Tower of Pizza he'd already taken off the tray to get out of the way of the Skeleton Crew. Ghostly hands that only Psychic Mediums and Death Magi could see removed the empty box. They'd replace it with another one in the not too distant future. Ghost employees unlived all over the PPC campus. According to the Psychic Mediums that was a good thing. It kept them busy until they could move on and was one of the reasons fewer hauntings happened on College Hill than most other areas of a city as old as Providence.

Nox grabbed cups and a bottle of root beer, following Fred and me back to the mezzanine. I'd known Fred since preschool. Even though we never went to each other's house after school or anything, we ran in lots of the same circles. I wasn't allowed to call him a friend but knew we would have been if my parents didn't run the two most important packs in the city. Mom headed the Extrahuman Task Force for the city police and Dad ran PPC Campus Police. The only way they'd need to be more impartial was if they worked for the DA.

We sat at Henry's table. It was quieter there when the Night Creatures practiced. We could actually hear each other talk in that corner. I let Fred eat half of his pizza first, then explained how I'd been dragged out of bed and ended up here. He chewed thoughtfully for a few moments. I sat waiting for his reaction, sipping root beer and wishing it had a shot of Jägermeister in it. No one could bust me for drinking. The gap year I'd taken before starting at PPC meant I was twenty-one in my sophomore year.

"Sounds like a mutiny. Better lie low and stay out of it." Fred adjusted the red Paw Sox cap he always wore, then chomped down another slice of pizza with eerily perfect teeth. "Worst that can happen is your folks get busted down from Alpha and have to run as part of the regular pack for a while, right?"

"Not exactly." I sighed into my root beer. "Thing is, they could get kicked out altogether depending on whether whoever did this gives them a fair challenge."

"That's nuts. It's not like they killed someone, right?" Fred brushed his hands over the now empty plate. I wondered where he'd put it all. He was about the same size as most bear shifters, but without the metabolism drain of shifting, I couldn't imagine how he used all those calories.

"No. No killing since before they took over, during an assignment at the Boston Internment." I put my hands flat on the table in front of me.

"It sounds more like a raid than a mutiny" I heard a plastic crack from Nox's direction, punctuating her statement. She held a brown paper bag over my cup and tilted it. "Shh. Don't tell or everyone will want some."

As she repeated the process over Fred's cup and then her own, I smelled rum. It wasn't Jaeger, but it'd do. I tried not to smile too much, just topped us all off with more root beer. I sipped, my shoulders instantly relaxing. My mind cleared too, letting me think more about what she'd said. A raid? There sure had been enough people in the house for that.

"Maybe you're right, Nox. It was like a raid, like the ATF or the FBI came in. Except it wasn't those agencies. I didn't smell flash-bangs or guns." I took another sip of the oddly satisfying drink.

"Anyone in your parents' pack have connections to those?" Fred gulped down half his spiked root beer.

"No. Not that I know of." I shrugged. "Everyone's police of some kind, but no Federal anything. This is Rhode Island, after all."

"Yeah, local focus." Nox chewed on her lower lip. "Not so easy to deal with some iffier elements if they think RICO's watching."

"Huh. You sound like my dad." Fred grimaced around another mouthful of pizza. He swallowed that before continuing. "And everyone knows he used to be connected a million ways from Sunday."

"Yeah. Gives my folks a nice headache because there's nothing to balance that out on the other side of things if you catch my drift." I knew better than to say the word Seelie out loud in the Nocturnal Lounge.

"Hey, we can't help it if we're better at that kind of thing than they are, in this neck of the woods." Fred held his hands out palms up, then frowned down at his empty plate. "They're too hidebound for anything but high society, and around here Hertha Harcourt has that element locked down."

"Dragon shifters don't let go of anything once they've got their hooks in. Tenacious." Nox seemed to look everywhere but at me. Neither of us was about to tell Fred how the dragon lady's son and heir was in my pack. "The whole Faerie population's unbalanced lately. Unseelies deal with change way better than they do."

I had to keep quiet while I swallowed my anger. Blaine Harcourt was one of the smartest people I knew, but still vying for Omega in Tinfoil Hat. He'd figured out that some disruptive element was messing with PPC and maybe all the Extrahumans in Providence months ago. He'd also decided to try to make Nox his latest conquest. She was a big girl and could make her own decisions, but nothing said I had to be happy about it. Blaine was a playboy and would stay that way until his mother told him who to marry. Some guys might have been okay with that, knowing he'd move along once he was done with her. I wasn't. Nox deserved better than to be treated like a toy. But I had no right to complain. It wasn't like I could offer her anything myself. Forbidden relationships were forbidden.

Fred glanced back and forth between us like he watched a tennis match, or maybe Forrest Gump playing ping pong. Probably the ping pong. I sighed, then kicked back all my rum and root beer. Nox didn't look at me, but she gave me a refill. I drank that, too, straight. I saw her take a shot directly from the bottle out of the corner of my eye.

"Whatever that was, I'm staying out of it." Fred picked up his plate. "Pizza calls. Maybe those ghosts will surprise me with a stack of bacon cheeseburgers instead some night."

The silence Fred left behind was the opposite of comfortable. I sat in it with Nox for a little while because nothing I could break it with was what I really wanted to say.

CHAPTER TWO

Nox

I was about to pass the rest of the rum to Josh and leave when Tony showed up with Blaine in tow. The dragon shifter smiled at us, then dropped me a wink. I'd have to sit there and let Josh's hackles rise and fall without comment. We needed Blaine's brain on this, so Josh would just have to deal with his jealousy issues. I wasn't interested in the dragon shifter, but any time I tried to talk to Josh about it, he shut me down. It was one of the most confusing things I'd ever seen, and being a Kelpie meant my ancestors' attitudes were constantly humming in the background.

"You called, we answered." Blaine sat down across from me, leaning his elbows on the table. "What did you need me for, Nox?"

"We'll need the rest of Tinfoil Hat when they wake up, too. Josh has a problem." I put the bottle to my lips, killing the rum myself. Liquid courage. I might be a Kelpie, but a magical Unseelie horse was small potatoes next to a dragon.

"You mean a problem besides thinking pajamas go with combat boots instead of a smoking jacket?" Blaine waggled his eyebrows.

"Knock it off." Tony sat down next to Blaine, rolling his eyes. "He had to bug out in the middle of the night. I bet you'd look even sillier." Tony put his head in his hands. "I can't believe I'm sticking up for a wolf shifter in public like this."

I laughed instead of sharing with the group that I'd never texted Tony. Well, it was sort of me covering for the cat shifter. I only half wanted to. The other half of that reaction came from Grandpa. He was the most recent and strongest influence on my magic pelt. Being a Kelpie was kind of a bum deal because someone parental was always watching unless you put the pelt away for a while. It took endless amounts of compromise and battle picking. Laughing at a joke was one I'd gladly lose if it meant I could fight him on something more important later. It was also hell on any attempt at feminine grooming. Styling my hair or makeup was as futile as resisting the Borg. A constant frizz-inducing dampness clung to my scalp, and even waterproof mascara ran like the wind under the pelt's influence.

"Oh. You texted Tony, too?" I wondered why Josh sounded so relieved about that. Why would it make any difference whether I got in touch with Tony or Blaine? I let cat-boy answer.

"Yeah. Guaranteed to be awake all night, you know." Tony Gitano was lucky none of us were Telepathic Psychics. I only knew he was lying because I'd forgotten to message him.

"Yeah. Unless you're bird watching." Someone would have to be the butt of Blaine's jokes tonight. After Intersession, the whole pack knew Tony had a soft spot for a certain owl shifter.

"What's that supposed to mean?" Tony blinked, his pupils narrowing into something resembling catlike slits.

"Nothing at all. Just groggy. Too bad you couldn't just let sleeping dragons lie." Blaine pulled an iPad out of his backpack. "Ah, the curse of being the brainiac."

"Thought that was Frampton's nickname, Trogdor." Josh gave a Lynn-worthy snort.

"True enough." He powered up the tablet, propping it up in its case so he could use the attached keyboard. "Can't we lose the old Strongbad moniker, though? Call me Smaug or something a little more classic?"

"How about Puff? You are magic and live by the sea, after all." I smiled mildly.

"Trogdor's fine." Blaine cracked his knuckles and started typing. "Okay, Josh. What happened?"

I listened to Josh's story again, trying to think of anything that hadn't occurred to me before. A mutiny still seemed most likely, but why? Could it be the alliance he'd made with Henry? No. The response to that had been overwhelmingly supportive. Since Henry had been a Psychic, wasn't an old vampire, and had no Faerie heritage, he was an excellent choice for the first new alliance since the Big Reveal. Coincidence had been on our side this winter. I gently knocked on the wooden bottom of the table, hoping that trend would continue as we moved into spring.

"Tell me again about wolf shifter politics and moon phases." Blaine scratched his chin. "I know there's something about moon phases and leadership, but can't remember what, exactly."

"See, this is why Lynn's the brainiac and you're Trogdor the dragon man. She'd remember that." Josh leaned back in his chair, glancing down at my now empty rum bottle. "It's the new moon tonight. I've been so out of it I didn't even think. That changes things by a mile."

"How so?" I tossed my dearly departed rum bottle into the wastepaper basket in the corner by the bookcases. "Three points. Anyway, continue."

"New moons are the one time packmates can apprehend an Alpha, but then it makes no sense for them to take my sister and stomp into my room. My parents are the real Alphas. No offense, guys, but Tinfoil Hat's not considered the real thing in wolf shifter terms."

"What could it be, though?" Tony scratched his head, then tucked a strand of hair behind one ear. He seemed stumped, but my ancestors noticed something flat in his voice. I wondered whether he shared my suspicion. Now I understood why Grandpa wanted to cover for him.

Maybe he'd cover for me now. "Couldn't be about that whole Summoner problem over winter break, could it?"

"Well, your parents did arrest that Summoner for murder. What did they find at his house? Anything that might be a problem for the pack or police?" Blaine tapped his fingers on the table. "He had Anchors for pure Faeries, both, um…not the variety that comes in here."

"Huh." Josh leaned forward, palms on the table. "I'm not sure what they found. There'll be a list down at Campus Police, though."

"Good. Then someone can check in the morning." Blaine blew a smoke ring.

"Don't you mean I can check in the morning?" Josh clenched his jaw.

"That might be a bad idea." Blaine raised an eyebrow. "Unless you want to end up wherever they've got the rest of your family. The moon's technically still new for a couple more days. Anyway, since you're not a real Alpha. You have to lie low. They could snatch you anytime. Might want to avoid the general campus until you know it's safe."

"That's one week. I can't do anything to defend my family's honor until the half-moon." Josh put his head in his hands. "I'm going to flunk a mid-term."

"Why?" Blaine typed something on his iPad. "Haven't you been studying?"

"No." Josh sighed. "I slacked off, and our brainiac, Lynn, can't help me. This exam is shifter-specific and physical."

"I'll do whatever I can." I wanted to put my arm around him. I fought with Grandpa until he let me punch Josh's shoulder instead. My ancestors always fought me on displays of affection toward men. "School of hard Nox is in session."

"I'll help, too." Tony grinned, his eyes going back to normal. "School of homework fetching over here, for the other classes. Also, a little more neutral than Kelpie school, just in case."

"Oh, good point." Blaine tapped the table again. His toothy grin reminded me more of a crocodile than an oligarch. Grandpa thought those were almost the same thing.

"Maybe." I peered across the table at Blaine. "What time is it, anyway? I have an early class on Tuesdays."

"Almost five." Blaine shut down his iPad. "I should get out of here, head back to the dorm. I have a plan about how to get the information from Campus Police involving Olivia, but I need to find her before breakfast. Extrahuman Law students can access their files. Where are you staying, Josh?"

"With me." Fred loomed behind Tony. "Dad's at a job on Block Island. Only people home all week are me, Mom, and my kid brother. They're Psychics and I'm untithed, so all good on the Faerie neutrality front just in case."

"How did you know all that? You were down there in that noise stuffing your face." Tony glanced up, doing his cat shifter bristle.

"Ears." Fred stuck his hand under the table and pulled something off. "See?" He held up a small gray triangle, then stuck it on the side of his head. I watched the shimmer of falling Glamour as it dropped, revealing his true appearance.

Everyone else besides me gasped. Tony's reaction was slightly delayed. Redcaps had gray skin, red eyes, slightly pointed ears, and a set of perfectly even teeth so white they were almost blue. Fred almost looked like one, a sign he'd used faerie magic so much he'd need to tithe to a Monarch soon. Once he'd put the top of his ear back on, Fred's Glamour came back, rounding his ears and changing his skin back to its usual Mediterranean olive tone. I tried not to look at Tony, wondering why he'd covered for himself like that. With the amount of time he spent in the Nocturnal Lounge and his Nocturnal History major, he'd have studied Changelings by now, surely?

"Wow. How much longer are you going to be able to put off tithing and taking your Mantle?" Grandpa's question slipped out before I could censor myself. He'd done that to me all through Magic Theory during Winter Intersession. At least Chuck, Ian, and Maddie had taken it in stride. It wasn't something I liked doing in front of Josh, though.

"Maybe summer." Fred didn't even grin. "I was hoping to get through the Fall semester before I have to spend a year and a day in the Under. Now I'll be lucky to make it through Spring."

"We'll miss you." Tony's voice cracked a little. "Whenever it's time, I mean." I wondered what the cat man wasn't saying.

"That's mutual, squirt." Fred flicked Tony on the side of the head. "Anyway, we'd better get going before the sun comes up, Josh. You probably don't want to be on the street in your PJs in broad daylight."

"Yeah." Josh got up, shouldering his bag. He looked me right in the eye. "I'll call you later." He ignored the light haze of smoke coming from Blaine's direction. "Got to let you know what I need help with."

I nodded, not breaking eye contact with him even though Grandpa wanted me to. He didn't much like how interested I was in Josh. I didn't care. I waited to break eye contact until he had to turn and follow Fred. Blaine packed up and left, too. Tony sat diagonally from me across the table. I kept my eyes on Josh until he was out of sight, making the cat wait.

"Why are you still here, Tony?" I finally looked at him, startled at the anger flashing in his bright green and vertically slitted eyes. I'd gotten his inner cat up, but had no idea why.

"Because you need to know Josh's biggest problem, and I didn't want to deal with him freaking out over it." I studied him. His face, posture, and voice all seemed genuine enough. I gave in to Grandpa, this time, and let him nudge me into using a little Kelpie charm. Tony's pupils dilated slightly, still cat-vertical but more relaxed.

"All right. I'm listening." I folded my hands on the tabletop.

"Faerie neutrality." Tony took a deep breath. "It's his part in releasing that Sprite over Intersession that's screwing things up for his family."

"But that's on me. Josh didn't do anything but stand there." I'd been the one to undo the enchantment on the poor creature. I'd even stolen the means to do it right out of Blaine's backpack. Grandpa made me shudder. Risky business, stealing from a dragon shifter, even a young one.

"He stood by and let you do it. As your Alpha, he's responsible."

Tony made a noise halfway between a sigh and a hiss. "And whose idea was it, anyway?"

"Mine." I would have fidgeted, but Grandpa kept me still.

"Bull." Tony's eyes narrowed.

"All right, you got me." I shrugged the shoulder Grandpa had relinquished to my control. "Josh actually had the idea that freeing the Sprite would stop it. So what?" He'd thought of it right after I saw that funny little Gnome, but Tony didn't have to know that.

"Josh took a side. He's heir to two of the biggest shifter authorities in the city. He's supposed to be neutral, but he sided with you, an Unseelie shifter. And then, he let you take a Gnome's advice." He stared, unblinking.

"He did it to save his Beta. Nothing more." I gripped the edge of the table, wondering how he knew about the Gnome with the metal teeth. "We stopped a murderer. No one should complain about that."

"If that's true, why didn't he turn the Sprite in?"

"That Sprite owes us all. He'd have lost favors from a Pure Faerie." That should have been perfectly reasonable as far as the Faerie Courts were concerned.

"You tell me how that looks." Tony put his hands flat on the table.

"Bad." I closed my eyes. "Like he's the Alpha they were actually after, not his parents." I held my breath for a moment. "But he said they don't consider him a real Alpha, right?"

"Not right. That idea lives in Understatement City." Tony dragged his nails against the tabletop, leaving faint grooves. "Him trusting your judgment has to be the reason for all this. Josh's problem is you. Dump him."

"Huh?" I blinked and swallowed at the same time.

"Break up with him, Yoko." Tony's glare was almost palpable.

"But we're not even going out. I don't even think he likes me that way." I knew I was wrong the second the words came out of my mouth. Why else would he be jealous of Blaine?

"Bull." I heard a muffled squeak as Tony ground his teeth. "Leave the pack then."

"What's the big deal about it for you anyway, Tony Gitano?" I leaned back in my chair, unable to stop Grandpa from saying what he wanted. "You're the shadiest, dodgiest person I've ever seen. There's an awful lot of rule-bending in your family. Plus, you knew about the Gnome. I never breathed a word of that to anyone. What if you're the problem?"

Tony's eyes got big, and his face paled. Something between a hiss and a growl rumbled at the back of his throat. He opened his mouth, then closed it again without saying anything. His nails made a splintery sound against the table. He lifted them up, holding his hands palms out in a gesture of concession, possibly even surrender. He stood, backing away from me. The mantle on his duster drooped as though he'd been out in the rain. I didn't understand why right away until I felt water dripping from my hair to my shoulders.

"Jeez Tony, I'm sorry." I struggled to get my hand to my stomach, fighting Grandpa every step of the way to release myself from the grasp of my pelt. I pulled it off, rolled it up, put it away in the oilcloth in my rucksack. "Look, it's just me now. No more ancestors."

"Are you sure that was all them?" He shivered a little. I didn't blame him. Grandpa's spell would freak out any feline. Kelpie Water magic was one reason I'd enrolled at PPC. I needed to learn how to control it. Cat shifters were scared of water, and all my ancestors knew it. Still, Tony seemed even worse off than expected, like he'd come close to drowning before.

"Almost all. Look, it's obvious you're hiding something most of the time, but I don't think you're the problem. And that was an unfair low blow, mentioning your family like that. I'm sorry, Tony."

"Yeah. And I'm sorry, too." He sat back down, but only on the edge of the seat. "Look, if we're going to get Josh out of this and avoid a huge Extrahuman conflict, we need to be honest without attacking each other."

"You sound like a diplomat."

"I kind of am. Supposed to be if I can ever—" He blinked, eyes redder than they should be. Was he on the verge of tears? "But anyway." He cleared his throat. "I wouldn't be surprised if this has something to do with Blaine's Extramagus. Remember what Henry found in his amulet? An Extramagus around his age, with a possible connection to that Stanhope family. We need to look at that, find out what happened to them."

"If they're Magi, what would they have to do with wolf shifters?"

"Could be plenty. That kid Henry described was blond. So was Stanhope. So's Josh for that matter. Maybe there's a relation there. Magi used to marry into any Extrahuman family they could back in the day. Have you ever seen his parents? Pictures of his siblings?"

"He has siblings?" I blinked. He'd never mentioned them.

"Two. One's been missing for years. The other's missing a leg, the sister he mentioned. That's why he inherits the packs even though he's the youngest." Tony spoke without quite meeting my eyes, head tilted slightly to the side as though hearing something I couldn't.

"How do you know all this?"

"Coincidence, convergence, and conniving. One of the reasons all that stuff you said freaked me out so much is because it's a little true. I am dodgy and shady. I have too many secrets to keep that aren't mine. The ones that do belong to me…well. Voices carry. I can't risk mentioning them."

"The cat man who knew too much?" I quirked an eyebrow.

"Yeah. Curiosity kills." His lips stretched into a thin, flat line.

"Let's hope satisfaction works like an AED." I sighed. "So, what do we do now?"

"Go to class. Get information. Help Josh study. Wait for Trogdor and the brain to puzzle it out."

"All that in a week, huh?" I shook my head.

"Yeah. Let's hope it's a long one." Tony got up, stretching and clearly more at ease than he'd been just a few minutes before. "It'll be a long day, at least. Maybe I'll have time to catch a cat nap this afternoon."

"Same here, minus the cat part." I stifled a yawn. "Hopefully, Josh won't call in the middle of that."

He did, of course.

CHAPTER THREE

Josh

I thought I'd gotten the wrong number when a huge yawn answered. I checked the screen to find I hadn't.

"Whoozat?" Nox's slurred voice came in crystal clear. I tried to imagine her just after a nap, fluffing sleep-tousled hair and stretching limber arms over her head. What would she wear to sleep? I cleared my throat, ending that line of thought as fast as I could.

"Just Josh. Calling about homework." I held my tongue. Couldn't say much of anything else. "I can read you a list whenever you're ready."

"Go ahead." I heard the clack of a keyboard and a muffled conversation over the clink of silverware.

"Wait a minute, Nox." I felt my brow ridging like a Ruffles potato chip. "Were you sleeping in the dining hall?"

"No." I heard her hand cover the phone as she told someone she didn't want any more coffee. "Why would I do a thing like that?"

"Dunno. Are you in a cafe or something? You know what, never mind." I sighed. I'd have to call Bobby or Lynn and ask them to check on her. Or maybe Maddie once she got back from Vermont. I'd even call Jeannie if I had to. I rattled off the list of classes, Professors, and office hours I'd prepared earlier.

"Okay. I'll talk to Tony. He can bring your homework for everything besides Shifter Mastery." I heard her take a sip of something. "For that, we should meet. I don't think Tony will give you much of a challenge sparring."

"But where?" I ran a hand over my head, spiking up my hair. "I'm not supposed to go to campus, remember?" There was a long pause like Nox was thinking or struggling with some idea.

"I'll think of something."

"Fine." I wondered why she didn't just ask Bobby for help with that and then remembered. He'd be taking the freshman version of Shifter Mastery. If he practiced with me, he'd get too worn out to handle his coursework. "I gotta go."

"Bye." She hung up.

I wished I could talk to Beth. I'd tried, but her phone went straight to voicemail, and there was no response to my texts. I shook my head, still unable to think of a reason they'd take her. Beth's losses meant she wasn't even in the running for Beta of either pack in the future. I missed her, even more than when she'd been down the hall. At least I knew she could hear my knocking on the door and requests to come out and do something. If any of them hurt my sister, they'd be outcasts the minute I took over. She'd been through enough. I got up and headed toward the door of the Redfords' attic guest room. I nearly bumped into Fred's younger brother in the doorway.

"Sorry, kid." I felt like a jerk because I'd forgotten his name.

"You need to say more of what you mean and mean more of what you say." The kid's eyes were round as saucers. I could barely see his irises, they were so dilated. Did the Redford family Psychic ability come with fortune cookie one-liners and involve mainlining eyedrops?

"Um, okay." I shrugged, still looking down at him. Had I ever been that tiny? "Anything else?"

"Oh! Sorry." The kid blinked and shook his head. His eyes went back to normal. "Mom says there're sandwiches downstairs if you're hungry." He stepped out of the doorway.

"Thanks, kid." I stepped into the hall and headed toward the stairs.

"My name's Ed." He smirked up at me, looking like he knew I couldn't remember his name.

"Awesome." So, the Redfords were the type of people who made their kids' names rhyme. Who'd have thought?

Downstairs was cozy but well-crafted like the rest of the house. Fred's dad didn't own the most successful Extrahuman contracting business for nothing. Redford Renovations did everything from building entire houses with magical accouterments to outfitting old homes with magical devices to accommodate disabilities. He'd sent a crew over to re-do half our estate after Beth lost her leg. That had been harrowing because she'd also lost her fiancé, Ren Ichiro. He'd been from a Tanuki family, though not a shifter. Tanuki and their kin were supposed to be the luckiest people on the planet. I wondered whether he'd given up all his Luck so she could live through the wreck on the Newport Bridge.

In the kitchen, the dining table, sideboard, island, and every counter was covered with plates of sandwiches. I spotted just about every combination of bread and filling you could think of. I almost told Mrs. Redford she didn't have to go to that kind of trouble for little old me when Fred walked in. He sat at the table, pulling six plates close to him and glancing up with a territorial spark in his eye.

"*Mangia!*" Mrs. Redford's accent was deep Cranston, with long, nasal vowel sounds. Unexpected, considering her hair was much smaller than most ladies from that part of Rhode Island. "Sit. Eat. You're skinny, even for a wolf shifter. At least you've got more meat on you than that scrawny Gitano boy my Fred works with."

"Yes, ma'am." I picked up a ham and swiss on rye and sat across from Fred, noticing he'd already polished off five plates. He pulled the sixth toward him. I wasn't going to bother asking where he put it all. Redcaps ate even more than their untithed Changeling offspring. Mrs.

Redford was probably used to making more than twice this much lunch.

"You call Nox yet?" Fred enunciated surprisingly well around the mouthful of sandwich.

"He did." Ed sat on a stool by the island, a bologna sandwich on Wonderbread clutched in one pint-sized hand.

"Well, that's good." Fred swallowed a mouthful of the meatball sub. "Except for the part where you listened in on a guest."

"Sorry, but Rob wanted me to." Ed glanced up toward the lazily spinning ceiling fan.

"Rob, schmob." Mrs. Redford was there, looming over Ed. "How many times have I told you to be careful of that one? Loves to get you into trouble."

"I know Mom, but he said it was important." Ed sighed, looking at something or someone near the ceiling. "Rob says Josh has a big problem. He needs to do everything right, or he's going to be in serious danger."

"Is this true, Rob?" Mrs. Redford looked right where Ed did. She waited, reminding me for all the world of someone using a Bluetooth earbud. Her eyes dilated just like Ed's had. After a moment, she sighed and turned to pat the kid on the head. "You're right this time, bambino. But next time, don't just go taking Rob's word for anything without asking me first, okay?"

"All right, Mama." Ed crammed the last of his sandwich in his mouth. "Can I go play now?"

"Sure." She glared at the spot I assumed Rob occupied instead of her younger son's retreating form. "You stay here with me. Let the boy be a boy, not a conduit." She glanced at me. "You, too." How had she known I'd been about to escape with a second sandwich?

"What's up, Mrs. Redford?" I took a bite of this new confection of bread and filling, waiting for her to talk. Velvet Elvis. My tongue stuck to the roof of my mouth.

"Rob's connected to the ghost of a Precognitive. He doesn't usually see things happening to the living, but he did this time. You want to know why?"

"Sure. Go ahead." That's right, the mom and the kid were Mediums. I hadn't paid much attention to Psychic wooj before making one of the vampiric variety my Beta.

"You or someone you care about will die if you don't correct your course." She picked what looked like prosciutto and provolone on ciabatta off the top of one of the plates. "Maybe both."

"I'll take that into account." My voice came out all mushy because the peanut butter still stuck to the roof of my mouth. What a canine predicament. I glanced around for a drink. I moved toward a glass and the water pitcher. "Thanks."

"Whatever Ed said to you upstairs was important." Mrs. Redford got between me and the water, her gaze intense over the top of her bread, cheese, and meat. "Do whatever he told you, and you might come through this in better shape than your sister did the last time Rob declared a dire prediction."

"Wait, what?" I almost dropped my sandwich. "What's Beth got to do with this?"

"She didn't listen, even though I warned her myself." Mrs. Redford shook her head. "Thought a bad foretelling would go away because the Ichiros are what they are. But you know how that turned out. Don't let it happen to you, too. Coincidence only makes it more likely that prediction will come true."

"Ugh." Fred reached for a BLT on multigrain. "Coincidence is a bitch, and then you die."

"Language, Frederick Raymond Redford, or you eat outside." Mrs. Redford reached one hand toward a rack of wooden spoons.

"Sorry, Mama." Fred put the sandwich down and folded his hands on the crumb-strewn table in front of him.

"First strike today. Just be good." She dropped her hand, then poured three glasses of water.

"I will, Mama." Fred picked his half-eaten sandwich up and ate it in one bite. Then, he gulped his water down in one go. "And thanks for lunch."

"Don't forget who else you should thank." Mrs. Redford glanced at the stack of plates floating toward the sink. They seemed to rinse and place themselves gently in the dishwasher.

"Thanks, crew." He nodded at the empty air around the floating china and flatware. Mrs. Redford grinned, then headed out the door to the parlor.

"Yeah, thanks." I finally understood why it wasn't such a big deal for Mrs. Redford to handle a Redcap diet. She had unseen help.

"So, Nox is getting your homework?" Fred reached and grabbed more plates of sandwiches from a counter. He held a bacon, egg, and cheese in one hand and a Reuben in the other.

"Yeah. Well, she's giving most of it to Tony. He's bringing it over here later." I propped one elbow on the table and leaned on my hand.

"Not her?" Fred's eyebrows lifted as he chewed. "Huh."

"Yeah, I know." I swallowed the last of the Velvet Elvis sandwich. "Does anyone know if she's been off campus except for the night she ran into me on Camp Street?"

"Off-campus? It's rare to see her *on* campus unless there's a class." He polished off both sandwiches, then snagged a roast beef and horse-radish. "At least, that's the way she was last semester. Only went to the Nocturnal Lounge for orientation. She's been there practically every night since it got fixed up."

"I wonder why?" I eyed a plate with mostly tuna, egg, and chicken salad sandwiches. Fred grabbed some when he saw I'd passed them up for a turkey with cranberry on wheat.

"Maybe she's taking a lot of classes this Spring." Fred made quick work of the smooshy sandwiches.

"Maybe." I had a feeling that wasn't all. "But she might be hiding." I told Fred about the apparent napping in the cafeteria. "One thing I can't figure, if she's hiding, why would she be out on Camp Street instead of on campus?"

"Depends on who she's hiding from, don't you think?" Invisible hands shuttled empty plates off the table, replacing them with the rest from the counters. Fred inhaled through his nose, smiling when he caught the aroma of steak bomb grinders.

"Oh. You think it's the Sprite thing?" I passed over the grinders, opting for a veal parm panini instead.

"Yeah. I know for sure they're in hiding." Fred polished off the grinders. "Why wouldn't Nox be, too?"

"I hadn't thought of that. But really, what could either Court do to her?" I chewed thoughtfully, relishing the tender texture of the sandwich. "She's not a Changeling who has to pick a side and tithe."

"The magic that lets her shift comes from the Unseelie Court. The King could conscript her and slap her with a punishment." The rest of the pressed sandwiches vanished before Fred continued. "But he probably won't. Dad says he's been in an amazingly good mood since that enchantment got undone. Thinks it's good press for his side, makes Unseelies look like the rule-benders they are instead of creepy evildoers."

"But that's just him, not, um, her." I raised an eyebrow. If the King was cool with letting Nox's transgression slide, the Queen would definitely think the opposite.

"Right." Fred glanced at the half-full plate on the kitchen island. "And good call not saying that name in here. Dad has alarms. Anyway, she'll claim Nox owes her. Probably something big, too."

"That's lame." I tried to hide my shock at the near extinction of edible items. "The Sprite was serving a Summoner. It's not like she could have used them herself until he kicked the bucket or their contract ran out."

"You'd have to talk to Blaine in order to understand that." Fred shrugged. "He's got a much better idea of how virtually immortal people feel about losing things they expect to keep forever."

"Good point." I set my unfinished half panini down on the empty plate in front of me.

"What did Ed say to you upstairs, anyway?" Fred set his elbows on the table, leaning forward.

"He wants me to be more honest." Ironic how my answer halfway ignored the kid's advice.

"Well that's a good idea for anyone, you think?" Fred smirked. I couldn't remember whether Redcaps were any good at detecting lies.

Even if they weren't, with a Psychic mom, Fred might have a leg-up on hunches and woojy feelings.

"For most." I nodded. "Not always for an Alpha, or someone hiding from people with excellent senses of smell."

"And that's why it's really for the best that you stayed here." Fred stood, reaching across the table to clap me on one shoulder. "Whole house has glamour on it. They won't smell you here. Unseelies don't dare piss my dad off, and the other Court would get fried if they got within fifty feet of the door."

"Yeah. But I'll have to leave at least once to practice with Nox." I sighed, hoping I didn't sound as Emo as I felt. "Not sure where we'll be able to go that's not on campus and safe for her."

"Someone will think of something." Fred stuffed the last ten sandwiches into a lunchbox in his rucksack. "That's the advantage of having a pack, right? When I get to campus, I'll check with one of your crew."

"Is it that late already?" I also stood, instinctively reaching for my bag before remembering I couldn't go to class all week.

"What do you mean, late?" Fred chuckled. "It's early. This was breakfast."

"Don't tell me you have Second Breakfast and Elevensies, too?" I laughed.

"Hey, no Hobbit meals jokes. Those just go places I don't even want to contemplate." Fred slung the rucksack over one shoulder. "I'll be back later tonight. This is where our Fellowship parts ways."

We laughed, and he left me alone with the remains of my tuna melt on pumpernickel.

CHAPTER FOUR

Nox

I shook off my desire to sleep even though I'd need energy for class later. I couldn't let anyone know I had no place to go. Seelies and Changelings likely to tithe that way went to PPC, but the entire campus was neutral ground. That wouldn't prevent them from following me if I left, however. My apartment didn't have an underground tunnel like Henry's. It wasn't warded because I didn't have enough skill to protect more than a broom closet. Most of my studies had been focused on shifting instead of magic. It's one reason I'd taken Magic Theory 101 as a Junior.

In the ladies' room, the mirrors above the sink gave me bad news. I splashed cold water on my face, hoping to reduce the puffiness under my eyes. At least I wasn't high-maintenance with makeup or hair or anything. That had turned out to be a blessing in disguise while hiding out. This limited wardrobe and bare minimum toiletries thing would have been intolerable for someone like Jeannie the Resident

Assistant, or even hair-iron addicted Lynn Frampton. People on campus were used to me looking unkempt, but my weariness was unmistakable now.

I had to find a place to get actual sleep if I wanted to keep my secret and help Josh. I'd checked the Alternative Therapies lab, hoping to find a hospital bed. There was one, but I couldn't risk breaking in. They locked that entire building between classes, and I'd get caught. The dorm basement lounge might still have the air mattress from Henry's stay. I'd just have to find a way to check it out while keeping my homelessness on the down-low.

I headed to the library, remembering how Blaine had mentioned meeting Olivia about an errand. They'd be in there right now. If they had to stop at the dorm before their next class, I could just follow them. A little ice in the lock would hold the main door long enough for me to sneak in later. I walked up the library steps and went inside.

The musty smell of old books and the static crackle of new computers surrounded me. I heard Blaine blathering on about a boat circling the harbor since Christmas, punctuated by Olivia's artificially perky vocalizations of agreement. The owl shifter might be the only person on campus more sleep-deprived than me, but that was her own damn fault. She'd taken meds to go against her natural nocturnal patterns. I wondered why. Extrahuman Law offered courses at all hours. I dismissed the question for the umpteenth time. It was her life and no business of mine unless she decided to share.

Thinking of life got me thinking about Maddie. She was the closest thing to a female friend I had. Lynn was so cerebral, it was hard to talk to her about much besides academics. If she'd been around over the weekend, maybe I could have gotten her help. Umbral magic could hide anyone from most Seelie things unless they watched Maddie casting her spell. But I couldn't expect her to hang around for hours while I slept or chaperon me all over town. I had to keep my big girl pants on and do things for myself. At least, that's what Grandpa kept twisting my internal arm about, anyway.

My nose wrinkled when I stepped up to the table. Instead of just taking the closest seat, the power of Grandpa compelled me to go all the way around the long table to avoid sitting next to Blaine. He had a beef against the dragon shifter for some reason, maybe even a whole entire cow. I slouched in probably the most uncomfortable chair ever made, nodding at Blaine and Olivia. The corners of my mouth twitched. More battle picking. I let Grandpa stop me from smiling.

"Hi, Nox." Olivia blinked a few times, then rubbed her eyes. When she opened them again, they had unusually large pupils, even for a gal who could turn into an owl. One of my other ancestors, a former doctor, inwardly cringed. I hoped she didn't have a stroke or a heart attack.

I nodded, keeping all the concern to myself. Blaine's lips curled, then parted. His smile was like neon in a 1970s roller rink. I couldn't decide whether he liked me or liked baiting Grandpa even more. Since he studied magic artifacts and anthropology, he had to know a little something about the ancestors all Kelpies and Selkies carried around in their pelts.

Blaine couldn't be old enough to have actually met my grandfather, but his mom might have. Rumor painted Mrs. Harcourt as an honest to goodness warrior princess. Her involvement in stamping out the post-Reveal violence all over Rhode Island only reinforced that reputation. Her son, on the other hand, was a genius-variety entitled brat.

"What's wrong, Nox?" Blaine's voice had a little lilt that let me know a sarcasm bomb was incoming. "Feeling a little hoarse?"

My nostrils flared as I tried to lock myself down and somehow stop the tidal-wave of magical anger Grandpa and all the rest of my ancestors unanimously agreed on unleashing. I stared at a knot in the wooden table in front of me. I imagined roots plunged deep in the soil, siphoning water out, leashing that force to use for nourishment and protection. When the ends of my hair started dripping, I clenched my fist, trying to move my arm across my gut so I could disengage the pelt. No luck. I'd given Grandpa an inch, and he'd taken five hundred miles.

"Miss Phillips, be still." I couldn't place the man's voice even though it was familiar.

The air chilled until icicles brushed my shoulders. I didn't dare turn my head or move. The hair on my arms and the back of my neck stood on end as Grandpa tried to force a shift right there in the library. Across from me, Blaine froze but not with the cold. His wide eyes and hoisted eyebrows meant whoever had me literally on ice was an unexpected visitor to the library. The chair beside me creaked slightly before he spoke again.

"There will be no further outbursts of this nature in my library. Are we clear, Mr. Harcourt?"

"Yes, sir." Blaine folded his hands on the table in front of him, then pulled his arms back as he realized he'd put his elbows on it. Whoever had taken the seat next to me was important enough for Blaine to worry about old-money table manners.

Whatever lowered the temperature eased up enough for me to do more than shiver. I scratched my skin beside my navel when I pulled the pelt free, but that was a small price to pay. I clutched it in one hand, waiting until I could stop my hands from shaking before putting it away in its enchanted oilcloth pouch. That had been a close call. You could get expelled for shifting indoors.

"You will apologize to Miss Phillips and then leave with your minion, Mr. Harcourt." The voice was formal but lacked the stern edge it carried earlier.

"Sorry, Nox." The left corner of Blaine's mouth tilted up, an unconscious signal of insincerity.

"You will do better than that." The voice chilled down to absolute zero.

"I apologize, Miss Phillips. It won't happen again." Blaine collected his jacket and backpack, then backed away, bowing slightly at the waist. He glanced nervously at Olivia. "Um, let's go to one of the dorm lounges, Olivia, okay?"

"Oh. Okay." Olivia bolted up from her seat like she'd had seven shots of intravenous espresso. "Hoo boy," she said over her shoulder. They left the library like a flight of arrows.

"Thank you, sir." I turned in my seat, giving the distinguished-looking man next to me a little bow like Blaine had. I wasn't sure who or what he was, but Blaine's best behavior was a good template for formality with the elderly fellow.

"If only the young men on campus acted with half the decorum of the young women, you'd have no need to thank me." His smile made his eyes twinkle like chips of obsidian embedded in terra-cotta clay. "I'm Taki Waban. Headmistress Thurston asked me to care for this library now that it's been rebuilt."

"Well, I think you're doing a wonderful job so far, Mr. Waban." I couldn't find my smile. Something about the new librarian was profoundly unsettling even though he looked like a harmless little man of Indigenous heritage. He carried a weight of ages that didn't match even his apparent fifty-something appearance.

"Do you, really? My talents lie less with tomes and more with confounding trouble though I suppose you could call me a book-worm." Something between a chuckle and a rumble rattled in his throat as though he had bronchitis. "Miss Frampton insists quite adamantly that the stacks are organized like a—" He tilted his head. "How does she put it? Ah yes, like a nerf-herder stampede handled the shelving." His lips tilted up in a trace of a smile.

"She doesn't take well to change." I felt most of the tension leave my no-longer-shivering shoulders. He had master-level control of his magic if he'd frozen my pelt's water and cut it back that fast. But he seemed friendly enough to me.

"Unlike some of her cohorts." He indicated me with a flat hand, palm up. "I'll be blunt. Miss Phillips, your will is stronger than the iron that bans your kind, but even you need to sleep sometime."

"I know, sir." I glanced at the door, realizing there was no one to follow into the dorm. "It's just that, besides the Lounge, I haven't got anywhere to go." My eyes stung, whether from lack of sleep or because, once spoken, the fact finally had the power to wound me.

"I understand your predicament all too well." He nodded. "That's why I always carry some of these. I have some spares. Take them." He held out his other hand, revealing a trio of what looked like lead crystal keys. They flickered blue even in the yellow incandescent light of the library. I recognized them immediately, even without the magic sight of my pelt.

"Church-keys? You really want to give that many of these away?" This kind of church-key didn't open beer bottles. Instead, they turned the space behind ordinary doors into heavily warded panic rooms. I'd have to bring something to sleep on every time, but what Mr. Waban offered were three chances at absolute safety for as long as I needed. I wondered how he'd got so many. They could only be made from ice dragon tears.

"They aren't mine to give." He placed them on the table in front of me. "They're yours, Miss Phillips. I've only been holding on to them for you."

"I don't know how to thank you." I pressed the palms of my hands flat against the table, not even daring to hope this wasn't some kind of weird joke.

"Use one of them today. I'll consider that sufficient thanks." The corners of his eyes crinkled again.

"But sir, what do I owe you? You've held onto them all this time." My gaze dropped down to the glimmering keys on the table. My hope was tarnished around the edges with unexpected guilt.

"Nothing. That price was paid before you were born." His voice lowered, whether from a desire for secrecy or sadness, I'd never know. I couldn't bring myself to look back up at him, meet that jet gaze.

"Oh." My exhausted mind couldn't make sense of his statement, only the fact that I didn't owe him anything. "Well, I'll go and use one, then, like you said. Thanks again, Mr. Waban." I stood, only realizing then that I hadn't even bothered to put down the extra-large bag I'd been lugging around with me. I headed toward the narrow hall leading to the stairwell. Pocketing two of the keys, I pointed the third at the door to a broom closet.

It opened on a bare room, narrow but long and wide enough for me to lie down comfortably with my things. There was even space for me to take off my shoes and jacket. I set the alarm on my phone, surprised that it had three bars in here. I lay on my back, hands laced under my head. After that, I couldn't do anything besides fall asleep.

CHAPTER FIVE

Josh

I was up to my elbows in homework on Wednesday night when Fred showed up with Maddie. They checked over every corner of the room I'd been staying in, making sure there weren't any spy devices like there'd been in the Nocturnal Lounge. Then, Fred pulled down the window shade and closed the curtains. Maddie called up her magic, gathering shadows around the both of us. I'd seen her do it before when she'd hidden herself and Nox outside Professor Brodsky's apartment. Being in the shadows was way different. I wondered why Nox hadn't mentioned how weird it was, seeing everything in muted purple hues. Then again, I'd tried to avoid her.

"Okay, Maddie. Follow me out. I'll get the mail. You just go over to that place Olivia showed you earlier." Fred opened the door and headed into the hall.

Maddie was too smart to answer. Clearly they'd already discussed the plan earlier. I was just along for the ride, so I went with it. That felt natural, unfortunately. How was I supposed to head up two powerful packs in the future if I kept letting myself get dragged along by Magi and Redcaps and bears, oh my?

Maddie walked fast for such a short girl. She beat feet like a champion power-walker, heading all the way down College Hill to North Main Street. On the corner outside RISD, we passed some hipsters. I would have loved to pop out at them, shock them out of their blasé broken-hip hangout poses. Too dangerous. Henry had already pranked the lumbersexuals and the shabby chics this way.

Maddie took a right and headed up the street. A few blocks later, Maddie stopped in front of a dojo. The sign up top was red with little pink flowers and the words Cherry Blossom School. A kanji I assumed to be a translation squatted beside the English lettering. Maddie stood at the door, waiting. I sighed, wishing for a fraction of the patience she seemed to possess. After what seemed like an hour but was probably more like sixty seconds, the door opened.

A stream of kids, mostly in the awkward 'tween age-bracket, trotted out. Their pimply little faces wore smiles for the most part. I almost missed slipping through the door as I watched them hop into waiting cars or shuffle toward their expectant adult counterparts. I made it through thanks to a sharp gust of cold wind slowing the door's trajectory. Once it closed behind us, Maddie relaxed, releasing her shadow magic.

"Less lollygagging on the way home, Josh," Maddie ordered, tapping one small foot on the linoleum. "We wouldn't have made it here on time for the class to let out otherwise. And we need to get you back to Fred's in time for his mom to let the cat out."

"Wait, an actual cat?" I scratched my head. "I haven't seen one the entire time I've been there."

"No, Tony." She smiled. "He'll be heading out after he swaps your homework."

"Oh. Okay, then." I looked around. Trophies lined the shelves in front of whitewashed wood-paneled walls. The wall behind the small reception counter held framed teaching credentials, some Extrahuman. The space was unfamiliar, but the trophies reminded me of something. I hadn't been to this martial arts school before, but Beth's dead beau had run one on the other side of town. I shivered for no good reason. "Where's Nox?"

"I brought her over before I got you. She said to just head on in there." Maddie waved her hand, sitting with her back to the wall between the practice space and waiting room, facing the street entrance. "I've got reading to do while you two spar. Have fun." The coy little smile the Umbral magus gave me was the first sign that strange things were afoot at the Cherry Blossom School.

I stepped through the bisected black and white flag that served as a door. At a glance, it seemed empty. The faint shimmer in one corner told me otherwise. Even if I hadn't seen that, the low, mossy scent of a pond during a thunderstorm gave her away. I headed straight for the corner with the shimmer, lunging at the approximate height of Nox's waist.

I got an arm full of nothing and a face-full of wall when she swept my leg. Blood dripped from my nose, landing on a gray scarf I'd last seen draped around Nox's neck. I sold more pain than her unexpected attack actually caused, trying to fake her out. Fail city. She caught me by the upper arm as I staggered away from her. I found myself looking at the drop-ceiling just a moment later.

I kipped up, ducking out of the way of the left hook she'd aimed at my already healed nose. Nox or one of her ancestors must have fought wolf shifters before. Going for the nose gave any opponent with glamour or cloaking an advantage since we relied on scent for accuracy. I kept my chin tucked, darting past her almost all the way back to the flag-draped door. She outpaced me. I should have expected a faerie horse shifter to be speedier than Gonzales.

I spun on my heel, aiming an uppercut at her chin. It connected, throwing her off balance. Her wobbly attempt at steadying herself gave me time to get behind her and grapple her under her arms. I thought I had her, but the wet, mossy scent intensified and her skin got all slippery. How she perspired that much in a chilly dojo was beyond me until I realized it was water magic. I tried to hold on, wrapping my hands in the damp fabric of her shirt.

We staggered halfway across the room together in what could have been some kind of post-modern interpretive dance-fight. I pushed against her back as hard as I could, trying to get her on the ground. Thoughts that had nothing at all to do with sparring flashed through my head, a completely inappropriate set of carnal images transmitted by my wolf. I banished them from my mind, but couldn't do a damn thing about my body. It seemed to distract her, at least. Nox's knees buckled, making me think I'd won. But then, the sound of tearing fabric told me I got served.

I ended up on my back again but didn't dare kip up this time. My hands were in the indecipherable tangle of the tattered remains of Nox's tank top. She had the whole mess pinned to the floor above my head. Her thigh was in an extremely inconvenient location, too. It felt like my face caught fire when I glanced down to see flashes of pale skin through the black lace of her bra. A chuckle halfway between a whicker and running water sounded in my left ear, and a low, velvety growl joined it. My wolf wasn't nearly as embarrassed with this round's outcome as I'd been.

"Someone likes a good match." Nox let go of my hands, smiling down at me. She licked her lips then shook her head, sending drops of water out in a nimbus.

"More than one someone." I brought my hands down, glad to have the torn shirt to deal with so I didn't have to get up right away. Not that I had any illusions that Nox hadn't noticed the state I was in.

"Wow. You borrowed that ego from Blaine?" Nox stood, turning her back to me as she headed over to a huge rucksack I hadn't noticed by the scarf. She got out a white tank and pulled it over her head. Shouldn't have bothered. It got soaked through in moments. The bra was even more distracting now.

"What?" I sat up, still failing miserably in my effort not to ogle her. "Ego?"

"You just go ahead and—" Nox let out a low grunt of effort. "Of course. You meant you and your wolf. And there I went, about to accuse you of assuming something." She turned around again, her face relaxed except for one line between her eyebrows. "Sorry for the outburst, Josh. Not for wiping the floor with you. That was fun."

"Fun?" I untangled my hands, then used them to spike up my hair. "That's all I am to you?" I winked to cover for my inside voice getting out. Maybe she'd think it was a joke.

"Maybe." She put her hands on her hips. "Want to go again?"

"No Glamour this time." I could have asked instead of ordered, but dammit, I was her Alpha, even though our pack was strictly of the rinky-dink variety.

"Why not?" She raised an eyebrow, pursing her lips. They glistened like the rest of her. I wasn't sure I'd be able to find another woman attractive again after that. Nox Phillips was ruining me just by standing there, waiting for an answer.

"No one in the class I'm practicing for can do that." I had to clear my throat, grateful my voice hadn't actually cracked like a lame teenager.

"Hmm." She put her hands together, lacing her fingers and cracking her knuckles. "Okay. We'll do it your way this time."

I just nodded. Either Nox didn't care that my family had to stay impartial, or she was using banter as a distraction. There was no way she didn't know nothing should happen between us. A couple of months ago, I'd have just assumed she just wanted to jump my bones. After the whole business over Winter Break, I'd never think something like that about Nox Phillips. She was a fighter, not a lover. She shut down unwanted flirting more handily than she'd just trounced me.

We circled the middle of the room, facing each other, stances combat-ready. I watched her eyes like every fight coach worth his salt had told me. Nox did no such thing. She stared just above the space between my eyes. It was unfamiliar, unsettling too. She'd already bested me once that night. I shouldn't let it happen again but had no idea what she was up to.

It felt like stalemate city the way we both held our ground. My patience ran out, the wolf inside making the biggest racket in the universe as it urged me to go ahead and grab her. I clenched my jaw, held my wolf by the throat, pushed it down. Raw ferocity would do nothing for me here even if my wolf had something on its mind besides fighting.

Nox leaped forward, full center. No faking one way or the other for her. Her arm came up at the last second, clunking me in the chin. If my jaw hadn't been clenched, I might have bitten the tip of my tongue. The blow knocked me back, but not over. I noticed she'd lifted her chin, so I went for her throat with my hands. My wolf, riled up at being held down all that time, had other ideas.

I ran her to the wall, one hand on her neck and the other clamped on her shoulder. Nox gasped as my mouth met her throat, teeth grazing her flesh. Despite her flirtatious talk earlier, she reacted to it like a threat instead of a come-on. Definitely a fighter. I wasn't entirely sure which I'd meant myself and she gave me no time to figure it out.

Nox used magic again, making me kick myself for not banning that, too. My mouth filled with water so cold it could have come off a glacier. I had to let go and spit it out or risk it going up my nose and cutting off my air. She managed to get her hands around my wrists, pushing against me as she tried to break my grasp. Then, the lights purpled and went out.

A rustle of fabric and an icy breeze told me someone had come through the front entrance. The lights came on again along with the sound of one footstep and a puzzlingly familiar dragging sound. Nox and I broke it up, both turning toward the flag covering the doorway.

"Oh—" Maddie sounded like someone who'd just seen an injured animal. Her footsteps joined the visitor's. Moments later, the flag parted to reveal who'd interrupted our practice.

"Beth!" I rushed forward to help my sister as she hobbled forward on her remaining leg and a rickety wooden crutch.

"Josh." She sighed like the last autumn leaf dropping to the ground. Her knee buckled. "Never thought I'd find you. 'Specially not here."

"How did you get away?" I let her lean on me, led her back through the curtain to settle her on a chair next to Maddie.

"I didn't. They let me go." She tried to prop the crutch against the wall, but it slid sideways. Beth looked like she was near tears until Nox caught and righted it. "Thanks."

"Wait. Without your prosthetic?" I knelt on the floor in front of my formerly reclusive sister. "Who do I have to kill?"

"Uncle Jake." She leaned her elbows on her thighs, resting her head on her hands. That's how she used to sit in the tree fort back when we were kids. My heart nearly split open with rage.

"Son of a bitch." I made a fist, about to ventilate the wall with it. Nox stopped it with a palm. Something crunched, pain flashing in my knuckles, but it'd heal in a minute. "I should have known." Jake was Mom's brother. He'd always been pissed that she hadn't given him her pack once she married Dad.

"Yes, you should have." Beth peered up at me through damp eyelashes, a muscle in her jaw twitching. My sister always got teary when she was angry. But why'd she direct it at me?

"So this is somehow my fault?" I paced toward the desk, then back again.

"Not completely." Beth shook her head. "But it's your responsibility. You're the heir."

"Funny how that goes, isn't it?" I ran a hand through my hair.

"I didn't want this either, you know." She glanced at the spot where her right knee should be.

"Yeah, I know." The accident hadn't been her fault, or Ren's. Drunk drivers suck. Missing older brothers suck, too.

"It's weird being here." Beth shook her head at the wall behind the counter. "Seeing him again."

I followed her gaze. I'd been so focused on meeting Nox, I hadn't checked the name on all the credentials, or the small photo far to the right and at the bottom of the display space. Ichiro. Ren's father hadn't shut down the dojo. He'd just renamed and moved it. I looked up at the trophies on the other wall. The three biggest had the name Phillips on them. No wonder I hadn't been able to beat Nox. Small world.

"Yeah, weird." I sighed, trying to focus. "So they let you go. Why?" Since that damned accident, talking to my sister was like pulling teeth sometimes.

"Got a message to give you." Beth reached into her jacket, rummaging in the interior pocket. "Here. I'm not sure what it says."

I broke the seal, trying not to look surprised that it was formally addressed and composed like a letter to the Alpha of a rival pack. Nox read it over my shoulder. I couldn't figure out why Uncle Jake would bother with this level of formality. I hadn't inherited my place at the head of either of my parents' packs yet. I leaned back, feeling the weight of my half of the alliance medallion tap me on the breastbone.

"Oh." My right hand flew to my chest, clutching the metallic object along with the fabric covering it. "They wanted me, not you guys. Tinfoil Hat's more important than I thought."

"You're so dense sometimes." Beth shook her head. "I mean, really? You think they didn't want you as bad as they wanted our folks after you went and made a vampire your Beta?"

"Yeah, well, they didn't get me on the New Moon." I turned the letter around so she could see it. "Sucks to be them."

"That alliance makes you a real Alpha." Nox slapped me on the shoulder. "Good for you. Not so good for me."

"We'll figure something out." I blinked, not daring to even look at Nox. I tried not to notice Beth staring at me like I'd suddenly turned green or something. "My Uncle can try to negotiate a prisoner exchange, but since I'm a real Alpha, I can fight him instead."

"But it's not Uncle Jake and company who want her." Beth pointed to some fine print below the second signature line. "He must owe something big. Do you see who witnessed this?"

"Oh, no." Maddie gulped.

"Yeah, well." Nox snorted. "You piss off the Sidhe Queen enough, she gets involved. When's this happening?"

"Half-moon." Beth looked at Nox, then at me. She sighed. "That's Monday."

"And things will just get more dangerous for me after that. She's more powerful when the moon's on the wax." Nox crossed her arms over her chest. "Maybe I should just agree to stand trial."

"Do you get a lawyer in Faerie trials?" Maddie stood up, stepping next to her friend. She didn't touch Nox, though.

"Yeah, but only for sentencing. Guilt's determined by magic. I definitely did it, nothing will say otherwise. No Faerie will touch this. Probably not any other Extrahuman lawyer, either."

"We'll think of something." Maddie tapped her chin with one finger. "Maybe Olivia...hmm. But she's just a student, not even interning until summer." She scratched her head.

"You need to think of nothing as far as legal issues go." I jumped up at the unexpected voice. Beth covered her mouth. Maddie turned. Nox's shoulders straightened. "I will represent you."

"Ichiro-San." She bowed at the waist. "Thank you."

"Thank me when your trial is complete." The middle-aged man who'd walked through a hidden door behind the counter peered at each of us in turn. "I'm more than qualified to plead your case. And as you know, I've got an extra advantage. Luck will be on your side." He winked at Nox, and she smiled nearly as widely as she had the night she'd found me wandering the streets in my pajamas.

"What's he mean?" Maddie blinked, then squinted at Mr. Ichiro. I already knew, of course. So did Beth. I kept my mouth shut to let Nox tell her friend the awesome news.

"Ichiro-san isn't just the owner of Cherry Blossom School or a lawyer. He's a Tanuki."

CHAPTER SIX

Nox

Grandpa's happiness at Ichiro-san's offer had me so pumped up I barely noticed Beth put her head in her hands. A keening so high pitched it was almost inaudible came from between her palms. I tried to batter down the solid wall of gloating that came from him and the rest of my ancestors but barely made a dent.

Ichiro-san went straight to Beth just as I finally realized why Josh's last name had seemed so familiar when we'd met. It had been in the obituary my last year of High School. Ren Ichiro, survived by his father, sister, and fiancée Beth Dennison. I glanced away from the stump of her leg, thankful my grandfather had seen worse and didn't want to stare. She'd lost her mate and her leg. No wonder Josh had to be Alpha. Losing Ren was probably worse for her than losing the limb. Wolf shifters got unstable and volatile without a mate, sometimes needing to be locked up by their packs. Beth might be able to find another fellow. Coincidence wasn't so cruel as to only have one potential mate in the world for each person. But she didn't seem like she wanted to look even after three years.

Josh was by the counter, checking out the hidden door. I knew about it but had never actually seen it. His fists clenched, posture stiffening. I watched the back of his neck redden as I approached him. Grandpa wouldn't be happy if I did anything to comfort him physically, so I just walked near enough to brush his shoulder with mine.

"Did you know he could see us that whole time, Nox?" Josh jerked his chin at a bank of glass inside the narrow room. One-way mirror, of course.

"No. Is the fact that he did going to be a problem?" I felt my cheeks heat up as I realized my late sensei's dad had seen me shirtless and using a sparring match as a crude form of flirtation.

"Luna's Light." He let out his remaining breath slowly. "I shouldn't let it be. Yeah, that'd be for the best. Not a problem."

"I'm glad." I took a step away, but Josh caught me by the arm. "But I didn't mean—"

"Listen." His whisper carried a hint of a growl. "I don't know what your deal is, but I'm letting the fact that he saw you beat me slide for my sister. You will tell me what this is all about later. Understand?"

"Perfectly." I turned my head, not having to tilt it down to look him in the eye. His usually honey-brown eyes brightened to a yellow-amber color. I put one hand over my stomach, gasping as I pulled my pelt free. "I'll explain. I couldn't with this thing on and now is definitely not the time."

"When, then?" Josh's eyebrows slanted frown-ward as his eyes narrowed. "Seems like there'll be none with classes and trials."

"I don't know." I shrugged, my fist tightening on the slippery pelt. "If it's important to you, then make time."

"Swan Point. Memorial Grove." The reason for his choice stung my eyes with threatening tears. Ren Ichiro's body had never been found, and Josh's brother was also presumed dead. The Grove was a place to mourn those who'd never come home. Like my father.

"The Megalith?" I wanted to shut my eyes, but couldn't. The giant stone had been brought over from South County back before the Big

Reveal. I'd been there every year since Dad died, but he still hadn't moved on.

"Yeah. Midnight work for you?" Josh's eyebrows went back to their usual level.

"I'll make it." I nodded. This time, when I pulled away, he let me go. It'd take a covert effort to get over there, but our entire situation had gotten loads more complicated. Refusing to talk about what might be between us would be the height of idiocy.

I heard Ichiro-San call a cab for Beth. I sighed, worried I'd be on my own on the way back to campus. The old Tanuki would want to get Beth somewhere safe immediately. His ability to choose the luckiest route wouldn't be available to me, and Maddie would need to bring Josh back to Fred's. But she surprised me by linking her arm through mine.

"Mr. Ichiro will bring Josh with him. It's okay. They can't nab him now that it's not the New Moon, anyway." She glanced at Beth, who nodded.

"Yeah, they said he's off-limits. Made it abundantly clear they think that's only temporary." She looked so tired, I wanted to give her a hug. Almost. Beth's inability to get over losing Ren only made things more difficult for Josh. I softened. It wasn't right to judge her about losing her mate when I didn't even know what it was like to have one .

I took a deep breath, watching Mr. Ichiro help Beth from her seat to the door, Josh following closely. Maddie had already drawn her shadows around us, so we followed them out. As my head cleared, I wondered why Josh's troubles were such a big deal to me, anyway.

"You're super protective of him suddenly, huh?" Maddie glanced at me as we walked arm-in-arm up the street.

"Um." My teeth squeaked as I clenched my jaw. "Him who?"

"Oh, come on, Nox." Maddie shook her head, making her curls bounce. I couldn't get mad at her. She was just being a friend.

"Yeah, Maddie. Fine." I rolled my eyes. "Josh is driving me batty. I can't make any sense of how he acts around me, mostly because I can barely think straight around him. I don't know if I want to kick him or kiss him half the time."

"Well, I think he likes you." She grinned. "Maybe you two should give things a shot."

"At least you getting together with Henry didn't start a war." I sighed. Maddie's dad was a vampire, and her mom had had a license to get turned. They were happy for her as long as she finished school before applying for a license of her own.

"You really think that's where this is headed?" She patted my arm with one brown hand. "War between who?"

"If the trial was just his uncle trying to take over, then maybe not." We walked another half a block up the hill before I spoke again. "But it looks like Josh and I screwed something up when we helped you guys over winter break. His uncle might just be trying to fix things. The way Beth talked about the Queen getting involved almost seems like she had a hand in their pack politics. Or maybe someone else did."

"But why?" Maddie's curls bounced as she shook her head. "If the Queen has a problem with you, why would she involve the Dennisons?"

"Maybe she wants to work through someone else at this time of year. And maybe she didn't, like I said. She might just have seen the pack problem and decide to use it to her advantage." I listened to her boots and my sneakers tap and squeak against the damp pavement. "If she lets Unseelies get away with stuff like what I did, the Seelies will lose power. She can't afford that."

"Sounds like a big mess." Maddie stopped, tugging on my arm. We'd gotten to Thayer Street. "Want me to have the Tinfoil Hat brainiac society look at it?"

"They can try." I tugged back, urging her to keep on walking with me. "There's not going to be much for them to go on until we know what she's aiming to sentence me with."

"Make me a list of possibilities. I'll get Lynn and Blaine in on it with me." She chuckled. "Lynn says they read at warp factor nine."

I actually laughed but remembered to keep it quiet enough not to break out of the shadow magic she'd hidden us with. We turned down toward the Thayer Trolley Tunnel, where I did the special knock to open the secret door. Maddie said goodbye at the bottom of the stairs to go finish her homework. Once through the doorway, I was on campus and safe. The Nocturnal Lounge was emptier than usual. Checking a flier on the wall by the coffee and snack station told me why. Night Creatures were playing down at The Living Room. The usual crowd here would all be over there supporting them. I sighed, sinking into one of the new-to-PPC cushy chairs, relishing some alone time. Maybe I could even take a short snooze.

The clunk and tap of worn boot-heels told me I wasn't completely alone. I sat up, turning most of the way around in my seat to find Bianca the Psychic Medium smiling at me. She grabbed a cup of tea as she came , the bag tag fluttering in the breeze of her passage like a tiny moth around a flame. Except that when she sat down and set the cup on the end table next to her, the tag just kept on flapping.

"You look atypically mournful tonight." Bianca didn't usually notice the living too much unless the place was empty like now, or they seemed down in the dumps. She twirled some of her pink-tipped blonde hair between her fingers absently.

"Yeah. Got a lot to think about." I rubbed my eyes. "Not enough time as I'd like, either."

Most people would have taken my words as a strong hint to just get lost already, but not Bianca. She didn't have much people sense unless the people in question weren't exactly in this world anymore. It had to be odd, seeing an entire city full of ghosts when no one else could. Weird enough to make her weird, too. Then again, maybe it took an already out-of-touch person to make the kind of contact Mediums could with the Other Side. I decided to let my overtired mind drop the whole idea like the chicken and egg argument it seemed to be. Regardless, Mediums kept ghosts from freaking out. Most people appreciated them, but usually from afar to avoid the flakiness that went with talking to invisible dead people.

"Well, I'd leave you to it, but if I did, he wouldn't leave me alone." Bianca glanced at the fluttering tea tag. "Horace, that is. Usually, he's a great ghost to have around." Her usually vacantly kind face took on an expression that would have looked more at home on Headmistress

Thurston. "Tonight, he's being an absolute pest because there's something you need to know about your ancestors."

"So what's Horace on about then?" I figured handling this situation with Grandpa's ornery abruptness might be for the best.

"Well, he says your father's been bothering him. Keeps going on about how your grandpa makes you deny everything, whatever that means."

"Wait, what?" I blinked, leaning forward. "No way Dad's here."

"Oh, of course, he's not. He's contracted down at the Reservoir like he's supposed to be. But part of Horace's job is to go around and check on ghostly workers all over the state." Bianca rolled her eyes in the direction of her tea. "And that's how your father gave him an earful. He's so agitated, it's causing problems with the piping at the water treatment plant."

"So, Horace." I set my gaze vaguely at the spot Bianca had looked at. "What's my dad's problem, anyway?"

Bianca smiled. She nodded at the empty space as though listening to something.

"Horace says thanks for talking to him instead of me. He also says your dad's worried you're ruining your chances of finding your mate. Something about listening to your heart instead of your grandfather, whatever that means."

"And how would he know, anyway?" I slapped a hand over my mouth. "Ugh. That was supposed to be my inside voice."

"Why not have a nice cup of peppermint or chamomile tea and then relax?" Bianca's eyebrows made light-brown arcs. "You seem like you're on edge. No wonder your dad's worried about you."

"Bianca, I know you and Horace mean well, but you have no idea." I shook my head. "The last thing I need right now was a scolding from the hereafter that doesn't make any sense."

"Sorry if that message is unclear." Bianca turned, glancing at where the tea bag tag fluttered against the side of the cup even more rapidly. "What's that, Horace?" She made her listening face again, this time with extra forehead crinkle. "Huh."

"What is it now?" I glanced between her and where I thought the ghost was.

"Okay. He wants me to tell you that your dad knows what he's talking about. Your grandpa's going to get you in trouble. Horace says to remember how strong his influence is. You need to make peace with him, or you might lose part of yourself."

"What is Horace anyway, a ghostly Precog?" I raised an eyebrow. Precog ghosts were rare. Since most of them saw their own death coming, they'd usually finish any business before death.

"No. He's a Ghostly Medium, my mentor since I almost died." Bianca sighed. "Look, all I know myself is, your dad must have been upset. There was worry ectoplasm all around Horace when he came back from the reservoir."

"This is pretty confusing for me." I shook my head. "We don't take anything but Psychic Ways 101 in my major."

"Sorry, Nox. We tried to make it simple. The main thing I guess is, your dad wants you to be happy. He's worried you're about to walk into a situation where that won't happen if you don't stand up for yourself. Something about coincidence."

"Gah, not coincidence again." I ran my hands through my hair. "At least that's something I understand, though. Look, Bianca. Thanks for the chat. And thanks, Horace, for the information. I'm just not sure there's much I can do with it."

"Yeah, I kind of figured." Bianca stood up and reached into the hammock-shaped tie-dye bag she always carried. "Have some of these. They're better than tea when things get really rough." She dropped a few foil-wrapped packages on the table next to me. Then, she collected her cup. "Come on, Horace. We've got library ghosts to check in on."

"Thanks." When she turned at the top of the stairs to flap a hand in farewell, I waved back.

The packages were chocolates, so dark milk or cream couldn't have been within miles of the factory that made them. I bit into one, the bittersweet taste reminding me of my meeting and that load of explaining to do. If only any of this made sense.

Grandpa was always a troublemaker. I'd never realized how much until Dad died protesting water privatization and I inherited the pelt that made me a Kelpie. I wasn't sure I'd be able to stand up to Grandpa without Dad's help. But until his ghost moved on, the part of him that belonged to the pelt was stuck in limbo. I wondered whether helping Dad finish his business would help me with the Old Boy's Club I had to handle every time I put my pelt on.

But what was Dad's unfinished business? That's what I should have asked Horace. I grabbed another chocolate, frowning at my failure to think of such an obvious question. As the candy melted slowly in my mouth, I sighed. I shouldn't beat myself up over it. I'd had maybe six hours of sleep in as many days. His unfinished business had to have something to do with me. If I really wanted to know, there was one way I might find out.

I pulled my phone from my rucksack, tapped it out of sleep and swiped away the screen-saver. My finger hovered over the dial button next to the entry marked Mom. I hadn't heard her voice since the middle of summer when she made her annual trip to Block Island. After Dad died and my brother Uri moved out, she'd sold everything and moved to Key West. It was always islands with her. My brother and I had done nothing but disappoint her, neither of us inheriting her Water magic.

She'd never made her feelings secret but didn't use them against either of us like she could have. Mom was a sour woman, but self-aware. She kept her distance instead of unleashing a torrent of abuse like some other people might have. I tapped the yellow text icon instead of the green call one.

Dad have any unfinished business I should know about? I set the phone next to the last piece of chocolate and got up to fix some coffee instead of the tea Bianca suggested. It looked like I wasn't going to get that nap after all, so it was caffeine jitters time for me. I tapped one foot, stirring cream in the coffee. I didn't understand how Maddie could put so much sugar in hers. Light and bitter was my constant coffee order. After one sip, I sat back in the chair to wait. Less than a minute later, I got my mother's blunt reply.

You. He always wanted to see you happy. Find your mate, and he'll move on. I waited to reply, absolutely sure I didn't want to play one of her blame games while sleep-deprived.

Thanks, Mom. It was the only safe reply. Still, she wasn't about to leave it at that.

Find and accept. Why ask this now? I glared at the words. It'd take too long to tell, and the last thing I wanted was Mom involving herself in this. She'd help, but do it while looking down her nose the entire time. If I didn't answer, she'd call. I wasn't sure I could handle that in crisis mode.

Busybody Psychic. It felt wrong to throw Bianca under the bus like that, especially after she'd given me chocolate. I could apologize to her some other time. There was no question it'd get back to her. The skeleton crew loved her, and any of them could read my texts.

Is there a boy? Even though I'd turn twenty-one in the summer, Mom still talked to me about boys instead of men.

Maybe.

Complicated?

A little bit.

You'll handle it, you're a big girl. Night, Nox.

I sent back a similar sentiment, glad the conversation was over. I closed out of the messaging screen, revealing the time. Was it really eleven already? I'd have to head out now to make it to Swan Point in time. I pulled the oilcloth bag from my pack, glad I could shift with it. Only magical shifters could take something with them. I chose the woolen blanket in my rucksack, tying it around me in what I hoped was a modest enough fashion. I undressed under it, thankful I had water magic to warm me the whole way. Shoes were out of the question, and I had a long tunnel to traverse before I could shift.

I pressed the pelt against my bare stomach until it melded with the skin there, then tucked the pouch between two of the knots holding my improvised dress together. Why we couldn't have met on campus had me baffled until I stowed my things in one of the lockers under the emergency sun blankets.

I stared at the Campus Police logo. Who'd been running the

department since Josh's dad had been detained? He must want to keep the details of our conversation out of their ears. I engaged the combination lock, then headed through the underground door, raising a bubble of glamour around myself as I stepped through. Unseelies would be able to see through it, but only a traitor would report me to the Seelies. I let muscle memory and instinct lead me toward fresh water. Then, I settled in for what I hoped would be a productive internal conversation. I sighed, remembering that quote of Albus Dumbledore's. "Of course it is happening inside your head, Harry, but why on earth should that mean that it is not real?"

Grandpa, what's your problem? He piped up right away.

You know. I expected a boy. Phillips Kelpies are always boys. You make all this more difficult than it should be. I got an impression of shaggy salt-white hair atop a grizzled face, an untidy contrast to the photographs that always showed him clean-shaven. I realized he mustn't have had time to clean himself up before he died.

So blame Uri for getting Earth magic. I am what I am. Are you sure you're not the one making this difficult? I can't change, and it's either me or get locked up in a vault or a hoard.

We might as well have been stored for the next generation. Everyone behind me thinks you won't be brave enough to do what has to be done. Images of tall men dying in combat flickered through my mind.

Times are different now. We're not secret anymore. And how dare you imply I'm not brave? I projected my own image of the morning I removed the Sidhe Queen's magic from a poor, tormented creature.

You're admirably defiant, we'll give you that. But we're not convinced you're capable of sacrifice. Your rebellious streak is part of the problem. All you do is fight us when we're the ones who really know what being a Kelpie is all about. This time, he showed me placid lake shorelines, pristine riversides, ponds kept safe from the ravages of the modern age.

You're angry that I'm not Greenpeace Eco-Warrior enough? That's your big issue? I shook my head.

The King gave us our magic so we could protect these places, not so we could anger his Queen. They were in love then, remember? You need to start applying yourself to those ends. Make amends to her. His face in my mind's eye suddenly looked more tired than I felt. *And get rid of the idea I'm so hidebound that I can't understand modern sacrifice will look different from what it was in my day.*

Okay, Grandpa. Can we stop fighting each other so much of the time now? I sighed, startling myself as the sound echoed against water at the end of the tunnel. I'd come to the place where I could shift.

One more thing, and we'll try to settle down. Your mate.

I don't have one yet, remember? I stepped to the water's edge, letting my toes touch the rime of ice where it met the pavement.

Resolve that as soon as you can. This time, the voice coming through my mind was smoother and heavily accented with nasal vowels. *Time is short. We need your father here.* The impression of this ancestor's face was bleary with time, but still recognizable as my great-great-great-grandfather. He'd been born a Precognitive psychic.

Working on that. I visualized Josh. *Stop fighting me on it.* The sounds of eleven different laughs mingled in my mind's ear, finally resolving into words spoken in near-perfect unison.

Silly girl. We weren't fighting you. We've been testing him. The voices of my ancestors mingled and faded as my arms and legs elongated. My neck thickened and lengthened. The wool blanket became a piebald marking across my back. I stepped into the water, ducking under as I swam out of the tunnel and upstream toward Swan Point Cemetery.

CHAPTER SEVEN

Josh

Most of the way to the Ichiro house on Angell Street, Beth stared out the window. I didn't blame her. The grubbiness of her face, hair, and clothes plus her missing prosthetic equaled neglect wherever she'd been kept. Having to track me on one rickety crutch all the way to her dead mate's dojo must have made it even worse. And now, she'd have to spend the rest of the time until Monday at his father's house. This sucked more for her than it did for me.

I watched her for a while, hoping maybe all these straws would break the back of my sister's depression camel. No such luck, even while riding in a cab next to a Tanuki. They were luck-masters. People had been shocked when Ren Ichiro vanished into Narragansett Bay, never to be seen again. I hadn't. I'd watched their courtship. Ren hadn't inherited his dad's powers. He'd just had a general magic affinity, able to sense and activate devices like a psychic could. Still, people thought he should have lived. He'd been popular in the community, way more so than Beth. The public reactions to his death had been almost as bad for her as losing him. Some people even blamed her.

The old lawyer caught me looking. He gave me a wan smile, shaking his head slightly. I swallowed my sigh. I couldn't help Beth. All I could do was wish her well and hope she helped herself one of these days.

Mr. Ichiro had painted the house white since the last time I'd been there. The shutters were still the same light gray they'd been when the siding was red. But now, the entire place looked like bleached bone under the orange glare of an old sodium lamp that still hadn't been replaced with LEDs. Hairs on the back of my neck stood up as we got out of the car. Something wasn't right at the house.

Mr. Ichiro made me and Beth wait on the sidewalk as the cab pulled away. The way he left us made me think I should be on guard though nothing smelled out of the ordinary for a Tanuki's house. He pushed the door open without taking his house keys out or even touching the latch. It had been unlocked and ajar already, then.

My nostrils flared, letting me scent the air he stirred as he crossed the threshold. Someone else was in there with him, another Tanuki, female, if my nose hadn't been too busted up by Nox earlier. A muffled squeal became a hissing rush of whispers. Beth cocked her head, finally interested in what was going on. Good thing, too. Her hearing always was better than mine.

"Help me up those steps." Beth leaned on the wobbling crutch, and I took her free arm. We went as fast as we could, which meant a regular human pace. In the doorway, the crutch snapped in half. Beth tossed the pieces aside, gripping the door jamb instead.

My sister hopped on one foot through the near pitch-black hallway. I followed along, trailing her by scent through a door at the end. Beth stumbled headfirst into the brightly lit white-tiled kitchen. She caught herself on a long island in the middle, bellying up like it was a bar instead of her dead fiancé's family gathering place.

"Kim!" I stepped around Beth to see who she was greeting. "Why didn't you tell me she'd come back to town, Mr. Ichiro?"

"I didn't know she was here until just a minute ago." Mr. Ichiro's mouth was a thin, straight line. His eyes gleamed, but not with any kind of positive emotion. I felt like we'd walked into a shark tank instead of a homey kitchen.

"Nice to see you again, Beth." Kimiko Ichiro gave her a lopsided grin, then brushed right past my sister. "This is Josh? Why didn't anyone ever introduce us?" She flipped a lock of platinum-tipped brown hair over one shoulder.

Before I could even flinch, her hands slid under my jacket. I stepped back so fast she got caught by surprise. I tapped my foot, glaring down at her hands. Then, I snatched my wallet and phone away from her, stuffing them back in my pockets.

"That's why." I snarled.

"She was just having a little fun, Josh." Beth rolled her eyes. "It's what young Tanuki do. Chill out."

"I'll chill out when she apologizes for lifting an Alpha's wallet."

"Oops." Kim's mouth made a little round 'o' as she gasped. I did not know whether she was kidding. "Had no idea you leveled up. Sorry."

"It won't happen again." Mr. Ichiro locked gazes with his daughter. She looked away first. "Now, Kimi. You'll tell me why you broke into the house instead of calling your old father."

"That's sort of personal." Kimiko looked everywhere except at her father. "You know, the kind of private matter a girl wants to keep between herself and her dad. It's not something a nice girl should discuss in front of a shiny new Alpha."

"Kimiko." He stepped closer to her. "Did you get kicked out of the Academy again?"

"I wouldn't say kicked out, exactly." She shrugged, then flipped her hair. "It's just that I came to the understanding with the help of a new friend. I had more important things to do than sit in the same class-room every day doing drills just like everyone else." The set of her chin hadn't changed, but the corners of her eyes looked slightly misty. "Also, I can't stand being stuck there while you're here all alone."

"Kimi." Mr. Ichiro sighed, shaking his head. "You're at the Academy because you need the discipline."

"And I can't learn that at the dojo, why?" She glanced at me, then at Beth. "See? This isn't the time or place. We're being the worst hosts in the known universe."

Beth's lean had morphed into a slump. She scratched the patch of hair behind her left ear, a clear tell she was exhausted. The juggernaut of a yawn that burst through her lips made that unquestionable. I shook my head, pissed off at myself all over again at letting her get locked up for days in a place where they hadn't even given her water to wash with.

"Kimiko, help Beth to the back parlor. Then, go upstairs and get her fresh linens and some of your clothes."

"I can't give her a Cherry Blossom gi instead?" Kim couldn't withstand her father's severe glare. "Fine. I have some pajamas she can wear tonight." Her sullen pout morphed into a smile, as shiny and brittle as gilt leaf. "But tomorrow, I'm taking you shopping."

"As long as I can get the apparatus replaced, that sounds awesome." Beth flapped a hand at her stump, then put her arm over Kimiko's shoulders, unfazed by the attempted robbery of her brother and the Tanuki's fickle attitude. All I could do was watch them go, listening to the sound of three legs walking across the hall outside the kitchen.

"I apologize for my daughter's behavior." I turned back to Mr. Ichiro. All the stern tension in his face had melted away, leaving an emptiness I had a hard time looking at.

"It's okay." I shrugged. "She apologized. Girls will be girls."

"She wasn't like this before her brother vanished." He sat at the small table next to a bay window. "But then, you know how that sort of thing can change a person."

"Kind of. I was younger than her when Derek went missing." I took the seat across from him. Somehow, he looked smaller and older than back at the dojo. It made me feel like an even bigger jerk for what I was about to say to him. "Life gets harder. More pressure from the family. No longer a spare, but a full-on heir."

"She was always my heir, young one." His eyes flashed, and he held his head up higher. "Ren was born nearly mundane, just a touch of ability. He took after their mother, you know."

"Interesting how that goes." I leaned my head on my hand. "The boys take after Mom and the girls after Dad."

"You're just repeating words you've heard parents say." His shoulders rolled back out of their slouch. "They'll have new meaning for you someday, with luck. Your mother and father must be in such a state, their son and daughter in this on their own."

"At least we've got each other now." I bowed my head slightly. "And some experienced help."

"I won't be able to do much more than offer Beth a place to stay, I'm afraid." He put his hands flat on the table. "Since I'm representing Miss Phillips once you surrender her to the Sidhe Queen, any assistance I might give you would be a conflict of interest. Yet another thing you have yet to understand fully."

"Surrender Nox? Never. What kind of Alpha would I be if I did something like that?" I tried to swallow my anger but knew its rising was as obvious as the dawn to someone like Mr. Ichiro.

"The just kind." He looked away. "But I suppose you could refuse the Queen, at that. Admit to witnessing Nox's crime, but refuse to make the trade."

"What's the point of that?" I raised an eyebrow. "That'd just make it look like I sided with the Unseelies."

"You mean, you haven't?" It was Mr. Ichiro's turn to raise an eyebrow. "Everybody knows what happened—that she stole a Seelie artifact and undid the Queen's enchantment. Besides, if you surrender Miss Phillips, it might look like you've sided with the Seelies this time. You'll get a reputation for unreliability."

"So this is one of those frying pan and fire situations." I sighed.

"It doesn't have to be. It's not the fact of your refusal that matters, but how prettily you do it." The corners of his mouth turned up slightly as though this was the kind of problem he liked contemplating. I wished I could just let him have it. "If your reason for refusing is to further distance yourself from any perception of bias, for example, your reputation will seem more straightforward."

"See, this kind of thing is why my folks were so happy about Beth and Ren getting official." I shook my head, glad to at least have the old

Tanuki's advice. "The two of them could have handled this way better than me."

"Perhaps. However, you're the one responsible for handling it now. I believe you and Miss Phillips will figure out what to do together, just as Beth and Ren may have."

"Wait. What makes you think I'll—" I sighed, shaking my head. "Of course. You saw that whole match."

"I did." His grin was wan but unmistakable. "She's been my student since her family realized she'd need discipline in order to carry on their legacy."

"But that can't happen if the Queen just takes it from her."

"It also can't happen if she doesn't find her mate. Kelpies aren't so different from wolves or Tanuki. We all need companionship, and at least one from each generation must settle down to continue the family line."

"And Nox's brother's an earth magus, so he can't." I shook my head, marveling at how magic could have made a mistake like that. But then again, maybe it hadn't. Coincidence was weirder than those three witchy sisters who harassed Macbeth.

"Yes. Nox's responsibility is double, like Kimiko's. Don't make it harder for both of you by denying even the most unconventional of possibilities."

"But inappropriate relationships are, um, inappropriate." I winced inwardly, hoping it didn't show on my face. "And for wolf shifters, forbidden."

"Perhaps they're not impossible. Coincidence may still have a role to play in all this, but you'll never discover its influence if you avoid the issue." Mr. Ichiro stood. "And now, I must ask you to leave. Please don't stop by again. If you'd like to visit with Beth, send word, and we'll help her meet you elsewhere."

"Thanks, Mr. Ichiro." The last thing I wanted was to leave Beth alone with an old man and a pick-pocketing delinquent, but since my parents had given their blessing when Ren asked for it, I had to be content trusting his family with her safety.

I headed out of the gray house on Angell Street and turned on my heel to make my way toward Swan Point. At least Nox wasn't the only one with explaining to do.

CHAPTER EIGHT

Nox

The air was cold as I set my left fore-hoof on the bank of the Seekonk River. I tossed my head, flinging water off the long slope of my face and through the air behind me. There was a battered-looking boat in the water, but it was almost on the opposite shore in Pawtucket. Glancing around told me I was alone except for a rabbit and a Gnome. The little bunny took off like it was turbo-charged. The Gnome smiled. Their teeth were all made of metal. They sat on top of a toad-stool, holding a pipe and snapping their fingers to light it. I didn't have a thing to worry about from them. Gnomes were the smallest Unseelie creatures, like ants to the Sidhe Queen. She'd sooner squash one than listen to a word they might say.

I trotted through denuded underbrush, a few twigs and burrs brushing against my sides. I loved Water magic, but being able to shift into horse form and run free under the moonlight was even more amazing. This wasn't the night for that as much as I might need it. I'd have to explain myself and then go. Lingering would be too danger-ous, especially now that I'd seen another Faerie in the area.

Once at the edge of Memorial Grove, I stopped. Shrinking back down to my bipedal shape was like getting out of a roller-coaster car at the end of the ride. Still, I got no protest from the ancestors in my pelt until I moved to disengage it. Echoes of scolds ranging from decades to centuries old rang through my head like the din of rival church bells. At least they all agreed on something—that I shouldn't be out and about without the extra strength and magic the pelt granted its owner. That was what I was, even though I felt like they owned me instead. Once someone took up a Kelpie pelt, it was theirs until they died or put on a different one. It worked the same way for Selkies, the Seelie seal shifters. I wouldn't want to say that five times fast.

I put the pelt away in its oilcloth pouch, adjusted the blanket's drape, and tucked the pouch in a fold. At least it'd be close at hand if something dangerous showed up. I shuddered, thinking about how PPC's own Professor of Summoning got twisted into attacking students. Blaine said he thought it was the Extramagus. It occurred to me, however, that sometimes people just went bad. They couldn't stand something about their lives and snapped. Could that be Josh's uncle's problem, or was he being influenced, too?

A pale sliver of moon came out from behind the clouds. A keening howl rose from the other side of the enormous rock in the middle of the grove. I didn't step into the light until a twig snapped somewhere in front of me. Nice of Josh to do that instead of sneaking up like he could have. When he walked around the other side of the Megalith, my breath caught in my throat. Barely there moonlight made his hair look almost silver instead of blond. His eyes glittered with the fading gold of his recent shift out of wolf form. He tugged at the hem of his shirt, which told me he'd just put it on. I wasn't much surprised to catch a glimpse of firm, defined muscle after sparring with him at the dojo. All the same, it was a nice finish to what had already been a gorgeous view.

"Nice, um—" Josh's eyes moved up, down, and all around. "I've never seen someone wear anything like that before. Is it a dress?"

"Nope," I grinned. My face felt like I'd been standing next to a fire instead of in a wintry breeze. "Blanket."

"There's no way anyone but you could make a blanket look that good." His teeth flashed white in the darkness. Had I been staring at his mouth?

"Thought you'd make some kind of horse joke or something." I barely managed a shrug.

"There's absolutely nothing going on here that's got me in a joking mood." He took a step closer.

"Oh." I found myself unable to move. Well, that's a lie. I trembled a little. Lame, I know, but that's what happens when you stand outside without your Water magic in the middle of February wearing a blanket and no shoes.

"So, you said you have some explaining to do." He tilted his head, peering down at me.

"I know. It's just not the easiest thing to say." It also wasn't easy standing there with this incredibly gorgeous man who pushed me away with one hand and dropped compliments like breadcrumbs from the other. "Listen, I don't like talking around things. I'm going to take a deep breath and just dive into this. This is the kind of stuff I can't unsay and you can't unhear. You still game?"

"Perfectly." He gazed into my eyes. I almost blinked when he used the same word I'd said back at the dojo before agreeing to this meeting. A dig, or coincidence?

"Look, I think you're my mate." I took a breath, ready to just voice all my reasons without thinking about them.

"Been thinking the same. There's one way to see if we're right." Josh put an end to any more talk on the subject.

He pressed closer against me than he'd done during the match, nearly knocking the wind out of me. Then, he touched his lips to mine. I put my arms under his, crossing them under his shirt and over his back. He turned, putting me between himself and the Megalith. His hands were everywhere at first, then they joined forces to try to untie the knot holding my blanket-dress together. He broke our kiss off, leaving me gasping for air. Just as his mouth lowered toward the spot on my neck he'd had me by during our second match, he froze and put one hand to my lips.

"Someone's here." He turned, looking over his shoulder. "Do you smell seaweed?"

I shook my head, not daring to speak. Seaweed this far inland might mean a Selkie, but it could just be a breeze off the harbor. I thought of the Gnome on the toadstool. Could they have been followed, or had a magical device to report that they'd seen me? But that Gnome with the metal teeth wouldn't sell me out. Not when I'd taken their advice about the Sprite business.

"Stay here." Josh whipped off his shirt, then his pants. I tried not to look, but couldn't help it. Fear and desire clashed in my body like fire and ice. I watched him shift, his limbs growing rangier as his run morphed into a lope toward the tree-line. He sniffed the ground, the air, and set off through the trees at full speed.

I heard a howl and a bark, punctuated by a heavy splash and a tiny squeal. Spindly limbs of shrubs in the underbrush shook as Josh returned, something small held in his mouth by the scruff. I recognized it immediately. Even better, I finally remembered where I'd heard of a Gnome with metal teeth before.

"Put them down." I pointed at the little creature. "Maddie and Henry know this Gnome." I did, too, but I wasn't about to tell Josh about that.

Josh dropped them in a heap at my feet, then sat back on his haunches, grinning. His gray fur looked like it was tipped with silver in the low light. I waited for the Gnome to compose themselves, then hunkered down to talk to them.

"Gee Nome." I raised an eyebrow. "Nice to see you, but it's awfully late for you to be out of Henry's apartment."

"I'm here to repay an old favor." They crossed their arms over their chest.

"Okay, well, you're sort of interrupting something important here." I felt my blush reach the roots of my hair.

"It was your wolf who interrupted me." Gee Nome tapped one tiny foot. "You're not the only people who meet here, you know."

"Somehow I doubt you're out on a date." I thought about tapping my own foot in an attempt to look authoritative. Given the blanket dress and the raging blush, I decided not to bother.

"All the same, he interrupted me." The Gnome's voice transitioned from indignation to a squeaky whine. "Can't repay when a wolf chases my debtor away."

"Well, we smelled something like seaweed, and you know how dangerous everything Seelie can be to our kind." I side-eyed the Gnome. They couldn't be too stupid to know that, but they might be drunk. They were lightweights when it came to alcohol.

"Not everything Seelie is Seelie all the time." Gee shifted their weight from one foot to the other, looking like one of those balls that bounce over the words on a karaoke screen. The seaweed smell had to be a Selkie. The Gnome couldn't be talking about anything else.

"That's fine and well, but still it's dangerous." I sighed. "I'll have to get back to campus as fast as I can. It's the only place that's safe."

I felt the displacement of air and rustle of clothing that meant Josh had shifted back. I glanced up at him, disappointed I'd missed the view despite the predicament I was in. I shook my head at the gnome.

"Sorry." Gee raised their hand. I knew they were about to vanish before I could claim a favor.

"Wait. You owe me now, Gee." I pointed at Josh. "Him, too. We're in the biggest bind of our lives, and you interrupted us before we could figure out how to fix it."

"Public place. Not my fault. Already apologized." Gee brought their fingers together.

"No way. She says you owe, you pay." Josh picked Gee up by their hand. "You Vanish us all out of here right away, over to the laundry room in the dorm basement. Then you won't owe me anymore, at least."

"Fine. But only because you're the Gentleman's friend." The moment Josh let go, Gee snapped their fingers.

I hated getting Vanished. It feels like turning to sand and being dumped out by a kid with a broken beach pail. I wondered why Josh was okay with going to campus all of a sudden. Maybe he thought the cemetery was more dangerous than the risk of running into Campus Police. I shook my head, running one hand through my hair as I collected myself. At least it wasn't something I had to do literally.

"And what do I owe the Kelpie?" Gee was fine after vanishing, naturally.

"Tell me who you were meeting with and why." Now I did tap my foot. The coziness of the laundry room had more to do with that than confidence.

"Can't. Prior agreement. You understand." The Gnome smiled. They had me there. They couldn't breach an old contract to fulfill a new one.

"Okay, then." I sighed. "I need a way to get a light sentence in this trial the Queen's got planned."

"Can't do better than a Tanuki lawyer." Gee grinned up at me. Smug little creature probably thought I'd just let them go without paying me if they refused enough times.

"Tell me how Blaine ended up with that sea float." That bit had been bothering me, since a Seelie artifact shouldn't have ended up with a dragon shifter like that, even with Luck magic on it.

"Prior agreement again. I can only tell you half of that story." Gee shook their head.

"I'll settle for that now and the rest when your agreement expires." I gave them one curt nod. It was good enough.

"Okay!" Gee Nome jumped up, giving themselves a high five behind their back. "I Vanished back in time to make sure the whelp got what you'd need to fight that Spite."

"Wait, what?" Josh blinked. He seemed more disoriented from the Vanishing than me but directed his question properly away from the Gnome. "Gnomes can time-travel?"

"Only a little, and it's weird. There's a whole debate about the fourth dimension." I shrugged, then adjusted my now-slipping blanket.

"It's wibbly-wobbly and timey-wimey, isn't it?" Josh gave me a half-grin.

"Oh, yeah. Especially since Gnomes don't use blue boxes and sonic screwdrivers." I snorted a laugh. "Anyway, I bet that's all Gee has to tell us." I looked down at the Gnome.

"Just one more thing you need to know." They gave me their full metallic smile. "You undoing that enchantment was Lucky. Trust it."

"I'd have to trust you first." I rolled my eyes. Gnomes were about as reliable as other pure Faeries, which meant you only trusted them when you had them under a deal. That last bit felt like an add-on, they might be trying to screw us over with. Then again, they were friends with Henry.

"Up to you." Gee shrugged one little shoulder. "That's it. I'll find you at the end of my prior agreement for the rest." They snapped their fingers and vanished with a faint pop.

"So, do we believe them or not?" Josh rubbed his temples.

"I say we do." I nodded.

"Why?" He shook his head, then blinked a few times.

"Because the sea float's a thing Selkies use. And who was Gee meeting tonight?"

"Once I got to the water, I knew for sure it was a Selkie." Josh frowned. "There were tracks and everything, but they got away before I actually saw them."

"Right. So, I bet that's Gee's prior agreement. Has something to do with that float and a Selkie." I ran a hand through my hair.

"But aren't the Seelies and the Unseelies enemies?" He scratched his head.

"Between pure Unseelies and Selkies, not so much. The King's rules are like a sapling; they bend in the breeze. And Selkies only have a duty to protect the oceans. The Queen counts them as part of her power base, but they're not as bound by her rules as other Seelies, especially when they take their pelts off."

"Makes some sense." He stepped closer to me. "We have, um, a conversation to finish."

"Yes." I stood still, aching for him to touch me again, but not sure whether I could handle it.

"Ahem." Jeannie, the bear shifter Resident Assistant, stood in the laundry room doorway, a basket of disheveled laundry tucked against one hip. "Okay, folks. You don't have to go home, but you can't stay here. Go back upstairs and hang out with whoever you're visiting."

"Okay." Josh took my hand. "Come on, Nox. Let's go find our friends."

I followed him out of the laundry room toward the basement stairs, wondering where he was really taking me.

CHAPTER NINE

Josh

I led her by the hand up the stairs to the first floor, then down the hall to the elevator. After that, I pressed the up button without saying anything, clenching my jaw shut. I wasn't sure I could have a verbal conversation with Nox on the subject of mates. I hadn't had this kind of reaction from my wolf since I was thirteen and dreaming about girls every night. It wanted what it wanted, and I'd have to get my brain around that without Nox around or our interaction on the subject would be purely physical. The way she'd stiffened up told me that might not be the best way to settle this after all. It was like part of her wasn't there or something.

I turned my head, glancing over at her. She stared at the stainless steel elevator doors as they parted, her neck and shoulders held with stiff tension as we stepped into the lift in tandem. She needed to talk to someone before acting on this. Fortunately, I knew just who to leave her with. So did she. We reached for the button marked 5 at the same time.

"You thought of Lynn and Maddie, too?" Her voice was low and soft, like water under a deck on a summer day.

"Yeah." I shrugged with one shoulder. "We told Jeannie we'd go back to our hosts."

The elevator dinged, then opened on an empty hall. I didn't know which room the girls lived in, but I could track humans with no problem. Since Lynn was the only one of those in the dorms, picking up her scent was easy. Almost all the way down the rows of doors, we stopped in front of 566. A gloomy-sounding voice crooned over some intense drum and bass beats, which was definitely Maddie music. Nox knocked.

Lynn Frampton opened the door, her fingertips smeared with about seven different colors of highlighter. Her grin turned into a smile, and her raised eyebrow reminded me of Dr. McCoy from Star Trek. She gave Nox a once-over, then ushered her into the room. I stuck my foot in the door before she could close it on me.

"What gives, Frampton?" I put one hand on the door frame. "Let me in."

"Not by the hair on my chinny chin chin." Lynn threw back her head and guffawed. Nox's throaty laugh and Maddie's barely there titter mingled with it. "This clubhouse is girls only right now, big bad wolf. Go find Bobby. He should be down in his room, editing a Shifter Regulations paper."

"Should have known Darth Lynn would tell me to get lost." I pulled my foot back across the threshold. "Later, ladies."

I headed back down the hall, opting for the stairs this time. Lynn might be a regular human, but she had nearly uncanny instincts when it came to gaging shifter behavior. I needed to blow off some steam, or someone might get hurt. I took the first two flights like a normal person, but the third two steps at a time. On the last, I lifted my feet and slid on my hands down the railings. It took nearly all my willpower to keep my wolf from just turning around, breaking into Lynn's room, and kicking her and Maddie out of there to be alone with Nox.

This time, I tracked a dragon. I stopped by the lounge and peeked in. Blaine was in there without Bobby. He had what looked like an overhead projector with sheets of some kind of parchment scattered all around it. I headed down the hall, checking names on tiny stickers next to the doors instead of using my nose. Too many bears on the first floor. I knocked, and when Bobby answered, he pulled the door all the way open. He waved vaguely at the chair in front of his desk, then picked up his phone to let his thumbs do the texting shuffle.

I turned the chair around and sat in it, pushing the door shut with my toe. I didn't want Blaine walking in on this conversation, especially since I suspected my wolf's ferocity might have something to do with potential competition from a dragon shifter for my mate. Bobby put down the phone and looked up at me.

"Henry's on his way over here. I can already tell your wolf's up. I've never seen your eyes go this gold before. Lynn just pinged to tell me you showed up with Nox wearing a blanket. What's going on?"

"She thinks she's my mate." I leaned my arms on the back of the chair. "My wolf is in extreme agreement with that idea."

"That's awesome!" Bobby's eyes lit up the way they always did when something reminded him of Lynn.

"Nope." I watched him blink and shake his head. Then, I explained about how wolf shifters have to stay neutral when it came to the Faerie Courts. Someone knocked politely on the door.

"Wow." Bobby got up, opening the door. Henry just stood there grinning with his hands in his pockets.

"Dude, you have to invite him in." I rolled my eyes.

"Oh. Sorry, Henry. Come on in." Bobby blushed a little, the boy scout. Half the time, he reminded me of Steve Rodgers in the Captain America comics.

"Thanks." My Beta, the vampire, closed the door most of the way, walked in, and sat on the edge of Blaine's bed.

"Sitting in a dragon's nest." I shook my head. "Aren't you a little flammable for that?"

"We have an understanding." Henry smirked. "I'm too useful for him to fry me. Memory Psychics generally are to history buffs. So Bobby says you're having wolf problems?"

"Yeah, well." I shrugged. My shoulders were getting a workout lately in that regard. "It's Nox."

"You know, I kind of figured." Henry grinned with his lips closed. He still worried about freaking us out with his fangs. "What is she, your mate or something?"

"Were you listening in?" My eyes felt like pinballs, the way they kept rolling.

"No way. You have any idea how annoying amping up my hearing is in a dorm? All the stereos and televisions." He wrinkled his nose. "It'd be like trying to hear a needle in a haystack. Look, it was just kind of obvious over intersession. Anyway, is she or not?"

"Still not sure. My wolf thinks so. But it's a problem." I repeated all the stuff I'd told Bobby and then added in what had happened over at the Megalith in Swan Point. "Once she said that it was like my wolf practically took over."

"Woah." Bobby blinked. "Well, that's what happened to my bear with Lynn. Except sleepier. Because of all the snow and that pesky hibernation stuff."

"Looks like Josh has more standing between him and Nox than you guys had, though." Henry rubbed his chin.

"What do you mean?" Bobby leaned forward, glancing from me to Henry. "You guys know the Extramagus was trying to kill Lynn, right?"

"No. I did not know that." I ran a hand through my hair. "Is that why you and Blaine were on about that theory even before the Summoner problem?"

"Yeah." Bobby's eyebrows crinkled. "Hey, do you think the Extramagus might have something to do with this whole thing too?"

"No idea." I tapped my chin with one finger. "The thing is, pack issues happen all the time. And what Nox did, well the Queen's reaction isn't out of the ordinary according to her or Fred." I looked at Henry, who seemed lost in thought. "What do you think, Henry?"

"I was at the bank this morning, you know." He blinked, then looked from Bobby to me. "Found an amulet with a memory about a Selkie pelt gone missing a few years back, right after PPC changed its admissions policy. The Queen accused a Troll family of stealing it, but nothing came from that. We should look that case up. It might just be a legal precedent, but it could have coincidental implications."

"Wait, a Troll family? I remember reading something about that case for Advanced Ecology." Bobby pulled open his laptop. I saw him navigate to the PLEXIS Nexus. "This is probably something we want Olivia to look at sometime. She's the Extrahuman Law major."

"Well, what've you got for now?" I tried to look at his laptop, but couldn't without getting up. I stayed put.

"Looks like these Trolls protect the Mount Hope Bridge, between Portsmouth and Warren. The Tollands, all Unseelie, it looks like. A thorough search of all their assets didn't turn up the pelt." Bobby scrolled down, skimming the text on the screen. Lynn's study habits must have rubbed off on him. "A Selkie died in an accident there, and his pelt went missing."

"Wait, a minute. What was the date of that accident?" I felt like the pit of my stomach had turned to ice.

"March 15, four years ago." Bobby glanced up, then leaned back when he looked at my face.

"My sister Beth lost her leg on that bridge the same night." I swallowed hard past the lump in my throat. "Her fiancé died, too. Ren Ichiro."

"Huh. Ichiro's the name of the attorney on this report. Yoshi Ichiro."

"That's Ren's dad." I shook my head. "Beth is staying with him."

"Sounds more and more like we should consider this coincidence." Bobby looked up, his eyes wide and his nostrils flared. "The Extramagus tried to use an old accident to attack Lynn and old hate crimes to hurt Henry. We'd better run this by Blaine."

"Nothing doing." I shook my head, crossing my arms over my chest. "It's none of his business."

"Josh. You've got to get over this whole rivalry with the dragon thing." Henry sighed. "He just flirts with everyone. I mean, you should have seen what happened every time he remembered Maddie for a while."

"I want to let it go, man. But my wolf can't get over it unless the mate thing's resolved." I shook my head. "And that's just not a good idea."

"But you also can't just avoid Nox and Blaine." Henry leaned forward, staring me down. The alliance medallion under my shirt grew cold against my skin. "They're part of your pack, remember? Plus Blaine's the one with all the Extramagus information, and we need to know whether his hand is in this."

"The fact he's my pack-mate makes it worse. I can't be around him right now without a conflict we can't afford." I clenched my fists on the sides of the chair back. "This Extramagus is a major douche. Almost as bad as Blaine himself."

Bobby's mouth dropped open at the same time Henry's did. Their expressions would have been mirror images if Henry hadn't had fangs. The vampire's hand moved slowly up to hide them from view. Hurried heavy footsteps headed away from the door down the hall. I leaped up, pushing through and leaning out to see Blaine turn the corner into the lounge, his head and shoulders down. When I turned to step back into the room, I almost bumped into Jeannie.

"Wow, Josh." The blonde bear shifter shook her head, reminding me of Beth's big sister act from before the accident. "You should go apologize."

"Maybe he should apologize for listening in." I put my hands on my hips like I would have if I'd been talking to Beth. "Smart guy like him should know better."

"This is his room you're talking about him in, you know." Jeannie tried to look down her nose at me, impossible since she was more than a head shorter. Her disdain shouldn't have shaken me, but it did.

"And I'm his Alpha," I growled.

"So act like it." She tilted her chin up, snarling. Was this really the same girl Lynn said reminded her of a Barbie doll? "You lay things on the line with him. It's one thing people say they admire about your mom, Dennison. Fill her shoes."

"Who do you think you are, telling me how to head my own pack?" I loomed over her.

"I'm the Resident Assistant tasked with keeping these kinds of problems from trashing the campus. Now get down to that lounge and have it out. Take it outside to the park if you've got to get physical. And you're welcome." Jeannie spun on her heel and stalked down the hall, reminding me for all the world of Fleur Delacour telling Mrs. Weasley off in the Harry Potter books.

"Well, that settles it, then." Henry brushed past me into the hall. "You want me to tell Blaine to meet you down at India Point?"

"No." I took a deep breath, leashing my wolf with the cold feeling that still hadn't left the pit of my stomach. "But you guys should come with me, anyway."

"Sure thing." Bobby shut his laptop and set it down on the desk.

We headed down the hall, me in front with Henry and Bobby flanking me on the right and left. The whole walk could have been filmed in slow-mo and put into a movie montage. I focused on what I'd have to say, the questions I'd need to answer to bury the mate competition hatchet with Blaine so we could move past the bullshit. Henry had been right. It was the reason I'd made him my Beta. I couldn't sideline Blaine for this. Even if the pack problems had nothing to do with that Extramagus, I'd still need them all by my side when we went to get my folks back. The way that letter was addressed meant I had to do things officially, and that meant bringing everyone in my pack, including the dragon shifter, as infuriatingly arrogant as he was most of the time.

"Blaine. We're talking now." I strode across the room, leaning on the patch of wall between two windows. "Shut the door, Henry." My Beta followed the order. Bobby sat on the arm of the sofa Blaine had sprawled out on.

"Oh, okay. Because what I really need on top of all my own stress is an interview with the Alphahole." Blaine's eyes narrowed, a red spark rising in them. They were also slightly bloodshot and shiny at the corners. I flared my nostrils, scenting a hint of salt and brimstone as he puffed out a smoke ring. Hadn't Lynn mentioned something about Blaine being as lonely as she felt sometimes?

"Yeah, I've been a douchecanoe." I held my hands out, palms up.

"But it's temporary. Part of the reason I'm here is to offer you an apology. But before you go thanking me and accepting it, we have to talk about my mate."

"What to the who now?" Blaine sat up, tapping his ear. "I thought I heard you say the word mate, but you don't have one of those."

"It's a recent development and nothing's final yet." I took a deep breath, summoning all my calm and applying it to keeping my wolf down. "But you'd better leave Nox Phillips alone if you want to keep things copacetic."

"Wait," Blaine smirked. Then he snorted. He put one hand over his mouth, snickering behind it. Bobby tilted his head, glaring at his roommate as though a bear stare could get a dragon to shut up.

My wolf practically caught fire, leaping up within me, daring me to shift and go for Blaine's throat. I clenched my jaw and fists, fighting to keep control. Even with all that effort, I could feel my eyes going gold, the hair on my arms and the back of my neck raising as a low growl clawed its way out of my throat.

"I think you need to explain things better than that, Blaine." Henry's words, delivered in a cool deadpan, helped me focus.

"No, I mean seriously." Blaine took a deep breath and let it out with a little trickle of smoke. "Hold on a minute. Nox? Do you have any idea why I even flirted with her in the first place?"

I shook my head, knowing that if I tried to speak my wolf might just bust out and attack.

"I was trying to get Maddie and Henry together." Blaine shook his head. "I mean, she's smoking hot in the looks department, but way too intense. Not my type at all. If she's your mate, go for it. You guys'd be awesome together."

Bobby punched Blaine in the shoulder. That one brotherly gesture instantly settled my wolf, reminding me of Derek's face as he went with the Shifter Registry Feds, leaving me hidden in the brush next to the rain shelter on the Blackstone Boulevard bike path. I never told Beth or my parents that his disappearance had been my fault. He'd taken the rap for me during my first change, which happened in public before it was legal. Somehow, the FBE had known exactly where to look for us. I hadn't thought about how weird that was since the night it happened.

"Where did you go, Beowulf?" At first, I didn't realize it was Blaine who'd spoken. I'd never heard him talk without a zing of sarcasm or the disdained Long Island lockjaw.

"Just thinking about how far back all this mess might go. I'm going to need your help." I dropped my hands to my sides, finally able to relax my shoulders. "So. I'm sorry for acting like an Alphahole when I should just be an Alpha."

"Apology accepted." Blaine smiled, like an actual smile instead of a jerk-smirk. Then, the Long Island lockjaw returned like Aragorn to Gondor. "Now what's all this about needing my help?"

CHAPTER TEN

Nox

Lynn's joke about the big bad wolf hadn't been that funny, but her laughter was downright infectious. Even Maddie came down with a bad case of the giggles. I wasn't left as breathless by laughter as I'd been by Josh's affections earlier, but it was a near thing. The tears at the corners of my eyes couldn't decide whether they were stress relief or anguish or the awkwardness of my mating predicament.

"Okey-doke." Lynn sat at her desk then ran one hand through her hair, pulling it back over her shoulder like a curtain. "Now that the fun's over, I have to ask you a personal question, Nox. Why were you out in the middle of the night with Josh Dennison in nothing but your undies and a military surplus blanket?"

"Well, I could tell you a long story or a short one." I took a deep breath, trying a relaxation technique to keep from blushing. "Which version do you want?"

"Oooh, both!" Maddie clapped her hands together. "Give us the short one first, though."

"Don't you have any respect for spoilers, sweetie?" Lynn rolled her eyes.

"Nope. Can't stand the suspense." Maddie tossed her head, curls cascading over the right side of her face. "Sit down and dish."

"Okay." I sat gingerly on the edge of Maddie's bed next to where she'd patted it, then crossed my ankles. "Well, I met Josh out at Swan Point. Told him I think he's my mate."

"Oh. My. God!" Lynn sprung up from her seat. "No way! So you are? I mean, he is? I mean. I can't even believe this right now; this is so crazy!"

"Um." I blinked, completely puzzled by Lynn's weird behavior. She never got like this over anything but an A+ grade. "Well, we're still not sure."

"Oh, boy. Well, I've been there. I can't believe it. So, Swan Point. Isn't it a bit, um, cold out there for, um—"

"Lynn, chill on all the gritty detail questions." I'd almost forgotten Maddie was there until she spoke up and put her hand on my arm. "She's not wearing her pelt. What went wrong, Nox?"

"Besides the fact that any relationship between Josh and me is kind of forbidden because wolf shifters keep it neutral with the Faerie Courts?" I sighed and blinked. Had I been this close to tears all the way over here?

"Oh, no. I forgot." Lynn put her head in her hands. "Me and my big mouth. I'm sorry."

"It's okay," I lied. Lynn meant well; her wit just worked faster than her heart sometimes. It wasn't her, but the situation that had me down.

"No, it's absolutely not okay." Lynn shook her head. "Hey, you don't have a bag or anything." She got up, making a beeline for her dresser. "You can't go home in a blanket on a night like this." Lynn rummaged around until she found a PPC sweatshirt. "This is too long on me, so it'll probably work for you."

Lynn was shorter than me and curvy. I took the shirt and held it against my chest. It'd fit me across the shoulders just fine. She kept looking through the drawers, but all her pants would have had trouble staying up on my lack of hips.

"I'll get her something for the bottom." Maddie went straight to the lowest drawer of her dresser, unrolling a pair of gray yoga pants that looked way too long for her. "They sent me a tall instead of a short, and I washed them before I figured it out."

"Thanks, guys." I pulled the pants on under the blanket and then the sweatshirt over my head. Before putting my arms through the sleeves, I undid the knot holding the makeshift dress together. The wool was stubborn, practically glued together after being in brackish water and mauled by a randy wolf shifter. My face heated as I flushed with the memory of Josh's urgency. I hadn't known what to do at the time and probably wouldn't if it happened again.

"Wow." Lynn shook her head. "That looks like how I feel when I think about Bobby." I looked up to see her pointing at my reddening face. "Is it really so impossible for the two of you to be together?"

"I don't know." I put my arms in the sleeves, then pulled the blanket out from under the sweatshirt. "I've never heard of a wolf shifter finding a Faerie mate, or even an untithed Changeling."

"But he has a sister, though." Maddie chewed her bottom lip. "And she's older than him. Can't she take the packs over instead of him? I mean, a mate is a huge big deal with wolf shifters. They go nuts if they don't find one by middle age."

"Her mate died, and she still hasn't found another. A single wolf shifter can't run an established pack. It's even worse that I'm unsuitable." I shook my head. "It's like coincidence saying Josh's Uncle Jake is the right leader after all."

"Wait a minute." Maddie tapped her temple with one finger. "Hold on and let me look something up." She reached over and pulled a textbook about coincidence off her desk. I'd forgotten she was taking a course on that already. Something like a growl sounded in the small room. It took me a few seconds to realize it went along with the empty feeling in my gut.

"While we wait, you need some food." Lynn opened the drawer on her nightstand and chucked a few Power Bars at me. "They taste like cardboard according to Bobby, but they do the trick when he's hungry after shifting." She watched me tear up the wrappers and chew on one of the bars. "Wait. How did you shift without your pelt?"

"I didn't." My words came out all muffled and garbled around the gluey wannabe food, but Lynn seemed to understand them, anyway. A side-effect of being a bear shifter's mate, probably. I pulled the oilskin pouch from a fold in the blanket while swallowing. "That's all part of the long story Maddie wanted me to skip." I gave them the full account of my trip down the tunnel and swim up the river while Maddie looked things up.

Lynn opened her mouth, about to ask a question judging by the look on her face. Three firm raps on the door interrupted her. She got up and opened the door just as Maddie scrawled notes down on a piece of loose-leaf paper. Jeannie stood in the doorway for just a moment before shouldering past Lynn without so much as an invitation.

"You ladies should take this whole show down to the first-floor lounge. Everyone's there except Tony and Olivia." Jeannie stood next to Lynn's desk with her hands on her hips. Maddie collecting her notes and the RA's tapping foot were the only sounds for a moment. Lynn grabbed her backpack and headed out, Maddie following close behind. Jeannie let me out but stopped me with a hand on my shoulder as she shut the door to 566 behind her. I turned and stared.

"What is it?" I lowered my eyebrows. The last thing I needed was a lecture from a bear shifter who looked like she belonged on a CW show.

"Settle down." Her eyes were wide with an empathy that stopped my anger in its tracks. "I only just realized you don't have a place to stay. Can't go back to your off-campus apartment, huh?"

"Yeah, you're right." I turned my head, eying her warily. "I've had a little help, though."

"Not enough, from the looks of it." Jeannie tilted her head to the side, looking more like a cocker spaniel shifter than a werebear. "You need a hot shower. A bathroom with a real mirror. An actual bed."

"So? I got myself in trouble." I shrugged, holding my hands palms up to either side. "What's your point?"

"I can put you up for the weekend," she said. "The RA up on three has to go home for a wedding tomorrow. I'll stay in her room, and you can have mine while she's gone."

"Wow, Jeannie." I blinked my suddenly stinging eyes. "Thank you. I really owe you one."

"No, you don't." She smiled.

"I don't understand." I ran a hand through my hair, suddenly almost too weary to stand.

"It's the least I can do. What you did for that Spite might have pissed off the Queen, but it was the right thing to do in my book." Jeannie reached out and patted my shoulder. "Besides, I work for Student Life. You're a student with a life, so why shouldn't I help you? Now, get down to the first-floor lounge and talk to your friends. I'll ask Olivia to bring you over after your class tomorrow, tell her you're room-sitting."

I nodded, stifling a yawn, then shuffled down the hall. I was too tired to do much besides lean against the elevator wall on the way down. After the chime went off a second time, I blinked, just barely getting my hand between the doors so I could stop them from closing. I stepped out of the elevator on the first floor, heading for the sounds of my friends' voices and almost ran headlong into Tony Gitano. I hadn't spoken to him since our odd conversation in the Nocturnal Lounge the night Josh fled his home.

"So, they're finally thinking the Extramagus has something to do with all this." Tony smirked.

"Are they?" I could have slapped him for not telling them sooner.

"Yup. Jeannie called me over here." He took a step back from me, covering for his fear by leaning against the wall.

"She's well informed, isn't she?" I turned, taking two steps toward the lounge. If he wanted to continue being hinky, he'd have to do it on the way down the hall.

"Less than I am." Hurried footsteps punctuated his words. "Her connections are mostly from out-of-town."

"You really are pretty shady." I tried to ignore the chilly tile against my bare feet as I listened to his squeaky sneakers.

"You're entitled to that opinion." Tony caught up, coming into view in my peripheral vision.

"It's going to catch up to you someday." I shook my head.

"I've still got some of my nine lives left." He chuckled, but his eyes stayed flat and weary.

"That's not a myth?" I rubbed my eyes in tandem with another tummy rumble.

"You're entitled to your opinion of my multiple lives. And some food. Bobby ordered pizza. Go on in, but not a word about our previous conversation." Tony poked me in the bicep with one index finger.

"Why should I keep my mouth shut about that? It's useful information." I was too tired and hungry to deal with Tony's dodgy hangups.

"Then don't credit the source." Tony glared up at me. "You almost drowned me like a three-legged kitten last week. You owe me."

"Fine." I mimed zipping my lips. "No credit for Tony G. For now."

"Appreciate it." The little jerk held the door for me.

I stepped in, walking past everyone else and heading straight for the unoccupied sofa in the corner. The cushions felt like heaven, but my empty stomach kept me from falling asleep. The mingled conversation was hard to follow, but I didn't mind. Everyone was busy catching each other up, Lynn filling the less sordid details of my story into Josh's account. Henry headed over, sitting on the other end of the couch.

"You okay?" The vampire's brow furrowed.

"Nothing some food and a nap won't fix. Thanks for asking." I blinked, hoping I didn't look sleepier than Olivia.

"Least I can do for someone who helped save my life." He set his elbows on his knees, then folded his hands to rest his chin on them "Speaking of which, you have Seelie problems. It might be time to call in one of those favors from the Sprite. What do you think?"

"Probably. I'll need a safe place to do that." I sat up. "Oh! I can make one."

"What do you mean you can make one?" I hadn't noticed Blaine was there until after he spoke.

"Mr. Waban gave me some church-keys." I yawned.

"Tiamat's Scales!" He sat. Well, not really. More like his knees buckled when he happened to be standing in front of a chair. "I haven't heard of the old serpent even selling one since the nineteenth century."

"Serpent?" I raised an eyebrow. "What do you mean?"

"You didn't know?" Blaine snorted out a couple of smoke rings. "Taki Waban's a tough old drake of the ice variety. He was here before Mother came to the continent. No one even knows how old he is."

"Wow." No wonder Blaine had been afraid of him. Dragon shifters only got more powerful with age. It was one reason Mrs. Harcourt was adored from afar and with no small measure of fear. Her husband was centuries younger than her. I wondered what the story was there.

"Mother will be so jealous if she finds out you got your hands on those." He leaned in like a conspirator. "She'll never let you hear the end of it. Literally. She's always wanted some church-keys for her hoard. It's one of the few magic items she's missing, and Mr. Waban refuses to sell them to her at any price she's offered."

"Well, maybe she should try pissing off a Faerie Monarch or two." Josh sat down next to me. "I bet Taki Waban's keys cost bold action, not gold."

"I bet that's true." Blaine gave Josh a huge grin. "What'll you wager?"

"I've gambled enough to last the rest of the year, thanks." Josh stood. "Pizza's here." He strode over and brought back a whole box. That was okay since Bobby had ordered six.

We sat in the lounge, sharing pizza and information for a couple of hours. Tony eyed me briefly when I brought up the Extramagus's family tree, but no one questioned where I'd gotten the idea, anyway. Lynn just made a note to add genealogy to the future research list.

I nodded off on the sofa. When Josh shook my shoulder to wake me, everyone but Henry had gone. Josh left for his house, which he could finally return to. I wanted to go with him, help straighten up the place, but it was too dangerous. Instead, Henry brought me to the Nocturnal Lounge. I curled up with the bedroll from the bottom of my rucksack in the corner behind the vampire's favorite study table, relieved that it might be the last time I'd have to sleep there.

CHAPTER ELEVEN

Josh

I needed help. Unfortunately, I couldn't admit that to anyone in my pack except Henry and the sun was up. I picked up the phone and told Siri I had to talk to Beth. Don't get the idea that I'm an iFanboy; my parents buy the phones, and that's what they like. I'd be switching to Android once I was the one pulling the purse strings.

The phone rang twice as I imagined Adele's "Hello" blaring out of Beth's speakers while my face popped up on the screen. Yeah, that's a freakily depressing song, but what else do you expect a girl with one leg and a dead fiancé to want to listen to? Even Maddie's old goth music was too upbeat for my sister.

"Beth's phone, Kim speaking. Can I direct you to call someone cuter and less of a downer instead?"

My sister's voice took on a strident tone I hadn't heard since the day before the accident. Beth had been nothing but exhausted or weepy in all that time. Maybe the pick-pocketing Tanuki wasn't such a bad influence after all. I held the expensive white rectangle away from my ear as the muffled whoosh soundtrack of their struggle for the phone continued.

"What is it?" Beth's voice just barely drowned out the sound of Kimiko Ichiro's juvenile raspberry.

"Gotta talk. Some new information and ideas came up last night, and I need someone to bounce them off of."

"As long as you don't ask me if I want to build a snowman." Beth actually snorted out an honest to goodness laugh after that. So she'd paid attention the year that Frozen movie came out and I stood outside on the back lawn below her window blasting the damn song out of Derek's old boom-box like I was John freaking Cusak. Good.

"I promise. No snowmen." I snorted back. "Just an interview with your kid brother about a bunch of crazy theories."

"No whiny vampires named Louis, either." I heard a muffled protest about Brad Pitt's hotness and then another raspberry in the background.

"Okay." We'd never get off the phone with all the side-chatter. "What in Luna's name is Baby Metal doing over there, pretending she's two?"

"Baby Metal?" Beth full out guffawed. "Oh, that is rich!" I heard another tussle for the phone, then a click as it went to speaker.

"Who do you think you are, calling me Baby Metal? You big jerk!"

"You should meet some of his friends." Beth's voice told me she was either waggling her eyebrows or winking. Kimiko let out a frustrated little squeak.

"So, where do we meet?"

"I got it!" Kimiko squealed, her voice closer as she grabbed the phone and took it off speaker. "I'll text the address." Then she hung up.

And that was how I ended up in a Wickenden Street nail salon. I walked in, blinking at the design choices. Yellow paint with pink trim gave the entire place a girly vibe, and the endless chatter of the staff as they held hands and feet with the all-female clientele provided constant background noise. At least they weren't playing junk pop.

I spotted Kimiko right away. She waved, bouncing up and down in her seat, splashing a little puddle on the floor next to the spa her feet were submerged in. I closed the distance between us, determined to grab her by the shoulders and shake them while giving her a stern lecture about bringing a woman with only one foot for a pedicure. Luckily, I glanced at Beth before doing any such thing.

My sister's smile was even bigger than Kimiko's. She may have had only one foot in the spa instead of the usual two, but the woman helping her didn't act any differently than the one with Kimiko. I couldn't smile, but my embarrassment evaporated the sour look off my face right quick.

"We can talk here?" I raised an eyebrow.

"Sure," Beth grinned. "No one expects wooj in a nail salon."

"Fine, then." I leaned against the wall. "So, our problem doesn't just come from what happened at the end of Intersession. It goes all the way back to the night of your accident. Maybe further than that."

"Wait, really?" Beth's eyebrows threatened to meet her hairline. I had no idea why Kimiko giggled with one hand over her mouth and one pinkie sticking up.

"Excuse me." An unfamiliar female voice came from somewhere near my elbow.

"Uh, sorry. Am I in your way?" The last thing I wanted was to stand in the middle of where the nail-doers had to walk.

"No…" The woman shook her head, placing one ironically unpainted finger on her cheek. "It's just that, um, this area's for paying customers only, sir."

"Here!" Kimiko waved a pair of twenties in the air. "Sit down. My treat!"

I turned, intending to just leave and wait until they walked out of that yellow and pink house of humiliation, but my knees buckled. An unoccupied staff member whisked off my combat boots and socks. Before you could say "annoying Tanuki brat," I had my feet in a whirlpool right next to my sister.

"At least there's no snowmen or vampires named Louis, huh Josh?" Beth's giggly delivery and the sparkle in her eyes was worth the embarrassment.

All I could do was roll my eyes and let out a low growl. Having to deal with Kimiko was nearly as bad as hanging out with Blaine. I'd never met her before, not even through the year Beth had dated Ren. They clearly knew each other pretty well, though.

"Okay, so like I was saying." I cleared my throat, trying not to laugh. The whirlpool tickled a little. "There's a report that the other car in the accident belonged to a Selkie."

"And we should care about that drunk bastard, why?"

"Because his pelt went missing." I blinked as the pink-smocked staff member pulled my foot out of the spa and went to work massaging some kind of lotion on it. "Friends of mine think that's the real problem here, the reason the um," I glanced around. You never knew who might be a Changeling, even in a nail salon.

"Okay, so the Queen's angry because she thinks someone has something of hers?" Beth nodded. "Makes sense. Also tells us why she's focused on Nox in particular. She had to use something Seelie in order to turn that Spite back into a Sprite. Maybe the Queen thinks she has the Selkie pelt."

"Oh yeah." Kimiko twirled her hair. "She'd want that back for sure. Especially since those Monarchs can't make any more pelts unless they get back together."

"Well, that's not happening." I crossed my arms over my chest. The massage felt pretty decent, but I was afraid I'd end up with neon toenails or something, so it was hard to relax. "Anyway, I was there. She used a glass sea float, not a Selkie pelt."

"Good thing, too." Kimiko nodded. I didn't like her grin. "Do you have any idea how much those pelts go for if you can find a buyer who won't talk?"

"Leaping Luna!" I glared at the Tanuki. "No wonder your dad sent you to the Academy." That place was like Extrahuman Community College on lockdown.

"Woah, kid bro." Beth patted my hand. "Chill. She happens to know something about magic items. Maybe you could use her help."

"Info, yes. Direct help, no thanks." I shrugged. "Look, sorry about the school remark, okay. But I already have a magical artifact expert in my pack."

"Oh yeah, the dragon shifter, right?" Beth scratched her head. "What was his name again? Blake?"

"No." I sighed. "Blaine Harcourt. His mom owns three Newport mansions and the biggest hoard in this hemisphere. He grew up around magic items."

"Wow." Kimiko's eyes lit up like a Mall Christmas tree. "You know the Harcourts?"

"Just one of them." Hopefully, she'd leave it at that.

"Do you get invited to their parties or anything?" Her interest seemed shady. Either that or the Harcourts were a bigger deal than I'd thought.

"No." I sighed through a clenched jaw. "Look, we're getting off the subject here."

"Okay, so how do you think this information about the pelt will help?" Beth chewed her bottom lip. "Nox still undid what she undid and everything, so she will get punished, regardless."

"Right, but it might be just a slap on the wrist if we can find that dead Selkie's pelt and turn it over."

"True." Kimiko nodded. "It'd be a fair exchange, one enchantment for another. Seelie law is all about balance."

"So what kind of thing might she ask for if we don't get the pelt, then?"

"Why's that so important to you?" Kimiko looked down her nose at me.

"Because I think Nox and I are mates." I might have answered Kimiko's question, but I directed my answer at Beth.

"I understand." Beth nodded. "You want to protect her as much as you can. If the Queen suspects Nox of hiding a Selkie pelt, she'll want a Kelpie pelt in return."

"I also can't stand the idea of her giving up a part of herself because she saved my Beta's unlife." I told them both the story. Kimiko hadn't been around, and Beth had acted more dead than Henry until today.

"Wow. I didn't know that's why she did it." Kimiko grinned a little, losing the bratty veneer. She looked troubled, maybe even a little sad. "Huh."

"So, what did they do to look for the pelt?" Beth had her phone out, swiping and tapping.

"Just about everything you can think of. They even had Maddie's dad out here scrying." I shook my head. "Human and Extrahuman effort for almost a year, all focused on finding an unattached Selkie pelt."

"Would it have degraded by now, though?" Beth gave me a wan smile. "I feel out of my depth on this. Got no idea how the magic pelts work."

"Well, they're all aligned with water. That's why they're stored in oilcloth. If they dry completely out, they're toast." The facts rolled out of Kimiko's brain like they usually did for Lynn Frampton. She ignored the woman dabbing gold paint on her toenails. "Kelpie pelts need to be in fresh water, and Selkie pelts need salt. That bridge was over salt water, so if it fell in, it'd be okay."

"It was, was it?" Something bothered me about Kimiko's little speech, but I couldn't put my finger on it. "Hey, what if the reason no one's been able to find the damn thing is because someone picked it up and put it on?"

"Huh." Beth chewed on that for a minute. "That'd explain why they couldn't find it. Well one of the possible reasons, anyway."

"What other reason can you think of?" It was my turn to scratch my head. I was stumped. That was the reason I had super-geniuses in my pack, after all.

"Theft!" Kimiko's outburst smacked of nervousness. "Either kind of pelt is super valuable like I said. Dragon hoard valuable, even. Isn't that bridge near Newport?"

"It is. But I don't think Blaine would have…I mean, he's not my favorite person in the world, but he's no thief."

"But what about his parents?" Kimiko twirled her hair again, looking just about everywhere except at my eyes. "They're supposed to be big-time opportunists, especially his step-dad. Did they help in the search?"

"Dunno. Have to look at the records again." I wondered if Kimiko was fishing for information about the Harcourts or deliberately misinforming me. "But value aside, they're awfully hidebound to do something that, well, underhanded. Hoards are full of trophies. If there isn't some kind of conquest or right of possession behind an item, dragons aren't all that interested in it."

"You're right." Beth scratched her head. "What makes more sense is, some regular Joe or Jane picked it up thinking this was their chance to be an Extrahuman."

"But that'd be so illegal they'd never be able to really benefit from it."

"Well, what if he or she had nothing much to lose?" Beth sighed. "A Selkie skin would make it easy to live off the grid. For a person running from something, or who thought they had no other choice, it'd be a pretty easy decision to make."

"Point and match, Beth." If anyone knew desperation, it was my sister. I looked down to find the nail lady drying my feet with a little towel. My feet looked...decent. They'd spared me the indignity of putting polish on, thank goodness.

I pulled on my socks and laced up my boots. The girls had already waited for their toes to dry. We headed across the street to the cafe where I let Kimiko and Beth gab over quadruple lattes or whatever. Somebody had that pelt. It'd be amazeballs with a side of awesome-sauce if I could find them and present them to the Queen before Nox's trial. Of course, I'd also have to get through an Alpha contest against my uncle. No pressure, right?

CHAPTER TWELVE

Nox

Staying awake in my Local Extrahuman History class was easier today than it had been since the Spring semester started. I had Watkins, of course. He was the only Professor who taught that here except Brodsky. Since it was kind of my fault Watkins got stuck teaching two sections of a Junior level course along with the Freshman level Ecology class he constantly complained about, I'd been determined not to give him any headaches.

"If you can't get through one of my lectures without double-fisting coffee, you'll be warming the same seat next semester, Phillips." Half the heads in the room turned in my direction. Lucky break, I guess.

"Sorry, Professor." I stifled a yawn and tucked one of the Styrofoam cafeteria cups under my seat.

"So, as I was saying before some genius down at the dining hall led a horse shifter to coffee, the hurricane barrier went up around the time most of your parents were born. What else went up with it?"

"Ooh! I know!" Only one hand shot up front and center in the room. It was pale, long-fingered, and not quite human.

"Does anyone besides Albert have a clue?" Professor Watkins tapped the toe of one wingtip shoe behind his podium.

"Wards." I yawned. "They went up all along the coast in a great big circle. But they cut off at Tiverton, right in the middle of the Pell Bridge."

"Well, this is a pleasant surprise. It seems Phillips cares more about passing than just about any of you." Watkins' smile reminded me of sharks and crocodiles. "So tell me, Phillips, who put those wards up, anyway?"

Unfortunately, I had no clue. I remembered the wards from Tinfoil Hat's chat the night before, not from the textbook. Sighing, I almost gave up and shook my head until I remembered something Blaine and Henry had mentioned the last week of Intersession. I had a snowball's chance in hell of being right but would take that over zero chance any day of the week.

"Stanhope. He was an Extramagus, right?"

"Are you right?" The smile on Watkins' face didn't budge. "You tell me."

"Yes." I nodded with as much confidence as I could muster. "Stanhope. He was an Extramagus. He's the guy who made the wards."

"And does anybody know why he didn't bother with Tiverton?" Watkins turned away, pacing along the front of the lecture hall in search of his next victim. I sighed into my coffee, relieved I'd been correct.

About halfway between my back-row seat and Albert down in front, a woman nearly as pale as he was stood up. Olivia the amazing diurnal owl shifter. Her birdlike frame was emphasized by the feathery layers of nearly white hair on her head. Leave it to a bookworm bird shifter to be blessed with the ghost of Farrah Fawcett's best hair days.

"Adler. Tell all the people who didn't bother with the assigned reading why Stanhope refused to ward Tiverton."

"Because back then, the biggest community of Unseelies in Rhode

Island lived over there, and he was trying to curry favor with the Queen." She shifted her weight from one foot to the other. "Sir."

"And she remembered to call me sir, which is more than the rest of you louts bother with." Watkins clapped slowly. "I'll let all you slackers go as long as you remember this little tidbit that's going on next week's quiz."

He leaned against the podium, lowering his voice so much everyone stopped packing their things away in order to hear him. "Extramagi are some of the most powerful people in the world. But history tells us all that power's still never enough for them. They'll do absolutely anything, even the last thing you'd imagine, in order to get more. Extramagi. Greedy fargin icehole bastiches." He straightened. "Anyone who emails me with the movie that catch-phrase is from and which character said it gets two extra credit points on the quiz. Now get out of here."

I gulped down the rest of the coffee in the cup still on the tiny swivel desk in front of me, then reached down and grabbed the still-full cup under my seat. When I sat up again, Olivia stood blinking down at me. It must have been a novel experience for her since the only person in Tinfoil Hat her height was Maddie, and she loved stompy platform boots. Olivia always seemed to wear Converse high-tops or ballet flats. Today, she had on the latter.

I yawned at exactly the same time she did, the drawn-out breaths turning into a chuckle and a giggle, respectively. I tucked the coffee in the crook of one arm, then slung my rucksack over the other shoulder. Before I could move the desk piece, a shadow fell over it. I looked up again.

"Professor Watkins." I tried not to blink or look away. I knew he was a Psychic but forgot what kind. "Hi." Ideas about what to say flitted around my head like moths around a porch light.

"Phillips. You and Adler have an interesting collection of information between the two of you." He stroked his salt and pepper goatee. "Interesting in the Confucian sense."

"Er. Okay?" I would have made some excuse, cut and run, but I couldn't get up with Olivia in the way, and Watkins was blocking her.

"Professor, Nox and I have been working with a few other students on some local history since last semester," Olivia smiled, her big amber eyes blinking periodically as she spoke. "It's kind of a fun thing we got together and did once we realized a bunch of us aren't from around here."

"Ah. You'd better not try to tell me either of you is the ringleader of this little project because I'd sooner buy the Newport Bridge than that idea."

"No way. It was Blaine Harcourt's idea originally." Olivia's smile faded as Watkins ignored her, keeping his eyes on me.

"I see." He gave one curt nod. "The textbook's a little dry for an extracurricular project." Watkins pulled a small notebook out of his back pocket and the ubiquitous pencil from behind his ear. "Go to the library. Find Taki Waban. Check these books out." He jotted a list on the paper, graphite scratching in spidery script with no care for the blue lines. "Whatever you do, don't discuss them around Changelings. Read the one about shifter pack history first." He tore the paper off the pad, holding it out to me. "And by first, I mean directly. Do not pass the dining hall. Do not collect your lunch."

"Ooookay?" As soon as my fingers pinched the raggedy top of the list, Watkins let go of it and stalked back to the podium to collect his own things.

Olivia and I got out of there like a couple of bats out of a belfry when the guy at the bottom pulled the rope. We passed the dorm and crossed the street to the library. Olivia headed for the card catalog, but we didn't find any of the books listed in it. Same results when we tried the computer.

"He said to find Taki Waban." I glanced around but saw no sign of the old dragon shifter.

"You mean that new librarian?" Olivia shrugged. "Lynn says he knows nothing about the Library of Congress or even the Dewey Decimal system."

"I don't think that matters." I strode away from the computer, heading back toward the staff areas of the library. Behind me, I heard the patter of Olivia's ballet flats against the hardwood as she jogged to keep up.

At the end of the hall, a counter stood between us and a set of double doors, the kind that swung either way and had little round windows in them at head height for everyone except Gnomes, Sprites, and Olivia. I peered through them, spotting motion way back near a stack of cardboard boxes. I thought I saw a head of black hair streaked with white.

"Mr. Waban?" I called out to him louder than usual library etiquette allowed. I didn't care. The book Watkins wanted me to read had something to do with wolf shifters. Maybe it could help Josh. I'd gotten him and his family into who knows what kind of trouble. I'd do anything I could to get them out of it. Apparently even risking the wrath of a dragon older than Blaine's mother, who'd come here with the Vikings.

"Miss Phillips. Miss Adler." The unassuming man pushed through the door, stepping up to the counter. "It seems Professor Watkins owes me fifty dollars. When he phoned, he told me to expect you at least half an hour from now."

"Well, he told us it was an emergency."

"He said no such thing to me." One corner of Mr. Waban's mouth tilted up in a half-grin. "However, he did go on for longer than I'd like about how none of his students know how to follow directions. So, it's an emergency now, is it?"

"Um." I'd blustered myself into a corner again. This seemed to be my new default mode since meeting Josh. I had the idea it didn't look good on me.

"Here, Mr. Waban." Olivia came to the rescue again, plucking the book list from my hand and passing it to the quasi-librarian. If only she didn't turn into a medically induced pumpkin at eight-thirty on the dot every night, she'd be a great person to have around through all this mess.

"Hmm. I've got two of these." Mr. Waban raised one eyebrow.

"Please tell me one is the shifter pack history book?" I put my now empty hands flat against the countertop.

"It is." He tilted his head. "But these books are part of my personal collection. They're not library copies. I could lend it to you, but I'd prefer it not leave campus."

"No problem. I'd prefer not to leave campus myself." I grinned.

"Excellent. Here you are." Mr. Waban pulled two books out from behind the counter, placing them between my hands. Both were bound in worn leather, wrapped around and tied with strong rawhide cord. They looked more like personal journals or a collection of research papers than anything published on a printing press.

"Thank you. I promise to have them back as soon as we're done." I picked the volumes up gently, tucking them together in the inside pocket of my jacket. Then, I turned and headed down the hallway.

"Very good." I glanced over my shoulder at the sound of his voice. His face was inscrutable, almost like a mask under a sheet of ice. "Please give Mr. Dennison my regards."

I just nodded, heading out into the cold bright sunlight of the winter midday. Then, I checked the time, realizing I had to meet Jeannie so I could get the keys to her room. I crossed the street to the dorm, almost forgetting Olivia was still following me.

"Go get lunch, my friend." After turning, I paused. "I'm room-sitting, remember? I have stuff to do in there."

"You catching a nap?" She blinked. If Olivia thought I needed one, I probably could use a full eight hours.

"Hopefully. After I talk to Jeannie."

"Okay, see you later." She opened the door for me, then trotted off toward the dining hall.

I stepped into the lobby. Jeannie came out from around the corner, beckoning to me. I followed her all the way down the hall to room 111. She opened the door to find a tidy single room. The bed had been stripped, but fresh linens were folded in a stack at its foot. The desk was clear, too. Jeannie yanked on the long handle of a suitcase with wheels, dragging it to the door. She handed me two keys on a ring with a tag that said I Love Boston. I'd almost forgotten that's where she was from.

"Thanks so much again, Jeannie."

"You don't have to thank me. Just rest and take care of yourself. I was where you are a long time ago, and someone helped my family and me." She shrugged. "Least I can do is pay it forward."

I'd never let anyone call Jeannie La Montagne a Barbie doll in my presence again. After she left, I went to work making the bed, then distributing some of my things around the room to make it more comfortable. I took off my pelt, placing it in the oilcloth. Then, I put that in my rucksack next to the desk. Just as I was about to sprawl out on the bed and crack open the shifter pack book, the buzzer went off. I wasn't sure how it worked, so I grabbed Jeannie's keyring and headed down the hall to the front door.

When Josh smiled at me through the wire-crossed glass, I tried not to let my knees knock together. I blinked, trying to remember whether I told him I'd be staying in Jeannie's room or not. A hot flash of jealous anger surged through my whole body, but I opened the door, anyway. Only the tightening of his jaw gave away the fact my mood was visible. At least I'd put away my pelt. I had a feeling Grandpa might have tried to drown him like he'd done with Tony.

"What's up, Nox?"

"Huh?" I strode down the hall, letting him follow me. I didn't want him seeing my face until I knew for sure he hadn't actually come here to see a busty blond bear shifter instead of me.

"Jeannie better still be letting you use her room, or I'll shave her head."

"How did you know?"

"What? That she's giving you a place to stay?" He stepped up his pace, so we walked side-by-side down the hall. "Olivia ran into me on the way from the dining hall. She thought maybe you'd want to see me."

"Oh, really?" I glanced at him from the corner of my eye. The fire in my belly cooled.

"Yeah, really. I think she's been reading too many romances lately." He chuckled. "Thinks she's a matchmaker or something."

"I saw a book by Jane Austen in her bag at class today." I stuck out my tongue.

"Could have been worse." He shrugged. "There's that best-selling book with the handcuffs on the cover.

"You really think someone like Olivia Adler would read mommy porn?" I shook my head.

"Why shouldn't she?" He actually winked, the sly dog.

"Well, she should if she wants to. I'd never." I leaned against the wall next to Jeannie's door, not quite ready to be alone behind a closed door with him yet. "But this is the twenty-first century."

"Girl's gotta get her kicks somehow, and I don't see anyone hanging around her door." He gave me a toothy grin. "Same can't be said for you." He put one hand on the wall above my shoulder, then leaned on it. Just as he bent his elbow to move closer, I stepped away, turning my back to him so I could open the door.

I headed in, standing in the middle of the room with my hands on my hips. He'd gone in after me, of course, before I could say goodbye and shut the door which was the exact opposite of what I really wanted. I rolled my eyes, opening my mouth to say something snarkily reminiscent of Lynn. He covered it with his, wrapping his arms around me.

The way his body felt against mine was even more intense than the night before. How could that be when we weren't out in a semi-public place, and I had more on than an old blanket? Josh's hands moved up my back, one stopping across my shoulder blades and the other sliding up the back of my neck. He twined his hand in my hair, not pulling, but still holding firmly. He broke the kiss. I'd never have been able to. Somehow, I felt on fire and frozen solid at the same time.

The heat of his breath misted my cheek as he moved to the side and down to nuzzle my neck. I tried to say something, hoping maybe whatever words I'd utter might give me an idea of what this feeling was. No luck. The only sound out of my mouth was a breathy moan. This was ridiculous. I'd been there and done that, even if it was all the way back with my High School boyfriend. Of course, that was ancient history. I hadn't even looked at a man since Dad died and left me with the pelt way too soon.

If this had been a fight, I would have had the upper hand. Any move he made, I'd react with the counter, know where to look in order to anticipate his actions. I could do nothing but shudder. It was like the rest of the world went away. The only thing that existed besides me was him.

That probably sounds more romantic than Olivia's recent reading material. It might have been for someone else. I'm used to hearing eleven voices in my head and sensing magic in everything. I couldn't move. Nothing was in context anymore with the rest of the world on vacation.

Josh sensed this somehow. He pulled back, still cradling me against him, then ushered me to the edge of the bed. He pulled the chair out from under the desk, turned it around, and sat on it like a normal person instead of backward, for once. He leaned forward, putting his elbows on his thighs and resting his head on folded hands. Even though his posture was the height of informality, his face wore an expression of deep concern. I'd expected a million questions, possibly some kind of outburst driven by wounded pride. He said nothing, just sat and let me collect myself.

"That's it. Of course." I stood up on shaky legs. "Collect myself. Of course. That's why this isn't working. How stupid could I be?"

He cocked his head to one side, watching as I crossed the room to the desk. He still looked puzzled when I opened my bag. After I retrieved the oilcloth and put on my pelt, his eyes glimmered with a hint of understanding. I turned to face him, finally feeling ready for something other than a fight. I didn't waste time wondering whether it had been stupid to use it. Only what happened next could answer that question.

"You weren't really yourself either time then, huh?" He looked up at me, comprehension in his expression.

"Nope." I smiled. "Am now." A little thrill of anticipation shivered up my spine. The nearly numb tingle left over from his earlier caresses ran swiftly from cold to hot. It was my turn to chuckle now. I shook my head, sensing the approval and then slow retreat of my ancestors. Even Grandpa quieted, the stormy force of his personality calming to leave me with more control over the pelt's powers than I'd ever experienced.

It only took a few steps to cross the distance between us. Josh sat up, gathering his legs under him as he prepared to stand. I didn't let him. Instead, I reached down and tilted his chin up. Then, I planted one on him. A kiss, of course. He reached up, and I let him pull me down against him.

Later, when I pulled the borrowed sheet up to cover us, I heard the murmur of a twelfth voice, the song it sang familiar and sorely missed. Dad. Everything but the piece of him that'd live in the pelt had moved on. My eyes closed, heavy with profound relief and weariness.

"We were right," I managed. Then, I followed Josh's even breath under the surface of consciousness.

CHAPTER THIRTEEN

Josh

Pins and needles in my arm woke me up. I blinked, then tilted my head so I could kiss the top of Nox's head. She'd completely shocked me by rocking my world half the night like that. I smirked, remembering how awkward a kid I'd been before my first shift. I should have realized that without her pelt, she wasn't her whole self. I'd met Magi who'd lost their powers before, from encounters with Spites. If she lost her pelt, Nox would lose part of herself just like those Magi.

Now I'd have to find that drunk asshole Selkie's pelt or die trying. Literally, because she'd been right just before she fell asleep. Our hunches had been correct. This was righter than anything had ever been before in my life. I wouldn't tolerate anyone turning my mate into a shell of herself, not even the Sidhe Queen. I guess I'd finally taken a side, chosen a Faerie Court after all. I huffed out a little laugh.

It should have felt more like a major fail. It didn't. Even though I'd been like a second spare tire in the family hierarchy, neutrality had been hammered so hard into Derek's and Beth's heads I couldn't have escaped the idea if I'd wanted to. Dad always said taking a side would mean betraying the trust people placed in wolf shifters. We'd been the first shifters in general law enforcement positions after the Big Reveal, so the pressure was higher on our family to work harder, be more upstanding than others.

But Mom always said it was even bigger than that. Taking one side weakened the other. An imbalance could tip the scales toward the first open Extrahuman war ever. But something always bothered me about that idea. Sometimes, conflict happened. You couldn't avoid it all the time, no matter how hard you tried. Someone somewhere wanted to screw things up until all the hard work and impeccable standards in the world couldn't prevent a fight. And that's exactly what was happening right here and now.

The Extramagus was smart. He or she knew that more young Changelings tithed to the King since the Big Reveal because the old rules Seelies had to follow didn't work in the new mingled world. The Kings Court grew while hers stayed the same. That Extramagus knew the Queen had more to lose if, say, a Spite got defeated and destroyed in combat, or a Selkie pelt went missing. Or the mortal police force aligned with the Unseelies.

But then, there was coincidence to worry about. I had no idea what Derek's mate might have been like as he hadn't told us about one before he'd gone missing. Beth had happened to make a nice appropriate match, but then he'd also gone missing. Was it my turn to disappear, or worse? Or did coincidence make things for Pack Dennison hard this time around because my mate happened to be Unseelie? Should I be waiting for some kind of accident? I shuddered.

"Okay." Nox wrapped her arms around me, holding me closer. One of her hands reached up to stroke my cheek. "We got this. Whatever it is."

"Might be coincidence calling in its marker." I sighed. "Whammied both my siblings. Still think we got this?"

"Yeah, actually." She sat up, beaming at me in the morning light.

Her black hair stood out against one pale shoulder, and a defiant twinkle lit her blue eyes like moonlight on water. "If Tinfoil Hat's Beta can give coincidence a one-finger salute, so can its Alpha."

"Thanks. I needed a magic horse shifter to encourage me to buck the odds." I winked. She laughed, then leaned down. When her lips met mine, my wolf surged forward in complete agreement with my state of arousal. I turned the tables on her, getting the upper hand in this round more handily than I'd done when we sparred at the dojo. The thought of what a challenging opponent she'd been just made me want her more.

The knock and music of female voices out in the hall was worse at that moment than taking the ice-bucket challenge. I groaned, getting up to grab my clothes and pull them on. Being a shifter had at least given me years of practice in getting decent quickly. Nox was right behind me, but slower. I smoothed out the bed while she went to the door.

"Who is it?" Her voice was higher-pitched than usual, the only indication I got that she might be as frustrated as I was just then.

"We're going for breakfast. Come on already, or I'll force choke you through the door."

"Okay, Darth Lynn." Nox peered in the mirror next to the door, detangling her hair with her fingers. "Give me a minute. Meet you at the front door."

"One minute, or Alderaan gets it." Lynn's quip faded, along with some giggling accompaniment that sounded like Maddie the Umbral Magus. Yeah, I remembered her. She was a packmate, which Alphas never forget. Kind of convenient that she was dating the Beta.

"Look, Nox. We still need to talk about what's happening on Monday. I made a promise to, um, your lawyer." I leaned one elbow on the wall next to the door and stuck the other out, scratching the back of my head. One glimpse in the mirror on the closet door put an end to that. No self-respecting guy wants to look like the awkward anime character trying to talk to his girlfriend.

"Yeah. Can you do it in a minute?"

"Talking, maybe. Anything else..." I shrugged and dropped her a wink. Nox threw back her head and laughed.

"Okay. I didn't much care about Alderaan anyway." Her smile made my breath catch in my throat.

"Look, at the end, when I win the match against Uncle Jake, I can't just trade you away to the Queen."

"But you have to." She crossed her arms over her chest. "That's the only way to make up for what I did."

"No. I don't have to. I'm going to refuse to order you around on this as either your Alpha or your mate." I tucked my chin, gazing into her eyes, fighting the urge to get lost in that bright steely blue. "I can't do anything but give an honest account of events and then leave it up to you."

"I don't understand."

"I'll explain it as best I can, then." I put my hands on her shoulders. "If I give in to the Queen, just hand over one of my most accomplished pack members who also happens to be my mate, I'll look like I'm siding with her. Wolf shifters mate. We have to, or we go nuts and can't be leaders. Someone as old as the Sidhe fricking Queen can't pretend to be ignorant about that. Coincidence makes mates, not Faerie or pack politics. If I roll over for her, I look weak. That and I couldn't live with myself if I cuffed you and handed you over like you did something wrong instead of being a hero. So, that's why it's going to be up to you. You go with her willingly, of your own volition and under your own power, or not at all."

"So you're letting me decide whether to stand trial?"

"Yup."

She closed her eyes, nodding. I smelled salt before I saw the glimmers at the corners of her eyes. When she opened them, a matched set of tears rolled down. Her lips parted, teeth stark and bared in a flavor of defiance I'd never seen before. She raised her hands to her shoulders, placing them firmly over mine. I'd shaken the hands of probably half the politicians, law enforcement officials, and society heads in the state of Rhode Island. None of them had possessed even half the strong confidence in Nox's grip.

"Then after you beat your jerk of an uncle, I'll turn myself in. Let the Sidhe fricking Queen figure out what to do about a Kelpie with a Tanuki lawyer." She closed her lips, letting them meet as she leaned in to press them quickly but firmly against mine.

If only that was how it went.

CHAPTER FOURTEEN

Josh

I met my pack on Monday an hour after sundown on the bridge near the Temple to Music in Roger Williams Park. They'd all had a look at Nox's local shifter history books over the weekend. Extrahuman affairs that had to be settled in front of an audience usually happened there. A crowd had already gathered. I spotted all the guys in the Night Creatures, plus Jeannie, Mr. Ichiro, and Kimiko. A smoky whisper from Blaine confirmed my suspicion that Taki Waban had shown up as well.

Henry pointed out the Redford family sitting far away from Albert the Sidhe Changeling. Maddie and Lynn put their hands to their cheeks at almost the same time when they spied Headmistress Thurston. Bobby scratched his head, then pointed out Professor Watkins next to a decrepit guy in a black Greek fisherman's cap, but when I blinked, the professor was alone again. Tony jerked his chin at Bianca the Medium. Pretty much everyone from PPC had shown. I didn't let it go to my head, though. The campus loved my dad.

And then I saw him. He and my mom were up on the dais, chained to one of the columns by shiny manacles around their wrists. My wolf snarled deep within, and I had to fight back hard to keep him from taking over. They'd used silver. Beth must have known and decided not to tell me because she knew how I'd react. Chaining a wolf shifter with silver, even something silver-plated, was pure torture. I'd always thought Uncle Jake had been kind of an asshole, but I'd never believed he'd do something that heinous.

A cool hand on my shoulder settled me for the moment. I didn't have to look; I knew the feel of Nox's hand by heart already. I nodded at her, then took a step forward and put my hands on my hips.

"Let's do this." I walked down off the bridge and down the gentle slope designed to let voices carry. The rest of Tinfoil Hat followed. Well, everyone except Olivia. She'd fallen asleep in the Harcourt family party bus on the way over from campus, the poor thing.

Everyone else stopped at the curved line in the grass that marked the division between the seats and the flat expanse of lawn in front of the white marble temple. I crossed it, continuing on until I stood in front of Uncle Jake in the middle. The mutineers, about two-thirds of the members of Mom's pack and a little less of Dad's, stood on the steps between my parents and me. I glanced over to see Beth hobble out of the audience and stand between Bobby and Blaine. The dragon shifter offered her his arm and she took it, somehow managing to look more like a girl posing for her senior prom picture than a woman who needed assistance to make up for the ill-fitting prosthetic on her missing leg. She caught my eye, and I nodded. If I couldn't beat Uncle Jake, she'd step up. It'd be a long shot, but if I injured him badly enough, she just might do it. Her leg was less of a liability in wolf form.

"So, you actually showed up." Uncle Jake jerked his chin, sneering over my shoulder at my pack. "Nice crew. Too bad none of them can fight worth a damn."

"You know what they say about people who assume." I glared down at him, glad I'd ended up being taller than Mom's little brother, even if he did have nine years on me. "None of them will need to fight anyway. I'll beat you alone."

"No, you won't." Uncle Jake whistled. A statuesque redheaded woman dressed in a long, flowing robe stepped out of the pack behind him. "I'm invoking the trial of mates. Laila will be fighting tonight, against whatever psychic waif you have that passes for a mate these days." He eyed Lynn and Maddie.

"Awesome." I'd seen Laila fight before. She was savage, brutal, and exploited any weakness she could find. She also answered to a whistle. Nox would wipe the floor with her. Well, the grass, okay? You know what I mean.

I heard the sound of muddled murmurs carry across the lawn from my uncle's side as I turned on my heel and walked away. Yup, I put my back to Jake. From the low growl, he was the opposite of pleased. I walked right up to Maddie May, who still might have given Laila a run for her money considering her Umbral magic. Then, I held out my hand to Nox, who'd been standing behind her.

I turned around, heading back the way I'd come, hand in hand with my mate. She stood half a head taller than Laila, although she was thinner. Nox's smile was nothing nice when she turned it first to Laila, then to Uncle Jake. A clammy chill emanated from her as she locked gazes with the man trying to usurp my parents.

"So this is your Uncle Jake?" Nox raised an eyebrow. "I thought the trial of mates was intended for use by pregnant female Alphas, Josh." By addressing me instead of my uncle, Nox's statement couldn't be taken as a direct challenge.

"Yup." I shrugged. "Mom did it last time something like this happened. That was before I was born." I gave Uncle Jake my best smile.

"No more ignorant questions from the human peanut gallery." Jake's lip curled up in a more severe sneer than before. "I called the trial and named my champion. Name her already and let them start."

"Fine." I let go of Nox's hand, then turned to her and gave her a slight bow. "This is a veteran member of my pack and my mate. You might have heard of her since she's a little bit infamous right now. I present the Kelpie, Nox Phillips."

Nox

There was no way I'd beat Laila, even though I'd spent half the weekend reading the local shifter history book. All the same, when Josh introduced me, I waved to the crowd. This wasn't my first public fight. Most of the Cherry Blossom School's trophies belonged to me, after all. Then again, that was before I became an Extrahuman.

I'd expected a reaction from both packs and the crowd in general, but nothing like what happened. A few boos started up behind Uncle Jake, but then an eerie trilling sound rose from Bobby Tremain's throat. Was it a Rebel Yell? It didn't matter. The moment of silence that followed it gave Tinfoil Hat time to start a huge cheer. Everyone in the general audience joined in, hollering their approval far and away beyond any low sounds of dissent. I even saw Headmistress Thurston with her fingers in her mouth, whistling.

I bowed to Laila just like Ren had taught me to do before any fight, and the cheers got more intense. Then I nodded at Josh. He took a step backward. Uncle Jake mirrored him. They backed away from the center of the lawn, leaving Laila and me facing each other on the dewy lawn.

We circled each other, and before I knew it, I'd cracked my knuckles. Stupid habit, but knowing I only had a ghost of a chance to win this duel had me on edge. At least it looked like Laila intended to start the fight in human form. I'd have to beat her fast, then, before she shifted. Shifting to horse form on dry land would weaken my magic. I couldn't spare a glance at the pond on the other side of the Temple to Music. If only this match had been over there, I'd be able to throw water spells around, along with my meager glamour.

I kept my gaze fixed on the space between my opponent's eyes, just like I'd been taught. That was why I missed it when she started shifting. By the time I realized what was happening, Laila's robe was a pile of gray fabric on the ground, and her face was the last human-looking feature she possessed. I murmured a few words of focus under my breath, hoping to cover my late shift with the illusion it was farther along. It didn't work. Laila clearly had some experience with Changeling or even Faerie opponents and the fact she hadn't moved yet meant the ephemeral shimmer of any Glamour had given me away.

Laila bolted forward, her head down. She faked left, then headed around me to the right. I'd just leaned all my weight forward to kick out with my hind legs when I felt the air of her passage under them. She'd been about to hamstring me. My nostrils flared as I blew out a misty breath in the chill night air. The half-moonlight silvered Laila's russet fur as she darted past on my left. I planted my feet, not daring to rear. She was fast enough to go for my gut before I could strike out with my hooves. Instead, I focused my energy on calling up the deeps.

The earth under me had moisture in the soil. I felt water slick my coat, drenching my mane and tail until they stuck to me. Laila snorted, clearly aware of what I was doing but not why. It took too much time for me to call water even at this short distance in horse form. The fact that some force in the shadows up on the dais pushed against my magic like Sisyphus's boulder made it all worse.

Laila circled me again, and I had to choose between countering her and continuing my spell. Slashes of pain crossed my back legs, throbbing as they buckled under me. I managed to prop my weight on my forelegs long enough to level a glare at my opponent, screaming out a defiant neigh as I unleashed the force of pent-up water directly at her muzzle.

She couldn't howl, bark, whine, or whimper. She couldn't breathe, of course, unless wolves had evolved gills. They hadn't. She paced back and forth twice as though held captive behind iron bars instead of an open lawn. Then, Laila shook her head, bending it to the ground so she could rub her nose and mouth against the damp grass. I'd only sort of defeated her. I had to stay conscious, or she'd win In the trial of the mate, victory went to the last shifter standing.

She'd cut my legs deeper than I'd thought. My head spun with magical effort and pain. The coppery scent of blood only made it worse until I glanced over at Josh. His fists clenched, and his arms shook. I let my gaze travel up to his face, wanting that to be the last thing I saw if passing out was inevitable. Renewed energy surged through me as our eyes met, either the fact of his love or the magical bond between us letting me dig deeper for more. Laila hadn't bothered looking back at Jake. My magic told me she'd waited too long before she slumped to the grass, her body slowly transitioning from wolf to human form as her body involuntarily tried to dislodge the water.

I called back my magic, letting go of the cohesive force damming up her airway. Water flowed from her nose and mouth. I dragged myself forward, tilting my head to listen for her breathing. It was slow, but even. I'd won. Shutting my eyes, I rested my now-hairless face against the cool, dank grass. I couldn't stand, so I wouldn't bother trying. A collection of hushed gasps from everyone but Uncle Jake's pack reminded me I was in the altogether. I hadn't worn a robe either, so one of my favorite outfits currently decorated the blood- and water-smeared battleground in tatters.

Something warm, dry, and slightly scratchy covered my back. A pair of long-fingered hands I'd recognize anywhere stroked my hair. A set of lighter footsteps squelched through the muddy grass behind me, and I felt a sting of antiseptic, then someone bandaging my legs.

"Don't turn her." Lynn always sounded bossy, but this time, her voice was tinged with concern. "The cuts are deep. I have to put a poultice and bandage on these. Even with her pelt, they might take a few hours to heal."

"Fine." Josh's voice was hushed and a little shaky. "Just hurry it up. She's coming."

I looked up, turning my head away from the suddenly solemn audience. At the top of the dais, Josh's parents stood rubbing their unchained wrists. That would have been nice to see, except for the presence of the person who'd freed them. I averted my eyes, but it was too late. They'd met hers.

"So this is the insolent scion of House Phillips." The Sidhe Queen's voice was lower-pitched than I'd expected, its vowels extended in a languidly musical drawl. She tilted her head, peering down at Josh. "Hand her over, young Alpha, or risk my displeasure."

"I'll do no such thing." Josh rose. Even though he was one of the tallest people I knew, he still had to look up to meet her gaze.

"Did you misspeak?" The Queen's sky blue gown somehow managed to make her figure look fashionably thin and lush at the same time.

"No, Your Highness." Josh stood as still as he had that night in the Memorial Grove, all his attention focused. "Nox isn't mine to hand over. She's done nothing to displease me either as a member of my pack or my mate. In fact, she saved my Beta's life and now has claimed this victory that freed my parents. She will go to face your justice of her own will or not at all."

"And does she realize what sort of catastrophe refusal will assure?" The Queen raised one amber eyebrow.

"She does." I propped myself up on my elbows, continuing the Queen's disregard for my presence by referring to myself in the second person. "And that's why she's agreeing to go with you as soon as her other packmate finishes tending her wounds." Lynn had a suspiciously sudden coughing fit, then finished taping the bandages to my calves.

"So, you agree to submit yourself to the custody of my guards immediately and surrender your pelt?"

"I'll let you imprison me, sure. But you can't have my pelt."

"I can't allow a prisoner to keep such a powerful magical item while in custody."

"That's okay." I glanced back toward the audience where Taki Waban sat. The left corner of his mouth tilted up, and he gave me a slight nod. "I've got a church-key. I'll use that to store it before you bring me in."

Before I could ask Josh to go back to the bus and get my pack,

Blaine stepped forward, one strap slung over his shoulder. I hadn't seen him leave, but that was what he must have done when it was clear I'd won the match. He approached as Lynn went back to stand with Bobby, helping him support Beth.

"Here you go, horsefeathers," Blaine grinned down at Josh and me. "Now, all you need is a door and someone trustworthy to leave that key with."

"I could leave it with Ichiro-san." I winced as my attempt to get up filled with fail. "He's representing me." The pack hit the dirt near my head. I rummaged inside, pulling out a warm sweater and a cozy maxi skirt. I pulled them on as best as I could under the blanket draped over me.

"I've got an appropriate custodian in mind already." The Queen clapped her hands. "Hertha!" Blaine's eyes widened. A steady but small stream of smoke wafted out of his nose.

I didn't look up. All I saw were a pair of red and black patent Christian Louboutin pumps step lightly over the grass, stopping in front of me. I rolled on my side, trying not to bend my knees. A tall woman with hair as black and polished as obsidian looked down her nose at me. She couldn't help it, really. It was the angle her head happened to be at when she bowed to the Sidhe Queen.

"My husband will convey you to my vehicle because it seems my son also has a conflict of interest in this matter." One of the woman's perfectly shaped eyebrows tilted as she scrutinized me. "The key will be safe in my hoard until the conclusion of the trial. I will see it delivered to the right party personally when the time comes." She directed her gaze to Blaine, eyes narrowing. "And we have a great deal to talk about once this is done, whelp."

I blinked. The Queen's clap had summoned none other than Hertha Harcourt, the most influential dragon shifter on the Eastern Seaboard. I knew the Queen ranked amongst the most powerful beings on the planet, but it hadn't really hit home before how dangerous defying her had been. I'd kind of just done it in the moment, only thinking about my friends and pitying that poor Spite. Finally, I understood exactly how screwed I was.

Mr. Harcourt held his hands palm up. I watched powder-blue scales cover them. He pointed the fingertips at me, blowing gently. I rose off the ground, carried by his Air magic as he strode to the limousine I'd ridden in with Maddie less than a month before. It beat trying to walk hamstrung.

I used the church-key on the passenger door, pulling off my pelt and sealing it in the oilcloth from my pack. Josh had followed us, and Mr. Harcourt must have had some compassion for young love, despite his emotionless facade. He stepped far enough away for us to have a few moments alone.

"Nox, I don't know what to say. I'll get you out of this."

"You can't. Nothing but information can help now. The Queen has trials with law and order, not by combat like your pack. That's the King's way, not hers."

"Information's exactly what I'm banking on." He grinned. "I've still got a question to ask a certain ex-Spite."

"You shouldn't use that for me." I shook my head. "Save it for a time when you really need it."

"Believe me, this is the right time." He put his arms around me, holding me as closely as the Air magic would allow. "I'll do anything in my power to save you."

"You shouldn't worry. She wants my pelt. After that, she'll let me go. You don't have to save me because I'll be fine. I might even be a better mate as a regular girl. Definitely more appropriate."

"I can't believe I'm hearing this after you just fought in the Trial of Mates for me. I love you, Nox Phillips. That includes all twelve ornery ancestors in that pelt of yours. I've done my homework. A piece of you is in there too, a piece that'll be missing the entire time you go without it. I'm not letting the Queen do that to you without a fight."

"But I told you, she doesn't fight with fang and claw."

"Even better. I like a challenge." He ran his fingers through my hair. "Just because I have fang and claw doesn't mean I can't learn to fight on her terms. I'm not giving up. Neither will Ichiro-san."

Mr. Harcourt cleared his throat. Josh gave me a quick kiss, then backed away a few paces before he turned and ran back to the rest of our pack. The magical air wafted me away, over toward the Temple the long way. I handed Mrs. Harcourt the key on the way, struck by how much neither she nor her husband resembled Blaine. As I prepared to be imprisoned at the Temple to Music for the night, I thought about what Josh had said. I hoped using the rebel sprite's last question was worth it. But even with recent insider information, how could Josh beat the Sidhe Queen herself at a game she'd been playing since the dawn of humanity?

CHAPTER FIFTEEN

Josh

Blaine's party bus dropped Lynn, Bobby, Tony, and Olivia back at the dorms. It took the rest of us back to my house, including my parents and Beth. My blood relations all went directly upstairs. I tried to catch the Ichiros before they left the park, but they'd gone while I was talking to Nox. Probably for the best, considering Mr. Ichiro's warnings about conflicts of interest.

I brought Blaine, Henry, and Maddie to the basement with me. The rec room was down there, complete with a bar. I needed a drink. I poured Jaeger over ice in three shot glasses, then used the boiling water tap to make Henry some Earl Gray. He peered at the wall behind me, then took down a bottle of Gosling's and tipped a shot in the cup.

"A Gunfire, huh?" Blaine sniffed, clinking the ice in his glass. "Haven't seen one of those since Grandpa visited Newport."

"Who drinks hot tea in the summer?"

"Air dragons."

"Ah. Well, that's odd. How did you end up Fire?"

"Well, he's my step-grandpa."

"Wait. Your dad's not your dad?"

"Not technically. Look, we have more important things to talk about than my home life." Blaine puffed out a smoke ring. "What are we going to do about Nox?"

"I have a few ideas, but we should talk before I pull the ace out of my sleeve." I headed over to the pool table in the middle of the room, turned, then leaned on it. "The Queen wants a Kelpie pelt to make up for losing a Selkie one. Trogdor here knows artifacts. I need to know what's comparable that we can offer her."

"Nothing." Blaine didn't have to check anything or even think before answering. "Well, the original Selkie pelt that got lost, or a different Kelpie's pelt. But those are so rare they're nearly priceless."

"So, I have one question I can ask an extremely knowledgeable creature. Should I ask where to get a Selkie's pelt?"

"No." Henry inhaled the vapor over his teacup. "I know who you're going to ask and they won't be able to tell you that."

"So what should I ask, then?"

"How about asking it to give you evidence to win the trial?" Maddie leaned on the bar. "There's nothing that says the question has to be tightly focused."

"The problem with that is there's no evidence to help us win." Henry sighed. "Nox is guilty as charged. She undid the enchantment and used a Seelie artifact to do it. What I don't understand is how she got that float in the first place when you had it, Blaine."

"See, that's the weird thing." Blaine sipped his Jaeger. "I blurted out the idea of using it like a moron. But she shouldn't have even seen it. My bag was closed, the float under other stuff. Somehow, it was sitting right on top of my backpack, outside it."

"I think that might be my fault." Maddie looked so down her curls even drooped. "I sort of asked for help that night. I think I know who moved it."

"Look, you did what you had to do." Henry put his arm around her. "Neither of us would be here if you hadn't."

"What exactly happened, Maddie?"

"I made an oath to a Gnome. I owe them now because they helped our allies get the right things to the right place at the right time."

"Makes sense." I shrugged. "Gnomes have a weird time-space ability that only affects themselves and stuff right next to them. Tell on."

"So, I think maybe the whole thing's coincidental." Maddie leaned back against the bar next to Henry. "I asked Lynn to look up some history stuff about pelts to see what kind of pattern we might need to break."

"Good." I nodded. "She's on that now?"

"Yeah. She just had to help Olivia get in her room. Anyway, she'll text us with whatever she finds."

Just as I was about to ask Maddie what other information she had about the Gnome, I heard a soft pop behind me and felt eyes on the back of my head. I pushed off from the table, reaching over to grab my drink. It wasn't where it should be. I turned around slowly. A tiny creature in a tall, pointy and shabby hat pushed a ball toward me. Speak of the Gnome, and they shall appear. I realized the little bastard was positioning the eight ball, so I was behind it.

"You're trespassing on dangerous territory, Gnome." I put my hands on my hips.

"Just here to call in my favor from the Lady over there." The little twerp pointed at Maddie, then smiled brightly. Well, not exactly. They smiled like Jaws. Their mouth was full of shark's teeth.

"Great. Because we didn't need her help at all on this." The sour tang of Blaine's sarcasm rang out over my shoulder, along with the scent and sound of more Jaeger sloshing into his glass.

"Coincidence helps those who help themselves." The Gnome held out their hand. Maddie walked over to the table, sighing.

"I know, Gee. But now's not a good time." Maddie shook her head. "We've got a crisis on our hands here."

"That's why I need your help right now, Lady." The gnome blinked, their eyes glittering.

"Oh, I get it." I narrowed my eyes. "You're trying to make us fail. You must want this to happen."

"No, wolf lordling." They shook their head. "I need the Lady's help to fulfill another obligation. It's better for you and the Kelpie if she comes with me."

"This is bullshit." I held one hand over my head, about to swat that Gnome like a cockroach.

"You should trust him." Henry's hand circled my wrist like an icy manacle. "I've known Gee Nome for nine years, now. Their timing's impeccable and they've never made my situation worse even when they could have."

"You aren't me." I broke his grip but lowered my arm to my side. "But I wanted you as Beta for exactly that reason. I need as full an explanation as you can give me."

"I don't remember why Gee helps me, but they say that's because I ordered them not to mention it. Must be something to do with an event I'm not supposed to remember. Anyway, the entire time I've known them, they had metal teeth. Now they're shark. Something's changed in Gee's situation. If Gee says they need the help now, they mean it. And think about shark's teeth for a minute. What does that bring to mind?"

"The ocean." I let out a breath I hadn't realized I'd been holding. "The float. Selkies." I stared down at the gnome. "Fine. You take Maddie and get out of here. Do your thing."

Gee Nome giggled, clapping their hands as they hopped from one foot to the other. Then, they snapped their fingers. They and Maddie vanished with a louder pop than before.

"I wonder what a Gnome needs an Umbral magus for, anyway." Blaine scratched his head. "Especially one powerful enough to Vanish a full-grown person."

"They weren't that powerful before." Henry shook his head.

"Guess he leveled up, then." Blaine sighed. "Anyway, we need to decide what to ask the ex-Spite. Let's write some ideas down." He got paper and a pen from the desk on the other side of the room, then brought it back to the bar and sat.

We worked on ideas for about an hour when Lynn sent a text. I turned on the TV, then used the remote to navigate away from all the streaming services and get to the Internet browser. The files Lynn had sent would be easier to share on the big screen. I selected the first one.

"Huh." Henry stepped forward, pointing to the date. "I remember hearing rumors about this. A Kelpie died with no relatives who could take the pelt. Why are all those spots blacked out?"

"Redacted records." I selected the next one, showing Henry more of the same. "Either someone in this case is still around, or someone pulled major strings to keep it covered."

"It says over there that the pelt got sent to an appropriate custodian for storage." Henry scratched his head. "That sounds familiar."

"It should, Memory Man." Blaine sighed, practically collapsing into the easy chair behind him. "The Queen said that about my mom."

"So this isn't your mom's first Kelpie pelt rodeo, huh?" I punched Blaine's shoulder. "Come on, man. It's actually a good thing you have an idea. Otherwise, all this black magic marker redaction crap would just be a dead end."

"No, it's not good. And it really is just an idea until I can check the hoard inventory." Blaine leaned his elbows on his knees and put his head in his hands.

"Wait. Let me look at the rest of the files Lynn sent." Henry held his hand out for the remote. I gave it to him. He scrolled through. "Okay, look. This one here, it's out of place. There's a missing page."

"Well, Lynn says she sent them all."

"Figures. She's thorough." Henry nodded. "But the missing page can only be the form that tells who has a claim on the item and where it is. Since that's gone, someone influential must have covered this up."

"Leaping Luna!" A surge of hope flooded my heart. "That means there's another pelt out there. If we had another church-key, we could switch them."

"So not only do you want me to check the hoard inventory, you want me to steal from it?" Blaine froze, the tension in his muscles making him look almost like a statue. "From my own mother?"

"Well, if this was your mate, wouldn't you do it?"

"That's kind of my point, Josh. She isn't my mate. She's yours." His narrowed eyes gleamed with some hard emotion. "You want a switcheroo, you do it."

"Look, we still don't even know if the pelt's there." Henry's level-headedness came to the rescue again. "We also don't know if that's what the Queen's going to want. We need to call the Sprite, and Blaine needs to check the inventory before we even know what's probable. Why not start there?"

"Makes sense." I held out my right hand at Blaine. "I promise not to ask you to actually take anything from the hoard. But I have another idea. Just check the inventory while I talk to the Queen's angry ex-servant."

"Fine. I need a hardwired Internet connection, though."

"Sure, no problem." I showed him the modem, and he plugged in.

Henry murmured something under his breath. A few moments later, a short, lanky figure crawled out from under the pool table. Unlike most others of its kind, this Sprite had lines around their eyes and extra hollowness below the cheekbones. The biggest difference was their wings. The bones were there, but only tattered remnants hung where bright windows should have been.

"The Son of Dennis wishes to ask his final question?" The Sprite peered up at me, then glanced at Henry and nodded.

"Yes. You know how the Queen has Nox. She's going to put her on trial, and she's going to be guilty."

"I know. I also know the Tanuki is her solicitor."

"Yup. So, in light of all that, what's the Queen going to sentence Nox with?"

"An enchantment of equal importance to the one she broke." The Sprite sighed, shaking their head. "For a Kelpie, that would mean she must surrender a pelt. She's lucky she's not Psychic or human. Otherwise, it'd be her life."

"I can't believe Ichiro couldn't get the charges dropped or negotiate something else."

"The Queen doesn't drop charges."

"Nox is my mate. I have to do whatever I can to save her."

"She will be saved. She will walk away from the trial alive."

"No, she'll only be half-alive without that pelt."

"Alive all the same," the Sprite fluttered one hand at their ruined wings.

"I understand." I sighed. "But that's not good enough for me."

"Wait. The lemon-lime soda said something interesting." Blaine looked over his shoulder. "The Queen will demand *a* pelt. Not Nox's, specifically. You don't have to do anything secret about switching it. It'd be totally in the rules to give her a different one. The Queen couldn't complain. And yeah, the one from the form is in the hoard all right. All I have to do is convince my mom to hand that one over instead of Nox's. She hates how the Queen orders her around. I bet she'd help just to stick it to her."

"Hey now, wait a minute." Henry shook his head. "There's one thing we didn't think about in all this. What about the actual owners of that other pelt? Are they around somewhere? I mean, we can't tell from all these redacted documents."

"If giving the pelt to the Queen would save Maddie, would you do it?"

"Not if that meant some other family would lose what's rightfully theirs. Maddie wouldn't stand for that sort of thing. Do you think Nox would?"

I sighed, at an impasse. I looked from Henry, the angel on my shoulder, to devilish Blaine. Both sets of eyes pleaded with me to do what each considered the right thing. I tapped one foot on the indoor-outdoor carpeting, unable to decide. I reached into my pocket, intending to just flip a coin and let luck decide. My phone buzzed. I flipped it over to find a message from a number I'd never seen before. I opened it.

Need help? ~K The end of the message was a string of emoji I couldn't decipher.

"What's this say?" I handed the phone to Blaine because Henry had a snowball's chance in Hell of translating that.

"Huh." Blaine smirked. "Is this K person a Psychic or something? Dog, bat, fire, an airplane and a castle on one line. After that, fangs, paper, a white house, an angel, and a raccoon." He handed the phone back. "They'd better be Psychic, or I'll think your basement's bugged."

"Nope, Tanuki." I pulled the quarter I no longer had to use from my pocket. "I was just about to flip this to decide things. Luck."

"Well, that explains a lot." Henry nodded. "All this was fallout from that lucky float. Blaine found it. I touched it, Nox used it. Your friend K must have been at the Temple tonight. I say we follow her instructions."

"Even though she's telling Blaine and me to head over to Newport and you to meet her about a paper?"

"I trusted Luck before, and it turned out for me. I'll trust it again." Henry let his arms drop to his sides, though his forehead was still all furrowed. "If she's got proof the family attached to that other pelt is all gone, no one can object to us letting the Queen have it."

"Look, man, if we had more time I'd wait until you verified it." I shook my head. "But Tanuki know what they're doing. If she says we have to work on things at the same time, then that's how we should play it."

"But aren't Tanuki supposed to be kinda shady?" Blaine raised an eyebrow. "I mean, I really want to see my mom get off her designer couch and actually do something for a change, but is this particular gal one we should trust?"

"You know the lawyer representing Nox?" Henry waited until Blaine nodded. "She's his daughter. Annoying, but I think she genuinely wants to help."

"If it's good enough for the dead guy, it's good enough for me."

"That's undead to you, Trogdor." Henry gave Blaine a sideways look. Then, they both chuckled. "Okay, let's get out of here. Where am I supposed to meet this Tanuki?"

"Her dad's house." I scrawled an address on a napkin, knowing how navigating by smartphones was a bitch for vampires. "That's what the house and the angel meant. It's on Angell Street. Let's head out."

Henry took the napkin and followed Blaine and me out the door that led to the side of the house. The vampire amped up his speed with blood, heading around the house and out of sight in a breath. Blaine and I walked at a more sedate pace toward the expanse of grass at the back of my family's property.

"Is this enough room?" I eyed the space. We used to play soccer on it back when Derek and Beth were still in High School. I had no idea how big Blaine was in dragon form.

"It'll do." He puffed out a smoke ring. "You'd better get in front of me, though."

I stepped around and turned my back. Instead of the expected rustle of fabric to indicate he'd disrobed, I heard a series of rips and pops. The rich ass bastard had just shredded his clothes shifting. I could have afforded that myself, but never did unless it was a huge emergency. The Harcourts sure seemed to have brought Blaine up with weird priorities.

I turned around to see a red and orange scaled reptilian face staring back at me with red eyes and vertical pupils. He jerked one thumb-like claw at a spot on his neck. Pretty obvious he wanted me to get up there and hang on all the way to Newport. I wasn't sure I liked the idea of freezing, but when I climbed on, I was surprised to find his leathery skin hot to the touch, like someone with a high fever. I remembered something from class about dragon shifters not actually being reptiles, more like echidna and the platypus. Before I could recall it all, Blaine leapt into the air.

It was easy enough for me while he ascended. That seemed to take forever and felt like gravity had a hand pressing down on my back. During the descent, the wind tried to knock me off like I was on the ropes at a Royal Rumble. I felt movement behind me as Blaine tilted his wings. We coasted, and the wind resistance got more tolerable. Still, by the time we landed, my nails were blunted, my shoulders stiff, and my knuckles white.

The outside of the Harcourt mansion was white marble, all lit up with floodlights. Blaine had landed near a gazebo. I turned when he shifted, waiting until I heard a hollow *thunk* of wood followed by rustling fabric. When I turned around, he was fully dressed and already striding across the lawn to the house. I shrugged and followed, ignoring the rudeness. At least it wasn't like I'd need directions or anything. The mansion was obvious.

The entrance was even more ostentatious than the one at my house. Everything was huge, of course. Blaine could have gotten in without shifting if he'd really wanted to, though everyone in the house would have heard him coming. As it was, I made more noise than him, the soles of my combat boots a hollow counterpoint to the soft sound of his bare feet.

I swallowed, increasing my pace to catch up with him. I reached one hand out to his shoulder, about to stop him and call things off. Nox wouldn't be okay with what we were doing. Making a magical pelt, pieces of some other family's ancestors, pay the price for her own actions was something she might not want to do. I couldn't think of any reason the Sidhe Queen would want an Unseelie magical item unless she intended to destroy it. Nox wouldn't stand by and let that happen.

"Let me tell you a story," Blaine increased his pace, escaping my imminent grasp, "about a man and a woman very much in love."

"Huh?"

"Just shut up and listen, Beowulf." Blaine sighed. "Fine, I'll give you the purple-proseless version. The Queen and the King had a hard time making babies, so they adopted mortals to carry pieces of their power, passed down through generations by blood or trinket. That was where Selkies and Kelpies came from, along with a few other things long since extinct.

"But some mortals got powers of their own. The Queen governed with a strict hand and swift punishments. The King tested with guidelines and reinforcement. They fought, cut their kingdom in half. The King got custody of all the children who carried his magic, likewise for the Queen. But the grandchildren didn't always choose the same way, except the Selkies and the Kelpies."

"Okay, so that's why a Redcap or a Sidhe or a Goblin can choose courts and a Kelpie's always Unseelie."

"Yup. The pelts can't switch sides because the power's not genetic."

Blaine sighed. "But all Faerie creatures are like kids to the monarchs, so she'd never destroy a Kelpie pelt. She'd just keep it."

"So this is more like a custody battle in a messy divorce than offering up a lamb to the slaughter?"

"Exactly." Blaine turned his head, raising an eyebrow. "Feel better?"

"Almost." I tapped the phone clipped to my belt. "I wish they'd find something and text."

"Look, nothing in this world is perfect." Blaine stopped, so I did, too. We faced each other in front of a door that could have been the side of a barn. "You find one perfect situation, everything else goes to hell so you don't take it for granted. Happened to Bobby and Lynn, Henry and Maddie. It's your turn, dog-man. Don't screw it up by failing to take a risk."

"But what if what I'm risking is Nox hating my guts?" I blinked a few times, clenching my jaw.

"Is the goal to get her to love you? Because I think you've got that covered. You're trying to keep her soul intact." It was Blaine's turn to blink. His eyes went red and reptilian, then faded back to their normal color. "At least, you'd better be."

"The Hell do you mean by that?"

"Do you care about her, or what she thinks of you?" Blaine's shoulders quivered slightly. I noticed he'd been clenching his fists. "Because you sound more like a dragon shifter than Alpha of the first pack to have a vampire alliance in umpteen years."

I glared, looking him right in the eye. Neither of us blinked. I reached out with my right arm, pushing against the door next to us. It opened a crack which for that door was enough space for us to walk in side by side.

"Let's go in there and tell your mom how awesome it'll be to stick it to the man with a switcheroo."

All the tension went out of Blaine's face, shoulders, and hands. He closed his eyes. Instead of relief, he looked exhausted. Worse than that, he reminded me of the time I'd seen a guy up on the Pell Bridge, surrounded by EMTs and Firefighters trying to stop him from jumping. I felt a tug at my sleeve. The Sprite with the tattered wings stood there, peering at Blaine. It looked up at me, then nodded. I understood.

"You went in here all gung ho, and you knew." I shook my head. "You're going to put your mother up to this and put yourself right in the way of the Extramagus. No wonder you got so pissed when I hesitated."

"I can handle a puny mortal, Beowulf." The small noise he made wasn't exactly a snort. There wasn't even a trace of smoke around him. "I bet even Extramagi are crunchy and taste good with ketchup."

"Thank you." I didn't know what else to say.

"Shut up and let's do this already." Blaine turned, disappearing past the doorway. I followed him, struck once again by how my seemingly haphazard pack kept turning out to actually be made of some seriously impressive people.

CHAPTER SIXTEEN

Nox

The stone looked pastel blue in the morning light. It reminded me of veins under pale skin. I breathed in the dewy air, the scent and feel of the nearby pond in my lungs and on my skin. None of that would do me any good without my pelt, but the humidity gave me some small measure of comfort. I shivered, sharpening the dull ache of the wounds on the backs of my legs.

Something warm and soft moved away from my back. At the same time, three soft hoots came from somewhere above. I looked up into the eaves of the Temple to Music. Instead of pigeons as I expected, something white and shaped like a small barrel perched. I rubbed my eyes, and when I blinked again, it was gone. I glanced down to see a huge fluffy cat with tufted ears like a lynx's. Except this was no lynx. Its fur was black and glossier than most long-haired felines. It blinked bottle-green eyes at me.

"There's no way you're—" The cat hissed, cutting off the name I'd been about to say. The tip of its tail flicked. It padded up beside me, bumping its head against my right front pocket. It sat, leveling a stare at the church-key in my pocket and then at the door to the electrical panel behind me. I glanced around. The Sprite guarding me was all the way down the steps, admiring the oncoming dawn. I'd never seen him shifted before, but I knew without a doubt that this was Tony, telling me to use the key and escape.

"No way," I whispered. "I won't run and hide for the rest of my life."

Tony's cat ears flicked, and he blinked. A flutter of wings and a single soft hoot came from the eaves again. Olivia? When Tony looked up and flicked his tail at me, I figured I was right.

"It's nice of you to visit and all, but the guard will be back soon." I waved the backs of my hands at them. "Now shoo."

They barely made any noise leaving. I wondered whose idea that had been, but it didn't matter. If the Queen had thought I'd use the third church-key, she'd have taken it from me. I'd agreed to imprisonment and the trial, and I wouldn't go back on my word. I didn't want to be punished, but if that was what happened, at least it was for something I'd done. People on trial in the mortal courts weren't always so lucky. I shuddered, thinking about Professor Brodsky. If the court couldn't find evidence he'd been mind-controlled, he could be executed for killing two vampires and attempting to murder a third. I hoped he didn't lose, and that the right criminal would be brought to justice.

No matter what happened today, I'd be losing something. If I was lucky, I'd walk away from this trial a Kelpie, but I couldn't be with Josh. If I was unlucky, I'd lose part of myself. At least Josh's parents couldn't object to us settling down. But I had to wonder what good that would be. I couldn't have accepted everything that went along with my magic if it wasn't for Josh. And I wasn't even sure I could be a proper mate to him without that missing piece. It wouldn't be right to make him settle for half a mate.

A hand, small and strangely padded, covered one of mine. I looked down to see something more like a paw, black, furry, but still five-fingered. Deep brown eyes glittered from a band of nearly black fur. A

Tanuki. The first rays of the dawn touched the back of my hand, lighting the paw resting against it with a golden glimmer. I blinked, feeling a small but steady flicker of warmth around my hand. It traveled up my arm, so ticklish I had to use all my martial arts training to sit still and bear it.

"Ichiro-san?" But no. It couldn't be. This Tanuki's ruff was long and lush, with less silver in its coat than I'd ever heard of an older Tanuki having, even when they'd used Luck charms to gain more years of life. "Kimiko. What are you doing here?"

The young Tanuki cocked her head to one side. Her mouth opened in a canine grin as she removed her paw from my hand.

"Got it. You were never here." I chuckled. "Thanks for the visit." Josh had obviously found her annoying, but she must have had a big, brave heart to come all the way over here. I watched her trot away, the black-tipped bushy tail bobbing along behind her comical enough to make me chuckle again.

It felt colder when she left, despite the sun. I pulled the single woolen blanket the Queen had ordered left with me more tightly around my legs. That's when I noticed the little box sitting where Kimiko had been. It smelled like food. I wondered how she'd managed to bring an item with her and leave it behind without shifting, then remembered. Tanuki didn't have elemental magic. Their talents varied individually. She must be able to hide objects. I opened the box to find three rice balls. I wolfed them down before my Seelie guard could notice them.

On the bottom of the box was a message in black ink. I read it silently. *Trust your mate.* I blinked and read it again, wondering what I should do with it. That message might just make things worse for me if it got discovered. But the box shimmered and dissolved once the full light of the sun hit it.

"What are you doing?" I turned to see a familiar bundle of bamboo sticks crackling as they leaned over me.

"I could ask you the same thing. Where's the Sprite?" I glanced down the steps at where they'd been earlier. They were gone.

"None of your business. I told you we'd be meeting again that night at the Summoner's home."

"Yes, under very different circumstances if I remember correctly." I narrowed my eyes. "Are you here on the Queen's business or the Summoner's?"

"The Summoner couldn't hold me once he'd been captured. The mortal authorities broke all his anchors." I wasn't sure how a creature who looked like a stick-bug could sound smug, but this one managed.

"Well, here's to different circumstances." I raised a mock glass to the Brownie. "Maybe I have a chance of walking away from this."

"You do." They stiffened. "This too shall pass, but likely not in the way you'd expect."

"You Brownies and your fortune-cookie psychobabble." I rolled my eyes.

They ignored my taunt and stood rigid, their entire body straight as a sapling, which meant they had relaxed. The Brownie swayed a little in the breeze coming off the pond. I turned to look down the lawn. The first few cars pulled up to the curb nearest the Temple to Music. One of them was a Campus Police car, followed by a Providence Police cruiser and a Psychic News Network van.

"The News is here? Seriously?" I sighed.

Something clattered on the marble in front of me. A small white bottle with a red and white label. Tylenol. I peered back up at the Brownie. I had no idea whether they were looking in my direction or not. Even a bona fide tree hugger would know where to start with a Brownie. They looked more like mini Ents than little elves.

"What's this for?" I popped open the cap, finding the foil seal underneath still intact. They weren't trying to poison me, then.

"Mortal pain relief. You are both mortal and in pain, are you not?"

"No, I mean the kindness routine." I peered up, the sun making me squint. "What gives?"

"You were wrong to undo the Spite, but if you and your friends hadn't investigated the Summoner, I'd still be his slave." It creaked and crackled a bit. "Giving you something of his is customary. After all, you defeated him. That means you are entitled to some spoils by our laws."

"Analgesic spoils." I snorted. "Any port in a storm." I rattled two pills out of the bottle, realized they weren't extra strength, and shook out two more. I dry-swallowed them.

Back at the curb, more vehicles had pulled up. It was going to be a long beginning to an unpredictable day.

CHAPTER SEVENTEEN

Josh

"I know why you're here." Mrs. Harcourt had her back to us, and still she had the upper hand. I wasn't surprised; this was her house, after all. "I noticed the item you searched for in the hoard database, Blaine."

Blaine put one finger to his lips, stopping at the end of the long hallway we'd walked down. I stood next to him in the doorway which was wider than the Thayer Trolley Tunnel back in Providence. The hall opened on a hexagonal room, something like a foyer by way of decoration. It was huge, just like the rest of the mansion. Dragons need their space, I guess. For a few moments, Blaine's mother arranged red-tipped purple roses in a vase. Then she turned around, a slight smile on her brick red lips.

"You have your dog friend well-trained, whelp." Mrs. Harcourt ignored me, walking toward her son. "Good. Maybe he can clean a mess up for me instead of making one like the Kelpie did."

"What did you have in mind, Mother?" Blaine's voice sounded completely different here than it did at school. Without the zing of sarcasm or nonchalant confidence, he sounded like a different person. I wasn't sure what to think of Newport Blaine.

"We've got a pest problem again." Mrs. Harcourt put a hand on one hip, leaning all her weight on the opposite foot. She didn't look much older than her son, but she was supposed to be from the tenth century or something. I tried not to get too creeped out by that.

"Oh, no." Blaine's hair flopped from side to side as he shook his head. "Not Pharaoh's Rats?"

"Nothing quite so dangerous." One corner of her mouth tilted up. "Only a cockatrice which is why I don't want you or your step-father taking care of this. I'll brook no threat to my husband's manhood or my future grandchildren."

"Eww, Mom." Blaine's nose wrinkled. He reminded me of the time I was fifteen and got grossed out by catching my parents necking.

"I don't get it." I gave Mrs. Harcourt the same kind of smile my mom gave the District Attorney and the mayor. "Why can't a dragon shifter fight a cockatrice?"

"They're bad for the male's fertility." Her smile glittered with brittle humor. She reminded me of how Lynn was before she got together with Bobby. "I might be ages older than either of you, but I've got a husband for a reason."

Her statement would have made me more uncomfortable if she hadn't glanced at the portrait of a man on the far wall. I almost had to squint to see it was Blaine's step-dad. Another portrait hung to its left. The guy in that painting looked like my packmate. I didn't have to wonder where Blaine's bio-dad was. Dragons were possessive, so he had to be dead, or Mrs. Harcourt wouldn't have moved along to another man. The guy's clothing looked old, like something out of a Civil War flick. But how could Blaine be his kid if the last time he'd been painted was 1863 or whatever? I couldn't afford to think about that right then, so I dropped the thought. There'd be time later.

"I managed to lock the pest in here." Mrs. Harcourt's voice was coolly commanding, like someone who expected to be obeyed. "Head on in and don't come out until you have a dead cockatrice to show me." Mrs. Harcourt gestured to the door opposite the one we'd entered through, looking like a younger, raven-haired Vanna White. "I suggest you shift. They're fast, and they have sharp claws and beaks. And mind its gaze."

I stared at the door she'd gestured to, only aware she'd left the hexagonal foyer by the fading click of her heels. I stood next to Blaine, hoping he'd say something. This was his stomping ground, not mine. I waited as long as I could, then tapped my foot.

"What?" Blaine's voice was softer, tiny somehow compared to the larger-than-life mask he usually wore on campus.

"Give me the supernatural geek squad rundown." I turned to look at him. "I know how to chase chickens, but a cockatrice is only half one of those. So, what do I do?"

"I can't believe she asked you to do this." When he turned, I noticed his sweaty brow. His pallid face was set in an expression more uneasy than the one he'd worn before we came down here. How was that possible? "I'm so sorry."

"But I don't get why you should apologize." I shrugged out of my jacket, letting it fall with a hollow thud to the floor. Then I kicked off my boots.

"Don't let it scratch you. Its claws and beak have a venom that acts fast enough to be a mortal threat for a shifter your size. And don't look into its eyes." Blaine shuddered. "Look, maybe you shouldn't do this. Maybe Ichiro will talk the Queen down from taking Nox's pelt. Maybe I can stomp the thing, and we can tell Mom you did it."

"Nope. I'm not going to lie to Hertha Harcourt. And Yoshi Ichiro might be a legendary lawyer, but this is the Sidhe Queen we're talking about here. I can't take chances that aren't on me." I pulled my shirt over my head. "When you find your mate, you'll understand."

"It won't matter when I do, but that's not important now." Blaine's lower lip trembled. Was he about to lose it or something? I couldn't fathom why. He turned his back before I could ask. "What's important is, don't meet its gaze. If you do, Mother will have a wolf statue to add to her hoard."

"You mean it can go Medusa on me?" I unbuckled my belt.

"Yeah. Not if it sees you. Only if you look it in the eye. That's going to be tough on your wolf." His shoulders shook. "I'm gonna ask you again not to do this."

"I'm gonna tell you again, I'm doing it." After I folded my pants, I put them on top of my jacket with my shirt.

"Last chance. Back out, Josh." Blaine sighed. "Mother made this sound like a cakewalk. It's not. She values that pelt, so she gave you a task you might not survive. You could get maimed worse than Beth. You could die. There's no coming back from getting turned to marble."

"I wonder if cockatrice tastes like chicken." I chuckled to cover up the fact that I didn't care whether I made it as long as Nox got to stay whole. "No more questions. I'm shifting." Joints bent, lining up for running on all fours. My skin itched as it stretched and sprouted gray fur. I shook my ruff, then stretched. My wolf was ready for a fight.

Blaine didn't say anything else. He ran both his hands over his head, then dropped them to his sides. I sat on my haunches, noticing there was a human-sized door-within-a-door. Blaine opened that, keeping his back to me. I leaped inside, letting him close the door fast behind me so the cockatrice wouldn't get out. He needn't have bothered. I only caught a trace of its scent, a feathery, leathery, wet-stone kind of smell, shot through with a faint rot that could only be the poison.

The room was full of glass-fronted bookcases, packed to the gills with scrolls, clay tablets, marked hides, and books. At least I wasn't there to get rid of a bookworm infestation. The cockatrice's scent wasn't anything like the shelf contents. It was somewhere on the other side of the room from me, but the place was laid out in stacks. I guessed it was the Harcourt family library. Lynn would have given her left arm to get in here. Not with a cockatrice around, but still. They supposedly had stuff from ancient Roman times, maybe even earlier.

I heard the hushed chuckle of a cluck before I realized the little monster was atop the stacks. I swerved out of the way just in time. Three of its claws caught my fur, pulling a clump out. I decided not to look up or back, running around the shelving in a circle instead to try to get behind it. No dice. The next aisle of shelves was empty, the cockatrice already either back up top or over in a different row.

I trotted along, wishing I could velvet my claws like a panther or lion shifter. Even when I was careful, they made a noise on the floor. Why couldn't the Harcourts have carpet like normal people? Oh, right. Carpet was flammable. But so were books. Crazy dragons. I'd have to tell Blaine that if his family wanted wolf shifters hunting down their library pests, they should get softer flooring in here. A rug would really tie the room together.

This time, I felt the rush of air as the weird creature swooped down. I finally got a decent look at it. It had a long, green, reptilian tail I didn't expect, along with taloned claws more like an eagle's than a chicken. It was bigger than the average Rhode Island Red, too. The feathers I dared look at on its neck and breast were red and green, giving it an ironically cheery Christmas look. I jumped out of its way, but it almost pecked me. Instead of running down another aisle, I circled it. When I leaped, it fluttered back, tail dragging along the floor behind its skinny little bird legs.

I had no idea what it'd do next. The whole fight would have been easier if I could have looked at its eyes like I'd trained for, but that'd be fatal. The eyes might not have even shown me where it'd go next, anyway. I'd figured one thing out, though. That tail was a weakness. Its weight slowed the cockatrice down and probably didn't do it much good in the flying department.

It attempted to peck me again. This time, I cut the corner close when I went around it, going for the tail. My teeth sank into scaly flesh, piercing it and drawing blood. My wolf jaws were strong, and once I'd gotten my teeth in, I knew the fight would be over soon. Shaking my head, I knocked the cockatrice against one of the shelves. It let out a loud cluck, then a screech as I jerked my head the other way to slam the creature against the floor.

Growling, I dragged it back the way I'd come in, toward the door. It got hard to breathe with my mouth full of its blood. At least, that was what I thought. Each time it struggled, I shook the cockatrice again. Once at the door, I let its tail go. A sad-looking heap of scales and feathers sat at my feet. I sniffed it, found it still breathing. I took the back of its neck in my jaws and twisted. Once I felt the snap, I scratched at the door.

Blaine stood in the doorway, then sank to his knees on the threshold. His eyes were bloodshot, his face even paler than before. His hands shook as he fumbled a phone from his pocket. I heard gasping breaths as he tapped the screen, so why wasn't his chest heaving to go along with them? I fell on my side. Oh. That was my chest, my breaths.

"Tiamat's Scales, Josh." His voice was a hoarse near-whisper. "I told you to be careful." Blaine glanced at his phone, then reached out to touch my left front shoulder. He parted fur, peering. "A shallow scratch. Shards of the first egg, why did you do this?" He picked up the phone again, holding it out to snap a picture. Then he tapped the phone again, sending another message.

I whined, trying to get up, get out of the library on my own. I couldn't. My front legs wouldn't hold my weight. I pushed with my back legs, scooting myself along. Once my tail was out, I stopped. My tongue lolled from my mouth. Voices I could barely understand came from down the long hallway across the foyer, sounding like the time Beth and I tried to have a conversation through a box fan.

"Hang on, Josh." Blaine patted me on the head. On a better day, I would have bitten him for that, or was that a worse day? The last thing I remembered was the most important. I'd done it. I'd saved Nox.

CHAPTER EIGHTEEN

Nox

The cuts on the backs of my legs felt like a hundred wasp stings. That was actually an improvement. Before the Tylenol, they'd felt like a thousand wasp stings. My stomach grumbled despite the rice balls, and still I waited. The Brownie stood nearby as they had for the past two hours, like a tree. They hadn't said a word. I didn't blame them. The Queen had arrived shortly after the Psychic News Network van. She'd spent the entire time sitting in her magical levitating carriage, though.

I spotted Ichiro-san's car. He got out, juggling a briefcase, a drink tray, and a brown paper bag. Beth came around from the other side of the car to help him, without a crutch. A gust of wind pressed her trousers, outlining the brace that held her prosthetic on. She took Ichiro-san's briefcase and then his arm. Together, they approached me.

The length of time their walk took made me remember just how big the lawn in front of the Temple to Music was. I wondered whether as many people would show up here as there'd been last night. I almost lost my appetite. Fighting in front of a crowd was one thing, but being on trial made my gut feel like an entire flock of butterflies lived in there. Even worse, the Psychic News Network people were setting their cameras up at the top of the hill, like caretakers for insect-flamingo hybrids, the lenses like gaping, toothless mouths. That was worse than contemplating a crowd to stare and gasp at my guilt.

Ichiro-san and Beth sat, opening the bag which smelled like heaven and erased my awareness of the cameras for a while. I had donuts and coffee with them, trying to ignore the news crew and the people who steadily filled the lawn like an army of ants marching on a picnic. Waiting for this trial was worse than waking up hours before an exam I hadn't studied for. But, like an exam, its beginning would come on like the tide. Nothing I could do would stop it.

I'd almost forgotten the Brownie was still on the dais with us until they crackled a few times. At the foot of the steps, a rowan wood platform appeared with a clear crystal hovering in the air above it. Clicks sounded and flashes flickered in the crowd as the audience took pictures. I tried to swallow the lump in my throat. It wasn't just the Psychic News Network I'd have to worry about. I'd probably go viral on YouTube before noon. Not the way I'd always imagined becoming Internet famous.

"We'll head down there as soon as the Queen arrives." Ichiro-san patted my shoulder. "When she makes a statement, the truth crystal's color will change to reveal how honest your agreement is."

"So when she asks whether I undid the enchantment, I just say yes, and that's it?"

"Not exactly." He sighed. "You'll need to address her properly as 'Majesty' or 'Highness.' I have a list of questions here that she might ask you, depending on the crystal's reaction."

"Can you tell me what they are?"

"No. That'd make you automatically guilty of anything she thinks you might have done."

"Wow, that sucks." Beth blurted out what I'd been thinking. "Nothing like a mortal trial."

"Are you truly so surprised?"

"Someone should negotiate to change that." Beth shook her head.

"Plenty try to do just that, but in the opposite way you'd imagine." Ichiro-san sighed again. "Many mortals think the Queen's way is better. More reliable."

"That's insane." Beth sighed, shaking her head. "With Extrahumans in Law enforcement now, it's way easier to analyze evidence and arrest the right person."

"And also one of the reasons your Headmistress opened her school to anyone with the grades. Extrahuman Law is a major anyone can take, and since the Reveal, we need more lawyers with that kind of education. If only more humans would enroll."

"Wait for it," I grinned. "Lynn Frampton's a pretty good poster-child to attract that kind of student. Maybe I will be, too."

"Don't resign yourself to defeat." Ichiro-san opened his briefcase, removing a lapel pin. He took the backing off and pressed the point through the striped wool of his suit. Beth leaned a little closer, sniffing. The corners of her mouth turned up.

"Yeah, don't give up." Beth patted my arm. "It's Mr. Ichiro's job is to negotiate the sentencing in your favor. He's got some tricks." She glanced at the pin again. It was probably magic, but without my pelt, I couldn't tell for sure or get an idea of what kind.

"But I'm definitely guilty."

"And the Queen will enact the law to its letter. But sentences are flexible. Have hope." He affixed the back of the pin behind the lapel, then patted it.

"Yeah, I've heard that recently."

"Good." He stood, smoothing his suit. Then he nodded to the Brownie.

The sticklike creature guided me down the steps, one of their twiggy ends hooked in the three-link chain between my manacles. I stopped two paces behind them, next to the truth crystal platform. They let go, then stepped behind me. Ichiro-san stopped beside me.

Beth went back to a chair on the lawn, next to Lynn, Bobby, and Olivia. A pair of empty seats made me wonder where Josh and Blaine were. I wanted to ask, but it was too late. The Queen stepped out of her carriage, gliding across on golden gossamer wings she'd kept folded the night before.

She wasn't alone this time either. A stream of Sidhe attendants trailed to each side of her. They moved together, synchronized like ballet dancers partnering their mirrored reflections. They arranged themselves prettily at the aisle points in the seating, but I wasn't fooled. These Sidhe didn't even have a Glamour up. Everyone could see their alabaster skin, pointed ears, white hair, longer-than-human limbs, the watchful glitter in rainbow eyes. Those who cared to check would note that the baubles at their wrists and ankles had blades, their earrings were hollow tubes, and their necklaces strung with elf-shot darts. These were militant guards, not showy attendants, and armed to the teeth.

The inside of my head was too quiet. I actually missed Grandpa's sound and fury. What would he think of all this? What about Dad? Would they call me foolish for risking them like this, or praise me for doing the right thing by owning my actions? The only way to find out was to get through this.

The Queen stopped opposite us. Unlike the other Sidhe, her hair was streaked with amber that matched her eyebrows. Whether that was natural or some cosmetic she used, no one knew. One of the attendant warriors flicked his wrist a few times, straightening the monarch's jet black gown. I wondered why she'd worn that color, then realized how it made her white skin stand out in stark contrast. Black and white, no gray. Seelie justice. I took a deep breath and let it out slowly.

"You are Nox Phillips." The Queen's voice was quiet but commanding.

"Yes, Your Highness." A faint trace of gray formed at the center of the crystal. I closed my eyes. Of course. I should have said no and stated my full name. I opened my eyes. "No, Highness. My full name is Equinox Delta Phillips." The crystal cleared and brightened again.

"We need no further test questions." The Queen narrowed her eyes. "You undid an enchantment of mine, a binding on a creature who betrayed my trust eons ago."

"Yes, Your Majesty." The crystal stayed bright and clear.

"You did this to stop their attack while they worked under the command of a Summoner." One of her perfectly shaped eyebrows went up, hinting that she doubted that statement.

"That's true, Your Majesty." My guilt and the reason for it was crystal-clear to everyone. I heard more shutter snaps, and flashes glittered like the wings of carpenter ants all over the audience.

"You let the Sprite, a convicted criminal amongst my people, leave without attempting to apprehend them or informing the Seelie court." She tilted her head slightly, and I noticed the tresses beside her face quivering although there was no breeze. Great Goblin's Garters, but she was angry. That was the exact moment my give-a-damn busted.

"Yes, Your Highness." I felt a flush of heat rise in my cheeks. I wasn't embarrassed. Instead, my anger matched hers.

"You will state your reasons for that decision." Her glare threatened to pin me to the spot, unable to speak. I couldn't just tell everyone here what I thought, but if I lied, the crystal would show it— and any falsehood would give the Queen a reason to slap me with the worst possible sentence.

"Fine, Your Highness. Your enchantment was torture. Looking at that Spite was like standing next to a polluted river. I'm a Kelpie. We don't abide that kind of thing. Water runs free, and I can't bear to see anyone or anything bound that way. So I broke the bonds, exactly like my ancestors used to break down dams. And then I saw how mangled the Sprite was. Their wings are just rags now. They'll never fly again. I couldn't bear to cause them any more anguish, even indirectly. Your Majesty."

The clear crystal gleamed so brightly I couldn't look at it. Neither could the Queen, judging by her lowered eyelids though I doubted the crowd could tell from a distance. But Ichiro-san noticed, too. I watched one side of his mouth tilt the tiniest bit and the corner of his eyes crinkle. No one spoke until the light dimmed back down to normal.

"Very well." The Queen turned sideways as though about to leave. Then she looked over her shoulder. "One more." I could tell from the flare of her nostrils and the set of her jaw that this last bit was the most important to her.

"Yes, Your Highness."

"A Selkie pelt went missing a few years ago. You know something of its whereabouts."

"No, Your Majesty." The crystal grayed out on the first syllable. My mouth dropped open. At least it wasn't black. A hush fell over the entire crowd. I began to understand. I did know something, but I'd thought it was all speculation until that moment.

"You will tell me all you have heard and deduced of the missing Selkie pelt."

"It got lost in a car accident on a bridge, Your Majesty. That was in the papers back then, which anyone can check. It belonged to a drunkard, the man who caused the accident. That pelt has nothing to do with me." The crystal stayed bright and clear this time.

"And where is it now?" The armed attendants fingered their necklaces and rubbed their bracelets. If I lied now, a fight might break out.

"I...hold on." I raised my chained hands to rub my forehead. I'd been about to say I didn't know, but maybe our guesses in the lounge had been correct. "I think someone has it. Someone could have picked it up that night. There's been a Selkie around lately, too." I had to think harder, figure it out. I wasn't Lynn Frampton or Blaine Harcourt, but neither of them had been at Swan Point that night. I'd have to rely on my own wits instead of borrowing theirs.

"You will tell me who has it." The Queen turned to face me again.

A flight of gasps escaped the crowd as two attendants guarding the nearest aisle moved aside for no one. It was like they'd been unaware they'd done it until other people noticed. Now that was a mystery I could solve because I'd seen it before. Umbral magic. More than one someone had just walked past the guards under its cloaking effects. Was this some attempt to break me out? I wouldn't go.

A murky shimmer appeared like a smudge in mid-air. It melted away until I could see Maddie May standing next to a smiling Kimiko and a man with beige skin, hazel eyes, tawny sun-bleached hair, and more lines than I ever thought I'd see on his face. The salty tang of the ocean met my nose so strongly I sneezed. Here was my answer.

"Ren Ichiro, Your Majesty. He's got the Selkie pelt. We thought he'd died in the accident, but he must have used the pelt to save his own life." Ren and Kimiko rushed to their dad's side for a big group hug.

"Equinox Delta Phillips, you are guilty as charged of breaking my enchantment and of no other crime. Your solicitor will negotiate your sentence with me before his family reunion progresses further." The Queen beckoned, and Ichiro-san followed her. The Brownie accompanied me as I hurried to talk to Maddie.

"Where's Josh?"

"I don't know." She glanced around and saw the two empty seats. "He should be here. I just came from repaying that favor to Gee Nome. I had to hide Ren and bring him here because Gnomes are at risk around this many Seelies. But I haven't seen Josh or Blaine since last night."

I shivered, peering at the empty seats. Over where the cars had parked, the Harcourt limousine had just pulled up. I squinted since the sun was in my eyes. A woman strode down the hill, holding a burlap sack in one hand and an oilcloth pouch in the other. Hertha Harcourt. She went straight to Lynn, whispering something in her ear. Lynn went deadly pale, her eyes flicking to me. Then, she shook her head. I saw her mouth the word "No." Hertha murmured, opening the bag. Lynn went an unhealthy shade of green. She shut her eyes and shuddered. Bobby put his arm around her. Olivia put her hands on her cheeks. Beth froze like a statue, hands gripping her elbows. Maddie nudged me, then jerked her chin at the limo.

Josh had finally arrived. Blaine and Mr. Harcourt supported him between them. His feet dragged furrows in the grass. He sweated despite the brisk temperature, lips an unhealthy shade of blue. His eyes met mine, and he gave me a grim grin. My injured knees wobbled, threatening to buckle. Maddie grabbed my arm. The Brownie snapped the chain between my manacles. I glanced up to see Mrs. Harcourt handing an oilcloth pouch out to the Queen. I couldn't bring myself to care. Josh looked like death.

"Go." The Brownie's voice was low and not unkind. Maybe they weren't just a stick bug.

By that time, it wasn't far to Josh's side. Blaine and his dad put him on the ground, and I stretched out next to him. My stupid leg wounds made it impossible to squat.

"You're a mess, Dennison."

"Just getting you out of one, Phillips." His voice was raspy, and his eyes looked hollow. He shivered. "Your sentencing done?"

"Not just yet."

"I need to see that, know you're okay."

"No. You need rest."

"I can rest when you're safe." He closed his eyes. When he opened them again, they were that amber wolf color. "And maybe I'll even haunt you for a while."

"Why are you talking like that?"

"I'm dying. Cockatrice venom. No antidote. Even the brainiac doesn't know of one." He shuddered. I reached out to smooth his hair.

"There has to be some way." I shook my head, tears cold against the hot rise of defiant anger.

"One." I looked up. Ren stood over us. "Water magic can purify his blood, but we'd need to be extremely lucky to pull that kind of spell off. And we have to work together, even with the opposing Faerie energy."

"I can't help." The words came out as a growl. "Queen's got my pelt."

"No, she doesn't." Blaine stood there, holding a familiar oilcloth pouch. "She's got *a* pelt. This one's yours. The one my mom's handing over, not so much." Blaine shrugged. "Put it on and save your man, Equinox." He smirked.

"What about the Luck?" I took the pelt out of the pouch and pressed it to my stomach.

"Covered." Kimiko held something small and gleaming in her hand. "Lifted it off Dad at just the right time. Lucky, huh?" She held the lapel pin. Of course, a Tanuki lawyer would wear a Luck charm at trial. Its golden glow confirmed my earlier suspicions.

"It better be." I called to the water nearby and under the ground as I had at the fight the night before. Ren had already put one hand on Josh's right wrist and the other on his ankle. I mirrored him. I knew from my coursework that the Seelie and Unseelie energies in our Water magic would act like opposing magnets. If we did this right, we'd flush the cockatrice's venom right out of Josh's system.

We focused, each murmuring words under our breath, Ren's in Japanese and mine in a surprising mix of Gaelic and some other tongue I didn't recognize. One of my ancestors had done this before, but he was so far back in line I'd never heard him until now. I shut my eyes, trying to see his face in my mind's eye to get a better grasp of his knowledge. He'd been an ocher-skinned man with gleaming straight black hair and high cheekbones. His eyes twinkled, so dark a brown they were nearly black, like chips of obsidian in terra cotta clay. Now I understood why Taki Waban had given me the church-keys. Somewhere way back, we were related.

Josh's sweating went into overdrive, now tinged with green. The poison and water we flushed it with had to go somewhere. The longer we worked, the more color came back into his cheeks, although his eyes were still hollow, and his lips stayed blue. My whole body drooped, limbs heavy. My pelt's magic had also gone toward healing my legs, enough to make me worry I'd run out of steam before Josh was out of the woods. I glanced at Ren, looking for some sign. He shook his head and looked at Kimiko.

She sat at Josh's feet, holding the pin in her cupped hands. She seemed to be waiting for something. When Josh started seizing, she acted. A gilt glimmer rose from her hands, dissipating as it went. She blew gently on the shimmering air in front of her, tilting her finger-tips to point at Josh's feet. Golden motes wafted down over him, Ren, and me. A renewed surge of magic rushed over me like a big roller down at Scarborough Beach. Josh threw his head back, then broke

Ren's grip. He turned on his side, brackish water gushing from his nose and mouth.

When he pushed up from the ground, he sighed. There was no more blue around his lips, and his skin was back to its normal shade. He still had those dark circles under his eyes, but I'd take it. He flung his arms around me. I hugged him back so tightly, Grandpa got on my case about not breaking his ribs.

"Why don't *you* bring girls like this home, Blaine?" I glanced up at Mrs. Harcourt. She wasn't looking at me. Josh pulled me in for a kiss before I could figure out who she was talking about.

"They turn me down." Blaine snorted. "They're right, too, Mother."

When I could look around again, the Queen and her attendants were gone, along with the truth crystal. So were the Ichiros. The Harcourts brought everyone back to campus. They dropped me, Beth, and Josh back at the Dennisons'. I could have slept for days, but only got until the next morning.

CHAPTER NINETEEN

Josh

"I can't believe you're stuck in my old wheelchair." Beth set the glass with vodka and orange juice in it on the table in front of me. I glanced up and around, glad I'd been able to get down to the basement in this contraption. I don't think I could have handled another minute of being coddled by my parents upstairs.

"Yeah, but only for a couple more days." I sipped the tart beverage, glad I wasn't on any painkillers. Vodka tasted so much better than horse pills. "Leaping Luna! I missed my exam."

"I think the Headmistress will insist they let you make it up." Bobby sat across from me, steadily putting away bagels with cream cheese and lox.

"Yeah, you were on the Psychic News Network and everything." Lynn made more bagels topped with cream cheese and lox, keeping one for herself and passing the rest to Bobby.

"That was a Hail Mary pass, Hertha Harcourt coming out of left field like that with another Kelpie pelt." Fred opted for donuts instead of the bagels, inhaling a half-dozen of them. "You'd have died if she'd taken Nox's."

"Equinox, you mean." Blaine leaned back in his chair, smoke rising steadily from his nose. "I can't let anyone forget that's her real name."

"Jeez, you're worse than my brother." Beth elbowed him, then pointed at the Dark and Stormy in front of him. "You're not drinking that?" She reached for the glass.

"Not right now." Blaine shooed her away. "Just watching the fizz go out of it."

"You're an oddball, you know that, right?" Beth rolled her eyes and headed over to the bar to make her own drink.

"So, I think it's time to let Fred in on all of this." I drummed my fingers on the table. "Tell it, Trogdor."

"I'll let someone else do it for a change if it's all the same to you, Grand High Poobah." Blaine's eyes tracked his glass. Up, down. Up, down. I'd leave him to it for now, considering he'd saved Nox.

"Fine." I filled Fred in on the Extramagus situation, Lynn and Bobby chiming in from time to time.

"So now that this is over and you and Nox are okay, who's next?" Fred reached for more donuts, but they were all gone.

"Don't go eating the furniture, Fred." Olivia swept in from the backyard with a handful of bags. "Looks like I made it back from Dunkin just in time. Hoo boy." She set the bags on the table in front of the Redcap. "What did I walk in on?"

"Evil bad guy out to get us." Fred only had eyes for the bags full of pastries. "I'm on board."

"And you're trying to figure out who's next?" Olivia blinked, perching on a chair at the bar. "That's easy. The Harcourts."

"Yup." Blaine still watched the bubbles rise and burst. "Smart owl is smart, but she doesn't know everything."

"So enlighten me, oh great and scaly one." Olivia turned toward Blaine, leaning over the arm of her chair. But the dragon only shook his head in answer.

"The Extramagus never goes after just one person." I hadn't heard Tony come in. He watched Olivia intently, his eyes moving from her to the space between her and Blaine, as though measuring it. "It can't just be our Trogdor he's after."

"Cat-man said it." Blaine's eyes stayed glued to the glass. "No idea who it'd be in all this mess, though."

"I've got one." Lynn swallowed her mouthful of bagel. "Ren Ichiro. Nox couldn't have saved Josh without him."

"No way." Beth leaned against the bar, sipping rum-laced ginger ale. "I read through your notes last night. The bad guy can't touch Ren or me. I think the bridge was his doing."

"Hmm. Good point." Lynn shrugged with one shoulder, swallowing more bagel. "Gee Nome? Other than that, I've got nothing for now. You must be relieved Ren's safe, huh?"

Beth opened her mouth. Before she could speak, Nox rushed through the door and up to me, flinging her arms around my neck. I wheeled the chair back from the table, then pulled her into my lap. I might be too weak to stand or walk for more than a minute or two, but that didn't stop me from appreciating my mate. And I almost forgot about everyone else until the sound of a slap rang through the room.

"I don't want to see your face around here, Ren Ichiro." My sister stood face to face with the man she'd have married last spring, staring daggers into his eyes. His face bore a distinct red hand-print. Nox pressed a finger to the bottom of my chin, pushing my jaw back to a more dignified closed position.

"I'm sorry, Beth." Ren didn't hang his head. He just kept on looking her in the eye. "I should have—"

"Should have what? Told me you were alive? Told your dad, so he didn't spend a fortune on your funeral? Told poor Kimiko, so she didn't have dead brother damage just like me? I can't believe you put us through all that for three years, and then you waltz in here like it never happened. I can't listen to this now." She took a step toward him, and he walked backward. "Don't bother leaving." My sister stepped around the only man she'd ever loved and headed out the way Olivia had come in. The door shook in its frame after her.

Ren stood there, looking more lost at sea than I'd imagined he'd been when I thought he was dead. He blinked a few times, then took a deep breath. He sat on one of the barstools, gazing wistfully at Beth's forgotten drink.

"So, you lived on that boat that's been in the harbor all winter, huh?" Tony shuffled over to sit next to Ren, pushing the drink down the bar. "Good call, all things considered. It's what I would have done."

"Um, yeah. Lived on it for three years, actually." Ren nodded. "Been all up and down the east coast in that old thing."

"For the record, I know why you didn't say anything." I sipped my screwdriver. "Wolf neutrality. Beth would have lost you, anyway."

"Um, you have a Kelpie on your lap, though." He scratched his head. "Aren't your parents going to have an issue with that?"

"None at all," I smirked. "With a Selkie and a Kelpie as in-laws, we have balance. Beth'll come around. She just needs time."

"Dude, she slapped him." Fred blinked. "You can't be serious."

"Yeah, and she also said she can't listen. *Right now.*" I shrugged. "I know my sister. So do Mom and Dad. She'll hash things out with you eventually, Ren. But I'm warning you, your apology had better be Oscar-worthy when she does."

"Okay, but what about your pack? No balance there."

"Coincidence will take care of that. We'll find a Seelie member soon enough."

"Might have to make that two." Fred grimaced. His stomach rumbled, and for a moment, his glamour dropped. His skin was grayer than only a week ago, his ears pointier. "I have to tithe by the end of the semester, and that might be pushing it."

"Yeah, and when you do, you'll be in the Under for a year and a day." All newly tithed Changelings had to serve their Monarch for that amount of time to prove their loyalty and learn to control the extra power that came with Court alignment. "I'll have time to find someone to balance you out."

"But you've got me." Nox snuck a sip of my drink, then wrinkled her nose. "Balancing out the bad Unseelie influence on your pack is a bit overdue."

"So, what do you say, Ren?" I raised an eyebrow. "You already work well with at least one of my packmates, and I heard you talking to Headmistress Thurston about resuming your studies. I know you'll be around, and we have the smartest students here if you need study buddies."

"Um, sure." Ren glanced around the room. "But I only see one genius at the table." I hadn't noticed until then that Blaine's seat was empty. The dragon shifter had left the building.

I couldn't blame him. I wasn't sure we'd see much of him until after spring break. Even though I hadn't hidden in my house when I thought the Extramagus was after me, Blaine Harcourt probably would.

Once everyone was full of donuts, bagels, and beverages, they trailed out one by one. Nox put bottles away while I wheeled around the room, gathering napkins and paper plates to put in the trash bin. Tony stood in a corner, so still and quiet I hadn't noticed him at first.

"Go on, cat man. Shoo." I waved toward the door. "Isn't someone opening a can of tuna somewhere?"

"Nice joke. I've never heard that one before." He shook his head. "Look, I might as well say this in front of Nox, too."

"Say what in front of me?" She clinked the rum bottle back on the shelf and strode over.

"Just dropping some information to keep a promise." He shrugged. "I'm the one who woke you up the night of the new moon, Josh."

"Wait, what?" I couldn't believe my ears. I'd had suspicions about who my benefactor had been, but couldn't imagine Tony Gitano doing anything to risk his neck for anyone else. "How?"

"Church-key." He nodded at Nox. "You're not the only one who's gotten a present or few from Taki Waban."

"But why?" I shook my head, trying to reconcile the idea of Tony as a hero while dismissing my suspicion that the dragon librarian had warned me.

"You still don't understand." He sighed. "Look, your uncle Jake has some scary connections. It's why your mom didn't give him the pack when she married your dad. I mean, haven't you ever thought it was weird she kept on running it even through having three kids?"

"I just thought she was a liberated woman?" I narrowed my eyes, uncomfortable with the fact that a cat shifter seemed to know more about my extended family than I did.

"I'm sure she is. But there's more to it than that. More than even I'm completely certain of."

"And why should I believe you?"

"You don't have to if you don't want to." He shrugged. "I'm just putting it out there. Your family's not so great at keeping secrets because your parents are so upstanding. It's rare around here."

I growled. Nox put her hands on my shoulders.

"Look, I mean no disrespect, but an Extramagus with a superiority complex isn't the only player in this game we keep getting caught up in. When the big fish are after chum, the bottom feeders follow them. I think maybe you should be informed about stuff Lynn and Blaine can't find out in the library."

"Not now." I shook my head, suddenly completely exhausted. Near-death-by-poisoning could do that to a person. "Some other time."

"Okay, boss." Tony stepped sideways, closing the distance between himself and the door. "Just don't wait too long. Not knowing what I have to say almost took you out of the game before it started this time. And I don't have any more church-keys to get you out if something like that happens again."

"I've got one." Nox's lips made a thin, straight line. "Tell me. But later. You get some rest, Josh. I have an exam to take."

"Sure, horsefeathers." I rubbed my eyes, trying to stay awake long enough to hear what Tony might say. When I took my hands away, he was already gone.

Nox helped me to the couch and got me comfortable. Then she left for her exam. Finally in the quiet, I slept.

CHAPTER TWENTY

Nox

I filled in the last bubble on the scantron sheet, then got up and left as quietly as I could. I'd never ace Watkins' test, but at least I'd pass it. There would be time to make up points after Spring Break. When I got outside, I looked up at the sky, amazed at how blue it was. I headed back toward Josh's house. On the way, I heard something so beautiful it stole my breath. I closed my eyes, feet moving along the sidewalk toward the sound of a violin sweeter than honey and more entangling than spider shifter silk. I'd heard it before, felt the same compulsion the night I ran into Josh. This time, he wasn't here to distract me from following it.

I opened my eyes, trying to stop. I couldn't. Despite the early spring sun and balmy temperature, I had a bad feeling, like the night Dad didn't come home. Instead of Hope Street, I'd turned down Camp toward Rochambeau. I made it all the way to the park where I'd gotten into all this mess, feeling like I was falling toward something.

And I had an idea this might be how a fly felt on its way to the bottom of a pitcher plant.

I crossed Rochambeau, turning up the drive of a yellow triple-decker house I'd been to before. At the door, I rang the bell with the name Kazynski next to it and waited. The music stopped, but before I could bolt the door opened. A frail and wizened man, bald except for a semi-circle of fuzz behind his ears greeted me.

"Miss Phillips, please. I must speak with you." His voice was heavily accented, either Russian or Polish.

"Haven't you ever heard of email?" I leaned in the doorway. "I don't appreciate being compelled. So talk already."

"This was the only safe way. You must bring this to your Alpha." He held out an old wooden box, carved all over with flowers. When I touched it, it tingled with enchantment I couldn't identify. I suspected the box itself wasn't enchanted, but the item inside absolutely was. Strong, too.

"What's it for?"

"Safekeeping. It'll open when the time comes, and he'll know what to do with it then." Old Mr. Kazynski reached out to close the door. His forearm was marked with a line of numbers. He couldn't be old enough to have been in a Concentration Camp, could he? I sniffed, realizing he was something more than just plain human.

Stopping to think had cost me the chance to ask anything else. I'd have rung again, but the old fellow seemed so frightened. Still, I hesitated. After the last few weeks, I'd gotten tired of enigmas and danger. As I lifted my finger to press the button next to his name, Mr. Kazynski started playing again. This time, the music moved me away, like the songs they play when a nightclub's about to close. I tucked the box inside my jacket and turned right onto the sidewalk.

I headed up Rochambeau toward Hope Street, crossing and making the turns down side-streets to take me to Josh's house. Men were working, replacing the old iron gates with steel replicas. I hurried up the driveway, then around the side of the house to the basement entrance.

Josh sat up on the sofa, looking around until he saw me. Then, he smiled. I went over, sitting next to him. He leaned in, kissing me. I almost forgot about the box until he pulled me closer and bumped it.

"What's that?"

I told him. He sat for a few moments, running his fingers over the wooden carvings. He set it on the coffee table. Josh put his arms around me, moving in for another kiss. When we came up for air, I leaned against his chest.

"Doesn't it drive you nuts, not knowing what's in there?" I held him close, but gently. I felt lucky to be able to hold him at all, considering he was the first wolf shifter I'd heard of to survive a cockatrice scratch.

"Nope." He ran one hand through my hair while the other caressed my back. "I'll see when it's time. For now, I've got everything I need right here."

I tilted my head to look up at him, understanding completely. Whatever came at us, we'd handle it together.

THE ACADEMY ISN'T

A PROVIDENCE PARANORMAL COLLEGE
SHORT STORY

THE ACADEMY ISN'T

"I'm not going back there, and you can't make me."

"You'll do as I say," Yoshi Ichiro crossed his arms, forcing his face into the sterner lines his daughter needed to see on it. "But it is up to you to tell me your side of things before I make my final decision regarding your attendance at The Academy."

"I hate it there." Kimi always led with her emotion, something she'd have to either outgrow or learn to use if she wanted to be a long-lived Tanuki instead of the kind that ran out of Luck in the prime of life.

"You know better than to let hatred rule your mind." Yoshi shook his head, letting a mask of disappointment hide his fear for her. "Give me better reasoning than that or back you go."

"They teach nothing there that I don't already know." Kim twirled a lock of her hair. "I can't stand how strict it is, but the worst part is that it's so..." She tugged the hair, grimacing. "*Remedial.*"

"So you are bored."

"The Academy isn't for someone like me."

"I'd say it's more that someone like you isn't for The Academy." Ren leaned in the doorway. Just seeing him there hurt Yoshi's heart. He'd changed so drastically without growing much.

His son had taken after his late wife, Sora, a Telepathic Psychic.

He'd been entirely mundane, too, a common occurrence in Tanuki families, but he'd come back with a Selkie pelt after going missing for three years. The Ichiro family dynamic had changed after Sora's death, and here it was, turning in an entirely different direction.

"Please, Ren," Yoshi indicated the empty space on the sofa. "Sit down and add to the discussion."

"Okay." After taking a seat, Ren leaned forward. He appeared more interested in this conversation than Kimi herself.

"I'm just dying to hear what the absentee brother thinks of the school he hasn't even seen." Kimiko rolled her eyes.

If her stinging remark bothered Ren, he didn't show it. "Well, it sounds like a fine institution. But from the way you talk about it, sending you there is like trying to make a bird live inside an aquarium."

"It's the only school that would have her, with the grades she made in her last two years of High School." Yoshi couldn't measure his tone. Something panged in his chest, on the left. Hiding that pain took more effort than he'd expected.

"See? Even Ren thinks it's the same difference, Daddy." Though she'd usually glance off to the side to accompany such a dismissive remark, Yoshi's daughter watched him like their cat watched the robins nesting in the yew bush beside the parlor window.

"It's not." Yoshi kept his mouth still and flat but couldn't stop the hidden smile from crinkling the corners of his eyes. Despite his pain, having both of his children back with him was a blessing he hadn't dreamed of. "Once you figure out why those are not precisely the same, you will understand why I sent you there to begin with."

"Why can't you just tell me?" This time, Kimi did look away.

"You gave me the impression you're bored at The Academy because all of its answers are too easy for you to get."

Kimiko opened and shut her mouth, saying nothing. His daughter was a brilliant trickster, exactly as he'd been at her age. And tradition demanded that Yoshi be as inscrutable and maddening as his own parents had been with him ages ago. Without the challenge of mystery, an intellect like hers would only stagnate. Too much depended on her putting all the right pieces together soon, including his own life. though neither of his children knew that as yet.

And he couldn't interfere without risking coincidence turning Luck in favor of the wrong people. He was stuck under the same restrictions as the other experienced adults connected to the Extramagus. Because they'd once been allies, coincidence dictated that none of them could directly cross the rising power again. If any of the older generation dared such a thing, they'd risk convergence altering all the Precognitive work done decades ago.

"Daddy, I want to learn more than what the Academy has to teach me. Isn't that enough of a reason not to send me back there?"

"So tell me then, what do you want to learn?" Yoshi's fresh bout of chest pain only made him sit up straighter, defying it.

"I'm not sure."

"Once you've figured that out, come and talk to me. I will allow you to take the rest of this semester off, but if you have not decided by the end of May, we'll have trouble planning another course of education for you."

"Okay, Daddy."

A buzzer went off, its low atonal hum stretching longer than it should have by Yoshi's estimation. The throbbing stab in his chest reached a tipping point, then ran like a stream from a mountain spring. A chill came to his bones, one he'd never quite felt before.

"That's the fish." Ren turned his head, his body following until he was halfway across the parlor to the kitchen.

The cat leapt into Yoshi's lap and from there to the arm of his chair. She clung, hissing to the velvet upholstery, raising all the hair on her back, her tail an exclamation of something gone horribly wrong. But Yoshi stood anyway.

Just one more meal, one more hour with my children. He pleaded with fate itself, wanting more than it had ever offered him before. But it wasn't meant to be.

"Daddy!" Kimi caught him, her enhanced shifter strength allowing her to sweep him up in her arms as he'd done with her as a little girl.

Ren's hand flew with Extrahuman speed to the phone on the wall, pressing three numbers.

"I need the EME!" Ren raised his voice into the phone, as though the volume would bring the Emergency Medical Extrahumans faster.

"He's already here." Yoshi raised one arm, pointing at the door. It trembled more than he'd expected it to.

Ren dropped the phone and pulled open the front door to find Taki Waban there. He stepped inside, carrying his old black bag. Aside from the gray at his temples, the ancient dragon appeared almost the same as Yoshi remembered him best, from their days on the Western Frontier. Taki removed his shoes and set them aside.

"Daddy, that's a dragon, not a doctor." Kimi held him closer.

"All the same, he can help."

"No, he can't." Her voice came low and soft, a murmur even her Selkie brother and the oldest dragon in the Americas might have trouble hearing. "It's your Luck running out."

Yoshi had figured he couldn't hide that from her. As Tanuki, the two of them alone could see the running and turning of Luck energies, a type of magic even dragons couldn't properly track.

"He can." Yoshi gripped his left arm, unable to stop a grimace.

"Set me down and let him do what he can, Kimi."

She brought him down the hall and to his bedroom. Ren turned down the covers, then put them back up, covering Yoshi from the waist down. They both made way for Taki Waban, who perched on the edge of the bed. After setting his bag down, he opened it and produced a magipsychically-enhanced stethoscope from inside.

"Your father needs a Luck charm." Mr. Waban turned grave eyes on Ren instead of Kim as Yoshi expected. The old dragon was a master of deflection.

"On it." Ren rummaged through the top drawer of Yoshi's dresser but came up empty-handed.

"Ren." Kim stared at her hands.

"Okay, maybe in the desk." Ren crossed the room in the blink of an eye, searched again without results.

"Ren."

"At the office then."

"Ren."

"Come on, Kimi." He tugged her wrist.

"No, Ren." Her shoulders shook. "They're all gone."

Yoshi let his eyes wander from his daughter's face to his son's. This would be harder on his Ren than Kimi. He'd been hiding alone so long, missing them, while she'd been shut away fuming with anger.

"Wait." He dropped her arm. "Gone? Because of your--"

"Yeah." When she turned her head up, Kimiko's eyes glowed with brash conviction and the gold light of Luck. "But don't worry. I got this."

Fury suited both his children better than solitude, something he'd never realized until the cancer took Sora. His son would go on missing him, shutting himself away with regret at missed years. Kimi would be the one to fight for him now. But he'd known that since the day she was born.

The Precognitive who'd consulted with Providence's Extrahuman elite hadn't been wrong yet. Lady Luck help them all if she proved fallible this time.

DRAGON MY HEART AROUND

PROVIDENCE PARANORMAL COLLEGE
BOOK FOUR

What's luck got to do with it?

Dragon shifter Blaine Harcourt is bewildered when he catches a woman robbing his parents' Newport Mansion. It gets worse when they leave him in charge of her punishment. His stepdad says it's time to prove he's worthy of his future inheritance. His mother blames him for the whole thing. Blaine's so angry he can't even.

Kimiko Ichiro only wanted to replace what she had stolen from her father. It wasn't her fault that the only luck charms powerful enough to stop his rapid aging were in the Harcourt hoard. Robbing powerful dragon shifters seemed like the only way. Besides, thievery was no big deal to Tanuki.

Blaine was used to dealing with books and artifacts, not brilliant, dishonest women. Is Kimiko just using her feminine wiles to hoodwink him, or is something else at play here? And how did she get into the Harcourt's magically sealed vault in the first place? Could Blaine's part in foiling an evil Magus be the reason for his bad luck, and can Kimiko help him turn it around?

CHAPTER ONE

Blaine

I couldn't sleep again. Wondering when the Extramagus would come and try to kill me was an extra pain in my tail. I managed a brash attitude while awake, but my dreams were filled with a shadowy figure force-choking me harder than Vader on a bad day. That sucked big time because I couldn't even watch Episode IV to take my mind off all of it. I just freaked out and shut it off instead, and I loved that movie. That Magi-supremacist bastard should get himself served extra-crispy for ruining my enjoyment of Star Wars. Getting the jump on someone that powerful was light-years above my pay grade, though.

Like I'd done for the first two nights of my Spring Break, I wandered the manse expanse. As I snorted about my rhyme time, that I was a poet and didn't even know it, the worst thing in the world happened. The alarm went off, first the one for the vault and then the hoard inside it.

Why in the nest of the first Broodmother did my mother and her dandified Air dragon husband have to be at a charity ball? Why had I been such a recluse and refused Bobby's offer to stay with me over Spring Break? Why hadn't I invited all of Tinfoil Hat over for a Poker night? Why weren't my legs moving? I'd frozen when I should have dashed. It was time to make like Queen Elsa and let it go so I could see what the problem was.

I sprinted down the dragon-wide hallway, remembering my nanny Zyra, and how she used to read me Robert Asprin's old *Myth* series. Skeeve's dragon, Gleep, had galloped down hallways toward the bad guys. So had I, as a kid, when the bad guys were pretend. Time to run straight into the danger, just like that stupid fictional dragon. Gleep did it out of loyalty. I did it because Mother would slay me herself if I didn't.

As I ran, I thought about shifting. My dragon slept. He didn't do insomnia, apparently. Once I unsealed the hoard trinket room, I was glad of that. The first thing I saw when I opened the door was a shapely set of legs. I ogled them, then smacked my face with my palm. I'd been a dunderhead, assuming the Extramagus was a guy who'd just send guys.

The itch of my skin going scaly as I started shifting almost distracted me from the woman's face as she turned around, her eyes wide. Once I did, it was hard not to look at her. She had perfect beige skin and melting amber eyes. I'd seen her somewhere before, and she was way too young to be the Extramagus. Besides, she smelled like a shifter. I dialed back on dragoning out, lulling the beast inside back to sleep. A petite Japanese girl couldn't be a threat to scaly old me, right? She looked more afraid than I felt.

"Please forgive me." I watched her lower lip tremble, eyes still wide as she stepped slowly toward me with her hands behind her back. And I could almost imagine she approached a unicorn instead of a dragon man like me, but unicorns didn't exist. I gazed down into her soft eyes, imagining what her lips might taste like. Thinking that about a girl who seemed so pure made me want to slap myself. Her arm moved faster than I could track it. Everything went black.

"Ow!" My cheek rested on something smooth and cold. Yup, the floor. My vision was still a little blurry, but when I went to rub my eyes, I found my hands tied behind my back. Whatever had poked the tender spot on my head had another go. This time, I could only muster a groan.

"Tell me how to lift the wards, or I'll hit you again, dragon boy." The girl's voice wasn't menacing at all, but whatever she'd hit me with sure was.

"I can't. Ow!"

"You can, and you will."

"No, it doesn't work for me. Only Mother can open it now."

"Ugh. Not another mama's boy."

"What?" I moved my shoulder, tilting so I could look at my captor. Her hair was long and nut-brown with platinum streaks and tips. I'd seen her before, after Nox's trial. "Didn't you help save my Alpha? Why are you robbing me?"

"I'm not robbing you." She flipped her hair back over her shoulder. "I'm just taking something that belongs to my people."

I glanced at the small heap of trinkets on the floor next to her. Narrowing my eyes and calling on my dragon, I scrutinized them for magic energy. Sure enough, they swirled with golden Luck energy I couldn't decipher. This girl could only be Yoshi Ichiro's daughter.

"Look, I get that Tanuki are the best with Luck magic. Really, I do." I shook my head once and had to stop. It hurt too much. "But you don't understand dragon shifters. Once something's in the hoard, you can't claim reparations or eminent domain or whatever lawyerese your dad sent you over here to recite. My mom's like Bruce Banner and Doctor Jekyll recombined themselves a lovechild way back in the dark ages. You won't like her when she's angry. Even I don't, and she sort of raised me."

"Your mother sort of raised you?" One perfectly curved eyebrow lifted. "That's a weird thing to say."

"I give you a warning about an irate dragon lady, and her parenting skills are what you focus on?" This girl was driving me crazy. Also, my hands were falling asleep. I focused on scaling them over with a partial shift. Maybe that'd make it easier to get out of whatever she'd used to tie them together. But my dragon didn't want to escape. Under other circumstances, I wouldn't want to either.

"I can't heed your warning, so I figured I'd take the fun in dysfunctional for five hundred, Alex." She shrugged, making the buttons on the front of her blouse strain a little. I looked away.

"You're an odd one." That was the understatement of the decade. This girl was battier than a bat shifter. She'd broken into a dragon hoard, for Tiamat's sake!

"Back at you, Trogdor." She smiled, batting her eyes.

"Hey, only my friends are allowed to insult me like that. And none of my friends would ruin my life by trying to break in here." That made me stop and think, a tough task while recovering from the knock on my noggin. How had she broken in, anyway?

"And if your friends jumped off the Pell Bridge, I wouldn't." She flipped her hair over one shoulder, batting her eyelashes. I paid attention in an entirely inappropriate way. She looked younger than Lynn Frampton, but a Tanuki could physically be nineteen and chronologically be fifty with a Luck charm. And there was a whole pile of them, right in front of her.

"Maybe you'd be better off jumping from a bridge. Mother doesn't pull her punches, but I'm her only child. I could put in a good word if you try being a little nicer to me." I hadn't just said something that smarmy? Oh, yeah, I had. I'd meant it that way, too.

"How about you keep these a secret from your mom?" She held up a pair of Luck-infused cufflinks, then tucked them down the front of her shirt. "That'd give me tons of motivation to be—" She leaned over, her face close to mine. "Nice."

"Hey!" I wriggled, trying to stop her from sitting on my lap. It was no use. My dragon had woken up and given her his full attention. He liked what he saw even more than I did. That only made things worse. I rolled my eyes. "Why do you need my help? Can't you just get out the way you came in?"

"No such luck with the wards up." She shrugged, then gazed into my eyes. Most girls flinched when they were dragonish, but not her.

"That's a striking shade of red, Blaine. You're very attractive. Why didn't anyone bother telling me that, I wonder?" She put one arm around my neck.

"Gah!" I pushed with my feet, forcing my weight against the wall I leaned on so I could stand. She fell off my lap with a shrill little shriek. Mother would be back soon, and I couldn't let her see me with the burglar on my lap. And there was something else, too. "Stop trying to distract me. You got in here. You get yourself out. It's not like there's a shortage of Luck charms in here."

I flexed my arms, hearing the purr of tearing fabric as my hands pulled free of whatever she'd tied me with. Smoke trailed from my nose, hazing my vision. I always hated that. I focused and turned it into a ring instead so I could see what in Tiamat's name I was doing. Then, I lowered my shoulder and rushed her.

She stepped out of the way at the last possible second. That was a good thing since I had to swerve to avoid smashing a vase worth over a million dollars. I turned to face her again, reaching out to grapple her this time. I got her blouse. Instead of trying to get away, she threw herself at me.

We went down together, rolling around the marble floor in a tussle, unlike any fair fight I'd had. She grabbed handfuls of my hair, pulling my head every which way. I tried to get a grip without seeming like I was copping a feel. The way she writhed in my grasp made that almost impossible.

I felt the air change before I realized the door had opened. I'd been crawling, trying to get off the floor from my hands and knees with the Ichiro girl clinging around my neck and waist with her arms and legs. Her skirt had flipped up, giving Mother and my stepdad a show she might have fully intended. She laughed, obliterating any vestige of innocent girlishness left in my opinion of her.

"Blaine Carter Harcourt, put that girl down this instant." Mother's voice was quiet, which rated Defcon 1 on the Hertha Harcourt warning system. I'd rather hear her shout than whisper any day of the week.

It took effort, but I got on my knees and held my hands up like I was in the weirdest jazz dance routine ever. The girl hung on, clinging even tighter. There were women I'd had one night stands with who hadn't held me that close.

"Miss Ichiro, I believe?" Super stepdad, Wilfred Harcourt, to the rescue. He walked around alongside us, staring down. Then, he did something wildly inappropriate. He stuck his hand down the front of the Ichiro girl's shirt. He plucked something from her cleavage, then held it up. The cuff-links gleamed from between his thumb and first finger.

I stared at Mother, my eyes so wide I felt they might pop out of their sockets and roll around on the floor. She smiled. Not at her weak fart of a socially appropriate husband. Not at her bewildered son. She stood there grinning at the Ichiro girl. I blinked, probably saving my poor eyeballs from a bug's squashed fate.

"Well, Wilfred, it seems Blaine's got something to do besides mope around the manor during his Spring Break."

"I beg your pardon?" Mother never called him Wilfred unless she had something devious spinning the hamster wheel I suspected of running her brain. She was about to drop some serious trouble in my lap on top of the Tanuki who wouldn't leave.

"Yes. My son is just the young man to handle this particular problem." Her smile brightened in wattage until it could have made the moon and stars give up and go home.

"What?" I didn't realize my jaw had dropped until the Tanuki chick's thumb pushed it closed. I ground my teeth and pushed her me before speaking again. "Handle this problem?" I pointed at the girl. "She broke into your hoard. Yours, not mine."

"True, but it's a pile of wealth you'll be in charge of someday." Her lips closed over her teeth, but the corners of her mouth tilted so much they could have been tied to her ears. "And I hear you've got quite the reputation for taking care of little mysteries like this when they crop up for your friends. The least you can do is help your beloved mother with this one small matter."

"Oookay?" I stood up, brushing myself off. Movement snagged the corner of my eye. I turned, my elbow swinging ahead of me. I knocked a delicately rounded shoulder. Trinkets clattered to the floor. The girl put both hands to her cheeks, her mouth making a little round "o" of whatever emotion thieves have when they get caught. I grabbed her arm, knowing I'd better keep a hand on her if she weren't in my direct field of vision.

"I understand the reason behind your choice, wife, but shouldn't we at least tell him—" My stepdad shut his mouth mid-sentence when Mother snapped her fingers.

"You know nothing. This is my hoard, the one that brought your title to this marriage." Mother snaked her arm through her husband's. "I'll borrow some of Miss Thurston's faculty and set up wards around the property instead of just the vaults. That way, she can only run far enough to provide some amusement."

My stepdad straightened, throwing his shoulders back. He let her escort him to the doorway, then paused. His sibilant whispers carried a hint of pleas. I couldn't look away because I knew Wilfred had provoked her instead of swaying her.

"I won't tell him or her. And I think Mr. Waban can also help with those wards, come to think of it." The sound of Mother's heels clicking away against the marble punctuated the finality of that last statement. I felt bad for Wilfred, whose shoulders sagged like half the hoard's contents rested on them. I didn't much like Taki Waban either, and I suspected the feeling was more than mutual. Make one horse joke at the wrong time, make an enemy of the new ice dragon librarian.

I turned, reaching out to grasp the girl's other arm. Her head bowed so low I could only see the top of it. She didn't make a sound. I rolled my eyes. This had to be more manipulation, an attempt to get me to let her go. I headed down past the display case I'd caught her climbing and across an aisle to another curio cabinet, much less ornate than the other one. Then, I let go of one of her arms, pulled open the glass-fronted door, and took out a pair of bracelets. I slapped one on her wrist and the other on mine. The magic activating felt like a static shock to the face. I sneezed. She didn't, but looked up.

"What did you do?" She reached for the bracelet, trying to unfasten the clasp. I chuckled.

"These are Faerie Tithing bracelets. You can't go further than an acre from me without passing out." I let go of her.

"Doesn't that mean you also pass out?" Her smile was gentler than Mother's, but no less charged with mischief.

"No." I lied. I hate lying about my knowledge.

"Oh, you." Her laugh cascaded like that string orchestral stuff my stepdad listened to. "You're not the only artifact expert in the world, you know."

"Think what you want." I turned, heading for the door. "That acre includes height, you know. I'm going to the third floor, and this is the basement. It's a building constructed for dragons the size of football fields. You do the math."

"Don't you want to know my name?" Soft footsteps hurried to catch up with me. I glanced down, relieved to see she wore moccasins instead of stilettos like Mother.

"I don't care." But that was another lie. I did. But I didn't want to give her the satisfaction of asking her for it.

CHAPTER TWO

Kimiko

We walked in silence through the dragon-sized halls and up two flights of stairs. This wasn't at all how I had imagined the evening going. I should have been in and out of there once I had my mitts on the luck charms I'd come for. I didn't understand why, either. The charm I'd burnt when Blaine came in should have let me slip out before the wards engaged. Instead, I got confronted by three dragon shifters for the price of one. And Blaine was nothing like what I'd expected. Either Beth had misrepresented him, or he was a giant scaly liar. After his attempt to fool me about the Tithing Bracelets, my money was on liar.

When he ushered me into a room almost as big as the entire first floor of my dad's house, I thought maybe my Luck would change. I put on my most vulnerable face, slouching a little to make my blouse look more disheveled. I wish I could say he didn't bother looking at me. He glared. I'd royally pissed him off. I shouldn't care, and told myself I didn't as the door closed behind him with a hollow thud. But

I was a giant furry liar. A pair of liars, then, but nothing at all like a matched set.

There were four sets of double doors, with mirrors lining the walls between them. It felt like being in a glass house. I wondered who or what this room had been designed for, then shrugged. It didn't matter. I was used to being trapped in a place I didn't want to be, although not when so much was at stake beyond my boredom.

I decided to check out the amenities. One set of doors led to the most luxurious bathroom I'd ever seen. The shelves held plush towels, the cabinets all the lotions and potions a girl could want. I ran a bath, knowing the time it'd take to fill that huge Roman-style tub gave me a chance to check out the rest of the room.

A walk-in closet the size of a regular person's bedroom held neat rows of clothing for every occasion. All of it was feminine, not all of it in the colors I favored, but enough to make me wonder what in the name of Lady Luck could be going on here. Everything was my size, even the shoes. I leaned over, sniffing a dress. It smelled new with still a trace of the plastic it must have been wrapped in during shipping. I ran to a dresser, relieved to find only stretchy bras and underwear. No one had measured me in my sleep or snooped through my closets to suss out what size I wore. Whoever had estimated my dress size had to have a tailor's eye, though. Or an appraiser's. Someone was creepy in the estate of Harcourt, and my gut told me it wasn't Blaine.

I went to one nightstand. It had a locking drawer, with the key still in it. Someone wanted to give me the illusion of privacy, then. The glass on the walls made me wonder, though. Before stowing anything, I went to one mirror and pressed a finger to the surface. I knew the test wasn't the be-all and end-all, but it'd work as step one. The mirrors were set into the walls, stretching half the height to the cavernous ceilings the entire Harcourt mansion had. Even though there was a visible gap between my finger and its reflection, it could still be transparent.

With my hands cupped, I leaned against the glass. Trying to peer into any room that might be behind it would give anyone watching a rude surprise, but I couldn't see anything. Knocking made a thud near my ear, but a hollow reverberation higher up. I had a theory. I rapped on every single mirror to test them.

Half of them made the hollow sound. I marked each one with a touch of magic in the lower corner. There wasn't anyone watching right behind the mirrors, but there were probably concealed cameras high up. It's what I'd do if I were head of a family of paranoid dragons. One thing I didn't bother with was looking for bugs. I already knew I didn't talk in my sleep from my time in The Academy dorms, and I could wait to try to communicate with my ally until a bit later.

If I stood just right at the locking nightstand, I could conceal what I did with my purse before locking it up. I twisted and hunched, then peeked into my handbag to make sure my secret weapon was still in there. Once locked, I brought the key to a jewelry box on one dresser. A simple gold chain worked to string it on around my neck. Someone else in the house might have a copy of the key, but this was the best I could do for now. I'd have to rely on my Luck to keep anyone from looking in the drawer and the bag. I went back and touched the drawer again, with Luck magic, this time, hoping it'd be enough.

Back in the bathroom, I tossed a raspberry bath bomb into the water and threw my clothes at a hamper, not caring when they missed. With my hair pinned against my head by a studded gold clip, I sank into the hot water I hoped would ease my body and mind. When I opened my eyes, a slender glass of something that smelled suspiciously like plum wine sat on the tile edging the tub. Someone knew I was over twenty-one, then.

I didn't dare emerge from the bubble-covered water, so I tried checking the bathroom for magic. I should have done that to begin with, in the bedroom, too. Some Tanuki I was, forgetting an important thing like that. I blamed Blaine Harcourt with his jerky attitude and dreamboat eyes instead of myself.

After a few moments, I realized that a decorative gilt bamboo stand in one corner was actually a hiding place for a Brownie. I'd known Hertha Harcourt and the Sidhe Queen were tight, but not enough to assume it merited pure Faerie servants painting themselves to match the decor. I chalked it up to dragon craziness and decided to be friendly for the moment.

"Um, hi." I nodded to the stick-like creature in the corner. "How did you know I like plum wine?"

"The same way I knew your dress size." The brownie swayed a little, creaking slightly. "Your hostess mentioned it."

"Huh. That's weird." I sighed, relaxing back into the bath. I didn't have to worry about a Brownie ogling me since they had no gender, like the other pure Faeries. But I shouldn't ask them any more questions. If they served the Harcourt family, I'd just be digging my own grave and owe them by accident. "Well, thanks again." I picked up the glass, raised it, and sipped.

"I—" The Brownie creaked and crackled, twisting in a nonexistent breeze. "You're most welcome, Miss Ichiro."

"None of that 'Miss' stuff. Call me Kim." I winked. "Anyone who brings me wine this good deserves to be on a first-name basis."

"I understand." They straightened, a sign that they were at ease. "You consider it advantageous to be friendly with the help."

"You have some experience with Tanuki guests, then." I sipped the excellent wine again, letting the fruity and lightly fuzzy taste roll over my tongue a few times. I breathed in to enjoy its bouquet as well. "And anyone serving the Harcourts who gilds themselves goes above and beyond. Kudos! You must be one of the most highly-valued servants here."

"There's a mortal saying about making assumptions."

"Yeah, yeah." I waved my free hand in a dismissive gesture. "I'm an optimist."

"Tread carefully, Kim." Their voice sighed like a breeze through branches. "Your hostess has been waiting for something like this to happen for decades."

I swallowed more wine because there was no other way to get around the lump forming in my throat. When the bathwater cooled, I got out and dried off. A robe on the inside of the bathroom door covered me until I could slip into a silky nightgown from the dresser.

I took a deep breath, closing my eyes to tighten my focus. When I opened my eyes, I scanned the room for magical listening devices. Then, I checked under furniture and in decorations for the kind garden-variety humans used. It seemed whoever installed the cameras hadn't worried about listening in. The bed was comfortable and warm, the room quiet and almost peaceful once I turned the lights off.

"Ismail?" I knew my ally could hear me, but he didn't answer. Why would he? The creature I'd roped into helping me was under one of the oldest kinds of Faerie contracts. I still had him on the hook for one more go, and I bet comforting a despairing Tanuki wasn't on his list of favorite pastimes. I rolled over, turning my back on the nightstand, and shut my eyes.

The Brownie's ominous words kept me awake for a while. I'd almost stolen the thing I broke into the hoard to get, but if Hertha Harcourt had plans for me, I might not get one of her Luck charms where it needed to be in time. I flushed with anger and shame, turning my head so my tears fell on the sateen pillowcase instead of all over my face. The Harcourts had plenty of Luck charms in just that one vault. And dragon shifters got to be immortal all on their own, but Tanuki needed those charms to survive. If we used too much Luck without a charm, we aged faster. If we used up the last charm, years we'd borrowed ran out like sands through an hourglass.

I'd had no idea Dad's lapel pin was his last Luck charm when I nicked it. And then, Josh Dennison lay dying in front of the Temple to Music. With my brother engaged to his sister, the wolf shifter was practically family. If I hadn't burned the Luck in Dad's pin, then Josh would be in the ground, dead from a cockatrice scratch.

The only thing I'd ever been good at was sneakiness. That meant Dad's best chance was me doing a little stealing. I'd broken into the hoard to save my father, even though he'd never ask me to. If he didn't live to give me away at my wedding or hold his grandchildren, it'd be my fault. I couldn't live with the guilt, and I'd thought for one brief shining moment that I wouldn't have to. But Blaine Harcourt had ruined my entire plan by walking in before I was done and then not telling me how to get out in time. And Hertha Harcourt never gave things away. Trying to negotiate with her would come at a steep price.

As I drifted off, it occurred to me that I wasn't dealing with the dragon lady. She'd put Blaine in charge of me and my attempted theft. A week earlier, I'd have hoped he'd understand my predicament. But that was before I learned the up close and in person truth about him. Blaine Harcourt was every bit as paranoid and possessive as any other dragon shifter on the planet. He had to be the type of person to expect something precious from me in exchange for what he had in abundance. I was convinced he wouldn't help me, not even if I could get him somewhere private and tell him everything.

CHAPTER THREE

Blaine

I leaned on the door frame, thinking about knocking again. Just as I'd raised my hand, it opened. The girl glared, still wearing a shimmery nightgown. Her face was just as flawless-looking as it had been last night, although her eyes looked a little red around the rims. She'd been weeping, of course. I felt guilty, realizing she must have cried herself to sleep. But she'd broken in here, then clocked me one on the noggin. Why should I feel bad for her just because she was beautiful? That seemed like something my roommate Bobby would do, the Boy Scout. Had sharing a room with him made me soft, or just soft in the head?

I stuck my hand out, stopping the door as she tried to swing it shut. She rolled her eyes before I could do it myself. I stopped the trajectory of my eyeballs, not wanting her to think I'd copied her.

"What do you want?" Her scowl made her lips all pouty. I blinked, looking away from them. To think, I'd almost kissed her before she brained me. Stupid dragon hormones, always getting me in trouble.

"Uh, to ask if you want breakfast?" I tried smiling, but with the door crunching my fingers, it probably looked more like I had gas.

"No." Her stomach growled louder than a wolf shifter chasing a Gnome. She sighed. "Yes. I don't know. Shouldn't the Brownie just bring it, so I don't inconvenience you?"

"You've got a lot to learn about dragon hospitality." This time, I did roll my eyes. "And what Brownie?"

She stood there, chewing her lower lip, then she opened the door, inclining her head and waving with one hand to indicate I could come in. I stepped across the threshold but waited until she moved halfway across the room before shutting the door behind me and heading in. I didn't want her to brain me again.

Even though it'd take a high-ranking Faerie courtier to remove the bracelets, I was worried she might do something drastic like dislocating my thumb to try to take them off. I knew nothing about the Ichiro girl except that she had a habit of breaking out of secure boarding schools and into my mom's hoard. And that she drove me nuttier than a fruitcake.

"I'll be out in a minute. She grabbed her handbag from the nightstand, then something from the top drawer of the dresser and headed into the closet. The light went on when she shut the door, just like it did in all the closets at this mansion. I wondered exactly what kind of paranoia motivated Mother to make that addition.

I waited, listening to the clack of wooden hangers and rustle of fabric as she dressed. Instead of asking her about the Brownie again, I checked. This guest room was a mirror image of mine, so it was easy to find the likely places. Nothing. I headed for the bathroom even though that wasn't a great hiding place for water-phobic creatures like Brownies. Turning on the light nearly dazzled my eyes. The bedroom mirrors were shiny, but the shimmery decor in this bathroom was even more over the top. Nothing but towels, bath stuff, and that lame gilded pot of desiccated bamboo Mother insisted on having all over the house.

As I turned to go back into the bedroom, something creaked. Though the floors were covered with cushy mats, they were marble underneath. Besides, the sound came from the corner, not under my feet. Could the bamboo hide a Brownie? They looked like sticks, but it would have to be covered in gold paint to escape notice here.

"Ahem." The girl tugged my sleeve.

I turned in the doorway again, forgetting all about the Brownie. She'd just put on a simple sundress, but it made her look like a goddess. I wondered how a dress like that had ended up in her closet. It definitely wasn't one of Mother's last season items. Mother never wore pastels or floral prints.

"Um, okay." I turned my back on her, striding as fast as I could toward the door. "Breakfast. Follow me."

She did, a pair of gold ballet flats making muffled taps against the hall floors. She kept pace with me, something most of the girls back on campus had trouble with. I wondered how she managed, considering she couldn't be much more than five feet tall. I felt like the world's biggest idiot for not knowing her first name. Pride was one of my worst habits but swallowing it hadn't been something I was willing to do without the threat of an emergency or a bigger dragon. So why did I want to gulp down the whole lump for this thieving Tanuki?

"Look, I'm sorry about last night." I didn't even glance at her. I was so nervous. "How I said I didn't care what your name was and all that. I'm a class-A jerk even according to my friends, but Mother's crazy-intimidating. We're stuck together for at least the rest of the week, so, let's call a truce. How about it?"

"A truce has terms, Harcourt." I glanced sideways at a sudden movement only to find her braiding a strand of that glossy tawny-tipped hair of hers. Braiding and walking at the same time? Dexterity hadn't been her dump stat.

"Okay. So, what will it take to get your agreement?"

"I know you won't take these bracelets off and let me go. How about something fun? This is a billionaire's mansion. There's got to be loads of things to do in here, and I need something to take my mind off my problems."

"I think maybe you should be thinking about your problems,

though." Where in Tiamat's name was all this eggshell-walking coming from? She was a girl with Luck magic who turned into a little furry creature. I was the son of a billionaire who turned into a fire-breathing dragon. And she'd broken in here. I should be all Rhett Butler, not giving a damn. But how could I deliver zingers and sick burns if I didn't even know her name? And why didn't I want to?

"You just assume I'm not thinking about them all the time already?" She sniffed.

I turned my head to look at her, noticing the liquid sheen in her eyes complete with moisture at the corners. It felt like someone had just dropped an anvil in my belly. She kept on walking alongside me, her eyes on the marble her feet had yet to cross. The section of lower lip that wasn't in her teeth trembled lightly. I couldn't look away, not from someone so beautiful and so miserable at the same time. Big stupid mistake.

I fell on my tail, a side-effect of walking right into one of the pedestal tables Mother insisted on putting at every hallway intersection. The glass urn full of red apples tilted toward me, so I flung my arms up to shield my face from the inevitable rain of ruined fruit and glass shards. Maximum dexterity Tanuki girl caught it, righted it, then took an apple to polish on her sleeve. If I hadn't been a shifter, I wouldn't have been able to track her movements. I'd have thought the urn hadn't fallen, and she just picked up an apple while I wasn't watching.

I looked up, blinking. She stretched a hand down to me, the mist of tears gone from her eyes and a small smirk playing at the corners of her mouth. Something was off about her. I'd seen a mask slip but wasn't sure which emotion was genuine, the sadness or the mockery.

I put my hand in hers, letting her try to pull me to my feet on her own. She tugged and strained, huffing out an upward breath that blew her bangs off her forehead. A small star-shaped scar hid under there, gone from view before I could be sure it was more than a trick of the light or my imagination. The mark was tantalizingly familiar, and my first impulse was to brush aside her hair to get a better look. I didn't. Instead, I got my feet under me and finally stood up. When she let go of my hand, I felt a warm tingle where it had been.

"Thanks." I tucked a lock of hair behind my ear. "Look, this is going to go better if—"

"Kimiko." She scrutinized the shiny red fruit. "You know these are poisonous, right?"

"Yeah, like my mother." I shrugged. "Well, technically, she's venomous, and her breath is poisonous."

"Oh?" She placed the apple gently atop the others in the glass urn. "Really? How did you end up—"

"My bio-dad was a Fire dragon." I beckoned, then headed around the stupid table and its container of quietly deadly apples. "Mr. Harcourt isn't this baby's daddy. This kid is not his son."

"Weird." She glanced at me, then paid more attention to where she was going. Good on her. "I thought she married him back in the 80s."

"She did. I took decades to hatch."

"Wait." She held the hand she'd helped me up with in front of her, palm facing in. "You don't feel like a reptile."

"Neither do platypi."

"Platypuses."

"Whatever." I rolled my eyes. I usually only tolerated grammar corrections from Lynn for Bobby's sake. "Anyway, we're more like those than reptiles."

"If you were a character in a novel, you'd be the chosen one." Kimiko chuckled. It was low and throaty, not squeaky like I'd imagined.

"Good thing I'm not, then." I turned left down a narrower hallway. The aroma of cinnamon waffles wafted along toward us.

The kitchen was spacious and spotless, as usual. Kimiko stopped by the door, looking around at all the empty space. I had no idea what kind of kitchen she was used to, but this clearly wasn't it. Hoping she'd follow, I moseyed over to the counter where Gomer stood finishing spiced pears to go with the waffles. I leaned on the marble at enough of a distance to let him work and waited.

"Morning, Gomer."

"Good morning, young Master Harcourt."

"Oh, come on, Gomer. You don't need to get all Alfred Pennyworth on me. Kimiko's not exactly a formal guest and Mother's out for the rest of the morning."

"Well, then. Morning yourself, Blaine the Pain." The old Goblin cackled. "You want a waffle, make it yourself." He opened the iron, then flipped his waffle on a plate, which he took with him to one of the six stools at the breakfast bar.

I splooshed batter on the hot cast iron, not quite filling it, then closed it, not caring. It was food. I cared about what it tasted like, not how it looked. I dragged it onto my plate when it was done. Flipping was the territory of master chefs like Gomer. Mother had given him a job back in the 60s when tithing to the Sidhe Queen instead of the Goblin King had gotten him disowned and kicked out of the house by his family. They shouldn't have been surprised. The Seelies liked their rules, and any good chef has to follow recipes or suffer the consequences.

When I turned to top my waffle with spiced pears and fresh whipped cream, I almost knocked into Kimiko. She was licking. The. Serving. Spoon. For the whipped cream. I had no idea how long she'd been at that, but it sent me headlong toward a feverish fit. I reached out, snatching the spoon away and holding it over my head where she couldn't reach. As if that'd do any good at that point.

"How's anyone else supposed to enjoy this whipped cream now?"

"What's your problem, anyway?" She crossed her arms over her chest, then raised an eyebrow. "Afraid of girl cooties, Young Master Harcourt?" She actually made air quotes around the title.

I mumbled something about no one deserving this kind of thing, then tossed that spoon in the sink and got another. Relief washed over me as I saw her flipping the waffle iron closed instead of licking the bowl. She was a Tanuki, not a cat shifter. That was who I'd expect to violate a bowl of whipped cream. I daubed some on top of the pears I'd already taken, then sat a few seats down from Gomer. He'd given me grief about sitting too close before, something about hidden cameras. Goblins were almost as paranoid as dragon shifters.

Kimiko sat down with a plate more cream than waffle. She dug in, taking my statement about her not being a formal guest seriously. She was done before I reached the halfway mark. Leaning on her elbow overlooking the empty plate, she grinned.

"So, what do you have planned for us?"

"Fun, as promised, Kimiko."

"I was having fun before with the bowl of whipped cream." She smirked. "Well, at least the most fun you could have alone with that sort of thing."

"Trust me, what I have planned is all fun all the time." I couldn't help but smirk back at her.

Gomer's throat cleared a warning, reminding me it shouldn't be fun. I was supposed to be Kimiko's warden, not her friend. I wasn't sure whether she'd let me be either.

CHAPTER FOUR

Kimiko

The game room was fantastic. I could almost forgive Blaine for being such a spoilsport about the whipped cream. It had a dartboard, billiards table, ping-pong, air hockey, even an arcade-style DDR console. But the best part was the setup on the west wall. A screen stretched from one corner to the other, towering over my head. It had just about every kind of console that had existed since Atari plus a gaming rig attached to it. I had to sit down for a moment and just stare.

"This fun enough for you?" Blaine turned to face me, leaning against a decorative pillar. His smirk curled his lips in a way I wished I didn't find so interesting. I hadn't been lying back in the hoard; he *was* the most attractive man I'd ever laid eyes on. But he was keeping me here against my will with a magical device, preventing me from saving my father's life. I had to take a deep breath before all my frustration rose to color my cheeks and gave my anger away. So, I closed my eyes and thought about the video games.

"I don't even know where to start." I stood up, tracing one finger along the satiny-smooth wood trim of the billiard table. I felt him watching me again, and this time, the heat that threatened to color my cheeks wasn't from anger. That sucked. I headed to the dartboard, turned my back to Blaine, and picked up one projectile.

"I'd prefer you choose our activity, but if you're that overwhelmed, I can think of—"

He ducked in time, but barely. The dart had pinned a strand of his hair to the wall when it hit. "Um, okay. Darts it is." He pulled the projectile out of the wall, his sauntering pace casual as he headed toward me.

How dare he saunter after an attack like that? How dare he dodge that fast? After being klutzy in the hall earlier, he should have been an easy target. Then again, he was a dragon. Maybe I shouldn't have underestimated him.

I clenched my fists at my side as he took my attack in stride like some kind of lame joke. It wasn't. He didn't know I'd stuck the tip of the dart into the sliver of poison apple up my sleeve. I had to either incapacitate him so he wouldn't see how I got us out of the mansion, or convince him to help me. I didn't think much of my chances with the latter.

I beat him handily at darts, scoring seven more points than he did. It was easy. All I had to do was imagine his mother's face on the bullseye. I got tired of it pretty quickly, though. I headed over to the games, reaching out for a controller shaped like a guitar. Behind me, I heard him pick something up, and the screen lit. He took one of the other guitar controllers and got the game on. He'd played through it, and everything was unlocked, of course. I went straight to the hardest song, chuckling with irony at the juxtaposition of the band name and my opponent.

"Um, Kimiko, maybe…"

I selected Expert and started the game. What followed can't be described. Well, I guess I can say that trying to describe it reminds me of that song *Tribute* by Tenacious D. You know the one? They tell a story about how they beat a shiny demon's challenge to play the greatest and best song in the world. They do it but forget the entire winning song afterward. The song they tell the story with is pretty epic, but they say it can't match that one glorious lonely-road concert. Playing expert-level *Through The Fire and Flames* with Blaine Harcourt was like that, even though it didn't sound anything like that song.

I used to quadruple my allowance game-sharking the kind of boys who go on about fake gamer girls on that song. Blaine might have done the same. Might. It was getting harder to hate him or even just his guts. I still couldn't trust him, though. He'd never help me save my dad. I wasn't one of those Tinfoil Hatters he ran with over at PPC. I couldn't pretend he'd choose to help me over following his mother's orders. But he shook my resolve even more when I set down my ersatz guitar.

Blaine threw back his head and laughed. His own controller hung from the strap around his neck, forcing me to imagine him as a big goofy kid playing pretend rock stars or something. Was this some other game, trying to make me like him? What was the point in that? I couldn't like him. He might want to act like my friend now, but once I got out of here with a Luck charm, he couldn't pretend to be anything else. Stealing from a dragon shifter's hoard would make me his enemy forever.

"You rock." He finally unslung the guitar and pointed at the screen. "That's the best score I've ever gotten, and it wouldn't have happened without you."

"Huh? But I beat you." I peered at the screen, realizing I'd been so caught up in my thoughts I hadn't bothered to look at anything besides my winning score. Blaine had beaten his old record by a respectable amount. "Well, you still lost. You big scaly loser." I stuck out my tongue.

"Hey, losing to you is better than sitting in here alone trying to outdo my old high score." He shrugged.

I had nothing to say to that. He'd grown up alone, then. It made more sense now, how he'd said his parents "sort of" raised him. I blinked, missing my brother, Ren, terribly all of a sudden. He'd be wondering where I was, maybe even thinking I'd taken off and left him alone to care for Dad as his aging drastically accelerated. I had to pull myself together. Before I could shake my head and snap myself out of it, a set of warmer than average hands were on my shoulders.

"Hey. I noticed you made a face like this earlier. You okay?" The unexpected warmth in his eyes had my knees wobblier than my first impression of the game room. I raised my hand halfway to the side of his face, twisting my wrist to rub my fingertips against the apple sliver up my sleeve. I could touch his lips, then move in and pretend I wanted to kiss him. He'd drop like a rock, and I'd be free to take him hostage to demand a Luck charm. I pulled away and headed for the door, blinking back tears.

"I'm just tired and thirsty. This building's sized for dragons the length of a football field. Come along, or let the tithing bracelets knock us out." I pushed the door open. "I don't care which happens."

I hurried down the hall, telling myself those weren't butterflies in my stomach as I hoped he'd follow. Then, I let the sliver of apple fall from my sleeve and wiped my fingers on my dress once he'd caught up with me. I couldn't poison him, especially since I wasn't sure how much apple would be enough to kill him in his human form. I tried to tell myself I was failing my father because Blaine behaved honorably and his mother was the real enemy, not because of those eyes and that smile.

I'd have to tell him Dad was dying, but not where Mrs. Harcourt had any chance of hearing. My father was running out of time, and I was the only one who could save him. I needed Blaine on my side.

CHAPTER FIVE

Blaine

I shouldn't have trusted a word Kimiko Ichiro said, but it was hard
not to admire her skill at games. I hadn't been trounced so soundly
since I played another dragon shifter in online mode. And I hadn't felt
her use any magic, either, just her natural shifter abilities. That's why I
was surprised to find her almost in tears after the win. I paced her
down the hall, shortening my steps to go at her speed. She found the
route leading to the kitchen on her first try, probably some kind of
side-effect of studying the blueprints in preparation for the robbery
or whatever. I shook my head. Why would such a talented girl like her
do something so impossible and take such a risk? Why hadn't she just
asked me?

I ignored the smell of slightly stale apple, catching a whiff of tea
and the honey-seed cakes Mother always served to guests she wasn't
just pretending to like. Before we reached the door, I held up a finger
to signal a stop and quiet. Kimiko didn't argue or question me.
Instead, I blinked as her ears furred over and rounded further out

from her head. When she tucked her hair behind them, I saw they had pale, fluffy tufts at the centers, which matched the tips of the locks on her head. She leaned closer to the door. I joined her in eavesdropping. That particular pastime had helped me avoid trouble throughout most of my childhood. It made sense to me that a thief like her was used to listening in.

"Now, Hertha, there has to be some reason you've asked me here besides a thank-you tea." That was Headmistress Thurston talking, thank goodness. The tightness in my shoulders eased. It might have been the Sidhe Queen visiting, and I'd definitely been dropped from her nice list. Besides, the Headmistress was good people. She'd been the one to open PPC admissions to anyone with the grades, including dragons.

"Ulterior motives are like scales to dragons. You know my kind well, Henny." My mother actually sighed. "The break-in happened at a delicate time, as I'm sure you're aware. I can't tolerate having hoard security breached with something so precious inside, so I must know more about how it happened and why. I need Edgar Watkins."

I blinked. Professor Watkins had the hardest nose of any professor to stalk the halls of PPC in all its centuries, but his given name was Nate, not Edgar. I listened on, wondering whether the person Mother asked for might be a ghostly ancestor of his or something.

"I need Edgar Watkins too, with all the trouble we've been having on campus, but no one's seen him since poor Dahlia died and Henry got turned. Some people don't even seem to remember he exists."

"Are you sure about that?" I heard a clink as Mother put down her teacup. "Is Henry Baxter sure about that?"

"Perhaps you ought to send him an invitation for tomorrow evening."

"You know the reason I'm unable to do that." Mother sighed. "This is no time to invite a vampire inside my house."

"Understood. Still, an Air Magus like me isn't the right sort of person to ask about memories." I heard the Headmistress rattle an empty cup against her saucer. "Why not hire him? Send him an item to read if you can't have him here."

"I need Edgar in particular." I heard a series of four wooden taps that could only be Mother thrumming her fingernails on the table. "Some old business has come up as well."

"Then hire him to search for information about Edgar." I smelled cream and sugar, heard a crisp pour as the Headmistress refreshed her tea. "Although I'm not sure what the difference is between the two in your case."

"The difference is, the item in question can't leave the estate, he's directly linked to the old business I mentioned, and Unliving energy is too dangerous for the most vulnerable member of this household." What in Tiamat's name could Mother be talking about? I was the youngest and weakest Harcourt, and I hung out with Henry all the time.

Kimiko put her hands to her cheeks as calculation invaded her face like the Huns in China 200 years before the common era. Her ears flicked, pointing toward the door so she could listen in more closely.

"I've got no idea where Edgar Watkins is. Neither does his brother." The Headmistress sighed. "We're lucky he left us able to remember his name."

"Why not call your ex-husband, then? Whatever was his name again?" Mother's voice carried an emotion I wasn't used to hearing. Fear. This was one of the weirdest conversations I'd ever listened in on. Headmistress Thurston had lowered her voice to the point where I could only make out a few words of her answer.

"...Richard's been elusive just lately..."

"I understand it was a bad split, Henny, but you know what they say. Keep your friends close and your enemies closer." I heard a rustle of fabric and faint creak as Mother sat back in her chair. "Hasn't he gotten around to Tithing, finally?"

My breath became like the vacuum of space in the silence that followed. I hadn't known the Headmistress's ex-husband was an untithed Changeling. According to rumor, the Headmistress and her husband had broken up over her open admissions policy. At his age, he had to be an extremely powerful Magus. No wonder the Queen kept on getting involved in College affairs. She'd want him to Tithe to her, not the King.

This was a development I had to tell the rest of Tinfoil Hat about as soon as possible, Spring Break or not. I reached for my phone, but Kimiko grabbed my arm. She pushed me against the wall next to the door, shaking her head to cover those Tanuki ears with her hair. I smelled Chanel Beige and realized Mother hadn't been sitting back. She'd been getting up.

I opened my mouth to tell Kimiko to get the heck out of dodge, but she had other ideas for camouflaging our eavesdropping. She pounced on me, toppling us both on to a small decorative fainting couch.

Well, that's a little inaccurate. I caught her. But I would have flung her away if Mother hadn't been about to walk through the door on my right. I wouldn't have let her get that close to me again unless it was another knock-down-drag-out like we'd had in the vault. So I closed my eyes, letting her put on whatever show she had planned. I felt her hair tickle my neck, her breath in my ear, and her hands in my back pockets. I stifled a sigh, fighting the urge to melt into her ministrations and let whatever happened happen. My dragon was all for that idea. Kimiko seemed to know what she was doing. It'd been a while for me, and she smelled like heaven. Well, except that hint of stale apple.

Apple? The only apples she'd been around that day were Mother's Evil Queen poison ones. I twisted my hands in her hair, anger at the fact she'd tried to slip me a mickey flip-flopping at the silken feel of her tresses against my skin. Like Forbidden Chocolate Ice Cream, Kimiko Ichiro was bad for me but felt so good at the same time. I needed help with the new information we'd overheard, but also some solid advice about how to outwit an alternately amorous and dangerous Tanuki.

"When you said you had another guest, I didn't think you meant this sort." Headmistress Thurston's arch tone could only go with an eyebrow position of the same name. I didn't dare look and find out, not even when Kimiko climbed off my lap to smile at the next two scariest ladies in my universe.

I couldn't look at Mother and wouldn't look at the Headmistress. That left me even more stuck with that Tanuki than the tithing bracelets made me. She'd managed to use our faux make-out session as cover for shifting her ears back to human shape. Her hair was still perfectly smooth though she rearranged her dress shamelessly. The flash of leg she showed made my throat dry. I thanked Tiamat that I was sitting down.

"It's good to see the two of you working things out." Mother sounded amused. For me, that was like hearing a funeral dirge. She'd think I'd charmed Kimiko and gotten some kind of information about how she'd broken in here. I had to get away long enough to give that another go.

"Yeah. We were looking for you, actually. I wanted to know if you'd let us through the wards later. You see, I'd like to take Kimiko out, show her around Newport a little." I didn't mention the bracelets, but Mother saw me twist mine around my wrist. I grinned down at my shoes. Mother would know I was fibbing if I looked her in the eye, but I always did the shoe stare when she caught me red-handed with a girl.

"We can arrange that." Mother's head tilted toward Kimiko instead of me.

I chanced a glance up and almost gasped. Headmistress Thurston looked like death. Her face was nearly as pale as a vampire's, and the circles under her eyes spoke of extreme exhaustion. She shouldn't have been so severely drained from putting up some wards with a few dragons and a handful of other Magi. She must have been casting like her Air magic was on an Everything Must Go Final Clearance Sale. But where and why? More stuff to talk over with Tinfoil Hat. I had to buy myself some time away from Mother and Kimiko though.

"How about we arrange it for dinner tonight, then?" I gazed at the back of Kimiko's head when Mother turned at the sound of my voice, trying to make my eyes look moonier than a werewolf's. "Maybe seven o'clock?"

"That sounds perfect. I'll have the car take you to Freebody Park and make your reservations at The Spiced Bear for eight-thirty. That gives you time to walk and talk together." I wasn't sure because I wasn't exactly looking, but Mother might have winked. At Kimiko. No wonder the girl was so infuriating. My mother actually liked her. But why? Too many mysteries.

"I'll have to be heading back to campus now, Hertha." Head-mistress Thurston pulled her handbag up to her shoulder.

Mother made pleasantries with her guest as she escorted her down the hall and away. Before I could turn to look back toward Kimiko again, she squealed and flung her arms around me for the second time that day.

"Oh, Blaine!" She pulled back, gazing into my eyes. "You're not nearly as big a jerk as I thought you were. Thank you! You have no idea how awful it is being locked up everywhere I go by just about everyone I meet."

Instead of insulting her, I couldn't stop a smile from growing on my face. Her joy was infectious. Even if she wouldn't have made my top ten choices for company this week, it was better than sitting alone with my paranoia the whole time, just waiting for an Extramagus attack. I wondered whether she was wrong, whether maybe I did actually know about being locked up. It sure felt that way, but for me, it was more figurative than for her.

She went on about checking the weather and looking up the restaurant, picking clothes, and getting ready. I let her until we parted at her door. Her hand on my cheek was almost like a peck and I almost damned the torpedoes and gave her an honest-to-goodness kiss. Almost, but that only counts in horseshoes. I locked the door to my room behind me and turned on the spyware interference devices I'd used everywhere since the Grim attacks on Campus during the inter-session.

It was time to phone a friend.

CHAPTER SIX

Kimiko

My stomach reminded me that we hadn't gotten snacks or a drink. Changing my ears to listen to the weird not-soccer-mom conversation had made me ravenous. I went into the bathroom, checking the decorative urn for my buddy the Brownie. They weren't there. In the bedroom, I found a panel on the wall next to the phone, with buttons by a list of names. One of them was that Goblin I'd met at breakfast, Gomer. Once my bag and the magical object hidden inside were locked in the nightstand, I pressed it.

"Gomer at your service." I chuckled, wishing I could risk replying with a cheerful "Bilbo Baggins at yours."

"Hi, Gomer." I wasn't sure whether his end of the console told him which room this was. "This is Kimiko Ichiro. I need some food. A snack, anything. If you don't mind, please." My stomach made a noise that reminded me of the time I lost one of my galoshes in the mud. Shifting made me wish I could go on the Hobbiton diet, with Elevensies, Second Breakfasts, and all that jazz.

"Of course. I'll whip something up and have it sent along to the gold room." He chuckled. "Since you haven't stayed here before, make sure nothing's in the mandala on the rug. We don't much like ending up with laundry in the kitchen."

"Okay." I saw the design he was talking about. It must be some tangible marker for Vanishing or teleporting things. Faerie magic users being employed by a dragon family only made sense if you knew that dragons could see that kind of magic, unlike Magi. "Thanks, Gomer."

The intercom clicked off, and I felt more alone with my thoughts. I had to use this quasi-date to get Blaine on my side. So I'd need to plead my case about Dad while we walked, not in a place where friends or admirers of his mother might overhear. I didn't much care whether that happened before or after dinner. Still, I wished I had someone to talk to about this. The Brownie wasn't in the bathroom anymore. The only other option hadn't answered me last night, but maybe trying today was worth a shot. I took my purse out of the drawer and brought it into the bathroom, then turned on all the faucets.

"Hello, Ismail."

"Yes?" The deep voice was muffled, coming from my bag.

"Thank Lady Luck!" I set the purse on the counter and sat on the toilet lid so I could hear him better. "I thought you'd stopped speaking to me or something."

"No. I was sleeping, silly."

"Oh. I wasn't sure whether lamp-bound Djinn had a bedtime." I didn't admit how much more I didn't know about Djinn, which was pretty much everything besides the fact that they only granted each person three wishes while doing time in their family lamp. And that they were Faeries, so asking them too many questions meant you'd owe them.

"It's self-imposed. Let's just say I prefer to keep to the hours outside as much as possible. The last thing I want is lamp-lag if I ever stop serving in here." I heard something that could have been a sigh, but the lamp made me unsure of that. In any event, it was hard to try to read Ismail the Djinn the way I did other people. Trying to talk through metal was like listening through an old analog phone.

"Well, okay, then." I folded my hands in my lap and took a deep breath before continuing. "So, I have a date. With Blaine Harcourt."

"No Luck charms, but a date. Hmm. Did you let the dragon shifter catch you on purpose? I was wondering why you didn't wish yourself back home last night."

"He caught me, but not because I let it happen. He's something else. Anyway, the wards came down before I could wish. You already warned me that I'd have to wish before that. And then, Mr. Harcourt took away the charm I'd, um, pocketed."

"I see. You were right not to try after that. We Djinn are limited to Faerie powers, and even those can't Vanish people through wards."

"I'll have to find a way to get a charm and be outside wards so you can get me out of here, then. That's going to be hard with this thing." I twisted the tithing bracelet around my wrist three times.

"Yes. You'll need Blaine Harcourt with you unless you don't care about being in a coma." He sighed. "Or you'll need a highly ranked Courtier of the Goblin King to take it off of you ahead of time. That's an Unseelie bracelet set."

"That's not likely to happen in a house where the Queen's people are servants, Ismail."

"Ouch. Well, I'm sure you'll think of something."

"If only someone older and wiser had some advice." I didn't bother batting my eyes. While Djinn could read magical energy from inside their lamps, they couldn't actually see things like facial expressions unless they came out. Ismail was probably the most introverted Djinn I'd ever heard of. He hadn't even come out to grant either of my first two wishes. Most of them took any chance they could get to poof out.

"Yeah, if only." He chuckled before I could splutter.

"Relax, Kimiko Ichiro. Wear something that makes you feel pretty. Smile. You're a Tanuki and a good looking girl. Luck and circumstance are on your side even though coincidence might be iffy."

"Thanks, Ismail." I sat up. "You've gone so far above and beyond to help me ever since I, um, picked up your lamp." We both knew I hadn't just picked it up. I'd stolen it, of course, from a lab cabinet at The Academy.

"I'd tell you to fill out the customer satisfaction survey after I'm done helping you, but that's not one of the perks of my job." His last bit of advice faded out like someone turned down the volume. "Try to have fun."

I scratched my head, still not sure exactly how a Faerie bound in a lamp for who knows how long could joke about something like his enslaved state. Maybe he wasn't joking about being an introvert, or perhaps he'd taken a turn in the lamp to spare a family member that fate. Hopefully, I'd get a chance to ask him someday when all this was over. I couldn't risk any questions while I was master of the lamp though. Once the purse and Ismail's lamp were back in the nightstand, I got to work.

I had to make sure everything about me was perfect. I went into the closet to undress, putting the dress and everything under it in a hamper, then sticking the shoes back on the rack. After that, I shrugged into a robe and headed for the bathroom. In the shower, I washed my hair. And then I used the array of styling products and tools to make it as beautiful as possible. My stomach growled again when I smelled food. Gomer had come through.

Chewing watercress and cucumber sandwiches interspersed with sips of tea, I thought again about Ismail and his lamp. Should I bring it out to dinner or leave it behind? If Blaine found it on me, he'd be suspicious for sure and maybe confiscate it. I couldn't afford to let him know I had a Djinn at my service until I also had a Luck charm and hopefully Blaine's cooperation or at least indifference. But how likely was I to win him over? Tapping my toe against the thick rug, I made a mental list of what I knew about him in particular versus dragon shifters in general.

Blaine was lonely. His joy at losing two different games in a row to me couldn't mean anything else. Dragon shifters supposedly liked their privacy. But everything I'd read on them had to do with the elders. I'd heard Blaine's mother call him a whelp which meant he was young. I knew nothing at all about young dragon shifters. Maybe the privacy preference had more to do with pre-Reveal society than dragon shifter instinct. Could dragons truly be misunderstood creatures, or was it just a tired old trope they used to get sympathy in this new age?

He also acted awkward around me even though Beth mentioned he was a huge flirt and a playboy. Physically, he seemed to be clumsier around me, too. He'd had trouble fighting me in the vault, fallen on his tail in the hall, and only just barely dodged my dart. Those things shouldn't have happened.

Of all the shifters on the planet, dragons were the most dangerous exactly because they had better enhancements than the other kinds. Why couldn't he handle a little Tanuki like me? Could it be Luck? Every Extrahuman and even a few humans had a trace of the magic I manipulated. I hadn't bothered checking Blaine's. Stupid of me. He might be low on Luck in general. But that was unlikely considering the number of Luck charms the Harcourts had stashed away here.

What if Blaine had Luck, but it had taken a turn for the worse? The implications of someone or something messing with a dragon's Luck were chilling. They had the best defenses of any shifter, both physically and magically. Only Tanuki could tamper with their Luck directly. Luck on its own just went where coincidence wanted it to. Only Magi could track coincidence, and barely any could nudge it. If Blaine hadn't been in direct contact with some other Tanuki, who wanted him dead instead of out of her hair, then he was at ground zero of a coincidence bomb greater and more terrible than Oz's reputation in that movie with the yellow brick road.

I put down the sandwich, appetite melted in the deluge of hunches like the Witch of the West in water. In the nearest mirror, I checked my own Luck. My throat went dry and my fingertips cold. Luck swirled around me as always, but in reverse. The usual light-gold glimmering swirls were laced with baleful red. My Luck had spun into one terrible twister. It wasn't in Kansas anymore.

I couldn't wait. I had to get eyes on Blaine right away and check his Luck. My hand curled tight and clammy around the cut-crystal doorknob. It didn't turn.

I was trapped. There had to be another way out of this room and over to the next. One set of double doors opened onto a tiny balcony. Blaine's room was to the right of that. The exterior wall had a decorative ledge. What could possibly go wrong?

CHAPTER SEVEN

Blaine

My anti-spyware devices stopped magical eavesdropping like Superman stopped trains, but I didn't want anyone overhearing mundanely. Usually, I'd blast some tunes, but that wasn't good for talking on the phone. So that's how I ended up sitting at my desk with an open laptop to see who could chat online. No Bobby, no Lynn. No Henry at lunchtime, of course. I put my head in my hands, abandoning all hope. The soft chime of an incoming message sounded, reminding me of GLaDOS. Maybe I should murder my useless computer before it threw me through a Portal or snuffed me. I sighed and stared at the screen instead. **Incoming message from Tony G**, it said.

Trogdor! Burninate any good books lately? Apparently, cat shifter families didn't bother going on out-of-town Spring Break vacations.

Va fa Napoli, Tony. My Italian might be rusty, but I used plenty of the most popular local swear words in the living languages I spoke.

Woah, dude. No need to bust out the potty mouth. Chill. Oh, wait, you can't. :p

Shut up and leave me alone. Tony Gitano was the last person I wanted to ask about this stuff.

No. I have news. Did you hear Ren's sister Kimiko's missing? Gossip and bird-watching were Tony's favorite pastimes.

She's not. If we'd been talking in person, he'd have gotten the hint that I didn't want to say more. Probably wouldn't have mattered. He didn't care about hints or me not wanting to talk to him most of the time.

Um, no. She is. Ren's freaking out. Just saw him two minutes ago. Why hadn't I thought of her older brother before now? The last thing we needed was a pissed off Selkie swimming over and scaling the cliffs outside.

Get offline and catch him, tell him she's fine.

OMG WTF. You. Did. Not. Not with your packmate's sister? Assumptions like that are why talking to a shady excuse for a LOLCat rankled so much.

He's your packmate, too, cat-man.

Yeah, but she ain't at my house while her brother's on the warpath. Josh'll have kittens.

Let him. I don't care what Beowulf thinks.

Wow, you really like this girl.

No. I don't. She's a giant pain in my ass. And nothing happened. She's just staying here.

Whatever. So, why are you online if you have a guest nothing happened with yet? Something hinky going down?

None of your business. It absolutely was not. But that sort of thing hadn't stopped Tony from butting in before.

Well, no one else is around. Henry and Maddie left for Vermont last night. Everyone's gone but me. They all went home.

Josh, isn't in Providence?

Negatory. He took Nox to Cape Cod.

Fewmets. Of course, Josh could go out of town. No Extramagus hunting him down anymore. But he knew I was next, and he just left?

After I bailed his mate out of losing her magic and everything? *I'm stuck with the guy who flips out over laser pointers.*

I'll overlook the extra helping of verbal abuse. So what gives? Maybe I can help.

You can't. I really thought he couldn't. I needed another brain on this mess, and Tony's was always on how to trick friends and be a bad influence on people.

You can spend all your time arguing or give me the 411 and let me try. I put my head in my hands before making a decision and putting my fingers back to the keys.

Fine. Mother wants to hire some Psychic named Edgar Watkins, The Headmistress's ex is a Changeling. Also, Kimiko's here because I caught her in Mother's hoard trying to steal Luck charms.

Wait, Rick Thurston's a Changeling? Thought he was a Magus. But I hadn't mentioned the ex's name to Tony. Hadn't remembered it until he mentioned it. How had he known? Hinky cat-bastard.

He's both. Apparently, that happens sometimes.

What kind?

I closed my eyes. I should know, but I just couldn't remember. I had to have either read it somewhere or overheard it, right? Why was the Headmistress's ex-husband slipping my mind like a greased pig? The messaging program chimed again.

You don't remember either, huh, Trogdor?

No. Feels like it's on the tip of my brain, though.

Same. Anything else?

You really are useless.

Hey, I was going to take what you gave me and go look Ricky up in the Extrahuman Registries.

Oh. Sorry. Well, do it quick. The Headmistress could be an extra on The Walking Dead. Not like Henry, the fictitious zombie kind. Something's got her magically exhausted to the point where she could end up in the hospital.

Madonn.

Hey, you make me quit the cuss words, and then you go and do it?

Go to Naples, Blaine. Look, I'm sending you an Extrahuman Registry link from Olivia's PLEXIS Nexus ID. I did not want to know how he'd gotten that. And then I gotta go. Goombas on the move.

Um, what are you doing, playing Super Mario?

No. It's way more important than that. Look, I'm out of contact for a bit. Keep messenger open on your phone if you go anywhere.

No. Go jump in a lake, Tony.

Seriously, promise you'll keep messenger open.

All right, fine. At that point, I was just glad Tony didn't make me promise to answer it.

I shut down Messenger on the laptop and logged in on my phone. Then, I stood up to pace the room. And that's when I saw Kimiko Ichiro dangling from the railing outside my window like the last autumn leaf in a breeze. I dropped the phone and bolted for the balcony doors, flinging them inward to open them. I caught her by the wrist just in time, but her hand was so clammy she almost slipped my grip, anyway. Her eyes were wide and glassy, and when I hauled her up over the rail, she trembled like a fracking earthquake. I put her on my bed before I realized she was wearing nothing but a shiny satin bathrobe.

Anger kicked up the furnace in my gut like someone had poured butane on it. Smoke hazed my vision, probably hers too since I grabbed her by the shoulders and leaned in until our noses almost touched. Kimiko's lips were slightly parted, her head tilted back, but the whites of her eyes and the pinpoint pupils meant she was afraid instead of amorous. Good on her. At least she was the kind of girl who respected the fact an angry dragon had her in his clutches. But her gaze was unfocused.

"What in the name of the First Egg were you doing out there?" I clamped down harder on her shoulders. "I let the poison apple attempts slide, but this. Is. Madness."

"Blaine, it's your Luck." She shook her head, eyes still wider than the stratosphere. "Your Luck's corrupted, gone bad."

"Oh. Sorry." I let go of Kimiko's arms, hoping I hadn't hurt her. "Huh. I can't think of anyone who'd want me to be unlucky." I blew more smoke from my nose, unable to find the focus needed to make rings. "Can you?"

"No. But whoever it is messed with mine, too."

My phone blasted *Werewolves of London* by Warren Zevon. Josh was calling. I took a deep breath, then released Kimiko's shoulders.

"I need to answer that." I stabbed a finger at the air between us then waggled my eyebrows. "Don't move from that bed or you're crispy critters." She blinked and put her hand over her mouth, shoulders shaking around a suppressed giggle.

"What's up, wolf?" I held the phone to my ear.

"Put me on speaker." Josh sounded more like his dad than himself. Something had him in adult mode, not the kind of "adulting" you did alone on Cape Cod with your mate, either.

"What?"

"You heard me. Your companion needs to listen to this, too."

"I don't have a—"

"Bullshit. Speaker or you don't get the information I have." The absolute worry in his voice damped down my fire like a wet blanket. I pressed the button. "The Sprite told me you were next the night I fought the cockatrice, Blaine. They just interrupted Nox and me in the middle of lunch to say the Extramagus's other target this time is Kimiko Ichiro. Nox burned their debt to her for this next part, so you better pay attention. They said that if you don't start communicating and cooperating with each other, you're both dead."

"But she broke into Mother's—"

"I don't care what she's gotten herself into."

"But he just threatened—"

"Honey Badger don't care, and neither does Alpha Wolf. Cut the crap, shoot the breeze, stay alive." I heard a long sigh. "Blaine, you tell her everything we've got. No matter what you think of her or what she might be doing in your house, Kim saved my life. She's a target now, and I owe her. You're paying it back for me. Nox and I will try to make it to your place by tomorrow."

"Don't bother." I blew a long stream of thinner smoke out my nose. "Mother's not letting anyone in except for the Headmistress, Mr. Waban, and the Queen. She'd just tell you guys to scram."

"Okay, then. Maybe Ren can get in with the Queen's entourage, then."

"No!" Kimiko was on her feet, but she sat back down right away when I glared at her. "I mean, Ren's busy. He's got some important family stuff going on. Don't ask him to do anything else, I beg you."

"The only other packmate in the state is Tony," Josh grumbled. "Not the most reliable, but maybe he'll help. Talk to him."

"I did. Cat-man's doing what he can already."

"Oh. Wow, so something already happened?"

"Just bad luck." I shook my head, not wanting to go into the details of my sluggish clumsiness since coming back home for Spring Break. "Little things."

"Little things that add up to big." I was about to interrupt Kimiko, but she didn't talk about my tumble in the hall or anything embarrassing. Instead, she told him about how she'd checked our Luck, and it had turned. "Anyway, I'll help. Just send what you have to my phone. There just happens to be an app for that."

"Yup. It sounds like it might be coincidence again. You two be careful. Together. Take care of each other."

Josh hung up before we could protest. I led Kimiko out the door and back down the hall to her room in silence. She didn't speak, just looked up at me with those eyes, pupils dilated normally now. I reached out a hand to her, intending I don't even know what. She shouldn't want me to touch her after I exploded at her. I let it drop, but she caught it, gave it a squeeze with a steely grip I didn't expect.

"Together, like he said." She opened the door with her other hand, only letting go as she shut it. She hadn't averted her gaze or even blinked either, letting the panel of reinforced wood break our eye contact instead.

I stood outside for longer than I should have. When I finally turned to head back to my own room, a thick stalk of decorative bamboo in an urn crackled lightly.

"You'd better stay away from her, or I'll singe you and toss you into the Bay. She's my prisoner, not yours or your Queen's." I let the disguised Brownie quiver and headed back into my room to send all the Extramagus info to Kimiko. At least I wouldn't have to worry about her getting bored enough to climb out a window again. She'd have plenty to do.

Tony's PLEXIS Nexus search turned up a garden-variety Fire Magus, Richard Hopewell, who'd been married to Henrietta Thurston from the mid-1980s until just a few years ago. My fingers itched. I wanted to do another search, but couldn't without the login. I messaged the Shady Neighborhood Cat-man, asking him to search for Richard Hopewell's primary school and apprenticeship records from before the Reveal, also to do a search for Edgar Watkins. But Tony didn't answer. I zoned out to Angry Birds for so long I had to scramble to get ready in time to leave for dinner.

CHAPTER EIGHT

Kimiko

I didn't worry about the perfect dress anymore. The ones in the closet were all pretty close at any rate. I still couldn't figure out how they seemed meant for me or who put them in there on the same night I got stuck at the Harcourt mansion. I didn't have time to think about that now, anyway. Blaine and his friends were involved in something big, judging from the time it took to download the files he'd sent.

I clicked to open LORA, the Lucky analysis app I'd created while bored at the Academy, then spent the next hour letting it upload facts from Blaine's reports. Then, I pinned my hair up and took another shower while I waited. I wasn't the kind of girl who didn't break a sweat while hanging from a balcony and dealing with Blaine's dragon aggro.

"LORA, list the most common factors in the case."

The app followed my voice command, popping up three things immediately. First of all, the coincidence changes happened to exactly two people every time. Second, all the incidents occurred in Rhode Island. And third, multiple forms of magic were involved. That pointed to an Extramagus, like Josh said on the phone. But in all the reports, no one had figured out what the Extramagus's limitation was. I had a few possibilities, thanks to LORA. At least I'd have something to tell Blaine. But there had to be more.

"Check identities of Extramagi in the files against external sources." I let LORA chew on that while I went to the closet. At least I didn't have to check the weather after hanging out the window.

I slid hangers along the rod, flipping through dresses like pages in a paperback novel. I tried to care, but couldn't think straight. Extramagi were serious business, and one of them was after Blaine and me. I turned to the other side of the closet, hoping to find an outfit with pants. No such luck. Either whoever filled this wardrobe could fight in skirts, or they wanted to keep me from fighting. I went practical, selecting a vintage-looking style with a full knee-length skirt. It was yellow with gold threading along the hems, sleeves, and collar. The only shoes that matched had those stupid kitten heels, also known as ankle breakers.

But I could outwit the Harcourt Family Fashion Police. There were some flat patent turquoise Mary-Janes and a matching clutch. I grabbed those and found a filmy blue scarf to hang around the collar of a woolen camel coat. It was perfect, an outfit that couldn't possibly tempt Luck gone bad with a heel breaking, a purse strap catching on my neck, or a skirt tripping me up or hobbling me. And everything I wanted to bring would fit in the clutch, too.

I checked LORA again and found too large a list. I smacked my head and narrowed the parameters to Rhode Island. Stanhope, Edgewood, Williams. Of course, the oldest families. I scrolled down to see one more. Thurston. But the last recorded Extramagus in that family had been back in Colonial times. Still, it was interesting. Blaine's report only mentioned the Stanhopes. I wondered whether that was bias. The PPC students seemed to genuinely like their Headmistress. Then again, it could be something more sinister. If I were head of a college and belonged to a family of Extramagi, I might try to remove the records from school resources.

But I'd seen Miss Thurston myself just that day. She didn't look like she had the energy to do much of anything, let alone keep the facts straight enough to lie like that. The thing about lying is you need to memorize the truth if you expect to do your falsehoods justice. Wise men say a lie with a grain of truth is more potent, but that's just a bunch of pretty words.

The truth is the rock you build your tower of lies on. If you don't know where the high tide stops, or whether that rock has a crack in it, that tower crashes down with you inside. The truth is a foundation, not something to ignore if you're the type of person who relies on embellishment. No, Henrietta Thurston wasn't in this, at least not intentionally.

LORA's next trick would take the rest of the night. I set my questions up, narrowing parameters to include only Rhode Island again and drank the rest of the tea on the food cart. After that, I put on some makeup and read through Blaine's reports from Fall Semester exam week when all this had apparently started. After reading for a while, I knew better.

Blaine blinked when I opened the door, shook his head, blinked again. The faint trail of smoke rising from his nose stopped cold. I stared. His eyes weren't narrowed, and his hair wasn't tied back, tangled, and dull. Instead, it hung just past his shoulders in chestnut waves I hadn't expected. He cleared his throat, then held out his arm. I reached for it, remembering the first time I'd been at the carousel in Roger Williams Park and managed to grab the ring. But Blaine wasn't a prize. He was a puzzle, a powerful ally or a dire enemy, depending on which way I tried to piece together my perception of him. Was his paranoia sea or sky, his bad Luck turn flora or fauna?

I kept pace with him down the hall. It was easy, even for someone as short as me. All I had to do was take two steps to each of his. Simple adaptation. Maybe that kind of thing doesn't come naturally to other people. I'll never know and don't really care because I'm me and perfectly fine with that.

Blaine turned left when I expected him to continue toward the back stairwell. Moments later, we stood at the top of a staircase swooping down from the third to the first floor like a pair of wings. An instant of vertigo and déjà vu threatened to overwhelm me. I felt I'd been here before, and under less pleasant circumstances for some reason. If it hadn't been for my hand on Blaine's arm, I might have found myself with my hand in his pocket, nicking his wallet. I also might have tumbled headfirst down the steps. Instead, I glanced to the side and up, my lips tilting to match what my eyes were doing.

Light flashed to my left and down. Gomer stood behind a tripod, wearing an unspoken apology on his wrinkled brow. So, Mrs. Harcourt approved of this little outing. I still had no idea why Blaine had decided to stick with the plan and take me out on the town, especially after the nastiness in his room earlier. I suspected he needed to get away from Mommie Dearest for some reason. The anti-spyware devices I'd seen in his room only supported that theory. Paranoid dragons were paranoid.

We made it down the stairs without any more weirdness. Mrs. Harcourt wasn't around, even though she'd clearly ordered her Goblin chef to record the momentous occasion of her son going out on an actual date. Gomer took another snapshot. Blaine cleared his throat instead of rolling his eyes, giving me the impression that this whole series of events was atypical. Once we were out the door, his arm relaxed, though he didn't shake off my grasp or change the angle of his elbow to make holding on awkward.

"Tiamat's Scales, I'm glad to be out of there." He let the chauffeur open the door for us but helped me into the car himself. "I can't believe Mother made Gomer break out the old camera."

"Does she do that every time you take a girl on a date?"

"I don't know." He settled in the seat across from me, his eyes fixed on my face.

"I don't understand." I did. He either hadn't taken a girl on a date before or not where his mother could have anything to do with it. I suspected Dad would have been challenging my dates to duels instead of snapping photos.

"I don't either." He puffed out a couple of smoke rings.

"So, why are we going?"

"Mostly, I needed to talk to friends from school this afternoon without you watching." His eyes made like little stars. "But that was then, this is now. Can't work together unless you're reading over my shoulder." He shrugged. "What did you think of the reports?"

"You and your friends have an entirely ineffective system for data analysis."

"Excuse me?" And there were those narrowed eyes I'd come to expect.

"Look, I'm not putting down your research. That's brilliant. It's the putting it together part I think needs work." I pulled out my phone. "I used this app, put your data into it. It's analyzing something now, but you can check the previous results."

He took the phone, swiping and tapping through the stuff I'd found out earlier. He blinked, shaking his head again like he did back in front of my door.

"Who did you steal this software from?" Blaine winked before I could slap him.

"I coded it."

"Wow. You're a coder?"

"It's a hobby. The Academy doesn't have much to do besides super easy homework." I shrugged. "You're lucky."

"Huh?"

"Getting into PPC." The laugh I intended came out more like a whimper. "I didn't have the grades."

"That's not luck, it's hard work." The words dropped out of his mouth like a bag of chips from a vending machine.

"Is that something you believe, or more programming from the Mom unit?" I didn't actually try to stop my eyebrow from gaining altitude, but maybe I should have.

"Look, no one gets away with insulting Mother. Not even me." He shook his head, then raised his chin. "But I guess a Luck expert would be able to properly question philosophies on blanket Luck statements. My grades are mine, not Mother's. Those came from busting my tail, and I won't let you tell me otherwise, Tanuki or no."

"People make Luck, you know. If Extrahumans like you didn't, there wouldn't even be Luck charms."

"And Josh wouldn't be here. Point taken." He actually smiled. I closed my eyes, unable to watch his relief at the event I'd doomed my father with. "Hey." Fabric rustled. His hand covered mine. The car stopped, and he pulled it away.

I could have just sat in that car for a few hours, forced Blaine to take me back to the mansion and haul me inside. Instead, I opened my eyes when the chauffeur opened the door. I got out like a good little date and stood at the curb as the car pulled away. Blaine took my hand this time instead of offering his arm, leading me slowly through a small park.

"What happened back in the car?"

"I just got reminded of something."

"Anything you need help with?"

"Wait." I tugged on his hand, stopping him. He turned. "You want to know why I broke in. This thing that's got me down. It's the reason."

"And it has something to do with Josh Dennison."

"So you know. You knew all this time?"

"I know nothing, Kimiko." He squeezed my hand. "I deduce."

"Well, do you still want to offer me help when you don't even know what my problem is?"

"I do. Whether I can or not is another story. Some tall orders are big as houses. Others are Mount Everest."

"I'm still not sure I should tell you, or anyone else." I sniffed, hoping he'd think it was allergies. I shut my eyes.

"I get it. You're used to doing everything for yourself. 'If you want something done right' and all that?"

"Yeah."

"Come on, then." He put an arm around my shoulders. "We can

talk about it when you absolutely have to." I shivered, but definitely not with cold. Blaine Harcourt was driving me crazy, one minute all smoke and angst, the next a chivalry most would expect from knights instead of dragons.

I hadn't seen a fraction of that yet as it turned out.

CHAPTER NINE

Blaine

I might not know why, but Kimiko Ichiro needed a Luck charm. And I wanted to help her, but Mother let nothing leave her hoard without some dangerous bargain or ironclad agreement. Then again, she'd given me the task of resolving Kimiko's break-in. Tanuki only needed Luck charms for life-saving magic, so if she was trying to steal one, it could mean someone was in mortal danger. But she was a consummate liar. I couldn't fault her for it, though, considering that was one of my own talents. I'd come to an understanding. She angered me so much because of what we had in common. Unexpected mirrors were startling.

While kicking myself for wasting time casually gaming instead of pinging Tony for advice on outwitting a Tanuki, I realized all I should do is figure out what I would do in her situation. I kept my arm around her as I walked through and out of the park and then down Memorial Boulevard. The streets were quiet, almost empty. Lights were on at the bed-and-breakfast up ahead. As we crossed the side-street and approached the converted Victorian house, a woman dashed down the steps. She tripped the contents of her pink suitcase spilling on the sidewalk in front of us. What I could see of her face behind strands of blonde hair reddened. I knew her.

"Jeannie?" I held out a hand to help her up. "Jeannie La Montagne?" The bear shifter was also a Resident Assistant at the PPC dorms.

"Ugh. It figures I'd run into someone I know on the worst night of my adult life." She brushed her hair off her face. Tears streaked mascara in trails down her cheeks.

"Are you okay?" Kimiko got down on the sidewalk, collecting items and stuffing them back in the suitcase. I watched her. No sleight-of-hand. "What happened?"

"Well, I kind of got stranded here unexpectedly." She sighed, looking like the last thing she wanted to do was talk about it. But then, a man stepped out on the porch.

"Jeannie, come on. Come back inside, and we'll talk about this."

"No way, Dale. Stay here alone or with your side piece for all I care." Jeannie snatched a can of hairspray out of Kimiko's hand and flung it at Dale. He ducked, and it hit the wall.

"She meant nothing to me."

"It would be better if she did." Jeannie's throat rumbled with a low growl.

"Woah." Dale paled. I would too if I was a regular guy with a jilted bear-shifter girlfriend.

Jeannie's pert nose darkened as she began shifting. She turned her head, looking away from Dale and out somewhere toward the street. Messenger on my phone beeped, then I heard a moped in the distance. A black sedan turned from the intersection we'd just crossed, the heavily tinted window opened a crack. I smelled oil and gunpowder. Kimiko stared at Jeannie, completely oblivious.

My skin scaled over and the seams at the back of my jacket popped. I took one step back and over to put myself between the car and Kimiko. My partially shifted wings opened, circling around her. The engine revved, and then the bullets hit.

Scales are slightly better than kevlar for stopping mundane bullets, but the semi-automatic rounds felt like that one time I'd flown in a hailstorm. The rain of pain stayed mainly on the Blaine. None of them touched Kimiko or Jeannie. Dale jumped, then ducked back inside. Slugs hit the steps, chewing holes through the wood like giant metallic carpenter ants on speed. Chips flew up from the sidewalk, bouncing off my wingtips. I stared at Kimiko as though I could will her to stay still. She trembled, covering her ears.

A roar and the screech of claws on metal made me lower the clear protective lid on my eyes to turn my head. A massive golden bear tore the rear bumper off the car. Jeannie. She bellowed again, and I heard the car's engine whine. The driver floored it harder, tires squealing in their bid for traction against damp pavement. It fishtailed, and part of me hoped it'd flip. It didn't. Instead, the sedan scurried down the street, its back end wiggling like a *cucaracha* escaping a descending shoe.

A few deep breaths and some concentration had my wings folded against my back and scales fading from red to beige. I shifted back to almost human but left my skin armored except for my palms and fingertips. I pulled my phone from my pocket, thankful to have left it in a front pocket instead of the back. There was a message from Tony.

Goombas

The moped I'd heard before the attack chugged by, a familiar trench coat flapping behind the driver. That damn cat. He'd been following the shooters, referred to them as Goombas in our messages that afternoon. That could only mean one thing.

"How did you manage to piss off the Gatto Gang?" Jeannie spoke to Kimiko, who'd just given the bear shifter her coat.

"No idea." She shivered again. Or maybe she hadn't stopped. "They hate my dad, though. You know those offers they say you can't refuse?"

"Yeah?" Police sirens dragged out behind her question.

"Well, my dad did refuse them. More than once."

"Ugh." Jeannie pulled mismatched clothes from her bullet-riddled suitcase and pulled them on. "Well, those particular guys won't be messing with you again tonight."

Red and blue lights swirled and strobed, making the primary color trifecta on this corner of Memorial Drive. We waited, letting the staff members at the Bed and Breakfast give official statements to the uniformed officers on the scene.

"What's up, dude?" A detective in a puffy orange vest and acid-wash jeans flashed his badge and a set of fangs. His partner rolled her eyes, then focused a blue steel glare right at Jeannie.

"Um, not much. Do you want me to fill out a form or something, Detective…"

"Klein. Naw, dude." The detective shook his head, then turned to glance at his partner. His mullet would have put MacGyver's to shame. "I want you to answer my partner's questions." He waved a hand in her direction. "Detective Weaver."

"Okay." I turned to face the much scarier looking of the two. Her hair was highly polished, held up in a clip at the back of her head. It shone with some kind of immobilizing styling product, looking almost bullet-proof. One thick streak of white stood out in the otherwise conservative dark brown hair. A faint scar marked the expanse of forehead under the streak. My nose twitched, and I blinked my still active inner lid. The scary detective was some kind of shifter, but not one of the magical type. She also had a hint of Psychic power around her. A device? Her clothes? I glanced at Klein again. Not a trace of any Psychic energy on him. I smiled at scary streak lady.

"Can you identify the shooter?" Her face was deader-pan than Ben Stein's voice.

"Nope, sorry." I shrugged. She stared at me without blinking.

"What if I told you we saw someone in the area we know you are acquainted with?"

"Yeah. Tony Gitano." I nodded. "I saw him, but he had nothing to do with this."

"Are you sure?" I wasn't sure how Detective Meat Cleaver Weaver managed to keep her eyes open without them tearing.

"Look, Tony's not my favorite person in the world, but he couldn't have been shooting at me from that sedan." I waved my hand. "He putt-putted by on a Vespa like the lamest excuse for Ghost Rider in the known universe."

Detective Klein chuckled. His partner snapped her fingers, and he stopped it on a dime. I wiped the smirk off my face. Apparently, any charm or wit was lost on Detective Weaver. I straightened my tie, and what was left of my shirt, trying to imagine I was talking to Mother. The last thing I wanted was to get taken down to the station for questioning, and this felt like some kind of test.

"We've been watching you, Harcourt." The detective pointed one claw-like finger at my chest. "You or any of your little friends make one wrong move here in Newport, and we're on you like spiders on flies."

"Yes, ma'am." I gulped. She nodded, apparently mollified for the time being.

"I got their statements." Detective Klein waved a couple of triplicate sheets marked with Kimiko's and Jeannie's names in the air.

Detective Weaver didn't say anything. Her face could have been on one of the marble statues in Mother's poison apple grove. She turned her back and stalked off to her car, Detective Klein following at a safe distance. What in the name of Tiamat could she be? I held my breath until they got in their unmarked sedan and pulled away.

"Creepy spider shifters you have on the police force here." Kimiko patted my arm. "I'm sorry. Not apologetically, but in the sympathy kind of way."

"So that's what she was. Spider shifter." I shuddered. Spiders freaked me out almost as much as Pharaoh's Rats. Tiny things were more dangerous to dragons than other dragons most of the time.

"Well, the big bad spider's gone now." Kimiko winked. "Why not head off to wherever we were going as long as we'll make it in time for the reservation?"

"Um, but I'm not really dressed for that anymore." I turned my back, letting Kimiko and Jeannie inspect my shredded jacket and the holes in my shirt. Even though my dress shirts had special flaps to accommodate my wings in an emergency, the bullets had done a number on it.

"It's not really that bad. Mostly, you'll need a jacket." Jeannie's voice came from behind me as she plucked at my shirt. "They have those at most restaurants here, for people who show up too touristy." She stepped back around in front of me, standing next to Kimiko.

"Yeah, I guess you're right." I sighed. "Still, Mother's going to hear about this, and she wouldn't want me to go ahead with dinner after a drive-by."

Jeannie nodded, of course. She was an RA after all, the kind of person used to passing the buck and respecting the sort of authority my mother represented. Kimiko raised an eyebrow, shaking her head. One of her turquoise-shod toes tapped the pavement.

"You mean to tell me you've been stuck in that house for half a week and you're going home just because some assholes who won't come back shot at your scaly ass?" She twirled her hair. "Well, if that's what Mother thinks is best, I guess you ought to do it, right?"

The zing of sarcasm under her words made me tingle all over. I blinked my clear lid, looking for anything out of the ordinary about her energy. Nothing. But the entire idea she'd presented, rebellion against the great and powerful Hertha Harcourt, apex dragon shifter of the Eastern Seaboard, hit me with more force than all the Gatto Gang's bullets. A west wind blew around me, brushing her bangs aside. I noticed the tiny star-shaped scar again, focused on it. It was paler than the rest of her skin, clearly old. I wondered again where had I seen something like that before.

"You're right." I took a step toward her, reaching one hand out, not entirely sure what I was about to do. Jeannie cleared her throat.

"Now that I'm a third wheel dressed in Flasher Couture, I'd better get to the bus station and hope no one calls the cops before they open in the morning."

"Wait, Jeannie." I turned, my hand still extended. I flattened my palm into an inclusive gesture. "You're always getting us out of trouble back on campus. The least I can do is pull a string and get you a smarmy ex-boyfriend free place to stay. Come on."

Jeannie nodded and said something, but I barely noticed. Kimiko gazed up at me like I was some kind of hero even though Jeannie had actually run the bad guys off. But that look on her face wasn't about the drive-by, or was it? It didn't really matter. What did was that girls didn't look at me like that. I was always the brainy buddy or the smart-aleck sidekick, or the also-ran rival to any women of substance.

I was the guy shallow girls brought home for kicks, not to their families. I recited a litany in my head about her mysterious break-in, her lies, her sticky fingers, the poison apple. She walked along next to me, so close our hands kept touching. I shut the litany off and put my arm around her again. She was my problem in so many ways already, what was one more?

We walked the rest of the way to the Spiced Bear, which was inside a swankier place to stay than the one Jeannie's cheating ex-boyfriend had booked for them. I got her a room, and she went up to it. We were just in time for our reservation. And of course, the restaurant had a tatty tweed they kept for vacationers who'd forgotten the jackets-required policy. It reminded me of Professor Watkins. As we sat down, I remembered all the information Kimiko's app had organized. It'd have to wait for another minute or three, though.

"Um, they're going to come over here to take our wine order, and I don't know whether—"

"I'm old enough to drink, Blaine." She winked. I imagined having wine and other things with her in an extremely unorthodox and messy fashion. I was so distracted I didn't notice the hostess standing at my elbow with the telephone.

"Sir, a call for you."

"No, thanks." I waved her away.

"But, sir, She insisted." The capital letter in her voice meant it was Mother on the line.

"That's lovely of her. Please tell her I'm handling the situation, per her orders." I smiled. "We would like a bottle of Cardinale. And we'll have my usual for dinner. Thanks."

"Very good, sir." The hostess gave a slight bow and carried the phone away.

The meal was phenomenal as usual, and the company matched. But the best part of all was knowing I was having dinner here tonight by my own choice, not Mother's. I'd been around more than one block in the physical sense with women, but this was different. I wasn't out on a date with Kimiko Ichiro because I could be, or because Mother wanted me to be. We sat in the Spiced Bear because we wanted to be there together, and that made more of a difference than I could ever have imagined it would.

We didn't have time to walk after dinner. So we kept the mealtime conversation light, focusing on the games we hadn't played earlier that day. After getting my scales filled with lead, I deserved to relax and have fun. Kimiko seemed to understand that didn't happen too often for me, or maybe she felt the same way. Lockdown at The Academy trapped her as surely as expectations and obligations caged me. But she'd gotten out of that prison. I could bust out of mine, too. She helped me see how when you break free once, you learn to watch the exits just in case you need one the next time.

The limo stood at the curb directly in front of the steps, and we got inside and let the driver take us back to the mansion. This time, I sat next to her instead of across. She turned, looking at me expectantly. But I couldn't put my arm around her like I had on the relatively anonymous streets. Going back home was like going back into battle after a respite. When she put her hand over mine, I should have shaken it off. I didn't.

When we got out of the car, Mother was waiting. She gave me a smile that glittered like fool's gold. I wanted to look back, give whichever servant assigned to escort Kimiko back to her room a little stink-eye motivation to leave me to it. Mother wasn't having any of that. She had her game face on. When she stalked up the staircase and turned left, I knew she meant to give me five kinds of nastiness, all in the spirit of Tiamat's five heads. I followed, clenching my fists.

I wasn't surprised when she brought me to her rage cage. She'd spent too much time lately in the saltine-box shaped room, lined in granite from floor to ceiling. This was where Mother always went when she thought her temper needed a release. The only decor was what appeared to be wall carvings, vaguely runic. I knew better. The whole chamber was big enough for four fully shifted dragons and warded more heavily than some prisons. She waved a hand, and the door closed behind me. I knew this drill well. I wouldn't be leaving until she either opened that door or conceded to any argument I might present.

"How dare you disobey your mother?" She put all her weight on one leg and crossed her arms over her chest.

"Are you serious, Mother?" I'd been shot at, interrogated by a spider shifter, and rescued two people. I would not just stand there and eat the helping of Guilt Trip Supreme she wanted to dish out.

"Deadly." She tossed her head, black hair falling behind her shoulder on the right.

"That's interesting because you're the one who wanted me to write the story of Kimiko Ichiro and the Mysterious Dragon Hoard Invasion." I narrowed my eyes, homing in on the corners of her mouth and her nostrils. That's where she wore all her human form tells. "I was handling that."

"You'd just been shot at. Why in Tiamat's name would you go out and have a leisurely dinner afterward?"

"To get the girl I shielded from gunfire and certain death to talk to me, of course." I rolled my eyes, but only after a pause. I hoped she didn't notice my own slip in the Tells You Don't Show And Expect To Win At Poker department. "It's a tactic I learned from the best."

"You haven't used what you've learned by watching me before. Why start now?"

"You haven't dropped a responsibility this big and important in my lap before. Why start now?"

Her only response was a low growl. Someone who'd never lived with her may have mistaken it for a warning or expression of anger. I didn't. I ducked. Good thing.

The hiss behind me meant Mother's acid breath was doing the Alka Seltzer Sizzle on solid rock. From experience, I knew that if she hit me, I wouldn't heal for days. The wall wouldn't heal at all, though. I didn't bother looking over my shoulder because I knew there'd be one more vaguely runic line etched back there. I straightened, mirroring her cross-armed pose.

"Don't question my judgment, whelp, until you're prepared to challenge me for this estate and everything in it."

"And how do you know I'm not?"

"Because even you have no idea exactly what and who will become your responsibility if you do." Mother tapped the toe of one five-figure price-tag shoe against the stone.

"A point that becomes more irrelevant every time we have an argument like this." My dagger-thin glare turned into more of a squint as the smoke rising from my nostrils thickened. "Be careful, or all the trouble you went to, using nurture to direct me away from Father's mistakes, will backfire. Literally." I took a deep breath.

One corner of her matte-red mouth twitched down, and her weight shifted to her other leg. I let the breath out with a laugh instead of the gout of flame she must have expected. Although Mother stood up straight after that and put on her most withering glare, she seemed smaller than usual, somehow.

"You don't know what you're talking about." Nothing moved besides her mouth. "Until you understand the full extent of what you're inheriting, you will never be ready to."

"Like you were ready when it happened for you?" I put my hands on my hips.

"You are not me." Her eyes shifted from round pupils to slitted, dark brown to poison-green.

"Good."

"I already know how you feel about that, and now it's time for you to understand that I agree." She closed her inner eyelid. "No one should have to do the things I've done, especially not you. And that's why I say again, you are not ready to inherit everything in this house, whether you do it by challenging me or some other way."

"You aren't having me investigate Kimiko because of any danger she presents." I tightened my grip on my own arms instinctively. "You're worried about something else." I blinked. "Some*one* else."

Mother didn't answer. Instead, she turned her back, walking slow and steady toward the windowless end of the room. Before she disappeared into the dim and cavernous end of the room, she waved one hand. The door unlocked, and stone ground against steel as it opened.

I'd won the argument but lost something else. The shield of feigned ignorance.

CHAPTER TEN

Kimiko

At the door, Gomer waited to escort me via the back stairs to my room while Blaine went up the showy staircase with Mrs. Harcourt. Usually, eavesdropping was one of my favorite pastimes. The thought of listening in on whatever chewing-out Blaine would get made me vaguely ill.

I ran the bath again, stepping out of the shoes and the dress. The contents of the turquoise clutch went back in my own handbag, locked in the drawer again. A search of the drawers didn't turn up anything like the cozy flannel pajamas I would have put on back home after a night like this. So I selected a raw silk nightgown in dusky pink and hung it on a hook in the bathroom. I would enter the data about the shooting and try talking to Ismail after my bath.

I'd fallen asleep in the tub. A knock on the bathroom door startled me out of the tepid water. I toweled off quickly, then slipped the nightgown on and opened the door. Instead of the Brownie or Gomer, or even Ismail, it was Blaine. He'd changed his pants but had no shirt on. His skin was smooth, no hint of scales. It was also flaw-less, like his well-defined muscles. I hadn't imagined a bookwyrm would look so manly without a shirt, dragon shifter or no.

"How did you get in?" I glanced past him, rubbing my arms at an unexpected chill in the air.

"Nature's hang-glider." He jerked his chin at the balcony doors. "Much safer than your Spider Kim act."

"Yeah." I brushed past him to grab the bathrobe I'd left on the bed, and our arms touching sent a shiver across my skin and a heated flush up from my center. I wasn't cold anymore, but I put the bathrobe on, anyway. "What did you come here for?" I couldn't look at him when I said it and fiddled with the key on its chain instead.

"That LORA app…you said it was running something." His gaze bounced around the room, alighting just about everywhere except on me.

"Oh." I shouldn't have been disappointed. "Okay." I headed to the nightstand, shielded it with my body, and reached in for my phone. I needn't have bothered. Blaine wasn't looking. I stepped in front of him, clasping the phone in my hands between us. "Um, can I ask you something?"

"Um, yeah. You just did." He smirked, finally meeting my gaze. He put his hands in his pockets. "But you can ask something else."

"You're supposed to find out why I'm here, and how I broke in." I took a deep breath, feeling like I was about to step off a cliff or out of a plane and plummet to my death. "And I just opened a locked drawer in front of you. You didn't try to peek. Why?"

"Because you were going to tell me something back at the park." Blaine pulled his hands out of his pockets and opened one, revealing a small black orb on a silver chain. He touched it, setting it alight with some kind of Extrahuman energy. Then he looped the chain over his wrist and held out his hand. I took the hint, let go of the phone, and put one of my hands in, too. He clasped my hand and gazed into my eyes. The tingle I felt had nothing to do with magic. "You can tell me now without anyone overhearing."

"It's my dad. He's got maybe a week to live without a Luck charm."

I closed my eyes. "And your mother's the only person in this hemi-sphere who has any."

"So you thought pissing off a dragon family was the way to go?" Smoke billowed from his nose and mouth, making me feel like I was in the belly of an impending thunderstorm. "Assumed I'm just like Mother and any other textbook dragon, even after what I did for Nox. I mean, come on. You were there. I got Mother to give up a pelt, but Josh almost died. And you. Don't. Bother. To. Ask." His hand gripped mine tighter, and the heat of his breath was like a furnace on my cheek as I tried not to quake in fear. I opened my eyes. But Blaine didn't look angry. His shoulders were too droopy for that.

"It's my fault, Blaine." I looked the dragon right in the eyes, wishing I could flame up like the extinct Phoenix and match the inferno of whatever emotion fueled his fire. All I got for my trouble was a torrent of tears rolling down my face. "If I hadn't swiped Dad's pin and used it on Josh, he'd be fine. It was his last Luck charm. If I can't get him another one, I've killed my own father, just because I'm a kleptomaniac who thought Luck was on her side."

Blaine blinked, his grip loosening. He reached out to brush my tears away, and I flinched at the heat coming from him. The tears evaporated before his hand made contact with my cheek. He took a deep breath, lowering the temperature around us by at least three degrees. Then, he took another, closing his eyes. When he opened them, they were ember-red and reptilian.

"You did no such thing." He pulled me closer, holding me against his chest as I shook and wept. "It's the Extramagus. Coincidence. You're the one who said our Luck's turned. I just checked, and our magic energy's all over the place. We're a mess, Kimiko, because some asshole has a vendetta against desegregating Providence Paranormal College. Not because you saved a life. And you couldn't have known ahead of time that was your father's last charm."

I couldn't say anything to that. He was right. Blaine just gave me the benefit of the doubt about the charm. His confidence in me was a bigger mystery than anything I'd ever encountered. I didn't dare look up at him;. My face had to be a puffy mess from the ugly crying that went with my confession. But I couldn't stay like that, melting against his bare chest in a more figurative sense than his earlier temperature might have meant.

Blaine pulled back, easing my face off his shoulder. He gazed down at me, his eyes that amber-brown again. My knees felt weak, and my lower lip trembled. His face bent closer to mine until our lips almost touched. We both turned our heads at the wooden crackling sound from the corner.

"Fewmets!" He let go of me, pulling the anti-spyware amulet off my wrist as he headed toward the decorative bamboo in the golden urn. He pulled back his arm, making a fist.

"No!" I ran up behind him, leaping up to drag down his elbow.

Blaine's punch went wide, colliding with the mirrored wall instead of the Brownie hiding with the decor. A spiderweb of cracks appeared on the fake glass, extending all the way up to the ceiling. That was one camera in the room down for the count.

"Why are you stopping me from taking out a spy?" Blaine's nostrils flared, smoke puffing out in a thin curl. The tilt of his head and his tone of voice told me he'd reined his anger in, waiting for a real answer.

"Are you sure they're not an ally?"

"Point." He reached out, grasping the Brownie with one hand and pulling them from the urn. Gold powder dusted his palm when he let them go. The natural muddy brown of their bark showed through their disguise. "But we can't question them without getting in their debt."

"They'll want to come out of this unscathed, though." I turned my head to look at the Brownie. "They'll tell us something on their own if they know what's best, and Brownies are supposed to be canny."

"I am." The Brownie's creaky voice was nearly lost in the rattle they made as they bent toward one of the concealed cameras.

"This has those taken care of." Blaine held up the amulet. "So give me a reason not to turn you into firewood."

"Your mother doesn't employ my kind. I'm not here to spy for your enemy."

"Go on." Smoke wafted toward the wooden creature with Blaine's words.

"I can't tell you who sent me or why. Prior agreement." The Brownie crackled again. "All I can tell you is, my debtor is your ally."

"Of course." He rolled his eyes, then offered me his arm. "Still, there are some things that just aren't anyone's business, not even some mysterious benefactor's." Blaine turned to face me, smirking. "Would you like to make a bit of a scene, Kimiko? I promise it's all in the interest of getting to the bottom of this predicament."

"Um, sure?" I took his arm more out of desire to touch him again than anything else, although curiosity was a close second. The feel of his skin under my hand was downright addictive. I took a deep breath as he walked me to the door. He dropped his arm, wrapping it around my waist.

"Prepare to meet a pretend scoundrel. I solemnly swear I'm not up to no good, but you ought to act like I am, anyway." I tittered in response. Blaine's wit was as quick as mine. The swoon I faked at him was more genuine than I wanted to admit.

I turned my laughter into an indignant shriek when Blaine kicked the door to my room open and slung me over his shoulder. I watched from my upside-down position as he hip-checked the door shut. He stormed down the hall, more smoke than I'd ever seen trailing over his head and behind him. A low growl in his throat underscored my shrieks.

"You infuriating woman." Blaine's voice was a strained snarl. I could imagine the sneer curling his upper lip. "You're mine, you hear me? Mine to deal with as I see fit. Yes, I'm entitled. You're just a thieving Tanuki at my mercy. You will do as I say."

I cased the hallway, realizing he was putting on a show for the audio and visual recording devices spaced at regular intervals. I let myself tremble and whimper, knowing that whoever monitored those feeds would have no idea all my fuss came from a giggle fit instead of abject terror. A few tears rolled over my forehead, meeting the marble floors with soft plops. Only a Memory Psychic would be able to tell those came from the biggest laugh of the year and not Blaine's snarly threats.

We kept it up all the way to the end of the hall and through the outward swing of the door, the slam of it shutting, and the bolt being thrown.

After that, Blaine dropped me on the foot of his bed and collapsed on a little bench in front of it, clutching his sides. It took several minutes for me to catch my breath or remember that he'd carried me over his shoulder in nothing but a flimsy nightgown.

CHAPTER ELEVEN

Blaine

Making a truckload of smoke with Kimiko Ichiro over my shoulder: easy. Putting her down and letting her go afterward: nearly impossible. The bench creaked under me as I tumbled against it, not wanting to actually get on the bed with her. That was a crock of bull. I wanted nothing more than that but had told her the threats and the carrying on down the hall were all for show. When I gave my word, I kept it. There was no way a girl like her would want a pile of anxiety like me for anything but a fling. That near-miss kiss and the way she'd looked at me after the shooting could only be a flash-in-the-pan kind of thing. I wouldn't take advantage of a girl whose father was on borrowed time. I wouldn't even try courting her unless I could think of a way to help her first.

Before she composed herself, I got up and went through my audio surveillance negating routine. I wondered why Mother even bothered spying on me that way when I knew how to get around it so handily. Maybe she just had it set up in case anything happened in here while I was asleep. But that meant she thought someone in the house might be a danger to me. I shivered, suddenly chilled. It might just be paranoia. It sort of ran in dragonish families, after all, and I knew for sure I'd gotten a hefty dose of it myself. But just because you're paranoid doesn't mean someone's not out to get you.

And I knew for sure now. Kimiko Ichiro was not out to get my family or me. She was just dealing with the worst string of Luck a Tanuki could have encountered. If I thought Mother would believe me and let her go, I'd go tell her that instant. It'd never work. Mother had her jaws clamped around the idea that Kimiko's way in meant some heinous enemy could figure out how to break in and murderate the place. If she hadn't softened her paranoid stance during our after-dinner argument, she probably never would.

A bright guitar riff erupted from the speakers I'd placed around the room to achieve surround-sound. Oh, no, this was not the playlist I wanted to subject other people to. Before I could reach out to skip the embarrassingly outdated pop-punk music, Kimiko slapped my hand away. I blinked down at her smile.

"Leave it. This band is super corny, but I always loved this song." She grabbed my hands and pulled me back to the bench, swaying in time to the music as we went. Then she did the last thing I expected: she belted out every word of Simple Plan's *Addicted*. I sat down, watching her pick up a hairbrush and give an American Idol-worthy rendition for an audience of one.

"Did anyone ever tell you that you ought to do that kind of thing professionally?" She had one of those signature voices, the kind that wouldn't be mistaken for anyone else's. I hadn't been able to take my eyes off her the entire time. She'd nailed the song to my heart, mind, and attention span as blatantly as Martin Luther nailed his Ninety-Five Theses to the door of the Castle Church. I was the most fervent kind of believer, a convert.

"Yeah." She put the hairbrush down. "Ren." She shrugged, then plopped down on the bench next to me. "I gave up after that car accident, though."

"Oh." I got up and started pacing—anything to keep away from her. I was addicted, all right, like the song said. And still a dick, although trying not to be a giant one. "Well, you should take it up again, now that it turns out he's alive after all."

"Love to, if I could find the time. Breaking out of the Academy and stalking my dad got pretty time-consuming, you know. So's this lovely stay in the Newport Mansion." Kimiko twisted the tithing bracelet on her wrist. "Anyway, don't we have some investigating to do?"

"Yeah." I headed over to my desk, grabbed a couple of tablets from the top drawer. I tossed one on the bed near her and fired up the other. "Can you load your LORA app on these?"

"Sure I can, but should I?" She tilted her head, making her hair fall away from her chest. The nightgown she wore had a plunging neckline. I looked away as fast as I could, straining something in my neck.

"Ow." I winced. My muscles started trying to knit back together around the stupid knot. I tried rubbing it, but the damn thing was on the back of my shoulder.

"Sit." She gestured to the floor in front of the bench.

I sat. Didn't have much choice. Stupid accidents like that sucked for shifters, especially any flying ones. If I didn't get the knot worked out, it could carry over when I shifted and mess with my wing on that side. I put my hands on the floor, tucking them under my legs. That'd force me to keep them to myself. I wish I could say her touch melted all the tension away, but it didn't. If anything, it got worse.

"You're super tense." Her fingers pressed against both my shoulders, which probably felt like concrete. She gave up trying to rub or even prod and started punching instead. I sighed, leaning back.

"Yeah. Been a rough couple days for both of us."

"Wow." Her fists beat harder. "So big lizards are capable of empathy. Who knew?"

"It's the big secret of my people. We care." I snorted a laugh past my gritted teeth. It hurt, but she was breaking down the knot. "Little Tanuki girls have magic punches. Who'd have thought?"

"No one. Being easily underestimated is all part of my charm." She took her hands away, and I failed at not whining about it. "Okay, LORA's loaded up on these. Data's synced, too."

"I hear he's also fully functional." There was no way she'd get that reference.

"And anatomically correct." She tapped my much more relaxed shoulder with the corner of one of the tablets. I turned around and instantly regretted it. Well, no, I didn't. I regretted my reaction to her legs at eye-level. Anatomically correct didn't begin to describe. Anatomically amazing, astounding and a million other adjectives raced through my brain, not necessarily in alphabetical order. Maybe. I don't really remember. All I know for sure was I couldn't stand up.

"Look, I'm having a hard time here. Focusing, I mean. On stuff."

"Oh?" Kimiko blinked wide eyes, but I knew better than to assume her innocence was anything but a facade. She had to be deliberately teasing me. It felt like my head would explode in more ways than one if you get my drift.

"Yeah. Look, I shouldn't have dragged you out of there before you could get decent."

"Maybe, maybe not. But you did." Her smile was gentler than I'd expected. She stepped down from the bench, joining me on the floor. She left the tablet up there, then plucked mine from my hands and set it on top of hers. I thought the innuendo in the gesture couldn't possibly be intentional. I. Thought. Wrong.

Before I could say anything, Kimiko was in my lap, arms around my neck and legs around my waist like she'd been in the vault. This time, she wasn't fighting me, though. She pressed her forehead against mine, the tips of our noses touched, and our breath mingled. She sat, waiting. I tilted my head until our lips met instead of our foreheads, and then everything changed.

It wasn't what you think. The kiss was barely a brush of our lips. Nothing else happened because I was swept away. A memory, tiny but bright, like a light at the end of a tunnel, grew closer as I rushed toward it. If I'd been on the PPC campus, I'd think I'd been whammied by one of Henry's memory amulets or something. But I knew that wasn't the case. Once I got to the corner of my mind the kiss had pushed me toward, I understood.

I recognized myself from old photographs. The nearly blond hair of my early childhood graced the top of my head, and I was dressed all in red, sitting across from a little brown-haired girl with furry ears wearing the same color. Gomer was there, knife poised over an undecorated cake. Mother's voice instructed me to hold hands with the girl, and then an invisible force wrapped a cord made of twisted paper around our wrists. We sat with our hands tied together like that, listening to a man's voice drone out a phrase in what I now recognized as bastardized Latin. Memory me glanced up, seeing only a rotund figure, face obscured in the shadow cast by his black Greek fisherman's hat. A sudden, sharp pain pricked the top center of my forehead and thin twin cries welled up shrilly from child-throats.

I shook my head, snapping myself out of it. Kimiko still sat in my lap, but her eyes were glassy and far away, still lost in the hidden memory our first kiss had returned. I studied her face, finally reaching out to brush aside her bangs. The tiny star-shaped scar there was familiar because it mirrored mine. I finally understood why Mother had passed the responsibility of dealing with our intruder to me, and why she seemed to approve of and even like our would-be burglar despite her actions.

Kimiko Ichiro was my betrothed, had been since we were barely out of diapers. I could have someone take the tithing bracelets off, but I'd be stuck with her forever. And it didn't matter one bit to either of our families whether or not we liked it.

CHAPTER TWELVE

Kimiko

Blaine Harcourt was my betrothed. And someone had erased our memories of the whole entire event. I opened my eyes to find myself in his arms, his face bent over mine. Blaine's eyes softened with concern, the amber-brown color reminding me of scotch. I reached up, touching the side of his face. My thumb strayed to the corner of his mouth and stopped. I felt my heart thud in my chest. Should I get so intimate with him right after finding something like that out? Maybe he wasn't okay with being betrothed in general, or maybe not to me in particular.

"Thank Tiamat you're okay." Blaine stood up, carrying me to a chaise in the corner near his desk. "I wasn't sure you'd come out of that trance on your own."

"Well, I did. Sucks to be you." I blinked. "What happened?"

"Memory suppression broke is my guess." Blaine sat at his desk, fingers hitting the keys on his laptop. "But I'm asking the expert right now."

"Expert?"

"Henry Baxter, Psychic vampire. He's a Memory Psychic and a student at PPC, so if there's some type of Magus who can take a memory like that and make it come back, he'd know about it."

"Wait, you think the guy in the hat was a Magus and not a Psychic, even after the conversation we overheard this morning?"

"Um." His fingers froze, hovering over the keyboard like a pair of umbrellas. "Huh. Good question, good point." He stood, cracked his knuckles, and paced a couple of times in front of the chaise. "It's just that, you know, when you've watched six of your friends go through near-death experiences at the hands of a mysterious Extramagus, you jump to conclusions."

"I understand. But Occam had a Razor, and he knew how to use it. Simpler is better. Doesn't it make sense that at least one of our parents wouldn't want us to remember we were betrothed until we were old enough to lip-lock on our own? Maybe our parents hired him."

"Oh, definitely. Thanks for pointing out my paranoia." He glanced back at the screen. "Ha! Are you a Ravenclaw or a Gryffindor?"

"Um, Slytherin." I rolled my eyes. "Duh."

"Oh. Well, nobody's perfect. I forgive you. Also, ten points to Slytherin!" Blaine chuckled. "Henry's a Hufflepuff, but he totally agrees with your idea. It's most likely a Psychic because Magi with that kind of power are extremely rare. Except, he says, it's got to be a master-Level psychic. Someone who'd be qualified to teach doctoral-level stuff at PPC. And he only knows of one person like that who was around back then. His old mentor."

"Awesome, so Henry can tell us if he looks like the guy in that vision thing we both got, and we can rule out the Extramagus." I caught myself twirling my hair. Thinking about the Extramagus and our wrong-way Luck had me more upset than I wanted to admit.

"No such luck." Blaine ran a hand through his hair and sighed. "Ten more points to Slytherin if you can tell me why Henry can't give us a description."

"Master-level Mentor Man decided to wipe himself out of bunches of memories and hide for some reason."

"Bingo." Blaine pointed one finger at me, then winked. If I hadn't been sitting, I might have fallen over in a swoon. He was downright sexy when he got studious like that. "Damn, girl. You're going to win the House Cup for Slytherin all by yourself."

I smirked, thinking of at least seven other things I'd rather win than some fictional award from a series of novels about a magical school. Blaine slowly opened his eyes, the smile draining from his face. I watched his Adam's apple bob as he took one step closer to me, but he stopped and turned back to his computer.

"So, how are we going to find out who the black-hat guy is if Henry doesn't know?"

"He's got memories stockpiled somewhere." Blaine rattled a few more messages out on the keyboard. "He's been checking them, but it's a tiring thing. Might take him years."

"We don't have years." I sighed.

"I know." He looked over his shoulder. "We also don't have much help. No one's in town. Henry and Maddie are in Vermont, and they can only take the night bus back, Josh and Nox won't get here until tomorrow, and Bobby and Lynn are in Louisiana. All we have is Tony, and he's hinkier than a hinkfest in Hinktown."

"What about Jeannie?"

"She's not part of the pack." He shook his head. "Knows nothing about the whole Extramagus thing."

"Are you sure?" My question made Blaine freeze.

"She shouldn't." He ran a hand through his hair. Loud music or no, I still couldn't tell him about Ismail, and where I'd found his lamp in the first place.

"She's a Resident Assistant." I shrugged. "The ones at The Academy seem to know everything all the time about all of us. Shouldn't isn't the same thing as doesn't."

"She did put Nox up in her room during all that Faerie trial business." Smoke trailed out of Blaine's nose. He opened his mouth, and a siren went off.

When he bolted for the door, I followed him. There wasn't any reason to take off after him besides the bracelets, but I did it anyway.

Before he ran past me, his face went as white as chalk. Whatever had caused this alarm was beyond serious business.

During the running, I started recognizing my surroundings. We were headed back to the vault, the part of the hoard Blaine had caught me in at the beginning of this whole mess. I almost turned back, feeling like the biggest idiot in the universe for not bringing my bag and Ismail's lamp. I'd come to realize Blaine wanted to help me, but he didn't know how. I had the answer to that in the drawer of the nightstand, but I'd never find my way up there and back in time, even if I didn't get lost on the way. I'd thought maybe it was the perfect situation to get back on track for saving Dad, but I was wrong.

The door was open, sculptures toppled, displays broken, jewelry strewn like bright bits of shattered armor on a silenced battlefield. Blaine didn't stop for that, and neither did I. Instead, I followed in his wake like a small craft trailing an ocean liner on a collision course with an iceberg. We heard the scuff of shoes on marble scant seconds after the scrabble of little claws.

"Friggin' cockatrice again already?" Blaine muttered under his breath. I understood. One of those had almost killed Josh Dennison.

But I didn't smell a cockatrice. I wondered why he didn't realize that, although whatever had gotten in here was small. It smelled like dank, muddy fur and chitin, with no hint of venom. Almost at the back of the vault, a ring of bookcases towered like Stonehenge. They all faced away from us, plain oaken backs giving a starker and more forbidding feel than if they'd been placed with the book side in view. The space they encompassed was large enough to hold a full-grown dragon shifter and a half. Even Blaine hesitated, an homage to the fact that this was a place even he hadn't been, and likely shouldn't go even in an emergency.

A deep growl of frustration came from the other side of stacks weird enough to grace a Scottish heath. That got Blaine moving again. I followed him, dodging around one bookcase and then another until we stood together inside the ring. At the center was an egg the size of a year-old human baby. Its shell was mottled, sky-blue and poison-green. The man on the other side was hardly recognizable as Blaine's stepfather. His clothing was in tatters, and his hair was gone. All his visible skin was covered in skim-milk-white scales with blue edging. I watched him duck and bend, missing something that skittered across the floor.

And that was the source of that smell. *Herpestidae ichneumon*, also known as a Pharaoh's Rat. I'd studied them for a report in my Fall semester, but I'd never seen one. It looked something like a mongoose, but with long fur standing up in muddy spikes. It had quills along its spine, reminding me of a shoddily-armored porcupine. Because I couldn't remember whether they had magic, I checked its energy. It gleamed with pure golden Luck as it faked to one side and another, baiting Mr. Harcourt. Movement by the egg caught my eye. The Pharaoh's Rat Blaine's stepfather faced wasn't alone. A second one was going for the helpless egg, and it had good Luck layered on its energy, too. I felt the air change, going warmer next to me. Blaine was either preparing to flame or shift, actions that could get him or the rest of us killed. Pharaoh's Rats were deadly to dragons, able to burrow in for a long, slow, inevitable kill by internal hemorrhage. I couldn't let that happen to Blaine.

So I pushed him. Blaine toppled directly into one of the bookcases, sending it crashing into the one beside it. He scrambled to stop the avalanche of shelves and tomes and I stepped between the second Pharaoh's Rat and the egg, taking the action Blaine and his stepfather shouldn't. *Herpestidae ichneumon* preyed on full-grown dragons and their eggs, a dragon shifter's only natural predator. They had little to fear, especially since they could make themselves look like a ferret or a weasel even to Psychics and almost every kind of Magus. But Pharaoh's Rats feared Tanuki. We saw through their illusions and were too small for their burrowing tactic to work. We also matched them in speed, but only when shifted.

My skin furred over, the old familiar itch covering every inch of my body. I felt myself change in the shoulders, hips, and hands. Losing my thumbs always sucked. If I'd been a raccoon shifter instead of a canine resembling one, we wouldn't be packing the kind of magic I'd need to defeat this weaselly little rat in time.

I dashed directly toward the Pharaoh's Rat going for the egg. It dodged just a hairsbreadth short of me, and I discovered it was female. One touch would be all I needed to turn her Luck bad. I might even be able to figure out where she and her mate had come from. Pharaoh's Rats weren't shifters, or even sentient. They couldn't manipulate magic. They also couldn't break into locked vaults, so someone must have sent them in here. Whether it was an inside job or magic, I didn't know. The rat tried to get past me again to the egg, and that was when I caught her by the tail.

I stared, watching the gold in her Luck energy tarnish, turning dull and brassy like mine. Bad Luck was contagious, and although she couldn't make hers affect mine, the reverse was not true. My Luck had tap-danced all over hers. She locked gazes with me, then looked over my head, and a trilled call something like a chuckle left her throat. I bit down harder and shook her. The creature's head hit the floor, rendering her an unconscious heap.

I shivered at the displacement in the air and a chilly breeze that couldn't have come from outside. When I turned to leap at the male, it was too late. Mr. Harcourt had fully shifted in order to use the full force of his magical Air breath on the male Pharaoh's Rat. His open mouth made him vulnerable, making me think he was either stupid or so desperate to save his egg that he didn't mind risking death.

I made one last desperate lunge at the creature's hindquarters and tail, but missed. It had gone down poor Wilfred Harcourt's throat.

Only one thing could save him now. I'd have to use one of the Luck charms I'd come here to steal.

CHAPTER THIRTEEN

Blaine

"Dad, no!" My tongue didn't care that Wilfred wasn't my bio-dad. Neither did the rest of me. I dashed across the room, unable to believe what I'd just seen. I could have been a victim, too, if Kimiko hadn't knocked me out of the way. Pharaoh's Rats could burrow into a dragon shifter in human form, though it was harder for them to get in.

My dragonish eyes had let me track her movements, so I knew she'd tried to stop the beast from entering my stepfather's belly. After that, Kimiko took off, a howling brown-beige streak, and I didn't know why. She sounded nothing like a wolf, more like a fox's high-pitched wail. My stepdad shuddered all over, then coughed. Blood dribbled from the corner of his mouth, but no gore stained his teeth. Wilfred hadn't been able to bite down on it in time, then. He flopped on his side and scrabbled at his chest as though something in there hurt him. I knew it did. I gulped.

My legs wouldn't hold me up anymore. I sank to my knees next to the wintry-scaled and twitching form of the guy who'd taught me to knot a tie and fold a pocket handkerchief. Living with Wilfred had been a little like living with a Vulcan most of the time. His lack of demonstrated emotion didn't make me immune to mine. Watching him die felt like watching an old and solid boulder on the cliff walk topple into the bay during a storm surge.

And he *was* dying. The Pharaoh's Rat was in his belly, tearing him up. My teeth gnashed, my fists clenched in my hair, my eyes searched the room as my mind cycled through every item in this vault that might save him. There had to be something, a magic trinket or an ancient device to stop this. I didn't understand why he'd shifted until I really looked at the egg. The pale blue splotches on the shell meant it was his. Wilfred had finally gotten the heir he'd always wanted. And if I failed to think of something, he'd never live to see his whelp hatch.

A flurry of light footsteps and the scent of Chanel Beige brushed past. Mother. Her face held a static expression as she took in the scene as immobile as an ancient Greek theater mask. Except hers wasn't Melpomene's tragedy or Thalia's comedy. Mother's features paused somewhere in between. And that's why I didn't see it coming in time to stop her.

A bright flash of reflected light, a sound like a ruptured tire, a smell like rusted-shut ingots pried open, and the acrid taste of bile in my mouth. Blood like a fountain from Wilfred's throat, Mother's hand embracing the hilt of a stardust-bladed dagger, more tightly than she'd ever clasped his in affection. He stilled immediately, except for the Pharaoh's Rat writhing beneath the thin flesh under his ribs. Mother drew her blood-soaked arm back, plunging the dagger against him one more time. A muffled shriek blossomed, unfolding in pitch and volume as she twisted, killing the rat. And it was over.

Kimiko lowered her head and crept practically on her belly toward me, dropping a pair of gold cufflinks between us. She quivered against my side, shifting back to her human shape, as shameless of her nudity as Eve that first day in Eden. She clung to me, eyes on Mother, who'd paced over to the egg. With her clean hand, she caressed the shell, humming some lullaby I wasn't sure I could recall. Maybe I didn't want to remember it. No one had ever told me how my father had died. If it'd been like this, I definitely didn't want to find out now.

"He wanted to disinherit you, you know." Mother's voice was husky, low but not sweet. "Cut you off completely once you gradu- ated, and all because of the little one in here. I was having none of that. But he wouldn't agree to an equal split. I found papers. He'd been trying to use his title as leverage with the Flights to get them changed behind my back."

I wanted to ask her so many things. Why the flurry of excuses? All I could think was, had she talked this way about my father when he died?

"Mother, you don't have to—" I couldn't listen to her trash Wilfred like this now.

"Oh, but I do since it should have been me." She turned, her eyes boring into mine but her hand still on the egg. She clenched her free hand, blood dripping from it. "I was supposed to be down here, but he gave me a break so you and I could have our discussion earlier. Other- wise, I'd have gone to my grave thinking it was he who did me in."

"Wait." Kimiko peered around me. "This is going to be a big problem for you, Mrs. Harcourt. You'll be a suspect in his death."

"I know." She turned that Eye of Sauron gaze on Kimiko. I wrapped one arm around her in an instinctive gesture of protection. "You won't, Kimiko." Mother kicked the unconscious Pharaoh's Rat. It was only then that I noticed her feet were bare. "In fact, I'd let you take those Lucky cufflinks you were burgling last night and let you go, but I can't now. At least, not until Blaine does something for me."

I glanced at the girl in my arms as the hope lighting her eyes plunged into a desert island despair. Her silence was an epic to rival *The Odyssey*. She had to save her dad, and I was more determined than ever to help her do it. I stood, scooping up the cufflinks and helping her up along with me. I dropped the Luck charms in the front pocket of my overshirt.

"What's your price, Mother?" I shrugged off my flannel shirt and wrapped it around Kimiko's shoulders. She put her arms in the sleeves.

"Take this thing and examine it for psychic and magical tampering." Mother kicked the weaselly little would-be killer harder, propelling it in my direction. "Go down to Newport PD and tell the police everything you find out about it. After that, she can take her prize wherever it needs to go."

She knew. Mother had known all along what Kimiko had been after, and maybe even why. She'd made an agreement with Mr. Ichiro to betroth us, wiped our memories, and let her future in-law suffer through rapid aging. I couldn't imagine a legitimate reason for even a woman as ruthless and hard-hearted as my mother to do those things.

My teeth squeaked as I ground them together. The smoke I'd been making softened her features and the gory sight of my dead stepfather like a silk filter on a camera from the Golden Age of Hollywood. I picked up the Pharaoh's Rat by its tail and put my other arm around Kimiko's waist.

"When she leaves, I'm going with her and not coming back."

"You can't." Mother's tone brooked no argument, but I wouldn't let her order me around like that. Not after all of this.

"I will." I turned my back on Mother, but Kimiko didn't come along with me like an obedient little Tanuki fiancée. She wasn't one, thank Tiamat.

"You won't leave forever." I glanced back to see my betrothed shaking her head. "I'll send you back, at least for a little while." She reached out and took my hand. "You need to mourn the man who helped kind of raise you. I'll be your plus one if you need that, too."

I almost argued with Kimiko but saw Mother's face blanch. The red of her lipstick stood out even more than the blood that soaked her right hand. She'd stayed composed all through mercy-killing her husband and making her little devil's deal with us. What could have her in a full-on freak-out mode now? I told myself I didn't care.

"Okay. We'll examine this, but I'm not heading to the PD. I'm calling them in. This is an Extrahuman crime scene, and they need to investigate it, not just take a statement from one witness." I held up the deadly rodent and shook it. "After that, we leave. I'll upload my report to the hoard database at my convenience. We'll be back in time for the Mourning Day. Even if Newport's Finest decide to lock you up, I'll be here, keeping up appearances and observing tradition."

This time, when I turned my back and paced away, Kimiko walked beside me.

$$CHAPTER\ FOURTEEN$$

Kimiko

When the detectives showed up, Klein stayed outside with us while Detective Weaver went to question Mrs. Harcourt. Blaine seemed relieved about that. The vampire detective grinned, hiding his fangs as he ran a hand through his mullet to fluff it. I held the cage we had the Pharaoh's Rat in, wearing jeans, a t-shirt, and the flannel I'd worn up to my room from the vault. I had my handbag and Ismail's lamp with me, too. Blaine stood with his back to most of the lawn along the cliff walk. He glared at the creature that had almost killed a whelp in its egg. When Blaine shifted, his eyes went red and slitted first.

"Watching this kind of thing never gets old." Detective Klein jerked his chin at Blaine's clawed feet, his lengthening snout, the wings unfurling like mainsails.

My breath caught in my throat at the sight of his orange scales glittering under the light from the mansion. I was struck by the fact of his physical presence, not in a romantic way. Looking at Blaine in dragon form was like watching a bonfire or a thunderstorm. He was a thing of natural beauty, powerful and barely constrained. I felt utterly defenseless, faced with the fact that I was expected to marry and produce heirs for two families with a creature like him. I wasn't anywhere near worthy. And then, he was inside my mind.

"Great Egg of Tiamat." The version of his voice in my head was softer than I could have registered it with even my Tanuki ears. "That's how you see me?" He shouldn't have known that.

But he did. Blaine was everywhere in my mind, able to see or hear or sense all my thoughts and feelings. I'd done nothing to shield my psyche, hide my secrets. I closed my eyes and thought of descending curtains, closing doors, the storm barrier shutting during Hurricane Sandy.

"Sorry." I imagined saying the word to him in the interrogation room I'd spent seven hours in the night before Dad decided to send me to The Academy. "Never done this before."

"Huh. Interesting choice. Never been in one of these." I felt his smirk instead of imagining it. "Anyway, this is good. It's a place where Klein can't hear us. Just be careful not to answer stuff I say in here out loud, okay?"

"Wow. Unfair advantage much?"

"There's a reason dragons are almost at the top of the Extrahuman food chain. Open your eyes. Klein's looking at you funny."

"Sorry, Detective." I opened my eyes, giving the vampire the same gracious smile my mom used to give Dad's clients. "Never had the dragon mind-meld before."

"Heavy, huh?" Klein nodded gravely, an ironic contrast with his slang. The moon had set already, a fact that had Klein shifting his weight from one foot to the other and glancing past Blaine's bulk toward the east. "Anyway, let's talk about what we all see here."

"There's something you can find that we won't?" Blaine snorted along with the snide telepathic question. His "voice" had an echo, like the reverberation on a microphone prone to feedback squeaks. I wasn't sure why but decided it was probably because both the detective and I could hear him.

"Ayup." The detective put his hands in his pockets. "There's a reason Newport PD hired me even after that bastard turned me back in '96. I was top of the heap at State PD as a regular mortal. And there's all the stuff that comes with the vampire senses, too."

"'Kay." Blaine puffed out a smoke ring Gandalf the Gray would have envied. "I'm going to come right out and talk about the elephant in the room. This rat's got some magic on her that shouldn't be there. Faerie. Seelie. Djinn."

I wrapped my arms tightly around my chest, shivering, but not with cold. I took a deep breath, reinforcing my mind's eye view of the interrogation room I'd locked Blaine in. He couldn't know I'd had a Djinn's lamp in my bag all along. I let the breath out. He didn't. Ismail was Unseelie. So, the Extramagus had one of his or her own. I wondered how many wishes they had left.

"You have something to share, Miss Ichiro." Klein's statement came complete with an extra-large helping of suspicion.

"Yeah." I decided to share something besides the ace up my sleeve, though. "It's also got way too much Luck energy on it, still. Like, coincidental levels."

"What do you mean by 'still,' Miss Ichiro?"

"I mean, back in the vault, it had coincidental levels of Luck magic on it, all going deosil in the good Luck direction. I turned its Luck widdershins to defeat it back there like we told you already. But all the Luck should have dissipated by now."

"It smells all wrong." Klein's nostrils flared. "Open the cage."

"No way!" I stepped between him and the Pharaoh's Rat. "If it gets loose, it'll kill him."

"It won't." Klein bared his fangs. "It can't, not anymore."

"Do as he says." The Blaine inside the interrogation room nodded, grinning and relaxed. The big dragon in front of me played at twitching his wings nervously.

"Then *you* open it." I stepped aside, deciding I wouldn't take orders from either of them. Klein was only slightly less infuriating than Blaine, mostly because I wouldn't have to deal with him for much longer.

The latch made a tiny squeak. When Klein moved his hand away, the creature looked up at him by rolling its eyes. It toppled to one side, wriggling the spikes on its back weakly. I watched its Luck energy swirl faster, like the sparse suds of tepid bathwater spiraling down a drain.

"It's poisoned." Klein tapped his ear. "I can hear its blood getting silty."

"Mother." The Blaine in my head paced along the two-way mirror, seething with anger. On the glass beside him, the image of Hertha Harcourt caressing the egg played like a movie. "She could have scratched it when she kicked it."

"I get it." I imagined myself leaning my elbows on the table in the middle of the room. "She's a poison dragon, so that plus the Seelie energy makes you think she really did mean to kill your stepfather. Don't say anything to Klein yet, though. I have another theory."

"Hold on. All this might add up to something." I pulled my phone from my handbag, tapped it, and opened LORA. I added "poison," "Pharaoh's Rat," and its taxonomic name, *"Herpestidae ichneumon"* to the existing data and parameters. Then I chuckled, which sounded like rain hitting a headstone. I zoomed in on the items it'd be safe to let Klein see, locked the screen, and held the phone out to him. "Check it out."

"This isn't the software we use." Klein tapped the tip of one of his fangs with his tongue. "Huh. Trolls found a whole nest of these critters poisoned under the Pell Bridge last year, Tiverton side."

"And check out the registered Precog prediction." I pointed. "Show it to Blaine, too."

Klein's eyes went wide. He shook his head, turned the phone around. Blaine peered at it, lashing his tail.

"Who's Joyce?" Blaine's voice reverberated.

"Joyce Watkins." Klein sighed. "She died during the Reveal. Her husband disappeared, and no one knows why.

"There's a Professor Watkins at my school," Blaine commented.

"Yeah, Joyce's brother-in-law." He shrugged. "For whatever reason, the husband's full name is escaping me."

"It can only be Edgar." I kept that back from Klein, telling it to the

Blaine in the interrogation room. "Your mom and the Headmistress were talking about needing him, remember?"

"Tiamat's Scales!" The words filled the little room. So did more of Blaine's ideas, half-formed and nonverbal alike. His excitement felt like static electricity crackling through the air.

I couldn't handle it. The flood of thoughts and feelings coming from him stormed my lame attempt at a mental fortress like a breaker might topple a sandcastle. I put my hands over my face, then pulled them away wet. I looked down to find tears and blood. Blaine withdrew from my mind, leaving behind a balm of regret and apology.

"Jeez, not blood. Not after the night I've had." Klein's hands shook. He took two steps backward, dropping my phone on the lawn. Then he took another step back toward me. He closed his eyes. "No."

"Good evening, Detective Klein. Miss Ichiro. Young Master Harcourt." A man with terra-cotta-tone skin, jet hair streaked with silver, and nearly black eyes stepped between the hungry vampire and me. "I am Taki Waban, a friend of the family. Forgive the intrusion. We're looking for Mistress Harcourt." One corner of his mouth turned up, and he glanced to his right.

"Hi, I'm Tony." I hadn't noticed the other guy at first. He held out his arm, and I was about to shake his hand until I realized he was handing me a handkerchief. Try saying that five times fast.

"Thanks," I managed. I dabbed my nose and pinched it to stop the bleeding. Klein got a grip on himself and pulled a bag of blood from inside his vest.

"Mother's inside, being questioned by Detective Weaver, sir." This time, there wasn't any reverb when Blaine communicated to us. "You're welcome to wait inside. Gomer will direct you to whatever room she's designated."

"That's just the thing, Young Master." Mr. Waban shook his head. "Gomer is nowhere to be found. I had my suspicions, but…"

"I should have turned that Brownie into a torch when I had the chance."

"You mean the Brownie in my debt since the night Professor

Brodsky was apprehended? The one I sent to keep an eye on the two of you?"

Blaine blinked. Tony gasped. I chuckled. Detective Klein scowled.

"It makes sense." I grinned at Mr. Waban. "Gomer's a Seelie Goblin. They're so unusual, the Queen wouldn't want them in her inner circle. No wonder he's a servant in a dragon shifter's house."

"So you think Gomer's been passing information to some flagrantly idiotic person who thinks it's a good idea to mess with the Harcourts?" Tony directed the question at me but pointed his crossed fingers at Blaine from behind his back.

"Yeah." I picked up a lock of my hair, twirling it. "There had to be an informant. It explains the timing of both attacks. The shooters knew exactly where we'd be walking. But they didn't know we'd have a bear shifter to help us. And they expected Mrs. Harcourt to be guarding the egg instead of her husband. Wilfred filled in for her at the last minute."

"I see." Detective Klein wiped his mouth, then gestured at me with the bag of blood. "So, Wilfred Harcourt wasn't a target, but collateral damage. It was Hertha, Blaine, and the egg they wanted. But why bother poisoning the Pharaoh's Rat?"

"Because that way, it'd look like Hertha was trying to bump off someone in the Harcourt family and it went wrong." I told Detective Klein all about Wilfred's attempt to change Blaine's inheritance. Blaine agreed that was the kind of thing his mother might mention to Gomer. "Big tragic mistake. Whoever did this has a mind like a million steel traps."

"And you're at PPC for Extrahuman Crime Investigation, Miss Ichiro?" Klein put his hands on his hips.

"Um, no." I felt my face flush, embarrassed about my actual academic circumstances.

"You should be." Klein tapped my phone and handed it back to me. "And where did you get this app? It's gorgeous."

"She programmed it." Blaine's telepathic words came with three smoke rings. The reverb was back. A nervously pacing human form Blaine appeared along with the interrogation room in my mind's eye.

"Your interpretation is nice and all, but it's not the only one. I have a bad feeling about how Weaver might have taken everything, plus the fact that Mother wanted me to go to the PD initially. Do you trust me?" I nodded out on the lawn to him and everyone else. "Good. Stay close and try not to freak out."

"Woah, cool." Klein's smile was like the flash on a camera, blinding and then gone an instant later. "Detective Weaver, hi."

I'd heard footsteps but had been too distracted to check whose they were. But Blaine had known, of course. The spider shifter Detective stepped right up to Blaine's snout, somehow looking down her nose at him even though he was enormous. She flashed her badge.

"Stop getting all buddy-buddy with the dragon, Cal." She narrowed her eyes.

"Wait, what?" Klein blinked at his partner. "I don't get it."

"The house is full of Hertha Harcourt's poison apples. This whelp's never been close to his stepfather, even though he married the mother before Blaine hatched. A sibling means he'll have to split everything if not lose it all. And, according to a note from the Goblin butler, he has connections to the Gitanos and has been entertaining this Tanuki. She's got a record of Grand Theft, you know.

"Blaine Harcourt, you're under arrest for the murder of Wilfred Harcourt, and the attempted murder of your younger sibling. You'll shift back down to human form now and come along peacefully."

But he did no such thing.

CHAPTER FIFTEEN

Blaine

I scooped Kimiko up in my left talon and took off. I didn't worry about Weaver or Klein shooting at us, because the backdraft from my wings knocked them both flat, Taki Waban, too. What I could hardly believe was that Tony Gitano was the last man standing down there. He pumped his fist in the air twice. Before I got out of telepathy range with him, he promised to clear things up. I had my doubts about his ability to do that until I remembered him on the Vespa after the shooting.

He knew things I didn't, especially about any fake Gitano Gang contacts Gomer could have cooked up. I let my wings continue the ascent. Once I was at apex over the Pell Bridge, I'd tilt them and head back down to land at India Point Park, where I had some clothes stashed.

"Blaine?" Kimiko's thoughts gave me double vision, pulling part of my focus back to the interrogation room her imagination had cooked up. "Blaine, why are you running from the police?"

"Because we have to get the Lucky cufflinks to your dad. It sounded like they wanted to bring you in for questioning, too. If I let Weaver and company hold us, he could die before we get out."

She didn't give me anything like a verbal answer. Instead, the drab cinderblock walls in that little made-up room melted away. I was with her in a woodland clearing, sunlit with early morning light. The trees had blossoms, pink and white. The grass was still short and speckled with star-shaped white flowers. A brass lamp sat on a tree stump in the middle, but I didn't care enough about it to examine it more closely. Her arms went around my neck, her body pressed against mine. The warmth of her embrace in my mind was nothing like the mocking playfulness she'd shown when we almost got caught listening in. It was leaps and bounds beyond the brief lip-lock that had spurred the hidden betrothal memories.

Kimiko wasn't just showing me a telepathic display of affection. She was giving me her trust. This sanctuary of her heart and mind opened to my presence, welcoming me in a way I never thought another person would. I'd always been kept at arm's length before.

I lowered some of my own barriers, giving as good as I got. Tiger-lilies sprang up at the tree line, orange like my scales. Fluffy little clouds made dragon shapes in the previously clear sky. The trees sprouted leaves and fruit alongside the blossoms. Our imagination collaboration amalgamated spring and summer, dawn and midday. I wondered whether we'd break into a musical number.

The clearing filled with her laughter, my eyes filled with tears. This place was perfect. She was perfect. Mother had gone and betrothed me to my destined mate after insisting my entire life that I'd be married to make an alliance and would have to pass on anything coincidence might present.

Whether this was some kind of colossal mistake on her part, the Ichiro family Luck, or deliberate misleading from the Precog who'd been standing with the man in the Greek fisherman's hat, I had no idea. All I knew was, Kimiko Ichiro was my destiny, and not some ill fate like I'd imagined earlier that same day. I'd do anything for her now.

"Back at you." Her words were everywhere, not just in my ears. It's hard to explain, but telepathy is like that. It's not just communicating but communion. Her words sang in the breeze, rustled in the branches. They were close enough to be mine, my feelings also hers, our actions like a mirror without glass between the images. I would have kissed her, worried it'd be weird to have our first real one be imaginary.

But just because it was happening in my head didn't make it unreal. We were in both our heads at the same time after all. And neither of us had any idea when we'd get a solid-state chance. What we were doing in the shared mind space was more intimate than kissing, or anything either of us had done with other people. Uncharted territory.

And that's why I didn't think to question the dimming of the sky, the fading of the colors, and the floral scent vanishing. I expected the world to go away, just not for the reason it did.

Kimiko

Letting Blaine into the sanctuary I'd made when my mom died had been a leap of faith to meet his heroic one. He had taken off, defying his mother and the police because he knew my father was almost out of time. If we hadn't already been betrothed, I would have asked Dad to consider him as a marriage prospect. I didn't care that he'd have a record for evading arrest. Neither would the rest of my family, all things considered.

I thought he'd faded away to concentrate on landing. Then I realized he couldn't be. We weren't anywhere near land, and I'd have sensed that in his thoughts and feelings. The meeting of our minds didn't reveal everything about him, but I'd sensed the part of him focused on flying us to India Point Park. When he faded, nothing indicated a change in course.

At first, I thought he was dropping me, but Blaine's talon had actually gotten smaller. We were close to a thousand feet above Newport Bay, the lights on the Pell Bridge gleaming below against waters too calm for March. His wings merged back into his body, and we fell. His eyes stayed shut. The telepathic link had faded with his consciousness. The miasma of bad Luck around him was almost as thick as what had surrounded that Pharaoh's Rat in the cage just before it died.

I could twist into a dive, but Blaine couldn't. I had just seconds to act before he hit the water with his neck and broke it. Instead of adjusting my fall, I stuck my hand in my bag and rubbed. Ismail appeared, tethered to the lamp inside my handbag. No matter what happened, he'd be okay, could get back into his lamp before impact. He looked from me to Blaine, then back.

"What do you wish?" Ismail's magic made his voice audible even through the rush of free fall. He sounded more dejected than he should have, considering this would be my third and final wish.

"Send us to my Dad immediately."

"No." But Djinn weren't supposed to say that. They were supposed to grant any wish. The Seelie ones did it literally, which is where stories like The Monkey's Paw came from.

"Why?" I had to know, especially since time was running out to make another wish.

"You'll die and take everyone at his house with you." Ismail sighed. I couldn't believe a Djinn could be this helpful without consequences. Him giving me this information was bound to get him in deep trouble. "I can only Vanish you there, but that won't change your movement speed. I'm limited in what I can do, remember?"

"Fine." I made a choice, hoping it was the right one. "I wish our impact and time in the water will leave us both unharmed."

"Done."

The syllable ended, and the thick Luck energy around Blaine brightened until I thought the three of us must look like a falling star. It expanded, encompassing Blaine, Ismail, and me in a bubble. The rushing air stopped whipping my hair into snarls, and it felt like we were floating instead of falling. I reached out to Blaine, holding him close. We hit the water near the Tiverton side at the north of the bridge, where my brother had almost died in a car accident a few years earlier. Actually, we didn't hit the water. It was more like flopping on a memory-foam mattress after a long day.

The bubble dissipated slowly, taking on water like a leaky canoe. We were still in the water though Ismail was gone. He'd be back in his lamp, of course. I reached into my bag, intending to hand it to Blaine so he could use the wishes to get us to Dad. But the lamp was gone, and he was still unconscious. I clung to him, trying to figure out why he wouldn't wake up, even with cold seawater seeping in around us. And then I noticed my wrist.

My tithing bracelet was gone, but Blaine still had his. Only a high-ranking member of the Sidhe Queen's or Goblin King's Court could have removed it. Only one type of Faerie had the power to do something like that from a distance—another Djinn. So, the Extramagus had been out-wishing us, as I suspected. And here I was, stuck with the consequences of having used my last wish to land us in the drink. Why hadn't I wished us into a boat? Of course. My thinking was better done with coding and logic puzzles than on my feet, or in the air, as it turned out. And now, we'd be stuck with the *Titanic* ending instead of the *Pretty Woman* one. I got on my back, holding Blaine's head above water as best as I could, otter-style. Ren might have been proud.

"Come with me if you want to live!" And there was a woman in an actual canoe that wasn't leaky at all holding out an oar.

"Can't, he's TKO!" I hollered back to the woman, who pulled the paddle back into the boat with her. Then she reached down and grabbed Blaine's arms. She hauled him up over the side, biceps and shoulder muscles bulging. That girl had some big guns!

I had to blink when she grabbed me. I thought I saw a shaggy red mane of hair, pointy ears, pallid skin, and clawed nails at the ends of her fingers. A crane couldn't have pulled me from the bay any more effortlessly. She tossed blankets at me. By the time I finished wrapping Blaine up in one of them, I figured it out. Her glamour had slipped. Our rescuer was a Faerie. The boat was heading back to the bridge, not to pass south, but under and perpendicular. We docked in the lee of the bridge on the Tiverton side.

"So you're a Troll."

"And you've got a brain on you. Good." She tied a rope to a cleat on the dock. "You look familiar."

"A few years back, my brother went missing after a car accident here."

"Oh, yeah, I read about the guy who came back from the dead as a Selkie. So you're his Tanuki sister, then."

"And you saved our lives." I smiled. "Thank you."

"Maybe. Don't thank me yet." She had her fingers pressed to Blaine's throat. "His pulse is weak. We have to get him inside." She hoisted him over her shoulder, then got out onto the dock. "Come on."

I followed the Troll until she got to a blank stone wall. She knocked on it, and a hidden door opened, the light a warm red and smoky. Inside was a cave, the ceiling high near the entrance but sloping almost too low for me at the back. A few cots, camp chairs, crates, and an old wood stove furnished the place. The walls were painted in intricate vine designs. A pile of blankets moved on the cot in one corner, and a guy who resembled our rescuer got up, leaving another, smaller bundle behind. He was the same height as her, but stockier and much older.

"Grandpa, this guy has something wrong with him, and it's only getting worse."

"Tithing bracelet. Shouldn't touch it. This is the Harcourt whelp. His mother won't be happy to hear he's with an Unseelie courtier like me. She's a friend of the Queen."

"But she'll be unhappier if he's in a coma." I stepped closer to the big fellow. "If you don't take it off, what'll happen?"

"Depends." Grandpa grunted. "These old Tithing Bracelets knock the wearers out if they get too far from each other. But there's a terminal range. Looks like your friend here ran too far." He turned his back, heading for the cot again.

"But he didn't." I circled, trying to get in front of him again. "The other bracelet was on me, and then it wasn't."

"Huh." He squinted at me, then at Blaine. "Gemma, get my spectacles."

Instead of a pair of glasses, she brought him a contraption that looked more like the lens testers at an Optometrist's office. He strapped it on his head and lowered one huge lens over his right eye and a tiny one over his left. Then, he peered at us again.

"You're telling me the truth. But what in the name of the King did you do to anger a Seelie Djinn?"

"Saved a life." I gazed down at Blaine. "And he saved a soul." I reached out and brushed a wet lock of hair off his cheek. A faint golden glow swirled over my hand. Luck. And it was turning in the right direction, finally. But Blaine had none around him at all. "And your question's a test because Djinn can't do anything like wishing a Tithing Bracelet off one person and on to another unless they're doing time in a lamp."

"See, Grandpa?" Gemma held Blaine's arm up. "I fished up a couple of heroes. Now, why don't you help them already?"

"Heroes?" Grandpa chuckled. "Hardly. Well, I always wanted to have a favor owed from Hertha Harcourt." But when he tried to unclasp the Tithing Bracelet, it wouldn't budge. "Now that's curious. Most curious indeed." He flipped down a few more lenses on his spectacle contraption. "It seems I'm not high-ranked enough to take this bracelet off."

"What?" I trembled, a sinking sensation starting in my gut that was even worse than the free-fall earlier.

"I'm an Admiral, equal to a Marquess, and it's still not good enough. You'll need someone else."

"But he's dying."

"I know." Grandpa shuffled across to the corner opposite from where he'd been sleeping. "Here." He threw a sack at Gemma. "Have it Vanish them to the Duke's house immediately."

I peered at the sack as it squirmed. What did he have in there, a kitten? But when Gemma opened it, a little creature with a pointy hat stuck its head out. A Gnome. She brought it over, muttering something in what sounded like a Middle Eastern tongue. It took one look at Blaine and then haggled with her. She rolled her eyes.

"It won't Vanish them unless we free it from all further obligation, Grandpa."

"Fine, whatever. Make the deal." Grandpa waved his hand. "It's worth losing a Gnome's favor in order to get one from the Harcourts."

I assume Gemma's next words were an agreement to the Gnome's terms. An instant later, I felt the weird sensation of disintegration as I vanished from the Tiverton Troll cave. When I properly had eyes again, I found myself on a meticulously crafted porch. Blaine was in front of me, laying on the planks. I sat, drawing his head into my lap in hopes that he'd be more comfortable. The mailbox had the name Redford engraved on it. Gemma stood at the front door to the most well-constructed house I'd ever laid eyes on. She rang the bell.

"Uh, hi?" The guy who answered the door looked familiar from when I'd cased the PPC campus. He wore a red Paw Sox cap and a t-shirt with the Coca-Cola logo on it.

"Fred, get your dad. This is some serious Unseelie business."

"Great Goblin's Garters, is that Blaine Harcourt?"

"Yes." I'd heard of Fred Redford being a stand-up guy, also friends with Josh Dennison. "He needs this Tithing Bracelet off ten minutes ago."

Fred didn't say a word, just took off running into the house. He was back in moments with his dad. Neil Redford looked like a regular guy until he hunkered down next to Blaine. After that, he let his glamour down. Tithed Faerie courtiers could control that kind of thing in a way their Changeling offspring couldn't. I glanced at Fred. His glamour slipped, revealing the same grayish skin, pointy teeth, and red eyes as his father's. Gemma's held for the most part, although her hair got wilder looking for a second or two.

"What happened?" Blaine rubbed his hands over his face. While I'd been distracted by the glamour, Duke Neil Redford had taken the life-threatening jewelry off.

"Not much." I reached for Blaine but hesitated. He met me halfway, taking my hand in both of his. "Fell out of the sky, got rescued by

Gemma the Troll from Tiverton, a Gnome Vanished us to Providence, and then Duke Redford here got rid of your Tithing Bracelet.

"How in Tiamat's name did we survive all that?" His eyes went wide. "You didn't burn the Luck charm—"

"No." I sighed. "That's a long story for another time. I have to get to Dad's."

"Okay, I'll drive you over." Fred jingled some keys in his pocket.

"I'll call Lyft for Gemma." Mr. Redford pulled a phone from his pocket. "Tell your grandfather our debt is settled now."

Fred and I helped Blaine into an extended-cab pickup truck. I held my betrothed's hand the whole way home.

CHAPTER SIXTEEN

Blaine

Fred's truck rattled over pavement sorely in need of repair. At least that was what it felt like for my poor head. Kimiko and Fred both seemed immune to all the jostling. My wrist tingled, fingers numb but coming back to life. How had the tithing bracelet become a danger when Kimiko and I were touching? It made about as much sense as anything else over the last twenty-four hours, which was absolutely none at all. There was one time I'd been close to figuring it all out. The mental merge with Kimiko had given me new inspiration, bigger insight. If only I could get some of that mojo back, but I was too weak to shift even partially.

"Long story or not, can you give me an elevator pitch?" I kept the request to a murmur. "Fred knows what's in the files I gave you."

"Yeah, I'd like to know what's going on, too." I'd forgotten about Fred's big, pointy Redcap ears.

"Fine." Kimiko tapped her fingers against the window. "All the trouble since I got to Newport came from Djinns. I had no idea that using wishes would let an Extramagus counter me with them, too."

"Of course not. You didn't even know there was an Extramagus until after the Gitanos shot at us."

"What!" Fred's shout went through my head like an ice pick. "Tony would never do something like that."

"And he didn't. He warned us, actually." Kimiko picked up my still numb hand and rubbed it. It was almost like she knew it bothered me. Her touch brought some warmth and sensation back, but it ached. "Anyway, we were flying along perfectly fine when you just passed out. I wished us a safe landing. It was my third wish, too, so the idea was to hand you the lamp. But even if you hadn't been unconscious, it was gone."

"So you think the Extramagus wished for your bracelet to move over to someone else?"

"Wow, that means his Djinn is a Duke or better. You can't just wish a Tithing Bracelet off with a low-ranking one." Fred turned left on Angell Street. "They get extra powers from whatever else used to be in the lamp, but Djinn still have limits."

"Yeah. I've got the feeling my Djinn was pretty low on the totem pole. He was Unseelie but still bent the rules way more than I expected. Gave me advice and stuff. Well, at least we don't have to worry about the Extramagus making any more wishes since we already got attacked three times."

"You know, I'm not sure all three of his wishes got used."

"No? Why?"

"Because the Gatto shooting and the Pharaoh's Rat attack might not have come from the Extramagus." I sighed. "The Gatto Gang hates your dad, remember? Plus, there's too much bad blood and paranoia between Mother's generation of dragon shifters. Our investigation only made things more confusing."

"Not really." Kimiko brought out her phone, but it wouldn't turn on, let alone open the LORA app again. "I didn't show Detective Klein the whole picture. But I'm still missing a piece. What did you realize before you got out of my head back on your lawn?"

"Okay, so there had to be something besides the guy who wiped our memories at our betrothal ceremony."

The truck's wheels screeched as Fred slammed on the brakes. He swerved, pulling over in front of a hydrant across the street from the Ichiro house. His arm moved jerkily, slamming the transmission into Park. Then, the Redcap unbuckled his seatbelt and turned to stare into the extended cab at us.

"Great Goblin's Garters!" He shook his head, Paw Sox cap bobbing. "You're betrothed? You two? That's insane! No one ever tells me anything."

"We only just found out ourselves tonight, okay? Chill out, man." I glanced at Kimiko. She rolled her eyes, of course. I rolled mine back, and she giggled. "You're perfect. You know that, right?"

Her jaw went slack, and she blinked. The rear door opened, and a chilly gust blew in with Fred's fake gagging noises.

"Okay, you two. Get out. You don't have to go home, but you can't stay here."

"Um, actually Fred, we do have to go home." Kimiko jerked her chin at the little white house on the other side of the street. "I kinda sorta live there, you know." She clutched her handbag tightly to her chest, looked both ways, and crossed the street.

I followed, steadier on my feet than I'd been getting into the truck. Fred pulled away, honking as he left. A light went on inside, and by the time I got to the bottom step, the front door opened.

"Kim?" Ren Ichiro stood in the doorway, eyes on his sister. He glanced at me, then did a double-take. "Harcourt. You'd better not be the reason she's been missing."

"Nope, not me. My mother."

"There's no time for this." Kim put her hands on her hips. "I need to see Dad."

"Fine. Go in and see him, but he's in a bad way." Ren stepped aside and she went down the hall, then up the stairs. I went after her, but her brother stopped me. "No. He's dying, you know. She should say goodbye to him alone. Sit in the kitchen with the others. That's the door to the right of the stairs."

Before I could ask what he meant by saying goodbye and others, Ren shut the front door and headed left into a darkened parlor. I didn't want to mess with an angry Selkie, so I turned right at the bottom of the stairs. Josh Dennison was standing in the middle of the modest kitchen with his hand stretched out toward his sister Beth. She faced what had to be the back door, one hand resting lightly on the doorknob. Josh's mate, Nox Phillips, sat on a stool at the kitchen counter, one hand pressed over her eyes.

"What did I just walk in on here?" I glanced from Josh to Beth. Neither of them looked at me.

"Impending wolfy challenge." At least Nox was in a talking mood.

"I'm too tired for this." I shuffled to the stool next to hers and sat. "Just. Too. Tired."

"Wait, why?" Something in my voice must have snapped Josh out of whatever wolfy angst state he'd been in. Or maybe there was some Alpha wolf wooj going on.

"Oh, the usual stuff for us mad Tinfoil Hatters." I didn't shrug, just stared at Josh. "Using my wings as a kevlar shield, watching Mother mercy-kill Wilfred, running from the detective trying to arrest me, the thousand-foot free-fall next to the Pell Bridge, Tithing Bracelets gone wild."

Nox gasped. Beth dropped her hand from the doorknob.

"Leaping Luna!" Josh took three steps back toward the counter and leaned, looking me in the eye. "Wilfred's dead? Your stepdad? How?"

"And kevlar? Did someone shoot at you?" Nox tugged my sleeve.

I didn't turn to look at her, wanted just to forget she and Beth were even in the room. This was all on Josh. Kimiko and I wouldn't have been in this kind of trouble if we hadn't helped him. Besides, even if I didn't feel like it was all his fault, Josh Dennison was the leader of my pack. Any Extrahuman would hold him accountable for my safety, even if that wouldn't hold up in a court of law.

"It's only been hours since we talked on the phone, but this is a long story." I didn't remember or care whether Beth knew about the Extramagus or not. Most of what I had to say would be all over the papers and the news apps in the morning, anyway. "You might not believe it all, and I don't blame you. I wouldn't if it hadn't happened to me."

I told him all of it, not stopping when Ren quietly entered the room and took a seat at the breakfast table. Despite my disclaimer, all four of them believed me.

CHAPTER SEVENTEEN

Kimiko

I didn't skip the seventh step or the thirteenth. Refusing to sneak upstairs felt like I'd defied myself for once instead of Dad. After all the rebellion and sass in the decade since Mom died and the fact that I might still be too late, letting the creaky stairs announce my presence could be the most adult thing I'd ever done.

Dad had lived in the room at the end of the hall since Mom died. Why was it always this way, a long walk and too much time to think when we didn't want it but not enough when we did? This collection of moments stretched out, bits and bobs of time I'd have preferred metered out during the free-fall above the Bay. But we have to take time however we get it. The universe gives us no other choice.

The fact that Blaine felt his own guilt over Wilfred almost as strongly as I felt mine over Dad might have been comforting to regular humans. For Extrahumans, parallels like this smacked of coincidence. He had still been in the egg when Blaine lost the man who had sired him, and he'd lost the next best thing tonight. I'd lost my mom ten years ago. Coincidence seemed to indicate that my dad would die this evening too.

The door was ajar. I pushed by just enough to pass, not wanting to risk disturbing anything that belonged to my family more than I already had. I wouldn't have needed my enhanced hearing to listen to the sound of Dad's breathing. The breaths were shallow, uneven, the spaces between them more terrifying than that free-fall over the Bay. And I wondered how much of the two centuries he'd been alive had tallied their marks on his face, his body, his health. But I cut the speculation and stepped to his bedside. I had no excuse but cowardice to wonder when I could see for myself.

And it didn't look as bad as I'd imagined. His face mapped out more lines than I'd seen framing Taki Waban's eyes and hairline, but not as many as Professor Nate Watkins. And his color was higher than Henrietta Thurston's. My mouth dropped open. I squinted, trying to detect magic. I couldn't, of course. All a Tanuki like me could see was Luck, and that was there, just barely a glimmer. I closed my eyes, wishing Ismail could still help me, or that the telepathic bond between Blaine and me hadn't been severed. Then I realized that someone could tell me what had happened. Dad. But first, he needed my help.

I'd stowed the cufflinks in the front pocket of my jeans when I'd changed, in case Hertha Harcourt changed her mind about letting me have them. Good call, considering my dip in the Bay had washed out half the contents of my handbag. The room brightened as I pulled them out and opened my fist, as though the Luck in them knew where it had to go.

Dad's hand felt like an old book, leathery and heavy. When I tipped the cufflinks into the cup of his palm and closed his fingers over them, the surrounding glow dimmed, but his eyes opened. Rheumy brown irises gave way to gold. Dry lips parted as he mouthed my name. His breath went in and out like the bellows he used to get the fireplace going in winter.

"Kimi, get the lights." His voice wasn't up to closing arguments volume, but it was close enough. I just barely made out his hand going to the front pocket of his pajama shirt, but my ears picked up the muffled clink of the cufflinks dropping in.

"Anything, Daddy." My eyes stung as I fumbled blindly at the panel. I'd gone through all that—wishing myself into a hoard, defying scary old dragons, being shot at, fighting Pharaoh's Rats and getting dropped from a thousand feet—and now here I was, unable to flip a light switch. Finally, I made contact, but by then, I was crying. The last thing I wanted to do was let Dad see that.

I leaned my forehead against the wall, mouth open and eyes shut, forehead pressed against cool plaster and a hot flood on my cheeks. I put a silencer on my vocal cords, but the rush of my breathing, intermittent like Morse Code, whooshed in my ears, drowning all other sounds. All the same, the renewed Luck energy around my father told me he'd gotten up and come to comfort me. His hand on my shoulder reminded me of the last time we'd been together this way, the night Mom died. I opened my eyes.

"I always knew you'd do it." The rubber tipped end of a cane dented the carpet to the left of his feet. I swallowed past the bottled up angst I'd been carrying since I realized Dad was aging without his pin.

"Do what?" I couldn't look at him yet, not anything but his feet, anyway.

"Come through this. Be a hero." He patted my shoulder. "Make me proud."

"But I almost killed you."

"I knew you wouldn't." He didn't lead me to any conclusions. But he never did. He always expected me to figure things out on my own.

"Joyce Watkins. The Precognitive."

"Yes. She was the best in Rhode Island. And one of her last predictions had to do with you and Blaine Harcourt."

"Our betrothal?"

"No. She fibbed on that one, said the two of you weren't destined. Otherwise, Hertha would never have agreed to the arrangement."

"Why?"

"She believes her son should be spared any chance of heartbreak."

"That's twisted. I mean, what if he met his mate after he'd gone and married someone else?"

"He'd be expected to ignore her, the same way she ignored coincidence's choice for her to marry Wilfred instead. Your future mother-in-law hasn't got a heart of stone, but she's encased it in ice nearly her whole life."

"How did you manage to stay alive? You look in better shape than I expected."

"I got help. Some old friends helped slow down my aging." He sighed. "I have more work to do."

"Brodsky's trial." Blaine was the only other person who could make me look away from my father at that moment. "You're defending him."

"Perhaps. But you don't work for me." Dad's chuckle turned into a cough. "Even if I didn't need rest, I can't discuss my clients or cases with anyone but my staff."

"I get it." Blaine put his arm around me. "You need sleep. And so does Kimiko if she's going to hold me to that promise I made back when we left the vault."

"Go. You're welcome to rest in my house." Dad limped back to his bed and got in it, then closed his eyes. His breathing sounded normal now.

"Come on." I took Blaine's hand and led him out of the room, closing the door behind me. We stopped at a room across from mine. When I opened the door, Blaine hesitated.

"A guest room? Really?" He blinked, eyes round. "After all we've been through?"

"Dad wouldn't mind, but Ren wasn't so happy to see you."

"That was before the discussion we had with Josh, Nox, and Beth in the kitchen." He sighed, shifting his weight from one foot to the other. Somehow he managed to look exhausted and nervous at the same time. "Actually, it was more like the Harcourt Family Roast. But anyway, Ren understands now. I couldn't believe it, but he said he thinks the betrothal's a good thing." He closed the door to the guest room and crossed the hall in one giant step.

"I'm a complete mess."

"So am I, in more ways than one."

"I'm exhausted and tomorrow will be a long day regardless of whether we get thrown in the Newport jail or go to a dragon funeral."

"Same here." He leaned against the wall as I stood in the doorway. "But I don't want to be alone."

"Neither do I." I stepped backward, letting him in.

Blaine headed for my desk, but I waved him at the bed and told him to rest. I needed to get Eau de Bay out of my hair, so I grabbed a towel and pajamas and went down the hall to the bathroom. On the way back, I grabbed a towel for him from the linen closet. A red backpack sat outside the door, so I brought that in with me, too.

"So, someone left this. Maybe it made an ass out of you and me, but I just assumed it's yours."

"It is. Josh brought it over from India Point Park." He got up from the bed, stretching.

"Isn't that where we were headed before?"

"Yeah. It's one of the few places in town where my dragon fits." Blaine stepped up to stand in the doorway.

"So he went all the way over there just to get you a change of clothes?"

"Yeah." His cheeks reddened as he reached for the bag. "I used to think they all just kind of tolerated me, you know?"

"I understand." I let my hand linger on his for a moment, and he rewarded me with a smile. "Tagging you in for the bathroom match."

"Awesomesauce."

I curled up on my bed with my dank handbag on top of the nightstand and my completely ruined phone in my hands. It wouldn't turn on, waterlogged as it was. All the data on LORA might as well have been on Pluto. I'd downloaded everything to the tablets in Blaine's room, but wouldn't be able to get them unless Detectives Klein and Weaver weren't waiting to snag us the second we set foot in their jurisdiction. Something occurred to me just as Blaine came back in, hair still damp from the shower.

"Why would Weaver try to arrest you when she had exactly the same story Klein did?"

"Woah, you don't waste any time." He lifted the towel off his shoulders and rubbed his hair with it. "Hmm. A gorgeous woman once told me how Occam had a Razor, and he knew how to use it. I'd say she didn't get the same story we gave Klein."

"But we told him the truth." I dropped my useless phone back in my handbag. It made a squishy sound.

"I know, which means Mother didn't." He rattled off a few words in a language I didn't recognize. Probably a list of things people who had normal mothers wouldn't call them.

"Look, there has to be a reason." I stood and held a hand out to him. "Maybe Weaver's hinky, connected to the Extramagus somehow?"

"Simplest is, Mother told a lie. It's what she does." He took my hand, using it to draw me closer. "And there doesn't always have to be a reason for her to do it."

"Well, either way, is it going to stop you from trying to attend your stepdad's Mourning Day?"

"No." Blaine put his arms around me. "That same gorgeous woman said I need to mourn him, and she was right. Also, just about everyone's coming with me."

"Everyone?"

"Yeah, all of Tinfoil Hat. Josh, Nox, Ren. Bobby and Lynn are flying up early. Tony the hinky cat. Fred. Olivia. Jeannie. Even Henry and Maddie will show up after sundown, despite the fact that they can't actually come into the house because of the egg." He walked me over to the bed and sat on the edge of it with me. "The people in that pack of misfit toys I hang around with are the real deal. I started talking, and Josh got everyone who was out of town on speakerphone. I told them everything, not just what happened in the vault with Wilfred dying. All of it. About Mother and the paranoia all those years. And once I was done talking, I saw their faces. Knew for sure nothing about my life growing up was normal. And you know what?"

"What?" I put my legs in his lap and leaned against his chest.

"The thing that scared me most about finding that out didn't happen. They believed me like real friends are supposed to, even when the basics of my life seemed impossible to them. And that is why they'll all be there tomorrow. Even if we're in a holding cell or something, people will still be there for Wilfred. And me."

There was nothing to say to that. Instead, I let him hold me close and hugged him back. Blaine's mom had said some choice words about Wilfred, but that didn't stop Blaine from caring that he'd died. And yeah, he might be angry at his mother for a long time, but I could tell he loved her anyway, even though she'd spent most of his life encouraging him toward callousness.

"Blaine Harcourt, you have the biggest heart in the world." I looked up at him until he met my gaze. His eyes shone with emotions too numerous to catalog.

"Congratulations. It belongs to you, Kimiko Ichiro."

He demonstrated, and I began paying him back for such a generous gift. I had the feeling it'd take a lifetime to equal it. After a while, we slept.

CHAPTER EIGHTEEN

Blaine

I didn't fly us into Newport. Dragon shifter Mourning Days lasted twenty-four hours, during which we couldn't eat or sleep. The last thing I needed was to be starved as well as exhausted. I sat in the back of the unmarked sedan Josh had borrowed from his parents with my arm around Kimiko. Her breath was light and even, telling me she dozed most of the way over. Nox elbowed him, not exactly distracting him from driving as she pointed out my public display of affection for the woman who'd broken vault security but spared my heart the same fate. I leaned my head against hers as Josh pulled the car into the long driveway.

"So, they're going to arrest me inside, then, I take it."

"No one's getting arrested, you big paranoid lunk."

"But Detective Weaver tried it last night."

"Detective Weaver was mistaken. The evidence supported your story."

"How'd she get that kind of evidence?"

"You taking off like that apparently put out the cat signal."

"You mean I have Hinky Neighborhood Cat-man to thank for not being in jail during my stepfather's Mourning Day?"

"That's pretty much the size of it, yeah."

No Newport PD vehicles guarded the entrance. All I saw was an unmarked one pulling away with Tony Gitano in the back and Detective Weaver driving. He looked tired, not angry or scared to be in the back of a cruiser like that. I wondered why he wasn't in the front if he'd been helping the police. Then I remembered. The Gatto Gang were all Italian shifters from Federal Hill in Providence, mostly big cats like lions and panthers. Tony might ride in the back so he wouldn't look like a rat. All the same, I was pissed that I owed my freedom to a wannabe vigilante who turned into a fluffy little kitty cat.

Kimiko woke up and covered my mouth before I could get around to colorful metaphors about Tony Gitano in English. I continued rattling off words in Italian, Spanish, French, Latin, Greek, waiting to see whether she'd catch the fact that I'd switched to terms of endearment about her. Judging by the blushing smile, she did. I gazed down at her, memorizing the exact color of her cheeks, the arc of her smile, the feel of her palm against my lips. I'd need to keep my mind on all of that if I expected to get through this day alongside Mother.

We got out of the car and headed down the path to the back where everything would be set up. There would be two crystal urns, one for Mother and the other for me. Mourning Day couldn't happen inside, at least not for Mother and me or any other dragonish guests. And when I rounded the corner, I saw that almost everyone was there for her. I took a deep breath and turned right, so the cliff walk was on my left. A salt-tinged breeze blew what remained of my hair flat against my skull when I approached the transparent containers where each guest would leave something behind, a literal paying of respects. I stepped beside the one with my name engraved on it and dropped my item in.

The clink of the lucite keepsake locket one important woman had given me attracted the attention of the other. When Mother looked up and saw what I'd done and how I'd paid, her nostrils flared, and she actually put a hand to her lips. She stopped just short of touching them, though. Of course, she wouldn't want to smudge that blood-red lipstick. Everything was about appearances for her. I'd cut that line of thinking off with my hair that morning.

I didn't avert my gaze even though the color of the paint on her lips had inspired a stream of smoke to rise above me. And I rose above my anger, forgave her in my heart even if I couldn't say the words that day. Forgiving Mother wasn't about her. It wasn't even about Wilfred. It was about me, and my sibling, who slept in the egg below the mansion. Kimiko had been right. My heart was big, more vast than I'd imagined. And it was like the sea I'd grown up alongside, prone to both calm and tempest. It was up to me to decide whether to be still or surge. I'd decided to reserve the latter for enemies only. Today, I'd be surrounded by friends.

"Nice haircut, Blaine." Lynn Frampton didn't sound sarcastic, for once. She placed a blue and white handkerchief in my urn.

"Um, thanks, I think?"

"Someone had to make up for the stink-eye over there." The human girl who'd probably beat my GPA this semester shrugged. Lynn was smart but not always wise. Still, she knew tons about dealing with people disliking her. "You look dapper. I mean that."

I nodded, then faked a wince as Bobby Tremain, Lynn's mate and my roommate, punched me in the arm.

"Sorry about all this, dragon-man."

"Thanks, Bobby."

"No, I mean it. We should have been here." Bobby dropped a whittled carving of a bear in. I could tell by its style he'd done it himself.

"No way, man." I ran my hand over my head, coming up short, just like my hair. "I let you all think Trogdor could handle burninating everything on his own."

"Yeah, well, I definitely should have known better." Josh paid his respects with a tin wolf figurine. Nox clung to his arm, adding an obsidian arrowhead after it.

"Don't beat yourself up, Dennison." I glanced over my shoulder at the unexpected voice. Fred Redford tipped his hat at me. No one cared that his Paw Sox cap was completely out of place at a Mourning Day. Redcaps and their Changeling kin literally couldn't go anywhere without their hats. "I should have known he'd need help, too. And I was just on the other side of a little water." He put a pin with the Pawtucket Red Sox logo on it into the urn.

"Hey, can we stop with the whole Worst Friend contest? I had help anyway." I gave Kimiko's hand a squeeze. "The important thing is, you're here now. Thanks, you guys. I've got to shift and get in place before the dirge starts."

"Hey, call me anytime you need to today." Kimiko tapped her right temple, then pressed her lips close to my ear. "You don't have to do this alone," she whispered.

I spent the rest of the day perched on the second-highest gable on the mansion. Through our psychic link, Kimiko let part of my heart and mind rest in our shared mindscape glade. She also showed me the fanfare surrounding the Sidhe Queen's arrival. She had one of her courtiers with her, another Sidhe Lady with her matching son Al in tow. I remembered him from a Fall semester class. He paid his respects by dropping a copper wire sculpture of a dragon into the urn. Kimiko let me hear Al's expression of sympathy and its unexpected sincerity resonated with the musical keening I had to maintain for the entire Mourning Day. I barely knew the kid, his mom was a peripheral friend of Mothers, and yet he'd still thought to bring something for me. I'd never forget that.

After sunset, I couldn't greet Henry and Maddie in person. Kimiko did it for me. Henry, who knew what it was like to lose someone close enough to be family, let his actions speak. He was a memory psychic, not a poet, after all. He pressed an old cassette tape labeled "marriage mix" into my mate's hand before adding it to the urn. Kimiko and I watched a memory snippet of Wilfred and Mother dancing to Billy Idol's White Wedding at Henrietta Thurston's reception. Maddie added a clear paperweight which I happened to know used to be the anchor for a Grim.

And then, Olivia Adler showed up. The owl shifter wore light blue to honor the element she shared with Wilfred. I'd almost forgotten he'd tutored her in Practical Flight last semester. Her wardrobe choice made her stick out so much I noticed from the roof. She had Jeannie La Montagne with her, which I thought was a big surprise until I saw what she carried. A brass lamp, old fashioned and tinged green with tarnish almost everywhere. Through Kimiko, I smelled seawater.

My mate kept me from listening in, telling me that some things Jeannie had to say weren't her secrets to tell. What she did let me see was Olivia leaving a white tail feather, its tip honed into a quill and shimmering like an opal. Jeannie dropped in what looked like the promise ring I'd seen her take off the night of the drive-by shooting.

I almost stopped my keening when the Djinn popped out of the lamp. Kimiko called him Ismail and thanked him for coming. He also put a ring into the urn, although his looked like an antique of Turkish design. Kimiko didn't let Ismail apologize. She and I both agreed that none of what had happened was his fault. He'd done the best he could under the circumstances.

I knew dawn was close even before Henry left. The sun tinged the eastern sky, signaling to the dragons on the roof that we could stop our keening and come down now. A glamour screen left behind by the Sidhe Queen gave us cover to dress after we shifted back to our human forms. I waited for Mother to say something, but she didn't. Neither did Taki Waban. I noticed they didn't talk to each other, either. Didn't even exchange glances. Once dressed, I walked away, leaving them to their strangely avoidant behavior.

Crossing the lawn to Kimiko was like coming home, even though I strode away from the house I'd grown up in. Josh's car was still in the driveway since he and Nox had fallen asleep inside it while waiting for us. When we got in, they woke up, and Josh started the car. About halfway back to Providence, Kimiko cleared her throat.

"So, that wasn't awkward at all."

I chuckled, and something broke in my chest. I shouldn't say that. It was as though all the pain that went with caring too much about the wrong people had gone out with the Mourning Day keening. That thing in my chest was love. It hadn't broken. Instead, it had hatched.

EDWARD REDFORD AND THE SINISTER SPINDLE

A PROVIDENCE PARANORMAL COLLEGE
SHORT STORY

EDWARD REDFORD AND THE SINISTER SPINDLE

Robert

Whenever Ed Redford came home from school, I made myself invisible. I knew what he was in for, how his life wouldn't have a normal span or a normal anything for that matter. And I hadn't needed a Precognitive Psychic to tell me so, either.

Ghosts like me, especially those of us haunting around for long enough to see a dozen generations born, then die and sometimes unlive, find patterns the Extrahumans don't. Mortality is limiting; everyone knows that, even the vampires and the Fae who live much longer than most. But they're still more limited than a ghost like me with a long memory. Solidity has a grounding effect that persists through the first few decades for most ghosts.

I'm not most ghosts.

I'll introduce myself to you the same way I did young Edward, even though he couldn't understand or speak any human language when he became my Medium. My name is Robert Crandall Lafayette the Second. The boy calls me Rob, but I only allow that because he will be the most powerful Psychic Medium since I was a solid. That was hundreds of years ago.

The boy was only five days old when he stopped breathing in his bassinet. He technically died for a moment through no fault of his own, but recovered due to the speedy response of a medical team. That's how we met. And no, it's none of your business why infant Edward stopped breathing. That tale is his to spin for you or not, as he chooses.

His mother Delilah is a Medium too, but I wanted nothing to do with her. My loyalty is to his patriarchal side, the Redfords, who contracted me to serve their family after one of them avenged my unfortunate demise at the Roanoke Colony. No, I won't tell you about it. The entire debacle is part of the government's Classified Extrahuman History files, and you haven't got the proper clearance levels for that.

I agreed to discuss young Edward Redford's strange discovery with you, however, so that's the focus for now. We spend a typical afternoon together thusly: the boy arrives home and tries to scrounge a snack amidst his lunkish Redcap brother's and father's near-constant feasting. I don't help him. I pretend this is a way of training him to be more assertive, but it's actually due to the fact that his mother has a veritable army of ghosts at her command, all devoting themselves to the task of conveying anything edible from the kitchen to the hungry Redcaps' gullets. Even a ghost of my age and potency isn't much good at bypassing that many of the more lowbrow variety. Working against their efforts is like trying to swim up a waterfall.

Once Edward has something resembling a snack, I follow him up to his attic bedroom and then down into the basement where he procrastinates on his homework by practicing Mediumship with me. This has always been our little secret, mostly because none of the other Redfords bother with the back stairs. Delilah Redford's ghosts use it as a sort of refuge, but they and the boy don't mind sharing it. Edward's family doesn't check on him in his room until at least an hour after the Redcap feeding frenzy ends.

On that particular afternoon, our practice focused on identifying items imbued with Psychic energy. I'd been down in the basement during the wee hours of the morning, memorizing the locations of any such thing in preparation. But Edward honed his attention to pinpoint one box in the corner by the root cellar, something that hadn't been there before. I let him pull the dusty drop cloth off its top and fold open the lid. But when I saw the item within, I couldn't stand by any longer.

"Stop," I said. "Step away from that box immediately."

"Okay, Rob." The boy did as he was told. He'd never been obviously willful, just quietly rebellious. And rarely against me in any event. "Is that thing bad news?"

"I believe it might be, though I'll need a closer look to be certain."

Floating over to the cardboard crate was easy, too much so, in fact. But that only confirmed my suspicions.

"That's a Soul Spindle in the box. It's extremely dangerous to anything incorporeal."

"So, ghosts and out-of-body Psychics?"

"Yes, and technically will-o'-the-wisps, although only the ones who have left the Under."

"Yeah." Ed shrugged. "I don't know much about the Under."

"Oh, worry not." As I mentioned, I am aware of many things my young protégé is not. "You'll learn it all exceedingly well someday."

"So, aren't devices like Soul Spindles supposed to be registered, with slips on file and everything?"

"You are correct." I floated away from it, a task that took more of my energy than getting there in the first place. "I want you to go back over there and close the box, then cover it up as close to the way you found it as possible. But before you do that, look inside and see what if anything, is in there with the thrice-accursed device. And don't touch it, mind."

Edward peered in at the thing, his lips twisting in that way I knew meant something both upset and intrigued him. He folded the flaps back over the Soul Spindle in the reverse order he'd opened them and then draped the cloth. It wasn't precisely the same, but in such a way that a mouse might have disturbed it instead of a curious boy.

"There was a slip in the box, Rob, but it didn't look right. There wasn't a seal like you see on a legally approved one."

"Then it's as I suspected."

"What?"

"You're a smart boy, smarter than that potty wizard in those fanciful tomes you read after lights out." He indubitably was, which was why I always spoke to him like an adult. He'd have to grow up fast. "Why don't you tell me what you can deduce about this highly regulated item hiding in your parents' basement?"

"Well, if the slip isn't approved, then maybe it hasn't changed hands since before the Reveal. Mom might be selling it."

"In all the time we've been coming down here, have you noticed that box in the corner before now?"

"No." The line I knew would become a constant feature on Edward's face in his later years grew between his eyebrows. "So it's a black market item. Whoever put it here is hiding it until they can get the slip embossed to make it look legit."

"Precisely the conclusion I made. Excellent work." I floated over to the door to the back stairs. "Now, we ought to postpone our lessons for today. Or perhaps longer. Until the box is gone in any event."

"I get it." The boy paced quietly toward me. "We steer clear because whoever puts the fake seal on that slip will come down here, and we don't want to tangle with shady characters. Because I'm too young to be a proper ghost like you, Rob."

"Exactly."

Edward didn't speak again until we got back up to his room. "I can't figure out whose it is, though."

"No?" It was my turn to let my thoughts run rampant.

It had been so long since I'd been a small mortal child, it would take a few minutes to put myself in Edward's place, during which he'd continue to sulk. Rather than observe that, I drifted into the wall, hovering in my favorite thinking spot behind the portrait everyone but the boy thought was of me.

The boy wouldn't want to believe the simplest explanation that the illegal Soul Spindle in the basement belonged to his parents. He also wouldn't want to let his mind make the next leap, to the conclusion that one or both were involved in some criminal enterprise.

Edward's father had a somewhat public history of doing magical contract work on buildings owned by the local mafia Boss, Gino Gitano. But that had been years ago before even Ed's college-age brother was born. Neil Redford had taken strictly legitimate jobs at the first sign there'd be a Great Reveal, abandoning Gino as a business contact.

That left the boy's mother, Delilah. But his parentally dominated brain came to a roundabout conclusion I hadn't anticipated.

"It's gotta be Fred."

At the sound of his voice, I stuck my head back through the wall. Edward flopped on his bed, staring at the ceiling.

"How?"

"Fred's been hanging out more with Tony Gitano ever since they went to PPC together." The boy sat up. "I bet Tony stole that thing from his dad and hid it here."

"Why would Tony do that?"

"I don't know. Because everyone thinks he's hinky?"

"What I meant to ask was, why would Tony Gitano jeopardize his scholarship over an item he can't even legitimize in order to sell?"

"Hormones?"

"Those don't work quite the way you think, Ed. It's not your brother or Tony. Neither of them can sense Psychic energies in any case. And I have it on the best authority that Gino does his son Tony no favors." I had, in fact, witnessed this myself on more than one occasion, but a full account would have frightened the boy out of his wits, so I refrained from relating it.

"Okay." The boy leaned forward, hanging his head. "It's Mom, then. She's Psychic and can actually use the thing. Didn't Mediums use them to get rid of Wraiths back before the Reveal?"

"Once upon a time, Ed, they did. But Soul Spindles are restricted magipsychic devices now. We discussed this before. Do you remember why?"

"Only government-employed Mediums can use them, checked out

from a Federal bank for each instance of Wraith removal. It's because the Spindles also hurt Projecting Psychics."

"Right. So why is an illegal Soul Spindle in your house?"

"It can't be because Mom needs a Wraith removed. There aren't any here, and the FBE comes within twenty-four hours on Wraith calls. She's called them before."

"So what does that imply?"

"My mom has a beef with a Projecting Psychic."

"Bingo."

"But why?"

"That's a mystery we lack clues to solve. But I'm sure more will reveal themselves in time."

"Okay."

After that, the boy actually pulled his schoolwork out of his knapsack and worked on it. Even mathematics. I could hardly blame him after the hard truths he'd just had to face.

I felt no guilt, only a vague sense of pride. Edward would go through worse than this soon. After that day, I had hope that he could handle what was to come. An auspicious conclusion on my part because he'd have to do it all without me.

DJINN AND BEAR IT

PROVIDENCE PARANORMAL COLLEGE
BOOK FIVE

What will you bear to survive?

Jeannie's heart broke when her ex-boyfriend's chick on the side confronted her during Spring Break. When she finds a mysterious brass lamp in the unlikeliest place, she's determined to use her wishes for good causes. But why is she, a bear shifter, suddenly a total klutz all of a sudden?

One hundred years ago, Ismail made a deal on the eve of a war he'd been conscripted to fight. He bound himself to a magic lamp, agreeing to serve three masters in exchange for safety, power, and time. He lost everything he should have protected.

Jeannie's luck is worse than the Rex Sox after the Bambino's curse. Ismail's thawing heart moves him to bend the rules of Djinn magic for her. But once he grants her three wishes, he'll be bound to that lamp forever unless a descendant exists who can take his place.

CHAPTER ONE

Jeannie

I'd been hanging around in a park by the water, minding my own business, which sucked. Staying in Newport after finding out my ex-boyfriend Dale cheated on me wouldn't have been possible if a friend hadn't paid for me to have a new room. And then, I'd found out his stepfather died in some kind of freak accident. So there I was, killing time until another friend picked me up for a jaunt by the Newport Police Station and then the funeral. So I sat there mentally preparing myself for the worst day ever. Unlike police interviews, I was used to funerals but hadn't ever been to one for a dragon shifter.

My suitcase and most of my clothes had bullet holes in them. Olivia Adler was bringing me something more appropriate for both occasions than retro pink acid-wash leggings with two suspiciously round rips and the old Night Creatures concert tee I usually slept in. I looked down at the shirt with its fanged design surrounding the letters "NC." Dale had bought me that shirt during better days in our relationship, before I'd gotten the acceptance letter to Providence

Paranormal's first open admissions and he didn't. He'd begged me not to leave, said he'd go crazy with me out of town so much. If only I knew at the time that meant he'd go crazy banging other girls until he knocked one up.

I sighed, putting my head in my hands. When Dale's girl on the side showed up in Newport to show me her baby belly in person, that was the end. I glanced out at the ocean, but couldn't bear looking at it and cast my eyes down instead. And that's when I saw the green thing on the other side of the rail. It looked like maybe copper or brass and wedged between some rocks on the shoreline. I leaned over the side to get a better look. Yup, it had to be some kind of metal, pretty badly tarnished, too.

Ducking under the rail was a much better idea than hopping it. I wore my least damaged shoes, white patent pumps with inch and a half heels. Even in flats I'd have had to tread carefully. With these shoes, getting over the rocks to snag whatever lost treasure waited among them was almost like trying to get around in those four-foot snowbanks we'd had over the winter.

"Ow!" My ankle strained as I snagged the handle on the back of the metal thing. I tiptoed back to the rail and under it again, glad I hadn't broken my neck. And finally, I had time to get a good look at my prize.

Well, not really. I held an old lamp, the oil-burning kind. I couldn't be sure, but I thought I'd seen it before when I toured The Academy and then again more recently. Yes, this could be the lamp I'd seen in the basement lounge during the Winter inter-session, but it was hard to be sure. Seawater only made green tarnish on certain metals, but was the lamp copper or brass? I figured there was only one way to find out.

I used the hem of my shirt to rub some of the tarnish off, and the lamp instantly warmed in my hands. I almost dropped it. A piece of metal washed up in mid-March should be cold, like it had been when I'd picked it up. And it shouldn't be spewing deep purple smoke from the end the wick's supposed to go in either. I took a deep breath and set it down on the bench next to me instead of dropping the dang thing. Good thing I did, too. The smoke coming from it got so thick that I couldn't see.

Even before the smoke cleared, I felt the presence beside me on the bench and knew I'd be meeting a Djinn. When I could look at the person who'd materialized to my right, the first thing I noticed was that the mostly tarnished lamp squatted between us like the world's weirdest chaperon. I almost giggled at that. I was nearly twenty-five and hardly qualified as the kind of girl who needed supervision. As a Resident Assistant, usually, I was the one doing that job.

"Ismail, at your service." He had a swarthy complexion that made the whiteness of his teeth stand out, and his hair was a smoky black. His dimple-framed smile was almost too bashful and cutesy to be traditionally handsome. "In case you weren't aware, I'm a Djinn, and you have claim to my lamp until I've completed three tasks for you."

"Hi, I'm Jeannie. Jeannie La Montagne." I stuck out my hand, wondering why I'd given him the lame Dorothy-Gale-from-Kansas self-introduction. Lamer than if I'd broken the heel off one of my pumps on the way over the rocks.

"Well, Jeannie Jeannie La Montagne, it is good to meet you." A different kind of man might have sounded like he was mocking me. Not Ismail. His big brown eyes held nothing but formality, so why did I have goosebumps? Could it be him?

"It's good to meet you, too, but I honestly don't think I need a Djinn." I winced a bit even though Ismail didn't seem unhappy to hear that. "I mean, I'm only a college student. We don't have too many life-or-death situations that we have to wish our way out of or anything."

"Coincidence never chooses wrong." Ismail's smile dimmed down into something more like a gentle grin. "I'm sure you'll think of something."

"Oh." I hadn't heard the crunch of shoes on gravel as Olivia approached. "Was I interrupting? It's just that we're already going to be late for your interrogation, and you still have to change. And then, there's the Air dragon's Mourning Day ceremony."

I sighed and shook my head, feeling like the world's biggest idiot. I'd just gone on about having no life or death problems, and Olivia had walked up and mentioned a dragon funeral. I should have expected as much. The owl shifter was helpful to a fault, but also unflinchingly honest. That was just peachy for her future career in Extrahuman Law but not so amazing for people like me. I wondered whether she'd ever heard of little white lies or even the concept of putting things delicately. Or maybe I was oversensitive because I'd had a rough week.

"Okay." I gazed out at the little parking lot, noticing that Olivia's car was one of those tiny Smart cars. Not the best vehicle for driving around with a woman who turned into a half-ton bear, or for carting extra Djinn passengers. Was Ismail solid when he came out of his lamp or more like a visible ghost? I wondered whether he'd need a seat belt.

"There can only be one air dragon having a Mourning Day in Newport." Ismail blinked gravely at me. "If you think it is appropriate, mistress, I would like to emerge from the lamp to pay my respects to Wilfred Harcourt."

"Um, okay." I winced inwardly at the term he used to address me, but the Djinn wouldn't know I'd been cheated on recently. Besides, his clothes and mannerisms told me he'd been in that lamp for a long time. Maybe "mistress" didn't mean the other woman back in his day. "But I think the car's too small for all three of us."

"I will return to my lamp for the drive, then, if that's acceptable."

"Look, Ismail." I stood up, smoothing out my t-shirt. "I don't want you to think you have to take my orders about something like that. I don't know much about claiming Djinn lamps, but I'm giving you permission to go ahead and decide for yourself when to come and go from your lamp. Also, I'm not a primary school teacher. You don't need a hall pass to use the restroom. And call me Jeannie, please."

"Thank you, Jeannie." He gave me a slight bow. "I will see you once we get to the Mourning Day ceremony."

Olivia and I watched him go back into his lamp. It was like the time in Chem lab when we did an experiment. The indigo beads of iodine in the flask turned into purple smoke, a reaction the professor called sublimation. Ismail did that. He went smoky, except that it was blue smoke instead of iodine's purple hue.

"Hoo, boy." Olivia flipped her hair over one shoulder. "Looks like you got yourself an Unseelie Djinn, Jeannie."

"Yeah, looks like it." I picked up the lamp in one hand and my bullet-scarred suitcase with the other.

"Believe it or not, the Unseelie kind is easier for folks who aren't used to dealing with Faeries." Olivia's trivia-filled chatter was one of the reasons I liked her.

"Really?"

"Yeah." She opened the driver-side door and got in. Olivia's obliviousness when on one of her tangents was one of the reasons not everyone liked her. "Unseelie Fae go by the spirit of the law, not the letter. They can give you a pass if they like you. And I think this one does. Like you, I mean."

I tucked the suitcase behind the seat and got into the car. Ismail's lamp went on the floor between my feet. Olivia drove us down the road to a gas station. When I went to the restroom to change, I left the lamp with my friend. I had no idea whether a Djinn could see me from inside his lamp if I brought it to the bathroom with me, but I didn't want to find out.

Once dressed and back in the car, I put the lamp in my bag and we rode along in silence. Olivia seemed to be on one of the ultra-focus trips her Adderal induced. Supposedly, the owl shifter took that so she could be diurnal. Whatever the reason, I always wondered what she'd be like if she kept to a night schedule like other nocturnally inclined Extrahumans. And then, I wondered why. It wasn't her Extrahuman Law major. PPC ran that one on both day and night schedules.

When we pulled up to the police station, I wiped my clammy palms on the rumpled t-shirt in my bag. Olivia noticed and tilted her head as she focused her eyes on me.

"It can't be that bad, Jeannie." She blinked big amber eyes. "If something were wrong, you'd be meeting Weaver and Klein at night when they're both powerhouses."

"Thanks." I got out of the car, leaving Olivia to wait as I tried to let her words comfort me. They didn't do much. Not that I didn't believe her, but spider shifters were scary. Most vampires, not so much.

The desk Sargent waved me along, gesturing down a hall. Detective Weaver stood there, six-foot-nothing and spindly. I looked up, not sure whether I should smile. I did it anyway and felt like an idiot when she brought me into the basement and then to an honest-to-goodness interrogation room.

Detective Klein ruined the effect by waving at me from the chair. He got up, pulled it out for me, and gestured at the cup of coffee within easy reach. Even though his smile bared his fangs, I could tell Klein was the good cop. I figured I'd better sit, so I did. When I took a sip of the coffee, my eyebrows felt like they'd actually go into my hair.

"We heard you liked mocha, so here it is." I almost gave myself whiplash turning my head to look at Detective Weaver. The dour expression she'd worn the night of the shooting and all the way down into the basement got replaced by a thread-thin smile.

"Wow, thanks." I sipped again, less tentatively this time. "I wasn't sure what to expect, but this wouldn't have been on the list."

"We're the Newport PD, not the Spanish Inquisition." Detective Weaver shrugged. "And don't tell anyone I spouted off a Monty Python line, or I'll take that mocha away." She actually winked. "I want to know why you think you're here."

"You have more questions for me." I blinked, not sure why what I thought about police procedure mattered.

"That's only part of it." Detective Klein half-sat on the table. He still wore the dorky orange puffy vest that looked like something from a cheesy 80s movie. I wondered whether he might actually be from the 80s, especially with his majestic mullet.

"Okay, then." I leaned back, cupping both hands around my coffee cup. My handbag strap caught on the back of the chair, and I almost tipped it over. "Woah!"

In a flash, Detective Weaver was there catching my chair. I knew spider shifters were fast but hadn't actually seen one in action. And then I realized she hadn't caught it with her hands. A handful of gossamer strands led from her fingers to my seat, steadying it.

"Thanks." I let out an exasperated breath. "I don't know what's going on with me today. Is it national bear klutzes day or something?"

Klein unleashed a belly-laugh. I felt like I was on campus with the other students instead of a police station. This wasn't supposed to happen, was it? I must have looked as confused as I felt because Weaver snapped her fingers at the threads, then put the serious back on her face.

"Look, we're mainly bringing you here to tell you things are still dangerous out there." She leaned against the wall by the doorway. "We're almost sure the shooters were part of the Gatto Gang. What we aren't sure about is who was the target. And that's where the questions come in. So, along the lines of why you think you're in here, why do you think a big cat shifter Mafia would want you dead?"

I froze for just a split second, nearly twenty years of guilt stopping me cold. And then it lifted, like it usually did. Too late, though. Both Weaver and Klein had noticed my reaction. I'd have to tell them something. I wracked my brain, knowing they'd think I was really a dumb blonde, despite being one of the first shifters accepted to PPC.

"Well, I was in the Boston Internment. That's pretty common knowledge since I let my classmates interview me about it for projects." I looked at Klein when I spoke, knowing he'd be the one checking the physical signs of lying. Vampires were good at that, of course.

"So you don't think it's got anything to do with the fact that you're friends with the Harcourt kid?" Klein had his hands in the pocket of his goofy vest.

"No. I mean, I'm the Resident Assistant in the dorm at school. It's not like we're bosom buddies."

"We know he paid for you to stay in Newport after the er, altercation with Dale Parker."

"Yeah, but that might be because I lent my room to one of his packmates a few weeks back."

"Huh." Klein pulled a ball-point pen from his pocket, the kind where the tip pops in and out with a button. He pressed it a few times, slowly. "Yeah, that checks out. He's in the Dennison kid's pack. Shifters with Hats or something like that."

"Tinfoil Hat," Weaver corrected. She eyed the pen warily. "So, can you think of anything else besides the Internment?"

"Actually, there is one thing." I shook my head. "I couldn't have been the target at all." I stared into my coffee, unable to block out the sound of Klein's pen clicking.

"And why is that?" Detective Weaver reminded me of Professor Watkins all of a sudden. I wondered whether they might be related.

"That car wasn't parked. It couldn't have been waiting for me." My explanation was peppered with Klein's noisy pen clicking habit. "I heard the engine, and it was active, not in idle. There's no way big cat shifters could have predicted the exact moment I'd be storming out of the bed-and-breakfast. But Blaine and his lady friend were walking to a dinner reservation. That's information someone could have gotten, nice and predictable. The shooter had to be after one of them."

"See, I told you." Weaver strode over to Klein and snatched the pen right out of his hand. "She figured it out. You owe me twenty bucks."

"Who'd have thought, huh?" Klein shook his head and produced a wallet from his back pocket. "On the same night, I met two ladies who could be detectives someday." He handed Weaver a twenty, then put the wallet away.

"Not me, I'm going into Social Services." I grinned. "I use my powers of deduction to help elderly Extrahumans. They can be a dodgy bunch, so there are probably some transferable skills there."

"Well, I look forward to seeing you in a more professional capacity in the future." Weaver smiled her thready smile again and opened the door. "You're free to go. Thanks."

I stumbled on the way out and spilled my mocha coffee all over the floor in front of the desk sergeant. If I didn't get it together, the Gitano Gang might just try to take me out for being a clumsiness menace in their territory.

CHAPTER TWO

Ismail

I paced the room I'd lived in for almost a century. My feet couldn't wear holes in the thick woolen carpets. That came with the power of serving in a lamp. Everything here would stay as I wished, the prison I'd agreed to do time in was utterly mine. And that's as it should be. The Goblin King wasn't the one who had to live in here. And I had more than enough power to bend it to my will.

I'd opted to serve, cut myself off from the world to escape being an Armenian man conscripted into the Turkish army. I could choose to see and hear events outside within a thousand miles. And I could even come out to be present with whoever mastered the lamp and the surrounding people. I spent more time outside the lamp than in, back then. I'd had a family out there.

And now, I believed I had no one of consequence to bother visiting with. Just a woman about the age I'd been when I got out of the Under after my time tithing to the King. I listened to her deliberately idle chatter with the girl who'd come to drive her away, noting how she guided the conversation to make the more awkward owl shifter comfortable.

At the police station, I thought she might make a wish to get out of trouble with the police, but she wasn't in any. Instead, they were concerned for her. Who was this Jeannie La Montagne, to engender such consideration, such camaraderie with Detectives used to second-guessing everyone around them? Dangerous, that's what. I'd have to be careful with someone like her as the lamp's master. She could call on me to use my power in ways I'd have trouble understanding.

In the foyer, when she spilled her coffee, I had almost caught it. But I wondered, why should I? I'd been paralyzed, unable to do anything for my family a century ago, so why rescue this girl? Hot coffee was nothing compared to the atrocities of war, after all. As with the lamp's last master, I acted with subtlety without leaving my safe place. I diverted the liquid, so none of it splashed her funeral attire. I found I had to draw on more power than expected in order to do it, as though something was working against me. But I thought it didn't matter.

The car ride to Wilfred's Mourning Day passed with no conversation over the woman on the radio singing about how when she calls, her former lover never seemed to be home. I stayed in my lamp until we were out on the Harcourt mansion's back lawn, watching my new master drop a ring in the urn and her owl friend leave a feather.

When Kimiko Ichiro brought me there only days before, I'd hoped to see Wilfred again, speak with him, pay him a visit and see the rare egg he and his wife had managed to get. All I had now to pay Wilfred Harcourt, the man who did what I couldn't by saving my children and neighbors, were respects. When I vanished myself out of the lamp in order to pay my token, everyone noticed.

"Ismail, I'm so glad you're not at the bottom of the bay!" The Tanuki girl grabbed my free hand before I could avoid her. I immediately sensed the telepathic link between her and Wilfred's stepson, although I had no idea what they conveyed through it, of course.

"I'd still be waterlogged if it hadn't been for Miss La Montagne." I nodded at my new master and tried my best not to stare. The dark suit became her, a far cry from the ragged clothing she'd worn when we met. I'd need to steel myself if I wanted to avoid falling victim to whatever unconscious charm she exuded, so I focused on the event at hand instead. "I'm sorry about—"

"Don't you dare, Ismail." Kimiko Ichiro let go of my hands and crossed her arms over her chest. "Coincidence sucks. I won't let you think what happened to Wilfred was your fault. Remember, I was the one with the wishes."

I nodded, unable to say anything else. She didn't know about Yeva, our children, or what the man we mourned meant to me. Explanations weren't part of the Djinn contract. I said nothing, just sighed and dropped a ring of my own into the urn. The old air dragon had always coveted it, so now his stepson could have it instead. Its front could open, the inside contained a note I'd written just that afternoon. Once Wilfred's own child hatched, Blaine would find instructions to pass that ring on.

I walked away across the lawn, back toward the tiny car I wouldn't fit in, not sure I wanted to be alone. As I was about to go back into the lamp, Jeannie stopped beside me. I stood next to her. She turned to face me, putting one hand on my arm. It tingled a bit, and I wondered why, especially because shifters didn't have magical energy unless in the process of changing forms.

"Ismail, I'm so sorry." Her big blue eyes held nothing but sincerity. I wasn't sure what to do with that. Most people had ulterior motives around a Djinn.

"Thank you." Giving the correct response to sympathy had become automatic since my wife's death. Wilfred used to trot me out whenever he wanted to tell the story of how he'd rescued Armenians during the Turkish genocide, though he'd done it less frequently after he saved Saul Kazynski from the Nazis decades later. Heroes weren't always the sort of people who did everything right. The Extrahuman kind were even more flawed than the ones non-magical folk wrote and read about in their comic books.

"I was just here because I know Blaine." She patted my arm a few times before taking her hand away. "Did you know he took a metric truck-ton of gunfire to protect Kim and me?"

"Yes. And I bet he complained about his clothes afterward, too." The corners of my mouth turned up. "Unsurprising, considering the example he had growing up."

"How did you know Wilfred, anyway?"

"It's a long story." I hadn't talked about it in my own words, so the fact that I wanted to answer Jeannie's question came as a surprise. A frightening one, at that. I tried not to narrow my eyes as I wondered whether she had Psychics in her family. "This isn't really the time or place for it."

"Some other time, then." She nodded without smiling. I wondered whether her air of sympathy was practiced, then stopped that train of thought. Jeannie La Montagne was too young to have much experience pretending at this sort of thing. She was a bear shifter, not a Sidhe or an immortal dragon, though she was lovely enough to have either in her ancestry.

"As you wish."

I vanished myself back into my lamp, both to cover for my sudden awkwardness and so we'd all fit in the tiny automobile. The last thing I heard was Olivia Adler's hooted exclamation.

"Hoo boy! That's weird."

Like most of her kind, the owl shifter was right in more ways than she'd intended. Serving Jeannie La Montagne just might turn out to be the strangest experience of my long life. It also might not end my servitude in the lamp. I'd scanned as many records as I'd been able to on the sly since Kimiko Ichiro wished herself out of the Academy and found nothing about my family. Without a tithed blood relative or Pure Faerie to take over, I'd be stuck in this lamp forever.

A week ago that might have suited me just fine. I wondered where my new, muddled feelings came from?

CHAPTER THREE

Jeannie

I shrieked as the water in the shower ran cold, unable to figure out why it happened every time I'd showered since I got back from Newport. I'd gotten tired of it after the first week. Here it was, the last week in April, and the cold water kept on going like the Energizer bunny.

No matter what time I tried, or which bathroom I used, I got what felt like six seconds of hot water and then the Ice Bucket Challenge. And to top it all off, I'd seemingly turned into the biggest klutz in the known universe since the end of Spring Break. Bumping, dropping, slipping, and tripping had taken a toll on my clothes and belongings, even if my fast shifter healing meant the bruises faded in minutes.

"Ow!" I slipped and fell, bruising my tailbone on wet tile. Even worse, I'd taken the shower curtain with me. Water ricocheted off it in a fine, cold spray, getting me right in the face. When I reached for the knob to shut the water off, I bumped my head. "I wish I was back in bed."

I flinched away as the bathroom filled with steam, thinking the water had gone scalding. It hadn't. A blue-suited figure stood between the shower and the sink. I stopped struggling to get untangled from the vinyl shower curtain, wrapping it around myself instead. I sighed, my shoulders shaking with laughter that walked the line between irony and frustrated tears.

"Sorry for saying with 'w' word." I hung my head, cold water dripping from my still sudsy hair to patter against the waterproof vinyl covering my nudity. "It's just a figure of speech."

"Understood. But lamp regulations mean I must respond somehow when you use it." Ismail averted his eyes and extended a hand. "I won't take it seriously unless you say otherwise. However, it looks like you could use some help."

"I won't be using up a wish, though?"

"No, not for something so simple as a hand up." He smiled, though still not directly at me. I hadn't expected a Djinn to be so charming, mostly because all the stories seemed to be about the Seelie ones. Ismail was handsome, polite, and here to grant wishes. Also mysterious. I realized I knew next to nothing about him, and decided that should change. After I was decent, of course.

"Okay." I took his hand. He managed to haul me up, shower curtain and all. Plastic rings clacked together. Ismail's hand was warm and soft, especially after the unintentionally ice-cold shower, and it lingered on mine long enough for me to think getting back under the spray was a good idea. I shouldn't be having thoughts like this about a guy, not after a messy breakup less than two weeks ago.

"I'll leave you to finish bathing." He inclined his head in something like a slight bow. "If you need me again, just call." He vanished in a puff of smoke, thank goodness. My thoughts and feelings were all over the place, and I still had shampoo in my hair.

I stuck my head back in the shower to rinse it out. Conditioning would not happen today. I wasn't a polar bear shifter. I didn't want to put my whole body back in the arctic spray, and the last thing I wanted to do was fall down in there again. When I shut off the water, I tried to hang the curtain back up. Lost cause. It had torn, making it hang almost drunkenly with one corner skewed. At least I hadn't bent the metal rod on the way down.

Finally dry and wrapped in my robe, I headed back to my room to dress and call the people down at Facilities. They'd send someone with a new shower curtain and to check the water. They'd done the latter for me twice already this week, so I apologized for being a nuisance. After I hung up, I wondered why they had found nothing wrong with the pipes or the water heater before. But I didn't have time for that kind of woolgathering. Instead, I headed out to my first appointment.

My major wasn't all that different from others at PPC for the first couple of years, but this final semester of mine would definitely be. While I still had two courses in the classrooms on campus, the rest of my time was split between meetings with my adviser and the volunteer outreach sessions she'd set up for the other four people taking Extrahuman Social Services with me.

The weather was brisk but sunny, so I walked up Thayer and took a right on Angell Street and walked the six blocks to the senior center. I waved at the care aides and their charges. None of those were my clients. I set up in a side room with a small tea table and waited. Minutes later, Mrs. Donato shuffled in and sat across from me, crossing her ankles and pouring tea into a china cup so delicate it looked like an extension of her fingertips when she held it to her lips for a sip. Her file said she was a precognitive psychic, but I'd never heard of her predicting anything. The older Extrahumans tended to be more reserved about using their powers than the ones who came of age around the Reveal, or my generation.

We chatted as usual after I'd asked all the questions on my form. Mrs. Donato told me stories about the days when she was my age, back during what she called "the humans' civil rights movement." I paid attention, not to the tales themselves, but how she told them. I had to look for signs of dementia, like repetition, using the wrong word for something, or mixing up names. I didn't take notes while we spoke, a technique I'd been lucky to master quickly. Clients felt better about confiding in a counselor whose hands weren't busy recording.

At the end of our time together, I bumped my purse with my foot and toppled it, sending lipstick, coins, and my wallet under the couch. I knelt to gather my things.

"Oh, dear," said Mrs. Donato. "Oh, my goodness me. Oh, I'm so sorry, Jeannie."

"Excuse me?" I looked up from stuffing everything back in my bag. Mrs. Donato peered into my empty teacup.

"Your leaves aren't good. No, not at all." The sigh that escaped her lips made the hair on the back of my neck stand up. She was making an honest-to-goodness prediction, all right. Why had I used loose-leaf tea that day? The last thing I needed right now was both of us getting freaked out by a scary premonition.

"Oh?" I hung my purse on the arm of my chair this time and got back in it, letting my conversation go back to the default mode I used with clients. "How's that, now?"

"The leaves here, they're telling me you've got an unlucky day in store for you." She lifted frail shoulders in a tiny shrug. "There's not much 'how' about it, though there may be a 'why.' You're a shifter, so you might not understand. I'm afraid it's entirely unavoidable, too."

"Well, thanks for the warning." I gave her what I hoped wasn't the lamest smile ever. "My day's over after two more chats like ours anyway. Hopefully, there won't be much room for bad luck to come get me while I study in my room."

"Whatever you say, dear." Mrs. Donato shook her head, then stood with the help of her aluminum cane. "Bye, now."

"Until next week." I smiled, hoping nothing in my voice or expression acknowledged her condescension.

My second appointment with Miss Agostino, a lion shifter, went well enough. She didn't make any weird predictions, anyway, although her nose wrinkled more than usual. She was generally ornery, being one of the older set who still thought shifters shouldn't mingle with Magi or tithed Faeries. Living in the PPC dorms meant I "smelled like magic" to her. I noted a slight decline in Miss Agostino's conversational patterns. Physically, she actually seemed to have improved. After our meeting, I made a note in her file about a new memory evaluation.

I waited almost twenty minutes before I realized my third and final client for the day wasn't showing up. I'd have to get out of here and head to his house. While I pushed the tea cart out of the room and down the hall toward the senior center's kitchen, the left wheel fell off. I sighed, wondering whether Mrs. Donato had noticed the loose wheel instead of actually reading the tea leaves.

While trying to snap the wheel back on the cart, I pinched the web of flesh between my thumb and forefinger, shrieking in pain. The wound healed almost immediately, a nice fringe benefit of being a bear shifter. And screaming like that had a fringe benefit of bringing help. Donna Murphy, one of the care aides, came running.

"Wow, I thought that cart looked shaky this morning. Mentioned it to the kitchen staff and everything." She made a clucking noise, then leaned over to jury-rig the wheel. "What do I need to do, give it a ticket and put a boot on it?"

I snickered. I liked Donna. She was one of the most experienced aides, with a snappy sense of humor and the ability to MacGyver things like the broken cart. I got up to give her some room but bumped the cart with my hip on the way up. The entire tea tray slid off the top of the cart, cups, and saucers tinkling in pieces on the hardwood floors. I reached out but missed the teapot by a centimeter. It hit the floor, going to pieces like a water balloon.

"Oh, now I'm teed off." The aide shook her bobbed dark brown hair out of her face. "Okay, maybe more 'teed on.'" The front of her scrub top was drenched.

Oh, Donna! I'm sorry!" I flared my nostrils but got no scent of blood. At least none of the broken china had cut Donna. I took a few steps back down the hall and opened the broom closet.

A long, wooden handle fell out and smacked me on the side of the head, stinging my dignity more than anything else. I bent to pick it up and got whacked in the back by the dustpan. All I could do was sigh and snag the cleaning utensils. Sweeping up the china shards wasn't easy, especially with some of them under the cart. But once Donna got the wheel back on, she pushed it forward so I could get the last of the mess. I dumped it all into a trash bin in the closet, then put out the sandwich-board sign to warn people about the wet floor until someone got a mop.

"*Piso mojado*." Donna smirked. "Seeing that always makes me want pizza, even though I know it has nothing to do with cheesy oven-baked goodness."

"Seriously, in total agreement with you." I laughed. "But no time for pizza now. Have you seen Mr. Kazynski?"

"Oh, no, I haven't." Donna looked up the hall and then down it. "He actually hasn't been here since last Friday. Mitzi said something about a stomach bug, I think."

"Oh, okay." Everyone knew Mitzi, a crow shifter, was the senior center's biggest gossip.

"Guess that means you've got to take a walk, huh?" Donna peered down at her still wet top. "And I need to go change. Don't want to go through the rest of the day smelling like bergamot, or people might think I'm having an affair with Captain Picard. I'll tell the House staff about the spill so they can mop."

"Thanks, Donna." I pushed the cart more carefully, this time, getting it back to the little alcove next to the kitchen where someone would bus what was left on the tray. Then, I headed out the door and down the steps.

My first mistake was not taking a left when I was supposed to. I didn't realize my mistake until I got all the way to Lippitt Park and the border of Providence and Pawtucket. I turned right around and marched back the way I came, bumping a woman coming out of a coffee shop. One of the coffees on her tray fell right off, lid popping to spill black coffee all over my pastel pink and white dress. At first, I was thankful it was iced instead of hot, but it felt like wearing ice later. I apologized and gave her five dollars before heading on my way.

Finally, I got to Rochambeau Avenue, the street Mr. Kazynski lived on. His building was halfway down a steep hill, so I had to walk carefully as I silently scolded myself for wearing four-inch platform heels.

I changed my internal tune when my right foot landed squarely in dog doo. In flatter shoes, I might have been splattered.

I stopped in front of Mr. Kazynski's building, hanging on to a fence as I tried to scrape the mess off my right shoe. I'd be mortified to track dog droppings into the old fellow's apartment. But the pavement was uneven. Scrambling to catch my balance on the fence, I felt something crack at the back of my left foot. I fell on my tail for the second time that day. What in the world was wrong with me? I wasn't a klutz normally, and there wasn't even a slippery shower with ice-cold water to escape here.

To make the whole culmination of public humiliation more complete, I saw curtains twitch on the first and second floors of Mr. Kazynski's building. Just what I always wanted, an audience. I shook my now sweaty hair off my face and reached into my handbag. I never went anywhere in platforms without a pair of ballet flats in my purse, or anywhere in pastels without a wrap dress right alongside it. And people wonder why ladies carry such big bags. It's for times like these, of course. For a bear shifter like me, those might happen even more frequently if I had to shift for some reason.

I couldn't change my dress, but the shoes were a must. I slipped the pumps off and replaced them with the flats, noticing a run in my right stocking, of course. On a day like this, what couldn't go wrong? I stood and sighed as I reluctantly dumped the platform pumps into a trash can. I had no choice. Not even a Faerie cobbler could fix something that broken.

The entrance was on the side of the building, so I walked halfway down the driveway and up the three steps to the stoop. The door buzzed, unlocking almost before my finger hit the doorbell. Mr. Kazynski had seen me coming, of course, but even though I should have expected the early buzzer, I didn't react fast enough to pull the door open in time. I rang again, he buzzed again. Finally, I got in.

"Miss La Montagne, good morning." Saul Kazynski's round figure took up most of the breadth of the doorway. He stepped back and aside, making room for me to get by.

"Good morning, Mr. Kazynski." I smiled, feeling like I could just about find the nearest patch of bare floor and go to sleep for the rest of the day. "I heard you've been home with a stomach bug, but we still need to have our visit."

"Yes, I know. Miss Murphy called while you were on the way over." He tilted his head, a scar at his jawline reminding me of all the stories he'd told about being a violinist over in Europe.

Instead of saying we ought to get started with the mandatory questions, I yawned. Mr. Kazynski shook his head and tut-tutted over me, offering lemon tea and jam on toast. My stomach rumbled in response before I could politely decline. I sat in his well-appointed but dusty parlor, watching him shuffle into the kitchen. The apartment was spacious but cluttered with furniture, curio cases, and nick-knacks. If Saul ever needed a wheelchair or even a walker, he'd have to redecorate or possibly even move. I made a mental note to tell my Professor about this. It was the kind of situation that could make an illness or injury lead to a rapid decline for a man his age.

Saul was in his nineties, an Empathic Psychic, and an immigrant. He'd come over alone, married and had children later in life than was typical, and set himself up as a violin instructor. He'd bought this building to house his whole family in. None of them had stayed. His paperwork said he had a granddaughter my age, but she'd moved out of Rhode Island the second she turned eighteen. Mr. Kazynski had lived alone since his wife died, and he'd retired from teaching music the year before we met. I was probably the only one who'd seen the inside of his house in all that time.

When he came back with the tray, I watched him, paying attention to his shuffling gait. He seemed steady enough. Like other people his age living at home, he had a system for navigating his living space that worked for him. I noticed there weren't any rugs or mats on the floors, and if there'd been doorjambs, they'd been removed. Someone had given him advice at some point, then. I didn't feel so bad about not visiting his home sooner.

He set the tray on the coffee table between us and served himself, leaving me to fix my own tea and toast. I started to give him a formal thank you, but he stopped me.

"Please, call me Saul, Miss La Montagne."

"Okay, Saul. And you can call me Jeannie."

It was as though some tightly coiled thing in him unwound. When he answered my questions, it was in a more relaxed fashion than I'd ever seen from him. When the conversation segued into the idly directed chatter I'd gotten used to, he stopped again.

"Today, Jeannie, I'd like to tell you a story you haven't heard." He settled his teacup down on its saucer, then leaned forward on his easy chair. "But first, I must show you something." He unbuttoned his right sleeve and began rolling it up.

I looked on, realizing I'd never seen him in a short-sleeved shirt. I took a deep breath, steeling myself for what I'd always suspected but hadn't confirmed. Because of this, when he turned his arm out, presenting the number like a line of graying ants inside, I didn't gasp or show any sign of shock.

"You always suspected this, Jeannie." Mr. Kazynski was stating a fact, not asking me a question. "And I know why."

"Please, Saul." I shut my eyes, opening them again after a short enough time to excuse the expression as a long blink. "I'm not supposed to talk about my time in the Boston Internment with clients. I wish I could—"

I put my hand over my mouth an instant before thick blue smoke filled the space on the sofa next to me. I had turned my head before it cleared, taking in Ismail's thick eyebrows, drawn together on his brow as he opened his mouth to question me.

"Ismail!" Saul's exclamation startled all the imminent excuses out of me, and Ismail turned to face the old psychic. "How long has it been?"

"Too long, my old friend." The Djinn's gentle smile did nothing to hide the tears threatening at the corners of his eyes. "I thought I'd never see you again."

I acted on my first impulse, reaching out to grab Ismail's hand and give it a squeeze. His eyes widened when he turned his gaze back on me. Then, he looked up, down, around the room with his cheeks coloring, pulling his hand away. What had I done wrong?

CHAPTER FOUR

Ismail

No one had dared touch me since I took up service in the lamp. Everyone else had known better. Even my own wife hadn't, though I thought that had more to do with using the lamp to escape front-line combat than the volatile and fickle power an Unseelie magic lamp represents. Jeannie had made a wish, and I'd greeted Saul instead of addressing that. Anything could happen if I didn't act fast.

"Did you mean to wish for such a thing, mistress?" I forced myself to look at Jeannie, unable to mold my expression into anything resembling a smile. I felt the buildup of magical potential behind her wish statement deflate like a slow leak in a tire.

"No, Ismail. Sorry about that." She pouted, making me struggle not to look at her lips. "Figure of speech again. And I'm sorry to you also, Saul. I'm not supposed to bring people to our meetings."

"*Dobre.*" Saul shook his head, as though clearing it of the impulse to speak in Russian. "Enough about what you are and aren't supposed to do. You're a guest in my house, both of you.

People visit so infrequently, and I won't let the college up the hill decide what we can and can't talk about in my home." He pushed the plate of toast and jam toward Ismail. "And you. I know you don't have to eat, but once upon a time, you liked to. Help yourself."

I looked at Jeannie. She blinked, and her lips parted as she realized just how much control she had over me and my actions.

"Wherever we go, Ismail, you can decide whether you want to eat or drink or, I don't know, even go get a haircut. I don't want you to wait for my permission for things like that."

It was my turn to drop my jaw in perplexity. This was the second such freedom Jeannie had granted me. It was almost as though she knew what it was like to be enslaved herself. But she wasn't a Djinn, nor a Faerie of any type. What's more, she was a woman living in a western country in the twenty-first century. If Saul were my master, I'd understand this sort of behavior. From someone like Jeannie, it made no sense.

"Yes, mistress," was all I could say. I poured a cup of tea and took a triangle of toast from the plate.

"I was about to tell Jeannie a story you already know, Ismail." Saul took up the conversational manner I remembered from the boat on the way over from Europe. The grin he wore wasn't exactly the same. It had a drawn and worn quality. Even time spent working while starved hadn't added to it back then.

"Oh?"

"Yes. About the rescue you mounted and its true purpose."

"It was never my rescue." I sighed. "Wilfred wished you and your fellow prisoners free." Instead of gasping as I expected, Jeannie grew even quieter. Her nostrils flared, and her brows drew down in thought.

"Yours was the face I saw at the window, yours the hand that cut the wire."

"I know, Saul. But if men doing evil excuse themselves by saying they were following orders, I can't claim goodness for doing the same."

"You can't tell me you wouldn't have broken down the walls of that prison on your own, Ismail. I won't believe that of you."

"I can neither confirm nor deny that for you, old friend." If dehumanization hadn't broken Saul Kazynski's belief, I surely wouldn't. "But perhaps this isn't the kind of story to tell a young woman."

Saul glanced at Jeannie, then looked down at the number on his arm. He rolled his sleeve down and closed the button at the cuff after only a few tries. He locked gazes with me, the depth of his stare trying to convey something to me, or maybe his intention was the reverse, to take some thought or feeling from me. Saul was an Empath, the kind of Psychic who held sway over feelings. The more emotional the state of the surrounding people, the more he could sway them. He'd never been harmless, and especially not now when age had given him wisdom and experience despite his continued lack of restraint.

"I disagree, but understand how it might be awkward to hear tales of heroics you don't believe you participated in." Saul stood more easily than his age should have allowed. "I can do better than that for my guests." He turned and shuffled over to a sideboard with a music stand beside it.

I knew what I'd see before he opened the weathered case, so I watched Jeannie instead. This time, she did gasp. The inside of Saul's violin case was embossed with the seals of both Faerie Monarchs, meaning he was one of the few mortals alive who'd been honored by both the Goblin King and the Sidhe Queen. Such a reputation gave him benefits many would envy, including the fact that his violin couldn't be destroyed. Even if it were shattered, the instrument would rebuild itself if the majority of the pieces got returned to the case. The enchantment was eternal as long as it remained the property of his blood relatives.

The music Saul made felt like it sent hooks into the very fabric of my heart. I'd thought it coated in steel until Jeannie's demonstration of compassion when I first appeared in the apartment. I swallowed as if that would banish the tears from my eyes. Then, I looked away, out a window, so neither of them would see how affected I was. But I already knew it was no use as far as Saul was concerned.

The whole reason he and the other prisoners at the German camp had remained alive long enough for Wilfred to find them was Saul and his violin. Empathic Psychics each had a talent, some art form with which they wielded their power to bend hearts. Every afternoon for nearly a year, the SS Commander wrote up orders to terminate all the prisoners come morning. Every evening, Saul played for the soldiers. Every night, the Commander tore up the papers that would doom the camp's denizens. I can't imagine the things Saul Kazynski had seen, heard, and endured in that year. I didn't want to. But his music wouldn't let me ignore my pain anymore.

Beside me, Jeannie seemed just as appalled and enthralled as I was. I wondered why, and when I tried to tell myself it was none of my business, Saul's music wouldn't let me. Maybe Jeannie thought her responsibility as an old man's caregiver meant she shouldn't trouble him. I was a Djinn, even more than that, her servant for the time being. I finally understood why she was so awkward a mistress. She was accustomed to being the one serving. Having someone else at her beck and call must be difficult for her.

As the notes spiraled out of Saul Kazynski's instrument, I understood that I hadn't done nearly enough. The time in the lamp had artificially extended my life, but I'd done nearly nothing with my extra time but sit and mourn. I'd gone about business as the lamp required, even though Unseelie rules meant I had so much more potential to act than that.

Wilfred Harcourt had been an opportunist, Kimiko Ichiro desperate. Jeannie La Montagne was an altruist. She couldn't think of real wishes because she wanted to make them count for others, not herself. Whatever crucible she'd been through as a youngling had forged a will bent on action and accountability. If all masters of Djinn since the beginning of our time in lamps had been like her, we'd live in a utopia.

I made a vow to myself. Jeannie La Montagne thought she didn't need wishes or even help. She was wrong. I would do everything in my power to help her until I couldn't anymore.

CHAPTER FIVE

Jeannie

Saul's unexpected performance left Ismail dumbstruck beside me on the loveseat. Me, not so much. The notes pouring like audible honey from that amber violin set my skin tingling with goosebumps. I didn't recognize the piece he played, but whatever it was had me wanting to get up, get out, go and do some good in the world, even more than my usual days entailed. The city was full of people struggling, hopeless, suffering. I'd helped a handful turn that around during my nearly four years in Providence. And I had to do better before I graduated and went back to Boston.

I could. I had Ismail. Three wishes, but I didn't understand the potential scope of his power. I'd need more information, some from researching magic lamps, but the rest from what I did best. Ismail would tell me. What was it Olivia had said? Unseelie Djinn had flexibility, loopholes, allowances built in by the Goblin King that would let him talk things over. After a hundred years inside a lamp, I'd be going nuts, wanting to chat nearly all day once I could. But Ismail didn't seem to share that trait. I'd need some confirmation and knew just where to get it.

When I said goodbye to Saul Kazynski at the door to his apartment, Ismail vanished himself instead of walking out with me. That sort of thing wouldn't do at all. I headed up Camp Street, this time, not wanting to retrace the unlucky steps I'd taken on the way here while going back to campus. Once back at the dorm, I washed up and changed into something more appropriate for the stomping around College Hill I'd do later. After that, I headed down the hall to knock on a door.

An orange origami paper dragon and a brown corrugated cardboard cutout bear rampaged across a construction-paper backed collage of buildings and shoreline. Each of them had a little crown made of Wrigley's wrappers. Scrawled across the bottom of the dorm door decor were the names Bobby and Blaine plus the tag-line "Team Tinfoil, blasting off again!" Neither of them had written that, but I didn't recognize the handwriting. I shrugged, then knocked.

"Come back in an hour." Even through the grumbling, I recognized Blaine's voice and the old movie quote. I chuckled.

"Housekeeping," I squeaked. "You want towel?"

"No towels, need sleepy." Blaine sounded more alert and also closer to the door.

"No sleepy." I gave up on the quotes since they'd done their job and gotten his attention. "I need some Tinfoil help."

"Oh, fewmets." I heard a rustle of fabric. "Hold on a minute."

I tried not to stare when Blaine Harcourt opened the door, but that was nearly impossible. There were just too many things going on in that doorway. He was in a set of Slytherin pajamas, eyes red and dragon-pupiled. I still wasn't used to seeing him with short hair, and he had a brunette girl in a yellow and black dress clinging to his waist, peeking out at me from under thick bangs. I recognized her.

"Kimiko, good to see you again." I tried not to smile because I knew most girls younger than me were reminded of Barbie dolls when I did.

"Yeah, nice to finally meet when we're not getting shot at and other unfun things." She giggled but looked up and down the hall a few times.

"Um." Blaine blinked, his eyes going back to their usual brown. "So, were there noise complaints or something?"

"Oh, no, nothing like that." I chuckled, watching Blaine's shoulders drop as the tension went out of them. "It's just that we have a mutual acquaintance who I'm not sure how to handle. And I wanted to ask if you'd chat with me about him."

"Ohmigod, Blaine!" Kimiko put one hand over her mouth. "She means Ismail!"

"Wait, what?" He rubbed his chin. "You mean your Unseelie Djinn? The one who paid respects to my stepdad with a stupidly rare antique?"

"Yeah, that's the one." I shrugged, knowing I couldn't possibly look nonchalant while blushing. "Can I come in?"

"Okay!" Kimiko bounced on her toes, shouldering Blaine out of my way. His lips made a grouchy frown, but his eyes twinkled. When I'd run into them in Newport, I hadn't thought they could seem more complementary to each other. I'd been wrong.

Blaine gestured to Bobby's desk chair. I sat, watching him toss the sheets and blanket back over his bed. He collected a tablet and sat down, tapping it to wake it up. Kimiko sat on the edge of the bed, dangling her bare feet off it. She smiled.

"So, Ismail the most introverted Djinn in the known universe, what do you want to know?"

"Introverted?" I blinked. "He pops out every time I say the 'w' word."

"Woah, really?" Blaine scratched his head.

"Yeah." I glanced from him to Kimiko, wondering why she hadn't been the one to answer. "What is that, weird or something?"

"Oh, yeah, it is." Kimiko twisted her hair between her fingers, then tapped the beige tips against her other hand. "He came out to talk to me twice. Like, he avoided doing that whenever he could. It was so bad, half the kids at The Academy thought his lamp was either empty or fake."

"But there's no such thing as an empty magic lamp." Blaine scoffed. He tapped the tablet a few times.

"Yeah, well, The Academy isn't selective about who it admits." She rolled her eyes. "So glad to be transferring here this summer. Anyway, those were all the students who didn't know better."

"Yeah, I almost forgot those lamps need an inhabitant, or they cease to exist." I took a regular-sized breath and counted to five. If they didn't stop going off on tangents, I might lose my patience. "But we're talking about Ismail in particular, not magic lamps in general."

"Oh, sorry." Kimiko dropped her hair. "Well, Ismail's pretty formal, except when he's not. He told me a couple of things, like how he'd been in the Harcourt hoard before when part of it was back in London. That was before Wilfred married your mom, Blaine. And also, he has kids. He gave me advice like only people with kids can, and when I called him on it, he said I sounded sassier than his son, but he'd let it slide because I reminded him more of his little girl."

"Well, Wilfred hasn't lived in London since the 1940s." Blaine sighed and bowed his head. "Hadn't." Kimiko threw her arms around his neck and leaned her cheek against his.

"I'm sorry, Blaine."

"No, it's okay. I'm just not used to thinking of any dragon shifter I've met in person in the past tense." He blew a smoke ring. "Anyway, you might think that means Ismail's from the 1940s, but he's not. I saw him on Mourning Day. His clothes are Turkish, from the turn of the twentieth century. Djinn can make their clothing look different with Faerie glamour, but I was in dragon form when I saw them. They were authentic, not magic. He must really be that old. And he was from a wealthy family, too, judging by his token of respect."

"Wait, you said he was in Wilfred's hoard, then the Academy, then you took the lamp?" I chewed on my lower lip. I wasn't Lynn Frampton or anything, but I wasn't stupid either. "So I'm the third master of Ismail's lamp. That means, when I'm done, he needs someone to replace him."

"That's going to be hard for a guy who's been locked up in a magic lab for decades. If he doesn't find one who's a tithed Faerie and get them to agree, he's stuck in that lamp forever." Kimiko's jaw clenched. "How many wishes did you make?"

"None." I shook my head. "Can't think of anything worth it, you know? It has to be something that'll have maximum impact."

"Wow, Jeannie." Blaine squared his shoulders. "If I thought you were a different kind of person, that'd be scary to hear."

"Don't mind the big paranoid ticklish dragon." Kimiko poked Blaine in the ribs until he snickered. "I totally understand. Even though Ismail's other weirdly un-Djinn trait is being helpful, I had a tough time deciding what to wish for too until I was in the moment."

"I bet he's not going to mind if you take your time deciding, either." Blaine tapped his tablet a few more times. "He wouldn't have the resources or knowledge to try to track down his family in the modern era, but I don't have that problem." He untangled himself from Kimiko. "I'll head to the library and look into it between classes. It shouldn't be anything too dire if you can't even think of stuff to wish for."

"Okay, but before you go, I wanted to ask Kimiko a couple more things."

"Sure!" She smiled. "Go ahead."

"Do you have any idea what he likes to do for fun?"

"Wow, hold on." Kimiko twirled her hair. "Um, no. All he mentioned was *choreg*, some kind of bread, I don't know. Oh, and he went nuts when he saw me drink kefir while I couch-surfed back in January. He said something about not believing it was sold in so many stores."

"Okay then, good to know." I nodded. "Thanks, you guys." I got up. "You're both super helpful."

They got up, too. I'd almost forgotten Blaine was heading to the library, and he almost forgot to change into regular clothes instead of his pajamas. I heard Kimiko ribbing him about that particular instance of absent-mindedness as the door shut behind me. After that, I almost walked out of the dorm, thinking I'd bring some kefir back from Whole Foods and then ask Ismail to talk, but then I got a better idea. I headed back to my room, got his lamp, and put it in my handbag. Then, I went out to Hope Street again, paying attention this time.

I had the perfect idea to try to help Ismail come out of his literal and figurative shell. All I could do now was try it and see what happened. I headed down to Kennedy Plaza and took the bus to Cranston. Not having a car in Rhode Island was way more inconvenient than it was in Boston, but public transportation was my jam. In the middle of the day like that, the bus wasn't crowded. I got a seat in the middle and pulled out my phone so I could read an eBook.

Picking up where I left off in the story that distracted me during the end of Spring Break in Newport was a little jarring. I'd picked out something gloomier than usual, a real tear-jerker. I couldn't keep reading it. Maybe I was as done with being down on myself as I'd been with Dale when that girl showed up. Donesville, capital of Alldone County.

In a month and change, I'd be one of the first shifters to graduate from PPC. I'd do it with honors and had several job offers all over New England from Extrahuman Social Services organizations, even without a graduate degree. I might be a bear shifter, but I'd risen from the ashes of the Boston internment camps like a phoenix. In three more years, my cousin Bobby would follow in my footsteps, just with a different major.

After visiting Mr. Kazynski's, I was absolutely sure Ismail was a survivor, even if I didn't know of what yet. He'd understand, and hopefully even be inspired to do something with his life after the lamp. During that bus ride, I had full confidence Blaine and Kimiko would track him down a replacement. I also thought Ismail was just like one of my clients, except in a younger-looking body. Now, I look back on the Jeannie La Montagne, who'd ridden the Cranston bus that day as a shortsighted ninny.

I had no idea what I was getting into.

CHAPTER SIX

Ismail

I knew Jeannie brought me along with her out of the dorm, down-town, then on the bus. But I had no idea why. I waited after she stepped off the intermittently stopping vehicle, pacing as she walked along a street somewhere. I could have checked our location, listened in on the surroundings, but I didn't. Long habits thicken like tree trunks. The more seasons they grow, the stouter they get. But when they fall, the more space they leave, and the impact with the ground is impossible to ignore. All I had going for me as a lamp-bound Djinn was the predictability of my power. The last thing I wanted was to risk losing it. Wherever she was going, whatever she meant to do, had my nerves spooked like a green colt.

The door Jeannie walked through squeaked, bells ringing with its movement. I could have guessed what kind of place this was, but the aroma gave it away entirely. I stopped pacing with one foot in mid-air. Fresh-baked sweetbread, not exactly like what I'd smell on the streets during celebrations, but close enough for climate and water source to excuse the difference. But what was a bear shifter with a French surname doing in an Armenian bakery? She'd stopped moving, too. I listened for her voice, thinking she'd be ordering something by now. But she didn't. I wondered what she was waiting for.

"Ismail?" Jeannie didn't whisper. I imagined she wasn't even trying to hide the fact that she was talking to her handbag. I didn't answer, a tactic that had worked with Kimiko. It hadn't with Wilfred, but Jeannie was a mundane shifter. She didn't have magic or much knowledge of how Faerie worked. If I kept waiting, she might even put herself in debt to me by asking thrice.

My face heated, my shame like wildfire. Who was I to take advantage of someone like her? She'd devoted her life to helping people when others would turn away. Maybe I'd done the same thing, but my so-called devotion came with being nearly indestructible and halted aging. No job could pay her like that. I put my foot down, closed my eyes to focus on modernizing my clothes, and took a deep breath.

"You called?" I opened my eyes as the smoke of my vanishing cleared. Either I'd put myself closer to her than I'd thought or she'd moved when I appeared. I tilted my head down, wondering whether her bear form was proportionate to her human size. I couldn't help but smile, imagining a petite bear. The air being filled with that sweet bread scent helped my mood even more.

"Yeah." The brilliance of her smile made me take a step back. I wasn't used to being smiled at like that, or at all, really. As I was wondering whether Jeannie had any notion of what personal space meant, I felt my elbow knock into something that wobbled.

The shift in gravity meant I didn't have to turn around, but I did anyway. A snap of my fingers righted all the cans, jars, and plastic-wrapped packages that threatened to clatter and shatter off the shelf. I blinked when I saw the labels had words in both Armenian and English. And then, I got a good look at where we were.

One-half of the space was a small specialty market selling various goods with import labels. The other half had a counter, tables, and chairs, and that's where the delicious bread smell came from. I didn't glance back at Jeannie but knew she watched as I looked around. I took a step toward the counter, peering up at the wall behind it to read the menu there. Foods I'd dreamed about but hadn't seen in decades were all on offer. A setup to the right of racks and rows of bread promised real coffee, the way I'd taken it before getting bound to the lamp.

I had to close my eyes, take a few deep breaths, clench my jaw. To say my feelings were mixed was like declaring the grass is green. Anger that someone who barely knew me would presume I'd want a reminder of lost days warred with relief at being surrounded by familiar sights and scents. Underneath that, an emotion I didn't recognize had taken root. Whatever else I might think of Jeannie La Montagne, I had to acknowledge that she'd brought something to my numb existence. What that was, whether it meant good or ill, remained to be seen.

"Do you like it?" She stepped to my right and stood beside me. "I'm sorry if this isn't right. We can go somewhere else."

"No. This is perfect." It was, too. A perfect storm of memory and the surge of thought that went with it. I'd weather it. It was more than what I deserved for abandoning my family.

"Okay, then." Jeannie's voice was light, but I knew she could tell I brimmed over with an emotion other than joy or even plain old happiness. "Why don't we order something, then sit down and talk?"

She didn't take my hand as she had in Saul's apartment. My fingers twitched, inappropriate. Even without the tether of joined hands, I let her lead me to the counter. The middle-aged woman behind it smiled, clapping floured hands when I greeted her in Armenian and made an order. She waved us at the seats, promising to bring everything over once it was ready. In moments, an aroma of coffee more plush than the carpets in my lamp permeated the store.

I gestured to the chair across from the one I stood behind. I shouldn't pull it out, or Jeannie might think this was a date. Lamp-bound Djinn shouldn't get emotionally invested in their masters, a mistake I'd had trouble avoiding the last two times. But none of that made any difference to Jeannie. She sat, beaming up at me as though I'd presented her with all the trappings of a modern romantic outing. I settled into my seat, folding my hands on the table in front of me.

"Why did you bring me here?" I studied her face, waiting for an explanation.

"Okay, that wasn't what I was expecting." She leaned her head on one of her hands. "I figured you could use some time out of the lamp. Someplace that's not as crowded as anything near campus. You're welcome."

"You do realize that once you make your wishes, you're not likely to see me again."

"That doesn't matter to me." Her eyebrows pulled together.

"I don't want you to waste your time."

"That's nonsense." Jeannie smirked. "You just want to hide in your lamp and avoid everyone. But you're going to have to get used to the outside world someday."

"Not likely. Or don't you know what happens when a Djinn has no successor after the lamp's third master?"

"Oh, I know. Eternal servitude." She nodded. "But that's not happening. You'll have one."

"How?"

"You should realize that Kimiko Ichiro thinks she owes you one. Blaine Harcourt, too." She smirked. "They're working on tracking down your family."

I froze, letting that sink in. The Tanuki and the young dragon shifter were both intellectual forces to be reckoned with. As a team, they'd surely find something, a fact that had me trembling. Jeannie tilted her head, lifting her hand as though about to reach across the table. And then our order came.

The smiles that stretched our faces felt tied on, like banners over a rained-out garden party. Sensing the tension, our hostess set everything down and made herself scarce. I gripped the edge of the table instead of a fork or my coffee cup, knuckles whitening. The fear that sang through me made no sense. But that was the worst part about anxiety. It robbed me of reason as surely as bandits ransacked unsuspecting travelers.

"Make them stop." The words came out low and soft, sibilant, reminding me of prayer more than the demand I'd intended.

"I'll do no such thing." Jeannie leaned on the table, reaching across on my left past the plates of pastry and the coffee things. Her fingertips brushed mine. "Anyway, no one could stop those two once they get into researching something. You're stuck with being helped. It's hard to accept, but that's what happens when you do things for other people. They want to return the favor."

"But I had to help Kimiko. Exactly like I have to help you." I shook my head, unable to move my hand away from hers. "I followed orders. She doesn't owe me anything."

"All the same, she thinks differently. Ismail, don't try to tell me you only do what's required." She locked gazes with me. Would it be dangerous to look away? That generally got shifter's hackles up. I stared back, not willing to chance it.

"Very well. I'll stop protesting their efforts. But you know the big flaw in the Golden Rule, right?"

"You're talking about that whole 'do unto others' thing. No, I don't. Tell me."

"It doesn't take into account that one man's trash is another man's treasure. And the reverse is also true." I imagined kicking myself. Why couldn't I just say right out that I feared to find any relatives I might have after all this time? I should be able to admit how what they might think of me was more paralyzing than a staring contest with a cockatrice.

"You'd rather be forced to live at the whim of whoever coincidence directs to your lamp than meet long-lost relatives, then." She nodded, withdrawing her hand, then picked up her cooling coffee and took a sip. "You're going to find this hard to believe, but I understand." She broke eye contact.

"You can't, possibly." I sighed, staring down at my *choreg*. Leaving it on the plate felt like a parallel to the rest of my existence since that day in the desert when I'd acted too late. Denial.

"You're not my client, or not officially, anyway, even though what we're doing here is exactly the sort of thing I'm devoting my career to." She picked up her fork and knife and began cutting a corner off her sweet bread. "Because we're not on the books, I can tell you about the Boston internment camp, how my family should have been able to get away before the round-up, and why they didn't. It was my fault, you see. If you want to know more, just ask. I'll tell you anything you want to know about that. You don't have to tell me why you'd rather not meet whoever they find. But it might be easier for you to accept if you dip your toe in the idea before it happens. I won't bring it up again. Just remember, I'm here if you want to talk."

I stared, finally unable to stop myself from gaping as she put the fork to her lips and took a bite of *choreg*. How could Jeannie La Montagne sit there enjoying herself, treating her senses to a delicacy I'd denied myself for a century? Maybe she did know I could have treated myself to a glamoured version of *choreg* at any time while in the lamp. But what uncanny instinct could have told her I hadn't? It was like she could literally see how I felt, like Saul.

"Are you Psychic?"

"I get that question all the time." She smiled around the mouthful of bread, then swallowed it and went to work cutting off another piece. "Not really. My grandma was, so I have hunches sometimes. Anyway, you ought to eat some bread before it gets cold. And have some coffee, first."

Ignoring her about the coffee might have looked like an immature act of rebellion. It wasn't. I had to know whether I could handle an outing like this before she tried to rope me into another one. I didn't bother with a fork and knife, letting my hands get sticky as I lifted the bread to my mouth.

At first, I'd worried the bread and company while eating it would take me back in time, sting with the sense of empty tables and sorely missed faces. It didn't, or at least not quite. Every time the flavors on my tongue threatened to whisk me away like a cyclone, the clink of metal on Jeannie's plate anchored me to the present. No one in my family had eaten their *choreg* with a fork. It was time to call her bluff.

"I want you to tell me." I picked up my coffee cup, the sticky heat on my fingertips making my mind wander to what it might be like to reach across the table, pick apart the rest of Jeannie's bread, and feed it to her by hand.

"Hmm?" She paused with her knife about to pierce the crusty, seeded hide of *choreg* again.

"The Boston Internment." I sipped, the brew frothy and bitter. It was time to hear a tale of the sort of survival I'd run from enduring, time to look the sins of my past in the face and stare them down. "Tell me everything."

CHAPTER SEVEN

Jeannie

"Okay, then." I set my fork down, laid the knife aside. With one hand, I turned my water glass in a circle, then took a deep breath. "You know how the Reveal happened, right?"

"I know the version they teach at The Academy."

"Then you know enough about that." What a relief. "Good. About a year after all the chaos, Registry laws went into effect. They started registration, getting a database together of all the Extrahumans. The Magi and Psychics did it freely for the most part. When you can hurl fireballs or make people forget you exist, having people know what you are isn't such a big deal. Most of the Faeries felt the same, especially the Seelies. They like their rules, and there's always the Under to escape to. But it was different for shifters and vampires, some of the Psychics, too."

"I remember overhearing a conversation about Psychics denying their abilities during the Registry. Something Kimiko spoke about with a Psychic vampire?"

"Oh, that'd be Henry Baxter." I smiled, remembering how good an influence he'd been on his girlfriend Maddie since they got together. "Yeah. They did. It's how they managed to help some of the most vulnerable Extrahumans survive the Reveal. But they could do that because there isn't a way to test a Psychic except by what they say. Only the Summoners are really noticeable. But anyway, that's not something shifters can get away with. There's a physical test for that, scientific, where they take a sample and know what we are in under a minute, no matter how sneaky we're trying to be about it."

"Did many shifters try to hide, though?" Ismail tented his fingers around the little coffee cup, gazing into it before taking another sip.

"Lots, especially in the southern half of the country." I stopped spinning my water glass, then dried my fingers on the napkin in my lap. "There was a ton of intolerance and backlash down there back then. My cousin Bobby's parents took off and lived out of a truck in the Ozarks for three years. But Boston was different, like most of the Northeast." I sighed. "Or so we thought."

Ismail stilled, reacting to something. I glanced around, trying to figure out what it could be. Tithed Faeries sensed all kinds of magic, so there could be danger nearby. I flared my nostrils and tilted my head, trying to scent or listen for any threat. But there was nothing. And then, I noticed his eyes were locked on me. Something about me or the story I told had alarmed him. I should have known. He was another survivor, after all. And now I understood the real reason an Extrahuman Social Services worker shouldn't talk about her personal troubles with clients. It wasn't for privacy, but so we wouldn't cause more harm than good.

"Are you all right, Ismail?"

"I will be." He set his coffee down in the saucer, then put his hands on the table. "Please continue."

"Okay." But I wasn't sure I could. I closed my eyes. "What should I tell you about first? How we thought it was perfectly reasonable for the Mayor to ask all the shifters to move into temporary housing on barges in Boston Harbor? How about when he had a Boston PD task force guarding us for our own safety? I was seven and thought the police were our friends, just like I'd been taught. We were like frogs in a pan on a slowly heating stovetop, and then we were like fish in a barrel."

"What do you mean?" Ismail had leaned forward until he was on the edge of his seat. He didn't blink, something I thought was impossible for anyone but dragon shifters.

"I mean there wasn't much we could do when people on the barges started disappearing. But my mom and dad had some ideas. They started a resistance, teamed up with some otter and walrus shifters. They snuck out and contacted Kelpies and Selkies. With that much Water magic, we would have been able to defend the barges and also find out where the missing people went. It would have been the first time since the Faerie Wars that many from both sides worked together too. Mom and Dad had what seemed like an ocean of hope. They thought for sure we'd get the lost shifters back."

"You didn't, of course." Ismail tilted his head, his steady stare interrupted by a sheen of tears and one long blink.

"No. The Kelpies and Selkies never made it. The Queen didn't want her people to help. She stopped them instead."

"But why?"

"She refused to risk her Selkies, so she locked them all in the Under until the Internment was over. Even worse, she put up a Ban to keep the Kelpies out. Without them, half the Extrahumans on the barges disappeared before the President sent the National Guard to stop the Internment."

"How did she find out, though?"

"I told her, of course. That's how it was all my fault." I shook my head, hiding all traces of guilt from my face by picking at the napkin under the table instead where Ismail couldn't see. "I sent her a message in a bottle, dropped it off the side of our barge. Because I thought she'd help us."

"Her decision is hardly your fault."

It was my turn to sit still. The napkin I'd let go of fluttered to the floor, and for once, I didn't lean down to pick it up. And just as he had earlier, Ismail turned his head, scanning the room for threats. I studied his face again, noticing things I hadn't the first time I'd seen him in Newport. Faint lines marked the corners of his eyes and the space between his brows and traveled the breadth of his forehead. The jet curls just above his ears mingled with scant silver strands. They matched what I saw in the mirror every morning, adornments etched by guilt and the yarn of penance spun from my life since I squealed on my parents.

Ismail didn't ask how I was. Instead, he retrieved my fallen napkin, placing it on the table between us like a white flag or a peace offering. He left his hand beside it instead of drawing away again. He waited until I met his eyes again, then turned his palm up. I reached across and took his hand, not caring about how it was still slightly sticky from the *choreg*.

"Well, now you know the worst thing I've ever done. Thank you."

"For what? Surely you've told this story before."

"Yes, I have. But no one I've told it to so far extended their hand to me afterward like you just did." I squeezed it. "So, thanks."

"I still wonder one thing." He looked down at our hands, then squeezed back. "What happened to the missing people?"

"You remember how I said we thought the police were protecting us?"

"Yes." He nodded once.

"There actually was a threat. Extrahuman trafficking." I took a deep breath before continuing. "Many of the families on those barges were found later in circuses, zoos, mines, factories, tourist attractions. Some of them were even okay afterward. But the rest they only found records of. Laboratory records. And ashes. Can't forget those."

"I'm sorry." Ismail reached across and placed his other hand over mine.

"You shouldn't be." I sniffed, shaking my head as the corners of my eyes leaked. "You couldn't have done anything."

"I should have asked Wilfred to pass my lamp to someone else."

"You were in The Academy by choice?"

"Yes." Ismail's grasp loosened, as though he expected me to pull away. "I didn't want a second or third master for my lamp. I wanted nothing more to do with people anymore, Extrahuman or not."

"I understand." I knew what he'd have to say to that. Even though no one else I'd shared this story with ever made it this far, I'd been where Ismail was right then. I had to decide how much I wanted to tell him.

"How could you?" He blinked. "What happened next for you was the opposite of my— well, I guess you could call it a life. But you devoted your life to helping others after making that mistake."

"Because I wanted to curl up and hide." I closed my eyes, taking a leap of faith in this Djinn I'd only just met yet felt like I'd known forever. "I had a whole plan about heading up to the Arctic circle and just hibernating until I didn't wake up." I kept my eyes closed, expecting the worst, since that was what I'd told him.

Ismail let go of my hand. I heard the scrape of the chair on tile as he stood. I tried not to listen for his footsteps, but my enhanced hearing got nothing, anyway. He'd Vanished himself, then. I knew I shouldn't tell anyone but a psychiatrist about contemplating suicide. I'd gone and scared him off like a jerk after promising to help him.

"Yes, you do understand." His words startled my eyes open. He sat beside me, in the chair he'd pulled around the table. "I'm sorry for doubting you, Jeannie."

My mouth dropped open. I could hardly believe he was apologizing to me when I'd gone and been inappropriate. He put his elbows on his knees, then folded his hands and leaned forward and gazed into my eyes. How had I failed to notice his, how they were brown but shot through with amber? Was that a Djinn thing? Why did I care about something like that when I'd decided to treat Ismail the same way I would a client?

But I hadn't been the same with him as with Mr. Kazynski or Mrs. Donato. Ismail wasn't like them even though he was technically older than either. He looked my age even though his mannerisms were from a different era and he talked like a high-society Harcourt. I wondered what he thought of me, but didn't dare ask, not while we locked gazes like this.

For once, I wasn't sure what to do or say. Usually, I was the one to break the ice or help people shake off their shock and the inaction that went with it. I thought back to catching Josh Dennison and Nox Phillips snogging in the dorm laundry, how I'd moved them along and given Nox a place to stay. Instead of the usual snickering that memory inspired, I got chills and shivered like it was December instead of the end of April.

Ismail reached out, pushing a lock of hair aside that had fallen out from behind my ear. His touch lingered as his fingertips brushed the side of my ear. Maybe it was an accident, maybe something else. His gaze was intense, penetrating. I'd spent the entire afternoon trying to get through to him so that I could help, and now he sat beside me, looking at me like a desert traveler might gaze at a glass of water. I knew I was looking at him exactly the same way. This kind of thing had happened to me before, but it had been one-sided. I took a breath again, trying not to prepare whatever words might come out with it and just speak to him in the moment. But the words didn't make it in time.

"Did you enjoy your *choreg* and coffee?" The woman from behind the counter shuttled our empty plates from the table to a large round tray.

"Very much, thank you." Ismail turned his head to smile at the woman. Had he smiled before this? I couldn't remember because that expression looked so natural on him. Familiar too, like I'd seen it before somewhere. I definitely had. Where, though? It was right on the tip of my brain but took off like a tomcat leaping down from the top of a fence.

I sat in silence, collecting my thoughts as Ismail chatted with the woman about *choreg* recipes in Armenian. She handed him a coupon card, the kind where you collect stamps each time you visit to exchange for a discount later. She'd filled half the spaces up for us already. After that, she faded back into the duties of running the cafe and left us to each other's company again.

"Would you walk with me for a while, Jeannie?" Ismail had stood and extended his hand to help me up. I took it, but couldn't take him up on his offer.

I explained that I had a meeting with my adviser and then a class. When he asked when we could talk again, I gave him a time later that night after dinner. His smile was the last thing to vanish as he went back into his lamp. Even though the bus back to Kennedy Plaza passed by some lovely spring scenery, all I could see was that last smile. It had touched his eyes, genuine.

CHAPTER EIGHT

Ismail

The only place a Djinn could go for advice besides whoever his master trusted was either his Monarch or the Under. Technically, that wasn't true. I couldn't leave the lamp unless she called me out of it, but I could communicate with anyone I knew who was in the realm opposite this one. I stood in front of the silver-backed mirror on the north wall of my lamp and willed it into a window. After that, all I had to do was imagine Neil Redford, and he'd appear on the other side of the glass—as long as he wasn't in the earthly realm, at least.

"Well, I'll be a monkey's uncle. Ismail! How you doing, old buddy?" Neil flashed his perfect teeth. Perfectly white, that is. They were sharp, almost like a shark's, double row included. Seeing any Faerie in the Under meant you got the real them without their glamour. Redcaps all had teeth like that, plus pointy ears and gray skin. I could also see Neil's mantle, the sign of rank in the Goblin King's Court.

"You've moved up in the court, I see." I smiled back. "Congratulations."

"I'd say thanks, but really you ought to compliment my son, Fred." Neil turned his smile down to a grin. "If he hadn't helped me fix the King's cleaning contraption, I'd never have made it past Marquess to Duke."

"Well, I'm glad you're not still a Page after all this time" I'd met Neil because that's what we both were during that first year and a day in the Under. Neil had been a pioneer on America's western frontier, but in the other realm, mortal nations and geography didn't matter. I'd been sent to help him out there on occasion. Only one thing divided Faerie, the rift between the King and his counterpart.

"Well, shoot. Has it really been that long?" He shook his head, a forelock of sandy blond hair streaked liberally with gray flopping over one of his gleaming red eyes. "You don't look like you've aged a day. But then, you've been in a lamp all this time, right?"

"Right."

"That's a bum deal, buddy."

"It has its bumless moments, however." I smiled and gestured at the opulent surroundings behind me.

Neil threw back his head and laughed. No, he guffawed. I had to wait nearly two minutes for him to compose himself again and by then his knees were sore from slapping. Watching a Redcap laugh would have been sheer terror for most mortals, but I wasn't one. Even though the insatiable maw he'd opened could have devoured my lamp, items ensorcelled by the Monarchs persisted. Because I'd tithed to the King, no Unseelie creature could truly destroy it. I was another matter entirely.

"So, you've been in there all this time. You didn't call, you didn't write, you didn't Magic Mirror your way over to see me." Neil narrowed his eyes. "Why?"

"I was tired." I shook my head. "Shell-shocked. That sounds like what you'd call yellow-bellied, I know."

"Now you look here." Neil set his jaw to the point where it was squarer than I'd thought it possible for jaws to get. "You've seen two wars up close and personal, and a couple of gunfights besides. These days, they call what had you in its teeth PTSD. It's serious enough to get any fighting man an honorable discharge. I won't hear you calling yourself yellow-bellied over hiding again."

"Fine. How about if I call myself a coward for agreeing to the lamp life to begin with?"

"I always thought you did it to protect your family."

"I wish it were that simple."

"Well, shoot." This time, Neil didn't laugh. "So why chew the fat about it with me now, after all this time? You join Alcoholics Anonymous or something?"

"I thought Prohibition ended eighty years ago?" The quip came automatically, with no wind in its sails. "As to why, I met someone important."

"Woah now there, Izzy." Neil's hands went up like he'd been outmatched on a dusty Main Street at high noon. "What did you do, meet another Djinn through this magic mirror thing like some kind of Under dating service?"

"No. And I think you've got the wrong idea. Maybe." I tried to shake off the memory of Jeannie's hand in mine. "I met my lamp's third master."

"Let me guess—you have no idea where any of your descendants are, or whether any of them are tithed."

"Correct." I didn't need to explain to Neil that I was facing eternity in this lamp.

"Does this new master know?"

"Yes, and it's not good. She's taking her time with wishing, and she wants to help me track down my family."

"Well then, how's that bad?"

"I don't know. It seems like it shouldn't be, but for some reason, I just can't shake the idea that something's not right."

"So is it the situation or the lady who's giving you that there case of the heebie-jeebies?"

"The lady is one of the most altruistic people I've ever met. It's the situation." I took a deep breath, figuring bluntness would be best. "I sense coincidence at work here."

"Shi—" A gong sounded somewhere off in the distance on Neil's side. He waited until it rang thirteen times. "Look, I gotta run. Duke duties over at formal court with His Majesty. But just so you know, it's not just you. Coincidence has been flapping its butterfly wings all over Providence for months now. We'll talk some other time, but I'm gonna give my oldest kid Fred a heads up. He'll have the time to help you out over the next week or two. Who's your master lady so I can put him in touch?"

"The bear shifter, Jeannie La Montagne, from Boston." I studied Neil's face, which had gone uncharacteristically blank and chalky-pale under the gray.

"Noted. You'll hear from him tonight. He's got some friends with time most of the rest of us don't have. They'll fill you in." My old friend was in such a hurry that he turned his back before the mirror had silvered back over.

I gazed into it at my own face. I wondered how anyone could see it as the face of a friend, let alone more than that. My wife and I had met and married years before either of us had any idea how little mettle I possessed. Once Yeva found out, she'd grown dissatisfied and shrewish. I'd made it worse by proving her right when I failed to confront her about it. Was my inaction truly this PTSD illness Neil had mentioned, or had it started with the wife I'd failed to protect?

I wasn't sure I wanted to find out, but I wasn't sure I had a choice.

I felt the pull of Jeannie's attention less than an hour later. My earlier indecision had me rethinking the whole thing. Maybe I could endure eternity in the lamp better than facing my past and trying to convince a stranger to take a potentially life-ruining turn in here. But that wasn't what I actually feared at all. The worst would be to find none of them were left at all, that there were no descendants, that Yeva had died to protect children who wouldn't survive to have their own someday. A close second would be to find them and discover they hated me.

"I wish I didn't have to do this research paper." Jeannie's statement made it impossible not to appear. I sighed, changing my clothing's appearance to the modern-looking t-shirt and jeans. The lamp's magic Vanished me into a scarred wooden chair beside a long table covered with papers and books. I turned my head to see her with one hand clapped over her mouth.

"That sounds like the least genuine wish I've ever heard." I almost covered my own lips after that utterance. My time talking with Neil had left my guard down. I placed my hand on the table, not wanting to reveal more than she'd already seen with that one slip.

"Good. I don't want you to actually grant it." Jeannie shuffled a few of the papers, some marked with a red pen. "This is the second draft. Third time's the charm, and at the rate I'm going, it'll be done early. It's easy enough, just mildly annoying busywork."

"You ought to be careful, though, with these fake wishes." I shook my head. "Even though I'll agree not to grant them, coincidence has a way of hearing."

"Silly Djinn, coincidence isn't sentient." Jeannie's giggle was soft enough not to anger the librarian, but still, it caught his attention.

"That may not be true." The librarian sauntered to the end of the Reference desk closest to us. "Since you're not in a major course of study which includes magical theory, I don't expect you to know that. But I thought you might benefit from some enlightenment on the subject under your specific circumstances."

"Thanks, Mr. Waban." I raised an eyebrow, startlingly intrigued by Jeannie's reaction to public correction.

"You can thank me by keeping that in mind later." As the librarian turned away, I noticed his eyes had slitted pupils, dragonish, confirming my guess about his identity. He'd been on the Frontier, too.

"So, Jeannie, if you didn't want me to complete your research paper, why did you call?"

"Fred Redford wants to talk to us. He's meeting us here after his class gets out. But first—" She turned her head, looking up at the cold gust of wind from the opening library door. "Well, they're here. I don't have to tell you."

"Hello again, old man." Blaine Harcourt sat down across from us, followed by a woman who definitely wasn't Kimiko Ichiro. This girl looked the same age as the other, but that's where the resemblance ended. She was slightly shorter, had a more generous figure, and tawny hair framed her smirking face. "I brought some extra help."

"Hi, I'm Lynn, A.K.A. Darth Sarcasm, A.K.A. the Tinfoil Brainiac." She grinned at me and winked at Jeannie. "You didn't tell me your Djinn looks more like Aladdin than a big blue guy. Nice. High five!" Lynn raised one hand, holding it up halfway across the table. Jeannie blinked, then reached out and slapped it.

"It's good to meet you, Lynn." I nodded, hoping I wouldn't have to slap the high five. She spared me the exercise. I looked at Blaine. "Jeannie told me you and your mate were doing some research. What did you find?"

"Not much yet, although there's a new lead." Blaine took a deep breath, then let it out with three smoke rings. He glanced warily over my shoulder at Mr. Waban. "We found out that your son went to Poland and your daughter to Italy. We lost track of him, but it seems she got married to a man from America. The problem is, Ellis Island naturalization did some funky things with people's names. I'll let Lynn take it from here."

"Yeah, okay, so…" She pulled her long hair over one shoulder, then pulled out her phone and put it on the table in front of her. "We didn't find any records of Armenians coming over from Italy, just Italians. But there were a bunch of women who came over with brand new husbands, married in Italy instead of stateside. A ton of them had no maiden names, just the names of the towns in Italy where they got married. And half of them were called 'Monalisa' which just means 'milady' in Italian."

"We'll have to go through all those records in more detail." Blaine leaned over, peering at Lynn's phone. "There are loads like that. We have to cross-reference some magical records, too, but we need to ask you a couple of questions. This might come down to genetics instead of records."

"Very well." I crossed my arms over my chest, instantly regretting the unconscious gesture when Lynn raised an eyebrow and nudged Blaine in the ribs.

"Okay. We know you're Faerie, born a Changeling. How far back is your family line as far as Faerie blood goes?"

"As far back as anyone can remember. Djinn mostly, but my grandmother's side was Sidhe all the way back."

"Okay, good. We'll look through the magical records for an immigrant with that kind of lineage. If your daughter was trying to find a match so she could come to America, she might have said that up-front and center. Magi families back then looked for that kind of thing. Might be hard if she married a human though." Lynn jotted something in a small notepad. "So, how about your wife's family?"

"Shifters, though she wasn't one." I closed my eyes. "Leopards. Kimiko told me they're almost endangered now."

"Wow, I'd love to look at a sample of your blood sometime." Lynn's eyes were wide. "Oh, sorry. It's just that we're working on Extrahuman genetics this semester. I'm an Alternative Therapies major."

"Our Lynn here is going to be a doctor." Blaine grinned.

"So's Jeannie, technically, if she goes to Grad School." Lynn winked. Jeannie didn't. She was looking past Lynn at the door again. "What's wrong?"

Jeannie didn't say anything. But when Blaine glanced over his shoulder, I knew there'd be some kind of trouble for sure.

CHAPTER NINE

Jeannie

A sudden pang of guilt got replaced with annoyance as Blaine Harcourt got up and left when Tony Gitano walked into the library with Fred Redford. The whole business over Spring Break had changed Blaine's attitude about lots of people, places, and things, but not as far as Tony the cat shifter was concerned. That was a shame in my book. I wasn't alone. I caught Taki Waban, the new librarian, shaking his head with a soft clucking sound.

"Fracking dragon shifters and their paranoid tempers," Lynn muttered as she shuffled the papers into a loose pile and dumped them on top of the books in her backpack. She looked over her shoulder as she headed for the door Blaine was tapping his foot next to. I saw her mouth a word that could only be sorry in Tony's general direction. She couldn't know the crazy local rumors about Tony's family or the fact that he was here on a full scholarship. Blaine might, but probably didn't care. He could be a snooty little jerk sometimes.

"Hey, Jeannie." Fred smiled and waved as he greeted me in library-appropriate tones. His mouth tilted sympathetically. "Eww, research paper. This is why I went with Engineering. All my research is math."

Ismail chuckled at that. I glanced over at him, wondering whether he'd gone to college back in Armenia and what he'd studied if he had. I'd have to ask him sometime.

"So's half of mine." I lifted one sheet after another of notes I'd been taking, flipping one over with each word. "Lies. Damn lies. Statistics."

"Oooh." Tony leaned over, peering at the numbers and their labeled columns upside-down. "This is the opposite viewpoint paper? Not looking forward to that one next year."

"Yeah." I shrugged. "It's a descriptive paper, mostly, with just a short survey this time. But it's a distraction, so I want to get it done quick. I'd rather be doing more of my clinical work." I raised an eyebrow at Tony. "You're taking Extrahuman Psych Research next year?"

"It's part of what they decided should go into my crazy major." He shrugged, not really looking at Fred or me. Tony got dodgy every time something unique about him came up, and I just happened to know he was pioneering a brand new major here at Providence Paranormal. The Headmistress herself had mapped it out for him.

"Okay." I didn't want to piss him off or freak him out. "You guys need help? I could use a break from this."

"Actually, that'd be awesome." Fred grinned. "We need a few books that aren't in the Nocturnal Lounge. It's for an Extrahuman History paper."

"Yeah, and after we get them, we're going back there." Tony looked down at his shoes. "To the Lounge, I mean. Because you never know when it will get knocked over, blown up, or set on fire again. Same goes for this library."

"If any of that happens, we'll fix it." Fred waved a hand absently as though Tony's remark was a gnat.

"I'll stay here and keep an eye on your things, Jeannie." Ismail gestured at the heavy bag I'd just zipped my draft and graphs into.

"Thanks, Ismail." I smiled. Fred nodded at the Djinn, almost like he'd expected to see him there. Before I could wonder what was up with that, Tony took a step back, looking for all the world like someone had dropped him headfirst into a room full of rocking chairs. "What's wrong, Tony?"

"Are you a Seelie Djinn or an Unseelie Djinn? And don't try pulling anything lame, like trying to tell me you're Dorothy Gale from Kansas." Tony wrinkled his nose.

"Unseelie. Not that it's any of your business." Ismail narrowed his eyes, looking scary for the first time since I'd met him. "And if you'd like me to hold my tongue about what you are, you'll stop asking me personal questions."

It was only then that I realized Ismail was at least as dodgy about giving answers as Tony, possibly more. One of these sides of him must be something rarely revealed. The cat shifter backed down, not exactly seeming to relax, still on guard. Ismail gave him a look that reminded me just how much magic power Djinn tended to pack, more than most professors here on campus. Taki Waban's presence probably did more to deter Tony than Ismail's, then again maybe not. If it were me on that end of this confrontation, I'd be more comfortable with the dragon I knew than the Djinn I didn't.

Fred cleared his throat, then handed me a slip of paper with some titles on them. I headed into the stacks without consulting the computer or the library ghosts. Fred probably asked me for help because he knew I had some firsthand information about his subject from more than a few of my clients. I stopped at a shelf near one of the back windows and stood on my toes. There they were, barely touched dust-jackets gleaming. I pulled two books down.

"There's one more on the top shelf, but you'll have to get it." I shrugged. "I can't reach that one." Ironic how I turned into a half-ton bear but stood just under average height in my human form.

"Thanks, Jeannie." Fred ran his finger along the spines until he got to the book he wanted. He slid it off the shelf but lost his grip. I started to raise my hands, but it'd be too late. That book was going to hit me right in the face. I'd be lucky not to have a broken nose.

And that's when Ismail decided to make another smoke-filled

appearance. Tony coughed. Fred gasped. I waved the smoke away from my eyes to find out what had happened. The Djinn stood there, wearing the clothes I'd last seen him in two weeks ago. The blue jacket made his gold sash and vest stand out, the red scarf around his neck creating an even sharper contrast. I'd forgotten how striking he was, and the guilt from earlier came back with a vengeance. He glanced down at the cover of the book he'd plucked from the air over my head.

"The Boston Extrahuman Internment," he read aloud. "Are you sure this is the right book?" Ismail handed the book to Fred. And then Ismail was glaring at one of the most easygoing Redcaps I'd ever heard of.

"Of course, he is." A flash of embarrassment raced through me, making my face burn with a flush. I didn't keep it a secret, the fact that I'd been there. I didn't advertise it either. "He wants to talk to me for a History project. It's nothing I haven't done before."

"So, how about it, Jeannie?" Fred didn't exactly look at me. I knew he was about to do something awkward. Then, he surprised me by looking me in the eye when he asked. "Do you have time for an interview?"

"Time, yeah." I nodded, suddenly so weary I could have gone back to the dorm and slept for sixteen hours. In my Freshman year, I'd talked to what felt like hundreds of other students, answering their questions about what it was like on the barges and whether we knew the human government would go that far before it happened. But then, those students published their papers. Instead of interviewing me directly, they started citing those older interviews to the point where I hadn't done one all year. Fred might be the last undergrad at PPC to interview someone who'd actually been there. It was completely unnecessary. There had to be some kind of ulterior motive.

"So how about it? Will you come down to the Nocturnal Lounge and answer a few questions? I can promise you the pizza's good." Fred sighed. "I hate to ask, but…" His shrug was shallow and half-hearted, but at least he didn't look away. The Redfords were stand-up people, even if they had been a little muddled with Gitano Gang business in the past. That was what decided me.

"Sure. Just let me grab my bag." I headed back through the stacks faster than I'd intended, leaving Fred and Tony behind. I tripped over my own feet, but Ismail caught me by the arm. He'd managed to keep up, shooting a final dirty look at Tony as he went.

"You talk about this freely with your classmates?" Ismail put his hands on the table, leaning down to try to look at my face as he spoke. I wondered whether that was a Djinn thing or just him.

"Not all of it, but yeah, I answer their questions for their papers and projects. Been doing it the whole time I've been at this school." I held the shoulder strap of my bag longer than I should have, staring at it for a moment. "Why would I stop now?"

"Because most people don't speak of times like that unless they have to." His brow furrowed.

"Well, I do." I sighed. "Have to, that is. If people like me who were there don't talk about it, people might forget how it happened." I turned away from him as I snagged my sleeve in the zipper on my backpack. I sighed and fixed it. His expression had been flat, mask-like. I glanced at his un-glamoured clothing again. I wondered exactly how long had he been in that lamp. What had he been through to make him like being locked in a vault?

"You're a brave woman, Jeannie La Montagne."

"Thanks, but I hope you don't mind if I disagree. It's just talking. Come along and listen, considering you already know the worst part of that particular story. I promise an Unseelie Djinn like you will fit right in at the Nocturnal Lounge."

"Oh, wow." Fred interrupted. I almost chewed him out for it. "Yeah, he totally will. Henry's going to love this guy. Did you know that he saves people from falling objects, too? And hey, I didn't catch your name. I'm Fred Redford." He stuck out his hand.

"I know. I am Ismail." The Djinn bowed instead of accepting the handshake, then raised an eyebrow as though he expected some other reaction from the Redcap.

"Cool." Fred scratched his head as though he was trying to think of something. Then, he bowed back. "We'd better hurry or we'll lose Tony."

He was right, too. I caught a glimpse of the cat shifter's trench coat as he headed out the door. We hurried after him and, of course, I tripped over my feet a few times in the process. Ismail caught me every time. It was only a few blocks away, but the entrance to the Nocturnal Lounge was partway down a creepy old trolley tunnel. I didn't mind walking down there with three other people but watched for Ismail's reaction. He seemed nervous at first though his eyes twinkled merrily when Fred did the secret knock to get the door to open.

I'd been in there before, but it had been almost two years since the last time. And I wasn't sure what to expect after the renovations over Winter Intersession, but they managed to make it almost the same again. I'd almost forgotten how many books were crammed into the mezzanine and how just about everything edible floated through the air in the hands of the ghostly Skeleton Crew. True to Fred's word, there was heavenly smelling pizza downstairs in the area upperclassmen had nicknamed The Pit. Fred shooed me over to a table already occupied by a dark-skinned Goth girl I thought I should recognize and Nox Phillips, a Kelpie one year behind me. Nox was mated to Josh, an Alpha wolf shifter who led the most diverse pack on campus. I sat at the far end of the table from them, not expecting much in the way of conversation.

"Hi, Jeannie." Nox picked up her coffee and moved to a seat next to mine. "So, Fred convinced you to show up?"

"Yeah, I don't like saying no to interviews about Boston unless I really have no time."

"Good, because after he asks his questions, we have a few things to talk to you about as well." The Goth girl had moved over, too. I peered at her, trying to place the name that went with the face.

"I'm Maddie, Lynn Frampton's roommate up in 566." She touched her chest and mumbled a few words in what sounded like Latin. "It's okay that you don't remember me. I'm an Umbral magus."

"Oh!" Memories flooded back from other times I'd met her. "Okay. You have an amulet that's helping me remember you now. Your parents are vampires, and you're from Vermont."

"Uh-huh." She gave me a cheery smile. "Hello again!"

"Okay, so now that's done." Nox grinned. "You're about to graduate, so you know what an Extramagus is."

"Oh, no. I mean, yeah I do, but they're like the baddest of bad news."

"The worst." I'd almost forgotten Ismail was there, standing at my right shoulder.

"You know, I always thought that was kind of biased. I mean, I can think of lots of people with big power who did the right thing most of the time." I chewed my bottom lip, not wanting to rehash my stance from almost every class that mentioned Extramagi but also not able to justify blanket fear and anger for an entire classification of people.

"Yeah, we know how you feel about stereotyping." Tony sat down with a cup of black coffee. Instead of drinking it, he pushed it over to Maddie. "That's why this is going to be hard."

"What's going to be hard?" I blinked. "I thought Fred just wanted an interview."

"Nope. He just thought that was the best cover for bringing you here. Convincing you all your recent klutziness and weird coincidences are because an Extramagus has his or her eye on you is what we're really after." Nox sighed. "I have to admit, it took me a while to believe it myself when it happened to me. But don't you wonder exactly what kind of trouble I was in back in February?"

"No, I don't." I shook my head. "I figured it was all about the Faerie Court conflict."

"Which got kicked up by the same Extramagus the lot of us think has been messing with the school for a long time." Nox ran a hand through her hair.

"That's disturbing, but it makes sense." Ismail sat down between Tony and me. "My last master thought one was causing her problems."

"Bingo." Maddie tapped her own nose. "That'd be Kimiko, and she was right. She and Blaine were lucky to escape with their lives. If you were her Djinn, then you know something about what a mess they were in. Nox already told you she and Josh were targets. Before them, it was Henry and I and before that, Bobby and Lynn."

"Whoever it is, seems to target two people at a time, folks who are either powerful or assets to the school, the community, or both." Henry Baxter, wearing an old black leather jacket, sat next to Maddie. "You two fit the bill."

"But Extramagi are so rare." I shivered, wondering why this felt like some kind of intervention. "I mean, there's a registry now. Everyone's accounted for, and there aren't any Extramagi on the books in Rhode Island anymore." I looked at Henry. "Not since you got turned, right?"

"We figured you'd say that." Maddie pulled out a tablet and tapped it twice to activate it. "That's why we talked it over with Josh. He gave us the okay to tell you about pack business, so we brought you this." She pushed it across the table at me.

The app running on the tablet looked like an interactive flowchart. Dates and names stood out, some of them instantly familiar. Tapping a listing gave a description of an event, sometimes a reference link to a public record, article, or book title. I'd almost been there for several of them, and others looked suspiciously like excuses I'd heard from a specific group of students. I might be blonde, but I wasn't dumb.

"Tinfoil Hat." I stared at Nox. "So that's the reason your whole pack even exists. You really think an Extramagus is after you guys?"

"Worse than that." Fred pushed a plate with one slice of pizza in front of me.

I picked it up and took a big bite, my stomach rumbling. Ismail cleared his throat, and Fred tossed another slice from his huge pile of bread and cheese to my plate. I might be petite in human form, but bear shifters got hungry, and my metabolism meant the calories burned up before they went to my hips.

"How could it be worse than all this?" I gestured with my free hand at the tablet. "I mean, most of you almost got killed, for crying out loud."

"We think the big bad is after the school, trying to get it shut down." Maddie tapped one of the entries. I saw an article about the arrest of Doctor Brodsky the Summoning professor in January, charged with two deaths. Then, she moved on to the Obituary for Wilfred Harcourt. "And he doesn't care who dies in the process, either."

CHAPTER TEN

Ismail

The conversation at the table went silent, although that didn't stop the Redcap Changeling and Jeannie from finishing their meals. That there was an Extramagus in the area wasn't news to me. I'd heard Kim and her mate, Blaine, discussing it, after all. But I hadn't realized this many people, an entire pack of shifters and others no less, were involved. I'd just assumed that, since Blaine Harcourt was a dragon shifter, he'd keep his troubles to himself. My servitude to Jeannie didn't require me to help her on this, or anything she hadn't explicitly asked of me. But an Extramagus could become the worst kind of tyrant. If left unchecked, they'd do anything to increase their power and lifespan or pay any cost. After that, there was no stopping them.

"I'm under no obligation to the rest of you or the school, but how can I help?" I leaned back in my chair.

"We didn't ask you here so you could help." Tony stared into his coffee. I gazed at the freakish aura of magic surrounding him. I'd never heard of a magical feline shifter before, and normal shifters didn't have magic energy unless someone else put it there. So I wondered whether he could be trusted considering the group was up against an Extramagus. But then I noticed that Tony's magic came from Faerie. Before I could scrutinize it further, he shot me a glare over the rim of his cup. I had to stop looking at a member of this pack that way or risk them all distrusting me.

"Okay, so why did you want to talk to Ismail, then?" Jeannie brushed crumbs off her hands and crossed her arms over her chest.

"You know how we said you're a target?" Fred swallowed his second-to-last mouthful of pizza, then frowned down at his plate.

"Yeah?" Jeannie tapped her foot under the table.

"Like Henry said, there's always been two." Tony shrugged. "We think Lamp Man's the other one."

"Seriously? An Extramagus would target a lamp-bound Djinn?" Jeannie scoffed. "That's insane. All they do is follow orders, and you can't get at them when they're in their lamps."

"No, it makes sense." I sighed. "I helped Kimiko and Blaine more than I should have. Being Unseelie means I can bend some rules while doing my job."

"Let me guess: that's the closest you're going to get to telling us exactly what you did to piss the bad guy off?" Tony's stare reminded me of a bristling tomcat.

"Wow, Tony. Just wow." Jeannie stood up. "You bring me over here, lay something this big on me, and then insult my friend?" I blinked at that. I was used to dealing with frightened folk, masters or people who wanted to become one. Did she consider me a friend? "Don't think that I'm soft because of how I look. Oh, and by the way, you're not one to talk about being cagey."

"She does have a point, Tony." Fred managed to speak coherently around a mouthful of pizza. "You're a pretty dodgy guy."

"Yeah, about my own personal life which is strictly my business and none of yours. I don't mince words about this." He slapped his hand down next to the tablet between Jeannie and me, then stared at me. "This is serious trouble, people. We're trying to figure out who this Extramagus is before an innocent man gets executed for crimes against Extrahumanity. A Summoning professor was Mind-controlled for crying out loud. What else can this bastard do? We don't know. They're always one or more steps ahead of us, and we still have no idea why anyone would want to mess with the school. Mark my words, it's about something much bigger than making students and faculty look bad."

Tony was right even though I refused to admit that out loud, after his outburst. I had to move the conversation along to something constructive. Heading off the potential social eruption with a question would be the best course. Luckily, I had plenty of those.

"Is there a list of the powers you think this Extramagus has?" I looked at the tablet, wary of touching it. I'd never used such a device before and wasn't sure how not to ruin their display.

The Umbral girl navigated to a different screen. I saw a few lists and scanned them. The rest of the information looked like a police dossier. I read that, too. When I shuddered, all eyes fell on me. I reminded myself that this was a group of students, young people with limited experience and without extra power from a lamp to help them. Neil had mentioned the older generation not having time, but I wondered whether he knew how dangerous this Extramagus might be. Right after that, I wondered whether I was overreacting. I composed myself, pushing down evidence of the cowardice that shaped my life when I was their age.

"How theoretical is this limitation you have listed for him?" I pointed at one of three guesses, careful not to touch the screen.

"Blaine, Lynn, and Olivia are our brain trust." Nox tossed her head. "They're the ones who checked into it. And Kimiko's the one who originally thought of the idea. You tell me how reliable she is."

"If his only limitation is being unable to use magic outside of Rhode Island, I'm not sure how you'll ever find an identity or a way to stop them." I sighed.

"Ismail, I wish to know who this Extramagus is." Jeannie pointed at the screen. There was no mistaking what she meant. I closed my eyes, focusing my magic like a drawn bow. But when I tried to loose it, send the bolt of my magic out to obey her command, it stopped.

"I can't grant that wish." My eyes flew open.

"Wait, what?" Jeannie's eyes widened. "I thought Djinn had huge cosmic powers but itty-bitty living space."

"The latter is true, the former not so much." I gestured at my face. "I went into the lamp when I was young. After tithing, but only weeks after my full year was up in the Under. And I got out at the same time as your father, Fred." I nodded at the young Redcap. "Also, I'm only a Marquess. Most Djinn are Dukes. I'm not as powerful as I could be."

"But what about the power from your lamp?" Henry scratched his head. "All the experience you have from however many years you've been in there? If it's a memory problem, I might be able to help."

"No need." I sighed. "I remember everything, including part of that extra power I mentioned before. But even a Djinn has limitations. For example, I'm limited in certain Faerie magics by my rank in the King's Court. In this case, something is blocking me, and the fact that I can't obey a direct command from the lamp's master tells me a few things."

"So, dish." Nox gave me a lopsided grin. "What's the four-one-one?"

"First, the energy blocking me is Faerie magic. Second, it's Seelie." A chorus of gasps sounded out around the table. I waited as they regained enough composure to silence their surprised murmurs. "Finally, the Extramagus is warded against Djinn. Do you understand what that means?"

"Ugh. It's right on the tip of my brain." Maddie put her head in her hands. "I'm not Lynn or Trogdor, and Olivia's asleep." She looked up again, peering at the rest of the group. "Anyone else?"

"Another Djinn." Nox tightened her hands into fists. "One in the um, other Court. The Extramagus must have one of his own."

"He definitely did when my dad had to rescue Blaine." Fred clenched his jaw, which was probably scarier for the others than me. None of them had worked with Redcaps in the Under, after all.

"But look here." Henry had slipped a glove on his right hand. He used it to tap the tablet's screen. "Kimiko made a note about how she thought all her wishes were countered by the Extramagus's own Djinn."

"Well, she *was* the one in the thick of that particular fight." Nox leaned her chin on her hand. "She must know what she's talking about there. But something about that explanation's not sitting well with the ancestors." Nox leaned back, rubbing her stomach and tilting her head as though listening to voices only she could hear. Kelpies got water magic and the ability to change into a horse, but that came with the input of anyone else who'd ever worn the pelt which gave them their magic. It seemed Nox was at peace with them, so their influence was probably a good thing.

"Of course, your ancestors are all riled up." Tony shook his head. "Kimiko was wrong. The drive-by shooting wasn't a Djinn wish; it was an Organized Crime hit. You don't need to make wishes for the big cat Mafia to shoot at Yoshi Ichiro's daughter. He's crossed them too many times in the courtroom."

Tony stood up. "Yeah, the Extramagus probably still has the same Djinn who knocked Blaine out over the Pell Bridge. But it's way more likely we've got a rat in Tinfoil Hat. Because the other thing that can ward against Djinn is a Monarch. Someone's carrying tales to Her. And I bet more than half of you right here think it's me. Probably for the best if I make myself scarce. Arrivederci."

Tony turned his back on the group, stalking down the length of the mezzanine. He looked back over his shoulder once. Directly at me, of course.

"He's been a real bag of cats lately," said Henry. "Don't take it personally."

"But he does have a point about a possible informant in or around your pack." I raised an eyebrow, intrigued that the vampire had brushed off the theory Tony had presented.

"Maybe, but that's for Josh to decide. He's the Alpha." Henry shrugged.

"Yeah, and he'll consider your opinion and mine as far as that goes, too." Nox stopped rubbing her stomach. "But I can tell you all right now, I think he's altogether wrong. And the Extramagus still has a Djinn on the line for a wish."

"Yup, I agree." Fred grinned. "And I bet it's for the same reason, too."

"You both saw something?" Jeannie looked from Nox to Fred, then back again.

"Yeah. Faerie magic energy surge." Fred winced. "I bet the only reason Ismail here didn't get any backlash is because of the wards we have here in the Lounge against that other unmentionable kind of Faerie magic."

"Is your whole school warded that heavily?" I blinked at Jeannie. "Surely there are students from the other side of the Under here."

"There are, so it isn't. They have their own Lounge. Spectral Magi and some diurnal shifters use it as well." She chewed her bottom lip. "I don't know how strong the overall school wards are, but they got increased after this Lounge and the library got wrecked."

"Is that why you have an ancient dragon for a librarian?" It was my turn to be bewildered.

"Wow. He's that old?" Nox shook her head. "I never knew. So many things make sense now." She chuckled. "No wonder Blaine's scared of him."

"Speaking of Blaine," Jeannie said, "shouldn't we bring him in on this now that Tony has left the building?"

"Nah, too late for him and Kimiko. Probably you guys, too."

"Don't dragon shifters need less sleep than the rest of us, though?" Jeannie glanced at Henry. "Well, besides our friendly neighborhood vampire, of course."

"Usually, yes. But he told us earlier that he has a big fancy dress formal shindig to go to tomorrow night." Nox wrinkled her nose. "Josh and I have to go, too, but I have time for a nap in the afternoon, and Blaine doesn't."

"Oh, no!" Jeannie shot out of her chair, putting her hands to her face for a moment. Then, she whirled and grabbed her bag. "I've got to go get some sleep, too. Sorry guys. Thanks for the heads-up, but I'll have to help you with it some other time."

"Wait!" Maddie reached out, tugging Jeannie's sleeve. "This is totally a life-or-death thing. It's not about you helping us, it's us offering to help you. I can hide you for a few days or something."

"Thanks, Maddie. I appreciate the offer, but I just can't take it." Jeannie somehow managed to look weary and frantic at the same time. "But the reason I have to jet is life or death, too."

"What do you mean?" Fred blinked.

"That hoity-toity costume shindig Blaine's going to." She turned to go as though that answered the question. When she scanned our faces, hers fell. "Look, you don't understand. It's a charity ball to benefit the Senior Center. I have to go and support it as part of my capstone class. If I miss it, I won't graduate. And even worse, the Senior Center's offerings could get cut if we don't raise enough. All those elderly Extrahumans would lose things like free medical screenings and temporary housing. I have to do my part."

I expected protests, but there were none. Maddie nodded, bouncing her dark curls. Henry shook his head and sighed, but grinned anyway. Fred's lips tightened, and he gave her some kind of salute. Nox stood up and shook her hand.

"Four of the pack will be there if you need us." Nox put her hand on one of her bony hips. "We're all rooting for you. Good luck, Jeannie."

But good Luck would be in short supply, as it turned out.

CHAPTER ELEVEN

Jeannie

"No way, Mom!" My fist hit the mattress so hard I dented a spring. "I'm not going to a formal event that my graduation depends on with Dale. Don't you remember? We broke up." I'd forgotten the morning of the ball was the same as Mom's weekly phone call from home.

"Well, I know that, Jeannie. It's a shame, really. I mean, he's such a catch." She sighed. "And stop grinding your teeth, dear. Those don't always regenerate so nicely if you crack them, you know."

"I shouldn't have told you." My finger hovered over the disconnect button on my phone.

"Well, of course, you should have, I'm your mother." Mom's airy tone clashed with that nasal Boston accent I'd struggled so hard to exorcise. "If you can't tell your own mother about breaking up with your high school sweetheart, who *can* you talk to about it?"

"I wish you'd maybe have some regular priorities for once, Mom." I took her bait instead of hanging up, flopping on my back and flinging my arm over my eyes like the long-gone Emo teenager I used to be.

Thank goodness for speakerphone. "I mean, seriously. I'm not like you, holding one of her man's hands while he throws money at his love children with the other." As usual, she ignored my insulting outburst.

"All the same, if you hadn't dumped him, you'd have a date tonight." She clucked more like a chicken shifter than a bear shifter. "Going alone to functions like these is bad form. I'm not wrong about that."

"Madam." Ismail's voice made me jump clear off the bed and over to the other side of the room in an instant. "Miss Jeannie La Montagne does not have to attend her function alone this evening. Just before your call, I asked her to accompany me. I still await her reply."

"Oh?" Nothing but the distant sound of church bells came from Mom's end of the phone after that. I imagined the temperature dropping in her immediate vicinity. "And you are?" Her frosty tone confirmed my musings.

"Marquess Ismail, centennial Djinn in His Majesty's Court." Ismail grinned and dropped me a wink. "If you check your mailbox, you will find my calling card, including my regrets that I can't pay you a proper visit until after the event in question."

I stood there with my back against the dorm-issue bookcase with my mouth hanging open. Formal-manners Ismail was way more impressive than jokey first-meeting Ismail, and light-years more intimidating than coffee shop confessional Ismail. His entire manner was authoritative, commanding. There was no way my mom didn't know which His Majesty he was talking about.

"Well, Marquess Ismail, I certainly hope you know what you're getting yourself into with my Jeannie." She tittered exactly like she had in the one recording we still had of her high school graduation. "She can be a handful."

"I can assure you that your daughter is exactly who I want on my arm at such an important event." One corner of Ismail's mouth turned up slyly. "The senior center was renovated by one of my dearest friends, Duke Redford. And the work Jeannie has been doing there this semester is invaluable. The chance to ask her is almost as much of an honor as the acceptance I hope she will grace me with."

"Well, of course, she accepts." Mom sounded positively breathless. "I mean, you're saying yes, right?"

"I'd go to a cleanup in Roger Williams Park if Ismail asked me to." My cheeks hurt. I hadn't been aware of smiling that hard. "So, yes. I'm Marquess Ismail's date this evening, Mom."

"Thank goodness. You've finally taken your mother's advice for once." She chuckled. "Have a lovely evening." The phone let out three low beeps when she hung up.

"Oh, no! I used a wish!"

"Not technically." Ismail handed me a notecard, the kind that folds over from top to bottom. The paper felt almost velvety. I opened it and read the words inked in delicate, flowing script.

"It's an invitation to accompany me dated yesterday. But why?"

"I heard you speaking to your friends about the ball, of course." He shrugged. "My intention was to leave it on your desk so you'd see it after breakfast, but…" He gestured at the dark screen of the phone.

"But I don't have anything even remotely appropriate to wear! Everything I own like that is back in Boston, and there's no time to drive up there and get it." I hoped that didn't sound like whining. If it did, Ismail didn't seem to mind.

"You have a Djinn. You always have something appropriate to wear while I'm around." He grinned again. "You can either show me a picture of a style you like or let me make one up for you."

"And that's not using a wish?"

"Not at all."

"Ismail, you're a complete and total lifesaver." I bounced up and down on my toes. "I could kiss you!"

"Er, ah, um." All the suave went out of him. Ismail suddenly only had eyes for his feet.

"That's just another one of those modern expressions." I'd sure put my foot in my mouth. I hadn't been lying about wanting to kiss him, but for an old fashioned guy like Ismail, that was probably a million miles from appropriate in his perspective.

"Oh." He looked up a smidgen, but not at me. "Well, perhaps you ought to go and have breakfast."

My rumbling stomach didn't let me protest. I thanked Ismail again, just verbally. Then, I headed down to the dining hall. He vanished back into the lamp instead of following me. Once my plate was piled high with pancakes and enough butter and maple syrup to respect Vermont and clog the arteries of its population, I headed toward an empty table in the corner.

"Hey, Jean-bean!" Lynn Frampton had other ideas. She stepped in front of me. "We have some stuff to talk to you about."

"Huh?" The aroma of my poor, neglected pancakes made it difficult to think. And besides, with my recent spate of clumsiness, the last thing I wanted to do was stand there holding them.

"Just come sit here instead of whatever lonely crag you had in mind to have your chow." Lynn smirked and beckoned me to a booth. She gave me plenty of room to make a beeline, too. But of course, she was used to dealing with bear shifters around food. She was my cousin Bobby's mate, after all.

So I cut into my pancakes and shoveled food into my mouth for a few moments before I even realized Tony Gitano was there, sitting in the corner with Lynn blocking him in. I blinked and kept on eating. I didn't have a problem with him myself, no matter how bad things seemed between him and Blaine or how he and Ismail were like oil and water. He was almost a survivor, like me, Ismail, and Mr. Kazynski. But whatever he was weathering still had him in its teeth.

"Yeah, okay, so." Lynn rolled her eyes and sighed, twirling her spoon in the bowl of Captain Crunch in front of her. "Blaine threw his computer across the room last night. Kimiko had to salvage the data on it. She's a computer whiz, who knew. But anyway, that's beside the point. Before I go any further with this discussion, is Ismail around?"

"Do you want him to be?"

"Not really. I think you and Tony should hear this first." She glanced at my bag, over my head, out at the rest of the dining room, even under the table. "I have to do something to be absolutely sure, but the results won't be back until maybe eight tonight."

"Absolutely sure about what, Frampton?" Tony thrummed his fingers on the table so hard he jostled the milk in Lynn's bowl and the extra syrup on my plate.

"Sorry, getting ahead of myself again. Maybe it's better if I show you." Lynn reached under the table again, producing a manila envelope. She pushed it between Tony and me.

"You open it, Tony." I held out my sticky hands. "I'll end up making it look like something that belongs to Winnie the Pooh."

"Fine, whatever." Tony lifted the flap, then slid some papers out. They had the grainy, gray speckled look of copies run off on a machine that leaked too much toner. He shook his head at one, sliding it across to me. But his eyes went wide at the second one. "How the Hell did you get a picture of my mother, Frampton? And why is she dressed like an extra from Kings of New York?"

"I didn't. That's your great-grandma. She's dressed like that because she just got off a ferry from Ellis Island."

"Let me guess, the big dude with her is great-grandpa Pasquale."

"Yes. And he was…"

"A lion shifter. I know." Tony kept gazing at the picture, seemingly enthralled with the image. "And great-grandma was a leopard." He ran one hand down the lower half of his face.

"Yup. We think she was a Persian leopard shifter, actually."

"But wait. That'd mean she wasn't Italian."

"Maybe." Lynn held up one hand, opened it to reveal a plastic tube with a long cotton swab sticking out of it. "We don't know for sure. So that's why I have this."

"Is that some Jerry Springer baby daddy test thingamabob?" Tony leaned back, shrinking further into the corner than I thought possible. He clutched the photocopied picture to his chest. "I'm not taking that. If it comes out wrong and word gets out, things will go even worse for me."

"Hey, Tony." Lynn tilted her head. "Don't be a fraidy cat."

Tony told Lynn to go do something by herself that she probably preferred doing with her boyfriend. I set down my fork and knife, making a little 'x' on my plate. Then, I wiped my hands on the napkin and picked up the paper he'd pushed across to me.

"This here is a family tree, Tony." I scanned the names, dates, and connections. "It's public knowledge on a genealogy website, and it says your great-grandma emigrated to Italy before she married and got on the boat to America. Her previous origins are unknown. Lynn's DNA test won't make a lick of difference to this record, especially since she's not even supposed to have access to that kind of magical medical technology in her Freshman year. She won't let it leak, and since she's smart, she'll destroy it along with the results as soon as she's done."

I had to give Lynn credit. She didn't wither under both our glares, but she sure did squirm.

"Guys, I'm just doing what I have to. No one else in Tinfoil Hat has access to that lab, anyway." She actually wrung her hands. "I promise I'll have Maddie or Henry get rid of anything left of the sample. That Sprite still owes them each a favor, so it'll be like it never existed."

"Fine. I'll open my mouth but I ain't saying aah." Tony waited for Lynn to uncap the collection vial, then dropped his jaw. She swabbed his cheek. He closed his mouth and rubbed the side of his face. "Now, what is it you're trying to find out? It better be related to our big magical problem."

"It sort of is, because all this family tracking has to do with one of the targets." Lynn tightened the cap on the vial, then tucked it away in her bag. "I'm going to either confirm or rule out your relation to someone." She stared at me.

"Wait, what?" Tony blinked across the table at me, then looked down at the paper in his hand, then at his own reflection in the chrome napkin holder on the table. "No way am I related to the La Montagnes. I mean, I'm sure you're a great family and all, but you're French, and I'm full blood It—"

"Ismail." I couldn't stand all the weird assumptions and tangents anymore. They were like something out of an old comedy flick.

"We're trying to find Ismail's descendants because I'm his lamp's third master. He'll be stuck in there forever if no one turns up."

Now that it was all laid out plainly like that, it seemed so simple and impossible. Even if Tony was a relation, he was a shifter, definitely not a Changeling. Only Magi or Psychics could be both. No way he could take over in any case. I shook my head, concerned about Ismail and the likelihood of his eternal service in the lamp. A guy like him shouldn't have to take orders like some kind of magical barista for the rest of time. And then Tony shockingly one-upped me on the plain speech front.

"And you finding out I'm his great-great-great something or other is going to help how?" Tony folded the paper and tucked it somewhere inside the trench coat he always wore. He looked away from us both. "Dammit, Lynn, I'm a shifter, not a Faerie."

"I know." She flipped her hair over one shoulder. "But you might have other relatives who are."

"Not from Great-grandpa Pasquale's side of the family, which is also my mom's." Tony shook his head. "Even if I'm your guy, that's a dead end."

"Hey, your mom might have had siblings, or maybe a brother or sister. Tell me about her." Lynn had utterly shattered the Tony Gitano code of asking too many questions without even realizing it.

"You let me up right now." Tony bristled. "You let me up or so help me, I'll tear you apart to get out of here. I don't give a whole bucket of rats that you're Bobby's girl, either."

Lynn slid out of the booth immediately, scrambling to get out of Tony's way. Something besides normal cat shifter stuff had me scrambling, too. Or maybe it was normal cat shifter stuff. Tony looked bigger than usual, his hair sticking out in all directions and his eyes gleaming bright green. My bear was up in a big way, enhancing my strength so I didn't know it. When I stood, I bumped the table. It tilted, then overturned like something out of a wrestling match.

Tony paid that calamity no mind, storming out the door without looking back. I caught a few mumbles about not trusting doctors or people who wanted to be them when they grew up.

"Well, that was unexpected."

"Lynn, never ask Tony about his family." I shook my head. "I mean, not ever. No one does."

"Well, I won't in the future. And you know, I think that didn't go so bad."

"Really? I can't think of a way it could have been worse."

"Hah." Her flat laugh made me look up from my attempt to right the table. "I can. Blaine could have been here, too."

I snorted, then gave up on the poor, wrecked booth. I hadn't just knocked the table over I'd demolished it. It'd torn from the base that welded it to the floor. My big, fat, unexplained klutz mojo had struck again, and I still had no idea how or why.

CHAPTER TWELVE

Ismail

My stomach fluttered as I waited for Jeannie to go about the rest of
her day. I didn't listen in or watch this time, confused by my uncus-
tomary nervousness. I'd check the hour, only to find the minutes had
crawled into stretches that felt like hours. When I tried to talk to Neil,
the mirror remained blank. I couldn't figure out why until I remembered that the charity event was partly his as well. The Senior
Center'd had all its renovations done by his company, after all.

When the silver timepiece I kept in the lamp chimed six, Jeannie
called to me. She'd decided to let me choose her attire. I stayed inside
as I worked, weaving magic to create and embellish a garment to fit
her from memory. I wasn't sure whether the new awkwardness
between us had lingered and was afraid to find out. Once it was
finished, I sent it out, along with a message that I would appear with
her once she arrived at the venue.

The Senior Center couldn't accommodate a function with dancing, so we'd be on the patio at the Capital Grille downtown. Fortu-

nately, it was a warm April for New England. With that in mind, I went to work on my own attire while I waited. The task didn't make the hour seem to pass any faster. Of course, there wasn't much for me to do besides make some embellishments to my century-old style of dress.

The next time Jeannie called, I vanished myself out of the lamp to be at her side. I offered her my arm before taking in my surroundings, then gaped like a fish at the man-made lagoon before me.

"I figured you'd want to get a good look at Water Place Park before we've got a more crowded view of it." She squeezed my arm.

"Thank you." I didn't look at her yet because I wasn't done taking in this place she called a park.

It was almost perfectly round, with a canal leading out from one side like a spoke. Braziers lit with red fire dotted the canal, with five interspersed around the lagoon like the points of an invisible star. All around in a circle was a cobblestone path, with steps up and down in places and the occasional bench. I peered at a brightly lit area one-quarter of the way from us, realizing it was a passageway leading out to street level. The lights shone on murals, mosaics, and sculptures. Providence city planners had taken a tunnel and turned it into an art display, a brilliant stroke. But none of it held a candle to the dazzling woman on my arm.

I'd dressed her in gold, to match the lowlights in her hair. I hadn't noticed before that her blue eyes were flecked with the same color. Her smile was more precious than a strand of diamonds, her touch on my arm as warm as the light from the fires. I'd dared something with her dress, making it less a replica from Turkish days gone by and more what the modern Western media would expect. Perhaps that had been a mistake. Jeannie shivered a little, probably chilled by her arms and midriff left bare by its design.

When she leaned against me, no doubt for warmth, I tried not to gasp or pull away. I couldn't help but tense up.

"I'm sorry." She tilted her head as she gazed up at me. "It's warm for April, but still. I should know you're not like guys who grew up in these times, even if we're physically about the same age."

"Please don't apologize." I rolled my shoulders, attempting to relax. "These are the times I live in now. I should get used to change, too. It comes with the lamp's particular brand of time-travel."

"Is that a not-so-subtle hint that you don't think we'll find you a replacement in time?" She started walking, and I followed her lead.

"I don't think one exists."

"Pure Faeries exist."

"Good luck finding one who wants to risk being at the whim of mortals without the ability to trick them into asking questions and placing them in debt."

"Who knows, maybe there's one out there who actually likes mortals."

"Doubtful," I sighed. "Even if there were, the Monarchs wouldn't like losing any of their Pure. It'd be a major act of rebellion."

"I've heard stories about Pure Faeries rebelling before."

"Is this from during the, er, Reveal?" I'd censored myself even though she'd explicitly told me not to. "I didn't mean that. What I intended to ask was whether those stories are from your time in the Boston Internment."

"I'm glad you asked what you'd meant to." Her grin was wry, but there. "Yes and no. I've heard it more than once, on the barges, from a client. The most recent was a story Nox told me. But any retellings will have to wait. We're here."

I let Jeannie show the hostess her passes. We followed her out to the patio where the function had just begun. Small groups sat, six to each round table. Blaine and Kimiko were at ours, in costumes based on the Japanese feudal era. The Tanuki girl kept looking at me sideways. I dismissed it as curiosity since I'd barely left the lamp the entire time she'd had it.

The rest of our table seemed to be reserved for professors from the College. I scanned the room, looking for Nox the Kelpie, and spotted her by one of the fire exits in a Security t-shirt. A lanky blond man only slightly taller stood on the other side of the door, wearing similar attire. He nodded at Jeannie, who murmured that he was Josh, the Alpha mentioned at the Lounge the night before.

The table closest to us was occupied by the entire Redford family, dressed like pioneers, Neil, his wife, Fred, and a boy of about ten. There were also two others I didn't recognize, an older Troll man with another young enough to be his granddaughter. Squinting at their place cards told me these were the Tollands, ranked Admiral and Captain in the King's Navy. I'd heard of them, but we hadn't actually met.

Off to the left of what looked like a dance floor was a string quartet tuning up. Two elderly women sat with a cello and a bass. An old man with a viola turned out to be Saul Kazynski. The violinist was a young woman with jet-black hair in a braid on one side of her neck. She looked so much like Saul had in his younger days, I knew this had to be the granddaughter in the photo I'd seen on his mantle. I blinked when she plugged her instrument into an amplifier, intrigued.

"Forgive me for my ignorance, Jeannie, but I didn't know that violins are electric now."

"Yeah. It's more of an internet pop culture thing. Unless you've been keeping up by reading newspapers or watching TV, you wouldn't know about Irina Kazynski. She's graduating from the Boston Conservatory next month. Already has a huge YouTube following."

"So, this is truly an important event, then." I raised an eyebrow. "A celebrity's donating her time to perform, Newport's first shifter family is sending a contingent even though they are allied with the Queen, and half the tenured faculty are here."

"Yeah, I told you." She patted my arm. "And I would have shown up in a cheap Halloween costume or a little black dress with a bunny ear headband if it weren't for you. Thanks again, Ismail." I glanced down at her, that smile of hers threatening to steal my breath again. Yeva never had that much of an effect on me.

"I'd do it again a million times over." Her blush was so deep a crimson that onlookers might have thought it made her look imperfect. To me, it only added to her charm.

Before I could say anything, a tired-looking woman with auburn hair and gray at the temples cleared her throat at the podium. There was no microphone, so she had to be an Air Magus. With those two clues, I knew this was Henrietta Thurston, Headmistress of Providence Paranormal College.

"Welcome, and thank you all for coming. It's been an interesting semester at the College, and eventful in an entirely different way than I could have expected."

Her voice rang out clear as a bell, but I could tell something in her energy was off. I'd heard the Headmistress worked hard, but that didn't account for the low level of magic around a woman of her age and skill level. I wondered whether some magic-leeching beastie or other hadn't been plaguing her as she slept. This distracted me so much I couldn't concentrate on the rest of her speech. At the end, she sat down at our table, across from Jeannie. A fellow about a decade older than her patted her arm from the seat reserved for a Professor Watkins. They grinned at each other.

Neil Redford took the podium next, talking about new improvements in the historic building which housed the Senior Center. Listening to him, I knew he'd found his passion in making things with his hands. The life Neil used to know, of wandering the frontier aimlessly, had never truly been him, a fact I remember shocking him with the night we met. And I remembered what he'd said to me in response, that I'd better find someone to love, or I'd turn into a whole heap of trouble.

When Neil introduced Jeannie, I understood exactly why attending this event was important enough for her not to go into hiding with Maddie, the Umbral Magus. If Neil's passion was building, Jeannie's entire reason for being was making sure the people in her care could get what they needed. She'd chosen the same path I had, but for all the right reasons. Instead of serving to run away from something, she'd made helping her life, to run toward people in need or at risk. That courageous concern lit the patio up more beautifully than the stars at her back.

At the end of her speech, Jeannie introduced the quartet, three of whom were seniors served by the Center. I could almost swear she could do magic because I felt almost like we took flight when she laced her arm through mine and led me to the dance floor. We waltzed among several other couples though I didn't bother much with looking at them.

"Jeannie, I think I want to tell you."

"Should we sit down?"

"No." I sighed as I spun her, watching as the spangles on her long skirt reflected light everywhere like a mirror ball. "It's better for me to be doing something while I speak about this, I think."

"Then go ahead. Say anything." She tilted her head again as she had on the way there. I took a deep breath and finally ran toward instead of away.

"After I came back from the Under, I told myself that my wife and children needed me in the lamp in case the unthinkable happened. And it did. The Young Turks rounded them up, but Yeva didn't summon me. They marched her into the deserts along with my son and daughter, and she didn't make a wish. I could have come out anyway, bent the rules like I've done for you. But I'd heard rumors. I couldn't bear to see them proved correct. I hadn't the stomach for it.

"And finally, Yeva wished to be rescued. But I couldn't bring myself to emerge beside her. I'd sensed some British Extrahumans on the other side of a dune. If they crested the ridge, they'd see everything. I left them a magical trail. After that, I dared to look. A massive rampaging dragon with blue and white scales spewed wind to rival a sandstorm from his mouth and rescued the victims."

"That was Wilfred Harcourt." The emotions in Jeannie's eyes mirrored mine: fear, sadness, a dash of guilt. She understood.

"I came to Yeva's aid too late to even see her fall. One of the guards stepped back, his scimitar red with blood. The children cowered back in fear as the man threatened them again. I knew what would come next, but I'd been a Magus as well as a Changeling before I tithed. My electrical magic was weak, but Yeva's death came with a surge of raw power. I burst free of the lamp, slinging a bolt of lightning at the murderer. The hair on the children's heads stood on end. The charcoal that was left of him clattered against the petrified lightning I'd made, then rolled down the dune."

"So it was Wilfred who brought your children and the others out of Turkey." She sighed. "No wonder you mourned him."

"Yes, and he took mastery of my lamp, as dragons do when they find something valuable. A Djinn serves three masters each time one takes a turn in a lamp, but because Yeva died after just one wish that went ungranted, she didn't count."

"What did he use his wishes on, if you don't mind my asking? And how did you end up at The Academy?" It was hard to think past the anguish, remembering it all caused, but Jeannie's questions helped me move along and change focus.

"Wilfred returned to Turkey, rescuing any Extrahumans he could find. He exchanged their freedom for heirlooms, but it didn't lower my opinion of him. A cowardly Djinn can't exactly judge a profiteering dragon. He did the same during the Second World War. I helped when I could without using a wish, granting three over a span of decades. After that, he could have passed me to anyone. Instead, he left me in a peace I sorely desired back in those days. And then, he married Hertha. She couldn't tolerate an Unseelie Djinn under her roof, so he donated my lamp to The Academy for study. When a certain Tanuki girl stole it and brought me back to Wilfred's home, I hoped to see him again, but coincidence had other ideas. I was left to pay my respects instead."

"Well, it's a good thing I haven't made any official wishes yet, then." She gazed up at me. "I can't even imagine being stuck in there forever, especially after you've been through all that. A profiteering dragon and a cowardly Djinn turned out to be heroes. You deserve your freedom. Besides," she grinned, "I'm not sure I want you designing gorgeous outfits for random women for the rest of time."

I didn't want to look away from her, but a tug at my sleeve meant I had to turn my head to see who dared vie for my attention. And I found myself frowning down at Kimiko Ichiro.

"Ismail, can I cut in? I have to talk to you."

"You see me out here, trying to actually live a little as you always said I should, and decide to interrupt it?" I softened the frown. Kimiko was wily but ultimately meant well. "Perhaps it can wait?"

Movement from behind her caught my eye. Blaine fidgeted at the edge of the parquet dance floor, glancing back and forth between Headmistress Thurston and the Professor with her, a man named Watkins. I couldn't see magic energy around him, so he had to be Psychic. But he looked almost as worse for wear as the Headmistress.

"It can't." Kimiko's eyes widened, and her mouth dropped open as she looked at Jeannie and me, then out at the lagoon the patio overlooked. "It's your Luck. Not you, your lamp's. It's turning the wrong way. That's why Jeannie keeps having accidents, and everything you try to do is harder. It's gone bad in a big—"

Before Kimiko could finish what she was saying, a shower of cold, brackish water rained down on us. Jeannie's foot slipped in it, sending us both to the ground in a heap.

A monstrous, hulking, amalgamated thing had risen out of the pool at the center of Water Place Park, and no one at that illustrious gathering seemed to have the slightest idea what to do about it.

CHAPTER THIRTEEN

Jeannie

I didn't know what that thing was besides ugly and enormous. It defied all Extrahuman or magical creature classification in my experience or education. Neil Redford stood up to it but got sent flying through the glass between the patio and the restaurant's main dining room for his trouble. If it could land a blow on a Redcap that old, it'd be able to smack me for sure.

I shifted anyway. The outfit Ismail had made me didn't tear into a million little pieces, just fell away like magic because that's what it was. I let out a roar, unleashing the universal sign for "angry bear." Josh Dennison had the same idea, howling up at the sky in what could only be a rallying cry. I never thought I'd hear hooves on parquet flooring, but Nox galloped beside us, her Water magic frothing up under her feet and flying from her mane in a shield against whatever that attacking creature was.

My ears twitched, and I wondered why both the Kazynskis were still playing. They'd gone from waltzes to The Devil Went Down to

Georgia. A sudden impulse to kick whatever passed for the mysterious creature's butt invaded my heart and mind like the aliens in The Day The Earth Stood Still.

"Luck tuuuuuuuurn!" Kimiko sounded like she was auditioning for a stage production of *Inu Yasha* and looked like she was doing the Macarena. Unfortunately, the whole effect and whatever Luck energy manipulation she'd intended failed when a ball of goo knocked her back. She floundered on the floor in her now-sodden costume. A heavy goblet rolled off the table above her and conked her on the noggin, and Kimiko went down for the count.

A rush of air whooshed behind me, and an angry reptilian cry rose in response to the Tanuki getting served. Blaine Harcourt's big red dragon body stood on the steps between the attacker and us. He opened his mouth and promptly got a throat full of slime. His head and neck swayed as his scales paled from red to his usual skin tone, then, he shrank back to his human form right there in the creature's path. I wondered how we were going to beat this thing if it had magic gunk that could knock us out of our shifted forms.

"The goo's enchanted!" I heard Maddie's voice coming from somewhere even though I couldn't see her.

I watched Captain Gemma Tolland try to run for the steps leading down to the middle of Water Place Park. She dropped her glamour completely, revealing wilder hair and eyes than usual, plus a set of delicate, pearly tusks protruding from her lower lip. I'd never seen a Troll get angry before. Spikes sprouted across her back and down her arms, growing along with her rage. But just before she could go full-out Troll Berserker, Admiral Tolland sent a beam of silver light straight at her. It lassoed her waist, and he dragged her back with him into the restaurant and out of the battle. It made sense. Admiral Tolland had a reputation for not getting involved in mortal affairs unless he got paid.

Without Gemma as a target of opportunity, the thing went straight for Fred's little brother.

"Not my baby!" Mrs. Redford was a Psychic Medium and thank goodness she'd brought her ghosts. "Get em' guys!"

When ghosts attacked, no one could see them unless they were Mediums or had some sort of Psychic device. I knew they were fighting because of the glasses and cups hurtling through the air, thrown by invisible hands. Even when they moved on to chucking chairs and tossing tables, the thing seemed unharmed. It just absorbed the furniture. But the thing turned away and left the Redford kid alone. That gave Josh Dennison and the rest of Tinfoil Hat's shifters exactly the opening they needed.

Josh darted forward, joined by a three-legged wolf bounding up from the bottom of the steps. That'd be his sister, Beth. A sleek, furry form splashed in the water, too, flanking the creature directly inside the lagoon. They dipped and weaved, distracting the thing long enough to protect Blaine and the Redfords until Fred got them out of the way. They all vanished into a patch of shadow in one corner of the patio, but Fred came back out almost immediately.

"It's some kind of golem!" Fred shouted in our general direction and past us. Golems took a concerted effort of mortal magic, Psychic energy, and Faerie powers. For all I knew, there could be an army of Extrahumans powering the thing. I remembered Ismail behind me. I could use a wish if only I knew what would get rid of the thing attacking us. Maybe I needed to think of something besides banishing it.

"On it, sonny boy!" Neil Redford picked bits of The Capital Grille's plate-glass window out of his sharp, pointy teeth and shook more off his now-massive and gray-skinned frame. He'd eaten the window he'd crashed into and gone full Redcap, dropping his glamour to call extra power from the Under. Fred's dad leaped and bounded across to where Professor Watkins and Headmistress Thurston lay prone on the floor. He reached for Watkins as Ismail extended his arm toward the Headmistress. At least the unconscious faculty members wouldn't get caught in the crossfire.

"No more ironic Unseelie heroics, Neil." Professor Watkins sat up, and I grunted in shock. His eyes were glassy and his limbs oddly limp, like he was either boneless or not moving under his own power. His voice was all wrong, too, like someone else was using his mouth to speak. I remembered Professor Brodsky, a Psychic Summoner victimized by Mind magic, and wondered if this was something similar.

Neil scratched his head, shrugging at the floppy professor as though he couldn't figure out what kind of threat he posed. That was when the thing from the lagoon slapped one of its long limbs across his face, knocking him out cold. Ismail jumped back and out of the way just in time. A renewed surge of music met my ears as the string quartet played faster. Something had amplified them, but I wasn't sure what. Their audio equipment looked fried. But Saul Kazynski had Psychic powers to affect emotions. That had to be it.

The strike against Neil was a sucker-punch, and I knew it. I looked for the other attack, wondering where the next blow would fall. But why hadn't the creature killed any of Tinfoil Hat, or Neil Redford, for that matter? Why would it pull its punches? And then I remembered that coincidence would slap any magic back on the caster. They'd all been attacked before, or in Neil's case, places he'd put his heart, soul, and magic into building. This had to be the work of the Extramagus.

I was too late to block it when the creature flung one of the tables it had absorbed at the string quartet. I watched Irina Kazynski turn her instrument toward the incoming barrage, amazed that her music changed its course. It would have crushed her grandpa if she hadn't. As it was, it slammed into his leg. I heard a wet snap, and he went down with a cry.

I snarled at Ismail, who crouched beside Headmistress Thurston. Wishes needed intent and words, but if I shifted, Josh and half his pack would be left to fight all by themselves. I used a claw to gouge two words in the slate of the patio, nonspecific and possibly a waste of a wish, but it worked. Ismail nodded, and a shield of crackling energy went up around the string quartet. Amazingly, Saul Kazynski and the rest kept on playing.

"Give me the lamp and the bear shifter and I'll let the rest of you escape with your lives." The voice coming from Professor Watkins' mouth was even more wrong than before, like he wasn't in his body anymore.

Josh growled, Nox snorted, and Beth barked, echoed by one which sounded like a seal from the lagoon. That had to be Ren Ichiro, Kimiko's Selkie brother. I refused to be left out or let the kids in Tinfoil Hat fight this battle for me, so I roared again and led the charge.

If the Extramagus wanted me, they'd have to deal with my fangs and claws first!

Ismail

I watched Jeannie leap from the top of the steps outside the patio, closing the gap between her and the creature. I couldn't let her grapple it. I knew what would happen. A golem like this had devoured an Allied platoon on the European Front in the Second World War before Wilfred and I stopped it. I'd held back this time because I told myself one of the high-status, wealthy guests would handle it, but they'd all either fled or fallen, and I had let a group of youngsters fight a battle I should have been at the front of. Two were unconscious, and the golem had injured one of my few remaining friends. Now it had hurt Jeannie. I couldn't let that happen. I wouldn't run away this time, even though I didn't have an Air dragon backing me up.

"Stop playing and fight!" I threw a punch toward the creature to direct my magic. I wasn't breaking any rules of the lamp to do it, either. This was the magic I'd grown up with—lightning. It struck, arcing over and around the golem in a blue and yellow honeycomb of lines and spaces.

Its surface rippled, the electricity jolting it. The pit of my stomach dropped when I remembered the Selkie in the water with it, but it was too late to take it back. It'd be too late for much of anything soon. If the golem devoured me with its acidic slime, I'd reform back in the lamp to grant Jeannie's last two wishes. After that, I'd die. I stood, holding lightning in my hands so at least I'd go down fighting, and maybe even take it with me. And then I heard Jeannie.

"I wish for no one in this entire state to suffer a golem's harm from this moment forward!"

"I call on the Under to help me grant this wish!" I took a deep breath, knowing her attempted wish would be useless. Only one of the Monarchs could make a ban that big and include a construct so powerful.

"My debt to you is paid, Marquess Ismail." The Goblin King stood between me and the golem. He snapped his fingers and the creature stopped, settling itself back in the lagoon. Whoever was controlling it mustn't know what to do with it now.

"Debt?" I blinked at his back, noting that he still wore the same dusty brown hunting boots, gray riding pants, and purple leather vest over a frilly shirt as he'd done a hundred years ago. "I had no idea you owed me anything but a place in your Court."

"Why, yes." He smirked, tapping the leg of his boot with a riding crop. "Your mistress saved my favorite bard's life, although you couldn't have known that at the time. That was the reason I gave him my favor, and the reason I can enable you to grant this shifter's wish tonight."

"Thank you, Your Majesty." I bowed to him as I'd done in the Under after I'd tithed.

"I must warn you, Marquess. You'll get no more direct help from me for the rest of the evening." He flicked his long black hair over one shoulder. "I like this new you, Ismail. Fare thee well, and let your heart lead you." With another snap of his fingers, he vanished much more neatly than I'd ever been able to do.

"Well, that was unexpected." Maddie emerged from the shadowy corner, holding one end of a big duffel bag. A golden-skinned man in surf shorts held the other. He ran a hand through his slightly singed brown hair and resembled Kimiko so closely that I knew my magic hadn't seriously injured the Selkie. They dropped articles of clothing near the other shifters so they'd have something to wear as they changed back. I saw what looked like a Sprite dashing toward the hole in the plate-glass window, then rubbed my eyes and looked again.

"That wasn't really a Sprite I just saw?" I looked around for an answer. Jeannie headed over, wearing a pink sundress. I put my arm around her, but before either of us could say anything, someone else did. We walked together toward the string quartet.

"Good old Ismail, questioning everything no matter what's happened." Saul's strained voice came from behind the Lightning shield I hadn't dropped yet. I took it down and headed over to him.

"It's too late for me to heal this, old friend." I placed my hand on his leg.

"I'll call an ambulance. This has pockets!" Jeannie grinned and pulled a phone out of the dress. Clearly, the bag was part of some preparation on the part of the Tinfoil Hat pack.

"Thank you." The lines on Saul's face lost some of their sharpness. "I know you can't reverse it after this much time." He was talking about the Gnomish magic that came with my lamp. One had lived in it before the Monarchs had split, so with a wish, I could have reversed the injury during the first five seconds after it took place. "But what will you do about the golem?"

"I'm not sure." The thing was still in the middle of Water Place Park. Jeannie sat with Saul and the other two elderly musicians. Saul's granddaughter was nowhere to be seen.

"Well, we have to do something about it." Blaine Harcourt hobbled over, wearing a towel and leaning on Kimiko. "It's draining Professor Watkins and the Headmistress every minute it stays there. Whoever sent it must have done a major group casting before with their help because they're tapped into it. If we don't tear that thing down fast, the two of them will die."

"Does anyone happen to have an Air dragon they can call?" I stood and began pacing the exact dimensions of my lamp out of habit. "Because that was how we did it last time. It's the only way without a Null Magus."

"Well, no. We don't have either of those." Blaine shook his head, eyelids drooping. "Let me guess: my fiery halitosis won't do it."

"You're in no condition to shift right now anyway." Kimiko squeezed his hand. "It needs extreme cold, not an inferno."

"Perhaps I can be of service." The vaguely familiar voice came from behind me.

Blaine jerked his head up, straining to try to stand up straight or otherwise look presentable. I recognized who'd just spoken.

"You're the librarian." I turned to look at the older man.

"Yes. Taki Waban is my name, and I am an ice dragon. Will that do?" His smile set his black eyes twinkling.

"Even better than Air." I chuckled. "Wilfred had to use most of his strength to cool the golem enough for me to shatter it. With ice breath, it should go much quicker."

He walked down the steps to the area in front of the lagoon. In dragon form, Taki Waban was black with a silvery sheen of frost on his scales. He was also bigger than Blaine, but serpentine and able to fit in tighter quarters as a result. He breathed on the golem, freezing it in seconds. I went as far as the second step on the stone staircase, then focused my magic again. My Lightning blast sent bits of it hurtling into the air and then back down to splatter into the water like an extremely localized rainstorm.

Right there, amidst all that confusion, Jeannie stood on the top step, placed her hands on my shoulders, and kissed me. I embraced her, running my hands up her back and then through her hair. She left me so breathless, I almost tumbled down the stairs. We grinned, not caring when some of the strange rain missed the water and fell on us and the patio, too.

"Whahappen?" Headmistress Thurston stirred, reaching out with her hands as though trying to grasp something. She bumped one foot into Neil Redford, who lay there groaning and clutching his head.

Professor Watkins didn't move. Jeannie returned to my side. We sat and watched his chest barely rise and fall. I put my arm around her again. Kimiko turned the Luck on my lamp back in the right direction. The Redfords went home together. All the shifters got dressed. Maddie called back her shadows. We agreed to stay with the wounded.

When the ambulances got there, the EMEs did their triage. They rushed away with Saul Kazynski and the Headmistress but took their time with Professor Watkins.

"Do you know what that means?" I nodded at the response of the medical people.

"No, but there's someone we can ask." Jeannie got up and held a hand down to me. "Come on, Ismail. We're supposed to meet Lynn about your descendants. It's a pretty good walk, so we should start now."

CHAPTER FOURTEEN

Jeannie

We got all the way up to Hope Street before he said anything, but Ismail let me hold his hand the entire way.

"You used one of your wishes to protect the entire state, Jeannie." He didn't stop walking or even turn his head to look at me. "Why is that?"

"Because I'm a bear. I might have grown up in Boston, but this is the place I picked for myself." I shrugged. "So I won't just leave things so some nutcase Extramagus can attack people with something like that whenever they want."

"Did you know that I can see records of all the wishes made with my lamp?" We walked along in silence for almost a block because I was ashamed to give him the answer.

"No. Didn't have any idea." I forced a stiff chuckle. "Can you believe they're letting me graduate in a couple of weeks?"

"I doubt anything so complicated as the function of ancient Faerie artifacts was a required subject matter for your major."

"Still, I feel downright ignorant after dealing with all this." I sighed. "Like maybe I'm not ready."

"Are we ever ready, though?" This time, he did look at me. "I graduated from college, tithed and spent my time in the Under. And I thought I was ready for everything. But I wasn't. I still might not be."

We turned the corner and walked along the long side of the lot Josh Dennison's big giant historic house was situated on. I noticed the wrought-iron fencing had all been torn down. It sat in a pile near where Ismail stepped in front of me, stopping so we could finish this conversation before meeting the others.

"Okay, so what's your point about readiness, then?" I put my hands on my hips. After doing all that work to bring Ismail out of his figurative and literal shell, I felt like I wanted to take a turn in one myself.

"The point is, whether you feel ready or not, you can't stop." He held his hands out in front of him, palms up at waist height. "You can't run away, either, because the fear's inside. It'll just follow you wherever you go. So when you say you're not ready, I say it doesn't matter. You don't have to be ready, you only have to keep moving forward. You helped me learn that, Jeannie La Montagne. And that's only one of the things I love about you."

I dropped my hands off my hips, then reached out to take both of his. As our fingertips touched, a flare of light blinded me. All I could see was a slim silhouette of someone with what looked like a cane, but I was wrong about that last bit.

"Lovely speech. Excellent last words." I'd never heard that voice before but I knew right away it was male. "I've finally gotten one over on you meddling kids, and I didn't even have to use a spell to do it."

The part of the figure I'd mistaken for a cane turned out to be one of the iron spikes. I realized that when the bloody end of it protruded from Ismail's chest. I stared at the figure again, but it vanished with the light. Spots and shapes danced in front of my eyes, and my stomach fell like an elevator with a severed cable. I sank to the ground holding Ismail and screaming.

"I wish this never happened!" My tears wet Ismail's face along with the blood at the corner of his mouth.

"Your wish, my command." He smiled and closed his eyes. I couldn't look away. The bloody tinge around his teeth turned pink, then vanished. I heard a metallic clang and turned my head to see the fence post drop back on top of the pile with the rest. When I looked back, every trace of the fatal wound was gone. The only way I knew it hadn't just been my imagination was the fact that we were both on the sidewalk instead of standing.

"Oh, no." I put my hands on my cheeks, head rushing with the gravity of my mistake. "Oh, now I've done it."

"Done what?"

"Trapped you in that lamp forever. And after we've gone and fallen in love." I sniffled. Couldn't help it. The Extramagus had probably wanted me to watch Ismail die, but watching him lose his freedom forever because of me was almost as bad.

"We still have one hour before I'm trapped forever." Ismail got up and dusted himself off. It was his turn to give me a hand up, like I'd done for him back at Water Place Park. "It's not over yet. Let's see what your friend has for us."

"Which friend?" Josh Dennison looked from me to Ismail and back again. "You've got about ten of them up there at the house. And what was that light? Wait, never mind. Tell me up there because they'll all want to know, and it's no fun repeating a story that many times."

We followed him to the basement. Everyone was there. Ismail stopped on the threshold. I realized that not even the Ball had been this crowded. At least there, we'd been under an open sky. Here, every seat was taken, and every surface in use somehow, from drinks on the bar to a study station set up on a board atop the billiards table.

"You okay?"

"I used Gnomish powers from my lamp to time reverse an iron bar through my gut, and you ask if I'm okay walking into a crowded room." Ismail's chuckle was tiny and soft, but still there.

"I just wanted to be sure you could handle it."

"Of course. I'm with you."

Josh cleared his throat three times before the room quieted down enough for Ismail and me to tell them all what had happened on the sidewalk just over the Dennison property line. When we finished, I counted to three before the room erupted in outrage.

"—actually did that to a Djinn!"

"—timey-wimey mojo or he'd be—"

"Who even uses iron bars anymore, I mean seriously…"

"—drop flaming fewmets on his head!"

"—sure it's a dude now, thank Lady Luck."

"—should check him for iron fragments anyway—"

"Leaping Luna!"

"—liverwurst sandwich down his throat and pitch him headfirst into the Under!"

"And after the Goblin King showed up…"

"—just glad he's alive."

It all stopped when a sound like a gunshot rang out through the room. Everyone turned to look. Tony Gitano stood holding a broken pool cue and quivering with anger. I wondered how breaking a stick could have sounded remotely like a shotgun. Before I could figure it out, he spat two words.

"Shut. Up." The thinner end of the cue dropped out of Tony's right hand. He hefted the larger in his left, flipping it so he held the jagged end in his palm. "You all are forgetting something." He pointed the cue at me. "Miss Perfect here just sent her boyfriend up Shit Creek without a paddle and you're all acting like a typical bunch of spooked Millenials. Cut. It. Out!" He hit a barstool, a chair, and the pool table with each word.

"So, what do you think we should do then, Tony?" Even leaning against the bar, Josh's entire stance dripped authority.

"Actually solve some problems for once. Oh, and maybe quit freaking out and slacking off."

"Hey!" Lynn stared daggers and Tony sure as Hell felt it.

"I wasn't talking about you, Frampton." Tony waved his free hand in her general direction. "I may not like your nosy methods, but you're the only one besides me who isn't too scared or lazy to do something constructive."

"Shut up, Puss-In-Converse!" The smoke around Blaine's head

looked like Mount St. Helen's. "You have no right to tell me how to act. You haven't lost anyone!"

"Exactly. My. Point." He slapped the pool cue against his hand this time. "And none of you have any idea what I've been doing."

"You keep mentioning a point, Tony, so get to it." Josh thrummed his fingertips on the top of the bar. I saw that an empty beer bottle was in easy reach of his free hand.

"You all gotta do more than what you have been." He turned his back on Josh, "Here's the list of casualties so far, in case you haven't been keeping track. Two vampires, killed by the Grim. Professor Brodsky's sanity. Wilfred Harcourt, who should have been immortal. Kazynski's hip. Ismail's freedom. Professor Watkins."

"Wait, what?" Lynn blinked back tears. My own eyes stung, too.

"No!" Nox stood up. "That can't be true."

"I've been monitoring CB all night because I'm not fooling around here." Tony tapped the Bluetooth earpiece he always wore. "He's in a vegetative state. Brodsky's trial is this fall. If we can get more dirt on the Extramagus than that he's got cajones instead of teats, that's evidence. We could undo a little of the damage, at least, and prevent that slippery twit from killing anyone else."

"Granted." Josh nodded at Tony. "We'll step things up. Exams are almost over, and we're all free this summer. But what's this about Ismail's freedom? I thought our brainiac was on that."

"There isn't anyone." Lynn sighed, resting her head in her hands. "Ismail's only living relative is a shifter. Unless someone has a pure Faerie in their pocket, the Extramagus won on that front."

"Wait a minute." Henry smiled, which was like someone jumping out of a box at the Factory of Terror haunted house up in Fall River. Vampires got their blood from hospitals and Henry Baxter took pains to be sure he was well-fed at all times, but his fangs were still pretty unsettling. What he said next made me think he looked like an angel. "I actually have one of those."

"You don't mean Gee Nome?" Ren Ichiro shook his head. "There's no way Gee'd agree to live in a lamp forever. They like sneaking around too much."

"And it would definitely be forever, too, if a pure Faerie took my place." Ismail sighed. "They don't technically have relatives, so there's no way out unless both Monarchs agree to release them."

"No, not Gee. Ren's right, and besides, I like having that Gnome around." Henry chuckled. Maddie rushed to his side and hugged him.

"Oh, Henry, it's the perfect idea!" She bounced up and down on the balls of her feet, her wide, bright smile gleaming out from the dusky skin of her face. Maddie May was easily the happiest looking Goth girl I'd ever seen.

"Hoo, boy." Olivia's excitement got swallowed by her yawn. " The Spite. I mean, the ex-Spite. I mean the Sprite, they're a Sprite now, right? The one hiding from the Queen?"

"Yup." Henry grinned this time, more aware now of the effect his smile had on the rest of the room. "I'll call them. Even gave them a name so we wouldn't have to say 'hey, you.' Hey, Sparky," he called, "come out and have a chat with me."

A spindly-limbed creature crawled out from under the billiards table. They had tawny skin and wore what looked like one of Josh's old PPC Security t-shirts, altered to fit. Two holes in the back let their wings out, but everyone could see the Sprite couldn't exactly fly anymore. The poor thing had only ragged tatters left where the delicate membranes of nearly transparent skin should have been. The Sprite held an ornately carved wooden box under one arm.

"I'm here, Henry Baxter." They nodded at the vampire. "Are you using the last of the favors I owe you?"

"Yes and no, Sparky." It hurt my heart a little that Henry had given the poor creature a nickname. That pain eased when I saw them give him a toothy grin.

"I see. This Djinn needs a replacement." It kept its distance from Ismail, which made sense considering Sprites were Seelie creatures. But, if they used to be a Spite, one of the Queen's vicious hunting hounds, no wonder they tolerated the King's subjects. "And I need a home, someplace where even the Queen can't harm me."

"Yeah, but I think that's too tall an order for what you owe me."

Henry shrugged. "Still, it's up to you. Are you willing to give up your freedom like that, Sparky?"

"Yes, but on one condition." They looked at Maddie when they spoke, not at Henry. "You hide the lamp in Billy Taylor Park, where the Kelpie freed me."

"Wait, what?" Maddie tilted her head, bouncing her curls. "But it's a public place."

"All the same," the Sprite replied, "those are my terms to make this agreement."

"That's so risky, though." Lynn shook her head. "Anyone who bumps into the lamp will know it's there and pick it up."

"No, I agree with Sparky." Tony tilted his head. "You have to put the lamp in the park."

"Why in Tiamat's name would *you* be cool with something like that, cat-man?"

"Because Sprites can see patterns in coincidence. If Sparky wants to be there, they have a reason." Tony cleared his throat, then mumbled, "and I owe them a favor."

"That would repay both debts, leaving me free to occupy the lamp without conflict of interest." Sparky's nod might have been sage if they hadn't looked like a hairless kid. "I will take Duke Ismail's place."

"Thank you." Ismail chuckled. "But I'm a Marquess, not a Duke."

"Nope." Nox squinted at Ismail. "Sparky's right. You must have seriously impressed the King back there at Water Place. You leveled up. Gratz!"

"Um, can we get this done, please?" I pointed at the clock above the bar. "We only have a few minutes left."

I took the lamp out of my bag, placing it on the billiards table and opening the top. Ismail and Sparky held it between them, each reciting in two different languages I couldn't understand. Purple smoke flowed out of the lamp toward Ismail, while yellow motes of light swirled around Sparky's side, entering through the lid I'd opened. Something I can only describe as a reverse flash ended with Sparky hovering above the lamp. They waved at us and vanished inside.

The smoke around Ismail had coalesced into shackles on his wrists and ankles, joined by lengths of chain. When Sparky vanished, the magical bonds flew into a billion dark purple pieces, then dissipated. Ismail was free.

CHAPTER FIFTEEN

Ismail

I stood there grinning at Jeannie as I rubbed my wrists. Then, I leaned down and kissed her full on the mouth, more deeply and passionately than the quick one back at Water Place Park. The room filled with cheers and whistles I was only vaguely aware of. When I pulled away, she flung her arms around my neck as though she'd never let go.

"What was that for?"

"I just wanted to see what it was like kissing you now that I'm a free Djinn."

"Did you like it?" She smiled.

"I can't even begin to describe how much."

"Enough to want to do it again?"

I gave her an encore which went longer than the performance it followed. I lost track of time, possibly even the rest of the world. It differed completely from forgetting the months or seasons in the lamp. Somehow the fact I knew it would be fleeting made it feel more eternal.

"Um, I don't want to break up the schmooping, so sorry." It was a woman's voice. "But we kind of promised to do something."

I felt a tug on my sleeve. Jeannie and I broke it off to see Maddie staring at my hand. I hadn't even realized I'd still been holding the lamp.

"Oops."

The Umbral Magus shrugged and gave me a half-smile, then held out her hands. I dropped my old home into them. She headed toward the door with Tony and Henry.

"You want me to go, too?" Nox strode toward the door. Josh stopped her.

"Don't. Henry's got enough on his plate, having to change three memories. Why add to it?"

"Good point." She went back to the bar and what looked like a root beer float but smelled like alcohol.

"Did you want a Jaeger and root beer float?" Jeannie led me over to the bar. "I could go for one myself right about now."

"Hmm. I'm intrigued, but I might be too much of a lightweight for that."

"I'll get you some wine, then." Jeannie went back behind the bar and poured.

With Tony gone, the rest of the room seemed to relax. I understood now that he wasn't a spy or untrustworthy. The cat shifter just didn't want everyone knowing everything about him. Perhaps he'd even gotten that trait from me. I'd have to keep as much of an eye on him as he'd allow. I was his thrice-great grandfather, after all. And from what I'd heard and seen so far, he trusted his family less than his packmates. He might need my help before long.

"Okay, so we have some more information now." Josh got his phone out and woke it up. "Let's tell LORA the Extramagus is male for sure." He kept on tapping, swiped, then put the phone back in his pocket. "Tony was right about something. We've been dropping the ball too many times, so let's put our heads together and keep it in the air. Any theories?"

"I have one." I twirled the wineglass between my fingers, watching the light play across the golden liquid inside.

"Shoot." Josh leaned against the billiard table.

"It's rare, but it does happen that Psychics and Magi have other powers." I took a deep breath, knowing how controversial my idea might be. "I think he might also be a Changeling."

"But he can't be." Josh shook his head. I hadn't expected an Alpha open-minded enough to befriend a flightless Sprite to protest. But it turned out he had an excellent reason. "All the evidence points to him being Henry's age or older. And he was born in the 1970s. How could a Changeling go that long being untithed?"

"Yeah. I'm a wreck over having to tithe this summer." Fred's forehead crinkled as he frowned. "It sucks. I hoped I'd at least make it through Junior year. Guess that's what I get for taking a year off to work for Dad."

"You're not a Magus—"

"You're not a Psychic—"

Lynn let out a belly laugh while Blaine chuckled at their conversational collision. I waited, hoping one of the so-called brains in the pack figured it out. Lynn spoke first, still slapping her knee.

"If the Extramagus has all those mortal powers, he'd be able to hold off using his Faerie magic just about all the time. Using that is what makes Changelings need to tithe young. He could still be Henry's age."

"Yeah, you're right." Fred sighed. "Guy has all that power, and he uses it for homicide. Just think of all the things he could be building."

"Hmm." Blaine scratched his chin. "Dragons waste their energy like that, too. But on paranoia."

"Hey, you resemble that remark." Kimiko punched him in the arm.

"Yeah, but everyone knows I'm a stereotype-defying dragon." He winked at her. "What I mean to say is, maybe we should make guesses about this guy more like he's a dragon than a Magus. I mean, he's definitely paranoid, uses other people or creatures to do his dirty work, keeps all his awesomesauce for his own waffles. Maybe that stuff will help us predict what he'll do next instead of just to whom."

I was beginning to get the idea that half of the group had paired off. That might be another source of the tension I'd sensed. I wondered why everyone was looking at Fred. Apparently, so did he.

"What are you all staring at?" His surly expression changed to one of alarm. "My glamour's not down again, is it?"

"Nope." Nox kicked back the dregs of her alcoholic float. "They think you're next."

"Wait, what? Why?" His eyes got almost as big as his mouth. It made sense to me once they mentioned it.

"Your father helped me, then went after the golem tonight," I answered because no one else had all the information, and it was my theory, anyway. "So did you. Needing to hold off tithing makes you vulnerable. And if the Extramagus is a Changeling, he's planning to go Seelie. You're a Duke's son. Neil's the King's man. Which way are you going?"

"GK, all the way." Fred waved one index finger in the air like a half-hearted cheer. His stomach rumbled in counterpoint.

"There you are, then." I raised my glass to him. "May you have more success against him than I did."

Glasses all around the room clinked. Fred stomped to the fridge, got out a can of beer, and bit it to guzzle down the contents.

"But who else is next?" Jeannie scratched her head. "Back in the lounge, you said he always targets pairs."

"That's curious." I sipped my wine, trying to keep a grin off my face. "Tell that to this Lora person you've got helping you and see what she comes up with."

"Silly, Djinn!" Kimiko smirked. "You know all about LORA."

"That I do." I winked. "Tell your program that the Extramagus might be embittered. Perhaps he's lost a mate or never found one. He's picking his victims by coincidence patterns, right?"

"Yeah, that's what we think." Blaine raised an eyebrow and blew a smoke ring.

"He's looking for destined lovers, then."

"How do you figure?" Fred crushed his now empty beer can and tossed it into the blue bin.

"Lynn and Bobby. Henry and Maddie. Josh and Nox. Kimiko and Blaine. And now me and Jeannie." I glanced at Olivia. She was sleeping in an easy chair. Fred hadn't looked at her once.

"Cool theory, bro." Fred laughed. "But you're wrong. My head's in school and work every hour I'm not sleeping or with my family. I don't have time for girls."

"As you say." I just smiled at him. Fred Redford had no idea what he was in for as far as romance went. Unsurprising, considering Neil had waited so long to find a bride. The apple didn't fall far from the tree in the Redford line. Fortunately, the conversation moved along to other ideas, with background given to Jeannie and me as they went. The group of them who'd been targeted by the Extramagus before me had some interesting stories to tell.

I might have found myself more at ease with this group than I'd felt in a century, but I wasn't about to discuss how I'd felt about love before getting to know Jeannie. That was for her ears only. I wanted another hundred years to tell my feelings to her. Looking in her eyes, I knew she shared my wish.

The End

Thank you for reading! If you loved this book, I would love a review.

Please be on the lookout for the next Providence Paranormal College collection, available soon at Amazon and through Kindle Unlimited.

CONNECT WITH THE AUTHOR

Find D.R. Perry Online

Website: https://drperryauthor.com/

Facebook: https://www.facebook.com/drpperry/

Twitter: https://twitter.com/DRPerry22